THREE COMPLETE NOVELS
MORRIS WEST

THREE COMPLETE NOVELS

MORRIS WEST

THE SHOES OF THE FISHERMAN

THE CLOWNS OF GOD

LAZARUS

WINGS BOOKS

NEW YORK • AVENEL, NEW JERSEY

This omnibus was originally published in separate volumes
under the titles:
The Shoes of the Fisherman, copyright © 1963 by Morris L. West.
The Clowns of God, copyright © 1981 by Compania Financiera
Perlina, S.A.
Lazarus, copyright © 1990 by Melaleuka East Investments Ltd. Pty.

This edition contains the complete and unabridged texts of the original
editions. They have been completely reset for this volume.

This 1993 edition is published by Wings Books,
distributed by Outlet Book Company, Inc., a Random House Company,
40 Engelhard Avenue, Avenel, New Jersey 07001,
by arrangement with St. Martin's Press.

Random House
New York • Toronto • London • Sydney • Auckland

Printed and bound in the United States of America

Library of Congress Cataloging-in-Publication Data

West, Morris L., 1916-
  [Novels. Selections]
  Three complete novels / Morris West.
     p. cm.
  Contents: The shoes of the fisherman—The clowns of god—Lazarus.
  ISBN 0-517-09390-1
  1. Catholic Church—Vatican City—Clergy—Fiction. 2. Vatican City
—Fiction. I. Title. II. Title: 3 complete novels.
PR9619.3.W4A6   1993
823—dc20   93-17740
                                                         CIP

8 7 6 5 4 3 2 1

CONTENTS

THE SHOES
OF THE
FISHERMAN

For
Christopher, Paul
and Melanie

AUTHOR'S NOTE

Rome is a city older than the Catholic Church. Everything that could happen has happened there, and no doubt will happen again. This is a book set in a fictional time, peopled with fictional characters, and no reference is intended to any living person, whether in the Church or out of it.

I cannot ask my friends to accept the responsibility for my opinions. So those who have helped me with this book must remain anonymous.

To those who gave me their stories, to those who placed their learning at my disposal, to those who spent upon me the charity of the Faith I offer my heartfelt thanks.

Thanks are due also to Penguin Books, Ltd., for permission to reprint three extracts from the Philip Vellacott translations of Euripides (*Alcestis, Iphigenia in Tauris, Hippolytus*).

Also to Reverend Father Pedro A. Gonzalez, O.P., for a passage from his thesis on Miguel de Unamuno, which is incorporated without quotes in the body of the text.

M.L.W.

I

THE Pope was dead. The Camerlengo had announced it. The Master of Ceremonies, the notaries, the doctors, had consigned him under signature into eternity. His ring was defaced and his seals were broken. The bells had been rung throughout the city. The pontifical body had been handed to the embalmers so that it might be a seemly object for the veneration of the faithful. Now it lay, between white candles, in the Sistine Chapel, with the Noble Guard keeping a deathwatch under Michelangelo's frescoes of the *Last Judgment*.

The Pope was dead. Tomorrow the clergy of the Basilica would claim him and expose him to the public in the Chapel of the Most Holy Sacrament. On the third day they would bury him, clothed in full pontificals, with a mitre on his head, a purple veil on his face, and a red ermine blanket to warm him in the crypt. The medals he had struck and coinage he had minted would be buried with him to identify him to any who might dig him up a thousand years later. They would seal him in three coffins—one of cypress; one of lead to keep him from the damp and to carry his coat of arms, and the certificate of his death; the last of elm so that he might seem, at least, like other men who go to the grave in a wooden box.

The Pope was dead. So they would pray for him as for any other: "Enter not into judgment with thy servant, O Lord . . . Deliver him from eternal death." Then they would lower him into the vault under the high altar, where perhaps —but only perhaps—he would moulder into dust with the dust of Peter; and a mason would brick up the vault and fix, on a marble tablet with his name, his title and the date of his birth and his obit.

The Pope was dead. They would mourn him with nine days of Masses and give him nine absolutions—of which, having been greater in his life than other men, he might have greater need after his death.

Then they would forget him, because the See of Peter was vacant, the life of the Church was in syncope, and the Almighty was without a Vicar on this troubled planet.

The See of Peter was vacant. So the Cardinals of the Sacred College assumed trusteeship over the authority of the Fisherman, though they lacked the power to exercise it. The power did not reside in them but in Christ, and none could assume it but by lawful transmission and election.

The See of Peter was vacant. So they struck two medals, one for the Camerlengo, which bore a large umbrella over crossed keys. There was no one under the umbrella, and this was a sign to the most ignorant that there was no incumbent for the Chair of the Apostles, and that all that was done had only an interim character. The second medal was that of the Governor of the Conclave: he who must assemble the Cardinals of the Church and lock them inside the chambers of the conclave and keep them there until they had issued with a new Pope.

Every coin new-minted in the Vatican City, every stamp now issued, bore the words *sede vacante,* which even those without Latinity might understand as "while the Chair is vacant." The Vatican newspaper carried the same sign on its front page, and would wear a black band of mourning until the new Pontiff was named.

Every news service in the world had a representative camped on the doorstep of the Vatican press office; and from each point of the compass old men came, bent with years or infirmity, to put on the scarlet of princes and sit in conclave for the making of a new Pope.

There was Carlin the American, and Rahamani the Syrian, and Hsien the Chinese, and Hanna the Irishman from Australia. There was Councha from Brazil, and da Costa from Portugal. There was Morand from Paris, and Lavigne from Brussels, and Lambertini from Venice, and Brandon from the City of London. There were a Pole and two Germans, and a Ukrainian whom nobody knew because his name had been reserved in the breast of the last Pope and had been proclaimed only a few days before his death. In all there were eighty-five men, of whom the eldest was ninety-two and the youngest, the Ukrainian, was fifty. As each of them arrived in the city, he presented himself and his credentials to the urbane and gentle Valerio Rinaldi, who was the Cardinal Camerlengo.

Rinaldi welcomed each with a slim, dry hand and a smile of mild irony. To each he administered the oath of the conclavist: that he understood and would rigorously observe all the rules of the election as laid down in the Apostolic Constitution of 1945, that he would under pain of a reserved excommunication preserve the secret of the election, that he would not serve by his votes the interest of any secular power, that if he were elected Pope he would not surrender any temporal right of the Holy See which might be deemed necessary to its independence.

No one refused the oath; but Rinaldi, who had a sense of humor, wondered many times why it was necessary to administer it at all—unless the Church had a healthy disrespect for the virtues of its princes. Old men were apt to be too easily wounded. So when he outlined the terms of the oath, Valerio Rinaldi laid a mild emphasis on the counsel of the Apostolic Constitution, that all the proceedings of the election should be conducted with "prudence, charity, and a singular calm."

His caution was not unjustified. The history of papal elections was a stormy one, at times downright turbulent. When Damasus the Spaniard was elected in the fourth century, there were massacres in the churches of the city. Leo V was imprisoned, tortured, and murdered by the Theophylacts, so that for nearly a century the Church was ruled by puppets directed by the Theophylact women, Theodora and Marozia. In the conclave of 1623 eight Cardinals and forty of their assistants died of malaria, and there were harsh scenes and rough words over the election of the Saint, Pius X.

All in all, Rinaldi concluded—though he was wise enough to keep the conclusion to himself—it was best not to trust too much to the crusty tempers and the frustrated vanities of old men. Which brought him by a round turn to the problem of housing and feeding eighty-five of them with their servants and assistants until the election should be finished. Some of them, it seemed, would have to take over quarters from the Swiss Guard. None of them could be lodged too far from bathroom or toilet, and all had to be provided with a minimum service by way of cooks, barbers, surgeons, physicians, valets, porters, secretaries, waiters, carpenters, plumbers, firemen (in case any weary prelate nodded off with a cigar in his hand!). If (God forbid!) any Cardinal were in prison or under indictment, he would have to be brought to the conclave and made to perform his functions under military guard.

This time, however, no one was in prison—except Krizanic, in Yugoslavia, and he was in prison for the Faith, which was a different matter—and the late Pope had run an efficient administration, so that Valerio Cardinal Rinaldi even had time to spare to meet with his colleague, Leone of the Holy Office, who was also the Dean of the Sacred College. Leone lived up to his name. He had a white lion's mane and a growling temper. He was, moreover, a Roman, bred-in-the-bone, dyed-in-the-wool. Rome was for him the center of the world, and centralism was a doctrine almost as immutable as that of the Trinity and the Procession of the Holy Ghost. With his great eagle beak and his jowly jaw, he looked like a senator strayed out of Augustan times, and his pale eyes looked out on the world with wintry disapproval.

Innovation was for him the first step toward heresy, and he sat in the Holy Office like a grizzled watchdog, whose hackles would rise at the first unfamiliar sound in doctrine interpretation or practice. One of his French colleagues had said, with more wit than charity, "Leone smells of the fire." But the general belief was that he would plunge his own hand into the flame rather than set his signature to the smallest deviation from orthodoxy.

Rinaldi respected him, though he had never been able to like him, and so their intercourse had been limited to the courtesies of their common trade. Tonight, however, the old lion seemed in gentler mood, and was disposed to be talkative. His pale, watchful eyes were lit with a momentary amusement.

"I'm eighty-two, my friend, and I've buried three Popes. I'm beginning to feel lonely."

"If we don't get a younger man this time," said Rinaldi mildly, "you may well bury a fourth."

Leone shot him a quick look from under his shaggy brows. "And what's that supposed to mean?"

Rinaldi shrugged and spread his fine hands in a Roman gesture. "Just what it says. We're all too old. There are not more than half a dozen of us who can give the Church what it needs at this moment: personality, a decisive policy, time and continuity to make the policy work."

"Do you think you're one of the half dozen?"

Rinaldi smiled with thin irony. "I know I'm not. When the new man is chosen —whoever he is—I propose to offer him my resignation and ask his permission to rusticate at home. It's taken me fifteen years to build a garden in that place of mine. I'd like a little while to enjoy it."

"Do you think I have a chance of election?" asked Leone bluntly.

"I hope not," said Rinaldi.

Leone threw back his great mane and laughed. "Don't worry. I know I haven't. They need someone quite different; someone"—he hesitated, fumbling for the phrase—"someone who has compassion on the multitude, who sees them, as Christ saw them—sheep without a shepherd. I'm not that sort of man. I wish I were."

Leone heaved his bulky body out of the chair and walked to the big table, where an antique globe stood among a litter of books. He spun the globe slowly on its axis, so that now one country, now another, swam into the light. "Look at it, my friend! The world, our vineyard! Once we colonized it in the name of Christ. Not righteously always, not always justly or wisely, but the Cross was there, and the Sacraments were there, and however a man lived—in purple or in chains—there was a chance for him to die like a son of God. Now . . . ? Now we are everywhere in retreat. China is lost to us, and Asia and all the Russians. Africa will soon be gone, and the South Americas will be next. You know it. I know it. It is the measure of our failure that we have sat all these years in Rome and watched it happen." He checked the spinning globe with an unsteady hand, and then turned to face his visitor with a new question. "If you had your life over, Rinaldi, what would you do with it?"

Rinaldi looked up with that deprecating smile which lent him so much charm. "I think I should probably do the same things again. Not that I'm very proud of them, but they happened to be the only things I could do well. I get along with people because I've never been capable of very deep feelings about them. That makes me, I suppose, a natural diplomat. I don't like to quarrel. I like even less to be emotionally involved. I like privacy and I enjoy study. So I'm a good canonist, a reasonable historian, and an adequate linguist. I've never had very strong passions. You might, if you felt malicious, call me a cold fish. So I've achieved a reputation for good conduct without having to work for it. . . . All in all, I've had a very satisfactory life—satisfactory to myself, of course. How the recording angel sees it is another matter."

"Don't underrate yourself, man," said Leone sourly. "You've done a great deal better than you'll admit."

"I need time and reflection to set my soul in order," said Rinaldi quietly. "May I count on you to help me resign?"

"Of course."

"Thank you. Now, suppose the inquisitor answers his own question. What would you do if you had to begin again?"

"I've thought about it often," said Leone heavily. "If I didn't marry—and I'm not sure but that's what I needed to make me halfway human—I'd be a country priest with just enough theology to hear confession, and just enough Latin to get through Mass and the sacramental formulae. But with heart enough to know what griped in the guts of other men and made them cry into their pillows at night. I'd sit in front of my church on a summer evening and read my office and talk about the weather and the crops, and learn to be gentle with the poor and humble with the unhappy ones. . . . You know what I am now? A walking encyclopaedia of dogma and theological controversy. I can smell out an error faster than a Dominican. And what does it mean? Nothing. Who cares about theology except the theologians? We are necessary, but less important than we think. The Church is Christ—Christ and the people. And all the people want to know is whether or no there is a God, and what is His relation with them, and how they can get back to Him when they stray."

"Large questions," said Rinaldi gently, "not to be answered by small minds or gross ones."

Leone shook his lion's mane stubbornly. "For the people they come down to simplicities! Why shouldn't I covet my neighbor's wife? Who takes the revenge that is forbidden to me? And who cares when I am sick and tired, and dying in an upstairs room? I can give them a theologian's answer. But whom do they believe but the man who feels the answers in his heart and bears the scars of their consequences in his own flesh? Where are the men like that? Is there one among all of us who wear the red hat? Eh . . . !" His grim mouth twitched into a grin of embarrassment, and he flung out his arms in mock despair. "We are what we are, and God has to take half the responsibility even for theologians! . . . Now tell me—where do we go for our Pope?"

"This time," said Rinaldi crisply, "we should choose him for the people and not for ourselves."

"There will be eighty-five of us in the conclave. How many will agree on what is best for the people?"

Rinaldi looked down at the backs of his carefully manicured fingers. He said softly, "If we showed them the man first, perhaps we could get them to agree."

Leone's answer was swift and emphatic. "You would have to show him to me first."

"And if you agreed?"

"Then there would be another question," said Leone flatly. "How many of our brethren will think as we do?"

The question was subtler than it looked, and they both knew it. Here, in fact, was the whole loaded issue of a papal election, the whole paradox of the Papacy. The man who wore the Fisherman's ring was Vicar of Christ, Vicegerent of the Almighty. His dominion was spiritual and universal. He was the servant of all the servants of God, even of those who did not acknowledge him.

On the other hand, he was Bishop of Rome, Metropolitan of an Italian see. The Romans claimed by historic tradition a pre-emption on his presence and his services. They relied on him for employment, for the tourist trade and the bolstering of their economy by Vatican investment, for the preservation of their historic monuments and national privileges. His court was Italian in character; the greater number of his household and his administrators were Italian. If he could not deal with them familiarly in their own tongue, he stood naked to palace intrigue and every kind of partisan interest.

Once upon a time the Roman view had had a peculiarly universal aspect. The numen of the ancient empire still hung about it, and the memory of the Pax Romana had not yet vanished from the consciousness of Europe. But the numen was fading. Imperial Rome had never subdued Russia or Asia, and the Latins who conquered South America had brought no peace, but the sword. England had revolted long since, as she had revolted earlier from the legions of Roman occupation. So that there was sound argument for a new, non-Italian succession to the papal throne—just as there was sound reason for believing that a non-Italian might become either a puppet of his ministers or a victim of their talent for intrigue.

The perpetuity of the Church was an article of faith; but its diminutions and corruptions, and its jeopardy by the follies of its members, were part of the canon of history. There was plenty of ground for cynicism. But over and over again the cynics were confounded by the uncanny capacity for self-renewal in the Church and in the Papacy. The cynics had their own explanations. The faithful put it down to the indwelling of the Holy Ghost. Either way there was an uncomfortable mystery: how the chaos of history could issue in so consistent a hold on dogma or why an omniscient God chose such a messy method of preserving his foothold in the minds of his creatures.

So every conclave began with the invocation of the Paraclete. On the day of the walling-in Rinaldi led his old men and their attendants into St. Peter's. Then Leone came, dressed in a scarlet chasuble and accompanied by his deacons and subdeacons, to begin the Mass of the Holy Spirit. As he watched the celebrant, weighed down by the elaborate vestments, moving painfully through the ritual of the Sacrifice, Rinaldi felt a pang of pity for him and a sudden rush of understanding.

They were all in the same galley, these leaders of the Church—himself along with them. They were men without issue, who had "made themselves eunuchs for the love of God." A long time since they had dedicated themselves with greater or less sincerity to the service of a hidden God, and to the propagation of an unprovable mystery. Through the temporality of the Church they had attained to honor—more honor, perhaps, than any of them might have attained in the secular state; but they all lay under the common burden of age—failing faculties, the loneliness of eminence, and the fear of a reckoning that might find them bankrupt debtors.

He thought, too, of the stratagem which he had planned with Leone, to introduce a candidate who was still a stranger to most of the voters, and to promote his cause without breaching the Apostolic Constitution, which they had sworn to preserve. He wondered if this were not a presumption and an attempt to circumvent Providence, whom they were invoking at this very moment. Yet if God had chosen, as the Faith taught, to use man as a free instrument for a divine plan, how else could one act? One could not let so momentous an occasion as a papal election play itself like a game of chance. Prudence was enjoined on all—prayful preparation and then considered action, and afterward resignation and submission. Yet however prudently one planned, one could not escape the uncanny feeling that one walked unwary and unpurged on sacred ground.

The heat, the flicker of the candles, the chant of the choir, and the mesmeric pace of the ritual made him drowsy, and he stole a surreptitious glance at his colleagues to see if any of them had noticed his nodding.

Like twin choirs of ancient archangels they sat on either side of the sanctuary, their breasts hung with golden crosses, the princely seals agleam on their folded hands, their faces scored by age and the experience of power.

There was Rahamani of Antioch, with his spade beard and his craggy brows and his bright, half-mystical eyes. There was Benedetti, round as a dumpling, with pink cheeks and candy-floss hair, who ran the Vatican bank. Next to him was Potocki from Poland, he of the high, bald dome and the suffering mouth and the wise, calculating eyes. Tatsue from Japan wanted only the saffron robe to make him a Buddhist image, and Hsien, the exiled Chinese, sat between Ragambwe, the black man from Kenya, and Pallenberg, the lean ascetic from Munich.

Rinaldi's shrewd eyes ranged along the choir stalls, naming each one for his virtues or his shortcomings, trying on each the classic label *papabile,* he-who-has-the-makings-of-a-Pope. In theory every member of the conclave could wear it; in practice very few were eligible.

Age was a bar to some. Talent or temperament or reputation was an impediment to others. Nationality was a vital question. One could not elect an American without seeming to divide East and West even further. A Negro Pope might seem a spectacular symbol of the new revolutionary nations, just as a Japanese might be a useful link between Asia and Europe. But the Princes of the Church were old men and as wary of spectacular gestures as they were of historic hangovers. A German Pope might alienate the sympathies of those who had suffered in World War II. A Frenchman would recall old memories of Avignon and tramontane rebellions. While there were still dictatorships in Spain and Portugal, an Iberian Pope could be a diplomatic indiscretion. Gonfalone, the Milanese, had the reputation of being a saint, but he was becoming more and more of a recluse, and there was question of his fitness for so public an office. Leone was an autocrat who might well mistake the fire of zealotry for the flame of compassion.

The lector was reading from the Acts of the Apostles. " 'In those days, Peter began and said, Men, Brethren, the Lord charged us to preach to the people and to testify that He is the one who has been appointed by God to be judge of the living and of the dead. . . .' " The choir sang, *"Veni, Sancte Spiritus . . .* Come, Holy Spirit, and fill the hearts of the faithful." Then Leone began to read in his strong stubborn voice the Gospel for the day of the conclave: " 'He who enters not by the door into the sheepfold, but climbs up another way is a thief and a robber. But he who enters by the door is the shepherd of the sheep.' " Rinaldi bent his head in his hands and prayed that the man he was offering would be in truth a shepherd, and that the conclave might hand him the crook and the ring.

When the Mass was over, the celebrant retired to the sacristy to take off his vestments and the Cardinals relaxed in the stalls. Some of them whispered to one another, a couple were still nodding drowsily, and one was seen to take a surreptitious pinch of snuff. The next part of the ceremony was a formality, but it promised to be a boring one. A prelate would read them a homily in Latin, pointing out once again the importance of the election and their moral obligation to carry it out in an orderly and honest fashion. By ancient custom, the prelate was chosen for the purity of his Latin, but this time the Camerlengo had made another arrangement.

A whisper of surprise stirred round the assembly as they saw Rinaldi leave his place and walk down to the far end of the stalls on the Gospel side of the altar. He offered his hand to a tall, thin Cardinal and led him to the pulpit. When he stood elevated in the full glare of the lights, they saw that he was the youngest of them all. His hair was black, his square beard was black, too, and down his left cheek was a long, livid scar. On his breast, in addition to the cross, was a pectoral ikon representing a Byzantine Madonna and Child. When he crossed himself, he made the sign from right to left, in the Slavic manner; yet when he began to speak, it was not in Latin but in a pure and melodious Tuscan. Across the nave Leone smiled a grim approval at Rinaldi, and then like their colleagues, they surrendered themselves to the simple eloquence of the stranger:

"My name is Kiril Lakota, and I am come the latest and the least into this Sacred College. I speak to you today by the invitation of our brother the Cardinal Camerlengo. To most of you I am a stranger because my people are scattered and I have spent the last seventeen years in prison. If I have any rights among you, any credit at all, let this be the foundation of them—that I speak for the lost ones, for those who walk in darkness and in the valley of the shadow of death. It is for them and not for ourselves that we are entering into conclave. It is for them and not for ourselves that we must elect a Pontiff. The first man who held this office was one who walked with Christ, and was crucified like the Master. Those who have best served the Church and the faithful are those who have been closest to Christ and to the people, who are the image of Christ. We have power in our hands, my brothers. We shall put even greater power into the hands of the man we elect, but we must use the power as servants and not as masters. We must consider that we are what we are— priests, bishops, pastors—by virtue of an act of dedication to the people who are the flock of Christ. What we possess, even to the clothes on our backs, comes to us out of their charity. The whole material fabric of the Church was raised stone on stone, gold on golden offering, by the sweat of the faithful, and they have given it into our hands for stewardship. It is they who have educated us so that we may teach them and their children. It is they who humble themselves before our priesthood, as before the divine Priesthood of Christ. It is for them that we exercise the sacramental and the sacrificial powers which are given to us in the anointing and the laying on of hands. If in our deliberations we serve any other cause but this, then we are traitors. It is not asked of us that we shall agree on what is best for the Church, but only that we shall deliberate in charity and humility, and in the end give our obedience to the man who shall be chosen by the majority. We are asked to act swiftly so that the Church may not be left without a head. In all this we must be what, in the end, our Pontiff shall proclaim himself to be—servants of the servants of God. Let us in these final moments resign ourselves as willing instruments for His hands. Amen."

It was so simply said that it might have been the customary formality, yet the man himself, with his scarred face and his strong voice and his crooked, eloquent hands, lent to the words an unexpected poignancy. There was a long silence while he left the pulpit and returned to his own place. Leone nodded his lion's head in approval, and Rinaldi breathed a silent prayer of gratitude. Then the Master of Ceremonies took command and led the Cardinals and their attendants with their confessor and their physician and surgeon, and the Architect of the Conclave, and the conclave workmen, out of the Basilica and into the confines of the Vatican itself.

In the Sistine Chapel they were sworn again. Then Leone gave the order for the bells to be rung, so that all who did not belong to the conclave should leave the sealed area at once. The servants led each of the Cardinals to his apartment. Then the prefect of the Master of Ceremonies, with the Architect of the Conclave, began the ritual search of the enclosed area. They went from room to room pulling aside draperies, throwing light into dark corners, opening closets, until every space was declared free from intruders.

At the entrance of the great stairway of Pius IX they halted and the Noble Guard marched out of the conclave area, followed by the Marshal of the Conclave and his aides. The great door was locked. The Marshal of the Conclave turned his key on the outside. On the inside the Masters of Ceremonies turned their own key. The Marshal ordered his flag hoisted over the Vatican, and from this moment no one might leave or enter, or pass a message, until the new Pope was elected and named.

Alone in his quarters, Kiril Cardinal Lakota was beginning a private purgatory. It was a recurrent state whose symptoms were now familiar to him: a cold sweat that broke out on face and palms, a trembling in the limbs, a twitching of the severed nerves in his face, a panic fear that the room was closing in to crush him. Twice in his life he had been walled up in the bunkers of an underground prison. Four months in all, he had endured the terrors of darkness and cold and solitude and near starvation, so that the pillars of his reason had rocked under the strain. Nothing in his years of Siberian exile had afflicted him so much nor left so deep a scar on his memory. Nothing had brought him so close to abjuration and apostasy.

He had been beaten often, but the bruised tissue had healed itself in time. He had been interrogated till every nerve was screaming and his mind had lapsed into a merciful confusion. From this, too, he had emerged, stronger in faith and in reason, but the horror of solitary confinement would remain with him until he died. Kamenev had kept his promise. "You will never be able to forget me. Wherever you go, I shall be. Whatever you become, I shall be part of you." Even here, in the neutral confines of Vatican City, in the princely room under Raphael's frescoes, Kamenev, the insidious tormentor, was with him. There was only one escape from him, and that was the one he had learned in the bunker—the projection of the tormented spirit into the arms of the Almighty.

He threw himself on his knees, buried his face in his hands, and tried to concentrate every faculty of mind and body into the simple act of abandonment.

His lips commanded no words, but the will seized on the plaint of Christ in Gethsemane. " 'Father, if it be possible, let this Chalice pass.' "

In the end he knew it would pass, but first the agony must be endured. The walls pressed in upon him relentlessly. The ceiling weighed down on him like a leaden vestment. The darkness pressed upon his eyeballs and packed itself inside his skull case. Every muscle in his body knotted in pain, and his teeth chattered as if from the rigors of fever. Then he became deathly cold, and deathly calm, and waited passively for the light that was the beginning of peace and of communion.

The light was like a dawn seen from a high hill, flooding swiftly into every fold of the landscape, so that the whole pattern of its history was revealed at one glance. The road of his own pilgrimage was there like a scarlet ribbon that stretched four thousand miles from Lvov, in the Ukraine, to Nikolayevsk, on the Sea of Okhotsk.

When the war with the Germans was over, he had been named, in spite of his youth, Metropolitan of Lvov, successor to the great and saintly Andrew Szepticky, leader of all the Ruthenian Catholics. Shortly afterwards he had been arrested with six other bishops and deported to the eastern limits of Siberia. The six others had died, and he had been left alone, shepherd of a lost flock, to carry the Cross on his own shoulders.

For seventeen years he had been in prison, or in the labor camps. Once only in all that time he had been able to say Mass, with a thimbleful of wine and a crust of white bread. All that he could cling to of doctrine and prayer and sacramental formulae was locked in his own brain. All that he had tried to spend of strength and compassion upon his fellow prisoners he had had to dredge out of himself and out of the well of the Divine Mercy. Yet his body, weakened by torture, had grown miraculously strong again at slave labor in the mines and on the road gangs, so that even Kamenev could no longer mock him, but was struck with wonder at his survival.

For Kamenev, his tormentor in the first interrogations, would always come back; and each time he came he had risen a little higher in the Marxist order. Each time, he had seemed a little more friendly, as if he were making a slow surrender to respect for his victim.

Even from the mountaintop of contemplation he could still see Kamenev— cold, sardonic, searching him for the slightest sign of weakness, the slightest hint of surrender. In the beginning he had had to force himself to pray for the jailer. After a while they had come to a bleak kind of brotherhood, even as the one rose higher and the other seemed to sink deeper into a fellowship with the Siberian slaves. In the end it was Kamenev who had organized his escape— inflicting on him a final irony by giving him the identity of a dead man.

"You will go free," Kamenev had said, "because I need you free. But you will always owe me a debt because I have killed a man to give you a name. One day I shall come to you to ask for payment, and you will pay, whatever it may cost."

It was as though the jailer had assumed the mantle of prophecy, because Kiril Lakota had escaped and made his way to Rome, to find that a dying Pope had made him a Cardinal "in the breast"—a man of destiny, a hinge-man of Mother Church.

To this point the road in retrospect was clear. He could trace in its tragedies the promise of future mercies. For every one of the bishops who had died for his belief, a man had died in his arms in the camp, blessing the Almighty for a final absolution. The scattered flock would not all lose the faith for which they had suffered. Some of them would remain to hand on the creed, and to keep a small light burning that one day might light a thousand torches. In the degradation of the road gangs he had seen how the strangest men upheld the human dignities. He had baptized children with a handful of dirty water and seen them die unmarked by the miseries of the world.

He himself had learned humility and gratitude and the courage to believe in an Omnipotence working by a mighty evolution toward an ultimate good. He had learned compassion and tenderness and the meaning of the cry in the night. He had learned to hope that for Kamenev himself he might be an instrument, if not of ultimate enlightenment, then at least of ultimate absolution. But all this was in the past, and the pattern still had to work itself out beyond Rome into a fathomless future. Even the light of contemplation was not thrown beyond Rome. There was a veil drawn, and the veil was the limit imposed on prescience by a merciful God. . . .

The light was changing now; the landscape of the steppes had become an undulant sea, across which a figure in antique robes was walking toward him, his face shining, his pierced hands outstretched, as if in greeting. Kiril Cardinal Lakota shrank away and tried to bury himself in the lighted sea, but there was no escape. When the hands touched him and the luminous face bent to embrace him, he felt himself pierced by an intolerable joy, and an intolerable pain. Then he entered into the moment of peace.

The servant who was assigned to care for him came into the room and saw him kneeling rigid as a cataleptic, with his arms outstretched in the attitude of crucifixion. Rinaldi, making the rounds of the conclavists, came upon him and tried vainly to wake him. Then Rinaldi, too, went away, shaken and humbled, to consult with Leone and with his colleagues.

In his cluttered and unelegant office George Faber, the gray-haired dean of the Roman press corps, fifteen years Italian correspondent for the New York *Monitor,* was writing his background story on the papal election:

". . . Outside the small medieval enclave of the Vatican, the world is in a climate of crisis. Winds of change are blowing and storm warnings are being raised, now in one place, now in another. The arms race between America and Russia goes on, unabated. Every month there are new and hostile probes into the high orbits of space. There is famine in India, and guerrilla fighting along the southern peninsulas of Asia. There is thunder over Africa, and the tattered flags of revolution are being hoisted over the capitals of South America. There is blood on the sands in North Africa, and in Europe the battle for economic survival is waged behind the closed doors of banks and board rooms. In the high airs above the Pacific, war planes fly to sample the pollution of the air by lethal atomic particles. In China the new dynasts struggle to fill the bellies of hungry millions while they hold their minds chained to the rigid orthodoxy of Marxist philosophy. In the misty valleys of the Himalayas, where the prayer flags flutter and the teapickers plod along the terraces, there are forays and incursions from Tibet and Sinkiang. On the frontiers of Outer Mongolia the uneasy amity of Russia and China is strained to the point of rupture. Patrol boats probe the mangrove swamps and inlets of New Guinea while the upland tribes try to project themselves into the twentieth century by a single leap from the Stone Age.

"Everywhere man has become aware of himself as a transient animal and is battling desperately to assert his right to the best of the world for the short time that he sojourns in it. The Nepalese haunted by his mountain demons, the coolie hauling his heart muscle into exhaustion between the shafts of a rickshaw, the Israeli beleaguered at every frontier, everyone all at once is asserting his claim to an identity; everyone has an ear for any prophet who can promise him one."

He stopped typing, lit a cigarette, and leaned back in his chair, considering the thought which he had just written—"a claim to identity." Strange how everyone had to make it sooner or later. Strange for how long one accepted with apparent equanimity the kind of person one seemed to be, the state to which one had apparently been nominated in life. Then all of a sudden the identity was called in question. . . . His own, for instance. George Faber, long-time bachelor, acknowledged expert on Italian affairs and Vatican politics . . . Why so late in life was he being forced to question what he was, what he had so far been content to be? Why this restless dissatisfaction with the public image of himself? Why this doubt that he could survive any longer without a permanent supplement to himself? . . . A woman, of course. There always had been women in his life, but Chiara was something new and special. . . . The thought troubled him. He tried to put it away and bent again to his typewriter.

"Everywhere the cry is for survival, but since the supreme irony of creation is that man must inevitably die, those who strive for the mastery of his mind or his muscle have to promise him an extension of his span into some semblance of immortality. The Marxist promises him a oneness with the workers of the world. The nationalist gives him a flag and a frontier, and a local enlargement of himself. The democrat offers him liberty through a ballot box, but warns that he may have to die to preserve it.

"But for man, and all the prophets he raises up for himself, the last enemy is time; and time is a relative dimension, limited directly by man's capacity to make use of it. Modern communication, swift as light, has diminished to nothing the time between a human act and its consequences. A shot fired in Berlin can detonate the world within minutes. A plague in the Philippines can infect Australia within a day. A man toppling from a high wire in a Moscow circus can be watched in his death agony from London and New York.

"So at every moment every man is besieged by the consequences of his own sins and those of all his fellows. So, too, every prophet and every pundit is haunted by the swift lapse of time and the knowledge that the accounting for false predictions and broken promises is swifter than it has ever been in history. Here precisely is the cause of the crisis. Here the winds and the waves are born and the thunderbolts are forged that may, any week, any month, go roaring round the world under a sky black with mushroom clouds.

"The men in the Vatican are aware of time, though many of them have ceased to be as aware as they need to be. . . ."

Time . . . ! He had become so vividly conscious of this diminishing dimension of existence. He was in his mid-forties. For more than a year he had been trying to steer Chiara's petition of nullity through the Holy Roman Rota so that she might be free from Corrado Calitri to marry him. But the case was moving with desperate slowness, and Faber, although a Catholic by birth, had come to resent bitterly the impersonal system of the Roman Congregations and the attitude of the old men who ran them.

He typed on vividly, precisely, professionally:

"Like most old men, they are accustomed to seeing time as a flash between two eternities instead of a quantum of extension given to each individual man to mature toward the vision of his God.

"They are concerned also with man's identity, which they are obliged to affirm as the identity of a son of God. Yet here they are in danger of another pitfall: that they sometimes affirm his identity without understanding his individuality, and how he has to grow in whatever garden he is planted, whether the ground is sweet or sour, whether the air is friendly or tempestuous. Men grow, like trees, in different shapes, crooked or straight, according to the climate of their nurture. But so long as the sap flows and the leaves burgeon, there should be no quarrel with the shape of the man or the tree.

"The men of the Vatican are concerned as well with immortality and eternity. They, too, understand man's need for an extension of himself beyond the limit of the fleeting years. They affirm, as of faith, the persistence of soul into an eternity of union with the Creator, or of exile from His face. They go further. They promise man a preservation of his identity and an ultimate victory even over the terror of physical death. What they fail too often to understand is that immortality must be begun in time, and that a man must be given the physical resources to survive before his spirit can grow to desire more than physical survival. . . ."

Chiara had become as necessary to him as breath. Without her youth and her passion it seemed that he must slide all too quickly into age and disillusion. She had been his mistress for nearly six months now, but he was plagued by the fear that he could lose her at any moment to a younger man, and that the promise of children and continuity might never be fulfilled in him. . . . He had friends in the Vatican. He had easy access to men with great names in the Church, but they were committed to the law and to the system, and they could not help him at all. He wrote feelingly:

"They are caught, these old and deliberate men, in the paradox of all principality: that the higher one rises, the more one sees of the world, but the less one apprehends of the small determining factors of human existence. How a man without shoes may starve because he cannot walk to a place of employment. How a liverish tax collector may start a local revolution. How high blood pressure may plunge a noble man into melancholy and despair. How a woman may sell herself for money because she cannot give herself to one man for love. The danger of all rulers is that they begin to believe that history is the result of great generalities, instead of the sum of millions of small particulars, like bad drainage and sexual obsession and the anopheles mosquito. . . ."

It was not the story he had intended to write, but it was a true record of his personal feelings about the coming event. . . . Let it stand, then! Let the editors in New York like it or lump it . . . ! The door opened and Chiara came in. He took her in his arms and kissed her. He damned the Church and her husband and his paper to a special kind of hell, and then took her out to lunch on the Via Veneto.

The first day of the conclave was left private to the electing Cardinals, so that they might meet and talk discreetly, and probe for one another's prejudices and blind spots and motives of private interest. It was for this reason that Rinaldi and Leone moved among them to prepare them carefully for the final proposal. Once the voting began, once they had taken sides with this candidate or that, it would be much more difficult to bring them to an agreement.

Not all the talk was on the level of eternal verities. Much of it was simple and blunt, like Rinaldi's conversation with the American over a cup of American coffee (brewed by His Eminence's own servant because Italian coffee gave him indigestion).

His Eminence, Charles Corbet Carlin, Cardinal Archbishop of New York, was a tall, ruddy man with an expansive manner and a shrewd, pragmatic eye. He stated his problem as baldly as a banker challenging an overdraft:

"We don't want a diplomat, and we don't want a Curia official who will look at the world through a Roman eyeglass. A man who has traveled, yes, but someone who has been a pastor and understands what our problems are at this moment."

"I should be interested to hear your Eminence define them." Rinaldi was at his most urbane.

"We're losing our grip on the people," said Carlin flatly. "They are losing their loyalty to us. I think we are more than half to blame."

Rinaldi was startled. Carlin had the reputation of being a brilliant banker for Mother Church and of entertaining a conviction that all the ills of the world could be solved by a well-endowed school system and a rousing sermon every Sunday. To hear him talk so bluntly of the shortcomings of his own province was both refreshing and disquieting. Rinaldi asked:

"Why are we losing our grip?"

"In America? Two reasons: prosperity and respectability. We're not persecuted any more. We pay our way. We can wear the Faith like a Rotary badge—and with as little social consequence. We collect our dues like a club, shout down the Communists, and make the biggest contribution in the whole world to Peter's Pence. But it isn't enough. There's no—no heart in it for many Catholics. The young ones are drifting outside our influence. They don't need us as they should. They don't trust us as they used. For that," he added gravely, "I think I'm partly to blame."

"None of us has much right to be proud of himself," said Rinaldi quietly. "Look at France—look at the bloody things that have been done in Algeria. Yet this is a country half Catholic, and with a Catholic leadership. Where is our authority in this monstrous situation? A third of the Catholic population of the world is in the South Americas, yet what is our influence there? What impression do we make among the indifferent rich, and the oppressed poor, who see no hope in God and less in those who represent Him? Where do we begin to change?"

"I've made mistakes," said Carlin moodily. "Big ones. I can't even begin to repair them all. My father was a gardener, a good one. He used to say that the best you could do for a tree was mulch it and prune it once a year, and leave the rest to God. I always prided myself that I was a practical fellow, just as he was —you know? Build the church, then the school. Get the nuns in, then the brothers. Build the seminary and train the priests, and keep the money coming in. After that it was up to the Almighty." For the first time he smiled, and Rinaldi, who had disliked him for many years, began to warm to him. He went on whimsically, "The Romans and the Irish! We're great plotters, and great builders, but we lose the inwardness of things quicker than anybody else. Stick to the book! No meat on Fridays, no sleeping with your neighbor's wife, and leave the mysteries to the theologians! It isn't enough. God help us, but it isn't!"

"You're asking for a saint. I doubt we have many on the books just now."

"Not a saint." Carlin was emphatic again. "A man for the people, and of the people, as Sarto was. A man who could bleed for them, and scold them, and have them know all the time that he loved them. A man who could break out of this gilded garden patch and make himself another Peter."

"He would be crucified, too, of course," said Rinaldi tartly.

"Perhaps that is just what we need," said His Eminence from New York.

Whereupon Rinaldi, the diplomat, judged it opportune to talk of the bearded Ukrainian, Kiril Lakota, as a-man-with-the-makings-of-a-Pope.

In a somewhat smaller suite of the conclave Leone was discussing the same candidate with Hugh Cardinal Brandon from Westminster. Brandon, being English, was a man with no illusions and few enthusiasms. He pursed his thin gray lips and toyed with his pectoral cross, and delivered his policy in precise, if stilted, Italian:

"From our point of view, an Italian is still the best choice. It leaves us room to move, if you understand what I mean. There is no question of a new attitude or a fresh political alignment. There is no disturbance of the relations between the Vatican and the Republic of Italy. The Papacy would still be an effective barrier to any growth of Italian communism." He permitted himself a dry joke. "We could still count on the sympathy of English romantics for romantic Italy."

Leone, veteran of many a subtle argument, nodded his agreement and added almost casually, "You would not then consider our newcomer, the one who spoke to us this morning?"

"I doubt it. I found him, as everyone did, most impressive in the pulpit. But then eloquence is hardly a full qualification, is it? Besides, there is the question of rites. I understand this man is a Ukrainian and belongs to the Ruthenian rite."

"If he were elected, he would automatically practice the Roman one."

His Eminence of Westminster smiled thinly. "The beard might worry some people. A too Byzantine look, don't you think? We haven't had a bearded Pope in a very long time."

"No doubt he would shave it."

"Would he still wear the ikon?"

"He might be persuaded to dispense with that, too."

"Then we should be left with a model Roman. So why not choose an Italian in the first place? I can't believe you would want anything different."

"Believe me, I do. I am prepared to tell you now that my vote will go to the Ukrainian."

"I am afraid I can't promise you mine. The English and the Russians, you know. . . . Historically we've never done very well together. . . . Never at all."

"Always," said Rahamani the Syrian in his pliant, courteous fashion, "always you search a man for the one necessary gift—the gift of co-operation with God. Even among good men this gift is rare. Most of us, you see, spend our lives trying to bend ourselves to the will of God, and even then we have often to be bent by a violent grace. The others, the rare ones, commit themselves, as if by an instinctive act, to be tools in the hands of the Maker. If this new man is such a one, then it is he whom we need."

"And how do we know?" asked Leone dryly.

"We submit him to God," said the Syrian. "We ask God to judge him, and we rest secure in the outcome."

"We can only vote on him. There is no other way."

"There is another way, prescribed in the Apostolic Constitution. It is the way of inspiration. Any member of the conclave may make a public proclamation of the man he believes should be chosen, trusting that if this be a candidate acceptable to God, God will inspire the other conclavists to approve him publicly. It is a valid method of election."

"It also takes courage—and a great deal of faith."

"If we elders of the Church lack faith, what hope is there for the people?"

"I am reproved," said the Cardinal Secretary of the Holy Office. "It's time I stopped canvassing and began to pray."

Early the next morning, all the Cardinals assembled in the Sistine Chapel for the first ballot. For each there was a throne and over the throne a silken canopy. The thrones were arranged along the walls of the Chapel, and before each was set a small table which bore the Cardinal's coat of arms and his name inscribed in Latin. The Chapel altar was covered with a tapestry upon which was embroidered a figuration of the Holy Ghost descending upon the first Apostles. Before the altar was set a large table on which there stood a gold Chalice and a small golden platter. Near the table was a simple potbellied stove whose flue projected through a small window that looked out on the Square of St. Peter.

When the voting took place, each Cardinal would write the name of his candidate upon a ballot paper, lay it first on the golden platter, and then put it into the Chalice, to signify that he had completed a sacred act. After the votes were counted, they would be burned in the stove, and smoke would issue through the flue into the Square of St. Peter. To elect a Pope, there must be a majority of two thirds.

If the majority was not conclusive, the ballot papers would be burned with wet straw, and the smoke would issue dark and cloudy. Only when the ballot was successful would the papers be burned without straw, so that a white smoke might inform the waiting crowds that they had a new Pope. It was an archaic and cumbersome ceremony for the age of radio and television, but it served to underline the drama of the moment and the continuity of two thousand years of papal history.

When all the Cardinals were seated, the Master of Ceremonies made the circuit of the thrones, handing to each voter a single ballot paper. Then he left the Chapel, and the door was locked, leaving only the Princes of the Church to elect the successor to Peter.

It was the moment for which Leone and Rinaldi had waited. Leone rose in his place, tossed his white mane, and addressed the conclave:

"My brothers, I stand to claim a right under the Apostolic Constitution. I proclaim to you my belief that there is among us a man already chosen by God to sit in the Chair of Peter. Like the first of the Apostles, he has suffered prison and stripes for the Faith, and the hand of God has led him out of bondage to join us in this conclave. I announce him as my candidate, and dedicate to him my vote and my obedience. . . . Kiril Cardinal Lakota."

There was a moment of dead silence, broken by a stifled gasp from Lakota. Then Rahamani the Syrian rose in his place and pronounced firmly:

"I, too, proclaim him."

"I, too," said Carlin the American.

"And I," said Valerio Rinaldi.

Then in twos and threes, old men heaved themselves to their feet with a like proclamation until all but nine were standing under the canopies, while Kiril Cardinal Lakota sat, blank-faced and rigid, on his throne.

Then Rinaldi stepped forward and challenged the electors. "Does any here dispute that this is a valid election, and that a majority of more than two thirds has elected our brother Kiril?"

No one answered the challenge.

"Please be seated," said Valerio Rinaldi.

As each Cardinal sat down, he pulled the cord attached to his canopy so that it collapsed above his head, and the only canopy left open was that above the chair of Kiril Cardinal Lakota.

The Camerlengo rang a small hand bell and walked across to unlock the Chapel door. Immediately there entered the Secretary of the Conclave, the Master of Ceremonies, and the Sacristan of the Vatican. These three prelates, with Leone and Rinaldi, moved ceremoniously to the throne of the Ukrainian. In a loud voice Leone challenged him:

"*Acceptasne electionem* [Do you accept election]?"

All eyes were turned on the tall, lean stranger with his scarred face and his dark beard and his distant, haunted eyes. Seconds ticked away slowly, and then they heard him answer in a dead flat voice:

"*Accepto. . . . Miserere mei Deus. . . .* I accept. . . . God have mercy on me!"

Extract from
the Secret Memorials of
KIRIL I, Pont. Max.

No ruler can escape the verdict of history, but a ruler who keeps a diary makes himself liable to a rough handling by the judged. . . . I should hate to be like old Pius II, who had his memoirs attributed to his secretary, had them expurgated by his kinsmen, and then, five hundred years later, had all his indiscretions restored by a pair of American bluestockings. Yet I sympathize with his dilemma, which must be the dilemma of every man who sits in the Chair of Peter. A Pope can never talk freely unless he talks to God or to himself —and a Pontiff who talks to himself is apt to become eccentric, as the histories of some of my predecessors have shown.

It is my infirmity to be afraid of solitude and isolation. So I shall need some safety valves—the diary, for one, which is a compromise between lying to oneself on paper and telling posterity the facts that have to be concealed from one's own generation. There is a rub, of course. What does one do with a papal diary? Leave it to the Vatican library? Order it buried with oneself in the triple coffin? Or auction it beforehand for the Propagation of the Faith? Better, perhaps, not to begin at all; but how else guarantee a vestige of privacy, humor, perhaps even sanity in this noble prison house to which I am condemned?

Twenty-four hours ago my election would have seemed a fantasy. Even now I cannot understand why I accepted it. I could have refused. I did not. Why? . . .

Consider what I am: Kiril I, Bishop of Rome, Vicar of Jesus Christ, Successor of the Prince of the Apostles, Supreme Pontiff of the Universal Church, Patriarch of the West, Primate of Italy, Archbishop and Metropolitan of the Roman Province, Sovereign of the Vatican City State . . . gloriously reigning, of course . . . !

But this is only the beginning of it. The Pontifical Annual will print a list two pages long of what I have reserved by way of abbacies and prefectures, and what I shall "protect" by way of orders, congregations, confraternities and holy sisterhoods. The rest of its two thousand pages will be a veritable Domesday Book of my ministers and subjects, my instruments of government, education, and correction.

I must be, by the very nature of my office, multilingual, though the Holy Ghost has been less generous in the gift of tongues to me than he was to the first man who stood in my shoes. My mother tongue is Russian; my official language is the Latin of the schoolmen, a kind of Mandarin which is supposed to preserve magically the subtlest definition of truth like a bee in amber. I must speak Italian to my associates and converse with all in that high-flown "we" which hints at a secret converse between God and myself, even in such mundane matters as the coffee "we" shall drink for breakfast and the brand of gasoline "we" shall use for Vatican City automobiles.

Still, this is the traditional mode, and I must not resent it too much. Old Valerio Rinaldi gave me fair warning when an hour after this morning's election he offered me both his retirement and his loyalty. "Don't try to change the Romans, Holiness. Don't try to fight or convert them. They've been managing Popes for the last nineteen hundred years and they'll break your neck before you bend theirs. But walk softly, speak gently, keep your own counsel, and in the end you will twist them like grass round your fingers."

It is too early, Heaven knows, to see what success Rome and I shall have with one another, but Rome is no longer the world, and I am not too much concerned—just so I can borrow experience from those who have pledged me their oaths as Cardinal Princes of the Church. There are some in whom I have great confidence. There are others . . . But I must not judge too swiftly. They cannot all be like Rinaldi, who is a wise and gentle man with a sense of humor and a knowledge of his own limitations. Meantime, I must try to smile and keep a good temper while I find my way round this Vatican maze. . . . And I must commit my thoughts to a diary before I expose them to Curia or Consistory.

I have an advantage, of course, in that no one quite knows which way I shall jump—I don't even know myself. I am the first Slav ever to sit on the Chair of Peter, the first non-Italian for four and a half centuries. The Curia will be wary of me. They may have been inspired to elect me, but already they must be wondering what kind of Tartar they have caught. Already they will be asking themselves how I shall reshuffle their appointments and spheres of influence. How can they know how much I am afraid and doubtful of myself? I hope some of them will remember to pray for me.

The Papacy is the most paradoxical office in the world; the most absolute and yet the most limited; the richest in revenues but the poorest in personal return. It was founded by a Nazarene carpenter who owned no place to rest His head, yet it is surrounded by more pomp and panoply than is seemly in this hungry world. It owns no frontiers, yet is subject always to national intrigue and partisan pressure. The man who accepts it claims divine guarantee against error, yet is less assured of salvation than the meanest of his subjects. The Keys of the Kingdom dangle at his belt, yet he can find himself locked out forever from the Peace of Election and the Communion of Saints. If he says he is not tempted by autocracy and ambition, he is a liar. If he does not walk sometimes in terror, and pray often in darkness, then he is a fool.

I know—or at least I am beginning to know. I was elected this morning, and tonight I am alone on the Mountain of Desolation. He whose Vicar I am hides His face from me. Those whose shepherd I must be do not know me. The world is spread beneath me like a campaign map—and I see balefires on every frontier. There are blind eyes upturned, and a babel of voices invoking an unknown. . . .

O God, give me light to see, and strength to know, and courage to endure the servitude of the servants of God . . . !

My valet has just been in to prepare my sleeping quarters. He is a melancholy fellow who looks very like a guard in Siberia who used to curse me at night for a Ukrainian dog and each morning for an adulterous priest. This one, however, asks humbly if my Holiness has need of anything. Then he kneels and begs my blessing on himself and his family. Embarrassed, he ventures to suggest that if I am not too tired, I may deign to show myself again to the people who still wait in St. Peter's square.

They acclaimed me this morning when I was led out to give my first blessing to the city and to the world. Yet so long as my light burns, it seems there will always be some waiting for God knows what sign of power or benignity from the papal bedroom. How can I tell them that they must never expect too much from a middle-aged fellow in striped cotton pajamas? But tonight is different. There is a whole concourse of Romans and of tourists in the Piazza, and it would be a courtesy—excuse me, Holiness, a great condescension!—to appear with one small blessing. . . .

I condescend, and I am exalted once again on wave after wave of cheering and horn-blowing. I am their Pope, their Father, and they urge me to live a long time. I bless them and hold out my arms to them, and they clamor again, and I am caught in a strange heart-stopping moment, when it seems that my arms encompass the world and that it is much too heavy for me to hold. Then my valet—or is it my jailer?—draws me back, closes the window, and draws the drapes, so that, officially at least, His Holiness Kiril I is in bed and asleep.

The valet's name is Gelasio, which is also the name of a Pope. He is a good fellow, and I am glad of a minute of his company. We talk a few moments, and then he asks me, blushing and stammering, about my name. He is the first who has dared to raise the question except old Rinaldi, who, when I announced that I desired to keep my baptismal name, nodded and smiled ironically and said, "A noble style, Holiness—provocative, too. But for God's sake, don't let them turn it into Italian."

I took his advice, and I explained to the Cardinals as I now explain to my valet that I kept the name because it belonged to the Apostle of the Slavs, who was said to have invented the modern Cyrillic alphabet and who was a stubborn defender of the right of people to keep the Faith in their own idiom. I explained to them also that I should prefer to have my name used in its Slavic form, for a testimony to the universality of the Church. Not all of them approve since they are quick to see how a man's first act sets the pattern of his later ones.

No one objected, however, except Leone, he who runs the Holy Office and has the reputation of a modern St. Jerome, whether for his love of tradition, a Spartan life, or a notoriously crusty temper I have yet to find out. Leone asked pointedly whether a Slavic name might not look out of place in the pure Latin of Papal Encyclicals. Although he is the one who first proclaimed me in the conclave, I had to tell him gently that I was more interested in having my encyclicals read by the people than in coddling the Latinists, and that since

Russian had become a canonical language for the Marxist world, it would not hurt us to have the tip of one shoe in the other camp.

He took the reproof well, but I do not think he will easily forget it. Men who serve God professionally are apt to regard Him as a private preserve. Some of them would like to make His Vicar a private preserve as well. I do not say that Leone is one of these, but I have to be careful. I shall have to work differently from any of my predecessors, and I cannot submit myself to the dictate of any man, however high he stands, or however good he may be.

None of this, of course, is for my valet, who will take home only a simple tale of missionary saints and make himself a great man on the strength of a Pontiff's confidence. The *Osservatore Romano* will tell exactly the same tale tomorrow, but for them it will be "a symbol of the Paternal care of His Holiness for those who cleave, albeit in good faith, to schismatic communions. . . ." I must, as soon as I can, do something about the *Osservatore*. . . . If my voice is to be heard in the world, it must be heard in its authentic tones.

Already I know there are questions about my beard. I have heard murmurs of a "too Byzantine look." The Latins are more sensitive about such customs than we are, so perhaps it might have been a courtesy to explain that my jaw was broken under questioning and that without a beard I am somewhat disfigured. . . . It is so small a matter, and yet schisms have begun over smaller ones.

I wonder what Kamenev said when he heard the news of my election. I wonder whether he has humor enough to send me a greeting.

I am tired—tired to my bones and afraid. My charge is so simple: to keep the Faith pure and bring the scattered sheep safely into the fold. Yet into what strange country it may lead me I can only guess. . . . Lead us not into temptation, O Lord, but deliver us from evil. Amen.

II

I**N the white marble lounge of the Foreign Press Club, George Faber
stretched his elegant legs and delivered his verdict on the election:

"To the East a stumbling block, to the West a foolishness, to the Romans a
disaster."

A respectful laugh fluttered around the room. A man who had spent so many
years on the Vatican beat had a right to make phrases—even bad ones. Sure of
the attention of his audience, he talked on in his calm, confident voice:

"Look at it any way you like, Kiril I means a political mess. He's been a
prisoner of the Russians for seventeen years, so at one stroke we wipe out any
hope of rapprochement between the Vatican and the Soviets. America is involved, too. I think we can expect progressive abandonment of neutralist policies and a gradual lining up of the Vatican with the West. We are back again to
the Pacelli-Spellman alliance. For Italy—" He flung out eloquent hands that
embraced the whole peninsula. "Beh! What happens now to the Italian miracle
of recovery? It was created in co-operation with the Vatican—Vatican money,
Vatican prestige abroad, Vatican help in emigration, the confessional authority
of the clergy holding the Left in check. What happens now? If he starts making
new appointments, the links between the Vatican and the Republic can be
broken very quickly. The delicate balance can be tipped." He relaxed again and
turned on his colleagues a smile of charm and deprecation, the smile of
kingmaker. "At least that's my story and I'm sticking to it. You may quote me
with acknowledgments, and if anyone steals my lead lines I'll sue!"

Collins, of the London *Times,* shrugged fastidiously and turned back to the
bar with a German from Bonn. "Faber is a mountebank, of course, but he does
have a point on the Italian situation. I'm quite staggered by this election. From
all I hear, most of the Italians were in favor of it—though none of them gave
any hint of it before they went into conclave. It's a wonderful weapon for Right
or Left. The moment the Pope talks about any Italian business they can label

him a foreigner, interfering in local politics. . . . That's what happened to the Dutchman—who was it, Adrian VI? The historical evidence shows him a wise man and a sound administrator, but when he died the Church was in a bigger mess than before. I've never liked the kind of baroque Catholicism which the Italians hand out to the world, but in affairs of state they have a great political value—like the Irish, if you understand what I mean."

". . . For a picture story the beard is wonderful." This from a hungry-mouthed brunette at the other end of the bar. "And it might be fun to have a few Greek and Russian ceremonies at the Vatican. All those odd robes and those lovely dangling ikons on their chests. One could start a craze with those —pendants for the new winter fashion! Quite a line, don't you think?" She gave a high-pitched braying laugh.

"There's a mystery about it," said Boucher, the fox-faced Frenchman. "A complete outsider after the shortest conclave in history! I talked with Morand and with some of our own people. The impression was of desperation—as if they saw the end of the world and wanted someone special to lead us toward it. They could be right. The Chinese have gone to Moscow, and the word is that they want a war now or they will split the Marxist world down the middle. They may get it, too, and then there is an end of politics, and we had all better begin to say our prayers. . . ."

"I heard an odd one this morning." Feuchtwanger the Swiss sipped a coffee and talked in a whisper with Erikson the Swede. "A courier arrived in Rome yesterday from Moscow, by way of Prague and Warsaw. This morning a personage from the Russian Embassy called on Cardinal Potocki. Of course, nobody is saying anything, but I wonder if Russia expects something from this man. Kamenev is in trouble with the Chinese, and he has always seen a lot farther than the end of his nose. . . ."

"Strange," said Fedorov the Tass man softly, "strange! Wherever you turn today, you feel the finger of Kamenev, even in this—name him or not, you see his touch."

Beron the Czech nodded wisely, but said nothing. The great Kamenev was beyond the reach of his humble pen, and after twenty years of survival he had learned that it was better to say nothing for a year than to permit himself a moment's indiscretion.

The Russian talked on with the quiet zeal of the orthodox. "Months ago I heard a rumor—it was only a rumor then—that Kamenev had organized this man's escape, and that the Praesidium would have his head for it. Now although we have been told to say nothing, the secret is out. It was Kamenev. And he must be laughing in his sleeve to see a man on whom he has left his mark sitting on the apostolic throne."

"And what does the Praesidium think of it?" asked the Czech cautiously.

Fedorov shrugged and spread his stubby fingers on the table. "They approve, of course—why should they not? Kamenev's mark is on every one of them, too. Besides, the man is a genius. Who else could have done what all the Five-Year Plans could not do—bring the Siberian plains into flower? From the Baltic to Bulgaria, look what he has done! For the first time, we have peace in the Western marches. Even the Poles don't hate us too much any more. We are exporting grain. Think of it! I tell you, whatever this man does the Praesidium and the people cannot fail to approve."

The Czech nodded soberly, and then asked another question. "This, this mark of Kamenev—what is it?"

The Tass man sipped his drink thoughtfully, and then said, "He spoke about it once, I believe. I was not there, but I heard echoes of it. He said, 'Once you have taken a man to pieces under questioning, once you have laid out the bits on the table and put them together again, then a strange thing happens. Either you love him or you hate him for the rest of your life. He will either love you or hate you in return. You cannot lead a man or a people through hell without wishing to share a heaven with them, too!' That's why our own people love him. He put them on the rack for three years and then suddenly showed them a new world." He downed his drink at one gulp and slapped the glass on the table. "A great man, the greatest we have had since Peter the Emperor!"

"And this Pope—this Kiril—what sort of a man will he be?"

"I don't know," said the Russian thoughtfully. "If Kamenev loves him, strange things may happen. Strange things may happen to both of them."

He was not yet crowned, but already Kiril the Pope had felt the impact of power. The shock of it was greater than he had ever dreamed. Two thousand years of time and all of eternity were now given into his hands. Five hundred million people were his subjects, and his tribute came in every coinage of the world. He could walk, as he walked each day now in the gardens of the Vatican, and measure the confines of his kingdom in a day's stroll; yet this narrow domain was only a foothold from which his power reached out to encompass the tilted planet.

The men who had made him he could now unmake with a word. The treasures of the centuries which they delivered to him with the Keys he could dispense at will or dissipate with a fool's gesture. His bureaucracy was more complex and yet more cheaply run than any other in the world. The toy soldiers who guarded his sacred presence were backed by thousands of levies bound to him by vow to serve with their talent, their hearts, their will, and all their celibate lives. Other men held dominion by the fickle voice of voters, by the pressure of party alignment, or by the tyranny of military juntas. He alone in all the world held it by divine delegation, and no one of all his subjects dared gainsay it.

Yet the knowledge of power was one thing, the use of it was quite another. Whatever his plans for the Church, whatever changes he might make in the future, he had for the present to use the instruments at his disposal and the organization which his predecessors had transmitted to him. He had to learn so much so quickly, and yet in the days before his coronation it seemed almost as if there were a conspiracy to rob him of the time to think or plan. There were moments when he felt like a puppet being dressed and rehearsed for the theatre.

The cobblers came to measure him for new slippers, the tailors to stitch his white cassocks. The jewelers offered their designs for his ring and his pectoral cross. The heralds presented their drawings for his coat of arms: crossed keys for Peter's charge, a bear rampant on a white field, above it the dove of the Paraclete, and beneath, the motto *"Ex oriente lux. . . .* A light out of the East."

He approved it at first glance. It appealed to his imagination and to his sense of humor. It took time to lick a bear into shape—but once he was full-grown he was a very formidable fellow. With the Holy Ghost to guide him, he might hope to do much for the Church. And perhaps the East had been dark too long because the West had given too local a shape to a universal Gospel.

The chamberlains led him through audience after audience—with the press, with the diplomatic corps, with the noble families who claimed place about the papal throne, with prefects and secretaries of congregations and tribunals and commissions. The Chancellery of Briefs and the Secretariat of Briefs to Princes kept his desk piled with replies in impeccable Latin to all the letters and telegrams of felicitation. The Secretariat of State reminded him daily of crisis and revolution and the intrigues of the embassies.

At every step he stubbed his pontifical toe on history, ritual, and protocol, and the cumbersome methodology of Vatican bureaucracy. Wherever he turned, there was an official at his elbow, directing His Holiness' attention to this or that—an office to be filled, a courtesy to be bestowed, or talent to be elevated.

The setting was grandiose, the stage management was sedulous, but it took him nearly a week to find out the title of the play. It was an old Roman comedy, once popular, but now fallen into some disrepute: its title was *The Management of Princes.* The theme was simple—how to give a man absolute power and then to limit his use of it. The technique was to make him feel so important and to keep him so busy with pompous trifles that he had no time to think out a policy or put it into execution.

When he saw the joke, Kiril the Ukrainian laughed privately and decided to make a joke of his own.

So two days before his coronation he summoned without warning a private meeting of all the Cardinals in the Borgia rooms of the Vatican. The abruptness of the call was calculated, and the risk of it was calculated, too.

The day after his coronation all but the Cardinals of the Curia would leave Rome and return to their own countries. Each could prove a willing adjutant or a discreet hindrance to papal policy. One did not become a Prince of the Church without some ambition and some taste of power. One did not grow old in office without some hardening of heart and will. They were more than subjects, these hingemen, they were counsellors, also, jealous of their own apostolic succession and of the autonomy conferred by it. Even a Pope must deal delicately with them and not strain too far their wisdom, their loyalty, or their national pride.

When Kiril saw them seated before him, old and wise and shrewdly expectant, his heart sank and he asked himself for the hundredth time what he had to offer to them and to the Church. Then once again it seemed as though power renewed itself in him, and he made the Sign of the Cross, an invocation to the Holy Ghost, and then plunged into the business of the Consistory. He did not use the "we" of authority, but spoke intimately and personally, as if anxious to establish a relation of friendship:

"My brothers, my helpers in the cause of Christ . . ." His voice was strong, yet strangely tender, as if he pleaded with them for fraternity and understanding. "What I am today you have made me. Yet if what we believe is true, it is not you but God who has set me in these shoes of the Fisherman. Day and night I have asked myself what I have to offer to Him or to His Church—I have so little, you see. I am a man who was wrenched out of life like Lazarus, and then drawn back into it by the hand of God. All of you are men of your time. You have grown with it, you have been changed by it, you have contributed to change it for better or for worse. It is natural that each of you should guard jealously that place and that knowledge, and that authority which you have earned for yourselves in time. Now, however, I must ask you to be generous with me and lend me what you have of knowledge and experience in the name of God." His voice faltered a little, and to the old men it seemed for a moment as if he were about to weep. Then he recovered himself, and seemed to grow in size, while his voice took on a stronger tone. "Unlike you, I am not a man of my time—because I have spent seventeen years in prison and time has passed me by. So much of the world is a novelty to me. The only thing that is not new is man, and him I know and love because I have lived with him for so long in the simple intimacy of survival. Even the Church is strange to me because I have had to dispense for so long with what is unnecessary in it, and I have had to cling the more desperately to that which is of its nature and its essence—the Deposit of Faith, the Sacrifice, and the sacramental acts."

For the first time, he smiled at them, sensing their uneasiness and trying to calm them. "I know the thought that is in your mind—that you may have for Pope an innovator, a man avid for change. This is not so. Though much change is necessary, we must make it together. I try simply to explain myself so that you may understand me and help me. I cannot cling as zealously as some to ritual and to traditional forms of devotion because for years I have held to nothing but the simplest forms of prayer and the bare essentials of the Sacraments. I know, believe me, I know, that there are those for whom the straightest road is the safest one. I wish them to be as free as possible inside the bond of the Faith. I do not wish to change the long tradition of a celibate clergy. I myself am celibate as you are. Yet I have seen the Faith preserved under persecution by married priests who have handed it to their children like a jewel in silk. I cannot grow hot over the legalities of the canonists or the rivalries of religious congregations because I have seen women raped by their jailers, and I have delivered their children with these consecrated hands."

Once again he smiled and threw out his crooked hands to them in a gesture of pleading. "I am perhaps the wrong man for you, my brothers—but God has given me to you and you must make the best of me."

There was a long pause, and then he went on more strongly still, not pleading, not explaining, but demanding with all the power that surged within him:

"You ask me where I want to lead you, where I want to lead the Church. I will show you. I want to lead you back to God, through men. Understand this, understand it in mind and heart and obedient will. We are what we are, for the service of God through the service of man. If we lose contact with man— suffering, sinful, lost, confused men crying in the night, women agonizing, children weeping—then we, too, are lost because we shall be negligent shepherds who have done everything but the one thing necessary." He paused and stood facing them, tall, pale, and strange, with his scarred face, and his crooked hands, and his black Byzantine beard. Then he handed them like a challenge the formal Latin question:

"Quid vobis videtur. . . . How does it seem to you?"

There was a ritual to cover this moment, just as there was a ritual to cover every act of Vatican life. The Cardinals would remove their red caps and bow their heads in submission, and then wait to be dismissed to do or not to do that which they had been counselled. A papal allocution was rarely a dialogue, but this time there was a sense of urgency and even of conflict in the assembly.

Cardinal Leone heaved his lion's bulk out of his chair, tossed his white mane, and addressed himself to the Pontiff. "All of us here have pledged to your Holiness and to the Church the service of our lives. Yet we should not discharge this service if we did not offer counsel when we believed counsel was necessary."

"This is what I have asked of you," said Kiril mildly. "Please speak freely."

Leone made a grave acknowledgment and then went on firmly. "It is too early yet to measure the effect of your Holiness' election upon the world at large, and especially upon the Roman and Italian Church. I mean no disrespect when I say that until we know this reaction there should be a prudence, a reserve in public utterance and public action."

"I have no quarrel with that," said Kiril in the same mild fashion. "But you must not quarrel with me when I tell you that I want the voice of Kiril to be heard by all men—not another voice, in another accent or another mode, but my voice. A father does not speak to his son through an actor's mask. He speaks simply, freely, and from the heart, and this is what I propose to do."

The old lion held his ground and went on stubbornly. "There are realities to be faced, Holiness. The voice will change, no matter what you do. It will issue from the mouth of a Mexican peasant and an English academician and a German missionary in the Pacific. It will be interpreted by a hostile press or a theatrical television correspondent. The most your Holiness can expect is that the first voice shall be yours and the first record shall be the authentic one." He permitted himself a grim smile. "We, too, are your voices, Holiness, and even we may find it hard to render the score perfectly." He sat down amid a small rustle of approval.

Then Pallenberg, the lean, cold man from Germany, took the floor and presented his own problem. "Your Holiness has spoken of changes. It is my view and the view of my brother bishops that certain changes are long overdue. We are a divided country. We have an immense prosperity and a dubious future. There is a drift of the Catholic population away from the Church because our women must marry outside it, since our males were decimated during the war. Our problems in this regard are legion. We can solve them only at the human level. Yet here in Rome they are being dealt with by Monsignori who cannot even speak our language, who work solely by the canons, and who have no sense of our history or of our present problems. They delay, they temporize, they centralize. They treat the affairs of souls as if they were entries in a ledger. Our burden is great enough, we cannot carry Rome on our backs as well—for myself and for my brethren, *Appello ad Petrum.* . . . I appeal to Peter!"

There was an audible gasp at so much bluntness. Leone flushed angrily, and Rinaldi hid a smile behind a silk handkerchief.

After a moment Kiril the Pope spoke again. His tone was as mild as ever, but this time they noticed he used the plural of royalty. "We promise our German brothers that we shall give immediate and full consideration to their special problems and we shall confer with them privately before they return to their homeland. We would urge them, however, to patience and to charity with their colleagues in Rome. They should remember, too, that often things are left undone from habit and from tradition rather than from lack of good will." He paused a moment, letting the reproof sink in; then he chuckled. "I have had my own troubles with another bureaucracy. Even the men who tormented me did not lack good will. They wanted to build a new world in one generation, but the bureaucracy beat them each time. Let us see if we can find ourselves more priests and fewer bureaucrats —fewer clerks and more simple souls who understand the human heart."

Now it was the turn of the Frenchman, and he was no less blunt than Pallenberg. "Whatever we do in France—whatever we propose from France— comes here to Rome under the shadow of old history. Every one of our projects, from the worker priests to studies in the development of dogma and the creation of an intelligent Catholic press, is greeted as if it were a new tramontane rebellion. We cannot work freely or with continuity in this climate. We cannot feel ourselves helped by the fraternity of the Church if a cloud of censure hangs over everything we plan or propose." He swung around angrily and flung out a challenge to the Italians. "There are heresies here in Rome, too, and this is one of them: that unity and uniformity are the same thing, that the Roman way is best for everyone from Hong Kong to Peru. Your Holiness has expressed the wish to have his voice heard in its true tone. We, too, wish to have our voice heard without distortion at the throne of Peter. Appointments need to be made, men who can represent us and the climate in which we live, truthfully and with understanding."

"You touch on a problem," said Kiril carefully, "which preoccupies us as well. We ourselves carry the burden of history so that we cannot always deal with the simplicity of a matter, but must consider a complexity of colorations and historic associations." He raised a hand to his beard and smiled. "Even this I understand to be a source of scandal to some, although our Master and the first Apostles were all bearded men. I should hate to think that the rock of Peter should split for want of a razor. *Quid vobis videtur?*"

In that moment they laughed and loved him. Their anger with one another subsided, and they listened more humbly while the men from the South Americas told of their own problems: impoverished populations, a scarcity of trained clergy, the historic association of the Church with the wealthy and the exploiters, lack of funds, the strength of the Marxist idea held up like a torch to rally the dispossessed.

Came then the men from the East, telling how the frontiers were closing one by one on the Christian idea. And how one by one the old missionary foundations were being destroyed while the idea of an earthly paradise took hold of the minds of men who needed it so desperately because they had so little time to enjoy it. It was a brutal balance sheet for men who had to make their reckoning with the Almighty. And when finally it was done, there was a silence over the whole assembly, and they waited for Kiril the Pontiff to make his final summation.

He rose then in his place and confronted them—a figure oddly young, oddly alone, like a Christ from a Byzantine triptych. "There are those," he told them solemnly, "who believe that we are come to the last age of the world because man has now the power to destroy himself from the face of the earth, and every day the danger grows greater that he will do it. Yet we, my brothers, have no more and no less to offer for the world's salvation than we had in the beginning. We preach Christ and Him crucified—to the Jews, indeed a stumbling block; and to the Gentiles, foolishness. This is the folly of the Faith, and if we are not committed to it, then we are committed to an illusion. What do we do, therefore? From this point where do we go? I believe there is only one way. We take the truth like a lamp and we walk out like the first Apostles to tell the good tidings to whoever will listen. If history stands in our way, we ignore it. If systems inhibit us, we dispense with them. If dignities weigh us down, we cast them aside. I have one commission now for all of you—for those who are going away from Rome and those who stay here in the shadow of our triumphs and our sins—find me men! Find me good men who understand what it is to love God and love His children. Find me men with fire in their hearts and wings on their feet. Send them to me, and I will send them out to bring love to the loveless and hope to those who sit in darkness. . . . Go now in the name of God!"

Immediately after the Consistory, Potocki, the Cardinal from Poland, presented a petition for an urgent and private audience with the Pope. To his surprise, it was answered within an hour by an invitation to dinner. When he arrived at the papal apartment, he found the new Pontiff alone, sitting in an armchair, reading a small volume bound in faded leather. When he knelt to make his obedience, Kiril stretched out a hand and raised him to his feet with a smile.

"Tonight we should be brothers together. The cooking is bad, and I haven't had time to reform the papal kitchens. I hope your company will give me a better dinner than usual." He pointed to the yellowed pages of the book and chuckled. "Our friend Rinaldi has a sense of humor. He gave me a present to celebrate my election. It is an account of the reign of the Dutchman, Adrian VI. Do you know what they called the Cardinals who elected him? 'Betrayers of Christ's blood, who surrendered the fair Vatican to foreign fury, and handed the Church and Italy into slavery with the barbarians.' I wonder what they are saying about you and me at this moment?" He shut the book with a snap and relaxed once again in the chair. "It is only the beginning, and yet I do so badly, and I feel myself so much alone. . . . How can I help you, my friend?"

Potocki was touched by the charm of his new Master, but the habit of caution was strong in him and he contented himself with a formality. "A letter was delivered to me this morning, Holiness. I am told that it comes from Moscow. I was asked to deliver it directly into your hands." He brought out a bulky envelope sealed with gray wax and handed it to Kiril, who held it a moment in his hands and then laid it on the table.

"I shall read it later, and if it should concern you as well, I shall call you. Now tell me . . ." He leaned forward in his chair, begging earnestly for a confidence. "You did not speak in the Consistory today, and yet you have as many problems as the others. I want to hear them."

Potocki's lined face tightened and his eyes clouded. "There is a private fear first, Holiness."

"Share it with me," said Kiril gently. "I have so many of my own, it may make me feel better."

"History sets snares for all of us," said the Pole gravely. "Your Holiness knows this. The history of the Ruthenian Church in Poland is a bitter one. We have not always acted like brothers in the Faith, but like enemies one to another. The time of dissension is past, but if your Holiness were to remember it too harshly it could be bad for us all. We Poles are Latin by temper and loyalty. Time was when the Polish Church lent itself to persecution of its brothers in the Ruthenian rite. We were both young then, but it is possible—and we both know it—that many might have lived who are now dead had we kept the unity of the Spirit in the bond of faith." He hesitated, and then stumbled awkwardly through the next question. "I mean no disrespect, Holiness, but I must ask with loyalty what others will ask with a false purpose: How does your Holiness feel about us in Poland? How do you regard what we are trying to do?"

There was a long pause. Kiril the Pontiff looked down at his gnarled hands, and then abruptly heaved himself from the chair and laid his hands on the shoulders of his brother bishop. He said softly, "We have both been in prison, you and I. We both know that when they tried to break us it was not with the love we had, but with the resentments that we had buried deep inside us. When you sat in the darkness, trembling and waiting for the next session with the lights, and the pain, and the questions, what tempted you most?"

"Rome," said Potocki bluntly, "where they knew so much and seemed to care so little."

Kiril the Pontiff smiled and nodded gravely. "For me it was the memory of the great Andrew Szepticky, Metropolitan of Galicia. I loved him like a father. I hated bitterly what had been done to him. I remembered him before he died, a hulk of a man, paralyzed, torn with pain, watching all that he had built being destroyed, the houses of education, the seminaries, the old culture he had tried so hard to preserve. I was oppressed by the futility of it all, and I wondered whether it was worth spending so many lives, so many more noble spirits, to try again. . . . Those were bad days, and worse nights."

Potocki flushed to the roots of his thin hair. "I am ashamed, Holiness. I should not have doubted."

Kiril shrugged and smiled wryly. "Why not? We are all human. You are walking a tightrope in Poland, I am walking another in Rome. Both of us may slip, and we shall need a net to catch us. I beg you to believe that if I sometimes lack understanding I do not lack love."

"What we do in Warsaw," said Potocki, "is not always understood in Rome."

"If you need an interpreter," said Kiril briskly, "send me one. I promise him always a ready hearing."

"There will be so many, Holiness, and they will speak in so many tongues. How can you attend to them all?"

"I know." Kiril's thin frame seemed suddenly to shrink, as if under a burden. "Strange. We profess and we teach that the Pontiff is preserved from fundamental error by the indwelling of the Holy Spirit. I pray, but I hear no thunder on the mountain. My eyes see no splendors on the hills. I stand between God and man, but I hear only man and the voice of my heart."

For the first time, the harsh face of the Pole relaxed, and he spread his hands in a gesture of willing defeat. "Listen to that, Holiness. *Cor ad cor loquitur.* Heart speaks to heart, and this may well be God's dialogue with men."

"Let's go to dinner," said Kiril the Pontiff, "and forgive my nuns their heavy hand with the sauce. They are worthy creatures, but I will have to find them a good cookbook."

They ate no better than he had promised, and they drank a thin young wine from the Alban Hills; but they talked more freely, and a warmth grew between them, and when they came to the fruit and the cheese Kiril the Pontiff opened his heart on another matter.

"In two days I am to be crowned. It is a small thing, perhaps, but I am troubled by so much ceremony. The Master came into Jerusalem riding on a donkey. I am to be carried on the shoulders of nobles between the plumed fans of a Roman emperor. All over the world are barefoot men with empty bellies. I am to be crowned with gold, and my triumph will be lit with a million lights. I am ashamed that the successor of the Carpenter should be treated like a king. I should like to change it."

Potocki gave a thin smile and shook his head. "They will not let you do it, Holiness."

"I know." Kiril's fingers toyed with the broken crumbs on his plate. "I belong to the Romans, too, and they must have their holiday. I cannot walk down the nave of St. Peter's because I could not be seen, and even if the visitors do not come to pray they do come to see the Pontiff. I am a prince by treaty, they remind me, and a prince must wear a crown."

"Wear it, Holiness," said Potocki with grim humor. "Wear it for the day, and do not trouble yourself. Soon enough they crown you with thorns!"

An hour away at his villa in the Alban Hills, Valerio Cardinal Rinaldi was giving his own dinner party. His guests made a curious yet powerful assemblage, and he managed them with the skill of a man who had just proved himself a kingmaker.

Leone was there, and Semmering, the Father General of the Jesuits, whom the vulgar called "the Black Pope." There were Goldoni, from the Secretariat of State, and Benedetti, the prince of Vatican finances, and Orlando Campeggio, the shrewd, swarthy fellow who was the editor of the *Osservatore Romano*. At the foot of the table, as if for a concession to the mystics, sat Rahamani the Syrian, soft, complaisant, and always unexpected.

The meal was served on a belvedere which looked down on a classic garden, once the site of an Orphic temple, and beyond it to the farmlands and the distant glow of Rome. The air was mild, the night was full of stars, and Rinaldi's assiduous servants had coaxed them into comfort with one another.

Campeggio, the layman, smoked his cigar and talked freely, a prince among the princes. ". . . First it seems we have to present the Pontiff in the most acceptable light. I have thought a great deal about this, and you will all have read what we have already done in the press. The theme so far has been 'in prison for the Faith.' The reaction to this has been good—a wave of sympathy —an expression of lively affection and loyalty. Of course, this is only the beginning, and it does not solve all our problems. Our next thought was to present 'a Pope of the people.' We may need some assistance with this, particularly from an Italian point of view. Fortunately, he speaks good Italian and therefore can communicate himself in public functions, and in contacts with the populace. . . . Here we shall need both direction and assistance from the members of the Curia. . . ." He was a deft man, and he broke off at this point, leaving the proposition for the clerics.

It was Leone who took it up, worrying it in his stubborn fashion, while he peeled an apple and sliced it with a silver knife. "Nothing is quite as simple as it sounds. We have to present him, yes, but we have to edit him and comment him as well. You heard what went on in the Consistory today." He thrust the knife blade at Rinaldi and Rahamani. "Print what he said baldly and without explanation, and it would read as if he were ready to throw two thousand years of tradition out the window. I saw his point, we all did, but I saw, too, where we have to protect him."

"Where is that?" Semmering, the spare blond Jesuit, leaned forward in his place.

"He showed us his own Achilles' heel," said Leone firmly. "He said he was a man who had dropped out of time. He will need, I think, to be reminded constantly what our times are and what instruments we have to work with."

"Do you think he is unaware of them?" asked the Jesuit again.

Leone frowned. "I'm not sure. I have not yet begun to read his mind. All I know is that he is asking for something new before he has had time to examine what is old and permanent in the Church."

"As I remember," said the Syrian mildly, "he asked us to find him men. This is not new. Men are the foundation of every apostolic work. How did he say it? 'Men with fire in their hearts and wings on their feet.' "

"We have forty thousand men," said the Jesuit dryly, "and they are all bound to him by solemn vows of service. We stand, all of us, at his call."

"Not all of us," said Rinaldi without rancor. "And we should be honest enough to confess it. We move familiarly where he must move for a while awkwardly and strangely, in the headquarters of the Church. We accept the inertia and the ambition, and the bureaucracy, because we have been bred to it, and in part we have helped to build it. You know what he said to me yesterday?" He paused like an actor, waiting for their attention to focus on him. "He said, 'I celebrated Mass once in seventeen years. I lived where hundreds of millions will die without having seen a priest or heard the word of God, yet here I see hundreds of priests stamping documents and punching time clocks like common clerks. . . .' I understand his point of view."

"What does he expect us to do?" asked Benedetti acidly. "Run the Vatican with IBM machines and put all the priests in the mission fields? No man can be as naïve as that."

"I don't think he is naïve," said Leone. "Far from it. But I think he may discount too readily what Rome means to the Church—for order and discipline, and a stewardship of the Faith."

For the first time, Goldoni, the gray, stocky man from the Secretariat of State, entered the argument. His harsh Roman voice crackled like twigs in a fire as he gave his own version of the new Pontiff. "He has been in to see me several times. He does not summon me, but walks in quietly and asks questions of me and of my staff. I have the impression that he understands politics very well, especially Marxist politics, but he is little interested in details and personalities. He uses one word often, *pressure.* He asks where the pressures begin in each country, and how they act on the people, and on those who rule them. When I asked him to explain, he said that the Faith was planted in men by God, but that the Church had to be built on the human and material resource of each country, and that to survive it had to withstand the pressures that were suffered by the mass of the people. He said something else, too: that we have centralized too much, and we have delayed too long to train those who can maintain the universality of the Church in the autonomy of a national culture. He spoke of vacuums created by Rome—vacuums in classes and countries— and local clergies. . . . I do not know how enlightened his own policies may be, but he is not blind to the defects of those which already exist."

"The new broom," said Benedetti tartly. "He wants to sweep all the rooms at once. . . . He can read a balance sheet, too! He objects that we have so much in credit while there is so much poverty in Uruguay, or among the Urdus. I ask myself if he really understands that forty years ago the Vatican was almost bankrupt and Gasparri had to borrow ten thousand sterling pounds to finance the papal election. Now at least we can pay our way and move with some strength for the good of the Church."

"When he spoke to us," said Rahamani again, "I did not hear him mention money. I was reminded how the first Apostles were sent out with neither scrip nor stave nor money for the road. As I heard the story, that is how our Kiril came from Siberia to Rome."

"Possibly," said Benedetti irritably. "But have you ever looked at the travel bills for a pair of missionaries—or worked out how much it costs to train a seminary teacher?"

Abruptly Leone threw back his white mane and laughed, so that the night birds stirred in the cypresses and the echoes rolled down over the starlit valley. "That's it. We elected him in the name of God, and now suddenly we're afraid of him. He has made no threat, he has changed no appointment, he has asked nothing but what we profess to offer. Yet here we sit, weighing him like conspirators and making ready to fight him. What has he done to us?"

"Perhaps he has read us better than we like," said Semmering the Jesuit.

"Perhaps," said Valerio Rinaldi, "perhaps he trusts us more than we deserve. . . ."

Extract from
the Secret Memorials of
KIRIL I, Pont. Max.

. . . It is late and the moon is climbing high. The Square of St. Peter is empty, but the rumor of the city still reaches me on the night wind—footsteps sounding hollow on stones, a scream of motor tires, the bleat of a horn, snatches of faraway song, and the slow clip-clop of a tired horse. I am wakeful tonight, and I resent my solitude. I want to walk out through the Angelic Gate and find my people where they stroll or sit together in the alleys of Trastevere, or huddle in narrow rooms with their fears and their loves. I need them so much more than they need me.

One day soon I must do this. I must shrug off the bonds which are laid upon me by protocol and precaution and confront this city of mine so that I may see it and it may see me as we truly are. . . .

I remember the stories of my childhood, how the Caliph Haroun disguised himself and walked out with his vizier at night to search the hearts of his people. I remember how Jesus the Master sat at meat with tax-gatherers and public women, and I wonder why His successors were so eager to assume the penalty of princes, which is to rule from a secret room and to display oneself like a demi-God only on occasions of public festivity. . . .

It has been a long day, but I have learned something of myself and of others, too. I made a mistake, I think, in the Consistory. When men are old and powerful, they need to be drawn by reason and calculation because the sap of the heart dries up with age. . . .

When one is in a position of power, one must not show oneself publicly humble because the ruler must reassure with strength and a show of decision. If one displays one's heart, it must be in private, so that the man who sees it will believe that he has received a confidence. . . .

I am writing like a cynic, and I am ashamed of it. Why? Perhaps because I was confronted with strong men who were determined to bend me to their opinions. . . .

Leone was the one who irritated me most of all. I had hoped for an ally, and instead I found a critic. I am tempted to appoint him to another office and remove him from the position of influence which he now holds. Yet this, I think, would be a mistake, and the beginning of greater ones. If I surround myself with weak and compliant men, I shall rob the Church of noble servants . . . and in the end I shall be left without counsellors. Leone is a formidable fellow, and I think we shall find ourselves opposed to each other on many issues. But I do not see him as an intriguer. I should like to have him for my friend because I am a man who needs friendship, yet I do not think he will surrender himself so far. . . .

I should like to keep Rinaldi by me, but I think I must consent to his retirement. He is not, I think, a profound man, though he is a subtle and an able one. I sense that he has come to grips with God very late in his life and that he needs a freedom to audit the accounts of his soul. This, fundamentally, is why I am here, to show men the staircase to union with God. If anyone stumbles on my account, then I shall be the one to answer for it. . . .

Kamenev's letter is open before me, and beside it is his gift for my coronation—a few grains of Russian soil and a package of sunflower seeds.

"I do not know," he writes, "whether the seeds will grow in Rome, but perhaps if you mix a little Russian earth with them they will bloom for next summer. I remember that I asked you during one interrogation what you missed most of all, and you smiled and said the sunflowers in the Ukraine. I hated you at that moment because I was missing them, too, and we were both exiles in the frozen lands. Now you are still an exile, while I am the first man in Russia.

"Do you regret us? I wonder. I should like to think so because I regret you. We could have done great things together, you and I; but you were wedded to this wild dream of the hereafter, while I believed, as I still believe, that the best a man can do is make barren earth fruitful and ignorant men wise, and see the children of puny fathers grow tall and straight among the sunflowers.

"It would, I suppose, be courteous to congratulate you on your election. For what they are worth, you have my compliments. I am curious to know what this office will do to you. I let you go because I could not change you, and yet I could not bring myself to degrade you any more. It would shame me now if you were to be corrupted by eminence.

"We may yet have need of each other, you and I. You have not seen the half of it, yet I tell you truly we have brought this country to a prosperity she has not known in all her centuries. Yet we are ringed with swords. The Americans are afraid of us; the Chinese resent us and want to drag us fifty years back in history. We have fanatics inside our own borders who are not content with bread and peace and work for all, but want to turn us all back into bearded mystics from Dostoievski.

"To you perhaps I am anti-Christ. What I believe you reject utterly. But for the present, I am Russia, and I am the guardian of this people. You have weapons in your hands, and I know, though I dare not admit it publicly, how strong they are. I can only hope you will not turn them against your homeland nor pledge them to a base alliance in East or West.

"When the seeds begin to grow, remember Mother Russia, and remember that you owe me a life. When the time comes to claim payment, I shall send you a man who will talk of sunflowers. Believe what he tells you, but deal with no others, now or later. Unlike you, I do not have the Holy Ghost to protect me, and I must still be wary of my friends. I wish I could say that you were one. Greetings. Kamenev."

. . . I have read the letter a dozen times, and I cannot decide whether it brings me to the fringe of a revelation or to the edge of a precipice. I know Kamenev as intimately as he knows me, yet I have not reached down to the core of his soul. I know the ambition that drives him, his fanatic desire to exact some goodness from life to pay for the debasement he inflicted on himself and others for so many years. . . .

I have seen peasants scoop up a handful of soil from a new plot and taste it to see whether it was sweet or sour. I can imagine Kamenev doing the same with the soil of Russia.

I know how the ghosts of history threaten him and his people because I understand how they threaten me, too. I do not see him as anti-Christ, nor even as an archheretic. He has understood and accepted the Marxist dogma as the swiftest and sharpest instrument yet devised to trigger a social revolution. I think he would throw it aside the moment he saw it fail of its purpose. I think, though I cannot be sure, that he is asking my help to preserve what he has already won of good for the people, and to give it a chance to grow peacefully into other mutations.

I believe that having thrust himself up so high, he has begun to breathe a freer air and to wish the same fortune for a people he has learned to love. If this be true, then I must help him. . . .

Yet there are events which give him the lie at every moment. There are invasions and forays on every frontier, under the banner of the sickle and the star. Men are still starved and beaten, and locked away from the free commerce of thought and the channels of grace.

The great heresy of the earthly paradise still creeps across the world like a cancer, and Kamenev still wears the robe of its high priest. This I am pledged to fight, and I have already resisted it with my blood. . . .

Yet I cannot ignore the strange working of God in the souls of the most unlikely men, and I believe I can see this working in the soul of Kamenev. . . . I see, though only dimly, how our destinies may be linked in the divine design. . . . What I cannot see is how to comport myself in the situation which exists between us. . . .

He asks for my friendship, and I would gladly give him my heart. He asks, I think, for a kind of truce, yet I cannot make truce with error, though I can ascribe the noblest motives to those who propagate it. I dare not, however, place the Church and the faithful in jeopardy for an illusion, because I know that Kamenev could still betray me, and I could still betray myself and the Church.

What do I do?

Perhaps the answer is in the sunflower—that the seed must die before the green shoots come, that the flower must grow while men pass by, heedless that a miracle is taking place under their noses.

Perhaps this is what is meant by "waiting upon the mercy of God." But we cannot only wait because the nature with which He has endowed us drives us to action. We must pray, too, in darkness and dryness, under a blind sky. . . .

Tomorrow I shall offer Mass for Kamenev, and tonight I must pray for light for Kiril the Pontiff, whose heart is restless and whose vagrant soul still hungers for its homeland. . . .

III

For George Faber the coronation of Kiril I was a long and elaborate boredom. The ovations deafened him, the lights gave him a headache, the sonorities of the choir depressed his spirit, and the gaudy procession of prelates, priests, monks, chamberlains, and toy soldiers was an operatic cavalcade which pricked him to resentment and gave him no entertainment at all. The exhalation of eighty thousand bodies, jammed like sardines into every corner of the Basilica, made him feel faint and nauseated.

His copy was already written and filed for transmission: three thousand glowing words on the pageantry and symbolism and religious splendor of this Roman festal day. He had seen it all before, and there was no reason for him to repeat the tedium except, perhaps, the snobbery of sitting in the place of honor in the press box, resplendent in a new frock coat, with the ribbon of his latest Italian decoration bright upon his chest.

Now he was paying for the indulgence. His buttocks were jammed tight between the broad hips of a German and the angular thighs of Campeggio, and there would be no escape for at least two hours, until the distinguished congregation broke out into the Square to receive the blessing of the new-crowned Pope with the humbler citizens and tourists of Rome.

Exasperated, he slumped forward in his seat and tried to find a grain of consolation in what this Kiril might mean to himself and Chiara. So far the Curia had kept him tightly in wraps. He had made few public appearances, and no pronouncements of any moment at all. But the word was already about that this was an innovator, a man young enough and strange enough to have a mind of his own and the vigor to express it in action. There were rumors of rough words in the Consistory, and more than one Vatican official was talking of changes, not only in personnel, but in the whole central organization as well.

If changes were made, some of them might affect the Holy Roman Rota, where the petition of nullity for Chiara's marriage had lain in the pigeonholes for nearly two years. The Italians had a wry-mouthed joke for the workings of this august body: *"Non c'e divorzio in Italia . . . There is no divorce in Italy—and only Catholics can get it!"* Like most Italian jokes, this one had more than one barb to it. Neither Church nor State admitted the possibility of divorce, but both viewed with apparent equanimity a large-scale concubinage among the rich and a growing number of irregular unions among the poor.

The Rota was by constitution a clerical body, but much of its business was in the hands of lay lawyers, specialists in canon law, who formed, for mutual profit, a union as rigid and exclusive as any in the world, so that the business of marital causes banked up in a bottleneck, regardless of the human tragedies which underlay most of them.

In theory the Rota must adjudicate equally for those who could pay and for those who could not. In practice the paying petitioner, or the petitioner with Roman influence or Roman friendship, could count on quicker decisions by far than his poorer brethren in the Faith. The law was the same for all, but its decisions were dispensed more swiftly to those who could command the best service from the advocates.

The tag of the joke made another point as well. A decree of nullity was much easier to obtain if both partners to the marriage consented to the first petition. If *error* had to be proved in the contract, or *conditio*, or *crimen*, it was much easier to do it with two voices. But if one partner only made a petition and the other presented contradictory evidence, the case was doomed to a slow progress and to very probable failure.

In such cases the Rota made a neat, if hardly satisfying, distinction: that in the private forum of conscience—and, therefore, in fact—the contract might be null and void, but until it could be proved so in the external forum, by documented evidence, the two parties must be regarded as married even though they did not live together. If the aggrieved party obtained a divorce and remarried outside the country, he or she would be excommunicated by the Church and prosecuted for bigamy by the State.

In practice, therefore, concubinage was the easier state in Italy, since it was more comfortable to be damned inside the Church than out of it and one was much happier loving in sin than serving a prison sentence in the Regina Coeli.

The which precisely was the situation for George Faber and Chiara Calitri.

As he watched the new Pontiff being vested by his assistants in front of the high altar, Faber wondered sourly how much he knew or could ever hope to know of the intimate tragedies of his subjects, of the burdens which their beliefs and loyalties laid upon their shoulders. He wondered, too, whether the time had not come to throw aside the caution of a lifetime and break a lance, or his head, for the most contentious cause in Rome, the reform of the Holy Roman Rota.

He was not a brilliant man, and certainly not a brave one. He had a capacity for close observation and urbane reportage, and a slightly theatrical knack for ingratiating himself with well-bred people. In Rome these things added up to a valuable talent for a correspondent. Now, however, with the climacteric looming, and the lonely years, the talent was not enough. George Faber was in love, and being a Nordic puritan and not a Latin, he needed at all costs to be married.

The Church, too, wanted him married, being concerned for the safety of his soul; but she would rather see him damned by default or rebellion than seem to call in question the sacramental bond which she counted, by divine revelation, indissoluble.

So whether he liked it or not, his own fate and Chiara's were held between the rigid hands of the canonists and the soft, epicene palms of Corrado Calitri, Minister of the Republic. Unless Calitri slackened his grip—which he showed no sign of doing—they could both stay suspended till doomsday in the limbo of those outside the law.

Across the nave, in the enclosure reserved for dignitaries of the Republic of Italy, Faber could see the slim patrician figure of his enemy, his breast resplendent with decorations, his face pale as a marble mask.

Five years ago he had been a spectacular young deputy with Milanese money behind him and a cabinet career already in promise. His only handicaps were his bachelor estate and a fondness for gay young men and visiting aesthetes. His marriage to a Roman heiress, fresh from convent school, had put the ministry in his pocket and set the Roman gossips laughing behind their hands. Eighteen months later Chiara, his wife, was in hospital with a nervous breakdown. By the time she had recovered, their separation was an accomplished fact. The next step was to file a petition for a declaration of nullity with the Holy Roman Rota, and from this point began the tedious dialogue of the tragicomedy:

"The petitioner, Chiara Calitri, alleges first a defect of intention," so the lawyers deposed on her behalf, "in that her husband entered into the bond of matrimony without the full intent to fulfill all the terms of the contract, with respect to cohabitation, procreation, and normal sexual commerce."

"I had the fullest intention to fulfill all the terms of the contract. . . ." Thus Corrado Calitri in reply. "But my wife lacked both the will and the experience to assist me to carry them out. The married state implies mutual support; I did not get support or moral assistance from my wife."

"The petitioner alleges also that it was a condition of the marriage that her husband should be a man of normal sexual habits."

"She knew what I was," said Corrado Calitri in effect. "I made no attempt to conceal my past. Much of it was common knowledge. She married me in spite of it."

"Fine!" said the auditors of the Rota. "Either of the pleas would be sufficient for a decree of nullity, but a simple statement is not proof. How does the petitioner propose to prove her case? Did her husband express his defective intentions to her or to another? Was the condition made explicit before the contract? On what occasion? In what form of speech or writing? And by whom can the condition be verified?"

So inevitably the wheels of canonical justice ground to a halt, and Chiara's lawyers advised her discreetly that it was better to suspend the case while new evidence was being sought than to force it to an unfavorable conclusion. The men of the Rota stood firm on dogmatic principle and the provisions of the law; Corrado Calitri was safely married and happily free while she herself was caught like a mouse in the trap he had set for her. The whole city guessed at the next step before she made it. She was twenty-six years old, and within six months she and George Faber were lovers. Rome in its cynical fashion smiled on their union and turned to the merrier scandals of the film colony at Cinecittà.

But George Faber was no complaisant lover. He had an itch in his conscience, and he hated the man who forced him to scratch it every day. . . .

He felt suddenly dizzy. A sweat broke out on his face and palms, and he struggled to compose himself as the Pope mounted the steps of the altar, supported by his assistants.

Campeggio cocked an astute eye at his queasy colleague, and then leaned forward and tapped him on the shoulder. "I don't like Calitri, either; but you'll never win the way you're going."

Faber sat bolt upright and stared at him with hostile eyes. "What the devil do you mean?"

Campeggio shrugged and smiled. "Don't be angry, my friend—it's an open secret. And even if it weren't, you have it written on your face. . . . Of course you hate him, and I don't blame you. But there are more ways than one to skin a cat."

"I'd like to hear them," said Faber irritably.

"Call me for lunch one day, and I'll tell you."

And with that Faber had to be content, but the hope buzzed in his head like a gadfly while Kiril the Pontiff chanted the Coronation Mass and the voices of the choir pealed around the dome of the Basilica.

Rudolf Semmering, Father General of the Society of Jesus, stood rigid as a sentinel at his post in the nave and addressed himself to a meditation on the occasion and its meanings.

A lifetime of discipline in the Ignatian exercises had given him the facility of projecting himself out of the terms of time and space into a solitude of contemplation. He did not hear the music, or the murmur of the concourse, or the sonorous Latin of the ceremony. His subdued senses were closed against all intrusion. A vast stillness encompassed him while the faculties of his spirit concentrated themselves upon the essence of the moment: the relationship between the Creator and His creatures, which was being affirmed and renewed by the installation of His Vicar.

Here, in symbol, ceremony, and sacrificial act, the nature of the Mystical Body was being displayed—Christ the God-man as head, with the Pontiff as His Vicar, enlivening the whole body by His permanent presence and through the indwelling of the Paraclete. Here was the whole physical order which Christ had established as the visible symbol and the visible instrument of His working with humankind—the *ecclesia,* the hierarchy of Pope, bishops, priests, and common folk, united in a single faith with a single sacrifice and a single sacramental system. Here the whole mission of redemption was summarized— the recall of man to his Maker by the dispensation of grace and by the preaching of the New Testament.

Here, too, was the darkness of a monstrous mystery: why an omnipotent God had made human instruments capable of rebellion, who could reject the divine design or deface it or inhibit its progress: why the All-Knowing should permit those whom He had made in His own image to grope their way to union with

Him on a knife-edge path, in daily danger of losing themselves forever from His face. Here finally was the mystery of the *ministerium*, the service to which certain men—himself among them—were called: to assume a greater responsibility and a greater risk, and to show forth in themselves the image of the Godhead for the salvation of their fellows.

Which brought him by a round turn to the application of his whole meditation: what he himself must do for service to the Pontiff, the Church, and the Christ, to whom he was bound by perpetual vow. He was the leader, by election, of forty thousand celibate men, dedicated to the bidding of the Pontiff in whatever mission he might choose to give them. Some of the best brains in the world were at his command, some of the noblest spirits, the best organizers, the most inspired teachers, the most daring speculators. It was his function not merely to use them as passive instruments, but to help each one to grow according to his nature and his talent, with the spirit of God working in him.

It was not enough, either, that he should present the massive network of the Society to the Pontiff and wait for a single command to set it working. The Society, like every other organization and every individual in the Church, had to seek and to propose new modes and new efforts to further the divine mission. It could not surrender itself either to the fear of novelty or to the comfort of traditional methods. The Church was not a static body. It was, according to the Gospel parable, a tree whose whole life was implicit in a tiny seed, but which must grow each year into a new shape and a new fruitfulness, while more and more birds made nests in its branches.

But even a tree did not always grow at the same rate or with the same profusion of leaf and flower. There were times when it seemed that the sap was sparse, or the ground less nourishing, so that the gardener must come and open up the soil and inject new food into the roots.

For a long time now Rudolf Semmering had been troubled by the reports that came to him from all over the world of a slackening of the influence of his Society and of the Church. More students were drifting away from religious practice in the first years after college. There were fewer candidates for the priesthood and for religious orders. The missionary drive seemed to lack impetus. Pulpit preaching had declined into formality—and this in an age when the whole world lived under the shadow of atomic destruction, and men were asking more poignantly than ever before to what end they were made, and why they should breed children into so dubious a future.

In his younger days in the Society, he had been trained as a historian, and all his later experience had confirmed him in the cyclic and climatic view of history. All his years in the Church had shown him that it grew and changed with the human pattern in spite of—or perhaps because of—its perennial conformity with the Divine One. There were seasons of mediocrity and times of decadence. There were centuries of brilliance, when genius seemed to spring from every lane and alley. There were times when the human spirit, burdened too long by material existence, leapt from its prison and went shouting, free and fiery, across the rooftops of the world, so that men heard thunders out of a forgotten Heaven and saw once more the trailing splendors of divinity.

When he looked up at the great altar and saw the celebrant, moving stiffly under sixty pounds of gilded vestments, he asked himself whether this might not be the forerunner of such a time. Remembering the Pope's plea for men with winged feet and burning hearts, he wondered whether this was not the first offering he should make out of the resources of the Society—a man who could speak the old truths in a fresh mode and walk as a new apostle in the strange world that had been born out of the mushroom cloud.

He had the man, he was sure of it. Even in the Society he was little known because most of his life had been spent in strange places, on projects that seemed to have little relation to matters of the spirit. Yet now it appeared from his writing and his correspondence that he was ready to be used otherwise.

His meditation over, Rudolf Semmering, the spare methodical man, took out his notebook and made a memorandum to send a cable to Djakarta. Then from the dome of the Basilica the trumpets broke out in a long, melodious fanfare, and he lifted his eyes to see Kiril the Pontiff raise above his head the body of the God whom he represented on earth.

On the night of his coronation Kiril Lakota dressed himself in the black cassock and the platter hat of a Roman priest and walked alone out of the Angelic Gate to survey his new bishopric. The guards at the gate hardly glanced at him, being accustomed to the daily procession of Monsignori in and out of the Vatican. He smiled to himself and hid his scarred face behind a handkerchief as he hurried down the Borgo Angelico toward the Castle of Sant' Angelo.

It was a few minutes after ten. The air was still warm and dusty, and the streets were alive with traffic and the passage of pedestrians. He strode out freely, filling his lungs with the new air of freedom, excited as a schoolboy who had just broken bounds.

On the Bridge of Sant' Angelo he stopped and leaned on the parapet, staring down at the gray waters of the Tiber, which had mirrored for five thousand years the follies of emperors, the cavalcade of Popes and princes, and the dozen births and deaths of the Eternal City.

It was his city now. It belonged to him as it could never belong to anyone else but the successor of Peter. Without the Papacy it could die again and crumble into a provincial relic, because all its resource was in its history, and the history of the Church was half the history of Rome. More than this, Kiril the Russian was now Bishop of the Romans—their shepherd, their teacher, their monitor in matters of the spirit.

A long time ago it was the Romans who elected the Pope. Even now they claimed to own him, and in a sense, they did. He was anchored to their soil, locked within their walls until the day he died. They might love him, as he hoped they would. They might hate him, as they had many of his predecessors. They would make jokes about him, as they had done for centuries, calling the hoodlums of the town *figli di papa,* sons of the Pope, and blaming him for the shortcomings of his Cardinals and his clergy. Provoke them enough, and they might even try to murder him and throw his body in the Tiber. But he was theirs and they were his, though half of them never set foot in a church and many of them carried cards which showed them to be Kamenev's men and not the Pope's. His mission was to the world, but his home was here, and like any other householder, he must get along with his neighbors as best he could.

He crossed the bridge and plunged into the network of lanes and alleys between the Street of the Holy Spirit and the Via Zanardelli, and within five minutes the city had engulfed him. The buildings rose on either hand, gray, pitted, and weather-stained. A pale lamp glimmered at the shrine of a dusty Madonna. An alley cat, scrabbling in a heap of refuse, turned and spat at him. A pregnant woman leaned in a doorway under the coat of arms of some forgotten prince. A youth on a clattering Vespa shouted as he passed. A pair of prostitutes, gossiping under a street lamp, giggled when they saw him, and one of them made the sign against the evil eye. It was a trivial incident, but it made a deep impression on him. They had told him of this old Roman custom, but this was the first time he had seen it. A priest wore skirts. He was neither man nor woman, but an odd creature who probably was *mal'occhio*. It was better to be sure than sorry and show him the horns.

A moment later he broke out into a narrow square at whose angle there was a bar with tables set on the sidewalk. One of the tables was occupied by a family group munching sweet pastries and chattering in harsh Roman dialect; the other was free, so he sat down and ordered an espresso. The service was perfunctory, and the other guests ignored him. Rome was full of clerics, and one more or less made no matter.

As he sipped the bitter coffee, a wizened fellow with broken shoes sidled up to sell him a newspaper. He fumbled in his cassock for change, then remembered with a start that he had forgotten to bring any money. He could not even pay for his drink. For a moment he felt humiliated and embarrassed, then he saw the humor of the situation and decided to make the best of it. He signaled the bartender and explained his situation, turning out his pockets as evidence of good faith. The fellow made a surly mouth and turned away, muttering an imprecation on priests who sucked the blood of the poor.

Kiril caught at his sleeve and drew him back. "No, no! You misunderstand me. I want to pay and I shall pay."

The news vendor and the family waited silently for the beginning of a Roman comedy.

"Beh!" The barman made a sweeping gesture of contempt. "So you want to pay! But when and with what? How do I know who you are or where you come from?"

"If you like," said Kiril with a smile, "I'll leave you my name and address."

"So I'm to go trotting all over Rome to pick up fifty lire?"

"I'll send it to you or bring it myself."

"Meantime, who's out of pocket? Me! You think I have so much that I can buy coffee for every priest in Rome?"

They had their laugh then, and they were satisfied. The father of the family fished in his pocket and tossed a few coins expansively on the table. "Here! Let me pay for it, Padre. And for the paper, too."

"Thank you. . . . I'm grateful. But I would like to repay you."

"Nothing, Padre, nothing!" Pater familias waved a tolerant hand. "And you must forgive Giorgio, here. He's having a bad time with his wife."

Giorgio grunted unhappily and shoved the coins into his pocket. "My mother wanted me to be a priest. Maybe she was right at that."

"Priests have their problems, too," said Kiril mildly. "Even the Pope has a few, I'm told."

"The Pope! Now there's a funny one." This from the paper vendor, who, being a seller of news, claimed the right to comment upon it as well. "They've really cooked us beautifully this time. A Russian in the Vatican! Now there's a story for you!" He spread the paper on the table and pointed dramatically to the portrait of the Pontiff, which covered nearly half the front page. "Now tell me if he isn't an odd one to foist on us Romans. Look at that face and the—" He broke off and stared at the bearded visage of the newcomer. His voice dropped to a whisper. *"Dio!* You look just like him."

The others craned over his shoulder, staring at the portrait.

"It's queer," said Giorgio, "very queer. You're almost his double."

"I am the Pope," he told them, and they gaped at him as if he were a ghost.

"I don't believe it," said Giorgio. "You look like him. Sure! But you're sitting here, without a lire in your pocket, drinking coffee, and it's not very good coffee at that."

"It's better than I get in the Vatican."

Then seeing their confusion and their trouble, he asked for a pencil and wrote their names and their addresses on the back of a bar check. "I'll tell you what I'll do. I'll send each of you a letter and ask you to come to lunch with me in the Vatican. I'll pay you back the money then, too."

"You wouldn't joke with us, Padre?" asked the news vendor anxiously.

"No. I wouldn't joke with you. You'll hear from me."

He stood up, folded the newspaper, and shoved it into the pocket of his cassock. Then he laid his hands on the old man's head and murmured a benediction. "There now. Tell the world you've had a blessing from the Pope." He made the Sign of the Cross over the little group. "And all of you, tell your friends that you have seen me and that I didn't have enough money for coffee."

They watched him, stupefied, and he strode away, a dark, gaunt figure, but oddly triumphant from his first encounter with his people.

It was a petty triumph at best, but he prayed desperately that it might be the presage of greater ones. If Creation and Redemption meant anything at all, they meant an affair of love between the Maker and His creatures. If not, then all existence was a horrible irony, unworthy of Omnipotence. Love was an affair of the heart. Its language was the language of the heart. The gestures of love were the simplicities of common intercourse, and not the baroque rituals of ecclesiastical theatre. The tragedies of love were the tragedies of a waiter with sore feet and a wife who didn't understand him. The terror of love was that the face of the Beloved was hidden always behind a veil, so that when one lifted one's eyes for hope one saw only the official face of priest or Pope or politician.

Once, for a short space in a narrow land, God had shown His face to men in the person of His Son, and they had known Him for a loving shepherd, a healer of the sick, a nourisher of the hungry. Then He had hidden Himself again, leaving His Church for an extension of Himself across the centuries, leaving, too, His vicars and His priesthood to show themselves other Christs for the multitude. If they disdained the commerce of simple men and forgot the language of the heart, then all too soon they were talking to themselves. . . .

The alleys closed around him again, and he found himself wishing that he could peer beyond their blank doors and their blind windows into the lives of their inhabitants. He felt a strange momentary nostalgia for the camps and the prisons, where he had breathed the breath of his fellows in misfortune and wakened at night to the muttering of their dreams.

He was halfway along a reeking lane when he found himself caught between a closed door and a parked automobile. At the same moment, the door opened and a man stepped out, jostling him against the panels of the car.

The man muttered an apology, and then catching sight of the cassock, stopped in his tracks. He said curtly, "There's a man dying up there. Maybe you can do more for him than I can—"

"Who are you?"

"A doctor. They never call us until it's too late."

"Where do I find him?"

"On the second floor. . . . Be a little careful. He's very infectious. T.B.— secondary pneumonia and haemothorax."

"Isn't there anyone looking after him?"

"Oh yes. There's a young woman. She's very capable—better than two of us at a time like this. You'd better hurry. I give him an hour at most."

Without another word he turned and hurried down the alley, his footsteps clattering on the cobbles.

Kiril the Pontiff pushed open the door and went in. The building was one of those decayed palaces with a littered courtyard and a stairway that smelled of garbage and stale cooking. The treads cracked under his feet, and the banister was greasy to the touch.

On the second landing he came on a small knot of people huddled around a weeping woman. They gave him a sidelong, uneasy stare, and when he questioned them one of the men jerked a thumb in the direction of the open door.

"He's in there."

"Has he seen a priest?"

The man shrugged and turned away, and the wailing of the woman went on, unchecked.

The apartment was a large, airless room, cluttered as a junk shop and full of the morbid smell of disease. In one corner was a large matrimonial bed where a man lay, fleshless and shrunken, under a stained counterpane. His face was unshaven, his thin hair clung damp about his forehead, and his head rolled from side to side on the piled pillows. His breathing was short, painful, and full of rales, and a small bloody foam spilled out of the corners of his mouth.

Beside the bed sat a girl, incongruously well groomed for such a place, who wiped the sweat from his forehead and cleansed his lips with a linen swab.

When Kiril entered she looked up, and he saw a young face, strangely serene, and a pair of dark, questioning eyes.

He said awkwardly, "I met the doctor downstairs. He thought I might be able to do something."

The girl shook her head. "I'm afraid not. He's in deep shock. I don't think he'll last very long."

Her educated voice and her calm professional manner intrigued him. He asked again, "Are you a relative?"

"No. The people around here know me. They send for me when they're in trouble."

"Are you a nurse, then?"

"I used to be."

"Has he seen a priest?"

For the first time, she smiled. "I doubt it. His wife's Jewish, and he carries a card for the Communist Party. Priests aren't very popular in this quarter."

Once again Kiril the Pontiff was reminded how far he was from being a simple pastor. A priest normally carried in his pocket a small capsule of the Holy Oils for the administration of the Last Sacraments. He had none, and here a man was dying before his face. He moved to the bed, and the girl made place for him while she repeated the doctor's warning:

"Just watch yourself. He's very infectious."

Kiril the Pontiff took the slack, moist hand in his own, and then bent so that his lips touched the ear of the dying man. He began to repeat slowly and distinctly the words of the Act of Repentance. When it was done he urged quietly, "If you can hear me, press my hand. If you cannot do that, tell God in your heart you're sorry. He's waiting for you with love; it needs only a thought to take you to Him."

Over and over again he repeated the exhortation while the man's head lolled restlessly and the fading breath gurgled in his gullet.

Finally the girl said, "No use, Father. He's too far gone to hear you."

Kiril the Pontiff raised his hand and pronounced the absolution. *"Deinde ego te absolvo a peccatis tuis . . .* I absolve you from your sins in the name of the Father, and of the Son, and of the Holy Ghost. Amen."

Then he knelt by the bed and began to pray passionately for the soul of this shabby voyager who had begun his last lonely pilgrimage while he himself was being crowned in the Basilica of St. Peter.

In ten minutes the little tragedy was over, and he said the prayers for the departed spirit while the girl closed the staring eyes and composed the body decently in the attitude of death. Then she said firmly:

"We should go, Father. Neither of us will be welcome now."

"I would like to help the family," said Kiril the Pontiff.

"We should go." She was very definite about it. "They can cope with death. It's only living that defeats them."

When they walked out of the room, she announced the news bluntly to the little group. "He's dead. If you need help, call me."

Then she turned away and walked down the stairs, with Kiril at her heels. The high mourning cry of the woman followed them like a malediction.

A moment later they were alone in the empty street. The girl fumbled in her handbag for a cigarette and lit it with an unsteady hand. She leaned back against a car and smoked a few moments in silence. Then she said abruptly, "I try to fight against it, but it always shakes me. They're so helpless, these people."

"At the end we're all helpless," said Kiril soberly. "Why do you do this sort of thing?"

"It's a long story. I'd rather not talk about it just now. I'm driving home—can I drop you off somewhere?"

It was on the tip of his tongue to refuse; then he checked himself and asked, "Where do you live?"

"I have an apartment near the Palatine, behind the Foro Romano."

"Then let me ride with you as far as the Foro. I've never seen it at night—and you look as though you need some company."

She gave him an odd glance, then without a word opened the door of the car. "Let's go, then. I've had more than enough for one night."

She drove fast and recklessly until they broke out into the free space where the Forum lay, bleak and ghostly, under the rising moon. She stopped the car. They got out together and walked over to the railing, beyond which the pillars of the Temple of Venus heaved themselves up against the stars. In the terse fashion which seemed habitual to her, she challenged him:

"You're not Italian, are you?"

"No, I'm Russian."

"And I've seen you before, haven't I?"

"Probably. They've printed a lot of pictures of me lately."

"Then what were you doing in Old Rome?"

"I'm the bishop of the city. I thought I should know at least what it looked like."

"That makes us both foreigners," said the girl cryptically.

"Where do you come from?"

"I was born in Germany, I'm an American citizen, and I live in Rome."

"Are you a Catholic?"

"I don't know what I am. I'm trying to find out."

"This way?" asked Kiril quietly.

"It's the only one I know. I've tried all the others." Then she laughed, and for the first time since their meeting she seemed to relax. "Forgive me, I'm behaving very badly. My name is Ruth Lewin."

"I'm Kiril Lakota."

"I know. The Pope from the steppes."

"Is that what they call me?"

"Among other things. . . ." She challenged him again. "These stories they print about you, your time in prison, your escape, are they true?"

"Yes."

"Now you're in prison again."

"In a way, but I hope to break out of it."

"We're all in prison, one way or another."

"That's true. . . . And it's the ones who understand it that suffer most of all."

For a long moment she was silent, staring down at the tumbled marbles of the Forum. Then she asked him, "Do you really believe that you stand in God's shoes?"

"I do."

"How does it feel?"

"Terrifying."

"Does He speak to you? Do you hear Him?"

He thought about it for a moment, and then answered her gravely. "In one sense, yes. The knowledge of Himself which He revealed in the Old Testament and in the New pervades the Church. It is there in the Scripture and in the tradition which has been handed down from the time of the Apostles, and which we call the Deposit of Faith. This is the lamp to my feet. . . . In another sense, no. I pray for divine light, but I must work by human reason. I cannot demand miracles. At this moment, for instance, I ask myself what I must do for the people of this city—what I can do for you. I have no ready answer. I have no private dialogue with God. I grope in the dark and hope that His hand will reach out to guide me."

"You're a strange man."

"We are all strange," he told her with a smile, "and why not, since each of us is a spark struck off from the fiery mystery of the Godhead?"

Her next words were uttered with a poignant simplicity that touched him almost to tears:

"I need help, but I don't know how, or where, to get it."

For a moment he hesitated, torn between prudence and the promptings of a vulnerable heart. Then once again he felt within him the subtle stirring of power. He was the Pastor and none other. Tonight one soul had slipped through his fingers; he dare not risk another. "Take me home with you," he told her. "Make me a cup of coffee, then talk it out. Afterwards you can drive me back to the Vatican."

In a small apartment huddled under the shadow of the Palatine Hill she told him her story. She told it calmly and gravely, and with no trace of that hysteria which every confessor feared in his relations with women.

"I was born in Germany thirty-five years ago. My family was Jewish, and it was the time of the pogroms. We were chased about from one country to another, until finally a chance came to enter Spain. Before we applied for visas we were told it might help if we became Catholics. . . . So my parents went through the motions and became converts—Moriscos might be a better name! We took the new identity and we were admitted.

"I was a child then, but it seemed that the new country and the new religion opened their arms to welcome me. I remember the music, the color, the Holy Week processions winding through the streets of Barcelona, while little girls like me, with white veils and flower wreaths in their hair, threw rose petals before the priest who carried the Monstrance. I had lived so long in fear and uncertainty that it was as if I had been transported into a land of fairy tale.

"Then, early in 1941, we were granted visas for America. The Catholic Charities Bureau took care of us, and with their help I was placed in a convent school. For the first time, I felt thoroughly safe and, strangely enough, thoroughly Catholic.

"My parents did not seem to mind. They, too, had reached safe harbor, and they had their own lives to rebuild. For a few years I was serenely happy; then—how do I say it?—my world and I myself began to crack down the middle. I was a child still, but the minds of children open more quickly than adults ever believe.

"In Europe millions of Jews were dying. I was a Jew and I was oppressed by the thought that I was a renegade who had bought my safety by forswearing my race and my religion. I was a Catholic, too, and my belief was identified with the freest and happiest time of my life. Yet I could not accept the freedom or the happiness because it seemed they had been bought with blood money.

"I began to rebel against the teaching and the discipline of the convent and yet all the time I knew that I was rebelling against myself. When I began to go out with boys, it was always with the rebels, the ones who rejected any kind of belief. It was safer that way. Perhaps in the end it would be better to believe nothing than to be torn apart by a double allegiance.

"Then, after a while, I fell in love with a Jewish boy. I was still a Catholic, so I went to discuss the case with my parish priest. I asked for the usual dispensation to marry someone outside the Faith. To my surprise and my shame, he read me a bitter lecture. I heard him out and then walked out of the rectory, and I have never set foot inside a church since. He was a foolish man, blind and prejudiced. For a while I hated him, and then I understood that I was really hating myself.

"My marriage was happy. My husband had no fixed belief, nor, it seemed, did I; but we had a common race and a common heritage, and we were able to live in peace with one another. We made money, we made friends. It was as if I had achieved the continuity which my life had lacked from the beginning. I belonged to someone, to a settled order, and at long last, to myself.

"Suddenly, and for no apparent reason, a strange thing happened. I became morbid and depressed. I would wander around the house disconsolate, tears rolling down my cheeks, sunk in utter despair. Sometimes I would break out into violent rages at the slightest provocation. There were times when I contemplated suicide, convinced that I would be better dead than inflicting so much unhappiness on myself and on my husband.

"In the end my husband forced the issue. He demanded that I see a psychiatrist. At first I refused angrily, and then he told me bluntly that I was destroying myself and destroying our marriage. So I agreed to begin treatment, and entered on a course of analysis.

"This is a strange and frightening road, but once you begin to walk it you cannot turn back. To live life is hard enough. To relive it, to retrace every step in symbol and fantasy and simple memory, is a weird experience. The person who makes the journey with you, the analyst, assumes a multitude of identities: father, mother, lover, husband, teacher—even God.

"The longer the journey, the harder the road, because each step brings you closer to the moment of revelation where you must face once and forever the thing from which you have been fleeing. Time and again you try to step off the road or turn back. Always you are forced forward. You try to defer, to temporize. You create new lies to deceive yourself and your guide, but the lies are demolished one by one.

"In the middle of my analysis my husband was killed in an automobile accident. For me it was another guilt added to all the others. Now I could never restore to him the happiness of which I had robbed him. My whole personality seemed to disintegrate under the shock. I was taken to a nursing home, and the therapy began again. Slowly the nature of my hidden fear became clear to me. When I reached the core of myself, I knew that I should find it empty. I should not only be alone, but hollow as well, because I had built a God in my own image and then destroyed Him, and there was no one to take His place. I must live in a desert, without identity, without purpose, since even if there were a God, I could not accept Him because I had not paid for His presence.

"Does this seem strange to you? It was a terror to me. But once I stood in the desert, empty and solitary, I was calm. I was even whole. I remember the morning after the crisis when I looked out from the window of my room and saw the sun shining on the green lawn. I said to myself, 'I have seen the worst that can happen to me, and I am still here. The rest, whatever it is, I can endure.'

"A month later I was discharged. I settled my husband's estate and came to Rome. I had money, I was free, I could plan a new life for myself. I might even fall in love again. . . . I tried it, too; but in love one must commit oneself, and I had nothing to commit.

"Then I began to understand something. If I lived for myself and with myself I should always be hollow, always in solitude. My debts to my people and my past were still unpaid; I could accept nothing from life until I had begun to pay them.

"You asked me tonight why I do this kind of service. It's simple enough. There are many Jews in Rome—the old Sephardic families who came from Spain in the time of the Inquisition, immigrants from Bologna and the Lombard cities. They are still a people apart. Many of them are poor, like the ones you saw tonight. . . . I can give them something. I know I do. But what do I give myself? Where do I go? . . . I have no God although I need one desperately. . . . You tell me you stand in His shoes—can you help me . . . ?"

Extract from
the Secret Memorials of
KIRIL I, Pont. Max.

. . . I am troubled tonight. I am solitary and perplexed. My installation in the See of Peter is complete. I have been crowned with the triple tiara. The ring of the Fisherman is on my finger. My blessing has gone out to the city and to the world. In spite of it all—because of it all, perhaps—I have never felt so empty and inadequate. I am like the scapegoat driven into the desert, with the sins of all the people on my back. . . .

I must ask Rinaldi to find me a wise priest to whom I can confess myself each day, not only for absolution and the sacramental grace, but for a purging of this pent, stopped-up spirit of mine. I wonder if the faithful understand that the Vicar of Christ has often more need of the confessional than they themselves. . . .

I have seen many men die, but the sad and solitary exit which I witnessed tonight in a Roman tenement afflicts me strangely. The words of the woman who saw it with me still ring in my ears: "They can cope with death. It's the living that defeats them." It seems to me that this defeat is the measure of our failure in the ministry of the Word.

Those who need us most are those who are bowed the lowest under the burden of existence—whose life is a daily struggle for simple sustenance, who lack talent and opportunity, who live in fear of officials and tax-gatherers and debt collectors, so that they have no time and hardly any strength to spend on the care of their souls. Their whole life becomes a creeping despair. . . . If it were not for the infinite knowledge and the infinite mercy of God, I, too, could easily despair.

The case of the woman Ruth Lewin gives me more hope. While I was in prison and under the long ordeals of interrogation, I learned much about the intricate functioning of the human mind. I am convinced that those who devote themselves to the study of its workings, and of its infirmities, can do a great service to man and the cause of his salvation. . . . We should not, as shepherds of souls, treat this infant science with suspicion or hasty censure. Like every other science, it can be wrested to ignoble ends. It is inevitable that many who explore the misty country of the soul will make mistakes and false guesses, but every honest research into the nature of man is also an exploration of the divine intent in his regard.

The human psyche is the meeting ground between God and man. It is possible, I think, that some of the meaning of the mystery of Divine Grace may be revealed when we understand better the working of the subconscious mind, where buried memories and buried guilts, and buried impulses, germinate for years and then break out into a strange flowering. . . . I must encourage competent men inside the Church to pursue this study, and to co-operate with those outside it, to make the best use possible of their discoveries. . . .

The sick mind is a defective instrument in the great symphony which is God's dialogue with man. Here perhaps we may see a fuller revelation of the meaning of human responsibility and God's compassion for His creatures. Here we may be able to illuminate the difference between formal guilt and the true status of the soul in the sight of God. . . .

It might scandalize many if I declared openly that in a woman like this Ruth I see—or think I see—a chosen spirit. The key to such spirits is their recognition that their wrestling with life is in reality a wrestling with God. . . .

The strangest story in the Old Testament is the story of Jacob, who wrestled with the angel and conquered him and forced the angel to tell his name. . . . But Jacob went away from the struggle limping.

I, too, am a limping spirit. I have felt reason and the foundations of my faith rock in the dark bunker and under the lights and the relentless inquisition of Kamenev.

I believe still. I am committed more completely than ever before to the Deposit of Faith, but I am no longer content to say, "God is thus. Man is thus," and then make an end of it. Wherever I turn on this high pinnacle, I am confronted with mystery. I believe in the Godly harmony which is the result of the eternal creative act. . . . But I do not always hear the harmony. I must wrestle with the cacophony and apparent discord of the score, knowing that I shall not hear the final grand resolution until the day I die and, hopefully, am united with God. . . .

This is what I tried to explain to Ruth, though I am not sure that I did it very well. I could not bring myself to present her with blunt theological propositions. Her troubled spirit was not ready to receive them.

I tried to show her that the crisis of near despair which afflicts many people of intelligence and noble spirit is often a providential act, designed to bring them to an acceptance of their own nature, with all its limitations and inadequacies, and of the conformity of that nature with a divine design whose pattern and whose end we cannot fully apprehend.

I understand her terrors because I have endured them myself. This I am sure she understood. I advised her to be patient with herself and with God, who, even if she could not believe in Him, still worked in His own fashion and His own secret time.

I told her to continue the good work she was doing, but not to regard it always as a payment of debts. No one of us could pay his debts were it not for the redemptive act consummated on the Cross by Christ.

I tried to show her that to reject the joy of living is to insult Him who provides it, and who gave us the gift of laughter along with the gift of tears. . . .

These things I think I should write for others because the sickness of the mind is a symptom of our times, and we must all try to heal one another. Man is not meant to live alone. The Creator Himself has affirmed it. We are members of one body. The cure of a sick member is a function of the whole organism. . . .

I have asked Ruth to write to me, and sometimes to come and see me. I dare not let this office separate me from direct contact with my people. . . . For this reason I think I should sit in the confessional for an hour each week and administer the Sacrament to those who come into St. Peter's.

The nearest I came to losing my faith and my soul was when I lay naked and solitary in an underground bunker. . . . When I was brought back to the huts, to the sound of human talk—even to the sound of anger and ribaldry and blasphemy—it was like a new promise of salvation. . . .

I wonder whether this is not the way in which the creative act renews itself daily: the spirit of God breathing over the dark waters of the human spirit, infusing them with a life whose intensity and diversity we can only guess. . . .

"*In manus tuas, Domine* . . . Into thy hands, O God, I commend all troubled souls."

IV

IT was nearly six weeks after the coronation before George Faber arranged his luncheon with Campeggio. He might have put it off even longer had not Chiara argued him into it with tears and tantrums. He was by nature a prompt man, but he had lived long enough in Rome to be suspicious of any gratuitous gesture. Campeggio was a distinguished colleague, to be sure, but he was in no sense a friend, and there was no clear reason why he should concern himself with the bedding and wedding of Chiara Calitri.

So somewhere in the offing was a *combinazione*—a proposition—with the price tag carefully hidden until the very last moment. When one lunched with the Romans, one needed a long spoon and a steady hand, and George Faber was still a little shaken by his quarrel with Chiara.

Spring was maturing slowly into summer. The azaleas made a riot of color on the Spanish Steps, and the flower sellers did a brisk business with the new roses from Rapallo. Footsore tourists found refuge in the English Tearoom, and the traffic swirled irritably around Bernini's marble boat in the Piazza.

To stiffen his small courage, George Faber bought a red carnation and pinned it jauntily in his buttonhole before he crossed the Square and entered the Via Condotti. The restaurant which Campeggio had named for their rendezvous was a small, discreet place, far away from the normal haunts of newsmen and politicians. . . . In a matter of such delicacy, he claimed, one should not risk an eavesdropper, though Faber saw little point in secrecy since the Calitri story was common property in Rome. However, it was part of the game that every *combinazione*, every *progetto*, must be dressed up with a little theatre. So he submitted with as much good grace as he could muster.

Campeggio entertained him for half an hour with a vivid and amusing chronicle of the Vatican, and how the clerical dovecotes were fluttering as the new Pope asserted himself. Then with a diplomat's care he steered the talk toward Faber:

". . . It may please you to know, my dear fellow, that your own dispatches have been very favorably noticed by His Holiness. I am told he is anxious to make more direct contact with the press. There is talk of a regular luncheon with senior correspondents, and your name is, of course, first on the list."

"I'm flattered," said Faber dryly. "One tries always to write honestly, but this man is an interesting subject in his own right."

"Leone, too, has a soft spot for you, and you are well regarded in the Secretariat of State. . . . These are important sources and important voices, as you know."

"I'm well aware of it."

"Good," said Campeggio briskly. "Then you understand the importance of preserving a good relation without, shall we say, embarrassing incidents."

"I've always understood that. I'm interested to know why you bring it up now."

Campeggio pursed his thin lips and looked down the backs of his long, manicured hands. He said carefully, "I make the point to explain my next question. Do you propose setting up house with Chiara Calitri?"

Faber flushed and said testily, "We've discussed it. So far we haven't made any decision."

"Then let me advise you very strongly not to do it at this moment. . . . Don't misunderstand me. Your private life is your own affair."

"I'd hardly call it private. Everyone in Rome knows the situation between Chiara and myself. I imagine the rumor has reached the Vatican long before this."

Campeggio gave him a thin smile. "So long as it remains a rumor, they are content to suspend judgment and leave you in the hands of God. There is no question of public infamy which could damage your case with the Rota."

"At this point," Faber told him bluntly, "we have no case. The whole business is suspended until Chiara can get new evidence. So far she hasn't been able to find any."

Campeggio nodded slowly, and then began to trace an intricate pattern on the white tablecloth. "I am told by those who understand the thinking of the Rota that your best hope of a verdict rests on the plea of defective intention. In other words, if you can prove that Calitri entered into the marriage contract without the full intention of fulfilling all its terms—and that intention includes fidelity—then you have a good chance of a favorable decision."

Faber shrugged unhappily. "How do you prove what's in a man's mind?"

"Two ways: by his own sworn statement or by the evidence of those who heard him express the defective intention."

"We looked for people like that. We couldn't find any, and I'm damn sure Calitri won't give evidence against himself."

"Put enough pressure on him, and I think he might."

"What kind of pressure?"

For the first time, Campeggio seemed uncertain of himself. He was silent awhile, tracing long, flowing lines with the point of his fork. Finally he said deliberately, "A man like Calitri, who holds a high position and who has, shall we say, an unusual private life, is very vulnerable. He is vulnerable to his party, and to public attack. He is vulnerable to those who have fallen out of his favor.

. . . I don't have to tell you that this is an odd world he lives in—a world of strange loves and curious hates. Nothing in it is very permanent. Today's favorite is rejected tomorrow. There are always bleeding hearts ready to tell their story to a good listener. I've heard some myself. Once you have enough stories you go to Calitri."

"I go to him?"

"Who else? You report the news, don't you?"

"Not that sort of news."

"But you know plenty who do?"

"Yes."

"Then I don't have to draw pictures for you."

"It's blackmail," said George Faber flatly.

"Or justice," said Orlando Campeggio. "It depends on the point of view."

"Even if we did frighten a testimony out of him, he could then allege undue pressure and the whole case would be thrown out of court for good."

"That's a risk you have to take. If the stakes are high enough, I think you might be wise to take it. . . . I should add that I may be able to give you a little help in your inquiry."

"Why?" asked Faber sharply. "Why should you care a row of beans what happens to Chiara and me?"

"You've become a Roman," said Campeggio with cool irony. "Still, it's a fair question. I like you. I think you and your girl deserve better than you're getting. I don't like Calitri. Nothing would give me greater satisfaction than to see him destroyed. That's almost impossible, but if your Chiara wins her case it will damage him a great deal."

"Why do you dislike him so much?"

"I'd rather not answer that question."

"We have common interests. We should at least be honest with each other."

The Roman hesitated a moment, and then threw out his hands in a gesture of defeat. "What does it matter, anyway? There are no secrets in Rome. I have three sons. One of them works in Calitri's department and has, shall we say, fallen under his influence. I don't blame the boy. Calitri has great charm, and he doesn't scruple to use it."

"A dirty business!"

"It's a dirty town," said Orlando Campeggio. "I'm the last man who should say it, but I often wonder why they call it the City of Saints."

While George Faber was still chewing unhappily over his luncheon dialogue, Chiara Calitri was sunning herself on the beach, at Fregene.

She was a small dark girl, lithe as a cat; and the youths who passed, idling along the beach, whistled and preened themselves for her attention. Safe behind her sunglasses, she watched them come and go, and stretched herself more decoratively on the colored towel.

A sense of comfort and well-being pervaded her. She was young, the admiration of the youths told her she was beautiful. She was loved. Faber in his uneasy fashion was committed to fight her battles. She was freer than she had ever been in her life.

It was the freedom which intrigued her most of all, and each day she became more conscious of it, more curious about it, and more eager for its enlargement. This morning she had wept and shouted like a market woman at poor George because he had seemed unwilling to risk a talk with Campeggio. If he wavered again, she would fight him again, because from now on she could not love without the liberty to be herself.

With Corrado Calitri she had felt herself torn apart, blown this way and that, like paper shredded on the wind. For a time—a terrifying time—it was as if she had ceased to exist as a woman. Now at last she had put herself together again—not the same Chiara but a new one, and no one ever again must have the power to destroy her.

Deliberately she had chosen an older man because such were more tolerant and less demanding. They asked a more placid life. They offered affection as well as passion. They moved with authority in a wider world. They made a woman feel less vulnerable. . . .

She sat up and began to toy with the warm sand, filtering it between her fingers so that it spilled out and made a small mound at her feet. Inconsequently she thought of an hourglass, in which time measured itself inexorably in a spilth of golden grains. Even as a child she had been obsessed with time, reaching out for it as she now reached for freedom, spending it recklessly, as if by so doing she could bring the future into today. When she was at home she had cried to go to school. At school she had wanted always to grow up. Grown up at last, she had wanted to be married. In marriage—the bitter fiasco of her marriage to Corrado Calitri—time had suddenly and dreadfully stood still, so that it seemed she must be anchored eternally to this union with a man who despised her womanhood and debased it at every opportunity.

It was from this terror of static time that she had fled finally into hysteria and illness. The future toward which she had reached so eagerly was now intolerable to her. She no longer wanted to advance, but only to retreat into the dark womb of dependence.

Even here time was still her enemy. Life was time; an unendurable extension of loveless years. The only ways to end it were to die or to stay forever in retreat. But in the hospital the vigilant nurses held death away from her, while the physicians drew her slowly and patiently back to another meeting with life. She had fought against them, but they, too, were inexorable. They stripped her illusions away one by one like layers of skin until the naked nerves were exposed, and she screamed in protest against their cruelty.

Then they had begun to show her a strange alchemy: how pain might transmute itself into a mercy. Endure it long enough, and it began to diminish. Run from it, and it followed, always more monstrous, like a pursuer in a nightmare. Fight it, and in the end you could come to terms with it—not always the best terms, not always the wisest, but a treaty that was at least bearable.

She had made her own treaty with life now, and she was living better than she had hoped under the terms of it. Her family disapproved of the bargain, but they were generous enough to give her love and a measure of affection. She could not marry, but she had a man to care for her. The Church condemned her, but so long as she preserved a public discretion it would withhold a public censure.

Society, in its paradoxical fashion, registered a mild protest and then accepted her with good enough grace. . . . She was not wholly free, not wholly loved, nor wholly protected, but she had enough of each to make life bearable, and time endurable, because each now held a promise of betterment.

Yet it was not the whole answer, and she knew it. The treaty was not half as favorable as it looked. There was a catch in it—a dragnet clause which, once invoked, could cancel all the rest.

She looked out at the empty water of the Tyrrhenian Sea and remembered her father's tales of all the strange life that inhabited its deeps: corals like trees, whales as big as ships, fish that flapped their wings like birds, jewels that grew in oyster slime, and weeds like the hair of drowned princesses. Under the sunlit surface was a whole mysterious world, and sometimes the waters opened and swallowed down the voyager who risked them too boldly. Sometimes, but not always. . . . The most unlikely sailormen survived and came to safe harbor.

Here precisely was the risk of her own contract with life. She believed in God. She believed in the Church's teaching about Him. She knew the penalty of eternal ruin that hung over the heads of those who rashly dared the divine displeasure. Every step, every hour, was a tightrope venture of damnation. At any moment the contract might be called in. And then . . . ?

Yet even this was not the whole mystery. There were others, and deeper ones. Why she and not another had been submitted to the first injustice of a false marriage contract. Why she and not another had been forced into the suicidal confusion of a breakdown. And this precipitate grasping at any straw for survival. Why? Why?

It was not enough to say, like the parish confessor, that this was God's dispensation for her. It was Corrado's dispensation first. Did God compound injustice and then hold damnation over the heads of those who wilted under its weight? It was as if the sea rose up and swirled her back into the confusion of her illness.

There was no cure for the untimely thought that came in nighttime or daytime, prickling along the flesh like a cold wind. One could not surrender to it for fear of a new madness. One could not blot it out except by the exercise of love and passion, which in a strange way seemed to affirm what the preachers said they denied: the reality of love and mercy, and the hand that helped the most hapless sailormen out of the damnation of the deep. . . .

She shivered in the warm air and stood up, wrapping the towel about her. A brown youth with the figure of a Greek god whistled and called to her, but she ignored him and hurried up the beach toward the car. What did he know of life who vaunted it like a phallic emblem in the sun? George knew better—dear middle-aged, uneasy George, who shared her risk and was at least working to rid her of it. She longed for the comfort of his arms and the sleep that came after the act of love. . . .

Rudolf Semmering, Father General of the Society of Jesus, sat in the airport at Fiumicino and waited for his man from Djakarta. To those who knew him well his vigil was of singular significance. Rudolf Semmering was an efficient man, adapted by nature and ascetic exercise to the military spirit of Ignatius Loyola. Time to him was a precious commodity because only in time could one prepare for eternity. A waste of time was therefore a waste of the currency of salvation. The affairs of his order were complex and pressing, and he might easily have sent a deputy to meet this obscure member who was already thirty minutes late.

Yet the occasion seemed to demand a more than normal courtesy. The newcomer was a Frenchman, a stranger to Rome. He had spent more than twenty years in exile—in China, in Africa, in India, and the scattered islands of Indonesia. He was a simple priest, and a distinguished scholar, whom Rudolf Semmering had held in silence under his vow of obedience.

For a scholar the silence was worse than exile. He was free to work, to correspond with his colleagues all over the world, but he was prevented by a formal obedience from publishing the results of his research or teaching on any public rostrum. Many times in the last decade Rudolf Semmering had questioned his own conscience about this prohibition laid on so brilliant a mind. Yet always he had come to rest on his first conviction, that this was a chosen spirit which discipline would only refine, and whose bold speculations needed a term of silence to found themselves firmly.

A man with a sense of history, Semmering was convinced that the effectiveness of an idea depended on the temper of the time into which it was first introduced. It was too late in history to risk another Galileo affair or the burning of a new Giordano Bruno. The Church was still suffering from the sad debates over the Chinese rites. He was less afraid of heresy than of a climate of thought which could make heresy out of a new aspect of truth. He lacked neither compassion nor understanding of the sacrifices he demanded of a noble mind such as this one, but Jean Télémond, like every other member of the Society, had vowed himself to obedience, and when it had been exacted of him he had submitted himself.

For Semmering this was the final test of the metal of a religious man, the final evidence of his capacity for a Godly work in a position of trust. Now the test was over, and he wanted to explain himself to Télémond and to offer him the affection that every son had a right to expect from his father in the spirit. Soon he would be asking Télémond to walk a new road, no longer solitary, no longer inhibited, but exposed, as he had never been exposed before, to the temptations of influence and the attacks of jealous interests. This time, he would need support more than discipline, and Semmering wanted to offer them with warmth and generosity.

Diplomacy was involved as well. Since the time of Pacelli the Cardinals of the Curia and the Bishops of the Church had been afraid of any attempt to introduce a Gray Eminence into the counsels of the Pontiff. They wanted, and so far they had had, a return to the natural order of the Church, where the Curia were the counselors of the Pontiff and the bishops were his co-workers, acknowledging his primacy as the successor of Peter, but holding equally to their own apostolic autonomy. If the Society of Jesus gave any appearance of attempting to push a favorite into the Papal Court, it would inevitably meet suspicion and hostility.

Yet the Pontiff had called for men, and the question was now how to offer this one without appearing to canvass for him. . . . The voice of the traffic-caller crackled over the amplifiers, announcing the arrival of a BOAC flight from Djakarta, Rangoon, New Delhi, Karachi, Beirut. Rudolf Semmering stood up, smoothed down his cassock, and walked toward the customs entrance to meet the exile.

Jean Télémond would have been a striking man in any company. Six feet tall, straight as a ramrod, lean of visage, with gray hair and cool, humorous blue eyes, he wore his clerical black like a military uniform, while the yellow malarial tinge of his skin and the furrows about his upturned mouth told the story of his campaigns in exotic places. He greeted his superior with respectful reserve, and then turned to the porter who was struggling with three heavy suitcases.

"Be careful with those. There's half a lifetime of work in them."

To Semmering he said with a shrug, "I presumed I was being transferred. I brought all my papers with me."

The Father General gave him one of his rare smiles. "You were right, Father. You've been away too long. Now we need you here."

A spark of mischief twinkled in Télémond's blue eyes. "I was afraid I was to be hauled before the Inquisition."

Semmering laughed. "Not yet. . . . You're very, very welcome, Father."

"I'm glad," said Télémond with curious simplicity. "These have been difficult years for me."

Rudolf Semmering was startled. He had not expected a man so brusque and aware. At the same time, he felt a small glow of satisfaction. This was no vague savant, but a man with a clear mind and a stout heart. Silence had not broken him, nor exile subdued him. An obedient spirit was one thing, but a man with a broken will was no use to himself or to the Church.

Semmering answered him gravely. "I know what you've done. I know what you've suffered. I have, perhaps, made your life more difficult than it needed to be. I ask only that you believe I acted in good faith."

"I've never doubted that," said Jean Télémond absently. "But twenty years is a long time." He was silent awhile, watching the green meadows of Ostia, dotted with old ruins and new excavations, where red poppies grew between the cracks of ancient stones. Suddenly he said, "Am I still under suspicion, Father?"

"Suspicion of what?"

Télémond shrugged. "Heresy, rebellion, a secret modernism, I don't know. You were never very clear with me."

"I tried to be," said Semmering mildly. "I tried to explain that prudence was involved, and not orthodoxy. Some of your early papers and lectures came under the notice of the Holy Office. You were neither condemned nor censured. They felt, and I agreed with them, that you needed more time, and more study. You have great authority, you see. We wanted it used to the best advantage of the Faith."

"I believe that," said Jean Télémond. "Otherwise I think I should have abandoned the work altogether." He hesitated a moment, and then asked, "Where do I stand now?"

"We have brought you home," said Semmering gently, "because we value you, and we need you. There is work for you here, urgent work."

"I have never made conditions; you know that. I have never tried to bargain with God or with the Society. I worked as best I could within the limits imposed on me. Now . . . now I should like to ask something."

"Ask it," said Rudolf Semmering.

"I think," said Télémond carefully, "I think I have gone as far as I can on this lonely road. I think what I have done needs to be tested by discussion and debate. I should like to begin to publish, to submit my thesis to open criticism. This is the only way knowledge grows, the only way the horizons of the spirit are enlarged. . . . I have never asked for anything before, but in this I beg for your support, and for the support of the Society."

"You have it," said Rudolf Semmering.

In the cramped seats of the speeding automobile they faced each other, superior and subject, the man under obedience, the man who exacted the fulfillment of the vow.

Télémond's lean face crumpled a little, and his blue eyes were misty. He said awkwardly, "I—I did not expect so much. This is quite a home-coming."

"It is better than you know," said the Father General gently. "But there are still risks."

"I've always known there would be. What do you want me to do?"

"First you have to pass a test. It will be a rough one, and you have less than a month to prepare yourself."

"What sort of test?"

"July thirty-first is the feast day of St. Ignatius Loyola."

"I was ordained on that day."

"It makes a good omen, then, because on that same day His Holiness will visit the Gregorian University, which, you know, owed its beginning to our founder and St. Francis Borgia. . . . I want you to deliver the memorial lecture in the presence of His Holiness, the teaching staff, and the students."

"God help me," said Jean Télémond. "God help my stumbling tongue."

As they turned into the clamor of the city, through the Porta San Paolo, he buried his face in his hands and wept.

Ruth Lewin sat under a striped umbrella on the Via Veneto, sipped an *aranciata,* and watched the lunch-time crowds disperse toward siesta. The soft air of summer lifted her spirits, and she felt as if all the weight of the world could be shrugged off with one long comfortable yawn. Even the city seemed to have taken on a new face. The clamor of the traffic was a friendly sound. The folk were better dressed than usual. The waiters were more courteous. The ogling of the men was a compliment.

Nothing had changed in her situation. None of her doubts or dilemmas had resolved themselves, yet their burden was lighter, and she wore it with a better humor. It was as if her long convalescence were over and she could take her place confidently in the normal commerce of the world.

It was not all an illusion. She had suffered too long the perilous alternations of exaltation and depression to deceive herself about her cure. But the swings were shorter now—the heights less dizzy, the deeps less terrifying. The pulse of life was returning to a regular beat. The fever had broken at last, and the moment of crisis had been her meeting with Kiril the Pontiff in a Roman back alley.

Even now the memory was lit by a kind of wonder. His aspect was so strange —the scar, the beard, the contrast between his office and his humble dress. Yet when she had confronted him in her own house, over the banality of coffee and biscuits, the impression was not of strangeness but of extraordinary simplicity.

Ever since her break with the Church she had had a creeping distaste for clerical talk and the forms of clerical convention. This man had none of them. He wore his belief like a skin, and his convictions were expressed with the gentleness of one who had acquired them at a price he would not ask others to pay. His words came out new-minted and ringing with sincerity:

". . . All life is a mystery, but the answer to the mystery is outside ourselves, and not inside. You can't go on peeling yourself like an onion, hoping that when you come to the last layer you will find what an onion really is. At the end you are left with nothing. The mystery of an onion is still unexplained because like man, it is the issue of an eternal creative act. . . . I stand in God's shoes, but I can't tell you any more. Don't you see? This is what I am here to teach—a mystery! People who demand to have Creation explained from beginning to end are asking the impossible. Have you ever thought that by demanding to know the explanation for everything you are committing an act of pride? We are limited creatures. How can anyone of us encompass infinity . . . ?"

In the mouth of another the words would have sounded dry and stilted, but from this Kiril they came endowed with a quality of healing, because they were not read from a book, but from the palimpsest of his own heart. He had not reproached her for the dereliction of a baptismal faith, but had talked of it with kindness, as if it were even a sort of mercy in itself.

"No two people come to God by the same road. There are very, very few who reach Him without stumbling and falling. There are seeds that grow a long time in darkness before they push up shoots into the sun. . . . There are others that come to the light at one thrust in a single day. . . . You are in darkness now, but if you want the light you will come to it in time. . . . The human soul, you see, meets barriers that it must cross, and they are not always crossed at one stride. The direction in which the soul travels is the important thing. If it travels away from itself, then it must ultimately come to God. If it turns back upon itself, this is a course of suicide, because without God we are nothing. . . . Everything, therefore, that urges you to an outward growth— service, love, the simplest interest in the world—can be a step toward Him. . . ."

Disturbed as she was on that night, she had not taken in the full import of all that he had said. But the words had remained imprinted on her memory, and each day she found in them a new meaning and a new application. If now she could sit calm in a summer sun, watching the folly and flirtation of the town, passing no judgment on it or on herself, it was because of this Kiril, who sat in the seat of judgment and yet withheld verdict. If love were possible again, it would be because of him who lived solitary in the celibate city of the Vatican.

Love . . . ! It was a chameleon word, and she had seen more of its changes and colorations than she could admit without blushing.

Every big city had its enclave of cripples and oddities and vagrants who sustained life on the best terms they could get and were grateful for the most temporary easement from lonely misery. Here in Rome the kingdom of the beggars of love was a weird and polyglot domain, and in her time she had wandered over most of it.

It was a treacherous journey for a widow of thirty-five with money in the bank and a heart empty of resources. Unhappy boys had wept at her breast for their mothers. Straying husbands and playing tourists had come knocking on her door. Men with noble names had made her the confidante of their exotic attachments. The secret sisterhood had offered her entry to the sapphic mysteries. In the end she had emerged, shaken and unsatisfied, knowing that even in the half-world of the odd ones there was no place for her.

Love . . . ! Here on the Via Veneto pretty girls with poodles on a leash sold it by the night's installment. In the clubs and bars any woman with a foreign accent could buy it for a smile and the flirting of a lace handkerchief. . . . But where and how did one find the person on whom to spend this newly discovered self—so fragile and suddenly so precious?

Miraculously, Humpty-Dumpty had been picked up and put together again. He was sitting back on the wall, smiling and clapping hands at the concourse. But if he tumbled again and the glue came unstuck . . . who then could patch the eggshell? O little white wandering spirit, please, please stay in one piece!

Out of the clamor of the traffic she heard her own name spoken. "Ruth Lewin! Where have you been hiding yourself?"

She looked up to see George Faber, gray-haired and dapper as any Roman dandy, looking down at her.

In his private study Kiril the Pontiff was closeted with two of his senior ministers: Cardinal Goldoni, his Secretary of State, and Cardinal Clemente Platino, Prefect of the Congregation for the Propagation of the Faith. The purpose of their meeting was a daylong stock-taking of the affairs of the Church, Holy, Universal, and Apostolic. The study was a large room bare of ornament save for a carved wooden crucifix behind the Pontiff's desk and, on the opposite wall, a case full of maps showing the distribution of Catholic communities throughout the world.

In another setting and another dress they might have been a trio of international businessmen: the Pontiff, dark, bearded, and exotic; the Secretary of State, gray, stocky, and harshly eloquent; Platino, tall, olive-skinned, urbane, with a great eagle beak inherited from some Spanish ancestor.

But in this place and in this time they were dedicated, each to the limit of his own talent, to a folly that promised small profit to any business: the preparation of all men for death and for union with an unseen God. Their talk ranged over a multitude of subjects: money, politics, military treaties, economic agreements, personalities in high places around the globe; yet the core of the discussion was always the same: how to spread throughout the world the knowledge of Christ, His teaching, and the society which He had set up to preserve and disseminate it.

For them every question—how a man married, how he was educated, what he was paid, his national allegiance—was at root a theological proposition. It had to do with the Creator and the creatures and the eternal relationship of one with the other. Everything that was done in the dimension of time had its roots and its continuity in eternity.

When the Secretary of State appointed an ambassador to Austria or a legate to Uruguay, his function was to maintain an official relationship with the government so that in a climate of accord between Church and State human souls might be led the more easily to the knowledge and the practice of a saving truth.

When Platino appointed this missionary congregation or that to go into the jungles of the Amazon, he did so with the fullest conviction that he was obeying a clear command of Christ to carry a Gospel of hope to those who sat in darkness and the shadow of death.

It was, however, a point of view that raised special problems of its own. Men who did a Godly work were apt to become careless about the human aspect of it. Men who dealt with the currency of eternity were apt to rest too hopefully on the future and let the present slip out of their control. Those who were sustained by the two-thousand-year-old structure of the Church were protected too softly from the consequence of their own mistakes. With so much tradition to rest on, they were often prickly and suspicious about new modes of Christian action.

Yet in spite of all, men like Platino and Goldoni had an acute awareness of the world in which they lived and of the fact that to do the work of God they had to come to terms with what man had done for himself or to himself. Platino was making this point now. His long brown finger pointed to a spot in Southeast Asia.

". . . Here, for example, Holiness, is Thailand. Constitutionally it is a monarchy. In fact it is a military dictatorship. The religion of the state is Buddhism. At one time or another in his life every male of the royal family, and every senior official, takes the saffron robe and spends some time in a monastery. We have schools here. They are run by nuns and teaching priests. They are free to give religious instruction, but not within normal school hours. Those who wish to be instructed in the Faith must come outside these times. This is our first difficulty. There is another. Government appointments—and any position of consequence is a government appointment—are only open to Buddhists. Officially, of course, this is not admitted, but in fact it is true. The country is underdeveloped. Most commerce is in the hands of Chinese, so that for all practical purposes, a man who becomes a Christian must give up all hope of economic or social advancement. . . . The temper of the people, which has also been conditioned by Buddhist belief, is resistant to change and suspicious of outside influence. . . .

"On the other hand, there is evident among the young men a growing interior conflict. They are being brought every day into closer contact with Western civilization through American military and economic aid, but there is little opportunity or work for them. I have been given what I believe is a reliable statistic, that twenty-five per cent of senior male students are addicted to heroin before they leave school. You see the problem. How do we move to make a real penetration of the minds and hearts of the people?"

"How do you summarize the work we are doing now?" asked the Pontiff gravely.

"Basically as a work of education and charity. On the human level we are helping to raise the standard of literacy. We run hospitals which are used as training centers. There is a home for the rehabilitation of girls who have been taken out of the brothels. . . . We serve the community. We display the Faith to those who pass through our hands. However, the number of conversions is small, and we have not yet entered effectively into the mind and heart of the country."

"We have a worse position in Japan," said Goldoni in his brisk fashion. "We have a concordat which gives us much more effective working conditions than we have in Thailand, but here again we have made no real break-through."

"Yet we did once make a break-through," said Kiril with a smile. "It was begun by one man. St. Francis Xavier. The descendants of his converts are still there—the Old Christians of Nagasaki and Nara. Why do we fail now? We have the same message. We dispense the same grace as the Church of the Catacombs. Why do we fail?" He heaved himself out of the chair and stood by the map, pointing to one country after another and measuring the failures and retreats of the Church. "Look at Africa. My predecessors proclaimed constantly the need for the swift training of a native clergy: men identified with their own people, speaking their language, understanding their symbols and their special needs. Too little was done too slowly. Now the continent is moving toward a federation of independent African nations, and the ground has been cut from under our feet. . . . Here in Brazil you have an immense industrial expansion, and a huge population of peasants living in the most grinding poverty. To whom are they turning to champion their cause? To the Communists. Do we not preach justice? Should we not be prepared to die for it as for any other Article of Faith? I ask you again. Where do we miss?"

Goldoni breathed a silent sigh of relief and left the answer to his colleague. After all, a Secretary of State had to deal with a situation as it was, with diplomats and politicians as they were—good or bad, pagan or Christian. Platino, on the other hand, was charged directly with the spread of Christian belief throughout the world. His authority was enormous, and inside the Church they called him "the Red Pope," as the Father General of the Jesuits was called the black one.

Platino did not answer directly, but picked up from the desk two photographs, which he held out to the Pontiff. One of them showed a fuzzy-haired Papuan in a white shirt and white lap-lap, with a small crucifix hung round his neck. The other was the picture of a native from the uplands of New Guinea with a headdress of bird-of-paradise feathers and a pig tusk thrust through his nose.

As the Pontiff examined the photographs, Platino explained them carefully: "Perhaps these two men will answer your Holiness' question. They both come from the same island, New Guinea. It is a small place, economically unimportant, but politically it may become so as the pivot of a federation of South Pacific islands. In two years, five at most, New Guinea will be an independent country. This man . . ." He pointed to the photograph of the man who wore the crucifix. "This is a mission boy. A teacher in one of our Catholic schools on the coast. He has lived all his life in a mission colony. He speaks English and pidgin and Motu. He teaches the catechism, and has been proposed as a candidate for the priesthood. . . . This one is a tribal chief from the mountains: a leader of twenty thousand men. He speaks no English, he understands pidgin, but speaks only his own upland dialect. He is wearing now a ceremonial dress. He still holds to the old pagan beliefs. . . . Yet when independence is granted to this country, he is the most likely leader, while our mission boy will have no influence at all."

"Tell me why," said Kiril the Pontiff.

"I have thought about it a long time, Holiness," said Platino deliberately. "I have prayed much. I am still not sure that I am right, but this is what I believe. With our mission boy we have in one sense succeeded admirably. We have educated a good human being. We have set him in the way of salvation. He lives chastely, deals justly, and displays in himself the example of a Godly life. If he becomes a priest, he will teach the Word and dispense the grace of the Sacraments to those with whom he comes in contact. In him and those like him the Church fulfills her prime mission—the sanctification of individual human souls. . . . In another sense, however, we have failed because in this boy—how shall I say it?—we have limited the relevance of the Faith. . . . In the mission we have created a small, safe world for him. A Christian world, yes, but one that has cut itself off from the larger world which is still God's vineyard. We have made him an apolitical individual, and man by his nature is a political and social animal who has an immortal soul. . . . We have left him, in large part, unprepared for the dialogue which he must sustain throughout his life with the rest of his fellows in the flesh. . . . Look at our friend here, the one with the tusk through his nose. He is a man of power because he practices polygamy and each wife brings him a plot of land and then cultivates it for him. He holds to the old beliefs because these are his ground of communication with his tribe. He is their mediator with the spirits as he is their mediator with men of other tongues. He understands tribal law and tribal justice. In the difficulty and confusion which will follow the granting of independence, he will speak with more authority and more relevance than our mission boy because he has not been divorced from the realities of social existence. . . . Your Holiness spoke of Brazil and the South Americas. There is an analogy between the two situations. The Church has to deal with man in the circumstances in which he lives. If he is hungry, we have to feed him; if he is oppressed, we must defend him so that he may have, at least, a minimum freedom to set his soul in order. We cannot preach from the pulpit, 'Thou shalt not steal,' and then stand by, inactive, while political or social injustice is done to those who sit and listen to our preaching. . . . We see a strange example in Poland, where the Church has had for very survival to enter actively into a conversation with elements hostile to it. It has had to prove itself relevant, and it has done so. It lives the more strongly for that very reason, even though it lives more painfully. . . ."

He paused and mopped his forehead with a handkerchief.

"Forgive me, Holiness, if I speak more strongly still. We have all seen the progress that was made under your predecessor toward a growth of unity between the separated Christian communities. Our work in this field has only begun, but it seems to me that where we have been defensive, where we have retreated, holding the Faith to ourselves as though it could be tarnished by contact with the world, there we have failed. Where we have held it up for a witness, where we have affirmed most boldly that the Gospel is relevant to every human act and every situation, there we have done well."

"You affirm it," said Kiril the Pontiff bluntly. "I affirm it, as do our brother bishops scattered across the world, but the affirmation does not reach the people with the same clearness and the same fruitfulness—it does not even reach my Romans here. Why?"

"I think," said the Secretary of State brusquely, "the world is educating itself more quickly than the Church. Put it another way. The knowledge that is necessary to make an Act of Faith, and an Act of Repentance, is not enough to found a Christian society or create a religious climate. In the last twenty years men have been projected into a new and terrifying dimension of existence. . . . The graph of human science from the invention of the wheel to the internal-combustion engine is a long, gradual slope. It covers—what?—five, ten, fifteen thousand years. From the internal-combustion engine to this moment the line leaps almost vertically, pointing to the moon. . . . 'Tempora mutantur . . .'" he quoted wryly. "'Times change, and man changes with them.' If our mission means anything, it means that each new enlargement of the human mind should be an enlargement of man's capacity to know, love, and serve God."

"I think," said Kiril the Pontiff with a smile, "I should send you both out on a missionary journey." He crossed to his desk and sat down, facing them. He seemed to gather himself for a moment, and then very quietly, almost humbly, he explained himself. "I am, as you know, an eager man. It has been my fear, since I have sat in the Chair of Peter, that I should act too hastily and damage the Church, which is given into my hands. . . . I have tried to be prudent and restrained; I have understood also that one man in his lifetime cannot change the world. The symbol of the Cross is a symbol of the apparent failure and folly of God himself. . . . But it is my office to teach and to direct, and I have decided now where I want to begin. . . . What you have told me confirms me in the decision. I am grateful to you both. I want you both to pray for me."

The two Cardinals sat silent, waiting for him to go on. To their surprise, he shook his head. "Be patient with me. I need time and prayer before I declare myself. Go in the name of God."

"I suppose," said George Faber in his uncomfortable fashion, "I suppose you're wondering why I'm telling you all this about Chiara and me."

Ruth Lewin laughed and shrugged. "That's the way it goes in Rome—everybody's got a story. And a stranger's usually the best listener."

"We're not really strangers, though. How many times have we met? Half a dozen, at least. At the Antonellis' and at Herman Seidler's and—"

"So I'm convinced we're not strangers. Take it from there."

"I was feeling low—and I was delighted to see you."

"Thank you, kind sir."

"And I don't tell my life story to every girl I meet on a street corner."

"I don't think it matters in Rome whether you tell it or not. People know it just the same—in different versions, of course!"

Faber grinned, and looked for a moment like a self-conscious boy. "I've never heard your story, Ruth."

She parried the probe with a smile. "I've never told it. And I don't belong to the cocktail set."

"Where do you belong?"

"I've often wondered that myself."

"Do you have many friends here?"

"A few. They call me for dinner sometimes. I visit them when I feel inclined. I do a little work amongst some lame ducks in Old Rome. For the rest . . . *Mi arrangio.* I get along one way and another."

"Are you happy?"

Once again she hedged the answer. "Is anyone? Are you?"

"I'm in a mess," said George Faber bluntly.

"That's not your reputation."

Faber looked up sharply, wondering if she was mocking him. He had a small humor, and banter always made him suspicious. "What's my reputation?"

"You have the tidiest life in Rome . . . and a beautiful mistress to round it out."

"That's not the way I see it. I want to get married. It seems the only way I can do it is to mix myself up with blackmail and backstairs politics, and a bunch of gay boys and Lesbians."

"Don't you think the risk is worth it?"

His heavy, handsome face clouded and he ran a nervous hand through his gray hair. "I suppose it is. I haven't really had time to think it out."

"That means you're not sure."

"No, I'm not sure."

As if to divert her attention he signaled the waiter to bring him another cup of coffee. Then he lit a cigarette and stared moodily at the shop front on the other side of the pavement. For all her detachment, Ruth Lewin felt herself touched by a pang of pity for him. He was no longer young, though most women would find him attractive. He had built himself a comfortable career and a respectable name in his trade. Now he was being asked to risk them both for a girl who, once free, might grow tired of him and look for younger loving. She dropped her teasing tone and questioned him more gently.

"What does Chiara want?"

"Freedom at any price."

"Even at the price of your career?"

"I'm not sure of that, either."

"Don't you think you should ask her?"

"That's what bothers me. . . . I'm not even clear myself what the risks are. All I know is that on the one hand, there's an element of blackmail and I'm to be the blackmailer . . . Don't misunderstand me. I've been in this game a long time. I know that every newsman is tempted at some time or another to use his position for his own profit. My experience is that those who do it always lose in the end. I've never been a muckraker, and I'm rather proud of it. . . . On the other hand, I'm fighting for something and someone very precious to me."

"If you start a fight with Corrado Calitri," said Ruth Lewin soberly, "I can promise you it will be a very rough one."

He stared at her, surprised. "Do you know Calitri, then?"

"I know some of the people he knows. They play very dirty when their feelings are hurt."

He hesitated a moment, and then faced her with the question. "Could you help me to meet some of them?"

"No." She was very definite about it.

"Why not?"

"I lived in that little Arcady for a while. I didn't like it. I don't want to go back. Besides, you're a newsman. You have your own contacts."

"Not too many I can trust. Would you be willing to give me names . . . information?"

To his surprise, she burst out laughing, and then seeing his discomfiture, she laid an apologetic hand on his wrist. "Poor George! I shouldn't laugh at you. But I wonder . . . I really wonder . . ."

"What?"

"About you and Chiara. Are you both so sure you can go through with this fight—win or lose? If you lose, you know, they'll tear you into little pieces and feed you to the lions like early Christians. The Church won't have either of you. You'll never be welcome again at the Vatican or on the Quirinale. Are you both ready for that? Do you have enough love for Chiara? Does she have enough for you?"

He shrugged and spread his hands in a Roman gesture of puzzlement. "Beh! Everybody in Rome talks about love. Everybody plays at it in his own fashion. I've played, too, but now it's late in the day for me. I don't want to make a mistake."

"I'd like to help you," she told him quietly, "but it's your life and your girl. . . . I should go now; it's getting late."

"Would you let me take you home?"

"Better not. I'll get a taxi."

"Could I see you again?"

"Why, George?"

He flushed unhappily. "I've enjoyed talking to you. I hope you'll decide to help me. And if I go ahead with this Calitri business, I'll need to talk to someone I can trust."

"What makes you think you can trust me?"

"You said yourself you don't belong to the gossip circuit. I'd like to add that you're a very grown-up girl."

"Is that the best recommendation you can give me?"

Once again his rare humor asserted itself. "Give me time, and I may think of others."

"If and when you do, you can call me. I'm in the telephone book."

On which indecisive note they parted. As she rode home through the clamor of the afternoon traffic, she remembered that it was late in the day for her, too, and she felt again the pang of treacherous pity for George Faber and his puzzled middle-aged heart.

Extract from
the Secret Memorials of
KIRIL I, Pont. Max.

. . . It is an hour after midnight—the beginning of a new day. An important day for me because for the first time I shall begin to address myself to the whole Church. Late last evening I asked my confessor to come to me so that I might purge myself from the sins of the day and purify myself for the task I am about to undertake.

Afterwards I begged him to stay with me a little while and serve the Mass which I wanted to celebrate immediately after midnight. . . . It is strange how much variety there can be for a priest in the offering of the Sacrifice. Sometimes one is dry and unmoved, one has to make an effort of will to concentrate on the familiar ritual and on the staggering significance of the Act of Consecration. At other times it is as if one is caught out of oneself and "into the spirit," as St. John puts it. One is aware of God. One is at the same moment humbled and exalted, afraid and rapturously glad. . . .

Tonight it was different again. I began to understand in a new fashion the nature of my office. When, at the moment of elevation, I lifted the Host above my head, I saw the real meaning of the "we" with which the Pontiffs have addressed themselves customarily to the world. It is not "I" who am to speak or to write, it is the Church through me and Christ through me and the Church. . . .

I am myself, yes. But if I speak only of myself, and for myself, I am nothing. I am like the wind bells, whose sound changes with every breeze. . . . But the Word cannot change. The Word is immutable. . . . "In the beginning was the Word, and the Word was with God, and the Word was God." Yet in another sense the Word must renew itself in me as the redemptive act of the Crucifixion renews itself at the hands of every priest when he says Mass. I am the reed through which the voice of the spirit must be blown so that men may hear it in the mode of their own times. . . .

The paper is blank before me, the pens are ready. Is Kiril ready? I pray that he may be. What must he write? And how and to whom?

My subject is education, the preparation of a man to take his place in this world and in the next. My letter will be a discussion of the educative office of the Church—its mission to "lead out" the soul of man from the darkness of ignorance, from the bondage of the flesh, into the light and the freedom of the sons of God. . . .

How shall I write? As simply as I can because the deepest truth is the most simply stated. I must write from the heart—*cor ad cor loquitur*. And I must write in my own tongue because this is the best fashion for every man to talk of God, and to Him. Later the Latinists will take my words and harden them into the antique form which will preserve them for a permanent record in the Church. After them will come the translators, who will turn them into a hundred other tongues in which the Word of God must be preached. . . . The world is a Babel Tower of conflicting voices, but inside the Church there is and must always be "the unity of the spirit in the bond of faith."

Outside the Church, too, there is a unity which we neglect too often. It is the unity of men who suffer together a common existence, delight in common joys, and share the same confusions, regrets, and temptations. . . .

I am reminded of something forgotten too often by us the shepherds, Tertullian's *Testimony of the Soul*. . . . "Man is one name belonging to every nation upon earth. In them all is one soul though many tongues. Every country has its own language, yet the subjects of which the untutored soul speaks, are the same everywhere."

There is another reason why I want to write in Russian. I want Kamenev to see my letter as it came from my own hand. I want him to hear through it the tones of my voice so that he may know that I love him and the people among whom I was born. If it were possible I should like him to have my manuscript, but it may be difficult to get it into his hands, and I could not risk compromising him.

To whom shall I write? . . . To the whole Church—to my brother bishops, to all priests and monks and nuns, to all the faithful, without whom our office is meaningless. I must show them how their mission is not merely to teach but to educate one another with love and forbearance, each lending of his own strength to the weak, of his own knowledge to the ignorant, of his charity to all. . . .

And when I have written, what then? I must begin to act through the administration of the Church to see that reforms are made where they are needed and that the inertia of a large and scattered organization does not stand in the way of God's intention. I must have patience, too, and tolerance, understanding that I have no right to demand of God a visible success in all I attempt. I am the gardener. I plant the seed and water it, knowing that death may take me before I see the bud or the flower. It is late and I must begin. . . .

"Kiril, the servant of the servants of God, to the bishops and brethren of all the Churches, peace and apostolic benediction. . . ."

V

THE home-coming of Jean Télémond, S.J., was a drab little affair that belied the warmth of his superior's welcome.

The headquarters of the Society, at No. 5 Borgo Santo Spirito, was a large gray building, bleak as a barracks, that nestled under the shadow of St. Peter's dome. Its furnishings were sparse, functional, and without discernible beauty. The only man to greet him was the brother porter, a gray and crusty veteran who had seen so many members come and go that one more made no matter.

The whole aspect of the place was cheerless and temporary, a shelter for men whose training was to divest themselves of comfort and human attachment and make themselves soldiers of Christ. Even the religious emblems were ugly and mass-produced, reminders only of the interior life which no symbol could properly convey.

After they had prayed together, the Father General led him to his room, a small, whitewashed box, furnished with a bed, a *prie-dieu,* a crucifix, a desk, and a set of bookshelves. Its dusty windows looked out on a courtyard, chill and deserted even under the summer sun. Jean Télémond had lived more harshly than most and in less friendly places, but this first look at the Mother House plunged him into a deep depression of spirit. He felt solitary and naked and strangely afraid. The Father General gave him the timetable of the House, promised to introduce him to his colleagues at suppertime, and then left him to his own devices.

It took him only a few moments to unpack his meager personal belongings, and then he set about the task of laying out the mass of notes, manuscripts, and bulky folders which represented his life-work. Now, when the time had come to make the tally of it and present it to the world, it seemed small and insignificant.

For twenty years he had worked as a paleontologist, in China, in Africa, in America, and the far Indies, plotting the geography of change, the history of life recorded in the crust of the earth. The best scientific minds had been his colleagues and co-workers. He had survived war and revolution and disease and loneliness. He had endured the perilous dichotomy between his function as a scientist and his life as a religious priest. To what end?

For years the conviction had been growing in him that the only intelligible purpose of so much effort and sacrifice was to display the vast concordance of Creation, the ultimate convergence of the spiritual and physical which would mark the eternal completion of an eternal creative Impulse. Many times he had pondered the significance of the old proverb "God writes straight with crooked lines," and he was convinced to the marrow of his bone that the final vector of all the diverse forces of Creation was an arrow pointing straight to a personal divinity.

Many another before him had attempted this justification of God to men. Their achievements and their failures were the milestones of human thought —Plato, St. Augustine, Albertus Magnus, Thomas of Aquin . . . Each had used the knowledge of his own time to build a theology or a philosophy or a cosmology. . . . Each had added another stage to the journey of unaided reason; each had elevated man thus much above the jungle that spawned him.

For Télémond the project presented itself in another form: to trace, from the text of the living earth, the journey from unlife to life, from life to consciousness, from consciousness to the final unity of Creation with its Creator.

The study of the past, he believed, was the key to the pattern of the future. The justification of the past and of the present lay in the tomorrow that would thrust out of them. He could not believe in a wasteful Creator or in a diffuse, accidental, purposeless Creation. At the root of all his thought and, he believed, at the root of every human aspiration was an instinctive desire for a unity and a harmony in the cosmos. Once men abandoned their hope for it, they condemned themselves to suicide or madness.

That the harmony did exist, he was convinced beyond doubt. That it could be demonstrated, he believed also—though in another mode of credence. The pattern was laid, but it was not yet complete. He believed he had grasped the main lines of it, but his problem was to explain them in terms intelligible and acceptable. So vast an exposure needed new words, new levels of thought, new analogies, and a new boldness in speculation.

For too long Western thought had been disinclined toward a unified knowledge of the world. Even in the Church the spiral thinking of the Eastern fathers, the traditional Christian *gnosis,* had been overshadowed by the nominalist and rationalist tradition of Western theologians. Now, if ever, the hope of the world's survival seemed to rest on a leap out of mere logic into a recognition of new and bolder modes of communication.

Yet the terror of this first moment in Rome was that under the first impact of this noisy, brawling city, where past and present rubbed elbows with each other at every step, his conviction seemed to be weakening. Rome was so sure of itself, so sophisticated, so skeptical, so certain that everything that had happened or could happen had been weighed and judged beyond dispute—that his own voice must sound small and meaningless.

A long time ago, from a hut on the fringe of the Gobi Desert, he had written, "I understand now how little mere travel gives to a man. Unless the spirit expands with the explosion of space about him, he returns the same man as he went out." Here in the Mother House of the Society, where all the rooms looked the same, where everyone was dressed in the same black cassock and attended the same exercises of devotion and ate at the same table, he wondered whether in truth he had changed at all, and whether the enlargement which he thought to have attained was not a bitter illusion.

With a gesture of impatience he stacked the last manuscripts on the desk, closed the door on them, and walked out to view the city which threatened him so vividly.

A few moments' walking brought him out onto the broad reach of the Street of Conciliation and in full view of the Piazza of St. Peter. The slim finger of the obelisk pointed to the sky, and on either hand Bernini's colonnades swept backward to the sunlit dome of the Basilica. The sudden majesty of it all—the towering cupola, the gigantic figures of windy stone, the rearing masses of columns and pilasters—oppressed him, and he felt drunk with the suddenness of sun and space.

Instinctively he lowered his eyes to the human aspect: the straggle of afternoon tourists, the coachmen gossiping at their horses' heads, the peddlers with their little boxes of rosaries, the buses and automobiles, and the slim jets of the fountains. Once again the cogs of memory slipped into gear, and he remembered what he had written after his first look at the Grand Canyon of the Colorado. . . . "I am either unmoved or tremendously troubled by the sight of natural grandeur, or even by a spectacular artifact deserted by its makers. As soon as man appears, I am comforted again because man is the only significant link between the physical order and the spiritual one. Without man the universe is a howling wasteland contemplated by an unseen Deity. . . ." If man deserted even this ageless splendor of St. Peter's, it would decay and rot into a goat-cropping, where tree roots grew out of the stones and animals drank from the muddy basins of the fountains.

Encouraged, he strolled across the Piazza toward the entrance of the Basilica, pausing to look up at the papal apartments and ask himself what manner of man now dwelt in them. Soon they would meet face to face, and Jean Télémond would have to justify his own life's work to a man charged to perpetuate the life of the whole Church. Already rumors were rife about the new Pontiff and his challenge to the reactionaries and the extreme traditionalists in the Vatican. There were those who saw him as the prime mover of a second renaissance within the Church, a new and unexpected link between the logical West and the illuminated East.

If the rumors were true, then there was hope that Jean Télémond might be freed at last from his exile. If not . . .

On the opposite side of the Piazza lay the Palace of the Holy Office, where the Hounds of God kept watch over the Deposit of Faith. To them Jean Télémond was known already. Once a priest came under their scrutiny he was never forgotten, and everything he wrote must pass through their hands before it could be printed. Cardinal Leone was still there, too, he of the white mane and the cold eye and the uncertain temper. It was an open secret that Leone had small liking for the Father General of the Jesuits and that he favored more the opinions and the manners of the older orders in the Church. Télémond wondered what had prompted Semmering to risk the displeasure of the old lion by bringing back to Rome a man of suspect opinions.

There were politics inside the Church as well as out of it. There were questing minds and reluctant ones. There were blind traditionalists and too eager innovators. There were men who sacrificed order to growth, and others who reached so boldly for change that they held it back for centuries. There were rank pietists and fierce ascetics. There were administrators and apostles —and God help any luckless fellow who was caught between the millstones.

There was only one refuge; one committal, which he had made a long time ago. A man could walk only the path he saw at his own feet or that which was pointed out to him by a lawful superior. After that he was in the hands of God. . . . And their compass was more generous, their hold more reassuring, than the hands of any man.

In spite of the warmth he shivered and quickened his steps toward the interior of the Basilica. Looking neither to right nor left, he walked down the echoing nave toward the sanctuary, and then knelt for a long time, praying at the tomb of Peter.

In the small, cold hours between midnight and dawn George Faber lay wakeful and grappled with his new situation. Beside him Chiara lay sleeping like a child, satiated and tranquil. Never in the months of their loving had he experienced a passion so tumultuous, a mating so abandoned as on this night. Every sense had quickened, every emotion had surged up and spent itself in a climax of union so intense that death itself had seemed only a whisper away. Never had he felt so much a man. Never had Chiara shown herself so generously a woman. Never had speech been stifled so swiftly by the outpourings of tenderness and the transports of desire. . . . Never in all his life had he been so suddenly overwhelmed by the sadness of the afterward.

When their loving was done, Chiara had given a small contented sigh, buried her face in the pillow, and lapsed immediately into sleep. It was as if she had left him without warning and without farewell to embark on a private journey —as if having touched the limit of love, he were left solitary to face the darkness and the terrors of an endless night.

The terrors were more real than they had ever been before. For so rich a pleasuring, sometime, somehow, a price must be paid. And he knew beyond the shadow of a doubt that he would be the one to pay it. What he had felt this night was a springtime flowering which might never repeat itself, because for him it was late summer, late harvest, with the taxman waiting at the gate to claim his due.

For Chiara life was still her debtor. Payment had been deferred too long and her body was greedy for the tribute. For himself, a man on the wrong side of forty, the case was far other. He knew where the price tags were hidden. He knew the needs that followed the brisk satisfaction of the act of union: the need of continuity, the need of children to be born of the seed so richly spent in lust or love, the need of quiet harbor and a morning sunlight after the storms of the night.

Even as he thought about it, Chiara stirred and turned toward him for warmth. It was a gesture made in a dream, but it was more eloquent than words. Until her marriage to Calitri she had been protected at every step—by rich and doting parents, by cosseting nuns, by the traditions of her class. When her marriage had failed, she had found another refuge, and now she had come to rest in his arms to forgetfulness in his practiced embrace. So long as he held her strongly and securely, she would stay. But the moment his grip slackened or his courage faltered, she would slip away.

The strange thing was that she saw nothing one-sided in the bargain. She had given him her body, she had given him her reputation; what else was there to demand? Had he told her, she would never have understood. Married and the mother of children, she would grow in the end to maturity, but in this halfway state she would always be the girl-woman, half delighted by the adventure, half afraid of its consequences, but never wholly understanding that the debt of love was not all paid in the coinage of the flesh.

For her even tonight's encounter, rich, ruinous and wonderful, was a kind of flight—and he was too old, too wise, or too calculating to make it with her. Instinctively he turned, threw his arms about her, and drew her to him, wondering even as he did so why the miraculous oneness of the flesh should last so short a time, and why in the end two lovers must lie so often and so long like islands in a dark sea. Her slack hand lay across his body, her hair brushed his lips, her perfume surrounded him. But sleep would not come, and he rehearsed over and over again their dinner-table talk, when he had told her of Campeggio's advice, and where it might lead the pair of them. . . .

She had listened attentively, chin cupped in her hands, her dark eyes bright with eagerness, intrigued by the prospect of a plot.

"Of course, darling! It's so simple. Why didn't we think of it before? There must be twenty people in Rome who'd be happy to give evidence against Corrado. All we've got to do is find them."

"Do you know any of them, Chiara?"

"Not really. Corrado was always fairly discreet with me. Still, I'm sure if we talked around we'd get a whole list of names."

"The one thing we mustn't do," he told her firmly, "is talk around. If word gets out about what we're doing, we're finished. Don't you understand? This is a conspiracy."

"George, darling, don't be so melodramatic. All we're trying to do is get justice for me. You couldn't call that conspiracy, surely."

"It wears the color of it. And in the eyes of the Church, and civil law, it comes to the same thing. There are only two things we can do—employ a professional investigator or I'll have to do the investigation myself. If we use an investigator, it will cost me more money than I can afford, and in the end he could sell me out to your husband. If I do the job myself . . . I'm immediately embroiled up to the neck."

She stared at him, wide-eyed and innocent. "Are you afraid, George?"

"Yes, I am."

"Of my husband?"

"Of his influence, yes."

"Don't you want to marry me, darling?"

"You know I do. But once we're married we have to live. If I lose my reputation in Rome I can't work here any longer. We'd have to go back to America."

"I wouldn't mind that. . . . Besides, what about my reputation? I didn't throw that in your face, did I?"

"Please, Chiara! Please try to understand this isn't a matter of morals, it's a matter of authority, professional status . . . the credit I live by. If I'm held up as a common blackmailer . . . where do I start again? This is the double standard, sweetheart. You can sleep around as much as you like. You can make a million by exploiting the poor. But if you pass a bad check for ten dollars or breach the code of professional ethics, you're dead and buried and there's no coming back. That's the way the world is, rough as guts. Do what you want. Take what you want. But if you trip—God help you! That's what we have to face —together."

"If I'm not afraid, George, why should you be?"

"I've got to be sure that you know what's involved."

"I wonder if you really know what's involved for me. A woman needs to be married, George. She needs to have a home and children, and a man who belongs to her. What we have is wonderful, but it isn't enough. If you won't fight for it, George, what can I do?"

. . . And there it was, the challenge that had taken him at one stride to her arms—a challenge to his virility, a challenge to the one folly he had never indulged—to count the world well lost for love. But George Faber was a man of his own world. He knew himself too well to believe that he could live without it. He had made the gesture, to be sure. He had flung his cap at the whirling windmills, but when the time came to assault them with sword and lance, how would he be then? A knight in shining armor with his lady's favor on his helm . . . ? Or an aging Quixote on a spavined nag, an object of laughter for men and angels?

Valerio Cardinal Rinaldi sat on the terrace of his villa and watched the day decline toward the sea. The folds of the land were full of purple shadows, the hills were touched with gold and bronze, and the rooftops of village and farmhouse shone russet in the glow. A small breeze stirred across the land, carrying the scent of lilac and roses, and mown grass. The sound of childish laughter rose from the garden below, where his niece's daughter played among the Orphic marbles.

This was the good time—the hour between day and dusk, when the eye was rested from the harshness of the sun and the spirit was not yet touched by the melancholy of twilight. The cicadas were still, and the crickets had not begun their mournful chirping. He picked up the book that lay on his lap and began to read the crabbed Greek characters which hid the magical words of Euripides:

> And O for that quiet garden by the Western sea
>   Where the daughters of Evening sing
> Under the golden apple-tree;
>   Where the bold sailor wandering
>   Finds the Ocean-god has barred
> His Westward path over the purple waste!
>   Where huge Atlas lives to guard
>   The solemn frontiers of the sky!

> Where Zeus' palace fountains of ambrosial wine
>   Flow by the festal couch divine,
>   While holy Earth heaps high
>   Her fruits of rarest taste
> To bless the immortal feast with bountiful supply!

He was a lucky man and he knew it. It was given to few to arrive at eminence and then survive it with a strong heart and a good digestion to enjoy the quiet garden where the Daughters of Evening sang. It was given to few in his profession to hear the voices of children in his own orchard close, to have them cluster about his knee for a story, to give them a kiss and an old priest's blessing at bedtime.

Others he knew had died before their time. Others, again, survived painfully, with blear eyes or palsied limbs or slow cankers, on the charity of the Church. Some lapsed into senility or a poverty of possession and spirit. But he sat here in the splendor of a fading day—prosperous, independent, the last of the princely Cardinals of the Church. He had few regrets, because regret had always seemed a vanity and alien to his nature. He was ready for retirement— prepared for it, too, by a curious and scholarly mind and a diversity of friendships and interests. He did not fear death because in the normal course it was still a long way off, and he had lived an orderly life, investing his talents as best he knew for the service of the Church.

Yet sometimes—in the twilight hour, in the wakeful nights of an old man, or when he watched the peasants bending over the tillage of his estate—the poignant question presented itself: Why have I so much? Why am I endowed so richly and others in so niggardly a fashion? Or is this all a divine irony whose point will be revealed only in eternity?

Old Euripides had raised the same question and yet answered it no better:

> They wander over the waves, visit strange cities,
>   Seeking a world of wealth,
> All alike sure of achievement; yet
> One man's aim misses the lucky moment,
>   Another finds fortune in his lap.

And there was another question still. What did one do with all this fruitage of life? Toss it away, like little Brother Francis, and walk the world singing the praise of Lady Poverty? It was too late in the day for that. The grace of abandonment had passed him by—if, indeed, it had ever been offered. For better or for worse, he was saddled with the career he had built.

He was neither gluttonous nor spendthrift. He was educating his sister's children, and a pair of needy students for the priesthood. When he died half his wealth would go to his family, the other half to the Church. The Pontiff himself had approved the disposition. For what, then, should he reproach himself? For nothing, it seemed, except, perhaps, a certain mediocrity of spirit, a need of his nature to have the best of both worlds. And yet God Almighty had made them both, the seen and the unseen, for man's habitation and benefit. He had made man, too, and it was the nature of His mercy to exact no more than a just return on the talent He had given to each one.

Valerio Rinaldi was wise enough not to rejoice too freely in his good fortune. Yet he could not weep because there was nothing to weep for. So he sighed a little as the shadows drew closer over the land and went on reading the story of Hippolytus, the son of Theseus:

> To go into the dark! Now let me die, and pass
> To the world under the earth, into the joyless dark!
> Since you, dearer than all, are at my side no longer,
> And the death you have dealt is more than the death
>   that has swallowed you.

When twilight came at last, he closed his book and went in to say evening prayers with his household, and then prepare himself for dinner with Cardinal Leone.

The white-haired inquisitor was growling and crusty as ever, but he softened instantly at the entry of the children. When they bobbed before him, three dark-haired little maids, to receive his blessing, his eyes clouded and his hands trembled as he laid them on their foreheads. When the children backed away respectfully, he drew them to him and talked gravely as any grandfather about their lessons and their dolls and the momentous event of a day at the zoo. Rinaldi smiled secretly to see the old lion tamed so swiftly. He was even more surprised when the man who was the guardian of so many mysteries fumbled his way through a jigsaw puzzle and begged for time for the children to finish it with him.

When at last the children were dismissed and dinner was announced, Leone was strangely subdued. He said soberly, "You're a lucky man, Rinaldi. For this you should be grateful to God all the days of your life."

"I am grateful," said Rinaldi. "It troubles me that I have done so little to deserve my happiness."

"Enjoy it, my friend. It's the purest one you will ever know." Then he added a poignant afterthought. "When I was in the seminary, one of my old masters said that every priest should be given a child to rear for five years. I didn't understand what he meant then. I do now."

"Do you have any relatives?" asked Rinaldi.

"None. I used to think that as priests we didn't need them. That's an illusion, of course. . . . One gets lonely in the cloth as well as out of it." He grunted and gave a wintry smile. "Eh! We all get sentimental when we're old."

They dined alone as befitted a pair of princes, men who were charged with the weightiest secrets of the Church. An elderly manservant waited on them and withdrew after each course was served, so that they might talk freely. Leone seemed oddly moved by his meeting with the children, and as he picked absently at his fish he reverted once more to the problems of a celibate life.

". . . Every year, as you know, we get a small crop of cases at the Holy Office: priests who get into trouble with women, unsavory affairs between teachers and pupils, and allegations of soliciting by priests in the confessional.

It's inevitable, of course. There are bad apples in every barrel, but the older I get the less sure I am of how to deal with them."

Rinaldi nodded agreement. He himself had served as a commissioner of the Holy Office and was privy to its most diverse deliberations.

Leone went on: "We have a very bad case in front of us now, affecting a Roman priest and a young woman of his congregation. The evidence is pretty conclusive. The girl has fallen pregnant, and there is possibility of open scandal. I felt bound to bring the affair to the personal notice of the Holy Father."

"How did he take it?"

"More calmly than I expected. The priest in question has, of course, been suspended from his duties; but His Holiness ordered that he be required to submit to a medical and psychiatric examination before the case is finally decided. . . . It's an unusual step."

"Do you disagree with it?" asked Rinaldi quizzically.

"The way it was put to me," said Leone thoughtfully, "I was in no position to disagree. His Holiness pointed out that no matter what a priest does he is still an erring soul in need of help; that punishment was not enough; that we had to help the man to mend his error and his life. He went on to say that modern research had shown that many sexual aberrations had their roots in a real sickness of the mind, and that the celibate life raised special problems for those of a psychotic disposition. . . . The ruling of the canons is guarded on this point, but not, of course, prohibitive. A priest may seek or be given psychiatric treatment only in grave cases and with the permission of the bishop. The authority of the Holy Father is supreme in the matter."

"You still haven't said whether you agreed with his decision," said Rinaldi in his mild, ironic fashion.

Leone chuckled. "I know, I know. I have a bad reputation. To the Church at large I am still the Grand Inquisitor, ready to purge out error by rack and fire. . . . But it isn't true. I am always in dilemma in these matters. I have to be so careful of discipline. I am torn always between compassion and my duty to enforce the law. . . . I've met this man. He's a sad, troubled creature. We can break him with a word, and set him with the same word in the way of damnation. On the other hand, what about the woman, and the child which is to be born?"

"What did His Holiness have to say about that?"

"He wants the child made a ward of the Church. He wants the girl provided with employment and a dowry. Once again, you see, there is a question of precedent. But I admire his attitude even though I am not sure I can agree with all of it. He has a soft heart. . . . The danger is that it may be too soft for the good of the Church."

"He has suffered more than we. Perhaps he has more right to trust his heart than we have."

"I know that. I could wish he trusted me a little more."

"I know he trusts you." Rinaldi made the point firmly. "I know he has a great respect for you. Has he moved against you in any way?"

"Not yet. I think the real test is still to come."

"What do you mean?"

Leone cocked a shrewd eye at his host. "Don't tell me you haven't heard. The

Father General of the Jesuits has brought this Télémond fellow back to Rome. He's arranged for him to speak in the presence of the Pope on the feast of St. Ignatius Loyola."

"I heard about it. I'm invited to be present. I don't think it means too much. Télémond is a distinguished scholar. I think it's only natural that Semmering should want to reinstate him and give him a wider field of action in the Church."

"I think it's a calculated step," said Leone bluntly. "Semmering and I rub each other the wrong way. He knows that Télémond's opinions are still suspect."

"Come, come, old friend! He's had twenty years to revise them, and you certainly can't call him a rebellious spirit. He submitted, didn't he, when silence was imposed on him? Even the Holy Office can't refuse him the opportunity to restate his position."

"The occasion is too public. Too symbolic, if you want. I think Semmering has committed an indiscretion."

"What are you really afraid of, my friend? A victory for the Jesuits?"

Leone growled and tossed his white mane. "You know that isn't true. They do God's work, as we try to do it, in our own fashion."

"What, then?"

"Have you met this Jean Télémond?"

"No."

"I have. He's a man of great charm and, I think, of singular spirituality. I think he may make a very favorable impression on the Holy Father. I believe that's what Semmering's expecting, too."

"Is that a bad thing?"

"It could be. If he has the patronage of the Pontiff, then he is much freer to promulgate his opinions."

"But the Holy Office is still there to monitor them."

"It would be much more difficult to move against a man under papal patronage."

"I think you're making two unfounded assumptions—that he will get papal patronage, and that you will have to move against him."

"We have to be ready for anything that happens."

"Isn't there a simpler way? Why not raise the matter with the Holy Father now?"

"And what do I tell him? That I mistrust his discretion, or that he doesn't trust me enough?"

"I can see that might be difficult." Rinaldi laughed and rang the bell for the next course. "I'll give you my advice. Relax. Enjoy your dinner, and let the affair take its own way. Even the Holy Office can't do as well for the Church as the Holy Ghost. . . ."

Leone smiled grimly and addressed himself to the roast. "I'm getting old, my friend—old and stubborn. I can't get used to the idea that a youngster of fifty is wearing the triple crown."

Rinaldi shrugged like a true Roman. "I think the tiara fits him very well. And there is nothing in the Faith which prescribes that the Church must be a gerontocracy—a government of old men. I have time to think now, and I am sure age doesn't always make us wiser."

"Don't mistake me. I see the good that this man brings to us. He goes out like a true shepherd among the flock. He visits the hospitals and the prisons. Last Sunday, believe it or not, he sat through three sermons, in three different Roman churches . . . just to hear what kind of preaching we had in our pulpits."

"I hope he was impressed."

"He was not," said Leone with tart humor. "He made no secret of it. He talked of 'turgid rhetoric' and 'vague devotion.' I think we may hear something of this in the encyclical which he is preparing now."

"Is it ready yet?"

"Not yet. I hear he is still working on the first Russian version. . . . We may be in for some surprises. . . ." He laughed ruefully. "I've already had a few myself. His Holiness disapproves of the tone of certain Holy Office proclamations. He feels they are too stringent, too harsh. He wants us to refrain from outright condemnation, especially of persons, and to adopt a tone rather of admonition and warning."

"Did he say why?"

"He put it very clearly. He said we must leave room to move for men of good will even when they are in error. We must point out the error, but we must not do injustice to the intentions of those who commit it."

Rinaldi permitted himself a thin smile. "I begin to see why you are worried about Jean Télémond."

Leone ignored the joke and growled, "I'm inclined to agree with Benedetti. This man *is* a reformer. He wants to sweep all the rooms at once. He is talking, I believe, of a reform of the Rota, of changes in seminary training, and even of separate commissions to represent the various national Churches in Rome."

"That could be a good move," said Rinaldi thoughtfully. "I think that everyone but us Romans agrees that we have centralized too much. We live in troubled times, and if there is another war, then the Churches of the world will be much more isolated than they have ever been. The sooner they can develop a vigorous local life, the better for the Faith."

"If there is another war, my friend . . . it may well be the end of the world."

"Thank God things seem to be a little calmer at present."

Leone shook his head. "The calm is deceptive, I think. The pressure is building up, and before another year is out I think we may see a renewal of crisis. Goldoni was talking to me about it only yesterday. He is making a special report to the Pontiff."

"I wonder," asked Rinaldi softly. "I wonder how the crisis looks to a man who has sat for seventeen years in the shadow of death."

To Kiril the Pontiff the crisis presented itself in a variety of aspects.

He saw it first in microcosm, on the battleground of his own soul. At the lowest level—the level at which he had lived in the prison bunker—there was the simple impulse to survival: the desperate effort to cling to that single spark of life which, once extinguished, could never be lit again. There was only one infusion of life into the frail vessel of the body. Once the vessel was broken, it would never be put together again until the day of the last restoration. So with the infusion of life was infused also the instinct to preserve it at all costs against whatever threatened, or seemed to threaten it, from within or without.

Every animal contained within itself a mechanism of survival. Only man, the last and noblest of the animal kingdom, understood, however dimly, that the mechanism must run down and that sooner or later he must make a conscious act of abandonment of the gift into the hand of the Creator, Who had first given it. This was the act for which all his living was a preparation; to refuse it was to commit the final rebellion, from which there was no recanting.

Yet every day of every man's life was a series of small rebellions against the fear of death or of sporadic victories for hope in the unseen. Even for Kiril, the Vicar of God on earth, there was no retreat from the daily war. The impulse to survival took many forms: the delight in power which gave a man the illusion of immortality; the fear of opposition which might limit the illusion; the desire for friendship to buttress the weak body and faltering spirit; the urge to action which affirmed a man's potency against threatening circumstance; the desire to possess what must in the end be foregone; the cowardice which thrust him into isolation as if he could close every crack against the ultimate invasion of death. Even for a Pontiff, who stood by presumption nearest to God, there was no guarantee of victory over himself. Each day brought its own tally of defeats which must be repented and purged in the penitential tribunal.

But what of other men, so much less enlightened, so much more vulnerable, so much more oppressed by the terror of bodily extinction? On them the pressures of existence built up to the breaking point every day. For them he must find in himself a strength to lend, and a charity to spend, lest they collapse utterly under the burden, or turn and rend each other in a feral war, which would blot them out quicker than the merciful death from which they fled.

This was the other aspect of the crisis which he read in every report which was laid on his desk, in every newspaper and bulletin which came under his notice.

When a man in a capsule was shot into a new dimension of space and time, the world exulted as if he were coming back with a promise of eternity in his pocket.

When a new program of armament was announced, it seemed that those who promoted it wrote with the one hand a new profit into the stock market while with the other they inscribed their own epitaph.

Each economic treaty brought advantage to those who signed it and a degree of injustice to those whom it excluded.

The populations of the East and the Africas were exploding into a new magnitude, and yet men put their trust in islands of color or race, as though they were endowed with a divine right of election to an earthly paradise.

Every new victory over disease made a corresponding drain on the diminishing resources of the planet. Every advance in science was another patch on the shabby cloak which man wrapped about himself against the cold wind of dissolution.

And yet . . . and yet this was the nature of man. This was the historic method of his progress—a tightrope walk toward a destiny dimly perceived, but profoundly felt. The Church was in the world, though not of it—and it was her function to hold up the truth like a lamp to light the farther shore of man's ultimate arrival.

So Kiril the Pontiff, caught like all his fellows in the human dilemma, sat at his desk and traced in the formal words of his Secretary of State the shadows of the gathering storm.

"The pivot of the present situation is China. The most reliable reports indicate that the agricultural program has again broken down and that there will be a very light harvest this summer. This will mean, almost inevitably, a military push toward the rice-bowl areas of Southeast Asia immediately after the next monsoons. Military training is already being stepped up, and there are reports reaching us every day of repressive measures against disaffected elements. Our own people are being subjected to new campaigns of surveillance and open persecution.

"In America the economic recession has eased, but this is largely due to an increase in the program of military armament. Our sources in the United States inform us that any new Chinese expansion toward Burma or Indo-China or Siam would create an immediate danger of war. . . .

"In Bonn and Paris there is new talk of France and Germany participating in a joint program for the development of atomic weapons. This is a logical outcome of their status as senior partners in the European bloc, but it is clear that it must present itself as an open threat to East Germany and Moscow. . . .

"It has been our hope for some time that Russia's fear of the Chinese might bring about a betterment of her relations with the West, but this situation introduces a dangerous and contrary element.

"It would seem timely for your Holiness to make some clear and public comment on the dangers of this new armament race, which is being justified as a strengthening of the Western alliance against communism.

"It is difficult to see how it could be done, but if it were possible for us to make any contact with the Praesidium in the Kremlin and to introduce ourselves as a mediating element in East-West relations, there would be no time better than the present. Unfortunately, our opposition to the doctrines of communism is all too easily interpreted as a political alliance with the West. We have instructed our legates and nuncios everywhere to emphasize, both in public and in their conversations with political personalities, the dangers of the present situation.

"As your Holiness knows, we are now maintaining friendly relations with representatives of the Orthodox Church, and with senior members of other Christian bodies. We may look with confidence to their cooperation in this matter. However, the creation of a moral climate always lags far behind the creation of a political one, and we do have to face the fact that the next six or twelve months may well bring the world to the threshold of another war. . . .

"In Africa . . ."

Kiril the Pontiff put down the typescript and covered his tired eyes with the palms of his hands. Here again in macrocosm was the struggle for human survival. The Chinese wanted a bowl of rice. The Russian wanted to hold the civilized comfort which had just become familiar to him. A hundred and eighty million Americans had to be kept working, lest the precarious consumer economy should collapse. France and Germany, stripped of their colonies, had to maintain their bargaining power in the European community of nations.

"What we have we hold, because it is ours, because we have earned it. All that increases us is a good. All that diminishes us is a threat. . . . Jungle law . . . Survival of the fittest . . . There are no morals in politics. . . ."

Yet, boil it down, survival even for the individual was never a simple equation. The definition of rights and duties had occupied theologians and legalists for two thousand years of the Christian dispensation, and for thousands of years before that. It was one thing to state the law, but to apply it, to bring all the diverse millions of mankind to see it with the same eye, to recognize it as a divine decree . . . this was, on the face of it, a rank impossibility. Yet there was the promise. "I, if I be lifted up, will draw all things to myself." And without the promise there was no foothold of reason left in the universe. If one did not believe that the spinning orb of the earth was held safe by the continuance of a creative act, then one might well despair and wish it dissolved in fire, to make place for a better one.

Once again memory struck off at a tangent, to a conversation he had had with Kamenev nearly ten years before!

"The difference between you and me, Kiril, is that I am dedicated to the possible while you are dedicated to a nonsense. . . . 'God wishes that all men should be saved and come to the knowledge of truth.' That's what you preach, isn't it? Yet you know it's folly. A sublime folly, I agree. But still—a folly. . . . It doesn't happen. It won't happen. It can't happen. What is your heaven but a carrot to make the donkey trot? What is your hell but a rubbish heap for all your failures—God's failures, my friend! And you say He's omnipotent. Where do you go from here? Do you come with me to achieve the small possible or go chasing after the great impossible? . . . I know what you want to say: God makes all possible. Don't you see? I am God to you at this moment because you can't even move from that chair until I give the order. . . . Here! God gives you a little gift. A cigarette. . . ."

He had taken the cigarette, he remembered, and smoked it gratefully while his tired mind grappled with the paradox which Kamenev had presented to him. . . . The little gain or the great loss? Which? The limited wisdom or the monstrous folly? He had chosen the folly, and been consigned again to stripes and starvation and solitude to purge it out of him.

And now the paradox had reversed itself. Kamenev was faced with a situation impossible to resolve, while Kiril, the abject prisoner, stood in the shoes of God, to whom all things were possible.

For a long time he sat pondering the gigantic humor of the situation. Then he lifted the receiver and called Goldoni in the Secretariat of State.

"I'm reading your report. I'm impressed. I'm grateful. I'm also very worried. Now tell me something. . . . If I wanted to get a message to the Premier of Russia—a private message—how would I do it?"

Extract from
the Secret Memorials of
KIRIL I, Pont. Max.

. . . It is well that I have kept a sense of humor; otherwise I should be harassed to madness by the consequences of my most trivial actions. When a man in my position asks a simple question, the whole Vatican begins to flutter like a nest of birds. If I make the smallest motion, it is as if I were trying to shake the foundations of the world. I can only do what I believe to be right, but there are always twenty people with as many reasons why I should not move at all. . . . And I am a fool if I do not at least listen to their opinions.

When I proposed to Goldoni that I should make a pastoral visitation of the whole of Italy, and see on the spot the problems of my local clergy, he was aghast. Such a thing had not been done for centuries. It would create problems with the Italian government. It would raise God knows what questions of protocol and logistics and local ceremony. He pointed out that I was a prince and that the paying of princely honors would impose hardship on poor and depressed areas. I had to be very firm with him on this point and tell him that I am first and foremost a pastor, successor to a fisherman who was executed like a common criminal in the City of the Emperors. Even so, we have not yet agreed how and when I shall make this journey; but I am determined to do it before very long.

I want to make other journeys, too. I want to cross the frontiers of Europe and the oceans of the world to see my people—where and how they live, and the burdens they carry on their journey to eternity. . . . This, I know, is a project not easily accomplished. It will involve opposition from governments, a risk to myself and to the administration of the Holy See. . . . But it would, I believe, restate as nothing else could the apostolic mission of the Pontiff. . . . For the present, however, I have a more pressing concern: to establish and maintain a personal contact with Kamenev.

Immediately after my telephone call Goldoni came rushing across from the Secretariat of State to talk with me. He is a shrewd man, much practiced in diplomacy, and I have great respect for his opinion. His first counsel was a negative one. He could see no possible ground of communication with those who preach an atheistic heresy and who are engaged in an active persecution of the faithful. . . . He made the point, too, that all those who are members of the Communist Party are automatically excommunicated from the Church. I could not help remarking that in the twentieth century excommunication was a blunt weapon and very possibly an outmoded one. . . . He offered then the very valid caution that even a private dialogue with the Kremlin might constitute a diplomatic affront to Western governments.

I could not disagree with him, but I am obsessed by the belief that the prime mission of the Church is a pastoral and not a diplomatic one. I showed Goldoni the letter which Kamenev had written to me, and he understood my anxiety to begin some kind of conversation. Goldoni gave me, however, another warning: any step that I take may be misinterpreted as a sign of weakness and may be used as a propaganda weapon by the Communists. . . .

Goldoni is right, of course; but I do not believe he is wholly right. The truth has a virtue of its own; the good act has a virtue of its own, and we must never discount the fructifying power of the Almighty. . . .

I have never believed that everyone who comes to Rome must come here by way of Canossa. This, I think, has been one of our historic errors. The good shepherd seeks out the lost sheep and carries them home on his shoulder. He does not demand that they come crawling back, draggle-tailed and remorseful, with a penance cord around their necks. . . . It was St. Augustine who said, "It takes a big mind to make a heresy." And there are noble minds and noble spirits from whom the gift of faith is withheld and for whom salvation comes by way of the uncovenanted mercy of God. With all such we must deal in patience, tolerance, and brotherly charity, humbled always by the gratuitous mercy of God in our own regard. For them we must exercise in a special fashion the *ministerium* of the Faith and not insist too harshly upon its magistracy.

So, finally, Goldoni and I agreed on a compromise. We would try to get a message to Kamenev, to tell him that I have received his letter and that I have nothing but the most friendly disposition toward him and toward my own people. The problem was, of course, how to deliver the message, but Goldoni in his subtle fashion proposed an amusing solution. A South American diplomat who has social contacts in the Kremlin will seek an opportunity to speak with the Premier at a cocktail party and tell him that a friend of his would like to talk more about the growing of sunflowers. . . . In this way neither one of us will be compromised and the next effective move will be for Kamenev to make. God knows where the move may point, but I must pray and rest in hope. . . .

It is curious, but I am more deeply perturbed by the case which Leone has transmitted to me from the Holy Office: a priest accused of soliciting in the confessional, who is now in danger of being cited in a civil paternity suit. . . . This sort of scandal is, of course, sporadic in the Church, but I am troubled by the spectacle of a soul in a mortal sickness.

There are men who should never be priests at all. The system of seminary training is designed to filter out unsuitable candidates, but there are always the odd ones who slip through the net. There are those whose sole hope of a normal and fruitful life is in the married state, yet the discipline of the Western Church imposes on all priests a perpetual celibacy.

It is within my power as the Pontiff to dispense this unfortunate man from his vows and permit him to marry. My heart urges me to do it, and yet I dare not. To do so would be to create a precedent which might do irreparable damage to clerical discipline and to a tradition which has its roots in Christ's teaching on the state of dedicated virginity.

I have the power, yes, but I must use it to build and not to demolish what has been given into my keeping. I am aware that I may be increasing the danger of damnation of this unhappy soul. I want to deal with him as mercifully as I can, but I dare not, for one soul, put ten thousand others in jeopardy. . . .

The Keys of the Kingdom are given into my hands, but I do not hold them absolutely. They are mine in trust under law. . . . There are times—and this is one of them—when I wish I could take upon myself the sins of all the world and offer my life in expiation for them. I know, however, that I am only a man, and that the expiation was made once for all on Calvary. Through the Church I administer the fruits of redemption. I cannot change the covenant of God with man which governs their distribution. . . .

It is late, and my letter to the Church is still unfinished. Tonight I am working on the text "A chosen generation, a kingly priesthood." A priest is only a man, and we have only a few short years to train him for the burden of kingship. . . . To those who stumble under its weight, we must extend the maternal love of the Church. For them we must invoke the patronage of the Virgin Mother of all men. . . .

It is warm tonight. Summer is coming in, but there are those who walk in a lifetime winter, lost and alone. Let me not fail them who have felt the winter in my own bones, who have cried at night for love in a loveless prison. . . .

VI

THE princess Maria Caterina Daria Poliziano was a small gray woman who admitted to seventy-five years and was prepared to sue anyone bold enough to dispute her accounting.

Her hair was thin, her skin was shrunken. Her sharp beak and her black agate eyes gave her the look of a mummified eagle dug from some ancient tomb. But the Princess Maria-Rina was very far from dead and was, on the contrary, a very formidable old lady.

She kept an apartment in Rome—which she rarely used "because all Romans are beginning to look like commercial travelers"—a villa in Fiesole, where she held habitual court, estates in Sicily, farms in the Abruzzi, and holdings in beets and rice in the Romagna and along the valley of the Po. Her portfolio, begun by her father and augmented by the fortunate deaths of two husbands, was full of the fattest stocks in Italy, and she traded them as shrewdly as a gypsy tinker.

Her bony finger stirred every political pudding north of Lazio, and those whispers of power which did not begin in her drawing room circulated there, inevitably, before they blew into a wind. A summons to her table was either a warrant for execution or a promise of promotion. And more than one too bold politico had braved her anger only to find himself running out of funds, favor, and votes at the next election.

Her dress was antique, her manner more tyrannical than regal. She drank Scotch whisky and smoked Egyptian cigarettes in a long gold holder. She had a scandalous tongue, a dangerous memory—and an unexpected discretion. She despised the old, and courted the young like a crotchety but humorous vampire who could pay richly for youthful blood. In her villa garden, among the fountains and the cypresses and the avenues of weathered marbles, it seemed, in very truth, as if time stood still at her aged but imperious bidding.

Her favorite resort was an arbor hung with maturing grapes and fronting a small fountain where an antique Leda was courted by languid swans to the sound of water music. In a younger time the Princess Maria-Rina had been courted there as well—now, instead, she bargained with the legacies of her youth: power, money, and prestige. Once a month the Archbishop of Florence came to drink coffee with her. Once a week someone from the Quirinale came to lunch and make a private report from the Premier. Where the dandies of another age had bent over her small hand, now the bankers and the stockbrokers came to pay her a reluctant homage, and a tribute of secret confidence.

She was sitting there now, this summer morning, reading a blunt lecture to a Minister of the Republic, her nephew, Corrado Calitri:

"You're a fool boy! You come a certain way and you think it is the end of the journey. You want to sit down and play with the flowers. It's delightful, I'm sure, but it isn't politics."

Calitri's pale classic face flushed, and he put down his coffee cup with a clatter. "Now listen, Aunt, you know that isn't true. I do my work. I do it very well. Only yesterday the Premier was good enough to say—"

"Was good enough to say!" Her old voice crackled with contempt. "Why should you care what he says? What is praise, anyway, but breakfast for the prisoner before they cut his throat? You disappoint me, Corrado. You're a baby. You can't see past your nose."

"What do you expect me to see, Aunt?"

"The future!" said the Princess crisply. "Twelve months from now, when the election comes. Are you prepared for it?"

"Of course I am. The funds are there. My committees are working day and night, even now. I don't think there is any doubt I shall be re-elected. . . . I think the party will have a reduced majority. We'll have to open out a little further in coalition with the Left, but even so I'm assured of a seat in the Cabinet."

"And that's the end of the story?" Her dark agate eyes bored into him; her withered lips twitched into a smile of pity.

Calitri shifted uneasily in his chair. "Do you see another ending, Aunt?"

"Yes!" Her old hands reached across the table and fastened like talons on his wrist. "You have twelve months left to plan it, but if you plan aright you can lead the country." He stared at her, gape-mouthed, and she gave a high, cackling laugh. "Never underrate your old aunt, my boy. When you're as old as I am, you've learned to see round corners, and I tell you without a doubt you can lead the Republic . . ."

"You really believe that?" Calitri's voice was almost a whisper.

"I never tell fairy tales, my boy—and I gave up listening to them a long while ago. At lunch today you will meet some people who will show you how you can do it. There will be a certain amount of"—she rubbed her fingertips together in the gesture that signified money—"but that part we can handle. I want to talk to you about something else. There's another price to be paid, and you're the only one who can pay it."

Corrado Calitri cocked a shrewd eye at his relative. "And what is the price, Aunt?"

She fixed him with a beady and predatory eye and told him. "You'll have to clean up your life, and do it quickly. Get rid of this bunch of pimps and playboys that you hang around with. Push this marriage business through the courts. Get rid of Chiara. She's no good to you. And get yourself married again, quickly and quietly. I'll find you a woman who can manage you. You need a strong one —not a dewy-eyed schoolgirl."

"I won't do it!" Corrado Calitri exploded into sudden anger. "I won't be bought and sold like a piece of merchandise!"

He heaved himself out of his chair and began to pace restlessly up and down the flagged pathway between the arbor and the fountain while the old Princess watched him with a calm and calculating eye.

When his anger had spent itself a little, she went to him and linked her arm in his and led him slowly round the circuit of the villa plantations. She was a different woman now. She made no effort to tease or provoke him, but talked soberly and quietly, as if he were her son:

". . . I told you I don't listen to fairy stories any more—even about myself. I know what I am, Corrado—a dried-up old woman with paint on her face, and her past a million years away. . . . But I've lived, my boy. I've lived every minute of every hour. I've sucked the orange dry and spat out the pips. So listen to me, please. . . . I know you're not like other men. You were always different, even as a little boy. . . . Watching you, I used to think of someone trying to rub out the world and paint it new and clean again. I could have made it different for you, I think; but your father would never have me near the house. . . ." She gave a short, bitter chuckle. "He thought I was a corrupting influence. He was a straitlaced fellow, with no sense of humor. I never could see what your mother found in him."

"Misery," said Corrado Calitri harshly. "Misery and loneliness, and no love at all. I hated that man from the bottom of my heart."

"But you can't run away from him any longer," said the old woman softly. "He's dead, and the daisies are growing out of his ears. I know what you look for—the love you didn't get from him. I know you find it sometimes, but it doesn't last. I know the dangers when you go on looking desperately and without caution." Her thin hands clutched at his arm. "You do have enemies, don't you?"

"Who hasn't in a job like mine?"

"Have you ever been blackmailed?"

"It's been tried a couple of times."

"Then you know what I'm talking about. The enemies get more numerous and they grow bigger—bigger than you realize. Take Campeggio, for instance—"

"Campeggio!" He swung round to face her, genuinely startled. "Campeggio! I've never done him any harm."

"You have his boy," said Maria-Rina gravely.

"So that's the story." Calitri threw back his patrician head and laughed, startling the birds in the olive trees. "The boy works for me. I like him. He has talent, and charm and—"

"Beauty?"

"That, too, if you want. But not for me. You think I want to fall foul of Campeggio and the Vatican?"

"You've already done it," said the Princess Maria-Rina. "And without the

Vatican you can't lead the country at the next election. Now—now do you see what I'm talking about?"

For a long moment he did not answer her, but seemed to shrink back into himself. His youthful face furrowed. His eyes misted with sudden emotion. Finally he said softly, "Life is very long, Aunt. Sad, too, sometimes, and solitary."

"You think I don't know that, boy? You think when Louis died I wasn't sad and solitary? You think I didn't know what it was like to be middle-aged and rich, and able to buy what I couldn't get for love? I tried it, too, for a little while. Does that shock you?"

"No. I understand it."

"Then I woke up, as you have to wake up. You can't get out of bed every morning fearing to lose what you don't own, anyway. You can't wait and weigh the risks of the blackmailer. You can't govern your life by the snap of a pretty boy's fingers. No! One day you have to say to yourself: 'What have I got that is really mine? How best can I enjoy it?' When you come to add it up, you find there's a great deal. And there may even be a little loving as well."

"In marriage?" he asked with heavy irony.

"In it or outside. It makes small matter. For you . . ." Her skeleton finger stabbed at him like a dagger. "For you marriage is necessary. Very necessary."

"I tried it, remember."

"With a baby who was still playing with dolls."

"And this time?"

"First," said the old woman briskly, "we must get you out of the mess you're in now, and this is where you make your first payment."

"How much?" asked Corrado Calitri.

"In money, nothing. In pride . . . a great deal, perhaps. You will have to approach the Rota and reverse all your previous testimony."

"How do I make them believe me?"

The Princess Maria-Rina laughed again. "You repent. There will be joy in Heaven and in the Vatican when you come to repair the grave injustice that you have done to an innocent girl. You will be mending your ways, too, and they will be happy to have you back in the fold."

"I can't do it," said Corrado Calitri heavily. "It's a monstrous hypocrisy."

"It needn't be," said the Princess. "And even if it is, the Quirinale is worth a Mass, isn't it?"

In spite of himself Calitri smiled and laid an affectionate hand on the old woman's cheek. "Sometimes, Aunt, I think you're descended directly from the Borgias."

"I am," said the old Princess, "but on the wrong side of the blanket! Now . . . Will you do what I ask?"

"I'll have to think about it."

"You have thirty minutes, boy. At lunch they will want your answer and mine."

In a third-floor tenement, a stone's throw from the Pantheon, Ruth Lewin was caught up in another of the daily dramas of Old Rome. From the evening Angelus until nearly midnight she had been working with a twenty-year-old wife to help her give birth to her first child. For the last two hours the doctor had been with her, a haggard young man who seemed far too embroiled in the drama for his own good, or for that of his patient.

When finally they had dragged the child into the light with forceps, it was a monster—a tiny, whimpering deformity with a human head and a penguin body, whose feet and hands were attached directly to the trunk.

Ruth Lewin stared at it in horror, and the young doctor swore savagely.

"Sweet Jesus! Sweet suffering Jesus, look at it!"

Ruth Lewin found herself stammering helplessly, "But why? What caused it? What—"

"Shut up!" said the doctor harshly. "Shut up and give me water and a towel."

Mechanically she did as he asked and watched in fascinated horror while he swaddled the deformed body and then poured a few drops of water on the head and muttered the ritual words: "I baptize thee in the name of the Father, and of the Son, and of the Holy Ghost. Amen."

Ruth Lewin found voice again. "What's going to happen now?"

"That's my business. You get the mother cleaned up."

Angry and near to tears, she set about the menial task, bathing the torn young body, comforting the girl as she struggled back, moaning, into consciousness. When finally it was done and the young mother lay composed and decent on the pillows, Ruth Lewin looked up. "What now, Doctor?"

He was standing by the table, his back towards her, fumbling with the wrapping that covered the child. He turned a stony face to her and said:

"It's dead. Get the father in."

She opened her mouth to ask a question, but no sound issued. She searched his face for an answer, but his young eyes were blank as pebbles. He repeated the order. "Please call the father."

Ruth Lewin went to the door and beckoned to a tall, muscular boy who was drinking a glass of wine and talking with a group of neighbors on the landing. "Will you come in, please."

Puzzled, the youth approached her with the neighbors at his heels. She drew him inside and closed the door against the other curious faces.

The doctor confronted him, holding the swaddled body in his arms. "I have bad news for you, my friend. The baby was born dead."

The boy stared at him stupidly. "Dead?"

"It happens sometimes. We don't really know why. Your wife is well. She will be able to have other children."

Dumbly the boy moved toward the bed and bent, crooning, over the pale, half-conscious girl.

"Let's go," said the doctor abruptly. "I want to deliver this to the general hospital."

To the boy he said, "I have to take the body away. It's the law. I'll be back in the morning to see your wife and give you a death certificate."

Neither the boy nor the wife seemed to hear him, and he went out, carrying the small pathetic bundle, with Ruth Lewin following like a professional mourner. The crowd on the landing stared silently at their passing, and then crowded into the door of the room, whispering excitedly among themselves.

When they reached the street, the doctor laid the body of the child on the back seat of his car and slammed the door. Then he faced Ruth Lewin and said abruptly, "Don't ask any questions. I'll deliver the cadaver to the general hospital and make a report."

"Won't there be an autopsy?"

"No. Even if there were, it would show nothing. The child died of asphyxiation. . . ."

In a single moment all his control seemed to drain away. His body was shaken with rigors, and his young face twisted as if with an intolerable pain. Suddenly in a fury of desperation he was pleading with her. "Don't leave me now. For God's sake, don't leave me. Come to the hospital, and then . . . then let's go somewhere. Somewhere sane. If I'm alone tonight I think I'll go mad."

"Of course I'll come with you. But you can't blame yourself for this. You're a doctor; you know these things happen every day."

"I know! Oh yes, I know." He tried to smile, but it was more like a rictus of agony. "I'll tell you something you don't know. I've got twenty more babies to be born in the next eight weeks, and at least half of them are going to be like that."

"Oh God," said Ruth Lewin softly. "Oh God Almighty, why . . . ?"

In her quiet house under the haunted shadow of the Palatine he told her the why. He told her savagely and brusquely, as if the whole paradox of the healing art—its half promise of perpetuity, its ultimate surrender to mortality—had proved too much for him.

". . . It's a crazy thought . . . but medical pharmacy always seems to come with the elixir of life in one hand and a phial of poison in the other. . . . There are antibiotics that cure some people and kill others. There was the French drug that boiled men's brains. There was thalidomide, which gave sleep and then grew monsters in the womb. Now there's another one. It came on the market about twelve months ago—a combination formula to prevent nausea in pregnancy and reduce the danger of toxaemia. . . . Three months ago we started to get the first warnings from Germany about deformities induced by the drug. . . . It looks like thalidomide all over again, only this time everyone's trying to hush it up. . . ." He lay back in his chair, an image of dejection, fatigue, and pure misery. "I used to think I was a kind of medical apostle. I paid for drugs for poorer patients out of my own pocket. I bought the bloody stuff for that girl tonight, and for all the others in the quarter."

"There's no hope that the other births will be different?"

"Some of them will be normal. But the rest . . ." He flung out his hands in passionate appeal. "What do I do? I can't murder them all."

"First, you must never use that word again. I saw nothing tonight. I heard nothing."

"But you know, don't you?"

"I don't know anything—except this. You mustn't blame yourself, and you mustn't ever again play God. There's a kind of madness in that."

"Madness is right." He ran a shaking hand through his hair. "It was a madness tonight, and yet . . . What equipment do those people have to cope with such a situation? You know what they would have said if they'd seen that birth tonight? *'Mal'occhio!'* The evil eye. Someone looked on the mother and laid a curse on her while the child was still in her womb. You have no idea of the power of superstition over the minds of these poor folk. What would they do with the child? Some few might care for it. Others might stifle it or try to throw it in the river. Some few might sell it to professional beggars who would make profit from its deformity. . . . What about all the others still to come? What do I do about them? Sweet Jesus, what do I do?"

Without warning he was racked by deep weary sobs, so that Ruth Lewin ran to him and threw her arms about him for comfort and soothed him with soft and helpless words. When he was calm at last, she made him lie down on her bed, and covered him with a blanket, and then sat beside him, holding his hand until he lapsed into the mercy of sleep. Then she was alone—alone in the mournful hours, confronted by the ultimate mystery of life and death and pain, and the bloody stinking mess of the world.

She had seen a monster come to birth as the result of an act of healing and kindness. She had seen murder done in the name of mercy and found her heart more than half approving the act. Here in little was the whole mighty tragedy of man, the whole bleak mystery of his existence and his destiny.

Confronted by that pitiful embryo, how could one say that the cogs of Creation did not slip out of kilter and grind into a monstrous confusion? How could one talk of Omnipotence and Omniscience and an ever present Goodness? How could one find a soul or spirit in the weak, puling, fishlike creature, swimming blindly out of the fluid of the womb to affront the light of day?

Where now were the foundations of faith, and hope, and love? Where was one vestige of sanity in this madhouse of sick, maimed, helpless victims of civilization? If there was none, then it was time to quit and be gone. The exit was easy enough, and once she had almost passed through it. One could not go on blundering wildly through a hall of mirrors, confused, disordered, purposeless, and afraid. If there was no resolution to the discord, then pack up the band and send it home. But if there was, then it must be soon, before the tattered nerves frayed themselves into a screaming horror.

The weariness of the vigil crept into her bones, and she stretched out on the bed beside the sleeping man. But the contact of his body troubled her, and when he muttered and turned to her in sleep, she withdrew and went into the kitchen to make herself a cup of coffee.

She remembered another night with another man in this same house, and how for a while she had glimpsed a beginning of light. She asked herself what he would have made of tonight's affair, and what would have been his answer for the horrors that were still to come. Then the thought struck her, cold and reviving. This was his city. He had claimed it for his own. He had named himself as the shepherd and servant of its people. . . .

Ruth Lewin was still awake when the gray of the false dawn crept across the Palatine Hill. And before the city had rubbed the sleep out of its eyes, she had written her letter, begging a private audience with Kiril the Pontiff.

His own letter to the Church was already finished, and the Russian draft was in the hands of the translators. Now that it was done, he felt strangely empty, oppressed by a sense of futility and frustration.

While he was writing he had felt seized as never before by the power of the

Word, by the conviction of its inevitable fruitfulness in the hearts of good men. Yet now he was faced with the cold fact that without the grace of God—and men co-operating with the grace of God—the seed might lie fertile but fruitless for a hundred years. Among the millions of believers who professed an obedience to the Word, and to his authority as its Supreme Preacher, how many were there from whom he could exact a full performance?

He saw all too clearly what would happen to his letter. It would be read within a few months in every Catholic pulpit in the world. He would receive acknowledgements from bishops pledging their loyalty to his counsels and promising to carry them out as best they could. But between the promise and the fulfillment stood a hundred obstacles: shortage of men, shortage of money, shortness of sight and courage sometimes, and the natural resentment of the man at the point of action, who wondered why he was being asked to make so many bricks with so little straw.

The best one could hope was that here and there the Word would take fire in the soul of a man, would brighten his eyes with vision, and set him striding out to achieve a divine impossible. For himself he knew there was no other choice but to go on preaching, teaching, urging to action, and to wait, empty of all but hope, on the promise of the Paraclete.

There was a knock on his door, and the Maestro di Camera entered to inquire whether His Holiness was ready to begin the morning's audiences. Kiril glanced briefly at the list and saw that the first name was that of Ruth Lewin.

Her letter had troubled him deeply because it had reached him in a moment of temptation—the temptation to immerse himself in the political aspects of the Church and to challenge, by a display of power, those men, like Leone, who made no secret of their disagreements with him. There were those, he knew, who found his encyclical something of a novelty. It was too personal, they felt, too specific. It was too openly critical of past policy. It called for new modes of action in the training of the clergy and in the direction of missionary education. For himself, the man at the top, it was all too easy to thrust his authority down the throats of his subordinates and stifle their criticism by a summons to religious obedience.

Ruth Lewin's letter reminded him that the real battleground was elsewhere —in lonely rooms and solitary hearts, among folk who had no theology, but only an intimate and frightening familiarity with the problems of living and dying. Ruth Lewin represented a contact with such people. If he could make the Faith efficacious for her, then whatever the outcome of his pontificate, he would not have failed utterly.

When she was ushered into his presence, he greeted her warmly and then, without preamble, addressed himself to the subject:

"I had you called as quickly as I could because I know that you must be suffering a good deal."

"I'm grateful to your Holiness," she told him in her blunt fashion. "I have no right to bother you, but this is a terrible affair."

"For you?" asked Kiril quizzically.

"For me it calls everything into question. But I want to talk about the others first."

"What others?"

"The women who are going to give birth to these children. Most of them, I believe, are quite unprepared for what is going to happen."

Kiril's lean face clouded, and a nerve began throbbing under the scar on his cheek. "What do you want me to do?"

"We . . . That is, the mothers need help. They need a place where they can leave these children if they're not capable of looking after them themselves. The children have to be cared for. I'm told the expectation of life is short, but they will need a special kind of care—a special kind of loving."

"You think the Church can provide it?"

"It has to," said Ruth Lewin flatly. "If it means what it teaches." She flushed, understanding that she had committed an indiscretion; then she hurried into an explanation. "I'm a woman, your Holiness. I asked myself the other night what I would do, how I would feel, if I were the mother of such a child. I don't know. I don't think I should behave very well."

Kiril the Pope gave a small wintry smile of approval. "I think you underrate yourself. You have more courage than you realize. . . . Tell me. How many of these births are there likely to be in Rome?"

"We expect about twenty in the next two months. There may be many more."

He sat for a moment, silent and thoughtful. Then he gave a crooked, boyish grin and said:

"Well! Let's see what sort of authority I have in the Church." He picked up the telephone and dialed the number of the Secretary of the Sacred Congregation of the Religious.

Crisply he explained the situation, and then asked, "Which of our nursing nuns in Rome are best equipped to look after these children?"

There was an indistinguishable clatter of talk from the other end of the line, and Ruth Lewin saw the Pontiff's mouth tighten in anger. He said sharply, "I know it is difficult. Everything is difficult. But this is an urgent work of charity, and it must be done. If money is needed, we will provide it. It will be your business to find the accommodation and the nursing aid. I want it arranged within the next twenty-four hours."

He put down the phone with a bang and said testily, "These people live in a little world of their own. One has to bounce them out of it into reality. . . . Anyway, you can take it for granted that we shall provide care and hospital accommodation for those who need it. You will be informed by letter and telephone of the details. Then I shall have an announcement published in the *Osservatore* and circulated to the Roman press."

"I'm very grateful to your Holiness."

"I'm grateful to you, young woman. Now, what can I do for you?"

"I don't know," said Ruth Lewin unhappily. "I've been asking myself the same question all the way to the Vatican. Why do these things happen? Why does a good God let them happen?"

"If I could tell you that," said Kiril the Pontiff soberly, "I'd be God myself. I don't know, though I sometimes wish I did. You mustn't imagine that the mystery of faith is any simpler for me than it is for you. The Act of Faith is an act of acceptance—not an explanation. I'll tell you a story about myself. . . . When I was first taken to prison, it was in the bad time in Russia. There was much torture, much cruelty. One night a man was brought back to my hut who had been handled more brutally than any other I had ever seen. He was in agony, and he kept crying over and over again for someone to kill him and put him out of his misery. I tell you truly I was tempted. It's a terrible thing to see so much suffering. It degrades and terrifies those who see it but cannot alleviate it. That's why I can understand, though I cannot condone, what your doctor friend did. It seems almost as though one would be bestowing a divine mercy with the gift of death. But one is not divine, one cannot dispense either life or death."

He seemed for a moment to sink back into a private contemplation.

Ruth Lewin prompted him gently. "What was the end of the story, Holiness?"

"The man died in my arms. I should like to tell you that he died in a Godly fashion, but I have no way of knowing. I could not penetrate through his pain to touch the springs of his will. He just died, and I had to commit him to God. . . . That's the only answer I can give you."

"It's a leap into the dark," said Ruth Lewin gravely. "I'm not sure I can make it."

"Is it any less hard to stay where you are?"

"It's harder, I think."

"But you have already made one step into the dark."

"I don't understand."

"You could not condone this murder, even of a monstrous birth."

"Not wholly, no."

"And you have turned to me for help, not for yourself, but for the children."

"I just felt so inadequate. I needed someone who could act . . ."

"Perhaps," said Kiril the Pontiff softly, "perhaps that is part of the meaning of pain—that it challenges our arrogant possession of life; that it confronts us with our own frailty and makes us aware, however dimly, of the sustaining power of the Creator."

"I wish I could believe that. But how do you see God in a human child that looks like a fish?"

"It's not a new mystery, Ruth. It's a very old one. How do you see God in a dying criminal nailed on a gallows tree?"

"It isn't enough to say that," said Ruth Lewin harshly. "There has to be some loving somewhere. There has to be."

"True. . . . There has to be some loving. If the mystery of pain is not a mystery of love, then all this . . ." His crooked hands embraced the ornate room and all the Sacred City beyond it. "Then all this is a historic nonsense. And my office is a role for a mountebank."

His bluntness took her by surprise. For a moment she stared at him, caught by the contrast between his crooked, quizzical face and the religious formality of his dress. Then she said:

"Your Holiness really believes that?"

"I do."

"Then why can't I?"

"I think you do believe it," said Kiril the Pontiff gently. "That's why you are here to see me. That's why you act within a context of belief, although you are still wrestling with God."

"If I could only know that I was loved—that I was worth loving."

"You don't ask that of someone you love—why should you ask it of yourself?"

"Your Holiness is too clever for me."

"No! I am not a clever man. I understand you, Ruth Lewin, better than you know, because I have walked on the same road that you are walking now. I'm going to tell you another story, and then I'm going to send you away because there are lots of people waiting to see me. . . . My escape from Russia was arranged, as you know. I was released from prison and sent to a hospital because I had been very ill for some time. The doctors treated me well, and I was nursed solicitously. After seventeen years of endurance it was a strange experience. I did not have to fight any more. It was as if I became another human being overnight. I was clean, and well fed. I had books to read, and leisure, and a kind of freedom. I enjoyed it. I was proud to be decent. . . . It took a little time to understand that I was being submitted to a new temptation. I felt loved again. I wanted to be loved. I used to look forward to the coming of the nurse, to her smile and her service of me. Then came a moment when I understood that what Kamenev my tormentor had not been able to do to me I was doing to myself. I was demanding an experience of love. In spite of my priesthood and my bishopric I was being tempted by this attraction of a simple human communion. . . . Do you understand what I'm trying to say?"

"Yes, I understand it. It's what I feel every day."

"Then you will understand something else. That the taking and the demanding is only one side of the medal of love. The giving is the side that proves the true minting. If I took, I should have nothing to give. If I gave, the giving renewed the resource, and it was this that had kept me whole for seventeen years of imprisonment. . . ."

"And the return of love?"

"You are part of it," said Kiril the Pontiff gently. "You and these children whom we shall love together, and those whom I shall reach here and there in the Church, because my voice echoes in their hearts. . . . I am still lonely often, as you are. But to be lonely is not to be unloved, but only to learn the value of love—and that it takes many forms, and is sometimes hard to recognize." He rose and held out his hand. "Now I must send you away, but we shall see each other again."

She had long since rejected the authority which he represented; yet she bowed her knee and laid her lips to the Fisherman's ring on his finger, and listened with gratitude to the words of the blessing:

"*Benedictio Dei omnipotentis descendat, Patris et Fili et Spiritus Sancti, super te et maneat semper. . . .*"

For Kiril the Pontiff it was a startling irony that his encyclical on Christian education made far less stir than his statement in the *Osservatore Romano* on the victims of the new drug. Every correspondent in Rome cabled the full text of the *Osservatore* release, which was interpreted in Europe and America as a clear papal command to place the medical and social resources of the Church at the disposal of mothers and offspring who were affected by the deadly medicine.

For a week afterwards his desk was piled with letters and telegrams from bishops and lay leaders, commending his action as a timely demonstration of the charity of the Church. Cardinal Platino wrote expansively:

". . . It seems to me that your Holiness has shown in a very special fashion the relevance of the Church's mission to every act and circumstance of human life. It may well be that your Holiness' pronouncement points the way to a missionary method of great importance—the reintroduction of the Church into private and public life through works of practical charity. Historically speaking, this method has been the beginning of the most permanent evangelical activity, and it is, in fact, a true copy of the work of the Master, who in the words of the Gospel, 'went about healing the sick and doing good. . . .' "

Another man might have been flattered by so spontaneous a response to an executive action, but Kiril Lakota was preoccupied by those aspects of the problem which the press either ignored or built into a factitious drama.

Day and night he was haunted by the picture of a woman waiting through nine months of fear and uncertainty to give birth to a deformity, of a doctor urged to intervene before the tragic moment, of the child itself, and what might happen to it when it grew to maturity. For all these the charity of the Church was at best a postscript, at worst an unwelcome prolongation of grief and despair.

The mission of the Church to all these people was far other than a dispensation of kindness. It was to confront with them the naked fact of their existence, with all its risks and all its terror, and another fact, that their existence set them in a precise relationship with the Creator, who had called them into being. The Church could not change the relationship. It could not eliminate one single consequence of it. Its sole functions were to interpret it in the light of reason and revelation and to dispense the grace by which alone the relationship was made workable.

In theory every one of the thousands of priests who trotted about the streets of Rome in platter hats and black skirts was an official interpreter of doctrine, an official dispenser of grace, and a shepherd with a sackful of compassion for his flock. In fact there were all too few with the talent or the understanding to participate truly in these intimate tragedies of humankind.

It was as if the symbiosis of the Church failed at a certain point and the lives of its people diverged thenceforward from the lives of its clergy. It was as if the interpretation of God to man became a didactic exercise and the realities of God's grace were blotted out by the realities of pain and loss.

In the methodology of the Church the priest was always available to the people of his parish. If they did not turn to him, it was because of their own negligence and want of faith. This at least was the text of many a Sunday sermon, but in truth the breakdown came because the cleric no longer shared the tragedy of his people, was even protected from it by his cloth and by his education. . . .

Education! He came back to it again by a round turn, seeing more clearly than he ever had before that the fruit of his mission to the world must never be judged by spectacle or acclamation, but only by its flowering in the secret heart of the individual.

Buried under the pile of congratulations there were other and more disquieting letters. Like the one from Cardinal Pallenberg, in Germany:

". . . With the greatest respect, therefore, I would beg your Holiness to undertake an examination of the present constitution and method of working of the Holy Roman Rota. Your Holiness is well aware that because of our special circumstances in Germany, a large number of marital cases are being referred each year to Rome. Many of these have been delayed for three and four years, with consequent hardship and grave spiritual danger to the parties concerned. It seems to me and my brother bishops that there is need of swift reform in this matter, either by way of fuller reference of powers to provincial courts or by an increase in the number of Rota officials and the institution of a speedier method of examination. It is suggested that instead of all documents being translated into Latin—a slow and expensive progress—they might be presented and examined in their original vernacular. . . ."

On the face of it the Holy Roman Rota was a far shout away from an act of infanticide in a third-floor slum. Yet the causes which found their way into the slow files of this august body were no less dramas of love and passion. The Holy Roman Rota was the last court of appeal for marital cases within the Church, and every marital case was a history of love or the lack of it, and of a human relationship—defective or not—which had to be measured beside the divine one.

To the theologian and the canonist the function of the Rota was very simple. It had to render a decision as to whether or no a marriage was valid according to the moral law and the prescriptions of the canons. To many inside the Church, it seemed that this view was altogether too simple. The Rota was meticulously careful that justice should be done. It cared not one whit that it should seem to be done. Its methods were antique and often dilatory. Every document and every deposition had to be translated into Latin. The number of personnel, both clerical and lay, was hopelessly inadequate to handle the volume of business with any degree of speed. The least sympathetic of men could not fail to guess at the hardship which such slowness inflicted on those who had appealed to the tribunal.

Kiril the Pontiff understood the problem more clearly than others, but he had already learned that to accomplish a reform in Rome one had to prepare slowly and act strongly at the right moment; otherwise one ended fighting the bureaucracy, which was tantamount to fighting oneself.

He penciled a note on his calendar to discuss the question with Valerio Rinaldi, who, having retired from the politics of the Church, might give him good advice about how to beat them.

From Ragambwe, the black Cardinal in Kenya, came a note of even greater urgency:

". . . Events in Africa are moving much more swiftly than would have seemed possible two years ago. Within the next twelve months I believe we may see a bloody uprising of black against white in South Africa. This is an almost inevitable consequence of the brutal repressive measures exercised by the South African government under the banner of Apartheid, and by the archaic feudal and often brutal methods of the Portuguese. If this revolution is successful—and with the support of other African nations there is reason to believe it will be—then it may well be the end of Christianity for a hundred years in the southern continent of Africa. We are training catechists as fast as we can, but we cannot hope to train even a minimal number of native priests in the time at our disposal. I know that this may well seem a revolutionary suggestion, but I ask myself whether we should not consider very seriously a new program of training in which the local language, and not Latin, will be the basis of instruction, and in which the whole liturgy will be celebrated in the vernacular. If this course were approved, it might be possible to train a native clergy in about half the time it takes now to train them under the system laid down by the Council of Trent.

"I understand very well that this would mean a clergy less well educated than that in other lands, but the question is whether we shall have such a clergy, preaching the Word and dispensing the Sacraments validly and religiously, or whether we shall have no clergy at all. Your Holiness will understand that I speak of desperate measures for a desperate time, and that . . ."

Once again he was brought back to the subject of his letter, the education of the ministers of the Word. Once again he was faced with the intangible *X* that dominated the whole thinking of the Church—the infusion of the Holy Spirit supplying what was defective in man so that the Mystical Body was kept always alive. How far, therefore, could one go in entrusting the Church to this dominating influence of the Spirit? How far was it lawful to risk the Word and the Sacraments to men partly instructed, trusting to the Paraclete to supply the rest? And yet who but himself was to say what was a partial and what was a sufficient instruction? Did the Holy Ghost work less strongly now, in the twentieth century, than in the primitive Church, when twelve fishermen were entrusted with the Deposit of Faith and the mission to preach it to all nations . . . ?

Outside, the summer day was dying. The bells of the city were tolling their vain cry for recollection and withdrawal. But the city was full of other sounds, and it was left to Kiril the Pontiff to gather his household about him for vespers and a remembrance of the hidden God.

"You've done a very thorough job, my friend." Campeggio laid down the typescript and looked at George Faber with a new respect. "That's the most complete dossier I've ever seen on Corrado Calitri and his friends."

Faber shrugged unhappily. "I was trained as a crime reporter. I have a talent for this sort of thing. . . . But I can't say that I'm very proud of it."

"Love's an expensive business, isn't it?" Campeggio smiled as he said it, but there was no humor in his shrewd dark eyes.

"I was going to talk to you about that. The information in that document cost me a thousand dollars. I may have to spend a lot more."

"On what?"

"To get a signed statement out of one or more of the people mentioned in the dossier."

"Have you any idea how much it will cost?"

"No. But from what I've gathered so far, several of them are short of money. The most I can afford is another thousand dollars. I want to know if you're prepared to put up any more."

Campeggio sat silent awhile, staring down at Faber's littered desk. Finally he said deliberately, "I'm not sure that I should discuss the proposition in those terms."

"What do you mean?"

"From the point of view of the Rota, and of civil law, it could amount to a subornation of witnesses."

"I've thought of that myself."

"I know you have. You're an honest man—too honest for your own comfort, or mine. Let's look at it from another angle. How do you propose to approach your prospective witnesses?"

"I've marked three names in the document. Each one of them has open animosity to Calitri. One is an actor who hasn't had a good part for twelve months. One is a painter. Calitri financed one exhibition for him, and then dropped him. The third is a woman. I'm told she's a writer, though I've never seen anything she's published. The two men always spend the summer at Positano. The woman has a house on Ischia. I propose to go south during the summer holidays and try to make contact with each one."

"Are you taking Chiara with you?"

"No. She wants to come, but I don't think it's good diplomacy. Besides I . . . I need to test myself away from her."

"You may be wise, at that." Campeggio's shrewd eyes searched his face. "I wonder if any of us knows himself before his middle years? . . . Now tell me something else. Why do you think your witnesses will ask for money?"

"It's the way of the world," said George Faber wryly. "Nobody really wants to be persecuted for justice's sake. Everybody wants to make a profit on the process."

"You're a Catholic, Faber. How do you feel in conscience about this transaction?"

Faber flushed. "My conscience is compromised already. I'm committed to Chiara; I can't afford the luxury of scruples."

Campeggio agreed sourly. "It's a very Nordic point of view. It's probably more honest than mine."

"And what is your point of view?"

"About the money? I'm prepared to give you another thousand dollars. But I don't want to know what you do with it."

Faber's rare wintry humor asserted itself for a moment. "And that leaves your conscience clear?"

"I'm a casuist," said Campeggio with a thin smile. "I can split hairs as well as the Jesuits. It suits me to be in doubt. But if you want the truth . . ." He stood up and began to pace up and down Faber's office. "If you want the truth, I'm in deep confusion. I think Chiara has justice on her side. I think you have a right to try to get it for her. I think there is justice on my side, too, when I want to remove my son from Calitri's influence. I'm doubtful about the means, so I don't want to question them too closely. That's why I'm co-operating with you while leaving you to carry the burden of moral and legal decision. . . . It's a very Latin trick. . . ."

"At least you're open with me," said Faber with odd simplicity. "I'm grateful for that."

Campeggio stopped his pacing and looked down at Faber, who sat slumped and vaguely shrunken behind his desk. "You're a soft man, my friend. You deserve a simpler loving."

"It's my fault more than Chiara's. . . . I have to work double time to be free for the vacation. I'm worried about money. I'm scared that I may not be able to control the consequences of what we are doing."

"And Chiara?"

"She's young. She's been hurt. She's in an uncomfortable position for a woman . . . So she wants to be diverted . . . . I don't blame her. But I don't have the stamina for five nights a week at the Cabala or the Papagallo."

"How does she occupy herself while you're working?"

Faber gave a small, rueful grin. "What does any young matron of fashion do in Rome? . . . Luncheon parties, mannequin shows, cocktails. . . ."

Campeggio laughed. "I know, I know. Our women make good lovers and good mothers. As wives, even as unofficial ones, they lack something. They resent their husbands and spoil their sons."

For a moment Faber seemed to lose himself in a private contemplation. He said absently, "The loving is still good. . . . But I have the feeling that we're both starting to calculate. When Chiara came to me first she was almost broken. I seemed to be able to supply everything she needed. Now she's back to normal and I am the one with the needs."

"Doesn't she understand that?"

"That's the sixty-four-dollar question. . . . By nature she's impulsive and generous, but living with Calitri has changed her. It's as if . . ." He fumbled uneasily for the words. "As if she thinks men owe her a special kind of debt."

"And you're not sure you can pay it all?"

"No, I'm not sure."

"Then if I were you," said Campeggio emphatically, "I should cut loose now. Say good-by, cry into your pillow, and forget the whole business."

"I'm in love with her," said Faber simply. "I'm ready to pay any price to hold her."

"Then we're both in the same galley, aren't we?"

"What do you mean?"

Campeggio balked a moment, and then explained himself deliberately. "In the beginning possession always seems the ultimate triumph of love. You have your Chiara now, but you cannot be wholly happy until you possess her by legal contract. Then, you feel, you will be safe. You pluck the rose and put it in a vase in the drawing room, but after a while the bloom fades, and it is no longer so important that you own a wilting flower. When children come, they are another kind of possession. They depend on you utterly. You hold them to you by their need of sustenance and security. As they grow, you find that the bond weakens, and that you no longer possess them as you once did. . . . I want my son. I want him to be the image and the continuum of myself. I tell myself that what I do is for his good, but I know, deep in my heart, that it is also for my own satisfaction. I cannot bear that he should withdraw himself from me and give himself to another—man or woman—whom I consider less worthy. . . . But in the end he will go, for better or for worse. . . . Look at me now. I am a man of confidence at the Vatican. As editor of the *Osservatore* I am the mouthpiece of the Church. I have a reputation for integrity and I believe I have earned it. Yet today I am beginning to compromise myself. Not for you! Don't think I'm blaming you! It is for my son, whom I shall lose anyway, and for myself, because I have not yet begun to come to terms with age and loneliness. . . ."

George Faber heaved himself out of his chair and stood facing his colleague. For the first time, he seemed to take on an unfamiliar strength and dignity. He said evenly, "I have no right to hold you to any bargains. You're in a more delicate position than I am. You're free to withdraw your offer."

"Thank you," said Orlando Campeggio simply. "But I can't withdraw. I'm committed . . . because of what I want and what I am."

"And what are you? What am I?"

"We should have been friends," said Orlando Campeggio with dry irony. "We've known each other a long time. But we missed the chance. So I'm afraid we're just conspirators—and not very good ones at that!"

Ten days before the feast of St. Ignatius Loyola, Jean Télémond received a letter from His Eminence Cardinal Rinaldi:

Dear Reverend Father,

This is not an official communication, but a personal one. Just before your arrival in Rome the Holy Father granted me permission to retire from office, and I am now living privately in the country. I am, however, invited to be present next week when you address the students and faculty at the Gregorian University. Before that day I should very much like to have the opportunity of meeting and talking with you.

Already I know a great deal—more, perhaps, than you realize—about you and your work. I judge you to be a man favored by God with what I can only call the grace of commitment.

This grace is a rare gift. I myself have missed it, but for this reason, perhaps, I am the more aware of it in others. I am aware, too, that it comes to the recipient more often as a cross than as a consolation.

I believe that your recall to Rome may be an event of great importance to the Church. I know that it is a decisive one for you. I should like, therefore, to offer you my friendship, my support, and perhaps my advice in your future activities.

If it is convenient, perhaps you would be good enough to visit me next Monday and spend the afternoon with me. You will be doing me a favor, and I hope sincerely I may be of some service to you.

Yours fraternally in Christ Jesus,
Valerio Rinaldi
Cardinal Priest

For a man in crisis it was a princely encouragement, and it touched Télémond deeply. It reminded him—when he needed the reminder most—that for all its monolithic faith, the Church was a habitation of diverse spirits amongst whom still dwelt a virtue of fraternity and compassion.

In the clattering, gregarious, clerical society of Rome he felt like an alien. Its conventions irked him. Its brusque orthodoxy troubled him as if he were being reproached for his twenty-year solitude among the mysteries of Creation. The melancholy of the climacteric weighed upon his soul. On the one hand, he found himself dreading the moment when he must present the speculation of a lifetime to the public view. On the other, he found himself approaching the moment with a kind of calculation which made the risks he had sustained, in flesh and spirit, seem futile and even guilty.

Now suddenly there was a hand stretched out to welcome him, and a voice that spoke with an accent of rare understanding and gentleness. He had not lacked friendship in his life. His work had not wanted patronage and encouragement. Yet no one had ever seen it so clearly for what it was. A gamble, a commitment to living and knowing and believing, with a complete conviction that every moment of existence, every extension of knowledge, every act of faith, was a step in the same direction, toward God-made-man and man made in the image of God.

What had troubled him most in Rome was the feeling that certain people in the Church regarded his work as an arrogance. Yet an arrogant man could not have embarked upon such a journey, nor risked so much in a single-minded search for truth.

He had never been afraid of error since all his experience had shown him that knowledge was self-corrective and that a search honestly pursued must bring a man closer to the shores of revelation, even though their outline remained forever hidden from his view.

There was an attitude of orthodoxy which was itself a heresy: that to state the truth, as it had been stated and restated in every century of the Church, was to display it forever in all its fullness. Yet the history of the Church was the history of an immutable revelation unfolding itself into greater and greater complexity as men's minds opened to receive it more fully. The history of spiritual progress for an individual was the history of his preparation of himself to co-operate more willingly, more consciously, and more gratefully with the grace of God.

For Jean Télémond the letter of Valerio Rinaldi wore the aspect of such a grace. He accepted it thankfully, and made an appointment to visit the Cardinal in his country retreat.

They were instantly at ease with each other. Rinaldi walked his guest round the pleasances of the villa and rehearsed its history from the first Etruscan tomb, in the orchard, to the Orphic temple, whose pavement lay uncovered in the sunken garden. Télémond was charmed by the urbanity and kindness of his host, and he opened himself more freely than he had done for a long time, so that the old man looked out through his visitor's eyes on exotic landscapes and a cavalcade of histories new and strange to him.

When they had finished the circuit, they sat beside a marble pond and drank English tea, and watched the fat carp browse languidly among the lily pads. Then, amiably but shrewdly, Rinaldi began to probe the mind of Jean Télémond.

"Rome is a chameleon city. It wears a different color for each visitor. How does it look to you, Father?"

Jean Télémond toyed with the question for a moment, and then answered it frankly. "I am uneasy. The idiom is strange to me. I am a Gaul among the

Romans, a provincial among the metropolitans. I came back sure that I had learned so much in twenty years. Now I feel that I have forgotten something— some essential mode of speech, perhaps. I don't know what it is, but the lack of it troubles me."

Rinaldi put down his teacup and wiped his fastidious hands with a linen napkin. His lined patrician face softened. "I think you rate yourself too humbly, Father. It's a long time since Gaul was a province of Rome, and I think it is we who have lost the art of communication. . . . I don't deny that you have a problem, but I am inclined to read it differently."

Télémond's lean, disciplined features relaxed into a smile. "I should be grateful to hear your Eminence's interpretation."

The old Cardinal waved an eloquent hand, so that the sunlight gleamed on the emerald ring of his office.

"There are some, my friend, who wear the Church like a glove. Myself, for instance. I am a man who was made to grow comfortably within an established order. I understand the organization. I know where it is rigid and where it can be made flexible. . . . There is no merit in this, no special virtue. It is at bottom a matter of temperament and aptitude. It has nothing to do with faith, hope, or charity. There are those who are born to be good servants of the State. There are those who have an aptitude for the government of the Church. . . . It is a talent, if you want, but a talent which has its own temptations, and I have succumbed to some of them during my life. . . ."

He stared down at the lily pond, where the fish swam gold and crimson and the flowers spread their creamy petals under the afternoon sun. Télémond waited while the old prince gathered the rest of his thoughts.

"There are others, my friend, who wear the Church like a hair shirt. They believe no less. They love perhaps more richly and more daringly; but they move, as you do, uneasily inside the discipline. For them obedience is a daily sacrifice, whereas for me and those like me it is an accommodation—often a rewarding accommodation—to circumstance. Do you understand what I mean?"

"I understand it, but I think that your Eminence underrates himself to be kind to me."

"No! No!" Rinaldi's answer was swift and emphatic. "I am too old to pay idle compliments. I have entered into judgment with myself and I know how much I am found wanting. . . . At this moment you are a troubled man. . . ."

"So very troubled, Eminence," said Télémond softly. "I came to Rome under obedience, but there is no peace for me here. I know that."

"You are not born to peace, my friend. This is the first thing you must accept. You will not come to it, perhaps, till the day you die. Each of us has his own cross, you know, made and fitted to his reluctant shoulders. Do you know what mine is?"

"No."

"To be rich and content and fulfilled, and to know in this twilight of living that I have deserved none of it and that when I am called to judgment I must depend utterly upon the mercy of God and upon the merits of others more worthy."

Télémond was silent a long time, touched and humbled by this glimpse of an intimate and private agony. Finally he asked quietly, "And my cross, Eminence?"

"Your cross, my son . . ." The old man's voice took on a new warmth and compassion. "Your cross is to be always divided between the faith which you possess, the obedience which you have vowed, and your personal search for a deeper knowledge of God through the universe which He has made. You believe that there is no conflict between the two, and yet you are involved in conflict every day. You cannot recant the Act of Faith without a personal catastrophe. You cannot abandon the search without a ruinous disloyalty to yourself and to your own integrity. Am I right, Father?"

"Yes, Eminence, you're right; but it isn't enough. You show me the cross, but you do not show me how to carry it."

"You have carried it for twenty years without me."

"And now I am staggering under its weight. Believe me, I am staggering. . . . And now there is a new burden—Rome!"

"Do you want to go away?"

"Yes. And yet I should be ashamed to go."

"Why?"

"Because I hope that this may be the time of resolution for me. I feel I have been silent long enough for my thought to take shape. I feel that I have a duty to expose it to debate and dialectic. This exposure seems as much a duty as all my years of study and exploration."

"Then you must do your duty," said Rinaldi mildly.

"That makes another problem, Eminence," said Télémond with a flash of humor. "I am not a publicist. I do not present myself very well. I do not know how to accommodate myself to the climate of this place."

"Then ignore it," said Rinaldi bluntly. "You come armed with a right heart and a private vision of the truth. That is armor enough for any man."

Télémond frowned and shook his head. "I mistrust my courage, Eminence."

"I could tell you to trust in God."

"I do, and yet—" He broke off and stared unseeing across the reaches of the classic garden.

Rinaldi prompted him gently. "Go on, my son."

"I'm afraid—desperately afraid!"

"Of what?"

"That there may come a moment when this conflict in myself splits me in two and destroys me utterly. I can't put it any other way. I lack the words. I can only hope that your Eminence understands."

Valerio Cardinal Rinaldi stood up and laid his hands on the bowed shoulders of the Jesuit. "I do, my son, believe me! I feel for you as I have felt for few men in my lifetime. Whatever happens after your address next week, I want you to count me your friend. I told you you would be doing me a favor if you allowed me to help you. I put it more strongly. You may give me the opportunity of winning some small merit for myself. . . ." His habitual humor asserted itself again, and he laughed. "It's a tradition in Rome, Father. Painters, poets, and philosophers all need a patron to protect them from the Inquisition. And I may be the last real one left!"

Extract from
the Secret Memorials of
KIRIL I, Pont. Max.

. . . All this week I have been besieged by what I can only call a temptation of darkness. Never since my time in the bunker have I been so oppressed by the wild absurdity of the world, by the wastefulness of man's struggle for survival, by the apparent idiocy of any attempt to change human nature or bring about a corporate betterment in the human condition.

To reason with the temptation was simply to create another absurdity. To reason with myself was to invite a new confusion. A spirit of mockery seemed to inhabit me. Whenever I looked at myself I saw a jester in cap and bells, perched on a mountaintop, waving his silly wand at the hurricanes. When I prayed, my spirit was arid. The words were like an incantation from some ancient witchcraft—without virtue and without reward. It was a kind of agony which I thought would never come my way again, yet this time I was more deeply wounded by it than ever before.

In my confusion I addressed myself to a meditation on the passion and death of the Master. I began to understand dimly the meaning of the agony in Gethsemane garden, when the trouble of His human spirit communicated itself so poignantly to His body that its mechanism began to break down and He suffered, as a leukemia patient does, the bloody sweat which is a foretaste of dying.

For a moment also I glimpsed the meaning of His final desolate cry from the Cross. . . . "My God, my God, why hast Thou forsaken me?" In that moment I think He must have seen—as I see now—the wild folly of a world gone mad, bursting itself asunder in a tangential flight from its center.

At that moment His own life and death must have seemed a vast futility, just as my life and all my effort as His Vicar seem to me. Yet He endured it, and so must I. If He, God-man, could suffer, uncomforted by the Godhead, shall I refuse the cup which He hands on to me? . . .

I held to the thought with a kind of terror, lest it should slip away from me and leave me forever a prey to blackness and despair. Then, slowly, the darkness dissipated itself and I found myself shaken, almost physically ill, but confirmed once again in the essential sanity of belief. I did, however, see something very clearly: the plight of those who have no God to infuse a meaning into the monstrous nonsense of the whole human effort.

For a believer life is at best a painful mystery, made acceptable by a partial revelation of a divine design. To an unbeliever—and there are hundreds of millions from whom the grace of belief has been withheld—it must present itself at times as a kind of madness, always threatening, at times almost unendurable. Perhaps this is the meaning of what I am and what has happened to me: that being poor in all else, I can offer to the world the love of an understanding heart. . . .

Today a second letter arrived from Kamenev. It was delivered in Paris to the Cardinal Archbishop and forwarded to me by special messenger. It is more cryptic than the first, but I sense a greater urgency in it:

> I have your message and I am grateful for it. The sunflowers are blooming now in Mother Russia, but before they come to flower again, we may have need of each other.
>
> Your message tells me that you trust me, but I have to be honest and say that you must not trust what I do or what I am reported to say. We live in different climates, as you know. You command an obedience and a loyalty impossible in my sphere of action. I can survive only by understanding what is possible, by yielding to one pressure in order to avoid a greater one.
>
> Within twelve months, even sooner, we may come to the brink of war. I want peace. I know that we cannot have it with a one-sided bargain. On the other hand, I cannot dictate its terms even to my own people. I am caught in the current of history. I can tack across it, but I cannot change the direction of the flow.
>
> I believe you understand what I am trying to say. I ask you, if you can, to interpret it as clearly as possible to the President of the United States. I have met him. I respect him. In a private dealing I could trust him, but in the domain of politics he is as subject to pressure as I am—more so, perhaps, because his tenure is shorter and the influence of public opinion is stronger. If you can communicate with him, I beg you to do so, but secretly and with the greatest discretion. You know that I should have to repudiate violently any suggestion that there is a private channel of talk between us.
>
> I cannot yet suggest a secure method by which you can write to me. From time to time, however, you will receive application for a private audience from a man named Georg Wilhelm Forster. To him you may speak freely, but commit nothing to writing. If you succeed in a conversation with the President of the United States, you should refer to him as Robert. Foolish, is it not, that to discuss the survival of the race we must resort to such childish tricks.
>
> You are fortunate that you can pray. I am limited to action, and if I am half right for half the time I am lucky.
>
> Again I repeat my caution. You believe you stand in God's shoes. I must wear my own, and the ground is very slippery. Trust me no further than I

can trust myself. Martyrdom is out of fashion in my world. Greetings. Kamenev.

No man remains unchanged by the experience of power. Some are perverted to tyranny. Some are corrupted by flattery and self-indulgence. Some very few are tempered to wisdom by their understanding of the consequences of executive action. I believe this is what has happened to Kamenev.

He was never a gross man. When I knew him he had surrendered himself to cynicism, but this surrender was never quite complete. This was proved by his action in my regard. I would say that there is in his thinking no truly spiritual or religious domain. He has accepted too fully a materialist conception of man and of the universe. However, I do believe that within the limits of his own logic, he has arrived at an understanding of the dignity of man and a sense of obligation to preserve it as far as he can. I do not think he is governed by moral sanctions as we understand them in the spiritual sense. But he does realize that a certain practical morality is essential to social order, and even to the survival of civilization as we know it.

I think this is what he is trying to tell me: that I can trust him to proceed logically in his own system of thought, but that I must never expect him to work inside mine. For my part, I must not forget that while man is limited to the covenanted channels of grace, made available to him by the redemptive act of Christ, God is not so limited, and that in the outcome Kamenev's logic may be turned into a divine one. Even in the human order Kamenev's letter has a historic importance. The man who embodies in his office the Marxist heresy, who has tried violently to extirpate the Faith from the land of Russia, now turns to the Papacy to provide a free and secret mode of communication with the rest of the world.

I see very clearly that Kamenev offers me nothing—no entry for the Faith into Russia, no slackening of oppression or persecution. Cardinal Goldoni points out that at this very moment our schools and seminaries in Poland, and Hungary, and East Germany, are in danger of being closed altogether by the imposition of new and savage taxation. He asks me what Kamenev proposes to offer either to the Church or to the United States by way of a down payment toward peace. . . .

On the face of it he offers nothing. One might even make a good case for the opinion that he is trying to use me to his own advantage. I have to weigh this opinion very carefully. Yet I cling to the deep conviction that there is a divine design in this relationship between us and that it must not be allowed to degenerate into a political gambit. . . .

It is a historic fact that when the temporal power of the Church was greatest her spiritual life was at its lowest ebb. It is dangerous to read divine revelation into every paragraph of history, but I cannot help feeling that when we are like the Master, poorest in temporality, then we may be richest in the divine life.

From me the occasion demands prayer and prudence. . . . Normally we should communicate with the Government of the United States through our own Secretariat of State. In this instance we dare not do so. I have, therefore, sent a cable to the Cardinal Archbishop of New York, asking him to come to Rome as quickly as possible so that I may brief him on the situation and have him communicate directly with the President of the United States. Once I have spoken with Cardinal Carlin, we shall all be walking on eggs. If any hint of the matter is revealed to the American press, this small hope of peace may be lost to us forever. . . . In the morning I must offer Mass as a petition for a favorable outcome. . . .

Today I held the first of a series of conferences with the Congregation of the Religious and with the heads of the major religious orders. The purpose of the conferences is to determine how they may best adapt themselves to the changing conditions of the world and participate more actively and more flexibly in the mission of the Church to the souls of men.

There are many problems involved, and we shall not solve them all at one stroke. Each order holds jealously to its tradition and its sphere of influence in the Church. All too often the tradition is a handicap to apostolic effort. Systems of training differ. The "spirit of the order"—that mode of thought and action which gives it a special character—tends too often to harden itself into "the method of the order," so that it reacts too slowly and too stubbornly to the demands of the times.

There is another problem, too. The rate of recruitment of new members has become dangerously slow because many willing spirits find themselves too limited and constrained by an archaic constitution and even by a mode of dress and life which separates them too sharply from the times in which they live. . . .

Once again I am faced with the fundamental problem of my office—how to translate the Word into Christian action; how to scrape off the overburden of history so that the lode of the primitive faith may be revealed in all its richness. When men are truly united with God, it matters little what dress they wear, what exercises of piety they perform, what constitution they live under. Religious obedience should set a man free in the liberty of the sons of God. Tradition should be a lamp to his feet, lighting his pathway into the future. To renounce the world is not to abandon it, but to restore it in Christ to the beauty of its primal design. . . . We inherit the past, but we are committed to the present and to the future.

It is time, I think, for a deeper exploration and a clearer definition of the function of the laity in the life of the Church. Anti-clericalism is a symptom of dissatisfaction among the faithful. For the fact is that rebellion against the doctrine of the Church is less common than the gradual desertion of a religious climate which seems to be at irreconcilable odds with the world men have to live in. Those whose aspirations exceed the dimensions of the local pastor's mentality gradually fade from the pews in search of substitutes and partial truths, which as a rule, bring them neither peace nor joy, but certainly a sense of dedicated integrity. The number of these cases has become large enough to achieve some sort of recognizable status in the Church, which, though ambiguous, is radically different from the category of those whose militant darkness attempts to eradicate from human consciousness the very notion of man's existence dependent on God. . . .

In this world of ours, when men are reaching swiftly for the moon, the dimension of time seems to narrow daily, and I am perturbed that we cannot adjust ourselves more quickly to the change. . . .

In a couple of weeks the holiday season will begin in Europe. It is customary for the Pontiff to leave the Vatican and spend a vacation at Castel Gandolfo. In spite of my impatience I find myself looking forward to the change. It will give me time to think, to sum up for myself the thousand diverse impressions of these first months in office.

I have not dared to mention it to the Secretary of State, but I think I shall take the opportunity to travel a little in private, round the countryside. . . . I shall need a good driver. It would be embarrassing to me, and to the Italian government, if we had any accidents on the road—it would make a wonderful picture if the Pontiff were discovered in the middle of a highway, arguing with an Italian truck driver. . . . I find myself wishing for an agreeable companion to spend the vacation with me, but I have not yet found time to cultivate any real friendship. My isolation is all the greater because I am so much younger than the members of the Curia, and—God help me—I do not want to become an old man before my time.

I understand now how some of my predecessors have lapsed into nepotism and surrounded themselves with relatives, and how others have cultivated favorites in the Vatican. It is not good for any man to be wholly alone. . . .

Kamenev is married and has a son and a daughter. I should like to think he has made a happy match. . . . If not, he must be much more isolated than I. I have never regretted my own celibacy, but I envy those whose work in the Church is with children. . . .

A sudden dark thought. If there is another war, what of the little ones? They are the inheritors of our misdeeds, and how will they fare in the broadcast horror of an atomic Armageddon? . . .

It must not be . . . it must not!

—— VII ——

I N his bachelor apartment on Parioli, Corrado Calitri, Minister of the Republic, was conferring with his lawyers. The senior advocate, Perosi, was a tall, spare man with a dry, academic manner. His junior had a round dumpling face and a deprecating smile. In the far corner of the room the Princess Maria-Rina sat withdrawn and wary, watching them with hooded predatory eyes.

Perosi laid the tips of his fingers together like a bishop about to intone a Psalm, and summed up the situation:

". . . As I understand it, you have been troubled in conscience for some time. You have taken counsel with a confessor, and he has advised you that it is your duty to change your testimony with respect to your marriage."

Calitri's pale face was blank, his voice devoid of expression. "That's the position, yes."

"Let us be very clear, then, where we stand. Your wife's petition for a decree of nullity is made under the terms of Canon 1086, which states two things: first, the internal consent of the mind is always presumed to be in agreement with the words or signs which are used in the celebration of the marriage; second, if either party or both parties, by a positive act of the will, exclude marriage itself, or all right to the conjugal act or any essential property of the marriage, the marriage contract is invalid." He rustled his papers and went on in his professional fashion. "The first part of the canon does not really concern us. It simply expresses a presumption of the law, which may be overcome by contrary proof. Your wife's plea leans on the second part. She claims that you deliberately excluded from your consent her right to the conjugal act, and that you did not accept the contract as unbreakable, but as a form of therapy to be laid aside if the therapy failed. If her plea could be sustained, the marriage would, of course, be declared invalid. You understand that?"

"I've always understood it."

"But you denied in a written and sworn statement that your intention was defective."

"I did."

"Now, however, you are prepared to admit that the statement was false and that, in fact, you perjured yourself."

"Yes. I understand that I have done a grave injustice, and I want to repair it. I want Chiara to be free."

"You are prepared to make another sworn statement, admitting the perjury and the defective intention?"

"I am."

"So far, so good. This will give us a ground to reopen the case with the Rota." Perosi pursed his pale lips and frowned. "Unfortunately, it will not be sufficient for a decree of nullity."

"Why not?"

"It's a question of procedure covered by Canon 1971, and by commentaries on the code dated March 1929, July 1933, and July 1942. A party to a marriage who is the guilty cause of the nullity is deprived of the right to impugn the contract. He has no standing in court."

"Where does that leave us?"

"We need one or more witnesses to testify that you expressed to them, clearly and explicitly, your defective intentions before the marriage took place."

The brisk old voice of the Princess intruded itself into the conversation. "I think you can take it for granted that such testimony would be available."

"In that case," said Advocate Perosi, "I think we have a sound case, and we may look with some confidence to a favorable outcome."

He sat back in his chair and began rearranging his papers. As if on a prearranged signal, the dumpling man added a footnote to the discussion:

"With respect to my senior colleague, I should like to make two suggestions. It would be an advantage if we had a letter from your confessor, indicating that you are acting under his advice in trying to repair the injustice done. It might help, too, if you wrote a friendly letter to your wife, admitting your fault and asking her to forgive you. . . . Neither of these two documents would have any value in evidence, but they might, shall we say, help the atmosphere."

"I'll do as you suggest," said Calitri in the same colorless fashion. "Now I'd like to ask a couple of questions. I admit default, I admit perjury. On the other hand, I do have a public position and a reputation to protect."

"All the deliberations of the Rota, and all the depositions made before it, are protected by rigid secrecy. You need have no fear on that score."

"Good. How long do you think the business will take?"

Perosi considered the question a moment. "Not too long. Nothing can be done, of course, during the holiday period, but if all the depositions were in our hands by the end of August, we could have the translation done in two weeks. Then, in view of your position and the long suspension of the case, I think we would get a speedy hearing. . . . I should say two months at the outside. It might even be sooner."

"I am grateful," said Corrado Calitri. "I'll have the papers ready by the end of August."

Perosi and his colleague bowed themselves out. "We are always at the disposal of the minister."

"Good day, gentlemen, and thank you."

When the door closed behind them, the Princess threw back her bird's head and laughed. "There, now. I told you, didn't I? It's as simple as shelling peas. Of course we have to find you a confessor. There's a nice understanding Monsignore who attends me from Florence. Yes, I think he'd be the one. He's intelligent, cultivated, and quite zealous in his own way. I'll have a talk with him and arrange an appointment. . . . Come on now, smile. In two months you'll be free. In a year you'll be leading the country."

"I know, Aunt, I know."

"Oh, there's one more thing. Your letter to Chiara. There's no need to be too humble about it. Dignity, restraint, a desire to make amends, yes. But nothing compromising. I don't trust that girl. I never have."

Calitri shrugged indifferently. "She's a child, Aunt. There's no malice in her."

"Children grow up—and there's malice in every woman when she can't get what she wants."

"From what I hear, she's getting it."

"With the dean of the foreign press. What's his name?"

"George Faber. He represents one of the New York dailies."

"The biggest one," said the old Princess firmly. "And you can't shrug him off like a cold in the head. You're too vulnerable now, my boy. You have the *Osservatore* against you and Chiara in bed with the American press. You can't afford a situation like that."

"I can't change it."

"Why not?"

"Campeggio's son works for me. He likes me and dislikes his father. Chiara will probably marry this Faber as soon as she gets the decree of nullity. There's nothing I can do about either situation."

"I think there is." She fixed him with a shrewd and rheumy eye. "Take young Campeggio first. You know what I should do?"

"I'd like to hear it."

"Promote him. Push him forward as fast as you can. Promise him something even bigger after the election. Bind him to you with trust and friendship. His father will hate you, but the boy will love you, and I don't think Campeggio will fight his own son. . . . As for Chiara and her American boyfriend, leave them to me."

"What do you propose to do?"

The old Princess gave her high birdlike chuckle and shook her head. "You have no talent with women, Corrado. Just sit quietly and leave Chiara to me."

Calitri spread his eloquent hands in a gesture of resignation. "Just as you say, Aunt. I'll leave her to you."

"You won't regret it."

"I'll take your advice, Aunt."

"I know you will. Give me a kiss now, and cheer up. You'll have dinner with me tomorrow night. There are some people from the Vatican I want you to meet. Now that you're back in the bosom of the Church, they can begin to be useful to you."

He kissed her withered cheek and watched her leave, wondering the while that so much vitality should reside in so frail a body, and whether he had enough to sustain the bargain he had made with his backers.

All his life he had been making deals like this one. Always the price had to be paid in the same coin—another fragment of himself. Each depletion made him less assured of his identity, and he knew that in the end he would be altogether empty and the spiders would spin webs in the hollow of his heart.

Depression came down on him like a cloud. He poured himself a drink and carried it over to the window seat from which he could look down on the city and the flight of pigeons over its ancient roofs. The Prime Ministry might be worth a Mass, but nothing—nothing—was worth the lifetime damnation to emptiness which was demanded of him.

To be sure, he had made a contract. He would be the White Knight without fear and without reproach, and the Christian Democrats would let him lead them into power. But there was room still for a footnote, and the Princess Maria-Rina had spelled it out for him. . . . Trust and friendship. . . . Perhaps even more! In the sour bargain he had made, there was suddenly a hint of sweetness.

He picked up the telephone, dialed the number of his office, and asked young Campeggio to bring the afternoon's correspondence to his apartment.

At ten-thirty of a cloudless morning Charles Corbet Carlin, Cardinal Archbishop of New York, landed at Fiumicino Airport. An official of the Secretariat of State met him at the steps of the aircraft and hurried him past the customs and immigration officials into a Vatican limousine. An hour and a half later he was closeted with Kiril the Pontiff and Goldoni the Secretary of State.

Carlin was by nature a peremptory man, and he understood the usages of power. He was quick to see the change that a few months of office had wrought in the Pope. He had lost none of his charm, none of his swift, intuitive warmth. Yet he seemed to have reached a new dimension of authority. His scarred face was leaner, his speech more brisk, his whole manner more urgent and concerned. Yet, characteristically, he opened the discussion with a smile and an apology:

"I'm grateful that your Eminence came so promptly. I know how busy you are. I wanted to explain myself more fully, but I could not trust the information even to a coded cable."

Then in crisp, emphatic sentences he explained the reason for the summons and showed Carlin the text of Kamenev's two letters.

The American scanned them with a shrewd and calculating eye, and then handed them back to the Pontiff. "I understand your Holiness' concern. I confess I am less clear on what Kamenev hopes to gain by this maneuver."

Goldoni permitted himself a faint smile. "Your Eminence's reaction is the same as mine . . . A maneuver! His Holiness, however, takes a different view."

Kiril spread his crooked hands on the desk top and explained himself simply. "I want you to understand first that I know this man. I know him more intimately than I know either of you. For a long time he was my interrogator in prison. Each of us has had a great influence on the other. It was he who arranged my escape from Russia. I am profoundly convinced that this is not a political maneuver, but a genuine appeal for help in the crisis which will soon be upon us."

Carlin nodded thoughtfully. "Your Holiness may be right. It would be folly to discount your experience with this man and your intimate knowledge of the Russian situation. On the other hand—and I say it with all respect—we have had another kind of experience with Kamenev and with the Soviets."

"When you say 'we,' do you refer to the Church or to the United States of America?"

"To both," said Carlin flatly. "So far as the Church is concerned, the Secretariat of State will bear me out. There is still active persecution in the satellite countries. In Russia the Faith has been totally extinguished. Our brother bishops who went to prison with your Holiness are all dead. The Soviet frontiers are sealed against the Faith. I see no prospect of their being opened in our time."

Goldoni added agreement. "I have already put this view very clearly to His Holiness."

"And I," said Kiril the Pontiff, "do not disagree with it. . . . Now tell me about the American view."

"At first blush," said Carlin, "this looks to me like another version of the old summit meetings. We all remember the arguments . . . 'Let's bypass the lower echelons and let the leaders talk freely and familiarly about our problems. Let's skip the details and get down to the fundamental issues that divide us. . . .' Well, we had the meetings. They were always abortive. In the end every discussion was wrecked by the details. Whatever good will existed before the meetings was diminished, if not wholly destroyed. In the end, you see, the lower echelons of government are more decisive than the upper ones because under our system, and under the Russian one, the leader is always subject to the pressures of political and administrative advice from below. No single man can sustain the burden of decision on major issues." He smiled expansively at the Pontiff. "Even in the Church we have the same situation. Your Holiness is the Vicar of Christ. Yet the effectiveness of your decisions is limited by the co-operation and obedience of the local ordinaries."

Kiril the Pontiff picked up the letters from his desk and held them out to his two counsellors. "So what would you have me do about these? Ignore them?"

Carlin side-stepped the question. "What does Kamenev ask your Holiness to do?"

"He is very clear, I think. He asks me to communicate the letters to the President of the United States, and communicate also my own interpretation of his mind and his intentions."

"What is his mind, Holiness? What are his intentions?"

"Let me quote again what he says. 'Within twelve months, even sooner, we may come to the brink of war. I want peace. I know that we cannot have it with a one-sided bargain. On the other hand, I cannot dictate its terms even to my own people. I am caught in the current of history. I can tack across it, but I cannot change the direction of the flow. . . . I believe you understand what I am trying to say. I ask you, if you can, to interpret it as clearly as possible to the

President of the United States. . . .' To me, in my knowledge of the man, the message is quite evident. Before the crisis becomes irreversible, he wants to establish a ground of negotiation so that peace may be preserved."

"But what ground?" asked Goldoni. "Your Holiness must admit that he is somewhat less than precise."

"Put it another way," said Carlin in his pragmatic fashion. "I go back home. I call Washington and ask for a private interview with the President of the United States. I show him these letters. I say, 'It is the view of the Holy See that Kamenev wants to begin secret talks to fend off the crisis we all know is coming. The Pope will be the intermediary of the talks. . . .' What, do you think, the President will say or do then? What would your Holiness do in his place?"

Kiril's scarred face twitched into a smile of genuine amusement. "I should say, 'Talk costs nothing. So long as men can communicate, however haltingly, then there is a hope of peace. But close all the doors, cut all the wires, build the walls even higher—then each nation is an island, preparing in secret a common destruction.' "

Abruptly Carlin challenged the argument. "There is a flaw in the logic, Holiness. Forgive me, but I have to show it to you. Talk always costs something —this kind of talk especially. Secret parleys are dangerous because once they are brought into the open—and inevitably they must be—then they can be denied by those who took part in them. They can be used as weapons in political dealings."

"Remember!" Goldoni added the potent afterthought. "There are no longer two grand powers in the world. There is Russia, and the United States. There is the European bloc. There is China, and there are the uncommitted nations of Asia and Africa and the South Americas. There is not only the arms race. There is the race to feed the hungry and the race to align vast numbers of mankind with one ideology or another. We dare not take too simple a view of this very complex world."

"I hesitate to say it, Holiness," said Carlin gravely, "but I should not like to see the Holy See compromised by offering itself as an intermediary in bilateral and probably abortive discussions. . . . Personally I mistrust a truce with the Russian bear, no matter how prettily he dances."

"You have him in the papal coat of arms," said Kiril tartly. "Do you mistrust him there, too?"

"Let me answer the question with another. Can your Holiness trust himself completely in this matter? This is not doctrine or dogma, but an affair of State. Your Holiness is as open to error as the rest of us."

He had been dangerously frank and he knew it. To be Cardinal Archbishop of New York was to sit high in the Church, to dispose great influence, to command money and resources vital to the economy of the Vatican. Yet in the constitution of the Faith the Successor of Peter was paramount, and in its history many a Cardinal Prince had been stripped of his preferment by a single word from an outraged Pontiff. Charles Corbet Carlin sat back in his chair and waited, not without uneasiness, for the papal answer.

To his surprise, it was delivered in a tone of restraint and real humility. "Everything you tell me is true. It is, in fact, a reflection of my own thought on the matter. I am grateful that you have chosen to be open with me, that you have not tried to bend me by diplomatic words. I do not want to bend you, either. I do not want to force you to act against your own prudence. This is not a matter of faith or morals, it is a matter of private conviction, and I should like to share mine with you. . . . Let us have lunch first, and then I want to show you both something. You have seen it before, but I hope today it may take on another meaning for you."

Then seeing the doubt and surprise on their faces, he laughed almost boy-ishly. "No, there are no plots, no Borgia subtleties. I've learned something in Italy. One should never discuss weighty matters on an empty stomach. I think Goldoni will agree that I've reformed the Vatican kitchens, if nothing else. Come now, let's relax for a while."

They ate simply but well in Kiril's private apartment. They talked discur-sively of men and affairs and the hundred intimacies of the hierarchic society to which they belonged. They were like members of an exclusive international club, whose fellows were scattered to every point of the compass, but whose affairs were common knowledge in all tongues.

When the meal was over and the Vatican had lapsed into the somnolence of siesta time, Kiril put on a black cassock and led his two guests into the Basilica of St. Peter.

The tourists were sparse now, and no one paid any attention to three middle-aged clerics halted by the confessional boxes near the sacristy. Kiril pointed to one of them, which carried on its door the laconic legend "Polish and Russian."

"Once a week I come and sit here for two hours, to hear the confession of anyone who chances to come. I should like to hear them in Italian as well, but the dialects escape me. . . . You both know what this ministry of the tribunal is like. The good ones come. The bad ones stay away; but every so often there arrives the soul in distress, the one who needs a special co-operation from the confessor to lead him back to God. . . . It's a lottery always—a gamble on the moment and the man, and the fruitfulness of the Word one plucks from one's own heart. And yet there, in that stuffy little box, is the whole meaning of the Faith—the private speech of man with his Creator, myself between as man's servant and God's. There, encompassed by the smell of blood sausage and cabbage water, and the sweat of a frightened man, I am what I was ordained to be: a sublime opportunist, a fisher of men, not knowing what I shall catch in my net or whether I shall catch anything at all. . . . Now come over here."

He beckoned to an attendant to accompany them. Then he took the arms of the two Cardinals and walked them across to the steps that led down to the confession of St. Peter, in front of the great altar of Bernini. They descended the steps. The attendant unlocked the bronze grille in front of the kneeling statue of Pope Pius VI. When they entered the recess, he closed the door on them and retired to a respectful distance. Kiril led his two counsellors to the space where a dark hole plunged down toward the grottoes of the Vatican. Then he turned to face them. His voice dropped to a murmur that echoed softly round the enclosure.

"Down there, they say, is the tomb of Peter the Fisherman. Whenever I am afraid or in darkness, I come here to pray, and ask him what I, his inheritor, should do. He was an opportunist, too, you know. The Master gave him the

Keys of the Kingdom. The Holy Ghost gave him the gift of wisdom and the gift of tongues. Then he was left, still a fisherman, an alien in the empire of Rome, to plant the seed of the Gospel wherever there was earth to receive it. . . . He had no method. He had no temple. He had no book but the living Gospel. He was conditioned by the time in which he lived, but he could not be bound by the condition. . . . Neither can I. Do you remember the story of Paul coming into the city of Athens, among the philosophers and the rhetors, and seeing the altar of the Unknown God? Do you remember what he did? He cried out with a loud voice, 'Men, brethren! What you worship without knowing, I preach!' Is not this an opportunist, also? He does not reason with the moment. He does not appeal to a system or a history. He gambles himself and his mission on a word tossed into a milling crowd. Don't you see? This is the meaning of faith. This is the risk of belief."

He turned a luminous face on Carlin, not commanding but pleading with him. "Before your Eminence came to see me, I was in darkness. I saw myself as a fool shouting a folly to a heedless world. So be it! That is what we preach: transcendent nonsense, which we trust in the end will make a divine logic. . . ."

Abruptly he relaxed and grinned at them mischievously. "In prison I learned to gamble, and I found that in the end the man who always won was he who never hedged his bets. I know what you're thinking. I want to navigate the barque of Peter by the seat of my papal breeches. . . . But if the wind is blown by the breath of God and the water is rocked by His hands . . . how better can I do it? Answer me! How better can I do it?"

In the narrow enclosure Goldoni shifted uneasily on his feet.

Carlin stood as obstinate and unshakable as Plymouth Rock. He said evenly, "This is perhaps the faith that moves mountains, Holiness. I regret that it has not been given to me in the same measure. I am compelled to work by normal prudence. I cannot agree that the affairs of the Church can be administered by private inspiration."

Kiril the Pontiff was still smiling when he answered. "You elected me by inspiration, Eminence. Do you think the Holy Ghost has deserted me?"

Carlin was not to be put off. He pressed his argument stubbornly. "I did not say that, Holiness. But I will say this: No one is large enough to make himself the universal man. You want to be all things to all men, but you can never truly succeed. You're a Russian, I am an American. You ask me to risk more on this Kamenev than I would risk on my own brother if he were President of the United States. I cannot do it."

"Then," said Kiril with unexpected mildness, "I will not ask you to do it. I will not ask you to risk anything. I will give you a simple command. You will present yourself to the President of the United States. You will offer him these letters, and one which I shall write myself. If your opinion is asked, you will be free to say whatever you wish, as a private cleric and as an American, but you will not attempt to interpret my mind or Kamenev's. This way I hope you will feel free to discharge your duty to the Church and to your country."

Carlin flushed. He said awkwardly, "Your Holiness is generous with me."

"Not generous, only logical. If I believe the Holy Ghost can work through me and through Kamenev, why should he not work through the President of the

United States? It is never wise to discount Omnipotence. Besides," he added gently, "you may do better for me in opposition. At least you will guarantee the good faith of the Holy See toward the United States of America. . . . I think now, perhaps, we should pray together. It is not expected that we should agree on what is prudent, only that our wills should be set toward the service of the same God."

As the month of July drew to a close and the summer exodus from Rome began, Ruth Lewin found herself caught up once more in the cyclic drama of mental distress.

The onset of the action was always the same: a deep melancholy, a sensation of solitude, a feeling of rootlessness, as though she had been set down suddenly on an unfamiliar planet, where her past was meaningless, her future was a question mark, and communication lapsed into gibberish.

The melancholy was the worst sensation of all. As a symptom it was familiar to her, yet she could neither reason with it nor dispel it. It drove her into fits of weeping. When the tears stopped, she felt empty and incapable of the simplest pleasure. When she looked in a mirror, she saw herself old and ravaged. When she walked out into the city, she was a stranger, an object of derision to the passers-by.

The flaw in her personality must be evident to everybody. She was a German by birth, a Jew by race, an American by adoption, an exile in the country of the sun. She demanded belief and refused it with the same gesture. She needed love and knew herself impotent to express it. She wanted desperately to live, yet was haunted by the insidious attraction of death. She was everything and nothing. There were times when she huddled helpless in her apartment like a sick animal, afraid of the clamorous health of her kind.

All her relationships seemed to fail her at once. She moved like a stranger among her protégés in Old Rome. She made expensive telephone calls to friends in America. When they failed to answer, she was desolate. When they responded with casual thanks, she was convinced she had made a fool of herself. She was oppressed by the prospect of summer, when Rome was deserted and the heat lay like a leaden pall over the alleys and the sluggish life of the piazzas.

At night she lay wakeful, with aching breasts, tormented by a fire in the flesh. When she drugged herself into sleep, she dreamed of her dead husband and woke sobbing in an empty bed. The young doctor with whom she worked came to visit her, but he was too immersed in his own problems, and she was too proud to reveal her own to him. He was in love with her, he said, but his demands were too blunt, and when she drew away he was quickly bored, so that in the end he stopped coming, and she blamed herself for his neglect.

A couple of times she tried the old prescription for unhappy widows in Rome. She sat herself in a bar and tried to drink herself into recklessness. But three drinks made her ill, and when she was accosted she was brusquely and unreasonably angry.

The experience was salutary. It made her cling with a kind of desperation to the last vestige of reason. It gave her a little more patience to support the illness which she knew must pass, even though she dare not wait too long upon the cure. Each petty crisis depleted her reserves and brought her one step nearer the medicine cabinet, where the bottle of barbiturates mocked her with the illusion of forgetfulness.

Then, one heavy and threatening day, hope stepped into her life again. She had wakened late and was dressing listlessly when the telephone rang. It was George Faber. He told her Chiara was out of town. He was feeling lonely and depressed. He would like to take her to dinner. She hesitated a moment, and then accepted.

The incident was over in two minutes, but it wrenched her out of depression and into an almost normal world. She made a hasty appointment with her hairdresser. She bought herself a new cocktail frock for twice the money she could afford. She bought flowers for her apartment and a bottle of Scotch whisky for Faber, and when he came to call for her at eight o'clock she was as nervous as a debutante on her first date.

He was looking older, she thought, a trifle stooped, a little grayer than at their last meeting. But he was still the dandy, with a carnation in his buttonhole, an engaging smile, and a bunch of Nemi violets for her dressing table. He kissed her hand in the Roman fashion, and while she mixed his drink he explained himself ruefully:

"I have to go south on this Calitri business. Chiara hates Rome in the summer, and the Antonellis have asked her to go to Venice with them for a month. They've taken a house on the Lido. . . . I hope to join them later. Meantime . . ." He gave a little uneasy laugh. "I've lost the habit of living alone. . . . And you did say I could call you."

"I'm glad you called, George. I don't like living alone, either."

"You're not offended?"

"Why should I be? A night on the town with the dean of the foreign press, that's an event for most women. Here's your drink."

They toasted each other, and then fenced their way through the opening gambits of talk.

"Where would you like to dine, Ruth? Do you have any preferences?"

"I'm in your hands, good sir."

"Would you like to be quiet or gay?"

"Gay, please. Life's been all too quiet lately."

"That suits me. Now, would you like to be a Roman or a tourist?"

"A Roman, I think."

"Good. There's a little place over in Trastevere. It's crowded and noisy, but the food's good. There's a guitar player, an odd poet or two, and a fellow who draws pictures on the tablecloth."

"It sounds wonderful."

"I used to like it, but I haven't been there in a long time. Chiara doesn't like that sort of thing." He blushed and fiddled nervously with his liquor. "I'm sorry. That's the wrong beginning."

"Let's make a bargain, George."

He gave her a quick, shamefaced glance. "What sort of bargain?"

"Tonight nothing is wrong. We say what we feel, do what we like, and then forget it. No strings, no promises, no apologies. . . . I need it like that."

"I need it, too, Ruth. Does that sound like disloyalty?"

She leaned across and placed a warning finger on his lips. "No second thoughts, remember!"

"I'll try. . . . Tell me about yourself. What have you been doing?"

"Working. Working with my *Juden* and wondering why I do it."

"Don't you know why?"

"Sometimes. At others it's pretty meaningless."

She got up and switched on the record player, and the room was filled with the saccharine tones of a Neapolitan singer. Ruth Lewin laughed. "Pretty schmaltzy, isn't it?"

Faber grinned and lay back in his chair, relaxed for the first time. "Now who's having second thoughts? I like schmaltz—and I haven't heard the word three times since I left New York."

"It's the Yiddish in me. It slips out when I'm off my guard."

"Does that worry you?"

"Occasionally."

"Why should it?"

"That's a long story, and it's not for now. Finish your drink, George. Then take me out and make a Roman of me, just for tonight."

At the doorway of the apartment he kissed her lightly on the lips, and then they walked, arm in arm, past the ghostly marbles of the Forum. Then for a final surrender to whimsy, they hailed a *carrozza* and sat holding hands while the tired horse carried them clippity-clop over the Palatine Bridge and into the populous lanes of Trastevere.

The restaurant was called 'o Cavalluccio. Its entrance was an old oaken door, studded with rusty nails. Its sign was a prancing stallion, roughly carved into the weathered stone of the lintel and picked out with whitewash. The interior was a large, vaulted cellar, hung with dusty lanterns and set with heavy wooden refectory tables. The clientele was mostly families from the quarter, and the spirit of the place was one of amiable tyranny.

The proprietor, a dumpy fellow in a white apron, set them down in a dark corner, planked a flask of red and a flask of white wine in front of them, and announced his policy with a flashing smile:

"As much wine as you can drink! Good wine, too, but no fancy labels. Two kinds of pasta only. Two main dishes—a roast of chicken and a stew of veal in Marsala. After that you're in the hands of God!"

As Faber had promised, there was a guitar player, a swarthy youth with a red bandana round his neck and a tin cup tied to his belt for an alms box. There was a bearded poet, dressed in blue denims, homemade sandals, and a sackcloth shirt, who turned an honest penny by mocking the guests with verses improvised in the Roman dialect. For the rest, the entertainment was provided by the clowning of the guests themselves and an occasional raucous chorus called by the guitar player. The pasta was served in great wooden bowls, and an impudent waiter tied a huge napkin round their necks to protect their noble bosoms from the sauce.

Ruth Lewin was delighted with the novelty, and Faber, plucked out of his normal ambience, seemed ten years younger and endowed with an unsuspected wit.

He charmed her with his talk of Roman intrigues and Vatican gossips, and she found herself talking freely of the long and tortuous journey which had brought her at last to the Imperial City. Encouraged by Faber's sympathy, she exposed her problems more freely than she had ever done, except to an analyst, and found to her surprise that she was no longer ashamed of them. On the contrary, they seemed to define themselves more clearly, and the terror they had once held for her was magically diminished.

". . . For me everything boiled itself down to a question of security and the need to put down some kind of roots in a world that had shifted too quickly for my childish understanding. I never seemed to be able to do it. Everything in my life, people, the Church, the happiness I enjoyed—and I did have moments of great happiness—everything seemed to have the look of 'here one day and gone the next.' I found that I could not believe in the permanence of the simplest relationship. The worst moments were when I found myself doubting that anything that had happened to me was real at all. It was as if I had been living a dream—as if I, the dreamer, were a dream, too. Does that sound strange to you, George?"

"No, not strange. Sad, yes, but rather refreshing, too."

"Why do you say that?"

He sipped his wine thoughtfully, and then gave her a long, searching look over the rim of his glass. "I suppose because Chiara is just the opposite. In spite of everything that has happened to her, she seems completely certain of what she wants in life and how she's going to get it. There's only one way to be happy—her way. There's only one way to be amused or content—the way to which she has been bred. Her marriage to Calitri shocked her dreadfully, but basically it didn't change her view of life. . . . I think in the end you may be more fortunate than she is."

"I wish I could believe that."

"I think you must. You may not be happy yet. You may never be truly secure. But you're more flexible, more ready to understand the thousand ways people live, and think, and suffer."

"I often wonder if that is a good thing—or whether it's just another illusion on my part. You know, I have the same dream over and over again. I talk to someone. He does not hear me. I reach out for someone. He does not even see me. I am waiting to meet someone. He walks right past me. I'm convinced that I don't exist at all."

"Take my word for it," said George Faber with a rueful smile. "You do exist, and I find you very disturbing."

"Why disturbing?"

Before he had time to answer, the bearded poet came and took his stand by their table, and declaimed a long rigmarole that sent the diners into roars of laughter. George Faber laughed, too, and handed him a bank note for reward. The poet added another couplet that raised another roar of laughter, then backed away, bowing like a courtier.

"What did he say, George? I missed most of the dialect."

"He said we weren't young enough to be single, but we weren't too old to look like lovers. He wondered if your husband knew what you were doing, and whether the baby would look like him or me. When I gave him the money, he said I was rich enough not to care, but if I wanted to keep you I'd better marry you in Mexico."

Ruth Lewin blushed. "A very uncomfortable poet, but I like him, George."

"I like him, too. I wish I could afford to be his patron."

They were silent awhile, listening to the clatter and the muted, melancholy music of the guitar. Then casually enough, Faber asked:

"What will you do with yourself during the summer?"

"I don't know. Just now I'm dreading it. In the end I'll probably take one of those CIT tours. They can be pretty dull, I know, but at least one isn't alone."

"You wouldn't think of joining me for a few days? Positano first, then Ischia."

She did not shrink away from the question, but faced it in her forthright fashion. "On what terms, George?"

"The same as tonight. No strings, no promises, no apologies."

"What about Chiara?"

He gave her a shrugging, uneasy answer. "I won't question what she does in Venice. I don't think she'll question me. Besides, what harm is there? I'll be working for Chiara. You and I are both grown-up. I'd like you to think about it."

She smiled and refused him gently. "I mustn't think about it, George. You're finding it hard enough to cope with the woman you have. I doubt you could handle me as well." She reached out and took his hand between her palms. "You have a rough fight ahead of you, but you can't win it if you split down the middle. I can't divide myself, either. . . . Please don't be angry with me. I know myself too well."

He was instantly penitent. "I'm sorry. I guess it sounded pretty crude, but I didn't mean it like that."

"I know you didn't, and if I try to tell you how grateful I am I'll cry. Now will you please take me home?"

Their driver was still waiting for them, patient and knowing, in the darkened alley. He roused his dozing horse and set him on the long way home: the Margherita Bridge, the Villa Borghese, the Quirinale piazza, and down past the Colosseum to the Street of St. Gregory. Ruth Lewin laid her head on Faber's shoulder and dozed fitfully while he listened to the clip-clop of the ancient nag and searched his troubled heart.

When they reached Ruth Lewin's apartment, he helped her alight and held her for a moment in the shadow of the doorway.

"May I come up for a little while?"

"If you want to."

She was too sleepy to protest, and too jealous of the little that was left of the evening. She made him coffee, and they sat together listening to music, each waiting for the other to break the dangerous spell. Impulsively George Faber took her in his arms and kissed her, and she clung to him in a long and passionate embrace. Then he held her away from him and pleaded without reserve:

"I want to stay with you, Ruth. Please, please let me stay."

"I want you to stay too, George. I want it more than anything in the world . . . But I'm going to send you home."

"Don't tease me, Ruth. You're not a girl like that. For God's sake, don't tease me."

All the needs of the years welled up in her and forced her toward surrender, but she drew away from him and pleaded in her turn. "Go home, George. I can't have you like this. I'm not strong enough for it. You'll wake in the morning and feel guilty about Chiara. You'll thank me and slip away. And because you feel disloyal I won't see you again. I do want to see you. I could be in love with you if I let myself, but I don't want half a heart and half a man. . . . Please, please go!"

He shook himself like a man waking out of a dream. "I will come back; you know that."

"I know it."

"You don't hate me?"

"How can I hate you? But I don't want you to hate yourself because of me."

"If it doesn't work out with Chiara—"

She closed his lips with a last light kiss. "Don't say it, George! You'll know soon enough. . . . Perhaps too soon for both of us."

She walked with him to the portico, watched him climb into the *carrozza,* and waited until the fading hoofbeats had died into the murmur of the city. Then she went to bed, and for the first time in months she slept dreamlessly.

In the Great Hall of the Gregorian University, Jean Télémond stood facing his audience.

His address lay before him on the rostrum, translated into impeccable Latin by a colleague of the Society. His back was straight. His hands were steady. His mind was clear. Now that the moment of crisis had come, he felt strangely calm, even elated by this final and resolute commitment of a lifetime's work to the risk of open judgment.

The whole authority of the Church was here, summed up in the person of the Pontiff, who sat, lean, dark, and oddly youthful, with the Father General on one side of him and Cardinal Leone on the other. The best minds of the Church were here: six Cardinals of the Curia; the theologians and philosophers, dressed in their diverse habits—Jesuits, Dominicans, Franciscans, and men of the ancient order of St. Benedict. The future of the Church was there—in the students with scrubbed and eager faces, who had been chosen from every country in the world to study at the seat of Christendom. The diversity of the Church was here, too, expressed in himself, the exile, the solitary seeker, the exotic who yet wore the black tunic of brotherhood and shared the ministry of the servants of the Word.

He waited a moment, gathering himself. Then he made the Sign of the Cross, delivered the opening allocution to the Pontiff and the Curia, and began his address:

"It has taken a journey of twenty years to bring me to this place. I must therefore beg your patience while I explain myself and the motives which prompted this long and often painful pilgrimage. I am a man and a priest. I became a priest because I believed that the primary and the only perfectly sustaining relationship was that between the Creator and the creature, and because I wished to affirm this relationship in a special fashion by a life of service. But I have never ceased to be a man, and as a man I have found myself committed, without recourse, to the world in which I live.

"My deepest conviction as a man—confirmed by all my experience—is that I am one person. I who think, I who feel, I who fear, I who know and believe, am a unity. But this unity of my self is part of a greater unity. I am separate from the world, but I belong to it because I have grown out of its growth just as the world has grown out of the unity of God as the issue of a single creative act.

"I, therefore, the one, am destined to participate in the oneness of the world, as I am destined to participate in the oneness of God. I cannot set myself in isolation from Creation any more than I can, without destroying myself, set myself in isolation from the Creator.

"From the moment that this conviction became clear to me, another followed it by inevitable consequence. If God is one, and the world is one issue of His eternal act, and I am a single person spawned out of this complex unity, then all knowledge—of my self, of Creation, of the Creator—is one knowledge. That I do not have all knowledge, that it presents itself to me by fragments and in diversity, means nothing except that I am finite, limited by time and space and the capacity of my brain.

"Every discovery I make points in the same direction. No matter how contradictory the fragments of knowledge may appear, they can never truly contradict one another. I have spent a lifetime in one small branch of science, paleontology. But I am committed to all sciences, to biology, to physics, to the chemistry of inorganic matter, to philosophy, and to theology, because all are branches of the same tree and the tree grows upwards toward the same sun. Never, therefore, can we risk too much or dare too boldly in the search for knowledge, since every step forward is a step toward unity—of man with man, of men with the universe, of the universe with God. . . ."

He glanced up, trying to read in the faces of his audience a reaction to his words. But there was nothing to read. They wanted to hear his whole case before they committed themselves to a verdict. He turned back to the typescript and read on.

"Today I want to share with you a part of the journey which I have made for the past twenty years. Before we begin it, however, there are two things I want to say. The first is this: An exploration is a very special kind of journey. You do not make it like a trip from Rome to Paris. You must never demand to arrive on time and with all your baggage intact. You walk slowly, with open eyes and open minds. When the mountains are too high to climb, you march around them and try to measure them from the lowlands. When the jungle is thick, you have to cut your way through it, and not resent too much the labor or the frustration.

"The second thing is this: When you come to record the journey, the new contours, the new plants, the strangeness and the mystery, you find often that your vocabulary is inadequate. Inevitably your narrative will fall far short of the reality. If you find this defect in my record, then I beg you to tolerate it and let it not discourage you from contemplation of strange landscapes which, nevertheless, bear the imprint of the creative finger of God.

"Now to begin . . ."

He paused, twitched his cassock over his thin shoulders, and lifted his lined face to them in a kind of challenge.

"I want you to come with me, not as theologians or philosophers, but as scientists—men whose knowing begins with seeing. What I want you to see is man: a special kind of being who exists in a visible ambience at a determinable point in time and space.

"Let us look at him in space first. The universe which he inhabits is immense, galactic. It stretches beyond moon and sun into an enormity of dimension which our mathematics can express only by an indefinite extension of zeros.

"Look at man in time. He exists now at this moment, but his past goes back to a point where we lose him in a mist. His future prolongs itself beyond our conception of any possible circumstance.

"Look at man by numbers, and you find yourself trying to count the grains of sand on a shore line without limit.

"Look at him by scale and proportion, and you find him on the one hand a minuscule dwarf, in a universe without apparent limits. Measure him by another scale, and you find him in partial control of the enormity in which he lives. . . ."

The most skeptical of his hearers—and there were many in the audience who were disposed to be dubious of him—found themselves being caught up and carried along by the strong current of his eloquence. The passion of his conviction expressed itself in every line of his weathered face, in every gesture of his thin, expressive hands.

Rudolf Semmering, the grim, soldierly man, found himself nodding approval of the noble temper of his subject. Cardinal Rinaldi smiled his thin, ironic smile and wondered what the pedants would make of this valiant intruder into their private domain. Even Leone, the harsh old watchdog of the Faith, leaned his craggy chin on his hand and registered a reluctant tribute to the unflinching courage of this suspect spirit.

In Kiril the Pontiff the conviction grew, swift as a conjuror's mango plant, that this was the man he wanted: a man totally committed to the risk of living and knowing, yet anchored firm as a sea-battered rock to belief in a divinely planned unity. The waves might tear at him, the winds might score his spirit, but he would stand unshaken and unshakable under the assault. He found himself murmuring a message to sustain him. "Go on! Don't be afraid. Your heart is right, and it beats in time with mine. No matter that the words stumble and the record falters. The vision is clear, the will points straight and true toward the Center. Go on! . . ."

Télémond was in full course now, expounding to them his view of matter—the material of the universe, which expressed itself in so many different appearances, and finally in the appearance of man.

". . . 'God made man of the dust of the earth'! The Biblical image expresses aptly the most primitive conviction of man—a conviction confirmed by the most advanced scientific experiment—that the stuff of which he is formed is capable of indefinite scaling down to particles infinitely small. . . . At a certain point of this scaling down man's vision of himself becomes blurred. He needs spectacles, then a microscope, then a whole array of instrumentation to supplement his failing sight. For a moment he is lost in diversity—molecules, atoms, electrons, neutrons, protons . . . so many and so different! Then suddenly they all come together again. The universe, from the farthest nebulae to the simplest atomic structure, is a whole, a system, a quantum of energy—in other words, a unity. But—and I must ask you to lean and linger and think upon this most important 'but'—this universe is not a static whole, it is in a constant state of change and transformation. It is in a state of genesis . . . a state of becoming, a state of evolving. And this is the question which I ask you to face with me now. The universe is evolving and man is evolving with it—into what? . . ."

They were with him now. Critics or captives of the idea, they were with him. He could see them leaning forward in their benches, intent on every phrase and every inflection. He could feel their interest projected toward him like a wave. He gathered himself once again and began to sketch, with swift, decisive strokes, the picture of a cosmos in motion, rearranging itself, diversifying itself, preparing itself for the coming of life, for the coming of consciousness, for the arrival of the first subhuman species, and the ultimate arrival of man.

He was on his own ground now, and he marched them forward with him, out of the misty backward of a crystallizing world to the moment when the change from life to non-life took place, when the megamolecule became the micro-organism and the first biotic forms appeared on the planet.

He showed them how the primitive life forms spread themselves in a vast network around the surface of the spinning globe; how they joined and dis-joined into a multitude of combinations; how some conjunctions were swiftly suppressed because they were too specially adapted to a time and a condition of the evolutionary march; how others survived by changing themselves, by be-coming more complex in order to guarantee their own endurance.

He showed them the first outlines of a fundamental law of nature—the too specialized life form was the first to perish. Change was the price of survival.

He did not shrink from the consequences of his thought. He took his audi-ence by the scruff of their necks and forced them to face the consequences with him.

". . . Even so early in the evolutionary chain we are faced with the brutal fact of biological competition. The struggle for life is endless. It is always accompanied by death and destruction, and violence of one kind or another. . . . You will ask yourselves, as I have asked myself a thousand times, whether this struggle necessarily transfers itself, at a later stage of history, into the domain of man. At first blush the answer is yes. But I object to so crude and total an application of the biological pattern. Man does not live now on the same level upon which he lived when he first made his appearance on the planet. He has passed through successive levels of existence; and it is my belief, supported by considerable evidence, that man's evolution is marked by an effort to find other, less brutal, and less destructive modes of competition for life. . . ."

He leaned forward over the rostrum and challenged them with the thought that he knew was already in their minds.

"You ask me why I do not invoke at this moment a divine intervention in the pattern of human evolvement. It is because we must continue to walk along the exploratory path which we have set ourselves. We are limiting ourselves only to what we see. And all we are seeing at this moment is man emerging as a phenomenon in a changing universe. If we are troubled by what we see, we must bear the trouble and not seek too easy an answer for it. I make this point although man has not yet appeared to our exploring eyes. We have leapt forward to meet him. Now we must go back."

He could almost feel their tension relax. He stole a swift glance at the front row of the audience. Leone was shaking his white head and making a whispered comment to a Cardinal on his left. Rinaldi was smiling, and he lifted one hand in an almost imperceptible gesture of encouragement. Kiril the Pontiff sat erect in his chair, his scarred face immobile, his dark eyes bright with interest.

Gently now Télémond led them back to the main stream of his story. He showed them the primitive life forms reproducing themselves, multiplying, joining and rejoining, groping ingeniously but indifferently toward stability and permanence. He drew for them the tree of life and showed how it branched and yet grew upwards; how certain twigs died and fell off; how certain branches ceased to grow; but how, always, the main thrust of growth was upwards in the direction of the large brain and the complex organism, and the most flexible mechanism of survival. He showed them the first subhuman species—the hominoid, which was the prelude to the human—and finally he showed them man.

Then, brusquely, he presented them with a puzzle.

". . . From where we stand now, we see a continuity and a unity in the evolutionary process. But if we look closely, we see that the line of advance is not always a firm and a definite stroke. It is dotted in places, or broken. We cannot say where, in point of time, life began. Yet we know that it did begin. We know that the pterodactyl existed. We have dug his bones out of the earth. But where and by what mutations he came to be is not wholly clear to us. We see him first as plural . . . many pterodactyls. But was there a first couple or were they always many? We do not know. . . . So, with man, when we first find him on the earth, he is many. Speaking as scientists, we have no record of the emergence of man as a single couple. In the historic record written in primal clay, men are suddenly present. I do not say that they came suddenly, any more than that the pterodactyl came suddenly. All the evidence points to a slow emergence of the species, but at a certain point in history man is there, and with man something else is there as well. . . . Consciousness. . . . Man is a very special phenomenon. He is a being who knows, he is also a being who knows that he knows. We have come, you see, to a very particular point of history. A creature exists who knows that he knows. . . .

"Now, my friends, I want you to address yourself to my next question only as scientists, only as witnesses of the visible evidence. How did this special phenomenon emerge?

"Let us step back from him a moment. Let us consider all those phenomena which preceded him, many of which still co-exist with him, from the micro-organism to the hominoid ape. All of them have something in common—a drive, a groping, an urge to fit themselves for survival. To use an overworked and imprecise term, it is an instinct to do those things, to enter into those combinations and those associations which will enable them to proceed along their proper line of continuity. I prefer to choose another word than *instinct*. I prefer to say that this drive, or this capacity, is a primitive but evolving form of what culminates in man. . . . Consciousness. . . ."

Once again he had brought them to a crisis, and he knew it. For the first time, he felt really inadequate to display to them the whole range and subtlety of the thought. Time was against him, and the simple semantic limitation and the rhetorical power to persuade them into a new but still harmonious view of the nature and origin of humankind. Still, he went on resolutely, developing for them his own view of the cosmic pattern—primal energy, primitive life, primitive consciousness, all evolving and converging to the first focal point of history, thinking man. He took them further yet, by a bold leap into their own territory, showing all the lines of human development converging to a final unity, a unity of man with his Creator.

More vividly than ever before he could feel the mood of his audience shifting. Some were in awe, some were dubious, some had settled themselves into complete hostility to his thought.

Yet when he came to his peroration, he knew that he had done the best he could and that for all its sometime vagueness, and sometime risky speculation, his address had been the true reflection of his own intellectual position. There was nothing more he could do but commit himself to judgment and rest courageous in the outcome. Humbly, but with deep emotion, he summed it up for them.

"I do not ask you to agree with me. I do not put any of my present conclusions beyond reconsideration or new development, but of this I am totally convinced: the first creative act of God was directed toward fulfillment, and not destruction. If the universe is not centered on man, if man as the center of the universe is not centered on the Creator, then the cosmos is a meaningless blasphemy. The day is not far distant when men will understand that even in biological terms they have only one choice: suicide or an act of worship."

His hands trembled and his voice shook as he read them the words of Paul to the Colossians:

" 'In Him all created things took their being, heavenly and earthly, visible and invisible. . . . They were all created through Him and in Him; He takes precedence of all, and in Him all subsist. . . . It was God's good pleasure to let all completeness dwell in Him, and through Him to win back all things, whether on earth or in Heaven, unto union with Himself, making peace with them through His blood, shed on the Cross.' "

He did not hear the thunder of applause as he stepped down from the pulpit. As he knelt to pay his respects to the Pontiff and lay the text of his address in his hands, he heard only the words of the blessing and the invitation—or was it a command?—that followed:

"You're a bold man, Jean Télémond. Time will tell whether you are right or wrong, but at this moment I need you. We all need you."

Extract from
the Secret Memorials of
KIRIL I, Pont. Max.

. . . Yesterday I met a whole man. It is a rare experience, but always an illuminating and ennobling one. It costs so much to be a full human being that there are very few who have the enlightenment, or the courage, to pay the price. . . . One has to abandon altogether the search for security, and reach out to the risk of living with both arms. One has to embrace the world like a lover, and yet demand no easy return of love. One has to accept pain as a condition of existence. One has to court doubt and darkness as the cost of knowing. One needs a will stubborn in conflict, but apt always to the total acceptance of every consequence of living and dying.

This is how I read Jean Télémond. This is why I have decided to draw him to me, to ask for his friendship, to use him as best I know in the work of the Church. . . . Leone is uneasy about him. He has said so very bluntly. He points, quite rightly, to ambiguities and obscurities in his system of thought, to what he calls a dangerous rashness in certain of his speculations. He demands another full examination of all his writings by the Holy Office before he is permitted to teach publicly or to publish his research.

I do not disagree with Leone. I am not so bold that I am prepared to gamble with the Deposit of Faith, which is, after all, the testament of Christ's new covenant with man. To preserve it intact is the whole meaning of my office. This is the task which has been delegated to Leone in the Church. . . .

On the other hand, I am not afraid of Jean Télémond. A man so centered upon God, who has accepted twenty years of silence, has already accepted every risk, even the risk that he can be mistaken. Today he said so in as many words, and I believe him. . . . I am not afraid of his work, either; I do not have the equipment or the time to judge truly of its ultimate value. This is why I have counsellors and experts learned in science, theology, and philosophy to assist me. . . .

I am convinced, moreover, that honest error is a step toward a greater illumination of the truth, since it exposes to debate and to clearer definition those matters which might otherwise remain obscure and undefined in the teaching of the Church. In a very special sense the Church, too, is evolving toward a greater fullness of understanding, a deeper consciousness of the divine life within itself.

The Church is a family. Like every family, it has its homebodies and its adventurers. It has its critics and its conformists; those who are jealous of its least important traditions; those who wish to thrust it forward, a bright lamp into a glorious future. Of all them I am the common Father. . . . When the adventurers come back scarred and travel-worn from a new frontier, from another foray, successful or unsuccessful, against the walls of ignorance, I must receive them with the charity of Christ and protect them with gentleness against those who have fared better only because they have dared much less. I have asked the Father General of the Jesuits to send Jean Télémond to keep me company at Castel Gandolfo during summer. I hope and pray that we may learn to be friends. He could enrich me, I think. I, for my part, may be able to offer him courage and a respite from his long and lonely pilgrimage. . . .

In an odd fashion he has given me courage as well. For some time now I have been engaged in a running debate with the Cardinal Secretary of the Congregation of Rites on the question of introducing the vernacular liturgy and a vernacular system of teaching into the seminaries and churches of missionary countries. This would mean inevitably a decline of the Latin liturgical language in many areas of the world. It would mean also an immense task of translation and annotation, so that the works of the Fathers of the Church would be made available to clerical students in their own language.

The Congregation of Rites takes the view that the merits of the change are far outweighed by its disadvantages. They point out that it would run counter to the decisions of the Council of Trent, and to the pronouncements of later Councils and later Pontiffs. They claim that the stability and uniformity of our organization depends much on the use of a common official tongue in the definition of doctrine, the training of teachers, and the celebration of the liturgy.

I myself take the view that our first duty is to preach the Word of God and to dispense the grace of the Sacraments, and that anything which stands in the way of this mission should be swept aside.

I know, however, that the situation is not quite so simple. There is, for example, a curious division of opinion in the small Christian community in Japan. The Japanese bishops want the Latin system preserved. Because of their unique and isolated position they are inclined to be timorous about any change at all. On the other hand, missionary priests working in the country report that work is handicapped when the vernacular is not used.

In Africa the native Cardinal Ragambwe is very clear that he wants to try the vernacular system. He is very aware of the risks and the problems, but he still feels that a trial should be made. He is a holy and enlightened man, and I have great respect for his opinion.

Ultimately the decision rests with me, but I have deferred it because I have been so vividly aware of the complexity of the problem and of the historic danger that small and isolated groups of Christians may, for lack of a common communication, be separated from the daily developing life of the Church. We are not building only for today, but for tomorrow and for eternity.

However, listening to Jean Télémond, I felt myself encouraged to make a decisive step. I have decided to write to those bishops who want to introduce the vernacular system and ask them to propose to me a definite plan for its use. If their plans seem workable, and if at the same time a certain select number of the clergy can be trained in the traditional mode, I am disposed to let the new system be tried. . . . I expect strong opposition from the Congregation of Rites, and from many bishops in the Church, but a move must be made to break the deadlock which inhibits our apostolic work, so that the Faith may begin to grow with more freedom in emerging nations.

They are all jealous of their new identity, and they must be led to see that they can grow in, and with, the Faith toward a legitimate social and economic betterment. We are not yet one world, and we shall not be for a long time, but God is one, and the Gospel is one, and it should be spoken in every tongue under Heaven. . . . This was the mode of the primitive Church. This was the vision which Télémond renewed for me: the unity of the spirit in the bond of faith in the diversity of all knowledge and all tongues. . . .

Today I held the last series of audiences before the summer holidays. Among those whom I received privately was a certain Corrado Calitri, Minister of the Republic. I had already received most of the Italian Cabinet, but I had never met this man. The circumstance was sufficiently unusual for me to comment on it to the Maestro di Camera.

He told me that Calitri was a man of unusual talent, who had had a meteoric rise in the Christian Democratic Party. There was even talk that he might lead the country after the next elections.

He told me also that Calitri's private life had been somewhat notorious for a long time, and that he was involved in a marital case presently under consideration by the Holy Roman Rota. Now, however, it seemed that Calitri was making serious efforts to reform himself and that he had put himself and his spiritual affairs into the hands of a confessor.

There was, of course, no discussion of these matters between myself and Calitri. An audience is an affair of State and has nothing to do with the spiritual relationship of Pastor and people.

Nonetheless, I was curious about the man, and I was tempted for a moment to call for the file on his case. In the end I decided against it. If he comes to power, we shall have diplomatic connections, and it is better that it should not be complicated by a private knowledge on my part. It is better, too, that I do not interfere too minutely in the varied functions of the tribunals and the congregations. My time is very limited. My energies are limited, too, and presently they are so depleted that I shall be glad to pack and go from this place, into the comparative serenity of the countryside.

I see very clearly the shape of a great personal problem for every man who holds this office: how the press of business and the demands of so many people can so impoverish him that he has neither time nor will left to regulate the affairs of his own soul. I long for solitude and the leisure for contemplation. . . . "Consider the lilies of the field . . . they labor not, neither do they spin"! Lucky the ones who have time to smell the flowers and doze at noonday under the orange trees . . . !

VIII

GEORGE Faber left Rome early on a Saturday morning. He headed out through the Lateran Gate and down the new Appian Way toward the southern autostrada. He had a five-hour drive ahead of him, Terracina, Formia, Naples, and then out along the winding peninsular road to Castellammare, Sorrento, Amalfi, and Positano. He was in no hurry. The morning air was still fresh, and the traffic was heavy, and he had no intention of risking his neck as well as his reputation.

At Terracina he was hailed by a pair of English girls who were hitchhiking down the coast. For an hour he was glad of their company, but by the time they reached Naples he was happy to be rid of them. Their cheerful certainty about the world and all its ways made him feel like a grandfather.

The heat of the day was upon him now—a dry, dusty oppression which made the air dance and filled the nostrils with the ammoniac stink of a crowded and ancient city. He turned onto the Via Caracciolo and sat for a while in a water-front café, sipping iced coffee and pondering the moves he should make when he reached Positano. He had two people to see: Sylvio Pellico, artist; and Theo Respighi, sometime actor—both of them, according to the record, unhappy associates of Corrado Calitri.

For weeks now he had been puzzling over the best method to approach them. He had lived long enough in Italy to know the Italian love of drama and intrigue. But his Nordic temper revolted against the spectacle of an American correspondent playing a Latin detective in raincoat and black fedora. Finally he had decided on a simple, blunt approach:

"I understand you knew Corrado Calitri. . . . I'm in love with his wife. I want to marry her. I think you can give me some evidence against him. I'm prepared to pay well for it. . . ."

For a long time he had refused to reason beyond this point. Yet now, three hours from Rome, and a long way further from Chiara, he was prepared to come to grips with the *if.* If all failed, he would have proved himself to himself. He would have proved to Chiara that he was prepared to risk his career for her sake. He would be able to demand a two-way traffic in love. If that failed, too . . . ? At long last he was beginning to believe that he would survive it. The best cure for love was to cool it down a little and leave a man free to measure woman against woman, the torment of a one-sided loving against the bleak peace of no loving at all.

One could not bounce a middle-aged heart, like a rubber ball, from one affair to another; but there was a crumb of comfort in the thought of Ruth Lewin and her refusal to commit his heart or her own to a new affliction without any promise of security.

She was wiser than Chiara. He knew that. She had been tested further and survived better. But *love* was a rainbow word that might or might not point to a crock of gold. He paid for his drink, stepped out into the raw sunshine, and began the last leg of his journey into uncertainty.

The Bay of Naples was a flat and oily mirror, broken only by the wake of the pleasure steamers and the spume of the *aliscafi,* which bounced their loads of tourists at fifty miles an hour toward the siren islands of Capri and Ischia. The summit of Vesuvius was vague in a mist of heat and dust. The painted stucco of the village houses was peeling in the sun. The gray tufa soil of the farm plots was parched, and the peasants plodded up and down the rows of tomato plants like figures in a medieval landscape. There was a smell of dust and dung, and rotting tomatoes and fresh oranges. Horns bleated at every curve, wooden carts rolled noisily over cobblestones. Snatches of music swept by, mixed with the shouts of children and the occasional curse of a farmer caught in the press of summer traffic.

George Faber found himself driving fast and free, and chanting a tuneless song. On the steep spiral of the Amalfi drive he was nearly forced off the road by a careering sports car, and he cursed loud and cheerfully in Roman dialect. By the time he reached Positano, the shabby, spectacular little town that ran in a steep escalade from the water to the hilltop, he was his own man, and the experience was as heady as the raw wine of the Sorrentine mountains.

He lodged his car in a garage, hefted his bag, and strolled down a steep, narrow alley to the city square. Half an hour later, bathed and changed into cotton slacks and a striped sailor shirt, he was sitting under an awning, drinking a Carpano, and preparing for his encounter with Sylvio Pellico.

The artist's gallery was a long, cool tunnel that ran from the street into a courtyard littered with junk and fragments of old marbles. His pictures were hung along the walls of the tunnel—gaudy abstracts, a few portraits in the manner of Modigliani, and a scattering of catch-penny landscapes to inveigle the sentimental tourist. It was easy to see why Corrado Calitri had dropped him so quickly. It was less easy to see why he had taken him up in the first place.

He was a tall, narrow-faced youth with a straggly beard, dressed in cotton sweatshirt, faded blue denims, and shoes of scuffed canvas. He was propped between two chairs at the entrance to the tunnel, dozing in the sun, with a straw hat tipped over his eyes.

When George Faber stopped to examine the pictures, he came to life immediately and presented himself and his work with a flourish. "Sylvio Pellico, sir, at your service. My pictures please you? Some of them have already been exhibited in Rome."

"I know," said George Faber. "I was at the show."

"Ah! Then you're a connoisseur. I will not try to tempt you with this rubbish!" He dismissed the landscapes with a wave of his skinny hand. "Those aren't important. They're just eating money."

"I know, I know. We all have to eat. Are you having a good season?"

"Eh! . . . You know how it goes. Everyone looks, nobody wants to buy. Yesterday I sold two little pieces to an American woman. The day before, nothing. The day before that—" He broke off and cocked a huckster's eye at George Faber. "You are not an Italian, signore?"

"No. I'm an American."

"But you speak beautiful Italian."

"Thank you. . . . Tell me, who sponsored your exhibition in Rome?"

"A very eminent man. A Minister of the Republic. A very good critic, too. Perhaps you've heard of him. His name is Calitri."

"I've heard of him," said George Faber. "I'd like to talk to you about him."

"Why?" He leaned his shaggy head on one side like an amiable parrot. "Did he send you to see me?"

"No. It's a private matter. I thought you might be able to help me. I'd be happy to pay for your help. Does that interest you?"

"Who isn't interested in money? Sit down, let me get you a cup of coffee."

"No coffee. This won't take long."

Pellico dusted off one of the chairs, and they sat facing each other under the narrow archway.

Crisply Faber explained himself and his mission, and then laid down his offer. ". . . Five hundred dollars, American money, for a sworn statement about Calitri's marriage, written in the terms I shall dictate to you."

He sat back in his chair, lit a cigarette, and waited while the artist cupped his brown face in his hands and thought for a long time. Then he lifted his head and said, "I'd appreciate an American cigarette."

Faber handed him the pack, and then leaned forward with a light.

Pellico smoked for a few moments, and then began to talk. "I am a poor man, sir. Also, I am not a very good painter, so I am likely to remain poor for a long time. For one like me five hundred dollars is a fortune, but I am afraid I cannot do what you ask."

"Why not?"

"Several reasons."

"Are you afraid of Calitri?"

"A little. You've lived in this country, you know the way things run. When one is poor, one is always a little outside the law and it never pays to tangle with important people. But that's not the only reason."

"Name me another."

His thin face wrinkled, and his head seemed to shrink lower between his shoulders. He explained himself with an odd simplicity. "I know what this means to you, sir. When a man is in love, eh! . . . It is ice in the heart and fire in the gut. . . . One loses for a while all pride. When one is out of love, the pride comes back. Often it is the only thing left. . . . I am not like you. . . . I am, if you want, more like Calitri. He was kind to me once. . . . I was very fond of him. I do not think I could betray him for money."

"He betrayed you, didn't he? He gave you one exhibition and then dropped you."

"No!" The thin hands became suddenly eloquent. "No. You must not read it like that. On the contrary, he was very honest with me. He said every man has the right to one trial of his talent. If the talent was not there, he had best forget it. . . . Well, he gave me the trial. I failed. I do not blame him for that."

"How much would you charge to blame him? A thousand dollars?"

Pellico stood up and dusted off his hands. For all his shabbiness, he seemed clothed in a curious kind of dignity. He pointed at the gray walls of the tunnel. "For twenty dollars, sir, you can buy my visions. They are not great visions, I know. They are the best I have. Myself I do not sell. Not for a thousand dollars, not for ten thousand. I am sorry."

As he walked away down the cobbled street, George Faber, the Nordic puritan, had the grace to be ashamed of himself. His face was burning, his palms were sweating. He felt a swift, unreasonable resentment toward Chiara, sunning herself in Venice, five hundred miles away. He turned in to a bar, ordered a double whisky, and began to read through the dossier of his next contact, Theo Respighi.

He was an Italo-American, born in Naples and transported to New York in his childhood. He was a middling-bad actor who had played small parts in television, small parts in Hollywood, and then returned to Italy to play small parts in Biblical epics and pseudo-classic nonsense. In Hollywood there had been minor scandals—drunken driving, a couple of divorces, a brief and turbulent romance with a rising star. In Rome he had joined the roistering bunch who kept themselves alive on hope and runaway productions and the patronage of Roman playboys. All in all, Faber summed him up as a seedy character who should be very amenable to the rustle of a dollar bill.

He ran Respighi to earth that same evening in a cliffside bar, where he was drinking with three very gay boys and a faded Frenchwoman who spoke Italian with a Genoese accent. It took an hour to prise him away from the company, and another to sober him up with dinner and black coffee. Even when he had done it, he was left with a hollow, muscular hulk who, when he was not combing his long blond hair, was reaching nervously for the brandy bottle. Faber stifled the wavering voice of his own conscience and once again displayed his proposition:

". . . A thousand dollars for a signed statement. No strings, no problems. Everything that goes before the Roman Rota is kept secret. No one, least of all Calitri, will ever know who gave the testimony."

"Balls!" said the blond one flatly. "Don't try to con me, Faber. There's no such thing as a secret in Rome. I don't care whether it's in the Church or Cinecittà. Sooner or later Calitri has to know. What happens to me then?"

"You're a thousand dollars richer, and he can't touch you."

"You think so? Look, lover boy, you know how films are made in this country. The money comes from everywhere. The list of angels stretches from Napoli to Milano, and back again. There's a black list here, too, just like in Hollywood.

You get on it, you're dead. For a thousand crummy bucks, I don't want to be dead."

"You haven't earned that much in six months," Faber told him. "I know, I checked up."

"So what? That's the way the cookie crumbles in this business. You starve for a while, and then you eat, and eat good. I want to go on eating. Now if you were to make it ten thousand, I might begin to think about it. With that much I could get myself back Stateside and wait long enough to get a decent start again. . . . Come on, lover! What are you playing for? The big romance or a bag of popcorn?"

"Two thousand," said George Faber.

"No deal."

"It's the best I can do."

"Peanuts! I can get that much by lifting a phone and telling Calitri that you're gunning for him. . . . Tell you what. Give me a thousand, and I won't make the call."

"Go to hell." He pushed back his chair and walked out. The laughter of the blond one followed him like a mockery into the darkened street.

"The longer I live," said Jean Télémond musingly, "the more clearly I understand the deep vein of pessimism that runs through so much of modern thought, even the thought of many in the Church. . . . Birth, growth, and decay. The cyclic pattern of life is so vividly apparent that it obscures the pattern that underlies it, the pattern of constant growth, and—let me say it bluntly—the pattern of human progress. For many people the wheel of life simply turns on its own axis; it does not seem to be going anywhere."

"And you, Jean, believe it is going somewhere?"

"More than that, Holiness. I believe it must go somewhere."

They had taken off their cassocks, and they were sitting, relaxed, in the shade of a small copse, with a bank of wild strawberries at their backs, and in front the flat, bright water of Lake Nemi. Jean Télémond was sucking contentedly on his pipe, and Kiril was tossing pebbles into the water. The air vibrated with the strident cry of cicadas, and little brown lizards sunned themselves on rock and tree trunk.

They had long since surrendered themselves to bucolic ease and the comfort of each other's company. In the mornings they worked privately—Kiril at his desk, keeping track of the daily dispatches from Rome; Télémond in the garden, setting his papers in order for the scrutiny of the Holy Office. In the afternoons they drove out into the country, Télémond at the wheel, exploring the valleys and the uplands and the tiny towns that had clung to the ridges for five hundred years and more. In the evenings they dined together, then read or talked or played cards until it was time for Compline and the last prayer of the day.

It was a good time for both: for Kiril, a respite from the burden of office; for Télémond, a true return from exile into the companionship of an understanding and truly loving spirit. He did not have to measure his words. He felt no risk in exposing his deepest thoughts. Kiril, for his part, confided himself fully to the Jesuit, and found a peculiar solace in this sharing of his private burden.

He tossed another pebble into the water and watched the ripples fan out toward the farther shore until they were lost in the shimmer of sunlight. Then he asked another question:

"Have you never been a pessimist yourself, Jean? Have you never felt caught up in this endless turning of the wheel of life?"

"Sometimes, Holiness. When I was in China, for instance, far to the northwest, in the barren valley of the great rivers. There were monasteries up there. Enormous places that could have been built only by great men—men with a great vision—to challenge the emptiness in which they lived. . . . In one fashion or another, I thought, God must have been with them. Yet when I went in and saw the men who live there now—dull, uninspired, almost doltish at times —I was afflicted by melancholy. . . . When I came back to the West and read the newspapers and talked with my brother scientists, I was staggered by the blindness with which we seem to be courting our own destruction. Sometimes it seemed impossible to believe that man was really growing out of the slime toward a divine destiny. . . ."

Kiril nodded thoughtfully. He picked up a stick and teased a sleeping lizard, so that it skitted away into the leaves. "I know the feeling, Jean. I have it sometimes even in the Church. I wait and pray for the great movement, the great man, who will startle us into life again. . . ."

Jean Télémond said nothing. He drew placidly on his pipe, waiting for the Pontiff to finish the thought.

". . . A man like St. Francis of Assisi, for instance. What does he really mean? . . . A complete break with the pattern of history. . . . A man born out of due time. A sudden, unexplained revival of the primitive spirit of Christianity. The work he began still continues. . . . But it is not the same. The revolution is over. The revolutionaries have become conformists. The little brothers of the Little Poor Man are rattling alms boxes in the railway square or dealing in real estate to the profit of the order." He laughed quietly. "Of course, that isn't the whole story. They teach, they preach, they do the work of God as best they know, but it is no longer a revolution, and I think we need one now."

"Perhaps," said Jean Télémond with a twinkle in his shrewd eyes, "perhaps your Holiness will be the revolutionary."

"I have thought about it, Jean. Believe me, I have thought about it. But I do not think even you can understand how limited I am by the very machinery which I inherit, by the historic attitudes by which I am enclosed. It is hard for me to work directly. I have to find instruments apt to my hand. I am young enough, yes, to see big changes made in my lifetime. But there will have to be others to make them for me. . . . You, for instance."

"I, Holiness?" Télémond turned a startled face to the Pontiff. "My field of action is more limited than yours."

"I wonder if it is?" asked Kiril quizzically. "Have you ever thought that the Russian Revolution, the present might of Soviet Russia, was built on the work of Karl Marx, who spent a large part of his life in the British Museum and is now buried in England? The most explosive thing in the world is an idea."

Jean Télémond laughed and tapped out his pipe on a tree bole. "Doesn't that rather depend on the Holy Office? I have still to pass their scrutiny."

Kiril gave him a long, sober look, then quizzed him again. "If you fail to pass, Jean, what will you do then?"

Télémond shrugged. "Re-examine, I suppose. I hope I shall have the energy to do it."

"Why do you say that?"

"Partly because I am afraid, partly because . . . because I am not a well man. I have lived roughly for a long time. I am told my heart is not as good as it should be."

"I'm sorry to hear that, Jean. You must take care of yourself. I shall make it my business to see that you do."

"May I ask you a question, Holiness?"

"Of course."

"You have honored me with your friendship. In the eyes of many—though not in mine—it will seem that you have given your patronage to my work. What will you do if it is found wanting by the Holy Office?"

To his surprise, Kiril threw back his head and laughed heartily. "Jean, Jean. There speaks the true Jesuit. What will I do? I shall always be your friend, and I shall pray that you have health and courage to continue your studies."

"But if I should die before they are done?"

"Does that worry you?"

"Sometimes. . . . Believe me, Holiness, whatever the outcome, I have tried to prepare myself for it. But I am convinced that there is a truth in my researches. . . . I do not want to see it lost or suppressed."

"It will not be suppressed, Jean. I promise you that."

"Forgive me, Holiness. I have said more than I should."

"Why should you apologize, Jean? You have shown me your heart. For a lonely man like me that's a privilege. . . . Courage now. Who knows? We may see you a Doctor of the Church yet. Now if it will not offend your Jesuit's eyes, the Pope of Rome is going for a swim."

When Kiril stripped off his shirt and made ready for the plunge, Jean Télémond saw the marks of the whip on his back, and he was ashamed of his own cowardice.

Two days later a courier from Washington delivered to the Pontiff a private letter from the President of the United States:

> . . . I read with lively interest your Holiness' letter and the copies of the two letters from the Premier of the U.S.S.R. which were handed to me by His Eminence Cardinal Carlin. I agree that we shall need to preserve the most rigid secrecy about this whole situation.
>
> Let me say first that I am deeply grateful for the information which you give me about your private association with Kamenev, and your views on his character and his intention. I was also deeply impressed by the frank disagreement of Cardinal Carlin. I know that he would not have spoken so freely without the permission of your Holiness, and I am encouraged to be equally frank with you.
>
> I have to say that I am very dubious about the value of private conversations at this level. On the other hand, I am happy to pursue them so long

as there seems the slightest hope of avoiding the explosive crisis which now seems inevitable in the next six or twelve months.

The problem as I see it is both simple and complex. Kamenev has expressed it very well. We are caught in the current of history. We can tack across it, but we cannot change the direction of the flow. The only thing that can do that is an action of such magnitude and such risk that none of us would be allowed to attempt it.

I could not, for example, commit my country to one-sided disarmament. I could not abandon our claims for a re-unification of Germany. I should very much like to be quit of Quemoy and Matsu, but we cannot relinquish them without a serious loss of face and influence in Southeast Asia. I can understand that Kamenev is afraid of the Chinese, yet he cannot abandon an alliance—even a troublesome and dangerous one—which guarantees a solid Communist bloc from East Germany to the Kuriles.

The most we can hope for is to keep the situation elastic, to give ourselves a breathing space for negotiation and historic evolution. We must avoid at all costs a head-on clash, which will inevitably cause a cataclysmic atomic war.

If a secret correspondence with Kamenev will help at all, I am prepared to risk it, and I am very happy to accept your Holiness as the intermediary. You may communicate my thoughts to Kamenev and make known to him the contents of this letter. He knows that I cannot move alone, just as he cannot. We both live under the shadow of the same risk.

I do not belong to your Holiness' faith, but I commend myself to your prayers and the prayers of all Christendom. We carry the fate of the world on our shoulders, and if God does not support us, then we must inevitably break under the burden. . . .

When he had read the letter, Kiril breathed a sigh of relief. It was no more than he had hoped for, but no less, either. The storm clouds were still piled, massive and threatening, over the world, but there was a tiny break in them and one could begin to guess at the sunlight. The problem was now to enlarge the break, and he asked himself how best he might co-operate in doing it.

Of one thing he was certain: it would be a mistake for the Vatican to assume the attitude of a negotiator, to propose grounds for a bargain. The Church, too, carried the burden of history on her back. Politically she was suspect; but the very suspicion was a pointer to her task—to affirm not the method, but the principles of a human society capable of survival, capable of ordering itself to the terms of a God-given plan. She was appointed to be a teacher, not a treaty maker. Her task was not to govern men in the material order, but to train them to govern themselves in accordance with the principles of the natural law. She had to accept the fact that the end product—if, indeed, one could talk without cynicism about an end—must always be an approximation, a stage in an evolutionary growth.

It was this thought that led him once more into the garden of Castel Gondolfo, where Jean Télémond, studious and absorbed, was annotating his papers under the shade of an old oak tree.

"Here you sit, my Jean, writing your visions of a world perfecting itself, while

I sit like a telephone operator between two men, each of whom can blast us into smithereens by pressing a button. . . . There's a dilemma for you. Does your science tell you how to resolve it? What would you do if you were in my shoes?"

"Pray," said Jean Télémond with a puckish grin.

"I do, Jean. Every day—all day, for that matter. But prayer isn't enough; I have to act, too. You had to be an explorer before you came to rest in this place. Tell me now, where do I move?"

"In this situation I don't think you move at all. You sit and wait for the appropriate moment."

"You think that's enough?"

"In the larger sense, no. I think the Church has lost the initiative it should have in the world today."

"I do, too. I should like to think that in my Pontificate we may be able to get some of it back. I'm not sure how. Do you have any ideas?"

"Some," said Jean Télémond crisply. "All my life I've been a traveler. One of the first things a traveler has to do is learn to accommodate himself to the place and time in which he lives. He has to eat strange food, use an unfamiliar coinage, learn not to blush among people who have no privies, search for the good that subsists in the grossest and most primitive societies. Every individual, every organization, has to sustain a conversation with the rest of the world. He cannot talk always in negatives and contradictions."

"You think we have done that?"

"Not always, Holiness. But of late, all too often. We have lived to ourselves and for ourselves. When I say *we*, I mean the whole Church—pastors and faithful alike. We have hidden the lamp of belief under a cover instead of holding it up to illuminate the world."

"Go on, Jean. Show me how you would display it."

"This is a plural world, Holiness. We may wish it to be one in faith, hope, and charity. But it is not so. There are many hopes and strange varieties of love. But this is the world we live in. If we want to participate in the drama of God's action with it, then we must begin with the words we all understand. Justice, for instance. We understand that. . . . But when the Negroes in America seek justice and full citizenship, is it we who lead them? Or we who support most strongly their legitimate demands? You know it is not. In Australia there is an embargo on colored migrants. Many Australians feel that this is an affront to human dignity. Do we support their protests? The record shows that we do not. In principle, yes; but in action, no. We proclaim that the Chinese coolie has a right to work and subsistence, but it was not we who led him toward it. It was the men who made the Long March. If we object to the price they put on the rice bowl, we must blame ourselves as much as we blame them. . . . If we want to enter once more into the human dialogue, then we must seek out whatever common ground is available to us—as I take it your Holiness is trying to do with Kamenev—the ground of human brotherhood and the legitimate hopes of all mankind. . . . I have thought often about the Gospel scene when Christ held up the coin of the tribute and proclaimed, 'Render to Caesar the things that are Caesar's, and to God the things that are God's.' To what Caesar? Has your Holiness ever thought about it? . . . To a murderer, an adulterer, a paederast. . . . But Christ did not abrogate the conversation of the Church with such a one. On the contrary, he affirmed it as a duty. . . ."

"But what you show me, Jean, is not one man's commitment. It is the commitment of the whole Church—Pope, pastors, and five hundred million faithful."

"True, Holiness—but what has happened? The faithful are uncommitted only because they lack enlightenment and courageous leadership. They understand risk better than we do. We are protected by the organization. They have only God's cloak to shelter them. They grapple each day with every human dilemma—birth, passion, death, and the act of love. . . . But if they hear no trumpets, see no crusader's cross lifted up—" He shrugged and broke off. "Excuse me, Holiness. I am too garrulous, I think."

"On the contrary, Jean. I find you a very serviceable man. I am glad to have you here."

At that moment a servant approached, bringing coffee and iced water, and a letter which had been received that moment at the gate. Kiril opened it and read the brief, unceremonious message:

"I am a man who grows sunflowers. I should like to call upon you at ten-thirty tomorrow morning."

It was signed: "Georg Wilhelm Forster."

He proved a surprise in more ways than one. He looked like a Bavarian incongruously dressed by an Italian tailor. He wore thick German shoes and thick spectacles, but his suit and shirt and his tie came from Brioni, and on his small, pudgy hand he wore a bezel ring, half as large as a walnut. His manner was deferent, but vaguely ironic, as though he were laughing at himself and all he stood for. In spite of his German name he spoke Russian with a strong Georgian accent.

When Kiril received him in his study, he went down on one knee and kissed the papal ring; then he sat bolt upright in the chair, balancing his Panama hat on his knees, for all the world like a junior clerk being interviewed for a job. His opening words were a surprise, too. "I understand your Holiness has received a letter from Robert."

Kiril looked up sharply, to catch a hint of a smile on the pudgy lips.

"There is no mystery about it, Holiness. It is all a matter of timing. Timing is very important in my work. I knew when Kamenev's letter would reach the Vatican. I knew when Cardinal Carlin returned to New York. I was told the date and time of his interview with Robert. From that point it was a simple deduction that Robert's letter would reach you at Castel Gondolfo."

Now it was Kiril's turn to smile. He nodded approval and asked, "Do you live in Rome?"

"I have lodgings here. But as you can guess, I travel a good deal. . . . There is an extensive business in sunflower seeds."

"I imagine there is."

"May I see Robert's letter?"

"Of course."

Kiril handed the paper across his desk. Forster read it carefully for a few moments, and then passed it back.

"You may have a copy if you like," Kiril said. "As you see, the President is perfectly willing that Kamenev should see the letter."

"No copy will be necessary. I have a photographic memory. It's worth a lot of money to me. I shall see Kamenev within a week. He will have an accurate transcript of the letter and of my conversation with you."

"Are you empowered to talk for Kamenev?"

"Up to a certain point, yes."

To Kiril's amazement, he quoted verbatim the passage from Kamenev's second letter:

" 'From time to time . . . you will receive application for a private audience from a man named Georg Wilhelm Forster. To him you may speak freely, but commit nothing to writing. If you succeed in a conversation with the President of the United States, you should refer to him as Robert. Foolish, is it not, that to discuss the survival of the human race we must resort to such childish tricks.' "

Kiril laughed. "That's an impressive performance. But tell me, if you know of whom we are speaking why do I have to refer to the President as Robert?"

Georg Wilhelm Forster was delighted to explain himself. "You might call it a mnemonic trick. No man can guard altogether against talking in his sleep, or against verbal slips when he is under questioning. . . . So one practices this kind of dodge. It works, too. I've never been caught out yet."

"I hope you won't be caught out this time."

"I hope so, too, Holiness. This exchange of letters may have long consequences."

"I should like to be able to guess what they may be."

"Robert has already pointed to them in his letter." He quoted again. " 'An action of such magnitude and such risk that none of us would be allowed to attempt it.' "

"The proposition contradicts itself," said Kiril mildly. "Both Kamenev and the President—excuse me, Robert—point to the need for such action, but each in the same breath says that he is not the man to begin it."

"Perhaps they are looking to a third man, Holiness?"

"Who?"

"Yourself."

"If I could promise that, my friend, believe me, I should be the happiest man in the world. But as our countryman Stalin once remarked, 'How many divisions has the Pope?' "

"It is not a question of divisions, Holiness, and you know it. It is at bottom a question of influence and moral authority. Kamenev believes that you have, or may come to have, such an authority. . . ." He smiled and added an afterthought of his own. "From the little I have learned, I should say that your Holiness has a greater stature in the world than you may realize."

Kiril considered the thought for a few moments, and then delivered himself of a firm pronouncement. "Understand something, my friend. Report it clearly to Kamenev, as I have already reported it directly on the other side of the Atlantic. I know how small are our hopes of peace. I am prepared to do anything that is morally right and humanly possible to preserve it, but I will not allow myself or the Church to be used as a tool to advantage one side or the other. Do you understand that?"

"Perfectly. I have only been waiting for your Holiness to say it. Now may I ask a question?"

"Please do."

"If it were possible, and if it seemed desirable, would your Holiness be prepared to go to another place than Rome? Would you be prepared to use another channel of communication than the Vatican radio and the Vatican press, and the pulpits of Catholic churches?"

"What place?"

"It is not mine to suggest it. I put the proposition as a generality."

"Then I will answer it as a generality. If I can speak freely, and be reported honestly, I will go anywhere and do anything to help the world breathe freely, for however short a time."

"I shall report that, Holiness. I shall report it very happily. Now there is a practical matter. I understand the Maestro di Camera has a list of those who may be admitted readily to private audience with your Holiness. I should like my name added to the list."

"It is already there. You will be welcome at whatever time . . . Now I, too, have a message for Kamenev. You will tell him first that I am not bargaining, I am not pleading, I am not making any conditions at all for the free passage of talk through me. I am a realist. I know how much he is limited by what he believes and by the system to which he is subject, as I am subject to mine. Having said this, tell him from me that my people suffer in Hungary and Poland and East Germany and in the Baltic. Whatever he can do to ease their burden—be it ever so small—I shall count as done to myself, and I shall remember it with gratitude and in my prayers."

"I shall tell him," said Georg Wilhelm Forster. "Now may I have your Holiness' leave to go?"

"Go with God," said Kiril the Pontiff.

He walked with the strange little man to the gate of the garden and watched him drive away into the bright and hostile world beyond.

The Princess Maria-Rina was a doughty old general, and she had planned her nephew's campaign with more than usual care. First she had set him to rights with the Church, without which he could neither arrive at power nor begin to rule comfortably. Then she had isolated Chiara for a whole month from her American lover. She had set her down in a gay playground, surrounded by young men, one at least of whom might be ardent enough to seduce her into a new attachment. Now she was ready for her next move.

Accompanied by Perosi, and with Calitri's letter tucked into her handbag, she drove to Venice, plucked Chiara off the beach, and hurried her off to lunch to a quiet restaurant on Murano. Then she added her own brusque commentary to Calitri's letter:

". . . You see, child, all of a sudden it is very simple. Corrado has come to his senses. He has set his conscience in order, and in a couple of months you will be free."

Chiara was still shocked and delighted by the news. She was prepared to trust the whole world. "I don't understand it. Why? What made him do it?"

The old Princess dismissed the question with a wave of her hand. "He's growing up. For a long time he was hurt and bitter. Now he has better thoughts. . . . For the rest, you need not concern yourself."

"But what if he changes his mind?"

"He won't, I promise you. Already his new depositions are in the hands of Perosi, here. The final papers will be ready for presentation to the Rota immediately after the holidays. After that it's just a formality. . . . As you will see from his letter, Corrado is disposed to be generous. He wants to pay you quite a large sum by way of settlement. On the understanding, of course, that you will make no further claims on him."

"I don't want to make any claims. All I want is to be free."

"I know, I know. And you're a sensible girl. There are, however, a couple of other matters. Perosi, here, will explain."

It was all so neatly done that she was totally disarmed. She simply sat there, looking from one to the other, while Perosi explained himself with smooth formality:

"You understand, signora, that your husband is a public figure. I think you will agree that it would be most unfair, after this generous gesture, to expose him to comment and notoriety."

"Of course. I wouldn't want that, either."

"Good. Then we understand each other. Once the affair is over, then we should let it die quietly. No publicity. No word to the newspapers, no hasty action on your part."

"What sort of action? I don't understand."

"He means marriage, child," said the Princess Maria-Rina gently. "It would be most undesirable for you and for Corrado if you were to rush into a hasty union as soon as the decree of nullity is granted."

"Yes, I see that."

"Which brings us to the next question," said Perosi with elaborate care. "Your present association with an American correspondent. His name, I believe, is George Faber."

Chiara flushed, and was suddenly angry. "That's my business. It doesn't concern anyone else."

"On the contrary, my dear young lady. I hope to persuade you that it is the business of everyone. The settlement, for example, would not be payable if you were to marry Faber—or, indeed, if you were to marry anyone within six months."

"Then I don't want the settlement."

"I shouldn't be too hasty about that, child. It's a lot of money. Besides . . ." She reached out a skinny claw and imprisoned Chiara's hand. "Besides, you don't want to make another mistake. You've been hurt enough already. I should hate to see you wounded again. Take time, child. Enjoy yourself. You're still young. The world's full of attractive men. Kick up your heels awhile. Don't tie yourself down before you've had three looks at what's offering in the marriage market. There's another thing, too. . . . Even if you did want to marry Faber, there might well be certain difficulties."

"What sort of difficulties?"

She was frightened now, and they read the fear in her eyes. Perosi pressed the advantage shrewdly. "You are both Catholics, so naturally, I presume you will want to be married in the Church."

"Of course, but—"

"In that case you both come immediately into conflict with canon law. You have, if I may put it bluntly, been living in sin. It is a delicate question whether in the terms of canon law this would constitute 'public and notorious concubinage.' My own view is that it might. In this case a principle applies: that a guilty person shall not be permitted to enjoy the fruits of guilt. In canon law this is called *crimen,* and it is an invalidating impediment to marriage. It would be necessary to approach the Church for a dispensation. I have to tell you that there is no certainty that it would be granted."

The old Princess added a final rejoinder. "You don't want this kind of complication, do you? You deserve better. One mess is enough for any lifetime. . . . You do see that, don't you?"

She saw it very clearly. She saw that they had her trapped and beleaguered and that they would not let her go without a struggle. She saw something else, too. Something that shamed and excited her at once. She wanted it this way. She wanted to be rid of an attachment which had already grown stale for her. She wanted to be free to hold hands and play love games with young Pietro Antonelli while the moon shone and the mandolins played soft music in a gondola on the Grand Canal.

The day after his encounter with Theo Respighi George Faber drove back to Naples. His self-esteem had been badly damaged—by a man with too much honor and by another with too little. He felt shaken and sordid. He could hardly bear the sight of himself in a shaving mirror. The image of the great correspondent was still there, but behind it was an empty man who lacked the courage even to sin boldly.

He was desperate for reassurance and the forgetfulness of loving. He tried to telephone Chiara in Venice, but each time she was out, and when she did not return his call he was filled with sour anger. His imagination ran riot as he pictured her carefree and flirtatious while he, for her sake, was making this drab and uncomfortable journey to the hollow center of himself.

He had one more person to see—Alicia de Nogara, authoress of Ischia. But he had to restore himself before he could confront her. He spent a day in Naples, hunting for copies of her books, and finally came up with a slim, expensive volume, *The Secret Island.* He sat in the gardens, trying to read it, and then gave up, discouraged by its florid prose and its coy hints of perverted love among the maidens. In the end he skimmed through it to get enough information for a conversation piece and then gave it to a ragged urchin who would pawn it for the price of a biscuit.

He went back to the hotel and put in a call to Ruth Lewin. Her maid told him she was on vacation and was not expected back for several days. He gave up in disgust, and then, in sullen reaction, he determined to divert himself. If Chiara could play, so could he. He set off for a three-day bachelor jaunt to Capri. He swam in the daytime, flirted sporadically in the evening, drank twice as much as he needed, and ended with an abortive night in bed with a German widow. More disgusted with himself than ever, he packed his bag the next morning and set out for Ischia.

The villa of Alicia de Nogara was a rambling pseudo-Moorish structure set on the eastern slope of Epomeo, with a spectacular view of terraced vineyards and blue water. The door was opened to him by a pale, flat-chested girl, dressed in a gypsy shirt and silk slacks. She led him into the garden, where the great authoress was at work in a vine arbor. The first sight of her was a shock. She was dressed like a sibyl, in filmy and flowing draperies, but her face was that of a faded girl and her blue eyes were bright with humor. She was writing with a quill pen on thick, expensive paper. When he approached, she stood up and held out a slim, cool hand to be kissed.

It was all so stylized, so theatrical in character, that he almost laughed aloud. But when he looked again into her bright, intelligent eyes, he thought better of it. He introduced himself formally, sat down in the chair she offered him, and tried to marshal his thoughts. The pale girl hovered protectively beside her patron.

Faber said awkwardly, "I've come to see you about a rather delicate matter."

Alicia de Nogara waved an imperious dismissal. "Go away, Paula. You can bring us some coffee in half an hour."

The pale one wandered away disconsolately, and the sibyl began to question her visitor:

"You're rather upset, aren't you? I can feel it. I am very sensitive to emanations. Calm yourself first. Look at the land and the sea. Look at me if you want to. I am very calm because I have learned to float with the air as it moves. This is how one should live, this is how one should love, too. Floating on the air, whichever way it blows. You have been in love, haven't you . . . ? Many times, I should say. Not always happily."

"I'm in love now," said George Faber. "That's why I've come to see you."

"Now there's a strange thing! Only yesterday I was saying to Paula that although my books are not widely read they still reach the understanding heart. I think you have an understanding heart. Haven't you?"

"I hope so. Yes. I understand you know a man called Corrado Calitri."

"Corrado? Oh yes, I know him very well. A brilliant boy. A little perverted, I'm afraid, but very brilliant. People say I'm perverted, too. You've read my books, I presume. Do you think so?"

"I'm sure you're not," said George Faber.

"There, you see. You do have an understanding heart. Perversion is something different. Perversion is the urge to destroy the thing one loves. I want to preserve, to nurture. That's why Corrado is doomed. He can never be happy. I told him that many times. . . . Before he was married, after his marriage broke up."

"That's what I wanted to talk to you about. Calitri's marriage."

"Of course. I knew it. That's what the emanations were telling me. You're in love with his wife."

"How did you know?"

"I'm a woman. Not an ordinary woman. Oh no! A sapphic woman, they call me, but I prefer to say a full woman, a guardian of the deep mysteries of our sex. . . . So you're in love with Corrado's wife."

"I want to marry her."

The sibyl leaned forward, cupping her small face in her hands and fixing him with her bright blue eyes. "Marriage. That's usually a terrible mistake. The air, remember! One must be free—to float, to rise, to fall, to be held or to be let go. Strange that men never understand these things. I was married once, a long time ago. It was a great mistake. Sometimes I think men were born defective. They lack intuition. They were born to be slaves of their own appetite!"

"I'm afraid we were," said George Faber with a grin. "May I tell you what I want?"

"Please, please do."

"I want evidence for the Holy Roman Rota. For Chiara to be free, we have to prove that Corrado Calitri entered into marriage with a defective intention. We have to prove that he expressed this defective intention to a third person before the marriage took place." He fished in his pocket and drew out a typewritten statement which he had prepared that morning. "That, more or less, is the thing we want. Would you be prepared to sign it?"

Alicia de Nogara picked up the paper with fastidious fingers, read it, and laid it down on the table. "How crude! How terribly crude of the Church to demand this sort of indignity. Freedom again, you see! If people fail in love, let them be free to begin again. The Church tries to close up the soul in a bottle as if it were a foetus preserved in formaldehyde. . . . So very vulgar and medieval. . . . Tell me, does Corrado know that you've come to me?"

"No, he doesn't. For a reason I can't understand, he wants to hold on to Chiara. . . . Not to live with her, of course, but to hold her like a piece of land or an apartment."

"I know, I know. I told you he was perverse, didn't I? This is how it shows. He likes to torment people. He tried to torment me even though I wanted nothing from him. All I wanted to do was teach him how to give and return love. I thought I had succeeded, too. He seemed very happy with me. Then he went away, back to his boys, back to his little game of promises and refusals. I wonder if he's as happy now as he was with me."

"I doubt it."

"Do you want to hurt him?"

"No. I just want Chiara to be free and to have the chance of making her happy."

"But if I sign this, it will hurt him, won't it?"

"It will hurt his pride, probably."

"Good! That's where he needs to be hurt. When one loves, one must be humble. When you commit yourself to the air, you have to be humble. Are you humble, Faber?"

"I guess I have to be," said Faber ruefully. "I haven't very much pride left. Are you prepared to sign that document? I shouldn't say this, but I was prepared to pay for the evidence."

"Pay?" She was dramatically insulted. "My dear man, you are desperate, aren't you? In love one must never pay. One must give, give, give! Freely, and from the full heart. Tell me something. Do you think you could love me?"

He had to swallow hard to get the thought down, but he did it. He twisted his mouth into what he hoped was a smile and answered elaborately, "It would be my good fortune if I could. I'm afraid I shouldn't deserve it."

She reached out and patted his cheek with a cool, dry hand. "There, there, I'm not going to seduce you, though I think you would seduce very easily. I'm not sure I should let you throw away your life in marriage, but you have to learn in your own way, I suppose. . . . Very well, I'll sign it."

She picked up the quill and subscribed the document with a flourish. "There, now. Is that all?"

"I think we should have a witness."

"Paula!"

The pale girl came hurrying to her cry. She set her signature at the foot of the paper, and George Faber folded it and put it into his pocket. The thing was done. He had soiled himself to do it, but it was done. He let them lead him through the rituals of coffee and endless, endless talk. He exerted himself to be gentle with them. He laughed at their pathetic jokes and bent like a courtier over the hand of the sibyl to say good-by.

As the taxi drove him down to the crowded port, as he leaned against the rail of the lake steamer that took him back to Naples, he felt the document crackling and burning against his breast. *Finita la commèdia!* The shabby farce was over, and he could begin to be a man again.

When he got back to Rome, he found Chiara's letter telling him that her husband had agreed to co-operate in her petition and that she had fallen in love with another man. *Finita la commèdia!* He tore the paper into a hundred shreds, and then proceeded, savagely and systematically, to get himself drunk.

Extract from
the Secret Memorials of
KIRIL I, Pont. Max.

I have had a wonderful holiday, the first in more than twenty years. I feel rested and renewed. I am comforted by a friendship which grows in depth and warmth each day. I never had a brother, and my only sister died in childhood. So my brotherhood with Jean Télémond has become very precious to me. Our lives are full of contrasts. I sit at the summit of the Church; he lies under the rigid obedience of his order. I spent seventeen years in prison; he has had twenty years of wandering in the far corners of the earth. Yet we understand each other perfectly. We communicate swiftly and intuitively. We are both caught up in this shining hope of unity and common growth toward God, the Beginning, the Center, and the End. . . .

We have talked much these last few days of the grains of truth that underlie even the most divergent errors. For Islam, God is one, and this is already a leap from paganism to the idea of a single spiritual Creator. It is the beginning of a God-centered universe. Buddhism has degenerated into a series of sterile formulae, but the Buddhist code, although it makes few moral demands, conduces to co-operation, to non-violence, and to a polite converse among many people. Communism has abrogated a personal God, but there is implicit in its thesis an idea of the brotherhood of man. . . .

My immediate predecessor encouraged the growth of the Ecumenical spirit in Christendom—the exploration and the confirmation of common grounds of belief and action. Jean Télémond and I have talked much about the possibility of the Christian idea beginning to infuse the great non-Christian religions. Can we, for example, make any penetration of Islam, which is spreading so quickly through the new nations of Africa and through Indonesia. A dream, perhaps, but perhaps, also, an opportunity for another bold experiment like that of the White Fathers.

The grand gesture! The action that changes the course of history! I wonder if I shall ever have the opportunity to make it. . . . The gesture of a Gregory the Great, or a Pius V. Who knows? It is a question of historic circumstance and the readiness of a man to co-operate with God and in the moment. . . .

Ever since the visit of Georg Wilhelm Forster, I have been trying to think myself into the minds of Kamenev and the President of the United States. It is true, I think, that all men who arrive at authority have certain attitudes in common. They are not always the right attitudes, but at least they provide a ground of understanding. The man in power begins to see more largely. If he has not been corrupted, his private passions tend to diminish with age and responsibility. He looks, if not for permanence, at least for a peaceful development of the system he has helped to create. On the one hand, he is vulnerable to the temptations of pride. On the other, he cannot fail to be humbled by the magnitude and complexity of the human problem. . . . He understands the meaning of contingency and mutual dependence. . . .

It is well, I think, that the Papacy has been slowly stripped of its temporal power. It gives the Church the opportunity to speak more freely, and with less suspicion of material interest, than in other ages. I must continue to build this moral authority, which has its analogies in the political influence of small nations like Sweden and Switzerland, and even Israel.

I have given instructions to the Secretariat of State to encourage the visit of representatives of all nations and all faiths to the Vatican. At the lowest they constitute a useful diplomatic courtesy; at their best they may be the beginning of a fruitful friendship and understanding. . . .

This week I had Cardinal Rinaldi to lunch. I like this man. I talked with him about the possible reform of the Roman Rota, and he gave me valuable information about its methods and its personalities. In his quiet fashion he administered a reproof as well. He told me that Cardinal Leone felt that I did not repose enough trust in him. He pointed out that for all his vigor, he was an old man who had deserved well of the Church, and that I should perhaps bestow on him a mark of favor and acknowledgment. I find it hard to like Leone; he is so very much a Roman. But I agree with Rinaldi. I have written a gentle letter to Leone, thanking him for his work and asking him to wait on me as soon as I return to Rome. I have also asked for his private advice on the appointment of a new Cardinal to take the place of the Englishman, Brandon, who died two days ago. Brandon was one of those who voted against me in the conclave, and our relations were always rather formal and distant. Yet he was an apostolic man, and one always regrets deeply the passing of a laborer from the vineyard. I said a special Mass yesterday morning for the repose of his soul. . . .

News from Hungary and Poland is bad. The new taxation laws have already put several more schools and seminaries out of existence. Potocki is ill in Warsaw. My information is that he will recover. But the illness is serious, and we shall have to think of appointing a new man to help him and later to take over his office as Primate of Poland. Potocki is a man of political genius and deep spiritual life. We shall not easily find another to match him. . . .

Jean Télémond's first volume, *The Progress of Man,* is now ready for publication. This is the crucial part of his work, upon which all the rest depends. He is anxious to have it assessed by the Holy Office as soon as possible. For his sake I am anxious, too. I have asked Cardinal Leone to appoint commissioners to scrutinize it and report to me as quickly as may be. I have suggested that these commissioners be different men from those who made the first examination. We shall then have two sets of opinions and there will be no question of a carry-over from earlier, and far less complete, works. I am glad to say that Jean is very calm about it. He seems to be well, although I notice that he tires easily and is sometimes out of breath after a small exertion. I have ordered him to submit to an examination by the Vatican physician as soon as we go back to Rome. . . .

I want to keep him by me, but he is afraid of doing me a disservice. The hierarchy and the Curia are suspicious and uncomfortable about a Gray Eminence in the Vatican. Cardinal Rinaldi repeated his invitation to have Jean work at his villa. Jean likes the idea, so I suppose I shall have to let him go. At least we shall not be far from each other, and I shall have the pleasure of his company at dinner on Sundays. Now that I have found him, I am loath to let him go. . . .

I learned so much with him during our journeys through the Italian countryside. The thing that impressed me most vividly was the contrast between entrenched wealth and the grinding poverty in which so many of the people still live. This is the reason for the strength and attraction of communism in Italy. It will take a long time—longer than I have at my disposal—to redress the balance. However, I have thought of a gesture which may become a symbol of what is needed.

The Congregation of Rites has informed me that they are ready to proceed to the beatification of two new servants of God. Beatification is a long and expensive process, and the ceremonies which conclude it are also very expensive. I am informed that the total cost may well be as much as fifty thousand American dollars. It could be that I shall be accused of diminishing the splendor of the liturgical life of the Church, but I have decided to reduce the ceremony to a simple formality and to devote whatever funds are available to the establishment of local works of charity. I shall take steps to see that my reasons are published as widely as possible so that people will understand that the service of the servants of God is much more important than their glorification.

Oddly enough, I am reminded at this moment of the woman Ruth Lewin and the work which she and others like her are doing, without encouragement and without apparent spiritual help in various places in the world. I am reminded, too, of the saying of the Master that even a cup of water given in His name is a gift made to Him. A thousand candles in St. Peter's mean nothing beside a poor man grateful to God because he is grateful to one of his fellows. . . .

Wherever I turn, I find myself being drawn irresistibly to the primitive thought of the Church, and I cannot believe that I am being drawn into error. I have no private inspiration. I am in the Church and of the Church, and if my heart beats in tune with its pulse I cannot be too far wrong. . . . "Judge me, O God, and distinguish my cause from that of the unholy."

IX

SUMMER was in decline. The first colors of autumn were showing across the land. There was a pinch in the air, and soon the cold winds would begin to blow from the steppes down along the Alpine ridges. But the Sunday crowds in the Villa Borghese were still jealous of the warmth, and they paraded themselves cheerfully among the sellers of sweetmeats and the peddlers of novelties while their children stood gaping at the antics of Pulcinella.

Ruth Lewin was among them, playing nursemaid to a child—a tiny spastic creature with bobbing head and slobbering mouth—whom she had brought out from the slums for an airing. They were sitting on a bench, watching a fiddler with a dancing monkey while the child crammed himself with candy and bobbed a grotesque balloon in happy ignorance of his misfortune.

For all the pathos of her mission, Ruth Lewin felt calm and content. Her illness was over. She had come back from her holiday refreshed. She had made, at long last, a landfall. After the years of confusion her mind was clear. She knew what she was and what she had a right to be. It was not a conversion but an arrival. If she was not fulfilled, at least she was no longer in flight. If she was not satisfied, at least she could rest in hope of a betterment.

She was a Jew. She had inherited a race and a history. She was prepared to accept them both, not as a burden, but as an enrichment. She understood now that she had never really rejected them, but had been forced into flight from them by the circumstance of childhood. The flight was not a guilt, but an affliction, and she had survived it, as her ancestors had survived the captivities and the dispersions and the obloquy of the European ghettos. By the simple fact of this survival, by the half-conscious act of accepting, she had earned the right to be what she wanted to be, to believe what she needed to believe to grow to whatever shape her nature dictated.

She understood something else: that joy was a gift which one accepted gratefully and should not try to pay for, any more than one tried to pay for sunlight and bird song. One held out grateful hands to take the gift, and then held up the gift for a sharing. Payment was too gross a word to describe a disbursal like this. Flowers grew out of the eyes of the dead, but because one picked the flowers one should not carry a corpse on one's back for all the days of living. Children were born maimed and misshapen, but to deny them beauty and love by way of personal penance was a monstrous paradox. Doubt was a burden on all questing spirits, but when the doubt was resolved one should not cling to it in the luxury of self-torment.

She had no doubts now. She had entered into the Christian faith in childhood. She had made it a refuge, and then launched herself out of it into terror and confusion. Now it was no longer a refuge but an ambience in which she wanted to live and to grow. Like the sunlight, the bird song and the flower, it was free. She had no right to it, but she had no reason to refuse it, either. Everyone had a claim to sleep on his own pillow, hard or soft, because without sleep one died; and dying paid no debts, but only canceled them.

So, quite simply, on this Sunday morning she found herself at home.

To the traveler tossing on a windy ocean, home-coming always presented itself as a drama, a moment of revelation or of conquest. But the moment, when it came, was usually very trite. There were no banners and no trumpets. One was there, walking down a familiar street, seeing familiar faces in the doorways, wondering if the passage of time, the cavalcade of events, were not an illusion after all.

The child tugged at her arm with sticky fingers, begging to be taken to a toilet. She laughed aloud at the irony. This was the true shape of life at last—a succession of simplicities: snotty noses and soiled linen, bacon and eggs for breakfast, some laughter, some tears, and hanging over it all the majesty of mere existence. She took the child's hand and led him, stumbling and crowing, across the grass to unbutton his breeches. . . .

When she reached home, it was already dusk and the chill autumn was settling down on the city. She bathed and changed, and then because her maid was out she made her own supper, put a stack of disks on the record player, and settled down to a comfortable evening.

Time was, not so long ago, when the prospect of a solitary night would have driven her to desperation. Now, at peace with herself, she was glad of it. She was not sufficient to herself, but life, with its small services and its occasional piquant encounters, might now be sufficient to her. She was no longer an alien. She had her domain of giving, and sooner or later there might be a time of receiving, too. She could commune with herself because she had discovered herself. She was one, she was real. She was Ruth Lewin, widow, Jew by birth, Christian by adoption. She was old enough to understand, and still young enough to love if love was offered. For one day and one new woman it was more than enough.

Then the bell rang, and when she opened the door she found George Faber, drunk and mumbling, at the top of the stairs. His shirt was limp. His clothes were stained, his hair was in disorder, and he had not shaved for days.

It took her nearly an hour to sober him with black coffee and make sense out of his story. Ever since Chiara had left him, he had been drinking steadily. He had done no work at all. His bureau was being kept open by a stringer and by the kindness of his colleagues, who filed stories for him, answered his cables, and kept him out of trouble with New York.

For a man so urbane and precise it was a sorry downfall. For one so prominent in Rome the tragedy could quickly develop beyond remedy. Yet George Faber seemed to have no heart left to help himself. He despised himself utterly. He poured out the story of his affronted manhood. He abandoned himself to maudlin tears. Ambition had deserted him, and he seemed to have no foothold left from which to grope his way back to dignity.

He submitted like a child when she ordered him to take a bath and then tucked him into her bed to sleep off the rest of the drink. While he slept, muttering and restless, she emptied his pockets, bundled up his soiled clothes, and then set off to his apartment to find a new suit, clean linen, and a razor. He was still sleeping when she returned, and she settled down to another vigil and a critical examination of her own role in the drama of George Faber.

It would be all too easy now to present herself as Our Lady of Succor, ready with salve and sticking plaster to patch up his wounded pride. It would be dangerously simple to wrap up her love in a candy box and offer it as a solace for the lost one. For her own sake and for his, she must not do it. Love was less than half the answer when the pillars of a man's self-respect were shaken and the rooftrees came tumbling round his ears. Sooner or later he had to walk out of the wreckage on his own two feet, and the truest recipe of love was to let him do it.

When he came down to breakfast, haggard but tidy, she told him so, bluntly:

"This has got to stop, George—here and now! You've made a fool of yourself over a woman. You're not the first. You won't be the last. But you can't destroy yourself for Chiara or for anyone else."

"Destroy myself!" He made a gesture of defeat. "Don't you understand? That's what I found out! There's nothing to destroy. There's no me at all. There's just a bundle of good manners and journalist's habits. . . . Chiara was shrewd enough to see it. That's why she got out."

"For my money, Chiara is a selfish little bitch. You're lucky to be rid of her."

He was still stubborn in self-pity. He shook his head. "Campeggio was right. I'm too soft. One push, and I fell apart."

"Comes a time when we all fall apart, George. The real test is when we have to put ourselves together again."

"And what do you expect me to do? Dust myself off, stick a flower in my buttonhole, and walk back into business as if nothing happened?"

"Just that, George!"

"Schmaltz!" He threw the word at her in angry derision. "Yiddisher schmaltz! Straight out of Brooklyn and *Marjorie Morningstar!* Rome is laughing its head off about Chiara and me. You think I can sit up and let them throw coconuts at me just for laughs!"

"I think you must."

"I won't do it."

"Fine! So what's the alternative? Drink yourself silly every day? On money that other men are earning for you?"

"Why the hell should you care what I do?"

It was on the tip of her tongue to say, "I love you," but she bit back the words and gave him a more brutal answer. "I don't care, George! You came to me! I didn't go to you! I've cleaned you up and made you look like a man again! But if you don't want to be a man, then it's your own affair!"

"But I'm not a man, sweetheart! Chiara proved it to me. Two weeks away, and she's playing kiss-me-quick on the Lido with someone else. I risked everything for her, and then she put the horns on me. So I'm a man already?"

"Are you more of a man because you drink like a pig?"

She had silenced him at last, and now she began to plead with him. "Look, George, a man's life is his own business. I'd like to make you my business, but I'm not going to unless you tell me clearly and soberly that you want it like that. I'm not going to pity you because I can't afford it. You've made a fool of yourself. Admit it! At least you'll wear it with more dignity than the horns. You think I haven't felt the way you do? I have, and for much longer. In the end I grew up. I'm grown-up now, George. It's late in the day, but I'm grown-up. You've got to grow up, too."

"I'm so damn lonely," said George Faber pathetically.

"So am I. I've made the round of the bars, too, George. If I didn't have a weak stomach, I'd be a lush three times over. It's no answer, believe me."

"What is the answer?"

"A clean shirt and a flower in the buttonhole."

"Nothing else?"

"Oh yes! But that's for afterward. Please give it a try."

"Will you help me?"

"How?"

"I don't quite know. Maybe"—for the first time he smiled ruefully—"maybe, let me wear you in my buttonhole."

"If it's for pride, George. Yes."

"What do you mean?"

"I'm half a Roman, too, you know. You lose one woman, you have to find another. It's the only way to get rid of the horns."

"I didn't mean that."

"I know you didn't, darling; but I do. The moment you can tell yourself that I'm trying to mother you, or make myself another Chiara, then I'm no good to you. You're up and away, and on the bottle again. So let's make me a buttonhole. Wear me to show the town that George Faber is back on the job. Is it a bargain?"

"It's a bargain. . . . Thanks, Ruth."

"*Prego, signore.*" She poured him a fresh cup of coffee, and then asked him quietly, "What else is on your mind, George?"

He hesitated a moment, and then told her. "I'm afraid of Calitri."

"You think he knows what you did?"

"I think he could know. There was a man at Positano who threatened to tell him. If there were money in it, he would have told him by now."

"But you haven't heard from Calitri."

"No. But he could be biding his time."

"For what?"

"Revenge."

"What sort of revenge?"

"I don't know. But I'm in a ticklish position. I've committed a criminal act. If Calitri wanted to, he could bring me to law."

She answered him resolutely. "You'll wear that too, George, if it happens."

"I'll have to. . . . Meantime, I think I should tell Campeggio."

"Is he involved in this?"

"Not openly, but he lent me money. He makes no secret of his enmity for Calitri. . . . And Calitri could easily guess at a connection between us. As a servant of the Vatican, Campeggio is even more vulnerable than I am."

"Then you must tell him. . . . But, George . . ."

"Yes?"

"Whatever happens, remember the clean shirt and the flower in the button-hole!"

He gave her a long, searching look, and then said softly, "You do care, don't you?"

"Very much."

"Why?"

"Ask me in a month, and I'll tell you. . . . Now you get yourself down to the bureau and start work. . . . Leave me your key, and I'll clean up your apartment. The place is like a barnyard."

When they parted, he kissed her on the cheek, and she watched him striding down the street to his first encounter with reality. It was too early to tell whether he would be able to restore his own dignity, but she had kept hers, and the knowledge was a strength. She went upstairs, dressed herself in a new frock, and half an hour later was kneeling in the confessional in the apse of St. Peter's basilica.

"He has beaten us," said Orlando Campeggio. "At our own game—and with nothing but profit to himself."

"I still don't understand what made him do it," said George Faber.

They were sitting together in the same restaurant where they had made their first conspiracy. Campeggio was drawing the same pattern on the table-cloth, and George Faber, grim and perplexed, was trying to fit the jigsaw together.

Campeggio stopped his tracing and looked up. He said evenly, "I hear you've been out of circulation for a while."

"I went on a bender."

"Then you've missed the beginning of a good story. Calitri is being groomed to lead the country after the next election. The Princess Maria Poliziano is handling the campaign belowstairs."

"My God!" said George Faber. "As simple as that."

"As simple and as complicated. Calitri needs the favor of the Church. His return to the confessional has been discreetly publicized. The next and most obvious step is to regularize his marriage."

"And you think he'll bring it off?"

"I'm sure he will. The Rota, like any other court, can deal only with the evidence presented to it. It can make no judgments in the internal forum of conscience."

"The clever bastard," said George Faber with feeling.

"As you say, a clever bastard. He's been clever with me, too. My son has been promoted. He thinks the sun, moon, and stars shine out of Calitri's backside."

"I'm sorry."

Campeggio shrugged. "You have your own problem."

"I'll survive it—I hope! I'm expecting Calitri to move against me at any moment. I'm trying to figure out what he may do."

"At worst," said Campeggio thoughtfully, "he could have you tried on a criminal charge and then expelled from the country. Personally I don't think he'll do it. He has too much to lose if there is a public scandal over his marriage case. At best—and it's not a very good best, I admit—he could make things so uncomfortable for you that you would have to go, anyway. You can't function as a correspondent if you are not on reasonable terms with the men who make the news. Also, he could embarrass you with a whole lot of minor legalities."

"Those are my thoughts, too. But there is a chance that Calitri hasn't heard of my activities. Our drunken friend in Positano may have been bluffing."

"That's true. You won't know, of course, until the verdict has been handed down from the Holy Roman Rota. Whether Calitri knows or not, he won't make any move until after the case is over."

"So I sit pat."

"May I ask you a question, Faber?"

"Sure."

"Have you ever mentioned my connection with you to anybody else?"

"Well, yes. To Chiara and to another friend. Why do you ask?"

"Because in that case I'm afraid I can't sit pat. I have to make a move."

"For God's sake! What sort of move?"

"I have to resign from the *Osservatore*. I told you I was a man of confidence at the Vatican. I could not compromise myself or my employers by continuing to work under a constant threat of exposure."

"But there may be no exposure."

Campeggio smiled and shook his head. "Even so, I find that I cannot come to terms with an uneasy conscience. I am no longer a man of confidence because I can no longer trust myself. I must resign. The only question is how I shall do it. . . . On the basis of full disclosure to the Pontiff, or on a plea of age and infirmity."

"If you make a disclosure," said George Faber, "you ruin me more quickly than Calitri can do it. The Vatican is my beat as much as the Quirinale."

"I know that. You have problems enough without me. So this is what I propose to do. I shall wait until after a decision on the Calitri case is handed down from the Rota. If Calitri does not move against you, then I shall go to the Holy Father and offer him my resignation, telling him simply that I am acting under doctor's orders. If on the other hand, Calitri moves against you, then I shall make a full disclosure. That way we may both salvage a little from the wreckage." He was silent a moment, and then in a more friendly tone he added, "I'm sorry, Faber, sorrier than I can say. You've lost your Chiara, I've lost my son. We have both lost something more important."

"I know," said Faber moodily. "I should do what you're doing. Pack up quietly and head back home. But I've been here fifteen years. I hate the thought of being uprooted by a son of a bitch like Calitri."

Campeggio waved an expressive hand and quoted gently, " *'Che l'uomo il suo destin fugge di raro.* . . . It's a rare man who dodges his destiny!' And you and I were born for a troubled one. Don't fight it too long. One should always save a little dignity for the exit."

In his office at No. 5 Borgo Santo Spirito, Rudolf Semmering, Father General of the Jesuits, talked with his subject, Jean Télémond. There were letters under his hand which contained the reports of the Vatican physicians. He held them out to Télémond. "You know what these say, Father?"

"I do."

"Your cardiographs show that you have already suffered one and possibly two heart attacks."

"That's right. I had a mild seizure in India the year before last, and another while I was in the Celebes last January. I understand I may expect another at any time."

"Why didn't you write and tell me you had been so ill?"

"It seemed of small consequence. There was nothing anyone could do about it."

"We should have given you an easier way of life."

"I was happy in my work. I wanted to go on doing it."

The Father General frowned and said firmly, "It was a matter of rule and obedience, Father. You should have told me."

"I'm sorry. I did not look at it like that. I should have known better."

The stern features of the Father General relaxed, and he went on more mildly. "You know what this means, Father? You're a man in the shadow of death. You may be called without warning at any time."

"I've known that for months."

"Are you ready for it?"

Jean Télémond said nothing, and the Father General went on quietly. "You understand, Father, that this is the essential meaning of my office—a care of the souls entrusted to me by the Society and by the Church. Rightly or wrongly, I have laid heavy burdens on you. Now I want to be as much help to you as I can."

"I am very grateful, Father," said Jean Télémond. "I'm not sure how I should answer your question. Is any man ever truly ready for death? I doubt it. The best I can say is this: I have tried to live a logical life as a man and a priest. I have tried to develop my talents to make them serviceable to the world and to God. I have tried to be a good minister of the Word, and of the grace of the Sacraments. I have not always succeeded, but I think my failures have been honest ones. I am not afraid to go. . . . I do not think God wants any of us to fall out of His hands."

Semmering's lined face puckered into a smile of genuine affection. "Good. I am very happy for you, Father. . . . I hope we shall have you with us a long time yet. I want to tell you that I was deeply impressed by your address at the Gregoriana. I am not sure that I can agree with all of it. There were certain propositions which troubled me and still do. But of you I am sure. Tell me something else. How firmly do you hold to what you propounded then, and in your other works?"

Télémond considered the question carefully, and then answered. "From a scientific point of view, Father, I should explain it this way. Experiment and discovery bring one by a certain line to a certain point of arrival. . . . Up to that point one is scientifically certain because the discoveries have been documented and the logic has been proved by experiment. . . . Beyond the arrival point, the line projects itself infinitely further. One follows it by hypothesis and by strides of speculation. . . . One believes that the logic will continue to prove itself as it has done before. . . . One cannot be certain, of course, until the logic of speculation has proved itself against the logic of discovery. . . . So —again as a scientist—one has to preserve an open mind. I think I have done that. . . . As a philosopher I am perhaps less well equipped, but I believe that knowledge does not contradict itself. It develops onto successive planes, so that what we see first as a symbol may enlarge itself on another plane into a reality which to our unfamiliar eyes is different. Again, one tries to keep the mind open to new modes of thought and knowledge. . . . One understands that language is at best a limited instrument to express our expanding concepts. As a theologian I am committed to the validity of reason as an instrument for attaining to a limited knowledge of the Creator. I am committed also by an Act of Faith to the validity of divine revelation, expressed in the Deposit of Faith. . . . Of one thing I am sure—as I am sure of my own existence—that there is no possible conflict of knowledge at any plane, once the knowledge is wholly apprehended. . . . I remember the old Spanish proverb 'God writes straight with crooked lines,' but the final vector is an arrow which leads straight to the Almighty. This is the reason why I have tried to live fully in and with the world, and not in separation from it. The redemptive act is barren without the co-operation of man . . . but man as he is, in the world in which he lives—" He broke off and gave a little shrug of deprecation. "Forgive me, Father, I didn't mean to read lectures."

"It's a very good lecture, Father," said Rudolf Semmering. "But I want you to add something else to it. By your vow you are a child of obedience, an obedience of formal act, of submissive will, and humble intellect. Have you conformed the terms of your vow with the terms of your personal search?"

"I don't know," said Jean Télémond softly. "I am not sure that I can know until I am put to a final test. Cardinal Rinaldi expressed it very clearly when he said that this was the cross I was born to bear. I admit that often its weight oppresses me. Of this, however, I am sure, that there cannot be in the ultimate any conflict between what I seek and what I believe. I wish I could put it more clearly."

"Is there any way in which I can help you now, Father?"

Télémond shook his head. "I don't think so. If there were, believe me I should ask it. I think at this moment I am more afraid of this dilemma than I am of dying."

"You do not think you have been reckless?"

"No, I do not. I have had to dare much because all exploration is a risk. But reckless? No. Confronted with the mystery of an orderly universe, one cannot be anything but humble. Confronted by death, as I am, one cannot be anything but truthful. . . ." A new thought seemed to strike him. He paused a moment to weigh it, and then said bluntly, "There is a problem, though, in one's relations with the Church—not with the Faith, you understand, but with the human body of the Church. The problem is this. There are some believers who are as ignorant of the real world as certain unbelievers are ignorant of the world of faith. 'God is great and terrible,' they say. But the world also is great and terrible and wonderful, and we are heretics if we ignore or deny it. We are like the old Manichees who affirm that matter is evil and the flesh is corrupt. This is not true. It is not the world which is corrupt, or the flesh. It is the will of man, which is torn between God and the self. This is the whole meaning of the Fall."

"One of the things which bothered me in your address is that you did not mention the Fall. I know it will bother the Holy Office as well."

"I did not mention it," said Jean Télémond stoutly, "because I do not believe that it has any place in the phenomenal order, but only in the moral and spiritual one."

"They will say," persisted Rudolf Semmering, "that you have confused the two."

"There has never been any confusion in my mind. There may be some in my expression."

"It is on your expression that they will judge you."

"On that ground I am amenable to judgment."

"You will be judged, and soon. I hope you will find patience to support the verdict."

"I hope so, too," said Jean Télémond fervently. "I get so very tired sometimes."

"I am not afraid of you," said Rudolf Semmering with a smile. "And His Holiness speaks very warmly of you. You know he wants to keep you at the Vatican."

"I know that. I should like to be with him. He is a great man and a loving one, but until I am tested I should not want to compromise him. Cardinal Rinaldi has invited me to work at his villa while the Holy Office is examining my work. Have I your permission to do that?"

"Of course. I want you to be as free and comfortable as possible. I think you deserve that."

Jean Télémond's eyes were misty. He clasped his hands together to stop their trembling. "I am very grateful, Father—to you and to the Society."

"And we are grateful to you." Semmering stood up, walked round his desk, and laid a friendly hand on the shoulder of his subject. "It's a strange brotherhood, this of the Faith and of the Society. We are many minds and many tempers. But we walk a common road, and we have much need of a common charity."

Jean Télémond seemed suddenly withdrawn into a private world of his own. He said absently, "We are living in a new world. But we do not know it. Deep ideas are fermenting in the human mass. Man, for all his frailness, is being subjected to monstrous tensions, political, economic, mechanical. Knowledge is reaching like a rocket toward the galaxies. I have seen machines that make calculations beyond the mind of Einstein. . . . There are those who fear that we are exploding ourselves into a new chaos. I dare not contemplate it. I do not believe it. I think, I know, that this is only a time of preparation of something infinitely wonderful in God's design for His creatures. I wish—I wish so much —I could stay to see it."

"Why wait?" said Rudolf Semmering with rare gentleness. "When you go, you will go to God. In Him and through Him you will see the fulfillment. Wait in peace, Father."

"On the judgment?" asked Jean Télémond wryly.

"On God," said Rudolf Semmering. "You will not fall out of His hands."

Immediately after his return from Castel Gandolfo, Kiril the Pontiff was caught in a press of new and varied business.

The Institute for Works of Religion had prepared its annual survey of the financial resources of the Papacy. It was a long and complex document, and Kiril had to study it with care and concentration. His reactions were mixed. On the one hand, he had to command the industry and acumen of those who had built the Papal State and the Vatican bank into stable and solvent institutions, with operations stretching all over the world. This was the nature of their stewardship. Five Cardinals and a staff of highly competent financiers administered the temporal goods of the Church. They bought and sold in the stock markets of the world. They invested in real estate and hotels and public utilities, and on their efforts depended the stability of the Holy See as a temporal institution, whose members had to be fed, clothed, housed and hospitalized so that they might be free to work with reference to eternity.

But Kiril was too much an ironist not to see the disparity between the efficiency of a financial operation and the doubt that hung over so many works for the salvation of human souls. It cost money to train a priest and maintain a nursing sister. It cost money to build schools and orphanages and homes for the aged. But all the money in the world could not buy a willing spirit or fill a slothful one with the love of God.

By the time he had finished the document and the financial conferences, he had come to a resolution. His stewards had done well. He would leave them be, but he himself must concentrate all his time and all his energy on the prime function of the Church: the leading of men to a knowledge of their relationship with their Creator. A God-centered man could sit barefoot under a tree and set the world afire. A huckster with a million in gold, and scrip stacked up to the roof, would leave the planet unmourned and unremembered.

There was trouble in Spain. The younger clergy were in revolt against what they considered the archaic and obscurantist attitudes of certain senior prelates. There were two sides to the question. Pastoral authority had to be maintained, and at the same time the vivid and apostolic spirit of the younger Spaniards had to be preserved. Some of the older men had become too closely identified with the dictatorial system. The new ones, identified with the people and their hopes of reform, found themselves repressed and inhibited in their work. A violent reaction was beginning to make itself felt against the semisecret work of Opus Dei, which was on the face of it an institute for lay action within the Spanish Church, but which many claimed was being controlled by reactionary elements in Church and State. This was the climate in which schism and rebellion were born, yet the climate could not be reversed overnight.

After a week of discussions with his advisors he decided on a double step: a secret letter to the Primate and the Bishops of Spain, urging them to accommodate themselves with more liberality and more charity to the changing times, and an open letter to the clergy and the laity, approving the good work done, but urging upon them the duty of obedience to local ordinaries. It was at best a compromise, and he knew it. But the Church was a human society as well as a divine one, and its development was the result of checks and balances, of conflicts and retreats, of disagreements and slow enlightenment.

In England there was the question of naming a new Cardinal to succeed Brandon. The appointment posed a neat alternative! A politician or a missionary? A man of stature and reputation who would uphold the dignity of the Church—and the place it had regained in the established order? Or a rugged evangelist who understood the ferment of a crowded industrial country, and the disillusion of a once imperial society, and its fading confidence in a social and humanitarian religion?

At first blush the choice was simple. Yet given the temper of the English, their historic mistrust of Rome, their odd reaction toward revivalism, it was not half as simple as it looked.

Cardinal Leone summed it up for him neatly. "Parker, in Liverpool, is the true missionary bishop. His work among the laboring classes and the Irish immigrants has been quite spectacular. On the other hand, he is often very outspoken, and he has been accused of being a political firebrand. I do not believe that. He is an urgent man. Perhaps too urgent for the phlegmatic English. Ellison, in Wales, is in a very good standing with the establishment. He's urbane, intelligent, and understands the art of the possible. His advantage to us is that he can prepare a situation in which more apostolic men can work with some freedom."

"How long do we have?" asked Kiril. "Before a new appointment is necessary?"

"Two months, I should say, three at the outside. England needs a red hat."

"If it were left to your Eminence, whom would you choose? Parker or Ellison?"

"I should choose Ellison."

"I'm inclined to agree with you. Let's do this. We shall defer a decision for one month. During that time I should like you to make another canvass of opinion among the Curia, and among the English hierarchy. After that we shall decide."

Then there were the reports from Poland. Cardinal Potocki had pneumonia and was critically ill. If he died, there would be two immediate problems. He was deeply loved by his people, and deeply feared by the government, against whom he had held out stubbornly for sixteen years. His funeral might well be the occasion for spontaneous demonstrations, which the government could use for provocative action against the Catholic population. Equally important was the question of his successor. He had to be named and in readiness to take office, immediately the old fighter died. He had to know of his appointment, yet it had to be kept secret lest the authorities move against him before Potocki's death. A secret emissary had to get from the Vatican to Warsaw and present the papal rescript of succession. . . .

So one by one the countries of the world came under review, and the memory of a summer holiday faded further and further into the background. Finally, toward the end of September, came a letter from Cardinal Morand, in Paris.

> . . . A suggestion was made to your Holiness' Illustrious Predecessor that a papal visit to the shrine of Our Lady of Lourdes might have a spectacular effect upon the life of the Church in France. There were at that time several obstacles to the project—the health of the Holy Father, the war in Algeria, and the political climate in metropolitan France.
>
> Now these obstacles do not exist. I am informed that the French government would look with great favor on a papal visit, and would be delighted to welcome your Holiness to Paris after the visit to Lourdes.
>
> I need not say how delighted the clergy and faithful would be to have the Vicar of Christ on the soil of France after so long a time.
>
> If your Holiness were prepared to entertain the idea, I should like to suggest that the most appropriate time would be the feast of Our Lady of Lourdes, on February 11, next year. The French government concurs heartily with this timing.
>
> May I beg your Holiness most humbly to consider our request, and the good which might come from it, not only for Catholic France, but for the whole world. It would make a historic occasion—the first journey of a Pope into this land for more than a century. The eyes of all the world would be focused on the person of your Holiness, and there would be for a while a public and universal pulpit available. . . .

The letter excited him. Here was the historic gesture ready to be made. After his first exit from Rome others would follow almost inevitably. In the convergent world of the twentieth century the apostolic mission of the Pontiff might be reaffirmed in a startling style.

Immediately, and without consultation, he wrote a reply to Morand in his own hand:

> . . . We are delighted by your Eminence's suggestion of a visit to France in February of next year. We have no doubt that there will be certain voices in the Church raised against it, but we ourselves are most favorably disposed. We shall discuss the matter at the earliest opportunity with Cardinal Goldoni and later with members of the Curia.
>
> Meantime, your Eminence may accept this letter as our personal authority to initiate preliminary discussions with the French authorities concerned. We suggest that no public announcement be made until all the formalities are concluded.
>
> To your Eminence and our brother bishops, to the clergy and all the people of France, we send from a full heart our apostolic benediction. . . .

He smiled as he sealed the letter, and sent it out for posting. Goldoni and the Curia would be full of doubts and consequential fears. They would invoke history and protocol, and logistics and political side effects. But Kiril the Pontiff was a man elected to rule in God's name, and in the name of God he would rule. If doors were open to him he would walk through them, and not wait to be led through them by the hand, like a petty princeling. . . .

The idea of a peripatetic Pope had, with the passage of time, become strange in the Church. There were those who saw in it a succession of dangers—to dignity, since a man who packed his bags and went flying round the world might look too human; to authority, since he would be required to speak extempore on many subjects, without study and without advice; to order and discipline, since the Vatican Court needed at all times a firm hand to hold it together; to stability, since modern air travel entailed a constant risk, and to lose one Pontiff and elect another was an expensive, not to say perilous, business. . . . Besides, the world was full of fanatics who might affront the august personage of Christ's Vicar, and even threaten his life.

But history was not made by those who shied away from risks. Always the Gospel had been preached by men who took death for a daily companion. . . . Above all, Kiril Lakota was an opportunist with a restless heart. If a journey were possible, he would make it, discounting all but the profit in souls. . . .

From Kamenev, holidaying by the Black Sea, came a letter delivered by the ubiquitous Georg Wilhelm Forster. It was longer and more relaxed than the others, and it carried the first clear expression of his thoughts on the approaching crisis:

> . . . At last I am in private conversation with the other side of the Atlantic. I am more grateful than I can say for your good offices.
>
> I have been resting for a while, thinking out the program for the coming year and asking myself, at the same time, where I stand at this moment of my public and private life. My career is in apogee. I can go no higher. I have perhaps five more years of full authority and activity; after that the inevitable decline will begin, and I must be prepared to accept it.
>
> I know I have done well for this country. I should like to do better. For this betterment peace is necessary. I am prepared to go far to maintain it, yet you must understand that I want to go farther than I shall be permitted by the Party and the Praesidium.
>
> First, therefore, let me show you the position as I see it. You can trace my thesis on a child's map of the world. China is in a bad way. That means six hundred million people are in a bad way. This year's harvests have been dangerously light. There is real starvation in many areas. There have been reports, hard to confirm because of rigid censorship, that bubonic plague has broken out in some coastal towns. We have taken a serious view of this, and we have imposed a sanitary cordon at all frontier posts along our borders with China.
>
> Her industrial development is slow. We have deliberately made it somewhat slower by withdrawing many of our construction teams and experts, because we do not want China to grow too quickly under the present regime.
>
> The present leaders are old men. They are subject to increasing pressures from their juniors. If the economic crisis gets any worse, they will be forced into action, and they will inevitably mount military moves in the direction of South Korea, and Burma, and the northeast frontier of India.

At the same time, they will ask us to provide a diversionary front by renewing our pressure on Berlin and by pressing for a solution to the East German question, even to the point of armed intervention.

Once these moves are made, America must set herself in battle order against us.

Is there any remedy for this hair-trigger situation? I believe there is. But we must not be naïve about its efficacy. Let us get a breathing space first, so that we may proceed with a little more confidence to a long-term solution.

The first and most obvious remedy is nuclear disarmament. We have been debating this for years now, and we are no nearer to agreement. I think it is still out of the question, because public and Party opinion can be so swiftly excited by the issue. I know I cannot risk a decisive move, and neither can my opposite number. So we must discount it for a while.

The second remedy might appear to be the admission of China to the United Nations. This, again, is complicated by the fiction of the two Chinas and the existence of a rump government-in-arms on Formosa. Again we are involved in a highly political situation, too easily complicated by catch-words and prepared attitudes.

It is my view that with some preparation and a minimum of good will, a remedy may be found elsewhere. If the miseries of China were fully exposed to the world, not as a political, but as a human spectacle, and if an offer were made by America and the nations of the West to resume normal trade relations with the Chinese, by exporting food to her, by allowing the free passage of vital commodities, then we might at least defer the crisis. Of course, China would have to be prepared to accept the gesture—and to get her to do it is a delicate problem. We, on our part, would have to put our weight behind the Western offer, and we should have to make some kind of proposal of our own.

How far can we go? More properly, how far can I go with any hope of support from the Party and the country? I must be honest with you. I must not promise more than I can hope to fulfill.

Here, I think, is my limit. We would put no further pressure on Berlin, and leave the East German question in abeyance, while we reach for a less rigid form of settlement. We would discontinue nuclear tests in return for an assurance that the United States would also discontinue. We would reopen immediately—with a more practical compromise formula—the question of nuclear disarmament, and I would add my own personal authority to any effort to achieve a settlement within a reasonable time limit.

I do not know whether the Americans will find this enough, but it is the best I could assure in any negotiations. Even so, both we and the United States will need a very favorable climate to bring off a settlement. There is not too much time to prepare it.

I can almost hear you ask yourself how far you can trust me now. I cannot swear an oath, because I have nothing to swear by, but what I have written here is the truth. How I comport myself in the public view, how I behave during the negotiation, is another matter. Politics is more than half theatre, as you know. But this is the bargain I propose, and even if the Americans hedge it a little we can do business and give the world what it desperately needs at this moment, a breathing space to measure the current value of peace against what may happen if we lose it.

I hope your health is good. Mine is fairly robust, but sometimes I am reminded sharply of the passing of the years. My son has finished his training and has now been admitted as a bomber pilot in our Air Force. If war comes, he will be one of the first victims. This is a cold thought that haunts me while I sleep. This, I think, is what saves me from the ultimate corruption of power. What do I want for him? In olden times kings murdered their sons lest they prove rivals—and when they got lonely they could always breed other ones. It is different now. There are those who say we have simply grown softer—I like to think we are growing at least a little wiser.

I am reminded of your request to ease some of the burdens of your flock in Hungary, Poland, and the Baltic areas. Here, again, I must be honest, and not promise more than I can perform. I cannot issue a direct command, nor can I reverse abruptly a traditional Party policy, to which, moreover, I am personally committed. However, there will be a meeting of premiers of the fringe countries in Moscow next week. I shall put it to them as a proposal to prepare the atmosphere for what I hope will be a discussion of the Chinese question between ourselves and America.

I am hoping your Cardinal Potocki will recover. He is a danger to us, but as things are I would rather have him alive than dead. I admire him almost as much as I admire you.

One more point, perhaps the most important of them all. If we are to negotiate along the lines I have suggested, we shall need to reach a settlement before the middle of March, next year. If the Chinese begin a military build-up, it will be early in April. Once they start, we are in real trouble.

I read a copy of your letter to the Church on education. I thought it excellent and at times moving, but we have been doing so much better than the Church for forty years. One would think that you had less to lose than we have. Forgive the irony. It is hard to lose bad habits. Help us if you can. Greetings. Kamenev.

Kiril the Pontiff sat a long time, pondering over the letter. Then he went into his private chapel and knelt in prayer for nearly an hour. That same evening after supper, he summoned Goldoni from the Secretariat of State and was closeted with him until after midnight.

"You are an embarrassment to me, Mr. Faber," said Corrado Calitri gently. "I imagine you are an embarrassment to Chiara as well. She is very young. Now that the Holy Roman Rota has pronounced her free to marry, I imagine she will quickly find a new husband. The presence of an elderly lover could make things very difficult for her."

He was sitting in a high carved chair behind a buhl desk, slim, pale, and dangerous as a medieval prince. His lips were smiling, but his eyes were cold.

He waited for George Faber to say something, and when Faber did not answer he went on in the same silken tone. "You understand, Mr. Faber, that under the terms of the Concordat the decision of the Holy Roman Rota takes effect in civil law as well?"

"Yes, I understand that."

"Legally, therefore, your attempt to suborn a witness is a criminal offense under the laws of the Republic."

"It would be very difficult to prove subornation. No money was passed. There were no witnesses. Theo Respighi is a somewhat disreputable character."

"Don't you think his testimony would make you look disreputable, too, Mr. Faber?"

"It might. But you wouldn't come out of the affair very well, either."

"I know that, Mr. Faber."

"So it's a stalemate. I can't touch you. You can't touch me."

Calitri selected a cigarette from an alabaster box, lit it, and leaned back in his chair, watching the smoke rings curl upward toward the coffered ceiling of his office. His dark eyes were lit with malicious amusement. "A stalemate? I rather think it is a checkmate. I have to win, you see. No government, and certainly no political party, can support a situation where a correspondent for the foreign press can determine the career of one of its ministers."

In spite of himself Faber laughed dryly. "Do you think that's likely to happen?"

"After what you have done, Mr. Faber, anything is likely to happen. I certainly do not trust you. I doubt whether you will ever be able to trust yourself again. Hardly an edifying sight, was it? The dean of the press corps offering a bribe to a broken-down actor to pervert the law—and all because he wanted to go to bed legally with a girl! You're discredited, my friend! I have only to say a word, and you will never again be received in any government office, or any of the Vatican congregations. Your name will be dropped from every guest list in Italy. You see, I've never made any pretense of what I am. People have accepted me on my own terms, just as the country will accept me again at the next election. . . . So it is checkmate. The game is over. You should pack up and go home."

"You mean I'm expelled from the country?"

"Not quite. Expulsion is an official act of the administration. So far we are speaking . . . unofficially. I am simply advising you to leave."

"How long do I have?"

"How long would you need to make other arrangements with your paper?"

"I don't know. A month, two months."

Calitri smiled. "Two months, then. Sixty days from this date." He laughed lightly. "You will note, Mr. Faber, that I am much more generous with you than you would have been with me."

"May I go now?"

"In a moment. You interest me very much. Tell me, were you in love with Chiara?"

"Yes."

"Were you unhappy when she left you?"

"Yes."

"Strange," said Calitri with sardonic humor. "I have always thought that Chiara would make a better mistress than a wife. You were too old for her, of course. Not potent enough, perhaps. Or were you too much the puritan? That's the answer, I think. One has to be bold in love, Faber. In whatever kind of loving one elects. . . . By the way, is Campeggio a friend of yours?"

"He's a colleague," said Faber evenly. "Nothing more."

"Have you ever lent him money?"

"No."

"Borrowed from him?"

"No."

"That's curious. A check in the amount of six hundred thousand lire—one thousand American dollars—was drawn by Campeggio and paid into your bank account."

"That was a business transaction. How the hell did you know about it?"

"I'm a director of the bank, Mr. Faber. I like to do my work thoroughly. . . . You have two months. Why don't you take a real holiday and enjoy our lovely country? . . . You may go now."

Sick with anger and humiliation, George Faber walked out into the thin autumn sunshine. He went into a telephone booth and called Orlando Campeggio. Then he hailed a taxi and had himself driven to Ruth Lewin's apartment.

She fed him brandy and black coffee, and listened without comment while he rehearsed his short and ignominious interview with Corrado Calitri. When he had finished, she sat silent for a moment and then asked quietly, "What now, George? Where do you go from here?"

"Back home, I suppose. Although after fifteen years in Rome it's hard to think of New York as home."

"Will you have any trouble with the paper?"

"I don't think so. They'll accept any explanation I care to give them. They'll give me a senior job in the home office."

"So your career isn't really finished, is it?"

"Not my career. Just a way of life that I liked and wanted."

"But it's not really the end of the world."

He gave her an odd, searching look. "No. But it is the end of George Faber."

"Why?"

"Because he doesn't exist any more. He's just a name and a suit of clothes."

"Is that the way you feel, George?"

"It's what I am, sweetheart. I knew it as soon as I sat down in Calitri's office this morning. I was nothing—a straw man. I didn't believe anything, I didn't want anything, I had nothing to fight with, I had nothing to fight for. The wonder is that I feel quite calm about it."

"I know that calm, George," she told him gravely. "It's the danger signal. The quiet time before the big storm. Next, you start hating yourself and despising yourself, and feeling empty and alone and inadequate. Then you start to run, and you keep running until you hit a brick wall, or fall over a cliff, or end up in the gutter with your head in your hands. I know. I've been there."

"Then you mustn't be around when it happens to me."

"It mustn't happen, George. I'm not going to let it happen."

"Buy out, girl!" he told her with sudden harshness. "Buy out and stay out! You've had your storms. You deserve better now. I've made a damn fool of myself, I'm the one who has to pay."

"No, George!" She reached out urgent hands and forced him to turn to her. "That's the other thing I've learned. You can never pay for anything you've done, because you can't change the consequences. They go on and on. The bill keeps mounting up by compound interest until, in the end, you're crushed and bankrupt. It isn't payment we need, George. It's forgiving. . . . And we have to forgive ourselves, too. . . . You're a straw man, you say. So be it! You can either burn the straw man and destroy him. Or you can live with him and—who knows?—in the end you may get to like him. I've always liked him, George. In fact I've learned to love him."

"I wish the hell I could," said George Faber somberly. "I think he's a pompous, windy, gutless snob!"

"I still love him."

"But you can't live with him for the next twenty years and then come to despise him as he despises himself."

"He hasn't asked me to live with him yet."

"And he's not going to ask."

"Then I'll ask him: he's a straw man, I'm a straw woman. I don't have any pride, George. I don't have any pity, either. I'm just so damn glad to be alive. . . . It's not leap year, but I'm still asking you to marry me. I'm not a bad catch, as widows go. I don't have any children. I still have some looks. I do have money. . . . What do you say, George?"

"I'd like to say yes, but I daren't."

"So what does that mean, George? A fight or a surrender?"

For a moment he was the old uneasy George, running his hands through his gray hair, half mocking, half pitying, himself. Then he said soberly, "It's the wrong thing for a man to say, but could you wait awhile? Could you give me time to get into training for the fight?"

"How, George?"

He did not answer her directly, but explained himself haltingly. "It's a thing hard to explain. . . . I—I don't want to lose you. . . . I don't want to lean on you too much, either. With Chiara I was trying to hold on to youth, and I didn't have enough of it left. I don't want to come to you as empty as I am now. I want to have something to give as well. . . . If we could be friends for a while . . . Hold hands. Walk in the Villa Borghese. Drink and dance a little, and come back here when we're tired. With you I don't want to be what I'm not, but I'm still not sure what I am. These next two months are going to be strange. All the town will be laughing up its sleeve. I'm going to have to rake up some dignity."

"And then, George?"

"Then maybe we can go home together. Can you give me that long?"

"It may take longer, George," she warned him gently. "Don't be too anxious."

"What do you mean?"

But even when she had explained, she was not sure that he had understood.

Extract from
the Secret Memorials of
KIRIL I, Pont. Max.

. . . Today has been long and troublesome. Early this morning Orlando Campeggio, editor of the *Osservatore,* waited upon me to offer his resignation. He told me an involved and sordid story of a conspiracy to introduce suborned evidence into the marital case of Corrado Calitri, which has just been decided by the Holy Roman Rota. Campeggio told me that he himself had been a party to the conspiracy.

The attempt was unsuccessful, but I was deeply shocked by this revelation of the tangled lives of people who are old enough and educated enough to do better. I had no alternative but to accept Campeggio's resignation. I had, however, to commend his honesty, and I told him that his pension arrangements would not be disturbed. I understand very well the motives which led him to this breach of trust, but I cannot for that reason condone the act.

When Campeggio left me, I called immediately for the file on the Calitri case, and went over it carefully with an official of the Rota. There is no doubt in my mind that on the evidence presented, the Rota acted rightly in issuing a decree of nullity. There was another side to the picture, however: Corrado Calitri, a man of power and influence in Italy, has been living for a long time in mortal danger of his soul. I have little doubt that his sincerity in this case is suspect, but the Holy Roman Rota can give judgment only in the external forum. A man's soul can be judged only in the tribunal of the confessional.

So I am brought to a curious position. As a Minister of the Republic, Corrado Calitri is not amenable to my authority. Our relationship in the temporal order is defined by treaty and limited by diplomacy. If we quarrel, I may do much harm to the Church and to Italy, especially as I am not an Italian. In the spiritual order, however, Calitri is subject to me. As Bishop of Rome, I am his pastor. And I am not only authorized, but obliged if I can to intervene in the affairs of his soul. I have, therefore, asked him to wait upon me at a suitable time, and I hope that I may be able to offer him a pastoral service in the regulation of his conscience.

I have had a short but cheerful letter from Ruth Lewin. She tells me that she has finally resolved her position, and has decided to return to the practice of the Catholic faith. She was kind enough to say that she was indebted to me for the enlightenment and the courage to make the step. I know that this is only half the truth, and that I am at best an instrument for the working of Divine Grace. I am consoled, however, that having stepped outside the rigid confines of my office, I was permitted to make contact with her and to co-operate in re-establishing her peace of soul. . . .

Once more I have been brought to see vividly that the real battleground of the Church is not in politics or in diplomacy or finance or material extension. It is the secret landscape of the individual spirit. To enter into this hidden place the pastor needs tact and understanding, and the very particular grace bestowed by the Sacrament of Holy Orders. If I am not to fail Corrado Calitri—and it is very easy to fail those who are framed differently from other men—then I must pray and consider carefully before I meet him. If I do fail, if he leaves me in enmity, then I shall have created a new problem since I shall have to deal with him in public matters for a long time.

The President of the United States has received Kamenev's letter and my commentary on it. His reply is before me as I write:

> . . . On the face of it Kamenev does seem to offer a feasible basis for a short-term solution to our problem. I think we must get a better bargain than the one he offers. He is too good a horse trader to offer everything at once. I am not prepared to say how much more we need without submitting the project to study and taking the advice of my counsellors.
>
> However, you may tell Kamenev that I am prepared to open negotiations at this point, but that in my view they should now be initiated at diplomatic level. And he must be the one to begin them. If he is prepared to co-operate in this fashion, then like your Holiness, I believe we may make progress.
>
> I, too, am very concerned about the political climate in which these negotiations are begun. One always expects a certain amount of skirmishing and propaganda. We have to use it as much as the Russians. However, it must not be allowed to go beyond a safe limit. We shall need an atmosphere of moderation and good will, not only in our own negotiations but in our talks with members of the European bloc and with the representatives of uncommitted nations. In a deal like this there are so many limiting factors that it is difficult enough to maintain patience and restraint without calculated provocation.
>
> I agree in the main with Kamenev's estimate of the political and military situation. It is broadly confirmed by my own advisors. They agree also that if the situation still remains unsettled at the end of next March, the crisis will already be upon us.
>
> I note with lively interest the fact that your Holiness is considering a journey to France early next February. This would be a very notable event, and I ask myself—as I ask your Holiness—whether it might not be possible to use it to good purpose for the whole world.
>
> I understand very clearly that the Holy See cannot, and does not wish to, enter directly or indirectly into a political negotiation between the great

powers. But if on this occasion your Holiness could sum up the hopes of all men for peace and a negotiated settlement of our differences, then at one stroke we might have the climate we need.

I know that it will not be so easy to do. The Holy See may well have to speak for those countries where she has suffered the greatest injustice, but a historic occasion calls for a historic magnanimity. I wonder whether something like this was not in Kamenev's mind when he wrote to you first. I know that it is now in mine.

With all respect I should like to make a suggestion. The churches of Christendom are still, unhappily, divided. However, there have been signs for a long time of a growing desire for reunion. If it were possible to associate other Christian bodies with your Holiness' plea for peace, then it would be an even greater advantage.

I understand that a decision has not yet been made. I understand the weighty and prudent reasons for the delay. I can only say that I wish and hope that your Holiness will finally decide to go to Lourdes. . . .

Goldoni has seen the letter, and I know that he is torn between the excitement of the project and a prudent wish to consider all the possible consequences before a decision is made.

He suggested, diffidently, that I might care to discuss the matter with members of the Curia. I am inclined to agree with him. My authority is absolute, but common sense dictates that in so large and consequential a matter I should get the best advice available to me. I think also that I should call Cardinal Pallenberg from Germany and Morand from Paris to take part in the discussion. We have decided finally to name Archbishop Ellison, Cardinal Archbishop of Westminster. This might be a suitable occasion to call him also to Rome and offer him the red hat. . . .

Jean Télémond came yesterday to have dinner with me. He looks thinner and rather tired. He tells me, however, that he is feeling well and working steadily. He is very happy with Cardinal Rinaldi, and the two of them have become good friends. I am a little jealous of Rinaldi's good fortune because I miss my Jean, and in all this press of business I could use a little of his wondering vision of the world. Rinaldi sent me a short note by his hand, thanking me for my kindness to Leone. I have to admit that it was not so much a kindness as a calculated gesture. However, it did not go unnoticed and I am glad.

I know that Jean is still worried about the verdict of the Holy Office on his first volume. However, it is impossible to hurry an examination like this, and I have urged him to be patient. Cardinal Leone has promised to let me have an interim opinion by the end of October. I notice that he is treating the matter with extreme moderation, and is displaying personally a careful good will toward Jean Télémond. However, he is most emphatic that we should not appoint him to any office of preaching or teaching until the conclusions of the Holy Office are known.

I cannot disagree with him, but I still wish I could learn to like him. I have a free and easy commerce with other members of the Curia, but between Leone and myself there is always a kind of inhibition and uneasiness. It is my defect as much as his. I am still resentful of his Roman rigidity. . . .

Georg Wilhelm Forster has been to see me, and I have passed on to him the reply of the President of the United States. Forster is a strange little man who lives a dangerous life in apparently untroubled good humor. When I asked him about himself, he told me that his mother was a Lett and his father a Georgian. He studied in Leipzig and Moscow, and borrowed his German name for professional purposes. He is still a practicing member of the Russian Orthodox Church. When I asked him how he squared his conscience with the services of a Godless state, he turned the question very neatly:

"Is not this what you are trying to do, Holiness? Serve Mother Russia in the best fashion available to you? Systems pass, but the land is always there, and we are bound to it as if by a navel cord. . . . Kamenev understands me. I understand him. Neither demands too much of the other. . . . And God understands us all, better than we do ourselves."

The thought has remained with me all day, mixed up with thoughts of the coming crisis, and Jean Télémond, and the pilgrimage to Lourdes, and the strange bargain of Corrado Calitri. My own understanding stumbles often. But if God understands, then we are still in hopeful case. . . . When the poet writes, the pen needs not to understand the verse. Whether the pot be whole or broken, it still stands witness to the skill of the potter. . . .

X

IN the last week of October, Cardinal Leone, in private audience with the Pontiff, presented the judgment of the Holy Office on Jean Télémond's book. Leone seemed embarrassed by the occasion. He took pains to explain the nature and form of the document:

"There has been a question of time, Holiness, and a question of the special circumstances of the life of Father Jean Télémond, and the private relationship which he enjoys with your Holiness. With reference to the time factor, the Fathers of the Sacred Congregation of the Holy Office have preferred to issue an interim opinion on the work in question rather than a formal judgment. Their opinion is brief, but it is accompanied by a commentary setting down certain propositions which are basic to the whole thesis. With respect to the person of Jean Télémond, the commissioners make a special note of the evident spirituality of the man and his submissive spirit as a son of the Church and as a regular cleric. They attach no censure to him and advise no canonical process."

Kiril nodded and said quietly, "I should be grateful if your Eminence would read me this interim opinion."

Leone looked up sharply, but the Pontiff's eyes were hooded and his scarred face was as impassive as a mask. Leone read carefully from the Latin text:

" 'The most Eminent and most Reverend Fathers of the Supreme Sacred Congregation of the Holy Office, acting under instructions from His Holiness, Kiril I, Supreme Pontiff, transmitted through the Secretary of the said Sacred Congregation, have made a diligent examination of a manuscript work written by the Reverend Father Jean Télémond, of the Society of Jesus, and entitled *The Progress of Man*. They take note of the fact that this work was submitted voluntarily and in a spirit of religious obedience by its author, and they recommend that so long as he continues in this spirit no censure should attach to him, nor any process be instituted against him under the canons. They recognize the honest intention of the author and the contribution he has made to scientific research, particularly in the field of paleontology. It is their opinion, however, that the above-named work presents ambiguities and even grave errors in philosophical and theological matters which offend Catholic doctrine. A full schedule of objectionable propositions is annexed to this opinion in the form of extracts from the author's work, and commentaries by the most Eminent and Reverend Fathers of the Sacred Congregation of the Holy Office. The major grounds of objection are as follows:

" 'One: The author's attempt to apply the terms and concepts of evolutionary theory to the fields of metaphysics and theology is improper.

" 'Two: The concept of creative union expressed in the said work would seem to make the divine creation a completion of absolute being rather than an effect of efficient causality. Some of the expressions used by the author lead the reader to think he believed creation to be in some manner a necessary action in contrast with the classical theological concept of creation as an act of God's perfect and absolute freedom.

" 'Three: The concept of unity, of unifying action, strictly tied to Télémond's evolutionary theory, is more than once extended and applied even to the supernatural order. As a consequence there seems to be attributed to Christ a third nature, neither human nor divine, but cosmic.

" 'Four: In the author's thesis the distinction and difference between the natural and the supernatural order is not clear, and it is difficult to see how he can logically save the gratuitous nature of the supernatural order, and thus of grace.

" 'The most Reverend Fathers have not desired to take, letter for letter, what the author has written on these points; for otherwise they would be forced to consider some of the author's conclusions as a true and real heresy. They are very well aware of the semantic difficulties involved in expressing a new and original thought, and they wish to concede that the thought of the author may still remain in a problematic phase.

" 'It is, however, their considered opinion that the Reverend Father Jean Télémond be required to re-examine this work, and those later ones which may depend on it, to bring them into conformity with the traditional doctrine of the Church. In the meantime he should be prohibited from preaching, teaching, publishing, or disseminating in any other fashion the dubious opinions noted by the Fathers of the Sacred Congregation.

" 'Given at Rome this twentieth day of October, in the first year of the Pontificate of His Holiness, Kiril I, Gloriously Reigning.' "

Leone finished his reading, laid the document on Kiril's desk, and waited in silence.

"Twenty years," said Kiril softly. "Twenty years demolished in one stroke. I wonder how he will take it."

"I'm sorry, Holiness. There was nothing else we could do. I myself had no part in this. The commissioners were appointed at your Holiness' direction."

"We know that." Kiril's address was studiously formal. "You have our thanks, Eminence. You may carry our thanks and our appreciation also to the Reverend Fathers of the Sacred Congregation."

"I shall do that, Holiness. Meantime, how is this news to be conveyed to Father Télémond?"

"We shall tell him ourselves. Your Eminence has our leave to go."

The old lion stood his ground, stubborn and unafraid. "This is a grief to your Holiness. I know it, I wish I could share it. But neither my colleagues nor I could have returned a different verdict. Your Holiness must know that."

"We do know it. Our grief is private to ourselves. Now we should like to be alone."

He knew it was brutal, but he could not help himself. He watched the old Cardinal walk, proud and erect, out of the chamber, and then sat down heavily at the desk, staring at the document.

They were caught now, Jean Télémond and himself. At one stride they had come together to the point of decision. For himself the issue was clear. As custodian of the Deposit of Faith he could not accept error or even risk its dissemination. If Jean Télémond broke under the weight of judgment, he had to stand by and see him destroyed rather than permit one single deviation from the truth transmitted from Christ to His Apostles, and from the Apostles to the living Church.

For Jean Télémond, he knew, the problem was far greater. He would submit to judgment, yes. He would bend his will obediently to the Faith. But what of his intellect, that fine-tempered, far-ranging instrument that had grappled so long with a cosmic mystery? How would it bear the immense strain laid upon it? And its tenement, the weakened body with its fluttering, uncertain heart. How would it tolerate the battle soon to be waged within it?

Kiril the Pontiff bent his head on his hands and prayed an instant, desperately, for himself and the man who had become a brother to him. Then he lifted the telephone and asked to be connected with Cardinal Rinaldi, at his villa.

The old man came on almost immediately.

Kiril asked him, "Where is Father Télémond?"

"In the garden, Holiness. Do you want to talk with him?"

"No. With yourself, Eminence. . . . How is he today?"

"Not too well, I think. He had a bad night. He looks tired. Is something wrong?"

"I have just had the verdict from the Holy Office."

"Oh! . . . Good or bad?"

"Not good. They have gone as far as they can to minimize their objections, but their objections are still there."

"Are they valid, Holiness?"

"Most of them, I think."

"Does your Holiness want me to tell Jean?"

"No. I should like to tell him myself. Can you put him in a car and send him to the Vatican?"

"Of course. . . . I think perhaps I should prepare him a little."

"If you can, I shall be grateful."

"How do you feel, Holiness?"

"Worried for Jean."

"Try not to worry too much. He is better prepared than he knows."

"I hope so. When he returns, take care of him."

"I shall, Holiness. I have a great affection for him."

"I know. And I am grateful to your Eminence."

"Who delivered the verdict, Holiness?"

"Leone."

"Was he distressed?"

"A little, I think. I have never been able to read him very well."

"Would you like me to telephone him?"

"If you wish. . . . How long will it take Jean to get here?"

"An hour, I should say."

"Have him come to the Angelic Gate. I shall leave orders that he is to be brought straight to my room."

"I shall do that, Holiness. . . . Believe me, I am deeply sorry."

When Jean Télémond came in, pale of visage but straight and soldierly, Kiril went forward to greet him with outstretched hands. When he went to kiss the ring of the Fisherman, Kiril drew him erect and led him to the chair by his desk. He said affectionately:

"I'm afraid I have bad news for you, Jean."

"The verdict?"

"Yes."

"I thought so. May I see it, please?"

Kiril handed the paper across the desk and watched him intently as he read it. His fine face seemed to crumple under the shock, and small beads of sweat broke out on his forehead and on his lips. When he had finished, he laid the document on the desk and looked at the Pontiff with eyes full of pain and perplexity. He said unsteadily, "It's worse than I thought. . . . They've tried to be kind, but it's very bad."

"It's not final, Jean; you know that. Some of it seems to be a matter of semantics. For the rest there is no censure. They simply ask for a re-examination."

Télémond seemed to shrink back into himself. His hands trembled. He shook his head. "There isn't time. . . . Twenty years' work depends on that volume. It's the keystone of the structure. Without it the rest falls apart."

Kiril went to him swiftly, laying his hands on Télémond's trembling shoulders. "It isn't all wrong, Jean. They don't say that. They simply challenge certain propositions. These are the only things you have to clarify. . . ."

"There isn't time. . . . At night I hear the knocking on the gate. I am being summoned, Holiness, and suddenly the work is undone. What am I to do?"

"You know what you have to do, Jean. This is the moment you were afraid of. I am here with you. I am your friend—your brother. But the moment is yours."

"You want me to submit?"

"You must, Jean; you know that."

Through his own fingertips Kiril could feel the struggle that racked Télémond in body and spirit. He felt the tremor of nerve and muscle, the dampness of sweat. He smelt the odor of a man in mortal torment. Then the tremor subsided.

Slowly Jean Télémond lifted a pain-racked face. In a voice that seemed to be wrenched out of him, he said at last, "Very well. I submit. . . . What now? I submit, but I see no light. I am deaf to all the harmony I used to hear. Where has it gone? I'm lost, left . . . I submit, but where do I go?"

"Stay here with me, Jean. Let me share the darkness with you. We're friends —brothers. This is the time of gall and vinegar. Let me drink it with you."

For a moment it seemed that he would consent. Then with a great effort he took possession of himself again. He heaved himself out of his chair and stood facing the Pontiff, ravaged, shaken, but still a whole man. "No, Holiness! I'm grateful, but no! Everyone has to drink the gall and vinegar by himself. I should like to go now."

"I shall come and see you tomorrow, Jean."

"I may need more time, Holiness."

"Will you telephone me?"

"Only when I am ready, Holiness. . . . Only when I see light. Everything is dark to me now. I feel abandoned in a desert. Twenty years down the drain!"

"Not all of it, Jean. Hold to that, I beg of you. Not all of it."

"Perhaps it doesn't matter."

"Everything matters, Jean. The right and the wrong as well. Everything matters. Take courage."

"Courage? You know all I have at this moment? A small pulse inside me that flickers and beats and tells me tomorrow I may be dead. . . . I have said it, Holiness. I submit. Please let me go now."

"I love you, Jean," said Kiril the Pontiff. "I love you as I have never loved another person in my whole life. If I could take this pain from you, I would do it gladly."

"I know it," said Jean Télémond simply. "I am more grateful than I can say. But even with loving, a man must die alone. And this, I have always known, would be ten times worse than dying."

When the door closed behind him, Kiril the Pontiff slammed his fists down on the desk and cried aloud in anger at his own impotence.

The next day and the next, and the day after, he had no word of Jean Télémond. He could only guess at what he must be suffering. For all his authority as Supreme Pastor, this was one drama, one very intimate dialogue, in which he dared not intervene.

Besides, he himself was besieged with business, from the Secretariat of State, from the Congregation for the Affairs of the Eastern Church, from the Congregation of Rites. . . . Every tribunal and commission in Rome seemed to demand his attention at once. He had to drive himself through the days with a relentless discipline, and at night his desk was still piled high with papers, and his soul cried out for the refreshment of prayer and solitude.

Still he could not put Télémond out of his mind, and on the morning of the fourth day—a day taken up with private and semi-private audiences—he called Cardinal Rinaldi at the villa.

Rinaldi's report was less than comforting:

"He is suffering greatly, Holiness. There is no doubt about his submission, but I cannot begin to count what it is costing him."

"How is his health?"

"Indifferent. I have had the doctor to him twice. His blood pressure is dangerously high, but this, of course, is the result of tension and fatigue. There is little to be done for it."

"Is he still happy with you?"

"Happier here than anywhere else, I think. We understand each other. He is as private as he needs to be, and strangely enough, I think the children are good for him."

"What does he do with himself?"

"In the morning he says Mass, and then walks for a while in the country. At midday he goes to our parish church and reads his office alone. He rests after lunch, although I do not think he sleeps. In the afternoon he walks in the garden. He talks with the children when they come home. At night we play a game of chess together."

"He's not working?"

"No. He is in deep perplexity. . . . Yesterday Semmering came to see him. They talked together for a long time. Afterwards Jean seemed a little calmer."

"Would he like me to visit him?"

Rinaldi hesitated a moment. "I don't think so, Holiness. He has a deep affection for you. He talks of you very often with gentleness and gratitude. But he feels, I think, that he must not ask you to bend yourself, or your office, to his personal problem. He is very brave, you know, very noble."

"Does he know that I love him?"

"He knows. He has told me. But the only way he can return the love is by maintaining his own dignity. Your Holiness must understand that."

"I do. And, Valerio . . ." It was the first time he had used the Cardinal's first name. "I am very grateful to you."

"And I to you, Holiness. You have given me peace and the opportunity to share my life with a great man."

"If he gets really ill, you will call me immediately?"

"Immediately, I promise."

"God bless you, Valerio."

He put down the receiver and sat for a while, collecting his energies for the formalities of the morning. He did not belong to himself any more. He could spend no more than a part of himself even on Jean Télémond. He belonged to God, then through God to the Church. No man's purse was deep enough to stand such a constant expense of body and spirit. Yet he had to go on spending, trusting in the Almighty for a renewal of the funds.

The audience list was on his desk. When he picked it up, he saw that the first name was that of Corrado Calitri. He pressed the bell. The door of the audience chamber opened, and the Maestro di Camera led the Minister of the Republic into his presence.

When the first formalities were over, Kiril dismissed the Maestro di Camera and asked Calitri to sit down. He noted the containment of the man, the intelligent eyes, the ease with which he moved in an ambience of authority. This was one born to eminence. He had to be dealt with honestly. His pride had to be respected, his intelligence, also. Kiril sat down and addressed himself quietly to his visitor:

"I am anchored to this place, my friend. I am not so free to move as others, so I have to ask you to come to see me."

"I am honored, Holiness," said Calitri formally.

"I shall have to ask you to be patient with me, and not resent me too much. Later I believe you will sit on the Quirinal Hill; I shall sit here in the Vatican; and between us we shall rule Rome."

"There is a long way to go before then, Holiness," said Calitri with a thin smile. "Politics is a risky business."

"So this morning," said Kiril gently, "let us ignore politics. I am a priest and your bishop. I want to talk to you about yourself."

He saw Calitri stiffen under the shock, and the swift flush that mounted to his pale cheeks. He hurried on. "The editor of the *Osservatore Romano* resigned a few days ago. I think you know why."

"I do."

"I was sufficiently concerned to call for the file on your case from the Holy Roman Rota. I examined it very carefully. I have to tell you that the record of the proceedings is completely in order, and that the decree of nullity handed down was fully justified by the evidence."

Calitri's relief was evident. "I'm glad to hear that, Holiness. I did a great wrong in attempting marriage. I'm not very proud of myself, but I'm glad to see justice done at last."

Kiril the Pontiff said evenly, "There was something else in the record which interested me more than the legal process. It was the evidence of a deep spiritual dilemma in your own soul." Calitri opened his mouth to speak, but the Pontiff stayed him with an uplifted hand. "No, please! Let me finish. I did not ask you here to accuse you. You are my son in Christ; I want to help you. You have a special and very difficult problem. I should like to help you to solve it."

Calitri flushed again, and then gave an ironic shrug. "We are what we are, Holiness. . . . We have to make the best terms we can with life. The record shows, I think, that I have tried to improve the terms."

"But the problem is still there, is it not?"

"Yes. One tries to make substitutions, sublimations. Some of them work, some of them don't. Not all of us are ready for a lifelong crucifixion, Holiness. Perhaps we should be, but we are not." He gave a small, dry chuckle. "Just as well, perhaps; otherwise you might find half the world in monasteries and the other half jumping off a cliff."

To his surprise, Kiril acknowledged the irony with a smile of good humor. "Strange as it may sound, I don't disagree with you. Somehow or other, we all have to come to terms with ourselves as we are, and with the world as it is. I have never believed that we have to do it by destroying ourselves. . . . Or even more importantly, by destroying others. May I ask you a question, my son?"

"I may not be able to answer it, Holiness."

"This problem of yours. This thing that drives you. How do you define it for yourself?"

To his surprise, Calitri did not balk the question. He answered it bluntly. "I defined it a long time ago, Holiness. It is a question of love. There are many varieties of love, and—I am not ashamed to say it—I am susceptible to, and capable of, one special variety." He hurried on urgently. "Some people love children, others find them little monsters. We don't blame them, we accept them for what they are! Most men can love women—but even then, not all women. I am drawn to men. Why should I be ashamed of that?"

"You should not be ashamed," said Kiril the Pontiff. "Only when your love becomes destructive—as it has done in the past, as it may do with Campeggio's son. A man who is promiscuous is not a true lover. He is too centered upon himself. He has a long way yet to grow to maturity. Do you understand what I am trying to say?"

"I understand it. I understand also that one does not arrive at maturity in one leap. I think I am beginning to arrive there."

"Sincerely?"

"Which of us is wholly sincere with himself, Holiness? That, too, takes a lifetime of practice. Let us say that perhaps I am beginning to be sincere. But politics is not the best training ground, nor is the world."

"Are you angry with me, my friend?" asked Kiril the Pontiff with a smile.

"No, Holiness. I am not angry. But you must not expect me to surrender to you like a schoolgirl at first confession."

"I don't expect that, but sooner or later you will have to surrender. Not to me, but to God."

"That, too, takes time."

"Which of us can promise himself time? Is your span so certain? Or mine?"

Calitri was silent.

"Will you think about what I have said?"

"I will think about it."

"And not resent me?"

"I will try not to resent you, Holiness."

"Thank you. Before you go, I should like to tell you that here, in this place three nights ago, I stood and suffered with a man who is as dear to me as life. I love him. I love him in the spirit and in the flesh. I am not ashamed of it because love is the noblest emotion of humankind. . . . Do you ever read the New Testament?"

"I haven't read it for a long time."

"Then you should read the description of the Last Supper, where John the Apostle sat on the right hand of the Master and leaned his head on His breast, so that all the others looked and wondered and said, 'See how he loves Him.' " He stood up and said briskly, "You are a busy man. I have taken up too much of your time. Please forgive me."

Calitri, too, stood up and felt himself dwarfed by the tall, commanding figure of the Pontiff. He said not without humor, "Your Holiness took a great risk calling me here."

"This is a risky office," said Kiril evenly. "But very few people understand it —besides, your own risk is much greater. Don't, I beg of you, underrate it."

He pressed the bell and handed his visitor back into the practiced hands of the Maestro di Camera.

When Corrado Calitri walked out of the bronze gate and into the pale sunshine of St. Peter's square, the Princess Maria-Rina was waiting for him in the car. She questioned him shrewdly and eagerly. "Well, boy, how did it go? No problems, I hope? You got along well together? Did he talk about the verdict?

About politics? This sort of thing is most important, you know. You are going to live with this man for a long time."

"For Christ's sake, Aunt," said Corrado Calitri irritably, "will you shut up and let me think!"

At eleven o'clock the same evening, the telephone rang in Kiril's private apartment. Cardinal Rinaldi was on the line. He was in deep distress. Jean Télémond had suffered a heart attack, and the doctors expected another at any moment. There was no hope for his life. Rinaldi had already administered the last rites and summoned the Father General of the Jesuits. Kiril slammed down the phone and ordered his car to be ready in five minutes with an escort of Italian police.

As he dressed hurriedly for the road, childish, simple prayers leapt to his lips. It must not be. It could not be. God must be kinder to Jean Télémond, who had risked so much for so long. "Please, please hold him a little longer! Hold him at least till I get there and can set him at peace. I love him! I need him! Don't take him so abruptly!"

As the big car roared out through the nighttime city, with the Vatican pennant fluttering and the police sirens clearing the traffic, Kiril the Pontiff closed his eyes and fingered the beads of his rosary, concentrating all the resources of his spirit in a single petition for the life and the soul of Jean Télémond.

He offered himself as a hostage—a victim, if necessary—in his place. And even as he prayed, he wrestled with the guilty resentment that thus incontinently the man he loved should be snatched away from him. The darkness that Jean Télémond had endured seemed now to come down on him, so that even while he wrenched his will into submission his heart cried out bitterly for a stay of judgment.

But when Rinaldi met him at the door of the villa, gray-faced and shaken, he knew that his petition had been refused. Jean Télémond, the restless traveler, was already embarked on his last voyage.

"He's sinking, Holiness," said Valerio Rinaldi. "The doctor's with him. He will not last the night."

He led the pontiff into the antique room where the doctor stood, with the Father General of the Jesuits, looking down on Télémond, and the candles burned for a last light to the departing spirit. Télémond lay, slack and unconscious, his hands at rest on the white coverlet, his face shrunken, his eyes closed deep in their sockets.

Kiril knelt by the bedside and tried to summon him back into consciousness. "Jean! Can you hear me? It's I, Kiril. I came as soon as I could. I'm here with you, holding your hand. Jean, my brother, please speak to me if you can!"

There was no sign from Jean Télémond. His hands were still slack, his eyelids closed against the light of the candles. From his cyanosed lips there issued only the shallow, rattling breath of the dying.

Kiril the Pontiff leaned his head on the breast of his friend and wept as he had not wept since his nights of madness in the bunker. Rinaldi and Semmering stood watching him, moved, but helpless, and Semmering, unaware of the trick of circumstance, whispered the Gospel words " 'See how he loves him.' "

Then when the weeping had spent itself, Rinaldi laid his old hand on the sacred shoulder of the Pontiff and summoned him gently. "Let him go, Holiness! He is at peace. It is the best we can wish him. Let him go!"

Early the next morning, Cardinal Leone presented himself unannounced in the papal apartments. He was kept waiting for twenty minutes, and then was shown into the Pontiff's study. Kiril was sitting behind his desk, lean, withdrawn, weary of mouth and eye after the nightlong vigil. His manner was strained and distant. It seemed an effort for him to speak.

"We had asked to be left alone. Is there something special we can do for your Eminence?"

Leone's craggy face tightened at the snub, but he controlled himself and said quietly, "I came to offer my sympathy to your Holiness on the death of Father Télémond. I heard the news from my friend Rinaldi. I thought your Holiness would like to know that I offered a Mass this morning for the repose of his soul."

Kiril's eyes softened a little, but he still held to the formality of speech. "We are grateful to your Eminence. This is a great personal loss to us."

"I feel guilty about it," said Leone. "As if in some way I were responsible for his death."

"You have no cause to feel that, Eminence. Father Télémond had been ailing for some time, and the Holy Office verdict was a shock to him. But neither you nor the Eminent Fathers could have acted differently. You should dismiss the matter from your mind."

"I cannot dismiss it, Holiness," said Leone in his strong fashion. "I have a confession to make."

"Then you should make it to your confessor."

Leone shook his white mane and lifted his old head in answer to the challenge. "You are a priest, Holiness. I am a soul in distress. I elect to make my confession to you. Do you refuse me?"

For a moment it seemed as if the Pontiff would explode into anger. Then slowly his taut features relaxed and his mouth turned upwards into a tired smile. "You have me there, Eminence. What is your confession?"

"I was jealous of Jean Télémond, Holiness. I did what was right, but my intention was not right while I did it."

Kiril the Pontiff looked at the old man with puzzled eyes. "Why were you jealous of him?"

"Because of you, Holiness. Because I needed but could not have what you gave him at a first meeting—intimacy, trust, affection, a place in your private counsels. I am an old man. I have served the Church a long time. I felt I had deserved better. I was wrong. None of us deserves anything but the promised wage for a worker in the vineyard. . . . I'm sorry. Now will your Holiness absolve me?"

As the Pontiff moved toward him, he went down stiffly on his knees and bent his white head under the words of absolution. When they were finished, he asked, "And the penance, Holiness?"

"Tomorrow you will say a Mass for one who has lost a friend and is still only half resigned to God's will."

"I will do that."

Kiril's strong hands reached down and drew him to his feet, so that they stood facing each other, priest and penitent, Pope and Cardinal, caught in the momentary wonder of understanding.

"I, too, have sinned, Eminence," said Kiril. "I kept you at a distance from me because I could not tolerate your opposition in my projects. I was at fault with Jean Télémond, too, I think, because I clung to him too strongly; and when the moment came to let him go into the hands of God, I could not do it without bitterness. I am empty today, and very troubled. I am glad you came."

"May I tell you something, Holiness?"

"Of course."

"I have seen three men sit in this room; you are the last I shall see. Each of them came in his turn to the moment where you stand now—the moment of solitude. I have to tell you that there is no remedy for it, and no escape. You cannot retire from this place as Rinaldi has done, as I hope you will let me do very soon. You are here until the day you die. The longer you live the lonelier you will become. You will use this man and that for the work of the Church, but when the work is done, or when the man has proved unequal to it, then you will let him go and find another. You want love. You need it as I do, even though I am old. You may have it for a while, but then you will lose it because a noble man cannot commit himself to an unequal affection. And a gross man will not satisfy you. Like it or not, you are condemned to a solitary pilgrimage, from the day of your election until the day of your death. This is a Calvary, Holiness, and you have just begun the climb. Only God can walk with you all the way, because He took on flesh to make the same climb Himself. . . . I wish I could tell you differently. I cannot."

"I know it," said Kiril somberly. "I know it in the marrow of my bones. I think I have shrunk from it every day since my election. When Jean Télémond died last night, a part of me died with him."

"If we die to ourselves," said the old lion, "in the end we come to live in God. But it is a long, slow dying. Believe me, I know! You are a young man. You have yet to learn what it is to be old." He paused a moment, recovering himself, and then asked, "Now that we are at one, Holiness, may I ask you a favor?"

"What is it, Eminence?"

"I should like you to let me retire, like Rinaldi."

Kiril the Pontiff pondered on it for a moment, and then shook his head. "No. I cannot let you go yet."

"You ask a great deal, Holiness."

"I hope you will be generous with me. You were not made to rusticate or wither away in a convent garden. . . . There are lions abroad in the streets, and we need lions to fight them. Stay with me awhile longer."

"I can stay only in trust, Holiness."

"In trust, I promise you."

"You must not flatter me, Holiness."

"I do not flatter you, Eminence," said Kiril gravely. "You have much courage. I want to borrow it for a while. . . . Just now, you see, I am very much afraid."

* * *

The fear was tangible, familiar, and mightily threatening. It was the same which he had endured in the hands of Kamenev, and he had been brought to it by the same process. . . . Months of self-questioning. Recurrent crises of pain. Sudden and spectacular revelations of the complexities of existence, beside which the simple propositions of faith seemed pitifully inadequate.

If the pressure was kept on long enough, the delicate mechanism of reflection and decision seized up like an overdriven motor. All the processes of the personality seemed to fall into syncope, so that one was left confused and irresolute—even grateful to be swayed by a stronger will.

Every day during these first months of his Pontificate he had been forced to question his motives and his capacities. He had been forced to measure his private convictions against the accumulated experience of the bureaucracy and the hierarchy. He felt like a man pushing a stone uphill, only to have it roll back upon him at every third step.

Then, just when the progress seemed easier, he had been faced with a deep and long-hidden weakness in himself: the need for love that had driven him to cling so urgently to the friendship of Jean Télémond that his detachment as a religious man had been almost wholly destroyed. The foundations of his confidence had been weakened still further by his indulgence of resentment against Leone. It was not he who had taken the first step to reconciliation, but the old Cardinal. It was not he who had helped Jean Télémond to the conformity in which he needed to die, but Rinaldi and Rudolf Semmering.

If he had failed so dismally in these simple relationships, how could he trust himself and his convictions under the complex demands of leadership in the Universal Church?

So even after seventeen years of endurance for the Faith, everything was called in question again, and he saw how easy it would be to shift the burden of action. He had only to relax, to let the system of the Church take over. He did not have to decide anything. He had simply to propose and suggest, and work according to the opinions tendered to him by the Secretariat of State, by the Sacred Congregations, and by all the administrative bodies, little and great, within the Church.

It was a legitimate method of government. It was a safe one, too. It rested itself firmly upon the collective wisdom of the Church, and could be justified as an act of humility on the part of a leader who had found himself wanting. It would preserve the integrity of the Church, and the dignity of his office, against the consequences of his own incapacity. Yet deep inside him—deep as the roots of life itself—was the conviction that the work to which he had been called was far other. He had to show forth in himself the faculty for renewal which was one of the marks of the living Church. The problem now was that he could no longer reason out the conviction. The fear was now that he was living an illusion of self-love, and self-deception, and destructive pride.

Daily the evidence was mounting up against him. The question of his visit to France and of his involvement in the political discussion of the nations was already being canvassed among the Cardinals and Primates of the Church. Daily their opinions were being brought to his desk, and he was troubled by the extent to which they differed from his own.

Cardinal Carlin wrote from New York:

So far the President of the United States has professed himself happy with what your Holiness has done to assist the opening of negotiations with the Soviet Union. However, now that the talks have begun at diplomatic level, there is a fear that the Holy See may try to color them by using its influence in the European bloc of nations, whose interests diverge at certain important points from those of America. Under this aspect your Holiness' proposed visit to France may wear a far different look from that which is intended.

From Archbishop Ellison, who had not yet received the red hat, came the cool comment:

Your Holiness must be aware that the Republic of France was the bitterest opponent of the participation of England in the European community of nations. If your Holiness goes to France, inevitably you will be invited to Belgium and to Germany as well. It might seem to many Englishmen that France is trying to use the Holy See, as she used her before, to strengthen her own position in Europe at the cost of ours.

Platino, "the Red Pope," had another point of view:

I am convinced, as is your Holiness, that sooner or later the Vicar of Christ must take advantage of modern travel to present himself in person to the churches throughout the world. I ask myself, however, whether the first gesture should be one which is free from historic association. Might it not be better to plan much further ahead for a visit, say, to South America or to the Philippines, so that the missionary work of the Church would receive an impetus which it so badly needs at this moment?

From Poland, where Potocki was dying and where his successor had already been secretly named, came a warning even more blunt. It was delivered by word of mouth from the emissary who had carried the papal appointment to the new incumbent:

There is a feeling, strongly expressed, that Kamenev, who is known as a subtle and ruthless politician, may be trying to create a situation in which the Holy See can be named as a co-operator with the Kremlin. The effect of this among Catholics behind the iron curtain could well be disastrous.

On the other hand, there was Kamenev's last letter, which, if it meant anything at all, meant a startling change in the rigid Marxist thought, and a deeper change working in the man himself. Man was not a static animal. Society was not static, nor was the Church. Whether in the sense of Jean Télémond or in another, they were evolving, shedding historic accretions, developing new attitudes and new potentials, groping consciously or instinctively toward the promise of more light and fuller life. They all needed time—time and the leaven of divinity working in the human lump. Every moment saved was a deferment of chaos. Every hint of good was an evidence of God's ferment in His own creation. . . . Kamenev wrote:

> . . . So, thanks to your good offices, we are enabled to begin at diplomatic level a negotiation with the United States which has at least some hope of success. There will be rough words and hard bargaining, but time is running out, and of this at least we are all convinced.
>
> I am interested in your plan for a visit to France in the first part of February. I agree—though the Party would have my head if they heard it —that you may do much toward preparing a suitable climate for our discussions.
>
> I shall be more than interested to read what you will say. Inevitably you must discuss the question of rights and duties between nations. How will you treat the rights of Russia, where you have suffered so much and whence your Church has been extirpated? How will you treat the rights of China, where your bishops and priests are in prison?
>
> Forgive me. I am an incurable joker, but this time the joke is against myself. If any man could convince me that there is a God, you, Kiril Lakota, would be the one to do it. But for me there is still an empty heaven and I must plot and plan, and lie and bargain, and close my eyes on terror and violence, so that my son and a million other sons may grow and breed without a canker in the guts or a monster in the cradle because of atomic radiation.
>
> The irony is that all I do may be proved a folly and a precipitant for what I am trying to avoid. You are more fortunate. You believe you rest in the providence of God. Sometimes I wish—how very much I wish—that I could believe with you. But a man carries his destiny written on the palm of his hand, and mine is written differently from yours. I am often ashamed of what I did to you—I should like to prove to you that you have some reason to be proud of what you have done for me. If we have peace for only a year, you will have earned a great part of it.
>
> Think of me gently sometimes. Yours, Kamenev.

They were all separate voices. Yet in their diverse accents they expressed a common hope that man, living under the shadow of the mushroom cloud, might yet survive in peace to fulfill a divine plan in his regard.

He had to listen to them all. He might hope that in the end the conflict of their opinions would resolve itself into a harmony. Yet for all his fears, he knew that this hope was an illusion.

He could not, without a grim risk, step outside the field of action set down for him by divine commission. But inside that field of action he was supreme. The government was upon his shoulders and upon no other's. In the end he must decide. . . . Yet knowing his own infirmities, he shrank away from the decision.

Only two things were guaranteed to him by divine promise—that standing in the shoes of the Fisherman, he would not err in doctrine and that whatever folly he might commit, the Church would survive. . . . In all else he was left to his own devices. He might augment the Church gloriously, or inflict upon it a terrible diminishment. And this was the prospect that terrified him.

He was free to act, but he had no promise of the consequences of his action. He was ordered to pray, but he had to pray in darkness and could not demand to know the form in which the answer might come. . . .

He was still wrestling with the dilemma when the Father General of the Jesuits telephoned and requested an audience with him. He had, he said, a mass of business to discuss with the Pontiff, but this could wait until the day set for normal audiences. This time, he wanted to convey to the Holy Father the substance of his last talk with Jean Télémond.

"When I went to see him, Holiness, I found him in deep confusion," Semmering began. "I have never known a man so shocked. It took me a long time to calm him. But of this I am convinced. The submission he had made to your Holiness was firm and true, and when he died he was at peace. . . ."

"I am glad to hear it, Father. I knew what he was suffering. I wanted so much to share it, but he felt he had to withdraw from me."

"He did not withdraw, Holiness," said Semmering earnestly. "The thought in his mind was that he had to carry his own cross and work out his own salvation. He gave me a message for you."

"What message?"

"He said that he did not believe he could have made this final and necessary Act of Faith without you. He said that when the moment came it presented itself to him as the greatest risk of his life. A risk of his integrity and of reason itself. It was almost—and I use his own words—as if he might be launching himself into insanity. He said that the only thing that gave him courage to make the leap was that your Holiness had already made it before him, and that you had not shirked a single risk of speculation or of authority. . . . I wish I could convey to your Holiness the intensity with which he expressed himself." He gave a grim, restrained smile. "I have learned to be very skeptical, Holiness, of displays of fervor and religious emotion, but I am convinced that in this struggle of Father Télémond, I was witnessing the very real battle of a soul with itself and with the powers of darkness. I felt myself ennobled by the victory."

Kiril was moved. "I am grateful, Father, that you have told me. I am myself facing a crisis. I am sure Jean would have understood it. I hope he is interceding for me now with the Almighty."

"I am sure he is, Holiness. In a way his death was a kind of martyrdom. He met it very bravely. . . ." He hesitated a moment, and then continued, "There is another thing, Holiness. Before he died, Father Télémond told me that you had promised that his work would not be lost or suppressed. This was, of course, before the Holy Office issued its opinion. All Father Télémond's manuscripts have now come into my possession. I should like an indication of how your Holiness would prefer us to deal with them."

Kiril nodded thoughtfully. "I've been thinking of that, too. I have to agree with the option of the Holy Office, that Jean's opinions require re-examination. Speaking privately, I believe that there is much of value in them. It would be my thought to submit them to new study, and possibly to publish them later with annotation and commentary. I should think the Society of Jesus admirably equipped to carry out this work."

"We should be happy to undertake it, Holiness."

"Good. Now I should like to ask you a question. . . . You are a theologian and a religious superior. How far was Jean Télémond justified in taking the risks he did?"

"I have thought about that a long time, Holiness," said Rudolf Semmering. "It is a question I have had to ask myself many times, not only with Father Télémond, but with many other brilliant men inside the Society."

"And your conclusion, Father?"

"If a man is centered upon himself, the smallest risk is too great for him, because both success and failure can destroy him. If he is centered upon God, then no risk is too great, because success is already guaranteed—the successful union of Creator and creature, beside which everything else is meaningless."

"I agree with you, Father," said Kiril the Pontiff. "But you ignore one risk— the one which I am facing now—that at any moment up to the moment of death man can separate himself from God. Even I, who am His Vicar."

"What do you want me to say, Holiness?" asked Rudolf Semmering. "I have to admit it. From the day we begin to reason until the day we die, we are at risk of damnation. All of us. This is the price of existence. Your Holiness has to pay it like the rest of us. I could judge Jean Télémond because he was my subject. But you I cannot judge, Holiness. . . ."

"Then pray, Father—and have all your brethren pray—for the Pope on a tightrope."

The meeting of the Roman Curia, which Kiril had called to discuss the international situation and his proposed visit to France, was set down for the first week in November. It was preceded by a week of private discussions in which each of the Cardinals was invited to explore with the Pontiff his private opinions.

He did not attempt to sway them, but only to expose to them his thinking and to give them the confidence which they deserved as his counsellors. They were still divided. There were the few who agreed, the many who doubted, those who were openly hostile. His own fears were no less, and he still hoped that when the Curia came together in assembly, they would find a common voice to counsel him.

To assist them in their deliberations he had called Cardinal Morand from Paris, Pallenberg from Germany, Ellison from London, Charles Corbet Carlin from New York. Cardinal Ragambwe was there by accident because he had flown from Africa to confer with the Congregation of Rites on the new liturgical proposals.

The place of their meeting was to be the Sistine Chapel. He had chosen it because it was numinous with memories of his own election and all the others which had taken place there. He himself spent the night of the vigil in prayer, hoping to prepare himself to interpret his thoughts to the Curia and to receive from them some clear and concerted expression of the mind of the Church.

He was no longer confused, but he was still afraid, knowing how much might hang upon the outcome. The proposition which Semmering had presented to him was devastatingly simple—that a man centered in God had nothing to fear. But he was still troubled by the knowledge that he had been all too easily separated from this center and led astray into egotism. It was not the enormity of the act that troubled him, but the knowledge that the small lapses might be symptomatic of greater and undiscovered weaknesses in himself.

So when the Cardinal Camerlengo led him into the Chapel and he knelt to intone the invocation to the Holy Spirit, he found himself praying with a vivid intensity that the moment would not find him wanting. When the prayer was done, he stood to address the Cardinals.

"We have called you here, our brethren and our counsellors, to share with you a moment of decision in the life of the Church. You are all aware that in the spring of next year there may well be a political crisis which will bring the world closer to war than it has been since 1939. We want to show you the shape of the crisis. We want to show you also certain proposals that have been made to us which may help to minimize it.

"We are not so naïve as to believe that anything we may do in the material order will effectively change the dangerous military and political situation which exists today. The temporal domain of the Holy See has been reduced to a small plot of ground in Rome, and we believe that this is a good thing because we shall not be tempted to use man-made instruments of intervention when we should be using those provided us by God Himself.

"We do believe, however, and believe with firmest faith, that it is our commission to change the course of history by establishing the kingdom of Christ in the hearts of men, so that they may establish for themselves a temporal order based firmly upon truth, justice, charity, and the moral law.

"This is our charge from Christ. We cannot abrogate it. We must not shrink from a single one of its consequences. We dare not neglect any, even the most dangerous, opportunity to fulfill it.

"First let us show you the shape of the crisis."

With swift, decisive strokes he sketched it for them—the world embattled as it looked to one man sitting on a pinnacle, with the nations spread below and the atomic threat hanging above. None of them disagreed with him. How could they? Each from his own vantage point had seen the same situation.

He read them Kamenev's letters and those from the President of the United States. He read them his own commentaries and his own assessment of the characters and the dispositions of both men. Then he went on:

"It may seem to you, my brethren, that in the intervention we have already made there is a great element of risk. We admit it. It is clearly defined even in the letters from Kamenev and the President of the United States. We as Supreme Pontiff recognize the risk, but we had to accept it or let slip out of our hands a possible opportunity to serve the cause of peace in this dangerous time.

"We are aware, as each of you is aware, that we cannot count wholly on the sincerity or the protestations of friendship of any man who holds public office, even if he be a member of the Church. Such men are always subject to the pressure of influence, and opinion, and the actions of others over whom they have no control. But so long as a light of hope flickers, we must try to keep it alight and shield it from the harsh winds of circumstance.

"We have always believed, as a matter of private conviction, that our connection with the Premier of Russia, which dates back seventeen years, to the time of our first imprisonment for the Faith, had in it an element of Divine Providence which might one day be used by God for Kamenev's good or ours, or for the good of the world. In spite of all risks and doubts this is still our conviction.

"You are all aware that we have received an invitation from the Cardinal Archbishop of Paris to visit the shrine of Our Lady of Lourdes on her feast day, February eleventh, next year. An invitation has also been added from the Government of France to make a state visit to Paris afterwards. We do not have to tell you the risks of one kind or another which such a historic step would entail. Nevertheless, we are disposed to make it. Immediately we do so, other invitations will no doubt be issued, to visit other countries of the world. We shall be disposed to accept these, also, as time and circumstances permit. We are still young enough, thank God, and transport is now swift enough to permit us to do so without too great or too disastrous an interruption to the work of the Holy See.

"We have said we are disposed to do it. Before making a final decision we are anxious to have your opinion as our brothers and counsellors. We point out that if we decide to make the visit an immense amount of work will have to be done in a short time to prepare the public mind and to secure, so far as is possible, a friendly attitude from our brethren of other communions in Christendom. We do not wish to make a barren spectacle of our office. We do not want to raise historic animosities. We wish to go forth in charity to show ourselves as a pastor and to proclaim the brotherhood of all men, without exception of nation, race, or creed, in the Fatherhood of one God.

"If we do decide to go out thus into the world—this new world, which is so different from the old—then we do not wish to insist on niceties of protocol and ceremony. These are affairs of court, and if we are a prince by protocol, we are still a priest and a pastor by the anointing and the laying on of hands.

"What more can we say to you? These first months of our Pontificate have been full of labor and full of problems. We have learned much more than we should ever have believed possible, about the nature of our office, the problems of our Holy Mother Church and Her constant battle to make Her human body a fit vessel for the Divine Life which infuses Her. We have made mistakes. We shall no doubt make many others, but we ask you, our brethren in the pastoral office, to forgive us and pray for us. Last week we suffered a grievous personal loss by the death of our dear friend, Father Jean Télémond, of the Society of Jesus. We beg you to pray for him, and we beg you to pray for us, also, who stand on this stormy eminence between God and man.

"The question is before you, dear brethren. Shall we go out from Rome and travel like the first Apostles to confront the twentieth century, or shall we stay at home here in Rome and let our brother bishops take care of their own vineyards in their own fashion? Shall we let the world look after its own affairs, or shall we, as Supreme Pontiff, risk our worldly dignity to step down into the market place and proclaim the Unknown God . . . ?

"Quid vobis videtur. . . . How does it seem to you?"

He sat down on the throne prepared for him and waited. Silence hung over the assembly like a cloud. He saw the old men looking one at the other as if they were exchanging a thought that they had already discussed in private.

Then slowly Cardinal Leone, senior among the seniors of the Church, stood up and confronted the assembly.

"I will not rehearse for you, brethren, the hundred and one reasons for or against this project. His Holiness knows them as well as we. I will not recount the risks because they are as vividly present in the mind of the Pontiff as they are in ours. There are those among us—and I say frankly that I am one of them—who have grave doubts about the wisdom of a papal visit to France, or anywhere else, for that matter. There are others, I know, who see such a visit as a gesture both timely and efficacious. Who is right and who is wrong? Only God can decide the outcome and history pass a verdict on it. I do not think that any of us here would wish to increase the burden of His Holiness by attempting to sway him this way or that.

"The position is very simple. The authority of the Holy Father is supreme in the matter. Now or later he must decide on what is to be done. Whether our votes are for or against, *he* must decide. . . ."

For a brief moment he stood doughty and challenging, and then flung the last words down like a gage in front of the Curia:

"*Placetne, fratres.* . . . What say you, my brothers? Does that please you or not?"

There was a moment of hesitation, and then one after the other the red caps came off, and the murmur of assent ran round the assembly!

"*Placet* . . . It pleases us. We are agreed."

This was something Kiril had not expected. It was more than a formality. It was a vote of confidence. It was a gesture, prepared by Leone and the Curia, to affirm their loyalty and to comfort him in his trial.

It was more yet—an irony like the handful of flax burned under his nose before they crowned him, so that he would always remember his mortality. It was a committal of the Church, not to him, but to the Holy Spirit, who, even in spite of him would keep Her whole and alive until Judgment Day.

Now everything that he had inherited, everything that he had secretly demanded in his office, was in his hands: authority, dignity, freedom of decision, the power to loose and bind. . . . And he had to begin paying for it. . . . So there was nothing to do but say the ritual words of dismissal and let his counsellors go.

One by one the Cardinals came and knelt before him and kissed his ring in token of fealty. One by one they left. And when the door closed upon the last of them, he rose from his throne and knelt on the altar step before the tabernacle.

Above him was the towering splendor of Michelangelo's *Judgment.* In front of him was the small golden door, behind which dwelt the hidden God. The weight of the Cross was on his shoulders. The long Calvary was about to begin. He was left, as he would be left henceforward for all the days of his life. . . .

Extract from
the Secret Memorials of
KIRIL I, Pont. Max.

. . . I am calm now because the moment of decision has come and passed, and I cannot rescind the choice I have made. But the calm is at best a truce: uncertain, embattled, dangerous to him who rests in it too confidently.

The next day or the next, the clash of arms will begin again: the battle of myself with myself, of man with his ambient world—and with his God, whose call to love is always and most strangely a call to bloody conflict.

The mystery of evil is the deepest one of all. It is the mystery of the primal creative act, when God called into existence the human soul, made in His own image, and presented it with the terrifying choice: to center itself upon itself, or to center itself upon Him, without Whom it could not subsist at all. . . . The mystery renews itself daily in me, as it does in every man born of woman.

Where do I go? Where do I turn? I am called like Moses to the mountaintop to intercede for my people. I cannot go down until they carry me down dead. I cannot go up until God elects to call me to Himself. The most I can expect of my brothers in the Church is that they will hold up my arms when I grow weary of this life-long intercession. . . . And here is the shape of another mystery: that I who am called to spend so much find myself so poor in the things that are of God. . . .

"Forgive us our trespasses, as we forgive those who trespass against us. And lead us not into temptation, but deliver us from evil. Amen."

New York, March 1961—Sydney, August 1962

THE CLOWNS
OF GOD

For
my loved ones
with
my heart's thanks

AUTHOR'S NOTE

Once you accept the existence of God—however you define Him, however you explain your relationship to Him—then you are caught forever with His presence in the center of all things. You are also caught with the fact that man is a creature who walks in two worlds and traces upon the walls of his cave the wonders and the nightmare experiences of his spiritual pilgrimage.

Who knows but the world may end tonight?

—ROBERT BROWNING,
"The Last Ride Together"

PROLOGUE

In the seventh year of his reign, two days before his sixty-fifth birthday, in the presence of a full consistory of Cardinals, Jean Marie Barette, Pope Gregory XVII, signed an instrument of abdication, took off the Fisherman's ring, handed his seal to the Cardinal Camerlengo and made a curt speech of farewell.

"So, my brethren! It is done as you demanded. I am sure you will explain it all adequately to the Church and to the world. I hope you will elect yourselves a good man. God knows you will need him!"

Three hours later, accompanied by a colonel of the Swiss Guard, he presented himself at the Monastery of Monte Cassino and placed himself under the obedience of the Abbot. The colonel drove immediately back to Rome and reported to the Cardinal Camerlengo that his mission was accomplished.

The Camerlengo breathed a long sigh of relief and set about the formalities of proclaiming that the See of Peter was vacant and that an election would be held with all possible speed.

BOOK ONE

*I was in the spirit on the Lord's day and
I heard behind me a great voice, as of a
trumpet, saying: . . . What thou seest write
in a book and send it to the seven churches.*

—Revelation of St. John the Divine
1:10–11

I

SHE looked like a country woman, stout, apple-cheeked, dressed in coarse woollen stuff, her wispy grey hair trailing from under a straw hat. She sat bolt upright in the chair, hands folded over a large old-fashioned handbag of brown leather. She was wary but unafraid, as if she were studying the merchandise in an unfamiliar market.

Carl Mendelius, Professor of Biblical and Patristic Studies at the Wilhelmsstift, once called the Illustrious College of the University of Tübingen, stretched his legs under the desk, made a bridge of his fingertips and smiled at her over the top of it. He prompted her gently:

"You wanted to see me, madame?"

"I was told you understand French?" She spoke with the broad accent of the Midi.

"I do."

"My name is Thérèse Mathieu. In religion I am—I was—called Sister Mechtilda."

"Am I to understand that you have left the convent?"

"I was dispensed from my vows. But he said I should always wear the ring from my profession day, because I was still in the service of the Lord."

She held up a large work-worn hand and displayed the plain silver band on the wedding finger.

"He? Who is *he?*"

"His Holiness, Pope Gregory. I was with the sisters who work in his household. I cleaned his study and his private rooms. I served his coffee. Sometimes, on feast days, while the other sisters were resting, I prepared a meal for him. He said he liked my cooking. It reminded him of home. . . . He would talk to me then. He knew my birthplace very well. His family used to own vineyards in the Var. . . . When my niece was left a widow with five young children and the restaurant to keep going, I told him about it. He was very sympathetic. He said perhaps my niece needed me more than the Pope, who had too many servants anyway. He helped me to think freely and understand that charity was the most important of virtues. . . . My decision to return to the world was made at the time when the people in the Vatican began to say all those terrible things—that the Holy Father was sick in the head, that he could be dangerous—all that. The day I left Rome I went to ask his blessing. He asked me, as a special favour, to come to Tübingen and give his letter into your hands. He put me under obedience to tell no one what he had said or what I was carrying. So, I am here. . . ."

She fished in the leather bag, brought out a thick envelope and passed it across the desk. Carl Mendelius held it in his hands, weighing it. Then he laid it aside. He asked:

"You came straight here from Rome?"

"No. I went to my niece and stayed for a week. His Holiness said I should do that. It was natural and proper. He gave me money for the journey and a gift to help my niece."

"Did he give you any other message for me?"

"Only that he sent you his love. He told me, if you asked any questions, I should answer them."

"He found himself a faithful messenger." Carl Mendelius was grave and gentle. "Would you like coffee?"

"No, thank you."

She folded her hands over the bag and waited, the perfect nun, even in her country homespun. Mendelius posed his next question with casual care.

"These problems, this talk in the Vatican, when did they begin? What caused them?"

"I know when." There was no hesitation in her answer. "When he came back from his visit to South America and the United States, he looked ill and tired. Then there were the visits of the Chinese and the Russians and the people from Africa which seemed to leave him much preoccupied. After they left he decided to go into retreat for two weeks at Monte Cassino. It was after his return that the troubles began. . . ."

"What sort of troubles?"

"I never really understood. You must know I was a very small personage, a sister doing domestic work. We were trained not to comment on matters which were not our concern. The Mother Superior frowned on gossip. But I noticed that the Holy Father looked ill, that he spent long hours in the chapel, that there were frequent meetings with members of the Curia, from which they would come out looking angry and muttering among themselves. I don't even remember the words—except once I heard Cardinal Arnaldo say: 'Dear God in heaven! We are treating with a madman!' "

"And the Holy Father, how did he seem to you?"

"With me he was always the same, kind and polite. But it was clear he was very worried. One day he asked me to fetch him some aspirin to take with his coffee. I asked whether I should call the physician. He gave me a strange little smile and said: 'Sister Mechtilda, it is not a doctor I need but the gift of tongues. Sometimes it seems I am teaching music to the deaf and painting to the blind.' . . . In the end, of course, his doctor did come and then several others on different days. Afterwards, Cardinal Drexel came to see him—he's the Dean of the Sacred College and a very stern man. He spent the whole day in the Holy Father's apartment. I helped to serve them lunch. After that, well . . . it all happened."

"Did you understand anything of what was going on?"

"No. All we were told was that for reasons of health and for the welfare of souls, the Holy Father had decided to abdicate and devote the rest of his life to God in a monastery. We were asked to pray for him and for the Church."

"And he made no explanation to you?"

"To me?" She stared at him with innocent surprise. "Why to me? I was a nobody. But after he blessed me for the journey, he put his hands on my cheeks and said: 'Perhaps, little Sister, we are both lucky to have found each other.' That was the last time I saw him."

"And now what will you do?"

"Go home to my niece, help her with the children, cook in the restaurant. It is small, but a good business if we can hold it together."

"I'm sure you will," said Carl Mendelius respectfully. He stood up and held out his hand. "Thank you, Sister Mechtilda. Thank you for coming to see me— for what you have done for him."

"It was nothing. He was a good man. He understood how ordinary folk feel."

The skin of her palm was dry and chapped, from dishwater and the scrubbing pail. He felt ashamed of his own soft clerkly palms into which Gregory XVII, Successor to the Prince of the Apostles, had consigned his last, most secret memorial.

He sat late that night, in his big attic study, whose leaded windows looked out on the grey bulk of the Stiftskirche of St. George. The only witnesses to his meditation were the marble busts of Melanchthon and Hegel, the one a lecturer, the other a pupil in the ancient university; but they were dead long since and absolved from perplexity.

The letter from Jean Marie Barette, seventeenth Gregory in the papal line, lay spread before him: thirty pages of fine cursive script, impeccable in its Gallic style, the record of a personal tragedy and a political crisis of global dimension.

> My dear Carl,
>
> In this, the long dark night of my soul, when reason staggers and the faith of a lifetime seems almost lost, I turn to you for the grace of understanding.
>
> We have been friends a long time. Your books and your letters have travelled with me always: baggage more essential than my shirts and my shoes. Your counsels have calmed me in many an anxious moment. Your wisdom has been a light to my feet in the dark labyrinths of power. Though the lines of our lives have diverged, I like to believe that our spirits have maintained a unity.
>
> If I have been silent during these last months of purgation, it is because I have not wished to compromise you. For some time now I have been closely watched and I have been unable to guarantee the privacy even of

my most personal papers. Indeed, I have to tell you that if this letter falls into the wrong hands, you may be exposed to great risk; more, if you decide to carry out the mission I entrust to you, the danger will double itself every day.

I begin at the end of the story. Last month, the Cardinals of the Sacred College, among them some I believed to be friends, decided by a large majority that I was, if not insane, at least no longer mentally competent to discharge the duties of Pontiff. This decision, the reasons for which I shall explain in detail, placed them in a dilemma both comic and tragic.

There were only two ways to get rid of me: by deposition or abdication. To depose me they must show cause, and this, I believed, they would not dare attempt. The smell of conspiracy would be too strong, the risk of schism too great. Abdication, on the other hand, would be a legal act, which, if I were insane, I could not validly perform.

My personal dilemma was a different one. I had not asked to be elected. I had accepted fearfully, but trusting in the Holy Spirit for light and strength. I believed—and I am still trying desperately to believe—that the light was given to me in a very special fashion and that it was my duty to display it to a world caught already in the darkness of the last hour before midnight. On the other hand, without the support of my most senior collaborators, the hinge-men of the Church, I was impotent. My utterances could be distorted, my directives nullified. The children of God could be cast into confusion or misled into rebellion.

Then Drexel came to see me. He is, as you know, the Dean of the College of Cardinals, and it was I who appointed him Prefect of the Sacred Congregation for the Doctrine of the Faith. He is a formidable watchdog, as you have good reason to know. In private, however, he is a compassionate and understanding man. He was at pains to be precise. He was the emissary of his brother Cardinals. He dissented from their opinion but was charged to deliver their decision. They required me to abdicate and retire to obscurity in a monastery. If I refused they would, in spite of all the risks, take steps to have me declared legally insane and placed in confinement under medical supervision.

I was, as you may imagine, deeply shocked. I had not believed they would dare so much. Then came a moment of pure terror. I knew enough of the history of this office and its incumbents to see that the threat was real. Vatican City is an independent state and for what is done within its walls there is no outside audit.

Then the terror passed and I asked, calmly enough, what Drexel himself thought of the situation. He answered without hesitation. He had no doubt that his colleagues could and would make good their threat. The damage, in a critical time, would be great, but not irreparable. The Church had survived the Theophylacts and the Borgias and the debauches of Avignon. It would survive the moon madness of Jean Marie Barette. It was Drexel's private opinion, offered in friendship, that I should bow to the inevitable and abdicate on the grounds of ill health. Then he added a rider which I quote for you verbatim: "Do what they ask, Holiness—but no more, not by a fraction! You will go. You will retire into privacy. I myself will challenge any document that attempts to bind you to more. As to this light which you claim to have been given, I cannot judge whether it is from God or whether it is the illusion of an overburdened spirit. If it is an illusion, I hope you will not cherish it too long. If it is from God, then He will enable you, in His own time, to make it manifest. . . . But if you are declared insane, then you will be totally discredited and the light will be quenched forever. History, especially Church history, is always written to justify the survivors."

I understood what he was telling me, but I still could not accept so trenchant a solution. We talked all day, examining every possible option. I prayed alone far into the night. Finally, in utter weariness, I surrendered. At nine the next morning I summoned Drexel and told him I was prepared to abdicate.

That, my dear Carl, was *how* it happened. The why will take much longer to tell; then you, too, will be forced to sit in judgment on me. Even as I write these words I fear lest your verdict may be against me. So much for human frailty! I have not yet learned to trust the Lord whose gospel I proclaim! . . .

The poignant appeal moved Mendelius deeply. The script blurred before his aching eyes. He leaned back in his chair and surrendered himself to memory. They had met in Rome more than two decades ago, when Jean Marie Barette was Cardinal Deacon, the youngest member of the Curia, and Father Carl Mendelius, S.J., was teaching his first course on the elements of scriptural interpretation at the Gregorian University. The young Cardinal had been a guest at his lecture on Judaic communities in the early Church. Afterwards, they had dined together and talked, long into the night. When they parted they were already friends.

In the bad days, after Mendelius had been delated on suspicion of heresy to the Congregation for the Doctrine of the Faith, Jean Marie Barette had supported him through long months of inquisition. When his priestly vocation no longer satisfied him he had asked to be laicized and dispensed to marry. Barette had pleaded his cause with a reluctant and irascible Pontiff. When he applied for the chair at Tübingen, the most glowing recommendation had been signed "Gregorius XVII, Pont. Max."

Now, their positions were reversed. Jean Marie Barette was in exile, while Carl Mendelius flourished in the free zone of a happy marriage and a full professional life. Whatever the cost, he must discharge the debts of friendship. He bent again to the study of the letter.

. . . You know the circumstances of my election. My predecessor, our populist Pope, had fulfilled his mission. He had centralized the Church again. He had tightened discipline. He had restated the traditional dogmatic line. His enormous personal charm—the charm of a great actor—had masked for a long time his essentially rigorist attitudes. In his old age he had become more intolerant, less and less open to argument. He saw himself as the Hammer of God, smiting the forces of the ungodly. It was hard to convince him that, unless a miracle happened, there might be no men left at all—godly or ungodly. We were in the last decade of the century and only a stride away from global war. When I assumed office, a compromise choice after a six-day conclave, I was terrified.

I do not need to read you the whole apocalyptic text; the plight of the Third World thrust to the brink of starvation, the daily risk of economic collapse in the West, the soaring cost of energy, the wild armament race, the temptation for the militarists to make their last mad gamble while they could still calculate the atomic odds. For me the most frightening phenomenon was the atmosphere of creeping despair among world leaders, the sense of official impotence, the strange atavistic regression to a magical view of the universe.

You and I had discussed many times the proliferation of new cults and their manipulation for profit and power. Fanaticism was exploding in the old religions as well. Some of our own fanatics wanted me to proclaim a Marian year, call for vast pilgrimages to all the shrines of the Virgin throughout the world. I told them I would have none of it. A panic of devotees was the last thing we needed.

I believed the best service the Church could offer was that of mediation with reason and with charity for all. It was also the task which I, as Pontiff, was best fitted to perform. I let it be known that I would go anywhere, receive anyone, in the cause of peace. I tried to make it clear that I had no magical formulae, no illusions of power. I knew too well the deadly inertia of institutions, the mathematical madness that makes men fight to the death over the simplest equation of compromise. I told myself, I tried to convince the leaders of nations, that even one year's deferment of Armageddon would be a victory. Nevertheless, the fear of an impending holocaust haunted me day and night, sapped my reserves of courage and confidence.

Finally, I decided that, to keep any sense of perspective, I must rest awhile and rebuild my spiritual resources. So I went into retreat for two weeks at the Monastery of Monte Cassino. You know the place well. It was founded by St. Benedict in the sixth century. Paul the Deacon wrote his histories there. My namesake, Gregory IX, made there his peace with Frederick von Hohenstaufen. More than all, it was isolated and serene. Abbot Andrew was a man of singular discernment and piety. I would place myself under his spiritual direction and dedicate myself to a brief period of silence, meditation and inner renewal.

So I planned it, my dear Carl. So I began to do it. I had been there three days when the event took place.

The sentence ended at the bottom of a page. Mendelius hesitated before he turned it over. He felt a faint shiver of distaste as though he were being asked to witness an intimate bodily act. He had to force himself to continue the reading.

. . . I call it an event, because I do not wish to colour your appraisal of it, and also because, for me, it remains a fact of physical dimension. It happened. I did not imagine it. The experience was as real as the break-fast I had just eaten in the refectory.

It was nine in the morning, a clear sunny day. I was sitting on a stone bench in the cloister garden. A few yards away, one of the monks was hoeing a flower plot. I felt very placid, very relaxed. I began to read the fourteenth chapter of St. John's Gospel, which the Abbot had proposed for that day's meditation. You remember how it begins, with the discourse of Christ at his Last Supper: "Let not your heart be troubled. You believe in God; believe also in me. . . ." The text itself, full of comfort and reassur-ance, matched my mood. When I reached the verse "And he that loveth me shall be loved of my Father . . ." I closed the book and looked up.

Everything about me had changed. There was no monastery, no garden, no labouring monk. I was alone, on a high, barren peak. All about me were jagged mountains, black against a lurid sky. The place was still and silent as the grave. I felt no fear, only a terrible, bleak emptiness, as if the kernel of me had been scooped out and only the husk remained. I knew what I was seeing, the aftermath of man's ultimate folly—a dead planet. For what happened next I can find no adequate words. It was as if I were suddenly filled with flame, caught up in a fiery whirlwind, hurtled out of every human dimension into the center of a vast unendurable light. The light was a voice and the voice was a light, and it was as if I were being impregnated with its message. I was at the end of all, the beginning of all; the omega point of time, the alpha point of eternity. There were no symbols anymore, only the single simple Reality. Prophecy was fulfilled. Order was completed out of chaos, ultimate truth made manifest. In a moment of exquisite agony I understood that I must announce this event, prepare the world for it. I was called to proclaim that the Last Days were very near and that mankind should prepare for the Parousia: the Second Coming of the Lord Jesus.

Just when it seemed the agony would explode me into extinction it was over. I was back again in the cloister garden. The monk was hoeing his roses. The New Testament was on my lap, open now at the twenty-fourth chapter of Matthew: "For as the lightning cometh out of the east and appeareth even into the west . . . so shall the coming of the Son of Man be." Accident or omen? It did not seem to matter anymore.

And there you have it, Carl, as close as I can come to it in words, with the closest friend of my heart. When I tried to explain it to my colleagues back in Rome, I could see the shock in their faces: a Pope with a private revelation, a precursor of the Second Coming? Madness! The final explo-sive unreason! I was a walking time-bomb that must be defused as quickly as possible. And yet I could no more conceal what had happened to me than I could change the colour of my eyes. It was imprinted on every fiber of my being, like the genetic patterns of my parents. I was compelled to talk about it, doomed to announce it to a world rushing, heedless, towards extinction.

I began work on an encyclical, a letter to the Universal Church. It opened with the words: *"In his ultimis annis fatalibus . . .* In these last fateful years of the millennium . . ." My secretary found the draft on my desk, photographed it in secret and distributed copies to the Curia. They were horrified. Separately and in concert, they urged me to suppress the document. When I refused, they put my apartments under virtual siege, and blocked all my communications with the outside world. Then they summoned an emergency meeting of the Sacred College, brought in a team of physicians and psychiatrists to report on my mental state, and thus set in train the events which led to my abdication.

Now, in my extremity, I turn to you, not only because you are my friend, but because you, too, have been under inquisition and you understand how reason rocks under the relentless pressure of questioning. If you judge that I am insane, then I absolve you in advance from any blame and thank you for the friendship we have been privileged to share.

If you can go halfway to believing that I have told you a simple, terrible truth, then study the two documents appended to this letter: a copy of my unpublished encyclical to the Universal Church and a list of people in various countries with whom I established friendly relations during my pontificate and who may still be prepared to trust me or a messenger from me. Try to contact them, make them aware of what they can still do in these last fateful years. I do not believe we can hold back the inevitable cataclysm, but I am commanded to continue to the end the proclamation of the good news of love and salvation.

If you accept to do this, you will be at great risk—perhaps even of your life. Remember the Gospel of Matthew: "Then they shall deliver you up to be afflicted and shall put you to death . . . and many shall be scandalized and betray one another and hate one another."

I shall soon leave this place for the solitude of Monte Cassino. I trust I may arrive safely. If not, I commend myself as I commend you and your family, to God's loving care.

It is very late. The mercy of sleep has long been denied me, but now that this letter is written, perhaps it will be granted.

I am, yours always in Christ,
Jean Marie Barette

Under the signature was scrawled a brief ironic addendum: *"Feu le Pape."* Lately the Pope.

Carl Mendelius was numb with shock and fatigue. He could not bring himself to read the close-written text of the encyclical. The long list of names and countries might have been written in Sanskrit. He folded the letter and the documents together, then locked them in the old black safe where he kept the deeds of his house, his insurance policies and the most precious portions of his research material.

Lotte would be waiting for him downstairs, knitting placidly at the fireside. He could not face her until he had composed himself and framed some kind of answer to her inevitable questions: "What did the letter say, Carl? What really happened to our dear Jean Marie?"

What indeed . . . ? Whatever else Carl Mendelius might be—failed priest, doting husband, puzzled father, skeptical believer—he was a scholarly historian, rigid in his application of the rules of internal and external evidence. He could smell a textual interpolation a mile away, trace it with meticulous accuracy back to its source, Gnostic, Manichean or Essene.

He knew that the doctrine of the Parousia—the Second Coming of the Redeemer which would mark the end of all temporal things—was the oldest and most authentic in tradition. It was recorded in the Synoptic Gospels, enshrined in the Creed, recalled every day in the liturgy: "Christ died, Christ is risen, Christ will come again." It represented the deepest hope of the believer for the final justification of the divine plan, the ultimate victory of order over chaos, of good over evil. That Jean Marie Barette, lately a Pope, should believe it, preach it as an article of faith, was as natural and necessary as breathing.

But that he should be committed to the narrowest, most primitive form of the belief—an imminent universal cataclysm, followed by a universal judgment, for which the elect must prepare themselves—was, to say the least, disquieting. The millenarian tradition took many forms, not all of them religious. It was implicit in Hitler's idea of the thousand-year Reich, in the Marxist promise that capitalism would wither away and give place to the universal brotherhood of socialism. Jean Marie Barette had needed no vision to shape his version of the millennium. He could have plucked it ready-made out of a hundred sources, from the Book of Daniel to the Cévenol prophets of the seventeenth century.

Even his purported vision was a familiar and disturbing element in the pattern. The minister of an organized religion was called and ordained to expound, under authority, a doctrine fixed and agreed long since. If he exceeded his commission he could be silenced or excommunicated by the same authority that called him.

The prophet was another kind of creature altogether. He claimed a direct communication with the Almighty. Therefore, his commission could not be withdrawn by any human agent. He could challenge the most sacred past with the classic phrase, used by Jesus himself: "It is written thus . . . but I tell thus and thus." So the prophet was always the alien, the herald of change, the challenger of existing order.

The problem of the Cardinals was not the madness of Jean Marie Barette, but that he had accepted the official function of high priest and supreme teacher, and then assumed another, possibly a contradictory, role.

In theory, of course, there need be no contradiction. The doctrine of private revelation, of a direct personal communication between Creator and creature, was as ancient as that of the Parousia. The Spirit descending on the apostles at Pentecost, Saul struck down on the road to Damascus, John caught up to apocalyptic revelation on Patmos—all these were events hallowed in tradition. Was it so unthinkable that in this last fateful decade of the millennium, when the possibility of planetary destruction was a proven fact and a vivid danger, God might choose a new prophet to renew His call to repentance and salvation?

In theological terms it was, at least, an orthodox proposition. To Carl Mendelius, the historian, called to sit in judgment on the sanity of a friend, it was a highly dangerous speculation. However, he was too tired now to trust his judgment on the simplest matter; so he locked the door of his study and went downstairs.

Lotte, blond, plump, affectionate and contented as a cat in her role as mother of two and Frau Professor Mendelius, smiled up at him and lifted her face to be kissed. Caught in a sudden surge of passion he drew her to him and held her for a long moment.

She gave him a quizzical look and said, "What was that for?"

"I love you."

"I love you, too."

"Let's go to bed."

"I can't go yet. Johann telephoned to say he's forgotten his key. I said I'd wait up for him. Would you like a brandy?"

"Well, it's the next best thing."

As she poured the liquor she asked exactly the questions he had dreaded. He knew he could not fence with her. She was too intelligent for half-truths, so he told her flatly:

"The Cardinals forced him to abdicate, because they thought he was mad."

"Mad? Dear God! I should have said no one was more sane."

She handed him his drink and sat on the mat beside him, resting her head on his knees. They toasted each other. Mendelius stroked her forehead and her hair. She asked again:

"Why did they think he was mad?"

"Because he claimed to them—as he has to me—that he had a private revelation that the end of the world was near and that he was the precursor of the Second Coming!"

"What?" She gagged on the liquor. Mendelius passed her his handkerchief to mop her blouse.

"It's true, liebchen. He describes the experience in his letter. He believes it absolutely. Now that he is silenced he wants me to help spread the news."

"I still can't believe it. He was always so—so French and practical. Perhaps he has gone crazy."

"A crazy man could not have written the letter he wrote to me. A delusion, a fixed idea—that I could accept. It can happen, as a result of stress, or even as a result of a defective exercise in logic. Sane men once believed the world was flat. Sane people run their lives by the horoscopes in the evening papers. . . . Millions, like you and me, believe in a God they can't prove."

"But we don't go round saying the world's going to end tomorrow!"

"No, liebchen, we don't. But we do know it could, if the Russians and the Americans press the red button. We all live under the shadow of that reality. Our children are as aware of it as we are."

"Don't, Carl, please!"

"I'm sorry." He bent and kissed the top of her hair and then she pressed his hand against her cheek.

A few moments later she asked, quietly, "Are you going to do what Jean Marie wants?"

"I don't know, Lotte. Truly I don't. I'll have to think about it carefully. I'll need to talk to people who were close to him. Afterwards I'll want to see him . . . I owe him that much. We both owe it to him."

"That means you'll have to go away."

"Only for a little while."

"I hate it when you're away. I miss you so much."

"Come with me then. It's ages since you've been to Rome. You'd have lots of people to see."

"I can't, Carl. You know that. The children need me. This is a big year for Johann and I like to keep an eye on Katrin and her young man."

It was the small familiar contention between them: Lotte's constant clucking over her grown children, and his own middle-aged jealousy of her attention. But tonight he was too tired for argument, so he deferred the issue.

"We'll talk about it another time, liebchen. I need some professional counsel before I move a step out of Tübingen."

At fifty-three, Anneliese Meissner had achieved a variety of academic distinctions—the most notable of which was to be voted unanimously the ugliest woman in any faculty of the university. She was squat, fat and sallow, with a frog mouth and eyes scarcely visible behind thick myopic lenses. Her hair was a Medusa mess of faded yellow and her voice a hoarse rasp. Her dress was mannish and always ruinously untidy. Add to all that a sardonic wit and a merciless contempt for mediocrity and you had, as one colleague put it, "the perfect profile of a personality doomed to alienation."

Yet, by some miracle, she had escaped the doom and established herself as a kind of tutelary goddess in the shadow of the old castle of Hohentübingen. Her apartment on the Burgsteige was more like a club than a dwelling place, where students and faculty perched on stools and boxes to drink wine and make fierce debate until the small hours. Her lectures in clinical psychology were packed and her papers were published in learned journals in a dozen languages. She was even credited in student myth with a lover, a troll-like creature who lived in the Harz Mountains and who came to visit her in secret on Sundays and the greater holidays of the university calendar.

The day after he received Jean Marie's letter, Carl Mendelius invited her to lunch in a private booth at the Weinstube Forelle. Anneliese Meissner ate and drank copiously, yet still managed to deliver waspish monologues on the administration of university funds, the local politics of Land Baden-Württemberg, a colleague's paper on endogenous depression, which she dismissed as "puerile rubbish," and the sexual lives of Turkish labourers in the local paper industry. They were already at the coffee before Mendelius judged it wise to ask his question.

"If I were to show you a letter, would you be able to offer a clinical opinion on the person who wrote it?"

She fixed him with a myopic stare and smiled. The smile was terrifying. It was as if she were about to gobble him up with the crumbs of her strudel. "Are you going to show me the letter, Carl?"

"If you'll accept it as a professional and privileged communication."

"From you, Carl, yes. But before you give it to me, you'd better understand a few axioms in my discipline. I don't want you to communicate a document that's obviously important to you and then complain because my commentary's inadequate. Understood?"

"Understood."

"First then: handwriting, in serial specimens, is a fairly reliable indicator to cerebral states. Even simple hypoxia—the inadequate oxygen supply to the brain—will produce rapid deterioration of the script. Second: even in the gravest psychotic illnesses, the subject may have lucid periods in which his writings or utterances are completely rational. Hölderlin died in this town of ours a hopeless schizophrenic. But would you guess it from reading *Bread and Wine* or *Empedocles on Etna?* Nietzsche died of general paralysis of the insane, probably due to syphilitic infection. Could you diagnose that, solely on the evidence of *Thus Spake Zarathustra?* Third point: any personal letter contains indications of emotional states or even psychic propensities; but they are indicators only. The states may be shallow, the propensities well within the confines of normality. Do I make myself clear?"

"Admirably, Professor!" Carl Mendelius made a comical gesture of surrender. "I place my letter in safe hands." He passed it to her across the table. "There are other documents as well, but I have not yet had time to study them. The author is Pope Gregory the Seventeeth, who abdicated last week."

Anneliese Meissner pursed her thick lips in a whistle of surprise but said nothing. She read the letter slowly, without comment, while Mendelius sipped his coffee and munched petits fours—bad for the waistline but better than the cigarette habit which he was trying desperately to abandon. Finally Anneliese finished her reading. She laid the letter on the table in front of her and covered it with her big pudgy hands. She chose her first words with clinical care.

"I am not sure, Carl, that I am the right person to comment on this. I am not a believer, never have been. Whatever may be the faculty that enables one to make the leap from reason to faith, I have never had it. Some people are tone-deaf; others are colour-blind. I am incurably atheist. I have often regretted it. In clinical work I have sometimes felt handicapped when dealing with patients who have strong religious beliefs. You see, Carl"—she gave a long, wheezing chuckle—"according to my lights, you and all your kind live in a fixed delusional state, which is, by definition, insanity. On the other hand, since I can't disprove your delusions, I have to accept that I may be the sick one."

Mendelius grinned at her and popped the last petit four into his mouth.

"We've already agreed that your conclusions will be subject to large qualification. Your reputation will be safe with me."

"So, the evidence as I read it." She picked up the letter and began her annotation. "Handwriting: no evidence of disturbance. It's a beautiful regular script. The letter itself is precise and logical. The narrative sections are classically simple. The emotions of the writer are under control. Even when he speaks of being under surveillance, there is no overemphasis to indicate a paranoid state. The section dealing with the visionary experience is, within its limits, clear. There are no pathological images, with either a violent or a sexual connotation. . . . Prima facie, therefore, the man who wrote the letter was sane when he wrote it."

"But he does express doubts about his own sanity."

"In fact he does not. He recognizes that others may have doubts about it. He is absolutely convinced of the reality of his visionary experience."

"And what do you think of that experience?"

"I am convinced that he had it. How I would interpret it is another matter. In the same fashion I am convinced that Martin Luther believed he saw the Devil in his cell and pitched an inkwell at him. That doesn't mean I believe in the devil, only in the reality of the experience to Luther." She laughed again, and went on in a more relaxed fashion. "You're an old Jesuit, Carl. You know what I'm talking about. I deal with delusional patients all the time. I have to start with the premise that their delusions are real to them."

"So you're saying Jean Marie is a delusional subject?"

"Don't put the words in my mouth, Carl!" Her reproof was instant and sharp. She thrust the letter towards him. "Take another look at the vision passage again, and the pieces before and after. It falls exactly into a daydream structure. He is reading and meditating in a sunny garden. All meditation involves some degree of auto-hypnosis. He dreams in two parts: the aftermath of the cataclysm on an empty earth, and then the whirling fiery passage to outer space. Both these images are vivid but essentially banal. They could have been culled from any good science fiction film. He has celebrated them many times before. Now he daydreams them. When he wakes he is back in the garden. It's a common phenomenon."

"But he believes it is a supernatural intervention."

"He *says* he does."

"What the hell do you mean?"

"I mean," said Anneliese Meissner flatly, "he could be lying!"

"No! It's impossible! I know this man. We're close as brothers."

"An unfortunate analogy," said Anneliese Meissner mildly. "Sibling relationships can be infernally complicated. Simmer down, Carl! You wanted a professional opinion, you're getting it. At least take time to examine a reasonable hypothesis."

"This one is pure fantasy!"

"Is it? You're an historian. Think back. How many convenient miracles can you name? How many most timely revelations? Every sect in the world has to provide them for its devotees. The Mormons have Joseph Smith and his fabulous golden plates; the Reverend Sun Myung Moon made himself the Lord of the Second Advent, even Jesus bowed down to worship him. So suppose, Carl— just suppose!—your Gregory the Seventeenth decided that this was crisis time for the institution and that the moment was ripe for some new manifestation of divine involvement."

"Then he was taking a hell of a gamble."

"And he lost it. Might he not now be seeking to recover something out of the wreckage, and using you to do it?"

"It's a monstrous idea!"

"Not to me. Why are you choking on it? I'll tell you. Because, though you like to believe you're a liberal thinker, you're still a member of the Roman Catholic family. For your own sake you have to protect the mythos. I noticed you didn't wince when I mentioned the Mormons and the Moonies. Come on, my friend! Where's your mind?"

"It seems I've mislaid it." Carl Mendelius was grim.

"If you take my advice, you'll drop the whole affair."

"Why?"

"You're a scholar with an international reputation. You want no truck with madness or folk magic."

"Jean Marie is my friend. I owe him at least an honest enquiry."

"Then you'll need a *Beisitzer*—an assessor to help you weigh the evidence."

"How would you like the job, Anneliese? It might give you some new clinical insights."

He said it as a joke to take the sting out of their discussion. The joke fell flat.

Anneliese weighed the proposition for a long moment and then announced firmly, "Very well. I'll do it. It'll be a new experience to play inquisitor to a Pope. But, dear colleague"—she reached out and laid her big hand on his wrist —"I'm much more interested in keeping you honest!"

When his last lecture was over, late in the afternoon, Carl Mendelius walked down to the river and sat a long time, watching the stately passage of swans on the grey water.

Anneliese Meissner had left him deeply disturbed. She had challenged not only his relationship with Jean Marie Barette, but his integrity as a scholar, his moral stance as a seeker after truth. She had probed shrewdly at the weakest point in his intellectual armour: his inclination to make more tender judgments about his own religious family than about others. For all his skeptic bent, he was still god-haunted, conditioned to the pavlovian reflexes of his Jesuit past. He would rather conform his findings as an historian with orthodox tradition than deal bluntly with the contradictions between the two. He preferred the comfort of a familiar hearth to the solitude of the innovator. So far, he had not betrayed himself. He could still look in the mirror and respect the man he saw. But the danger was there, like a small prickling lust, ready to take fire at the right moment with the right woman.

In the case of Jean Marie Barette, the danger of self-betrayal could be mortal. The issue was clear and he could not gloss or hedge it. There were three possibilities, mutually exclusive. Jean Marie was a madman. Jean Marie was a liar. Jean Marie was a man touched by God, charged to deliver a momentous revelation.

He had two choices: refuse to be involved—which was the right of any honest man who felt himself incompetent—or submit the whole case to the most rigid scrutiny, and act without fear or favour on the evidence. With Anneliese Meissner, brusque and uncompromising, as his *Beisitzer* he could hardly do otherwise.

But what of Jean Marie Barette, longtime friend of the heart? How would he react when the harsh terms of reference were set before him? How would he feel when the friend he sought as advocate presented himself as the Grand Inquisitor? Once again Carl Mendelius found himself flinching from the confrontation.

Far away towards the Klinikum an ambulance siren sounded—a long, repetitive wail, eerie in the gathering dusk. Mendelius shivered under the impact of a childhood memory: the sound of air-raid sirens, and after it, the drone of aircraft and the shattering explosions of the fire bombs that rained down on Dresden.

When he arrived home, he found the family huddled around the television screen. The new Pope had been elected in an afternoon session of the conclave and was now being proclaimed as Leo XIV. There was no magic in the occasion. The commentaries were without enthusiasm. Even the Roman crowd seemed listless and the traditional acclamations had a hollow ring.

Their Pontiff was sixty-nine years old, a stout man with an eagle's beak, a cold eye, a rasping Aemilian accent and twenty-five years' practice in Curial business behind him. His election was the outcome of a careful but painfully obvious piece of statecraft.

After two foreign incumbents, they needed an Italian who understood the rules of the papal game. After an actor turned zealot and a diplomat turned mystic the safest choice was Roberto Arnaldo, a bureaucrat with ice water in his veins. He would raise no passions, proclaim no visions. He would make none but the most necessary pronouncements; and these would be so carefully wrapped in Italian rhetoric that the liberals and the conservatives would swallow them with equal satisfaction. Most important of all, he suffered from gout and high cholesterol and, according to the actuaries, should enjoy a reign neither too short nor too long.

The news kept the conversation going at Mendelius' dining table. He was glad of the diversion, because Johann was moody over an essay that would not come right, Katrin was snappish and Lotte was at the low point of one of her menopausal depressions. It was an evening when he wondered with wry humour whether the celibate life had not a great deal to recommend it, and a noncelibate bachelor existence, even more. However, he was practiced enough in marriage to keep that kind of thought to himself.

When the meal was over he retired to his study and made a telephone call to Herman Frank, director of the German Academy of Fine Arts in Rome.

"Herman? This is Carl Mendelius. I'm calling to ask a favour. I'm coming to Rome for a week or ten days at the end of the month. Could you put me up?"

"Delighted!" Frank was a silver-haired courtly fellow, an historian of Cinquecento painters, who kept one of the best tables in Rome. "Will Lotte be coming with you? We've got acres of space."

"Possibly. It's not decided yet."

"Bring her! Hilde would be delighted. She needs some girl company."

"Thanks, Herman. You're very kind."

"Not at all. You might be able to do me a favour, too."

"Name it."

"While you're here the Academy will be playing host to a group of Evangelical pastors. The usual thing—daily lectures, evening discussions, afternoon bus rides. It would be a great feather in my cap if I could announce that the great Mendelius would give a couple of lectures, perhaps conduct a group discussion . . . ?"

"Happy to do it, my friend."

"Wonderful! Wonderful! Let me know when you're arriving and I'll pick you up at the airport. . . ."

Mendelius put down the receiver and gave a chuckle of satisfaction. Herman Frank's invitation to lecture was a stroke of good fortune. The German Academy was one of the oldest and most prestigious national academies in Rome. Founded in 1910 in the reign of Wilhelm II of Prussia, it had survived two wars and the mindless ideologues of the Third Reich and still managed to maintain a reputation for solid Germanic scholarship. It offered Mendelius, therefore, a base of operations and a highly respectable cover for his delicate enquiries.

The German contingent at the Vatican would respond happily to a dinner invitation from Herman Frank. His guest book was an elaborate tome resplendent with exotic titles like "Rector Magnificent of the Pontifical Biblical Institute" and "Grand Chancellor of the Institute of Biblical Archaeology." How Lotte would respond to the idea was another matter. He needed a more propitious moment to open that little surprise packet.

His next step was to prepare a list of contacts to whom he should write and announce his visit. He had been a denizen of the city long enough to assemble a miscellany of friends and acquaintances, from the crusty old Cardinal who disapproved his defection but was still generous enough to appreciate his scholarship, to the Custodian of Incunabula in the Vatican Library and the last dowager of the Pierleoni, who directed the gossips of Rome from her wheelchair. He was still dredging up names when Lotte came in, carrying a tray of coffee. She looked penitent and forlorn, uncertain of her welcome.

"The children have gone out. It's lonely downstairs. Do you mind if I sit up here with you?"

He took her in his arms and kissed her. "It's lonely up here too, liebchen. Sit down and relax. I'll pour the coffee."

"What are you doing?"

"Arranging our holiday."

He told her of his talk with Herman Frank. He enthused about the pleasures of the city in summer, the opportunity to meet old friends, do a little touring. She took it all with surprising calm. Then she asked:

"It's really about Jean Marie, isn't it?"

"Yes; but it's also about us. I want you with me, Lotte. I need you. If the children want to come, I'll arrange hostel accommodation for them."

"They have other plans, Carl. We were arguing about them before you came home. Katrin wants to go to Paris with her boyfriend. Johann is going hiking in Austria. That's fine for him; but Katrin . . ."

"Katrin's a woman now, liebchen. She'll do what she wants whether we approve or not. After all . . ." He bent and kissed her again. "They're only lent to us; and when they leave home we'll be left where we started. We'd better start practicing to be lovers again."

"I suppose so." She gave a small shrugging gesture of defeat. "But, Carl . . ." She broke off, as if afraid to put the thought into words.

Mendelius prompted her gently. "But what, liebchen?"

"I know the children will leave us. I'm getting used to the idea, truly I am. But what if Jean Marie takes you away from me? This—this thing he wants of you is very strange and frightening." Without warning she burst into convulsive sobbing. "I'm afraid, Carl . . . terribly, terribly afraid!"

II

"IN these last fateful years of the millennium . . ." Thus the opening line of Jean Marie Barette's unpublished encyclical. "In this dark time of confusion, violence and terror, I, Gregory, your brother in the flesh, your servant in Christ Jesus, am commanded by the Holy Spirit to write you these words of warning and of comfort. . . ."

Mendelius could hardly believe the evidence of his own eyes. Papal encyclicals, for all their portentous authority, were usually commonplace documents —stating traditional positions on matters of faith or morals. Any good theologian could frame the argument. Any good Latinist could make it eloquent.

The pattern was still that of the old rhetoricians. The argument was laid down. Scripture and the Fathers were quoted in support. Directives were given, binding the conscience of the faithful. There was a closing exhortation to faith, hope and continuing charity. The formal "we" was used throughout, not merely to express the dignity of the Pontiff but to connote a community and a continuity in the office and in the teaching. The implication was plain: the Pope taught nothing new; he expounded an ancient and unchangeable truth, simply applying it to the needs of his time.

At one stroke Jean Marie Barette had broken the pattern. He had abrogated the role of exegete and assumed the mantle of the prophet. "I, Gregory, am commanded by the Holy Spirit . . ." Even in the formal Latin, the impact of the words was shocking. No wonder the men of the Curia had blanched when they read them for the first time. What followed was even more tendentious:

. . . The comfort which I offer you is the abiding promise of our Lord Jesus Christ: "I will not leave you orphans. Behold I am with you all days, even to the end of the world." The warning I give you is that the end is very near, that this generation shall not pass until all these things be fulfilled . . . I do not tell you this of myself, or because I have predicated it upon human reason, but because it was shown to me in a vision, which I dare not conceal but am commanded to tell openly to the world. But even that revelation was no new thing. It was simply an affirmation, clear as sunrise, of what was revealed in the Holy Scriptures. . . .

There followed a long exposition of texts from the Synoptic Gospels, and a series of eloquent analogies between the biblical "signs" and the circumstances of the last decade of the twentieth century: wars and rumours of wars, famines and epidemics, false Christs and false prophets.

To Carl Mendelius, deeply and professionally versed in apocalyptic literature from the earliest times to the present, it was a disturbing and dangerous document. Emanating from so high a source it could not fail to raise alarm and panic. Among the militant it might easily serve as a rallying cry for one last crusade of the elect against the unrighteous. To the weak and the fearful it might even be an inducement to suicide before the horrors of the last times overtook them.

He asked himself what he would have done had he, like the secretary, seen it, new-written, on the Pontiff's desk. Without a doubt he would have urged its suppression. Which was exactly what the Cardinals had done: suppressed the document and silenced the author.

Then a new thought presented itself. Was not this the fate of all prophets, the price they paid for a terrible gift, the bloody seal of truth upon their soothsaying? Out of the welter of biblical eloquence another text echoed in his mind; the last lamentation of Christ over the Holy City.

"Jerusalem, Jerusalem, thou that killest the prophets and stonest them that are sent to thee! How often would I have gathered thy children as a hen gathers her chickens under her wings, but thou wouldst not! . . . Therefore the day will come when thine enemies will cast a trench about thee, and beat thee flat to the ground, and thy children who are in thee; and they shall not leave in thee a stone upon a stone, because thou hast not known the things that are to thy peace!"

It was an eerie thought for the midnight hour, with the moonlight streaming through the leaded windows and the cold wind searching down the Neckar valley and round the alleys of the old town where poor Hölderlin died mad and Melanchthon, sanest of men, taught that "God draws; but he draws the willing ones."

All his experience affirmed that Jean Marie Barette was the most willing, the most open of men, the least likely to fall victim to a fanatic's illusion.

True, he had written a wildly imprudent document. Yet, perhaps this was the core of the matter: that in the hour of extremity only such a folly could command the attention of the world.

But command it to what? If the final catastrophe were at hand, its date computed irrevocably into the mechanism of creation, then why proclaim it at all? What counsel could prevail against the nightmare knowledge? What prayer had potency against a rescript written from eternity? There was a deep pathos in Jean Marie's response to the questions:

. . . My dear brothers and sisters, my little children, we all fear death, we shrink from the suffering which may precede it. We quail from the mystery of the last leap, which we must all make, into eternity. But we are followers of the Lord, the Son of God who suffered and died in human flesh. We are the inheritors of the good news which he left with us: that death is the gateway to life, that it is a leap, not into darkness, but into the hands of Everlasting Mercy. It is an act of trust, an act of love, by which, as lovers do, we abandon ourselves to, become one with, the Beloved. . . .

The knock at the door startled Mendelius. His daughter, Katrin, entered, hesitant and timid. She was in her dressing gown, her blond hair tied back with a pink ribbon, her face scrubbed clean of make-up, her eyes red with weeping. She asked, "May I talk with you, Papa?"

"Of course, sweetheart." He was instantly solicitous. "What's the matter? You've been crying." He kissed her gently and led her to a chair. "Now tell me what's bothering you."

"This trip to Paris. Mother's still very angry about it. She says I have to discuss it with you. She doesn't understand, Papa—truly she doesn't. I'm nine-teen. I'm a woman now, just as much as she is and . . ."

"Take it easy, little one! Let's start from the beginning. You want to go to Paris for the summer. Who's going with you?"

"Franz, of course! You know we've been going together for ages now. You said you liked him very much."

"I do. He's a very nice young man. A promising painter, too. Are you in love with him?"

"Yes, I am." There was a note of defiance in the answer. "And he's in love with me!"

"Then I'm very happy for you both, little one!" He smiled and patted her hand. "It's the best feeling in the world. So what comes next? You've talked about marriage? You want to become engaged? Is that it?"

"No, Papa." She was very firm about it. "Not yet anyway. . . . And that's the point—Mama refuses to understand."

"Have you tried explaining it to her?"

"Over and over! But she just won't listen."

"Try *me* then," said Mendelius gently.

"It's not easy. I'm not good with words like you. The thing is, I'm afraid; we're both afraid."

"Of what?"

"Of always . . . just that. Of getting married and having children and try-ing to make a home, while the whole world could tumble round our ears in a day." Suddenly she was passionate and eloquent. "You older ones don't under-stand. You've survived a war. You've built things. You've had us; we're grown up. But look at the world you've left us! All along the borders there are rocket launchers and missile silos. The oil's running out so we're using atom power and burying the waste that will one day poison our children. . . . You've given us everything except tomorrow! I don't want my baby to be born in a bomb shelter and die of radiation sickness! All we've got is today and loving each other and we think we've got a right at least to that!"

Her vehemence shocked him like water dashed in his face. The little blond *Mädchen* he had dandled on his knee was gone forever. In her place was an angry young woman, filled with a deep resentment against himself and his whole generation. The grim thought struck him that perhaps it was for her and all the others like her that Jean Marie Barette had written his prescription for life in the last days. Certainly it was not the young ones who had suppressed it, but the men of his generation, the elders, the seeming wise, the perennial pragmatists, living, in any case, on borrowed time. He breathed a silent prayer for wisdom of the tongue and began softly and tenderly to reason with her.

". . . Believe me, little one, I understand how you feel, both of you. Your mother understands, too, but in a different way, because she knows how a woman can be hurt, and how the consequences can be longer for her than for a man. She fights with you because she loves you and she's afraid for you. . . . You see, whatever mess the world's in—and I've been sitting here reading how much more horrible it may get—you've had the experience of loving and being loved. Not the whole experience, yet, but some of it; so you do know what loving's about: giving and taking and caring and never grabbing the whole cake for yourself. . . . Now you're beginning the next chapter with your Franz, and only the pair of you can write it, together. If you botch it, the best your mother and I can do is dry your tears and hold your hand until you're ready to begin living again. . . . We can't tell you how to arrange your emotional lives, or even your sexual lives. All we can tell you is that if you waste your hearts and waste that special joy that makes sex so wonderful, it's something you can't renew. . . . You can find other experiences, other joys, too, but never again that first, special, very exclusive ecstasy that makes this whole confusion of living and dying worthwhile. . . . What more can I say, little one? Go to Paris with your Franz. Learn your loving together. As for tomorrow? . . . How's your Latin?"

She gave him a tearful smile "You know it's always been terrible."

"Try this. *'Quid sit futurum cras, fuge quaerere.'* Old Horace wrote it."

"It still means nothing."

"It's very simple. 'Forbear to ask what tomorrow may bring.' . . . If you spend your whole life waiting for the storm, you'll never enjoy the sunshine."

"O Papa!" She threw her arms round his neck and kissed him. "I love you so much! You've made me very happy."

"Go to bed, little one," said Carl Mendelius softly. "I've still got an hour's work ahead of me."

"You work too hard, Papa."

He gave her a small admonitory pat on the cheek and quoted lightly, "A father without work means a daughter without a dowry. Good night, my love. Golden dreams!"

When the door closed behind her, he felt the prickling of unbidden tears—tears for all the youthful hope in her, and all her threatened innocence. He blew his nose violently, picked up his spectacles and settled back to his reading of Jean Marie's apocalypse.

. . . It is clear that in the days of universal calamity the traditional structures of society will not survive. There will be a ferocious struggle for the simplest needs of life—food, water, fuel and shelter. Authority will be usurped by the strong and the cruel. Large urban societies will fragment themselves into tribal groups, each hostile to the other. Rural areas will be subject to pillage. The human person will be as much a prey as the beasts whom we now slaughter for food. Reason will be so clouded that man will resort for solace to the crudest and most violent forms of magic. It will be hard, even for those founded most strongly in the Promise of the Lord, to sustain their faith and continue to give witness, as they must do, even to the end. . . . How then must Christians comport themselves in these days of trial and terror?

. . . Since they will no longer be able to maintain themselves as large groups, they must divide themselves into small communities, each capable of sustaining itself by the exercise of a common faith and a true mutual charity. Their Christian witness must be given by spreading that charity outwards to those who are not of the faith, by aiding the distressed, by sharing even their most meager means with those who are most deprived. When the priestly hierarchy can no longer function, they will elect to themselves ministers and teachers who will maintain the Word in its integrity, and continue to conduct the Eucharist. . . .

"God Almighty! He's really done it now!" Mendelius heard his own voice echo round the attic room. Fiction or predestined fact, this, from the pen of a Pope, was the unsayable, the absolutely unprintable. If the press of the world got hold of it, they would make Jean Marie Barette look like the maddest of mad mullahs, the craziest of all prophets of doom. And yet, in the context of an atomic calamity, it was a matter of simple logic. It was a scenario which, in one form or another, every national leader kept locked in his most secret files, the script for the aftermath of Armageddon.

Which brought Mendelius, by a round turn, to the third and final document: the list of those who, Jean Marie thought, would be prepared to believe his message and his messenger. This was perhaps the most startling deposition of all. Unlike the letter and the encyclical it was typewritten, as if it had once formed part of an official file. It contained names, addresses, titles, telephone numbers, methods of private contact, and terse, telegraphic notes on each individual. There were politicians, industrialists, churchmen, leaders of dissident groups, editors of well-known journals, more than a hundred names in all. Two sample entries set the tone of the record.

U.S.A.

Name:	Michael Grant Morrow
Title:	Secretary of State
Private Address:	593 Park Avenue, New York
Telephone:	(212) 689-7611
Religion:	Episcopalian

Met at presidential dinner. Firm religious convictions. Speaks Russian, French and German. Respected in Russia but Asian relations weak. Deeply aware of hair-trigger situation on European frontiers. Has written a private monograph on the function of religious groups in a disintegrating social framework.

U.S.S.R.

Name:	Sergei Andrevich Petrov
Title:	Minister for Agricultural Production
Private Address:	Unknown
Telephone:	Moscow 53871

Private visit Vatican with nephew of Premier. Aware of need for religious and ethnic tolerance in U.S.S.R. and satellites, but unable make headway against party dogmatists. Concerned that Russia's problems with food supplies and oil may precipitate conflict. Close friends in high military; enemies in K.G.B. Vulnerable in event bad harvest or economic blockade.

On the last page was a note in Jean Marie's own handwriting:

All of the people on this list are known to me personally. Each in his own fashion has demonstrated an awareness of the crisis, and a willingness to confront it in a spirit of human compassion, if not always from the standpoint of a believer. Whether they will change under the pressure of coming events, I do not know. However, each has reposed a degree of trust in me and I have tried to return the gesture. As a private person you will be regarded at first with suspicion and they will be much more reserved with you. The risks of which I have warned you will begin at your first contact, because you will have no diplomatic protection, and the language of politics is contrived for the concealment of truth. J.M.B.

Carl Mendelius took off his spectacles and tried to palm the sleep out of his eyes. He had read his brief with the devotion of a friend and the care of an honest scholar. Now, in this lonely hour after midnight, he must pass judgment on the text, if not yet on the man who had written it. A sudden cold fear took hold of him, as if the shadows of the room were haunted by old accusing ghosts: the ghosts of men burned for heresy and women drowned for witchcraft and nameless martyrs bewailing the vanity of their sacrifice.

In these skeptical years of middle age, prayer did not come easily to him. Now he felt the need of it; but the words would not come. He was like a man locked in darkness so long that he had forgotten the sound of human speech.

"Now, we're really in cloud-cuckoo-land!" Anneliese Meissner munched on a pickled gherkin and washed it down with red wine. "This so-called encyclical is a nonsense—a hotchpotch of folklore and mysticism!"

They were sitting in her cluttered apartment, with the documents spread before them on the table and a bottle of Assmanshausen to keep down the dust that lay everywhere. Mendelius had refused to let the documents out of his sight, while Anneliese had demanded, with equal vehemence, the right of the assessor to read every line of evidence. Mendelius protested her curt dismissal of the document.

"Let's stop right there! If we're going to debate the issue let's be scientific about it. First of all there's a whole body of millenarian literature from the Book of Daniel in the Old Testament to Jakob Boehme in the seventeenth century and Teilhard de Chardin in the twentieth. Some of it is nonsense—yes! Some of it is high poetry like that of the Englishman William Blake. Some of it represents a critical interpretation of one of the oldest traditions in the world. Second, any serious scientist will tell you that there may be a term, by evolution or catastrophe, to human existence as we know it on the planet. What Jean Marie has written falls well within the saner confines of the codex. The scenario of catastrophe is already a matter of informed speculation by the scientists and military strategists."

"Agreed. But your man still makes a mishmash of it! Faith, hope and charity while the wolf-children are snarling at the gates! A loving God brooding over the chaos he himself has engineered. Balls, Professor!"

"What would happen if the text were published?"

"Half the world would laugh it out of court. The other half would catch the dancing madness and go waltzing out to meet the redeemer on his 'cloud of glory.' Seriously, Carl, I think you ought to burn the damned thing and forget it!"

"I can burn it; but I can't forget it."

"Because you're a victim of the same God-madness!"

"What about this third document—the list of names?"

"I don't see that it has any significance at all. It's an aide-mémoire pulled out of the filing cabinet. Every politician in the world keeps records like that. What does he expect you to do with it? Trot round the world visiting all these people? What will you say to them? 'My friend Gregory the Seventeenth, the one they tossed out of the Vatican, believes the end of the world is coming. He's had a vision about it. He thought you should have advance notice.' Come on, Carl! They'd have you in a straitjacket halfway through the first interview!"

Suddenly he saw the funny side of it and laughed, a great bellow of mirth that subsided finally into a helpless giggle. Anneliese Meissner splashed more wine into the glasses and lifted her own in salute.

"That's better! For a while I thought I'd lost a good colleague."

"Thank you, Frau Beisitzer." Mendelius took a long swallow of wine and set down his glass. "Now let's get back to business. I'm going to Rome in a couple of weeks."

"The hell you are!" She stared at him in disbelief. "And what good do you expect to do there?"

"Have a holiday, give a couple of lectures at the German Academy, talk to Jean Marie Barette and people who were close to him. I'll make tapes during or after each interview and send them back to you. Afterwards, I'll decide whether to drop the affair or not. At least I'll have discharged my duty as a friend—and I'll have kept my assessor honest, too!"

"I hope you realize, my friend, that even when you've done all that, your evidence will still be incomplete."

"I don't see why it need be."

"Think about it." Anneliese Meissner speared another gherkin and waved it under his nose. "How are you going to talk to God? Will you put him on tape, too?"

He was a tidy man by nature and he prepared for his visit to Rome with finical care. He made telephone calls to friends, wrote letters to acquaintances, armed himself with introductions to Vatican officials, made dates far in advance for lunches, dinners and formal interviews. He was careful to stress the overt purpose of his visit: a search in the Vatican Library and the Biblical Institute for fragments of Ebionite literature and a short series of discourses at the Academy on the apocalyptic tradition.

He had chosen the subject not only because it provided a cue on which to begin his enquiries about Jean Marie, but because it might elicit from his Evangelical audience some emotional response to the millennial theme. In his younger days he had been deeply stirred by the Jungian idea of the "great dreaming," the persistence of tribal experience in the subconscious, and its perennial influence on the individual and on the group. There was a striking similarity between this notion and that which the theologians called the "Infusion" and the "Indwelling of the Spirit." It raised also the question of Anneliese Meissner, his *Beisitzer,* and her obdurate rejection of any transcendental experience whatsoever. Her gibe about talking to God still rankled—the more because he had found no adequate answer to it.

He spent a long time over a letter to the Abbot of Monte Cassino, who was now Jean Marie's religious superior. This was a most necessary courtesy. Jean Marie had placed himself under obedience, and the exactions of authority could extend to his physical movements and even to his private correspondence. Mendelius, a onetime subject of the system, had a nice perception of religious protocol. His letter told of his long friendship with Jean Marie Barette, his diffidence about intruding upon his present privacy. However, if the Abbot had no objection and the former Pontiff were willing to receive him, Professor Carl Mendelius would like to pay a visit to the monastery at a mutually convenient date.

He enclosed a note which he begged the Abbot to deliver into the hands of Jean Marie Barette. This, too, he had composed with studious discretion.

> My dear friend,
>   Please forgive the informality, but I am ignorant of the protocol for correspondence with a retired Pope, who has made himself a humble son of St. Benedict.
>   I have always regretted that it was not possible for me to share the burdens of your final days in the Vatican; but German professors are two marks a dozen and their sphere of influence seldom extends beyond the lecture hall.
>   However, I shall soon be in Rome—still researching the Ebionites and giving some lectures on the doctrine of the Parousia at the German Academy—and it would give me a great pleasure to see you again, if only for a little while.
>   I have written to the Father Abbot asking his permission to visit you, provided always that you are in the mood to receive me. If we can meet I

shall be grateful and happy. If the time is not opportune, please do not hesitate to say so.

I trust you are well. With the world in such a mess I think you were wise to retire from it. Lotte sends you her most affectionate greetings and my children their respectful salutations. As for myself, I remain always

Yours in the Fellowship of the Lord,
Carl Mendelius

The answer came back in ten days, delivered by a clerical messenger from the Cardinal Archbishop of Munich: the Very Reverend Abbot Andrew would be happy to receive him at Monte Cassino, and, if his health permitted, the Very Reverend Jean Marie Barette, O.S.B., would be delighted to see his old friend. He should telephone the Abbot immediately upon his arrival in Rome, and an appointment would be arranged.

There was no response at all from Jean Marie.

The evening before he left for Rome with Lotte he asked his son, Johann, to have coffee with him in his study. They had been uneasy together for a long time now. The boy, a brilliant student in economics, was uncomfortable in the shadow of a father who was also a senior member of the faculty. The father was often clumsy in his eagerness to foster so obvious a talent. The result was secrecy on the one side, resentment on the other, with only a rare display of the affection that still existed between them. This time Mendelius was determined to be tactful. As usual he managed only to be heavy-handed. He asked:

"When do you leave on your trip, son?"

"Two days from now."

"Have you planned a route yet?"

"More or less. We go by train to Munich, then start hiking—through the Obersalzburg and over the Tauern into Carinthia."

"It's beautiful country. I wish I were coming with you. By the way"—he fished in his breast pocket and brought out a sealed envelope—"this is to help with the expenses."

"But you've already given me my holiday money."

"That's something extra. You've worked very hard this year. Your mother and I wanted to show our appreciation."

"Well . . . thanks." He was obviously embarrassed. "But there was no need. You've always been generous with me."

"There's something I want to say to you, son." He saw the boy stiffen immediately. The old mulish look came over his face. "It's a personal matter. I'd rather you didn't discuss it with your mother. One of the reasons I'm going to Rome is to investigate what brought about the abdication of Gregory the Seventeenth. As you know he was my dear friend. . . ." He gave a small wry smile. "Yours, too, I suppose, because without his help your mother and I might never have married and you wouldn't be here. . . . However, the enquiries may take a long time and entail a great deal of travel. There may also be certain risks. If anything happens to me, I want you to know my affairs are in order. Doctor Mahler, our lawyer, holds most of the documents. The rest are in the safe over there. You're a man now. You would have to step into my shoes and take care of your mother and sister."

"I don't understand. What sort of risks are you talking about? And why do you have to expose yourself to them?"

"It's difficult to explain."

"I'm your son." His tone was resentful. "At least give me a chance to understand."

"Please! Try to relax with me. I need you now, very much."

"I'm sorry, it's just that . . ."

"I know. We rub each other the wrong way. But I love you, son. I wish I could tell you how much." Emotion welled up in him and he wanted to reach out and embrace the young man, but he was afraid of a rebuff. He went on quietly, "To explain, I have to show you something secret and bind you on your honor not to reveal it to anyone."

"You have my word, Father."

"Thank you." Mendelius crossed to the safe, took out the Barette documents and handed them to his son. "Read those. They explain everything. When you're finished, we'll talk. I've got some notes to write up."

He settled himself at his desk while Johann sat in the armchair, poring over the documents. In the soft glow of the reading lamp he reminded Mendelius of one of Raffaello's young models, obedient and immobile, while the master made him immortal on canvas. He felt a pang of regret for the wasted years. This was the way it should have been, long ago: father and son, content and companionable, all childish quarrels long forgotten.

Mendelius got up and refilled Johann's coffee cup and brandy glass. Johann nodded his thanks and went on with his reading. It was nearly forty minutes before he turned the last page, sat for a long moment in silence, then folded the documents deliberately, got up and laid them on his father's desk. He said quietly:

"I understand now, Father. I think it's a dangerous nonsense and I hate to see you involved with it; but I do understand."

"Thank you, son. Would you care to tell me why you think it's a nonsense?"

"Yes." He was firm but respectful. He held himself very erect, like a subaltern addressing his commander. "There's something I've wanted to tell you for a long while. Now seems as good a time as any."

"Perhaps you'd like to pour me a brandy first." Mendelius smiled at him.

"Of course." He refilled the glass and set it on the desk. "The fact is, Father, I'm no longer a believer."

"In God, or specifically in the Roman Catholic Church?"

"In neither."

"I'm sorry to hear it, son." Mendelius was studiously calm. "I've always felt the world must be a bleak place without some hope of a hereafter. But I'm glad you told me. Does your mother know?"

"Not yet."

"I'll tell her, if you like—but later. I'd like her to enjoy this holiday."

"Are you angry with me?"

"Dear God, no!" Mendelius heaved himself out of his chair and clamped his hands on the young man's shoulders. "Listen! All my life I've taught and

written that a man can walk only the path he sees at his own feet. If you cannot
honestly assent to a faith then you must not. Rather you should consent to be
burned like Bruno in the Field of Flowers. As for your mother and me, we have
no more right than anyone else to dictate your conscience . . . But remember
one thing, son. Keep your mind open, so that the light can always come in.
Keep your heart open so that love will never be shut out."

"I—I never thought you'd take it like this." For the first time his control
cracked and he seemed about to burst into tears. Mendelius drew him close
and embraced him.

"I love you, boy! Nothing changes that. Besides . . . you're in a new country
now. You won't really know whether you like it until you've spent a winter
there. . . . Let's not fight each other anymore, eh?"

"Right!" Johann disengaged himself from the embrace and reached for his
brandy glass. "I'll drink to that."

"Prosit," said Carl Mendelius.

"About the other thing, Father."

"Yes?"

"I can see the risks. I know what Jean Marie's friendship means to you. But I
think you have to get the priorities right. Mother has to come first; and, well,
Katrin and I need you, too."

"I'm trying to keep things in their right order, son." Mendelius gave a small,
rueful chuckle. "You may not believe in the Second Coming, but if it happens,
it will change the priorities somewhat . . . no?"

From the air the Italian countryside was a pastoral paradise, the orchards in
full bloom, the meadows bright with wild flowers, the farmland flush with new
green, the old fortress towns placid as pictures from a fairy tale.

By contrast, Fiumicino Airport looked like a rehearsal for final chaos. The
traffic controllers were working to rule; the baggage handlers were on strike.
There were long queues at every passport barrier. The air was filled with a
babel of voices shouting in a dozen languages. Police with sniffer dogs moved
among the harassed crowd looking for drug carriers; while young conscripts,
armed with machine guns, stood guard at every exit, watchful and uneasy.

Lotte was near to tears and Mendelius was sweating with anger and frustration. It took them an hour and a half to barge their way through to the customs
room and out into the reception area, where Herman Frank was waiting,
dapper and solicitous as always. He had a limousine, a vast Mercedes borrowed
from the German Embassy. He had flowers for Lotte, an effusive welcome for
the Herr Professor, and champagne to drink during the long ride back to town.
The traffic would be hell as always; but he wanted to offer them a small
foretaste of heavenly peace.

The peace was granted to them at last in the Franks' apartment, the top
floor of a seventeenth-century palazzo with high frescoed ceilings, marble
floors, bathrooms large enough to float a navy and a stunning view over the
rooftops of old Rome. Two hours later, bathed, changed and restored to sanity,
they were drinking cocktails on the terrace, listening to the last bells and
watching the swifts wheeling around the cupolas and attics, russet in the
sunset glow.

"Down there it's murder. . . ." Hilde Frank pointed at the cluttered thoroughfares jammed with automobiles and pedestrians. "Sometimes real murder, because the terrorists are very bold now and the crust of law and order has worn thin. Kidnapping is the biggest private industry. We don't go out at night as we used, because there's always danger from purse-snatchers and motorcycle gangs. But up here"—her gesture embraced the whole ancient skyline—"it's still the same as it's been for centuries: the washing on the lines, the birds, the music that comes and goes, and the calls of the women to their neighbours. Without it I don't think we could bear to stay any longer."

She was a small dark woman, bubbly with talk, elegant as a mannequin, twenty years younger than the white-haired husband who followed her every movement with adoration. She was affectionate, too, cuddlesome as a kitten. Mendelius caught the flash of jealousy in Lotte's eyes, when Hilde took his hand and led him to the corner of the terrace to point out the distant dome of St. Peter's and the Castle of Sant'Angelo. She told him in a loud stage whisper:

"Herman's so happy you've agreed to lecture for him. He's getting near to retirement and he hates the idea. His whole life has been wrapped up in the Academy—both our lives really, because we've never had any children. . . . Lotte looks very well. I hope she likes shopping. I thought I'd take her to the Condotti tomorrow while you and Herman are at the Academy. The seminar people haven't arrived yet but he's dying to show you the place. . . ."

". . . And we've got fine things to show this year!" Herman Frank, with Lotte on his arm, walked into their talk. "We're giving the first comprehensive exhibition of Van Wittel ever held in this country, and Piero Falcone has lent us his collection of antique Florentine jewellery. That's an expensive venture because we need armed guards all the time. . . . Now let me tell you who's coming to dinner tonight. There's Bill Utley and his wife, Sonia. He's the British envoy to the Holy See. Bill's a dry old stick but he really knows what's going on. Also he speaks good German, which helps things along. Sonia's a cheerful gossip with no inhibitions. You'll enjoy her, Lotte. Then there's Georg Rainer, who's the Rome correspondent for *Die Welt*. He's a relaxed fellow who talks well. It was Hilde's idea to invite him because he's got a new girl friend whom nobody's seen yet. A Mexican, I believe, and reputed to be rich! . . . We'll sit down about nine-thirty. . . . By the way, Carl, there's a pile of mail for you. I asked the maid to leave it in your room. . . ."

It was the warmest of welcomes and a reminder of happier times before the oil war began, and the Italian miracle turned sour, and all the bright hopes of European unity were tarnished beyond repair. By the time the dinner guests arrived, Lotte was completely relaxed and chatting happily with Hilde about a trip to Florence and another to Ischia, while Carl Mendelius outlined, to an enthusiastic Herman, the schema of his discourses to the Evangelicals.

Dinner was a comfortable meal. Utley's wife was a scandalously entertaining talker. Georg Rainer's girl, Pia Menendez, was an instant success—a stunning beauty who knew how to defer graciously to the matrons. Georg Rainer wanted news; Utley liked to reminisce; so it was easy for Mendelius to steer the talk to recent events in the Vatican. Utley, the Britisher, who in his mother tongue had elevated obscurity to a fine art, was very precise in German.

". . . Even to the outsider it was plain that Gregory the Seventeenth had everyone in a panic. The organization is too big and therefore too fragile to support an innovator or even a too flexible man at the top. It's like the Russians with their satellites, and their comradely governments in Africa and South America. They have to preserve, at any cost, the illusion of unanimity and stability. . . . So Gregory had to go."

"I'd be interested," said Carl Mendelius, "to know exactly how they got him to abdicate."

"Nobody's prepared to talk about that," said Utley. "This was the first time in my experience when there were no real leaks from Monte Vaticano. Obviously there was some very rough bargaining; but one got the impression there were some very uneasy consciences afterwards."

"They blackmailed him!" said the man from *Die Welt* flatly. "I had the evidence; but I couldn't publish it."

"Why not?" The question came from Utley.

"Because I got it from a medical man, one of the doctors they called in to examine him. Obviously he was in no position to make a public statement."

"Did he tell you his findings?"

"He told me what the Curia wanted him to find: that Gregory the Seventeenth was mentally incompetent."

"Did they put it as bluntly as that?" Mendelius was surprised and dubious.

"No. That was the problem. The Curia were very subtle about it. They asked the medicos—there were seven in all—to establish, beyond reasonable doubt, whether the Pontiff was mentally and physically competent to carry on the duties of his office in this critical time."

"That's a catch-all brief," said Utley. "Why did Gregory fall for it?"

"He was caught in a trap. If he refused, he was suspect. If he accepted he was subject to the medical consensus."

"And what was that?" Mendelius asked.

"My man couldn't tell me. You see, that was the other smart thing they did. They asked each doctor to render an independent opinion in writing."

"Which left the Curia free to write its own assessment afterwards." Bill Utley gave a small dry chuckle. "Very smart! So what was your man's verdict?"

"Honest, I believe; but not very helpful to the patient. He was suffering from gross fatigue, constant insomnia and elevated, though not necessarily chronic, blood pressure. There were clear indications of anxiety and alternating moods of cheerfulness and depression. Obviously if these symptoms persisted in a man of sixty-five, there would be reason to fear graver complications. . . ."

"If the other reports were like that . . ."

"Or," said Mendelius softly, "if they were less honest and a shade more slanted . . ."

"The Cardinals had him in checkmate," said Georg Rainer. "They picked the choicest bits of the reports, constructed their own final verdict and presented Gregory with an ultimatum: go or be pushed!"

"Loving God!" Mendelius swore softly. "What choice did he have?"

"A beautiful piece of statecraft though." Bill Utley chuckled wryly. "You can't impeach a Pope. Short of assassination, how do you get rid of him? You're right, Georg, it was pure blackmail! I wonder who dreamed up the ploy."

"Arnaldo, of course. I do know he was the one who instructed the physicians."

"And now he's the Pope," said Carl Mendelius.

"He'll probably make a very good one," said Utley with a grin. "He knows the rules of the game."

Reluctantly, Carl Mendelius, the onetime Jesuit, was forced to agree with him. He also thought that Georg Rainer was a very smart journalist and that it would pay to cultivate his acquaintance.

That night he made love with Lotte in a huge baroque bed, which, Herman swore on his soul, had belonged to the elegant Cardinal Bernis. Whether it had or it hadn't made small matter. Their mating was the most joyous in a long time. When it was over, Lotte curled up in the crook of his arm and talked in drowsy contentment.

"It's been a lovely evening—everybody so bright and welcoming! I'm glad you made me come. Tübingen's a nice town; but I'd forgotten there was such a lot of world outside."

"Then let's start seeing it together, liebchen."

"We will, I promise. I feel happier now about the children. Katrin was very sweet. She told me what you'd said to her and how Franz had taken the news."

"I didn't hear about that."

"Apparently, he said, 'Your father's a big man. I'd like to bring him back one good canvas from Paris.' "

"That's nice to hear."

"Johann seemed happier, too; though he didn't say very much."

"He got a few things off his chest, including the fact that he wasn't a believer anymore. . . ."

"Oh, dear! That's sad."

"It's a phase, liebchen." Mendelius was sedulously casual. "He wants to find his own way to the truth."

"I hope you made him aware that you respected his decision."

"Of course! You mustn't worry about Johann and me. It's just the old bull and the young one sparring with each other."

"Old bull is right!" Lotte giggled happily in the darkness. "Which reminds me, if I catch Hilde playing pat-hands with you too often, I'll scratch her eyes out!"

"Nice to know you're still jealous."

"I love you, Carl. I love you so very much."

"And I love you, liebchen."

"That's all I need to finish a perfect day. Good night, my dear, dear man!"

She rolled away from him, curled herself under the covers and lapsed swiftly into sleep. Carl Mendelius clasped his hands under his head and lay a long time staring up at the ceiling, where amorous nymphs and rapacious demigods disported themselves in the darkness. For all the sweet solace of loving, he was still haunted by what he had heard at dinner and by the last letter in the pile which the maid had left on his dressing table.

It was in Italian, handwritten on heavy notepaper, embossed with the official superscription of the Sacred Congregation for the Doctrine of the Faith.

Dear Professor Mendelius,

I am informed by our mutual friend the rector of the Pontifical Biblical Institute that you will shortly be visiting Rome for the purpose of scholastic research, and that you will be delivering some discourses at the German Academy of Fine Arts.

I understand also that you plan to pay a visit to the recently retired Pontiff at the Monastery of Monte Cassino.

Since I have always had the greatest admiration for your scholarly work, it would give me great pleasure to entertain you to coffee one morning in my private apartment in Vatican City.

Perhaps you would be kind enough to call me at the Congregation any evening between four and seven so that we may arrange a mutually convenient day, preferably before you go to Monte Cassino.

I send you my salutations and my best wishes for a pleasant sojourn.

Yours in Christ Jesus,
Anton Drexel,
Cardinal Prefect

It was beautifully done, as always: a courteous gesture and a tart reminder that nothing, but nothing, that went on in the sacred circle escaped the watchdogs of the Lord. In the old days of the Papal States they would have sent a summons and a detachment of gendarmes to enforce it. Now it was coffee and sweet biscuits in the Cardinal's apartment and sweet seductive talk afterwards.

Well, well! *Tempora mutantur . . . !* He wondered which the Cardinal Prefect wanted more: information or an assurance of discretion. He wondered also what conditions might be laid down before they would permit him to visit Jean Marie Barette.

III

HERMAN Frank had good reason to be proud of his exhibition. The press had been generous with praise, compliments and illustrations. The galleries of the Academy were thronged with visitors—Romans and tourists—and there was a quite astonishing number of young people.

The works of Gaspar Van Wittel, a seventeenth-century Dutchman from Amersfoort, were little known to the Italian public. Most of them had been jealously preserved in the private collections of the Colonna, the Sacchetti, the Pallavicini and other noble families. To assemble them had taken two years of patient research and months of delicate negotiation. The provenance of many was still a closely guarded secret—witness the large number still denominated *"raccolta privata."* Together they constituted an extraordinarily vivid pictorial and architectural record of seventeenth-century Italy. Herman Frank's enthusiasm had the rare and touching innocence of childhood.

"Just look at that! So delicate yet so precise! Almost a Japanese quality in the colour. A magnificent draftsman, a complete master of the most intricate perspective . . . Study these sketches. . . . Notice how patiently he builds the composition. . . . Strange! He lived in a dark little villa out on the Appia Antica. It's still there. Terribly claustrophobic. Mind you, it was all meadowland in those days, so probably he had all the space and light he needed. . . ." He broke off, suddenly embarrassed. "I'm sorry, I'm talking too much; but I love these things!"

Mendelius laid a gentle hand on his shoulder.

"My friend, it's a delight to listen to you! Look at all these young people! You've lifted them out of their resentments and confusions and set them down in another world, simpler, more beautiful, with all its ugliness forgotten. You have to be proud of that!"

"I am, Carl. I confess it. But I'm also scared of the day when all these canvases are down, and the packers arrive to ship them back to their owners.

I'm getting old. I'm not sure whether I'll have the time, or the energy—the luck for that matter!—to do anything like this again."

"But you'll still be trying. That's the important thing,"

"Not for long, I'm afraid. I retire next year. I won't know what to do with myself. We can't afford to go on living here; and yet I hate the idea of going back to Germany."

"You could take up writing as a full-time occupation. You've already got an established reputation as an art historian. I'm sure you could get a better publishing deal than you've had. . . . Why don't you let me talk to my agent and see what he can set up for you?"

"Would you?" He was almost pathetically grateful. "I'm not very good at business and I worry about Hilde."

"I'll call him as soon as we get home. Which reminds me, can I use your telephone now? There is a call I must make before midday."

"Come to my office. I'll have some coffee sent in. . . . Oh, before you go you simply must look at this view of the Tiber. There are three versions of it: one from the Pallavicini collection, one from the National Gallery and this one came from an old engineer who bought it for a song in the flea market. . . ."

It was another fifteen minutes before Mendelius was free to make his call to the Monastery of Monte Cassino. It took an unconscionable time to find the Abbot and bring him to the telephone. Mendelius fumed and fretted and then reminded himself that monasteries were designed to separate men from the world, not to keep them in touch with it.

The Abbot was cordial, if not exactly effusive. "Professor Mendelius? This is Abbot Andrew. Kind of you to call so promptly. Would you be able to arrange your visit for Wednesday next? It's a feast day for us, and so we shall be able to offer you a little more generous hospitality. I suggest you arrive about three-thirty and stay to dinner. It's a long drive from Rome; so if you care to remain overnight we'll be happy to accommodate you."

"That's very kind. I'll stay then and drive back on Thursday morning. How is my friend Jean?"

"He's been unwell; but I hope he will be recovered in time for your visit. He looks forward to seeing you."

"Please give him my most affectionate greetings and say that my wife asks to be remembered to him."

"I'll do that with pleasure. Until Wednesday then, Professor."

"Thank you, Father Abbot."

Mendelius put down the receiver and sat a moment lost in thought. There it was again: the courteous response, the veiled caution. Wednesday was a week ahead—more than enough time to cancel the invitation, should circumstances change or authority intervene. Jean Marie's illness, real or diplomatic, would provide an adequate excuse.

"Something wrong, Carl?" Herman set down the coffee tray and began pouring.

"I'm not sure. It seems the Vatican is more than a little interested in my activities."

"I would have thought that was natural enough. You've given them a few headaches in the past; and every new book causes a flutter in the pigeon loft. . . . Milk and sugar?"

"No sugar. I'm trying to lose weight."

"I've noticed. I noticed also you were pushing a little last night, for information on Gregory the Seventeenth."

"Did it show that much?"

"Only to me, I think. Was there any special reason?"

"He was my friend. You know that. I wanted to find out what really happened to him."

"Didn't he tell you himself?"

"I hadn't heard from him in months." Mendelius hedged his answer. "I imagine he had little time for private correspondence."

"But you'll be seeing him while you're here?"

"It's been arranged. Yes."

The answer was a shade too curt. Herman Frank was too tactful a man to press the matter. There was an awkward moment of silence; then he said quietly, "Something's been puzzling me, Carl. I'd like your opinion on it."

"Tell me, Herman."

"About a month ago I was called to our embassy. The ambassador wanted to see me. He showed me a letter from Bonn: a circular instruction to all academies and institutes abroad. Many of them, as you know, have valuable material on loan from the Republic: sculptures, pictures, historic manuscripts, that sort of thing. . . . All directors were told to arrange secret safe-deposits in the host countries where these things could be stored in the event of civil disorder or international conflict. We were all given a budget, available immediately, to buy or lease suitable storage."

"It sounds like a reasonable precaution," said Mendelius mildly. "Especially since you can't insure against war or civil violence."

"You miss the point." Herman Frank was emphatic. "It was the tone of the document that worried me. There was a note of real urgency, and a threat of stringent penalties for neglect. I got the impression our people are genuinely worried that some terrible thing may happen very soon."

"Do you have a copy of the instruction?"

"No. The ambassador was very firm that it must not leave the embassy. Oh, and that's another thing. Only most senior staff were to know its contents. I thought that was rather sinister. I still do. I know I'm a worrier; but all the time I think of Hilde and what might happen to her if we were separated in some emergency. I'd like your honest opinion, Carl."

For a moment, Mendelius was tempted to put him off with some facile encouragement; then he decided against it. Herman Frank was a good man, too soft for a rough world. He deserved a sober and honest answer.

"Things are bad, Herman. We're not at panic stations yet; but very soon we may be. Everything points that way: public disorder, the breakdown of political confidence, the huge recession—and the fools in high places who think they can solve the problem by a well-timed but limited war. You're right to be concerned. What you can do about it is another matter. Once the first missiles are launched there's no safe hiding place anywhere. Have you talked to Hilde about it?"

"Yes. She doesn't want to go back to Germany, but she agrees we ought to consider moving out of Rome. We've got that little farmhouse in the Tuscan hills. It's isolated; but there's fertile ground around it. I suppose we could survive just on what we grew ourselves. . . . But it seems an act of despair even to contemplate such a thing."

"Or an act of hope," said Mendelius gently. "I think your Hilde's a very wise girl—and you shouldn't worry about her as much as you do. Women are much better at survival than we are."

"I suppose they are. I've never thought about it that way. . . . Don't you wish sometimes we could find a great man to take control and lead us out of the filthy mess?"

"Never!" said Carl Mendelius somberly. "Great men are dangerous. When their dreams fail, they bury them under the rubble of cities, where simple folk once lived in peace!"

"I want to be open with you, Mendelius. I want you to be open with me."

"How open, Eminence? And on what subject?"

The courtesies were over now. The sweet biscuits were all eaten. The coffee was cold. His Eminence Anton Cardinal Drexel, grey-haired, straight as a grenadier, stood with his back to his visitor, looking out on the sunlit gardens of the Vatican. He turned slowly and stood a moment longer, a faceless silhouette against the light. Mendelius said:

"Please, Eminence, why don't you sit down? I'd like to see your face while we talk."

"Forgive me." Drexel gave a deep growling chuckle. "It's an old trick—and not very polite. . . . Would you prefer we speak German?"

In spite of his name, Drexel was Italian, born in Bolzano, long a territory in dispute between Austria and the Italian Republic. Mendelius shrugged. "As your Eminence pleases."

"Italian then. I speak German like a Tyrolese. You might find it comical."

"The mother tongue is the best one to be honest in," said Mendelius drily. "If my Italian fails me, I'll speak German."

Drexel moved away from the window and sat down facing Mendelius. He arranged the folds of his cassock carefully across his knees. His seamed face, still handsome, might have been carved from wood. Only his eyes were alive, vivid blue, amused yet appraising. He said, "You always were a tough customer." He used the colloquial phrase: *un tipo robusto.* Mendelius smiled at the left-handed compliment. "Now, tell me. How much do you know about what happened here recently?"

"Before I answer that, Eminence, I should like an answer from you. Do you intend to set any impediment to my contact with Jean Marie?"

"I? None at all."

"Does anyone else, to your knowledge?"

"To the best of my knowledge, no one; though there is obviously an interest in the encounter."

"Thank you, Eminence. Now, the answer to your question: I know that Pope Gregory was forced to abdicate. I know the means that were used to exact his decision."

"Which were?"

"A series of seven independent medical reports, which were then consolidated by the Curia into a final document designed to cast grave doubts upon the mental competence of his Holiness. . . . Is that accurate?"

Drexel hesitated a moment and then nodded assent. "Yes, it's accurate. What do you know of my own role in the matter?"

"It is my understanding, Eminence, that while dissenting from the decision of the Sacred College you agreed to convey it to the Pontiff."

"Do you know why they reached their decision?"

"Yes."

There was a flicker of doubt in Drexel's eyes; but he went on without hesitation. "Do you agree with it or not?"

"I think the means of enforcing it were base: flat blackmail. As to the decision itself, I find myself in dilemma."

"And how would you express that dilemma, my friend?"

"The Pope is elected as Supreme Pastor and Custodian of the Deposit of Faith. Can that office be reconciled with the role of prophet proclaiming a private revelation, even if that revelation be true?"

"So you do know!" said the Cardinal Prefect softly. "And, fortunately, you understand."

"So where does that leave us, Eminence?" asked Mendelius.

"Facing the second dilemma: how do we prove whether the revelation is true or false?"

"Your colleagues have already resolved that one," said Mendelius tartly. "They judged him a madman."

"Not I," said Anton Cardinal Drexel firmly. "I believed, I still believe, his position as Pontiff was untenable. There was no way he could have functioned in the face of so much opposition. But mad? Never!"

"A lying prophet, then?"

For the first time Drexel's mask-like visage betrayed his emotion. "That's a terrible thought!"

"He asked me to judge him, Eminence. I had to consider every possible verdict."

"He is not a liar."

"Do you think he is deluded?"

"I would like to believe it. Everything would be so much simpler. But I cannot; I simply cannot!"

Suddenly he looked exactly what he was: an old lion with the strength ebbing out of him.

Mendelius felt a surge of sympathy for the anguish scored in his face. Still he could not relent in his own inquisition. He asked firmly, "How have you tested him, Eminence? By what criteria?"

"By the only ones I know: his speech, his conduct, his writings, the tenor of his spiritual life."

Mendelius chuckled. "There speaks the Hound of God."

Drexel smiled grimly. "The wounds still smart, eh? I admit we gave you a rough time. At least we taught you to understand the method. What do you want to know first?"

"It was the writing that finally damned him. I have a copy of the encyclical. How did you read it, Eminence?"

"With great misgiving, obviously. I had not a doubt in the world that it must be suppressed. But I agree it contains nothing, absolutely nothing, that is contrary to traditional doctrine. There are interpretations that might be considered extreme, but they are certainly not heterodox. Even the question of an elective ministry, when ordination by a bishop is totally impossible, is a very open one—if rather delicate for Roman ears."

"Which brings us to the tenor of his spiritual life." There was a faint hint of irony in Mendelius' tone. "How did you judge that, Eminence?"

For the first time, Drexel's harsh face softened into a smile. "It measured better than yours, my dear Mendelius. He remained faithful to his vocation as a priest. He was a totally unselfish man, all of whose thoughts were directed to the good of the Church and of human souls. His passions were under control. In high office he was humble and kind. His anger was always against malice and never against frailty. Even at the end he did not rail against his accusers, but went with dignity and accepted the role of a subject without complaint. I am told by the Abbot that his life in Monte Cassino is a model of religious simplicity."

"He is also silent. How does that conform with the obligation, which he says he has, to spread the news of the Parousia?"

"Before I answer that," said Drexel, "I think we should clear up one question of fact. Obviously he wrote to you and sent you a copy of the suppressed encyclical. Correct?"

"Correct."

"Was this before or after his abdication?"

"He wrote it before. I received it after the event."

"Good! Now let me tell you something which you do not know. When my brother Cardinals had secured Gregory's consent to abdication, they were sure they had broken him, that he would do whatever they wanted. First they tried to write into the instrument of abdication a promise of perpetual silence on any issue affecting the public life of the Church. I told them that they had neither a moral nor a legal right to do so. If they persisted I would fight them to the death. I would resign my office and make a full public statement on the whole sorry affair. Then they tried another tack. His Holiness had agreed to enter the order of Saint Benedict and live the life of a simple monk. Therefore, he would be bound to obey his religious superior. Therefore, said my clever colleagues, the Abbot would be instructed to bind him to silence under the vow."

"I know that one," said Carl Mendelius with cold anger. "Obedience of the spirit! The worst agony you can impose on an honest man. We've taught it to every tyranny in the world."

"So," said Drexel quietly, "I was determined they should not impose it on our friend. I pointed out that this was an intolerable usurpation of the right of a man to act freely in the light of his private conscience, that the most stringent vow could not bind him to commit a wrong, or to stifle his conscience in the name of good. Once again I threatened exposure. I bargained with my vote in the coming conclave and I instructed Abbot Andrew that he, too, was bound under mortal sanction to protect the free conscience of his new subject."

"I'm happy to hear it, Eminence." Mendelius was grave and respectful. "It's the first light I've seen in this dark affair. But it still doesn't answer my question. Why is Jean Marie still silent? Both in his letter to me and in the encyclical, he speaks of his obligation to proclaim the news that he claims has been revealed to him."

Drexel did not answer immediately. Slowly, almost painfully, he rose from his chair, walked to the window and stood again, staring out into the garden. When he turned finally, his face was in shadow as before; but Mendelius made no protest. The man's distress was all too evident in his voice.

"The reason, I think, is because he is now undergoing the experience of all the great mystics, which is called 'the dark night of the soul.' It is a period of utter darkness, of howling confusion, of near despair, when the spirit seems bereft of every support, human or divine. It is a replica of that terrible moment when Christ Himself cried out: 'My God! Why have you abandoned me?' . . . This is the news I hear from Abbot Andrew. This is why he, and I, wanted to speak with you before you see Jean Marie. . . . The fact is, Mendelius, I think I failed him, because I tried to compromise between the promptings of the Spirit and the demands of the system to which I have been committed for a lifetime. . . . I hope, I pray, you may prove a better friend than I."

"You talk of him as a mystic, Eminence. That seems to predicate a belief in his mystical experience," said Carl Mendelius. "I'm not ready for that yet, much as I love him."

"I hope you will tell him that first and ask your questions afterwards. . . . Perhaps you'll be kind enough to call me after you've seen him?"

"You have my promise, Eminence." Mendelius stood up. "Thank you for inviting me here. I hope you'll forgive me if I seemed rude at the beginning."

"Not rude, just robust." The Cardinal smiled and held out his hand. "You were much less reasonable in the old days. Marriage must be good for you."

Lotte and Hilde had driven out to Tivoli for lunch, so he was treating himself to a solitary meal in the Piazza Navona. When he left the Vatican it was a quarter to midday; so he decided to walk. Halfway down the Via della Conciliazione he stopped and turned back to look at the great basilica of San Pietro, with the encircling colonnades that symbolized the all-embracing mission of Mother Church.

For half a billion believers this was the center of the world, the dwelling place of Christ's vicar, the burial place of Peter the Fisherman. When the IBM's were launched from the Soviet perimeters, it would be obliterated in the first blast. What would happen to the half-billion faithful once this visible symbol of unity, authority and permanence was destroyed?

They had been conditioned for so long to regard this time-worn edifice as the navel of the world, its ruler as the sole, authentic legate of God to men; to whom would they look when the house and the man were reduced to a glaze on the pavement?

These were no idle questions. They were possibilities hideously imminent— to Jean Marie Barette, to Anton Cardinal Drexel, to Carl Mendelius, who knew the apocalyptic literature by heart and saw it rewritten in every line of the daily press. He felt sorry for Drexel, old, still powerful, but bereft of all his certainties. He felt sorry for all of them: cardinals, bishops, curial clerics, all trying to apply the Codex Juris Canonicus to a mad planet, whirling itself towards extinction.

He turned away and strolled, in leisurely fashion, through the crowd of pilgrims, across the Victor Emmanuel Bridge and down the Corso. Halfway along the thoroughfare he found a bar, with tables spread along the sidewalk. He sat down, ordered a Campari and watched the passing show.

This was the best time in Rome: the air still soft, the flowers fresh on the vendors' stalls, the girls flirting their new summer finery, the shops filled with bright baubles for the tourist season.

His attention was caught by a young woman standing on the curb a few paces to his left. She was dressed in dark blue slacks and a white silk blouse that displayed high-tilted breasts. Her black hair was held back by a red scarf. She looked like a southerner, slight and olive-skinned; with a calm, Madonna face, singularly beautiful in repose. She carried a folded newspaper in one hand, and in the other a small handbag of blue leather. She seemed to be waiting for someone.

As he watched, a small red Alfa backed into the space near her. The driver parked it awkwardly, with the nose pointing out into the traffic. He opened the door and leaned across to speak to the girl. For a moment it looked like a pickup; but the girl responded without protest. She passed her handbag to the driver and, still holding the newspaper, turned back to face the sidewalk. The driver waited, with the door open and the engine running.

A few moments later a man, middle-aged, fashionably dressed and carrying a leather briefcase, walked swiftly down the Corso. The girl stepped forward, smiled and spoke to him. He stopped. He seemed surprised; then he said something which Mendelius could not hear. The girl shot him three times in the groin, tossed the newspaper into the gutter and leapt into the car, which roared away down the Corso.

For a single, stunned moment, Mendelius sat shocked and immobile; then he lunged towards the fallen victim and rammed his fist into the man's groin to stanch the blood pumping from the femoral artery. He was still there when the police and the ambulance men pushed their way through the crowd to take charge of the victim.

A policeman dispersed the gaping onlookers and the photographers. A street sweeper cleaned the blood from the pavement. A plainclothes man hustled Mendelius into the bar. A waiter brought hot water and clean napkins to mop his bloody clothes. The proprietor offered a large whisky with the compliments of the house. Mendelius sipped it gratefully as he made his first deposition. The investigator, a young, poker-faced Milanese, dictated it immediately over the telephone to headquarters. Then he rejoined Mendelius at the table and ordered a whisky for himself.

". . . That was most helpful, Professor. The description of the assailant, detailed and closely observed, is very useful to us at this early stage. . . . I'm afraid, however, I'll have to ask you to come to headquarters and look at some photographs—maybe work with an artist on an identikit picture."

"Of course. But I'd like to do it this afternoon if possible. As I explained, I have engagements to fulfil."

"Fine. I'll take you down when we've finished our drinks."

"Who was the victim?" asked Mendelius.

"His name's Malagordo. He's one of our senior Senators, Socialist and Jewish. . . . A filthy business, and we're getting more of it every week."

"It seems so pointless—a gratuitous barbarity."

"Gratuitous, yes; but pointless, no! These people are dedicated to anarchy, a classic and total breakdown of the system by a destruction of public confidence. . . . And we're getting very close to that point now. You may find this hard to believe, Professor. At least twenty other people saw the shooting today; but I'll bet a month's salary yours will be the only deposition that tells us anything concrete . . . and you're a foreigner! The others have to live in this mess; but they won't lift a finger to clean it up. So"—he shrugged in weary resignation—"in the end they'll get the country they deserve. . . . Which reminds me, you'd better be prepared to see yourself spread all over the newspapers."

"That's the last thing I need," said Mendelius glumly.

"It could also be dangerous," said the detective. "You will be identified as a key witness."

"And therefore a possible target. Is that what you're telling me?"

"I'm afraid so, Professor. This is a propaganda game, you understand—black theatre. They have to shoot the leading man. The girl in the ticket office has no publicity value. . . . If you take my advice you'll move out of Rome, preferably out of Italy."

"I can't do that for at least a week."

"As soon as possible then. Meantime, change your address. Move into one of the bigger hotels where the tourists congregate. Use another name. I'll arrange the passport problem with the management."

"It wouldn't help much. I'm booked for lectures at the German Academy. So, I'm still exposed."

"What can I say then?" The detective shrugged and grinned. "Except watch your step, vary your routine, and don't talk to pretty girls in the Corso!"

"No chance of police protection, at least for my wife?"

"Not a hope. We're desperately short of manpower. I can give you the name of an agency that hires bodyguards; but they charge millionaire rates."

"Then to hell with it!" said Mendelius. "Let's go look at your photographs."

As they drove through the midday chaos, he could still smell the blood on his clothes. He hoped Lotte was having a good lunch at Tivoli. He wanted her to enjoy this holiday; there might not be too many more in the future.

Later in the afternoon, while he waited for Lotte and Hilde to return from their outing, he sat on the terrace and taped a memorandum to Anneliese Meissner. He set down the new facts he had learned from Georg Rainer and from Cardinal Drexel and only then added his own comments.

". . . Rainer is a sober and objective reporter. His medical evidence though secondhand proved reliable. Clearly Jean Marie Barette was under great mental and physical strain. Clearly, too, there was no consensus on his mental incapacity. . . . As Rainer put it: 'Had they wanted to keep him, the most he would have needed was a decent rest and a reduction of his workload.' . . .

"Cardinal Drexel's point of view surprised me. Remember I was under inquisition for a long time, and I knew him as a formidable and quite relentless dialectician. However, even in our worst encounters, I never had the slightest doubt of his intellectual honesty. I would love to see you and him lock horns in a public debate. It would be a sell-out performance. He rejects utterly any idea of insanity or of fraud on Jean Marie's part. He goes further and puts him in the category of the mystics like Teresa of Avila, John of the Cross and Catherine of Siena. By inference, Drexel commits himself to a belief—not yet clearly categorized—in the authenticity of Jean Marie's visionary experience. So now it is I who am the skeptic or, at least, the agnostic. . . .

"I am to see Jean Marie next Wednesday and Thursday and I shall report to my assessor after those meetings. I give my first Academy lecture tomorrow. I am looking forward to it. The Evangelicals are an interesting group. I admire their way of life. And, of course, Tübingen has always been one of the heartlands of the Pietist tradition, which has had such a huge influence in England and the United States. . . . But I forget. You are tone-deaf to this music. . . . None the less I trust you and am glad to have you as my *Beisitzer.* My most affectionate salutations from this wonderful, but now very sinister, city. *Auf wiedersehen.*"

The audience was already seated when he entered the auditorium; twenty-odd Evangelical pastors, most of them in their early thirties, a dozen wives, three deaconesses, and half a dozen guests whom Herman Frank had invited from the local Waldensian community in Rome. Carl Mendelius felt comfortable with them. The theological faculty at Tübingen had been one of the early forcing-grounds for the Pietist movement in the Lutheran Church; and Mendelius was personally attracted by its emphasis on personal devotion and works of pastoral charity. He had once written a long paper on the influence of Philipp Jakob Spener and the "College of Piety" which he founded in Frankfurt during the seventeenth century.

When Herman Frank had finished his introduction and the applause had subsided, Mendelius laid out his papers on the lectern and began to speak. His manner was relaxed and informal.

"I don't want to give a lecture. I should prefer, if you agree, to explore our subject in a Socratic dialogue, to see what we can tell each other and what the historical evidence can tell us all. . . . In broad terms we are dealing with eschatology, the doctrine of last things: the ultimate destiny of man, of social organizations and of the whole cosmic order. We want to consider these things in the light of both Old and New Testament writings, and the earliest Christian traditions. . . .

"There are two ways of looking at the Doctrine of Last Things. Each is radically different from the other. The first is what I call the consummatory view. Human history will end. Christ will come a second time, in glory, to judge the living and the dead. The second is what I call the modificating view. Creation continues, but is modified by man working in concert with his creator, towards a fulfilment or perfection, which can be expressed only by symbol and analogy. In this view Christ is ever present, and the Parousia expresses the ultimate revelation of His creative presence. . . . Now I'd like to know where you stand. What do you tell your people about the Doctrine of Last Things? Show hands if you want to answer and let's hear your name and your home-place. . . . You sir, in the second row . . ."

"Alfred Kessler from Köln . . ." The speaker was a short sturdy young man with a square-cut beard. "I believe in continuity and not consummation for the cosmos. The consummation for the individual is death and union with the Creator."

"How then, Pastor, do you interpret the Scriptures to the faithful? You teach them as the Word of God—at least, I presume you do. How do you expound the Word on this subject?"

"As a mystery, Herr Professor: a mystery which, under the influence of divine grace, gradually unfolds its meaning to each individual soul."

"Can you clarify that—perhaps express it as you would to your congregation?"

"I usually put in this way. Language is a man-made instrument and there-fore imperfect. Where language stops, music, for example, takes over. Often a hand's touch says more than a volume of words. I use the example of each man's personal consummation. Instinctively we fear death. Yet, as all of us know from pastoral work, man becomes familiar with it, prepares himself, subconsciously, for it, understands it through the universe about him—the fall of a flower, the scattering of its seeds on the wind, the rebirth of spring. . . . In this context, the Doctrine of Last Things is, if not explainable, at least conformable to physical and psychic experience."

"Thank you, Pastor. Next."

"Petrus Allmann, Darmstadt." It was an older man this time. "I disagree totally with my colleague. Human language is imperfect, yes; but Christ the Lord used it. I think we err when we try to turn His utterances into some kind of double-talk. Scripture is absolutely clear on this subject." He quoted sol-emnly: " 'And immediately after the tribulation of those days, the sun shall be darkened and the moon shall not give her light and the stars shall fall from the sky and the powers of heaven shall be moved. And then shall appear the Sign of the Son of Man in heaven. . . .' What else does that mean but consummation, the end of temporal things?"

There was a surprising burst of applause from one section of the audience. Mendelius let it run on for a moment, then held up his hand for silence. He gave them a good-humored smile.

"So now, ladies and gentlemen, who would like to decide between these two men of goodwill?"

This time it was a grey-haired woman who held up her hand.

"I am Alicia Herschel, deaconess, from Heidelberg. I do not think it matters which colleague is right. I have worked as a missionary in Muslim countries and I have learned to say 'Inshallah.' Whatever is the will of the Lord will be done, however we humans read his intentions. Pastor Allman quoted from Matthew twenty-four; but there is another saying in that same chapter: 'But of that day and hour no one knoweth; no, not the angels of heaven, but the Father alone.'

She was an impressive woman and there was more applause when she sat down. She was followed by a young man from Frankfurt. This time he ad-dressed a question to Mendelius.

"Where do you stand on this question, Herr Professor?"

He was pinned now, as he had expected to be; but at least it forced him to some kind of definition. He paused a moment, collecting his thoughts, then outlined his position.

"As you know, I was ordained a priest in the Roman Catholic Church. However, I left the ministry and engaged myself in academic work. For a long time, therefore, I have been absolved from the obligation of pastoral interpretation of Scripture. I am now an historian, still a professing Christian, but dedicated to a purely historical study of biblical and patristic documents. In other words, I study what was written in the past, in the light of our knowledge of that past. . . . So, professionally speaking, I should not make predications on the truth or otherwise of prophetic writings, only on their provenance and authenticity."

They were silent now. They accepted his disclaimer; but if he ducked the issue of a personal testimony they would reject him out of hand. The knowing was not enough for them. True Evangelicals, they demanded that it be fruitful in word and action. Mendelius went on.

"By temperament and training I have always been inclined to interpret the future in terms of continuity, modification, change. I could not come to terms with consummation. . . . Now, however, I find myself drawn to the view that consummation is possible. It is an experiential fact that mankind has all means to create a global catastrophe of such dimensions that human life as we know it would be extinguished on the planet. Given the other experiential fact of man's capacity for destructive evil, we are faced with the fearful prospect that the consummation may be imminent. . . ."

There was an audible gasp from the audience. Mendelius added a footnote to the affirmation.

"But whether it would be wise to preach such a message is another question altogether, and I confess that, at this moment, I am not competent to answer it."

There was a moment of silence and then a small forest of hands shot up. Before he called for more questions Mendelius reached for the water glass and took a long swallow of liquid. He had a sudden incongruous vision of Anneliese Meissner peering at him through her thick spectacles and grinning all over her ugly face. He could almost hear her mocking verdict.

"I told you, didn't I, Carl? God-madness! You'll never be cured of it!"

The session was scheduled to end at midday, but the discussion was so lively that it was a quarter to one before Mendelius was able to escape for a pre-lunch drink in Herman Frank's office. Herman was lavish with compliments; but Mendelius was less than happy with the headlines in the newspapers stacked on his desk.

They ranged from the extravagant to the malicious: "Hero of the Corso"; "Distinguished scholar in shooting affray"; "Ex-Jesuit chief witness against terrorist brigades." The photographs were lurid: Mendelius spattered with blood, kneeling beside the victim, Malagordo being hoisted into the ambulance, Mendelius and the detective huddled in talk over their whisky. There was also an identikit picture of the assassin, carefully captioned: "Impression of the assassin by Professor Carl Mendelius of Tübingen University." The copy was orchestrated in Italian operatic style: grandiloquent horror, high heroics and heavy irony. . . . "It is, perhaps, not without a certain poetic justice that a Jewish Senator should owe his life to a German historian. . . ."

"God Almighty!" Mendelius was pale with anger. "They've set me up like a decoy duck!"

Herman Frank nodded unhappily. "It is bad, Carl. The embassy called to warn you that there are strong links between local terrorists and similar groups in Germany."

"I know. We can't stay at your place any longer. Call back to the embassy, get them to use their influence to book us a double room in one of the better hotels, the Hassler perhaps or the Grand . . . I absolutely refuse to expose you and Hilde to danger on my account."

"No, Carl! I will not bend to this kind of threat. Hilde would never permit it either."

"Herman, please! This is no time for heroics."

"It's not heroics, Carl." Herman was surprisingly resolute. "It's simple common sense. I refuse to live underground like a mole. That's what these bastards want! Besides, it's only for a week. The girls can go to Florence as they planned. A couple of old stagers like you and me should be able to look after ourselves."

"But listen . . . !"

"No 'buts,' Carl. Let's put it to the girls over lunch and see how they feel."

"Very well. Thanks, Herman."

"Thank you, my friend. This morning was a special triumph for me. In all my years at the Academy, I've never seen such an animated debate. They can't wait for your next appearance. . . . Oh, I almost forgot. There were two telephone calls for you. One was from Cardinal Drexel. He'll be in his office until one-thirty. The other was from the wife of Senator Malagordo. She'd like you to call her back at the Salvator Mundi hospital. . . . Those are the numbers. Make the calls now and get them off your mind. I'd like you to enjoy your lunch."

As he dialled Drexel's number, Mendelius was filled with misgivings. The Vatican placed a high premium on discretion. Drexel might well see the threat to Mendelius as a threat to the privacy of Jean Marie Barette. He was surprised to find the old warrior cordial and solicitous.

"Mendelius? . . . I presume you've seen this morning's papers?"

"I have, Eminence. I've just been discussing them with my host. An embarrassment to say the least."

"I have a suggestion. I hope you'll accept it."

"I'd be happy to consider it, Eminence."

"For the rest of your stay I'd like you to have the use of my car and my driver. His name's Francone. He used to be in the Carabinieri. He understands security work and he's alert and capable."

"It's a kind thought, Eminence, but I can't really accept."

"You can. You must. I have a vested interest in your safety, my friend. I propose to protect it. Where are you now?"

"At the Academy. I'm going back to the Franks' for lunch. The address is . . ."

"I have the address. Francone will report to you at four and will remain at your disposal during the rest of your stay. . . . No arguments now! We can't afford to lose the Hero of the Corso, can we?"

Much lighter in heart, Mendelius called the Salvator Mundi hospital and asked for the wife of Senator Malagordo. He was put through first to a very brusque German nun and then to a male security man. After a long silence the Senator's wife came on the line. She wanted to tell him her thanks for saving the Senator's life. He was badly hurt but his condition was stable. As soon as he was in a condition to receive visitors he would like to see the Professor and offer his thanks in person.

Mendelius promised to call later in the week, thanked her for her courtesy and rang off. When he heard the news, Herman Frank was happy again.

"You see, Carl! That's the other side of the medal. People are kind and grateful. And the Cardinal's a canny old fox. You probably don't know it, but the Vatican has a staff of very tough security boys. They have no inhibitions about breaking heads in the service of God. This Francone is obviously one of them. I feel better now—much better! Let's go home to lunch."

During the meal, Lotte was very quiet; but afterwards, when the Franks had retired for their siesta, she made her position plain.

"I'm not going to Florence, Carl, not to Ischia or anywhere out of Rome, unless you're with me. If you're in danger I have to share it; otherwise I'm nothing but a piece of furniture in your life."

"Please, liebchen, be sensible! You don't have to prove anything to me."

"Have you never thought I might have to prove it to myself?"

"Why, for God's sake?"

"Because, ever since we married, I've been on the comfortable side of the bed; the wife of a notable scholar first, and then the Frau Professor at Tübingen. I've never had to think too much about anything, except having my babies and running the house. . . . You were always there, a strong wall against the wind. I've never had to test myself without you. I've never had a rival. It was wonderful, all of it; but now, looking at other women my age, I feel very inadequate."

"Why should you? Do you think I could have made this career without you, without the home you provided, and all the loving inside it?"

"I think so, yes. Not quite in the same way perhaps—but yes, you'd have made it without me. You're not just a stuffy scholar. There's an adventurer in you, too. Oh, yes! I've seen him peeping out sometimes—and I've shut the door on him because he frightened me. Now, I want to see more of him, know him better, enjoy him before it's too late."

She was weeping now, quiet tender tears. Mendelius reached out and drew her to him, coaxing her softly.

". . . There's nothing to be sad about, liebchen. We're here, together. I don't want to push you away. It's just that suddenly, yesterday, I saw the face of evil—real evil! That girl—she couldn't have been much older than Katrin— looked like one of Dolci's Madonnas. But she shot a man in cold blood, not to kill him but to maim him in his manhood . . . I don't want you exposed to that sort of cruelty."

"But I am exposed to it, Carl! I'm part of it, just as much as you are. When

Katrin went off to Paris with her Franz, I wished I were young again and going in her place. I was jealous; because she was getting something I never had. When you and Johann used to fight, a part of me was glad, because he would always turn to me afterwards. He was like a young lover with whom I could make you jealous. . . . There! It's out now; and if you hate me I can't help it."

"I can't hate you, liebchen. I've never ever been able to be angry with you for very long."

"That's part of the problem, I suppose. I knew it and I needed you to fight me."

"I still won't fight you, Lotte." Suddenly he was somber and remote. "Do you know why? Because, all of my early life, I was bound—by my own choice, I agree—but bound nonetheless. When I became free I prized it so much, I couldn't bear to impose a servitude on anyone else . . . I wanted a partner, not a puppet. I saw what was happening, but until you saw it yourself, and wanted to change it, I couldn't, I wouldn't force you. Right or wrong, that's how I felt."

"And now, Carl? What do you feel now?"

"Scared!" said Carl Mendelius. "Scared of what may be waiting for us out there in the streets; even more scared of what's going to happen when I meet Jean Marie."

"I was asking about us—you and me."

"That's what I'm talking about, liebchen. Every way we move now, we're at risk. I want you with me; but not to prove something to me or to yourself. That's like having sex just to show you can do it. . . . It may be magnificent but it's a long way from loving. In short, it's up to you, liebchen."

"How many ways do I have to tell you, Carl? I love you. From now on, where you go, I go."

"I doubt the monks will offer you a bed in Monte Cassino; but apart from that, fine! We go together."

"Good!" said Lotte with a grin. "Then come to bed, Herr Professor. It's the safest place in Rome!"

In principle, it was an excellent idea; but before they could put it into practice the maid knocked on the door to tell him that Georg Rainer was on the line from the bureau of *Die Welt*. Rainer's approach was good-humoured but crisp and businesslike.

"You're a celebrity now, Carl. I need an interview for my paper."

"When?"

"Right now, on the telephone. I have a deadline to meet."

"Go ahead."

"Not so fast, Carl. We're friends of a friend, so I'll give you the ground rules, once only. You can decline to answer; but don't tell me anything off the record. Whatever you give me I print. Clear?"

"Clear."

"This conversation is being recorded with your consent. Agreed?"

"Agreed."

"We're running. Professor Mendelius, your prompt action yesterday saved the life of Senator Malagordo. How does it feel to be an international celebrity?"

"Uncomfortable."

"There have been some rather provocative headlines about your act of mercy. One calls you the Hero of the Corso. How do you feel about that?"

"Embarrassed. I did nothing heroic. I simply applied elementary first aid."

"What about this one: 'Ex-Jesuit chief witness against terrorist brigades'?"

"An exaggeration. I witnessed the crime. I described it to the police. I presume they have taken testimony from many others."

"You also gave them a description of the girl who fired the shots."

"Yes."

"Was it accurate and detailed?"

"Yes."

"Did you not feel that you were taking a big risk by giving that evidence?"

"I should have taken a much bigger one by remaining silent."

"Why?"

"Because violence can only flourish when men are afraid to speak and act against it."

"Are you afraid of reprisals, Professor?"

"Afraid, no. Prepared, yes."

"How are you prepared?"

"No comment."

"Are you armed? Do you have police protection, a private bodyguard?"

"No comment."

"Any comment on the fact that you are German and the man whose life you saved is a Jew?"

"Our Lord Jesus Christ was a Jew. I am happy to have served one of His people."

"On another matter, Herr Professor, I understand you gave a very dramatic lecture at the German Academy this morning."

"It was well received. I shouldn't have called it dramatic."

"Our report runs as follows and I quote: 'Asked by one questioner whether he believed that the end of the world as foretold in the Bible was a real and possible event, Professor Mendelius replied that he considered it not only a possibility but an imminent one.'"

"How the hell did you get that?"

"We have good sources, Professor. Is the report true or false?"

"It's true," said Mendelius. "But I wish to God you wouldn't print it."

"I told you the ground rules, my friend; but if you'd like to amplify the statement I'll be happy to report you verbatim."

"I can't, Georg. At least not at this time."

"And what's that mean, Herr Professor? Did you really take yourself so seriously?"

"In this case, yes."

"All the more reason then to print the report."

"How good a journalist are you, Georg?"

"I'm doing all right so far, aren't I?" Rainer's laugh crackled over the wire."

"I'm offering you a deal, Georg."

"I never make them—well, hardly ever. What do you have in mind?"

"Kill the end-of-the-world story and I'll give you a much bigger one."

"On the same subject?"

"No comment."

"When?"

"A week from today."

"That's a Friday. What do you expect to give me—the date of the Second Coming?"

"You get lunch at Ernesto's."

"And the story exclusive?"

"That's a promise."

"You have your deal."

"Thanks, Georg."

"And I still have the tape to remind us of it. *Auf wiedersehen*, Herr Professor."

"Auf wiedersehen, Georg."

He put down the receiver and stood, brooding and perplexed, under the indifferent gaze of the fauns and shepherdesses on the ceiling. All unwittingly he had walked himself into a minefield. One more uncautious move and it would explode under his feet.

—————— IV ——————

DOMENICO Giuliano Francone, chauffeur and man of confidence to his Eminence, was, in looks and character, an original. He was six feet tall, with an athlete's body, a grinning goat's face and a mop of reddish hair kept sedulously dyed. He claimed to be forty-two years old, but was probably on the wrong side of fifty. He spoke a German he had learned from the Swiss Guards, an atrocious Genovese French, English with an American accent and Italian with a Sorrentine singsong lilt.

His personal history was a litany of variables. He had been an amateur wrestler, a champion cyclist, a sergeant in the Carabinieri, a mechanic of the Alfa racing team, a notable boozer and wencher until, after the untimely death of his wife, he had found religion and taken a job as sexton in the titular church of His Eminence.

His Eminence, impressed by Francone's industry and devotion—and possibly by his raffish good humour—had promoted him into his personal household. Because of his police training, his skill as a driver, his knowledge of weapons and his experience in hand-to-hand combat, he had assumed, almost by natural right, the duties of bodyguard. In these rough and godless times, even a prince of the Church was not safe from the sacrilegious threats of the terrorists. While a religious man dared not show himself afraid, the Italian government made no secret of its fears and demanded commonsense precautions.

All this and more Domenico Francone elaborated eloquently, as he drove the Mendelius' and the Franks on a Saturday afternoon excursion to the Etruscan tombs of Tarquinia. His authority established, he then laid down the rules:

". . . I am responsible to His Eminence for your safety. So you will please do as I say, and do it without question. If I tell you to duck, you get your heads down fast! If I drive madly, you hang on tight and don't ask why. In a restaurant you let me pick the table. If you, Professor, go on foot in Rome, you wait until I have parked the car and am ready to follow you. . . . That way you keep your mind on your own affairs and let me do the worrying. I know the way these *mascalzoni* work. . . ."

"We have every confidence in you," said Mendelius amiably, "but is there anyone following us now?"

"No, Professor."

"Then perhaps you'd take it a little more slowly. The ladies would like to look at the countryside."

"Of course! My apologies! . . . This is a very historic zone, many Etruscan tombs. There is, as you know, a ban on excavation without permission, but still there is looting of hidden sites. When I was in the Carabinieri . . ."

The torrent of his eloquence poured over them again. They shrugged and smiled at each other, and drowsed the rest of the way to Tarquinia. It was a relief to leave him standing sentinel by the car while they followed a soft-voiced custodian through the wheatfields, to visit the people of the painted tombs.

It was a tranquil place, filled with lark song and the low whisper of the wind through the ripening wheat. The prospect was magical: the fall of the green land to the brown villages, with the blue sea beyond, and the scattered yachts, spinnakers filled with the land breeze, heading westward to Sardinia. Lotte was entranced, and Mendelius tried to re-create for her the life of a long-vanished people.

". . . They were great traders, great seafarers. They gave their name, the Tyrrhenian, to this part of the Mediterranean. They mined copper and iron and smelted bronze. They farmed the rich lands from here to the Po valley and as far south as Capua. They loved music and dancing and made great feasts; and when they died, they were buried with food and wine and their best clothes, and pictures of their life painted on the walls of their tombs. . . ."

"And now they're all gone," said Lotte quietly. "What happened to them?"

"They got rich and lazy. They hid behind their rituals and trusted to gods who were already out of fashion. Their slaves and commoners revolted. The rich fled with their wealth to buy the protection of the Romans. The Greeks and the Phoenicians took over their trade routes. Even their language died out." He quoted softly the epitaph: " 'O ancient Veii! Once you were a kingdom and there was a golden throne in your forum. Now the idle shepherd plays his pipes within your walls; and, above your tombs, they reap the harvest of the fields . . . !' "

"That's pretty. Who wrote it?"

"A Latin poet, Propertius."

"I wonder what they'll write about our civilization?"

"There may not be anyone left to write a line . . ." said Mendelius moodily, "and there certainly won't be pastorals painted on the side of our sepulchers. At least these people expected continuity. We look forward to a holocaust. . . . It took a Christian to write the 'Dies Irae.' "

"I refuse to think any more gloomy thoughts," said Lotte firmly. "It's beautiful here. I want to enjoy my day."

"My apologies." Mendelius smiled and kissed her. "Get ready to hide your blushes. The Etruscans enjoyed sex, too, and they painted some very pretty reminders of it."

"Good!" said Lotte. "Show me the naughty ones first. And make sure it's my hand you're holding, not Hilde's!"

"For a virtuous woman, liebchen, you have a very dirty mind!"

"Be glad of it, my love." Lotte giggled happily. "But for God's sake don't tell the children!"

She took his hand and trotted him up the slope towards the beckoning custodian. He was a young fellow with agreeable manners, a recent laureate in archaeology and full of enthusiasm for his subject. Awed by the presence of two distinguished scholars, he devoted his attention to the women, while Mendelius and Herman Frank chatted quietly in the background. Herman was in the mood for confidences.

"I've talked things out with Hilde. We've decided to take your advice. We'll shift ourselves out to the farm—gradually of course—and I'll work out a program of writing. If I could get a contract for a series of volumes, it would give me a continuity of work and some sense of financial security."

"That's what my agent recommends." Mendelius encouraged him. "He says publishers like that sort of project because it gives them time to build a readership. When we get back to Rome, I'll call him and see what progress he's made. He always spends weekends at home."

"There's only one thing that worries me, Carl . . ."

"What's that?"

"Well, it's slightly embarrassing . . ."

"Come on! We're old friends. What's the problem?"

"It's Hilde. I'm a lot older than she is. I'm not as good in bed as I used to be. She says it doesn't worry her and I believe it—probably because I want to, anyway. We do have a good life in Rome: lots of friends, many interesting visitors. It . . . well, it seems to balance things out. Once we leave, I'll have my work; but she'll be stuck in a cottage in the hills like a farmer's wife. I'm not sure how that will work out. It would be easier if we had children or grandchildren; but as things are . . . it would kill me to lose her, Carl!"

"What makes you think you will?"

"That!" He pointed ahead to the two women and the custodian, who was just unlocking the next sepulcher. Hilde was joking with him and her high bubbling laugh echoed across the quiet hills. "I'm an old fool, I know; but I get jealous—and scared!"

"Swallow it, man!" Mendelius was curt with him. "Swallow it and keep your mouth shut. You have a good life together. Hilde loves you. Enjoy it, day by day! Nobody gets eternal reassurance. Nobody has a right to it! Besides, the more scared you get, the worse you'll be in bed. Any physician will tell you that."

"I know, Carl. But it's rough sometimes to . . ."

"It's always rough." Mendelius refused to bend to him. "It's rough when your wife seems to pay more attention to the children than she does to you. It's rough when the kids fight you for the right to grow up in a different way from yours. It's rough when a man like Malagordo walks out to lunch and a pretty girl puts a bullet in his balls! Come on, Herman! How much sugar do you need in a cup of coffee?"

"I'm sorry."

"Don't be. You've got it off your chest. Now forget it." He leafed through his catalogue. "This one's the Tomb of the Leopards, with the flute player and the lutanist. Let's go in and join the girls."

As they stood inside the ancient chamber, listening to the custodian expound the meaning of the fresco, Mendelius pondered another random thought. Jean Marie Barette, lately a Pope, was driven to proclaim the Parousia; but did people really want to know about it? Did they really want to listen to the gaunt prophet shouting from the mountaintop? Human nature had not changed much since 500 B.C., when the old Etruscans buried their dead to the sound of lutes and pipes, and locked them in a perpetual present, with food and wine and a tame leopard for company, under the painted cypresses.

That night Mendelius and Lotte dined out in a trattoria on the old Appian Way. The garrulous Francone drove them there, and when they protested his long hours he silenced them with the now familiar phrase: "I am responsible to His Eminence." He ordered them to sit with their backs to the wall, then retired to eat in the kitchen, whence he could survey the yard and make sure no one planted a bomb under the Cardinal's limousine.

Their host for the evening was Enrico Salamone, who published Mendelius' works in Italy; a middle-aged bachelor with a taste for exotic and preferably intelligent women. His escort for this time was one Mme. Barakat, the divorced wife of an Indonesian diplomat. Salamone was a shrewd and successful editor who admired scholarship but never disdained a topical and sensational subject.

". . . Abdication, Mendelius! Think about it. A vigorous and intelligent Pope, still only in his mid-sixties, quits in the seventh year of his reign. There has to be a big story behind it."

"There probably is." Mendelius was elaborately casual. "But your author would break his back finding it. The best journalists in the world got only stale crumbs."

"I was thinking of you, Carl."

"Forget it, Enrico!" Mendelius laughed. "I've got too much on my plate already."

"I tried to tell him," said Mme. Barakat. "He should be looking outward. The West is a small and incestuous world. Publishers should be opening new windows—to Islam, to the Buddhists, to India. All the new revolutions are religious in character."

Salamone nodded a reluctant agreement. "I see it. I know it. But where are the writers who can interpret the East to us? Journalism is not enough; propaganda is a whore's trade. We need poets and storytellers steeped in the old traditions."

"It seems to me," said Lotte ruefully, "everyone shouts too loud and too often. You can't tell stories in a mob. You can't write poetry with the television blaring."

"Bravo, liebchen!" Mendelius squeezed her hand.

"It's true!" She was launched now and ready to engage in combat. "I don't have many brains, but I know Carl's always done his best work in a quiet, provincial situation. Haven't you always told me, Carl, too many people argue their own books out of existence? You, too, Enrico! You said once you'd like to lock your authors up until they were ready to walk out with a finished manuscript."

"I said it, Lotte. I believe it." He gave her a swift sidelong grin. "But even your husband here isn't the hermit he pretends to be. . . . What are you really doing in Rome, Carl?"

"I told you: research, a couple of lectures, and having a holiday with Lotte."

"There's a rumor," said Mme. Barakat sweetly, "that you were given some kind of mission by the former Pope."

"Hence my suggestion for a book," said Enrico Salamone.

"Where the hell did you pick up that nonsense?" Mendelius was nettled.

"It's a long story." Salamone was amused but wary. "But I assure you it is authentic. You know I'm a Jew. It's natural that I entertain the Israeli ambassador and any visitors he wants to present in Rome. It's also natural that we talk about matters of mutual concern. So now! . . . The Vatican has always refused diplomatic recognition to the State of Israel. The refusal is pure politics. They don't want to quarrel with the Arab world. They would like, if they could, to assert some kind of sovereignty over the Holy Places in Jerusalem. Echoes of the Crusades! There was hope that this position might change under Gregory the Seventeenth. His personal response to diplomatic relations with Israel was believed to be favourable. So, early this spring, a private meeting was arranged between the Israeli ambassador and the Pontiff. The Pope was frank about his problems, inside his own Secretariat of State and outside, with Arab leaders. He wanted to continue exploring the situation. He asked my ambassador whether a personal and unofficial envoy would be welcome in Israel. Their answer was naturally in the affirmative. Yours was one of the names suggested by the Pontiff. . . ."

"Good God!" Mendelius was genuinely shocked. "You have to believe me, Enrico. I knew absolutely nothing about it."

"That's true!" Lotte was instant in support. "I would have known. This thing was never, never mentioned—not even in his last . . ."

"Lotte, please!"

"I'm sorry, Carl."

"So there was no mission." Mme. Barakat was soothing as honey. "But there was communication?"

"Private, madame," said Mendelius curtly. "A matter of old friendship . . . And I'd like to change the subject."

Salamone shrugged and spread his hands in surrender. "Fine! But you mustn't blame me for trying. That's what makes me a good publisher. Now tell me, how's the new book coming?"

"Slowly."

"When can we expect the manuscript?"

"Six, seven months."

"Let's hope we're still in business by then!"

"Why shouldn't you be?"

"If you read the papers, my dear Professor, you'll know the great powers are talking us all into a war."

"They need another twelve months," said Mme. Barakat. "I keep telling you, Enrico. Nothing before twelve months. After that . . ."

"Nothing ever again," said Salamone. "Pour me the rest of the wine, Carl! I think we could use another bottle!"

The bloom was already off the evening; but they had to sit it out to the end. As they drove home through the sleeping city, they sat close and talked softly, for fear of rousing Francone to another oration.

Lotte asked, "What was the meaning of all that, Carl?"

"I don't know, liebchen. Salamone was trying to be smart."

"And Madame Barakat is a bitch!"

"He does collect some odd ones, doesn't he?"

"Old friends and new bedmates don't mix."

"I agree. Enrico should have known better."

"Do you think it was true about Jean Marie and the Israelis?"

"Probably. But who knows? Rome's always been a whispering gallery. The hard thing is to put the right names to the voices."

"I hate that kind of mystery-making."

"I, too, liebchen."

He was too tired to tell her how he truly felt: a man caught in toils of gossamer, the trailing wisps of a nightmare from which he could neither flee nor wake.

"What are we doing tomorrow?" asked Lotte drowsily.

"If you don't mind I thought we'd go to mass in the Catacombs; then we'll go out to Frascati for lunch. Just the two of us."

"Couldn't we hire a car and drive ourselves?"

Mendelius gave a rueful chuckle and shook his head. "I'm afraid not, liebchen. That's another lesson you learn in Rome. There's no escape from the Hounds of God."

Garrulous he might be, but Domenico Francone was a very good watchdog. He drove twice around the block before dropping them at the Franks' apartment, then stood watch until the ancient door closed behind them, sealing out the dangers of the night.

In the garden of San Callisto the bougainvillaea was in flame, the rose gardens in first flush and the doves still fluttered in their cote behind the chapel, all just as he remembered it from his first visit, long years before. Even the guides still looked the same: old devotees from a dozen countries, who dedicated their services as translators to the pilgrim groups who came to pay homage at the tombs of ancient martyrs.

There were no ghosts in the tiny chapel, only an extraordinary tranquillity. There were no baroque horrors, no mediaeval grotesques. Even the symbols were simple and full of grace: the anchor of faith, the dove carrying the olive twig of deliverance, the fish that bore the loaves of the Eucharist on its back. The inscriptions all spoke of hope and peace: *Vivas in Christo. In pace Christi.* The word *Vale*—farewell—was never used. Even the dim labyrinths below held no terrors. The *loculi,* the wall niches where the dead were laid, held only shards and dusty fragments.

In the Chapel of the Popes, they attended a mass said by a German priest for a group of Bavarian pilgrims. The chapel was a large, vaulted chamber, where, in 1854, Count de Rossi had discovered the resting place of five of the earliest

Pontiffs. One had been deported as a mine slave to Sardinia and died in captivity. His body was brought back and buried in this place. Another had been executed in the persecution of Decius, yet another was put to the sword at the entrance to the burial place. Now, the violence in which they had perished was almost forgotten. They slept here in peace. Their memory was celebrated in a tongue they never knew.

As he knelt with Lotte on the tufa floor, responding to the familiar liturgy, Mendelius remembered his own priesthood and felt a pang of resentment that he should now be debarred from its exercise. It had not been so in the early Church. Even now, the Uniats were permitted a married clergy; while the Romans clung obstinately to their celibate rule, and reinforced it with myth and historic legend and canonical legislation. He had written copious argument about it, still fought it in debate; but, married himself, he was a discredited witness, and the lawmakers paid no heed to him.

But what of the future—the near future—when the supply of celibate candidates would dry up, and the flock would cry out for ministry—by man or woman, married or single, it made no matter, just so they heard the Word and shared the Bread of Life in charity? Their Eminences at the Vatican still ducked the issue, hiding behind a carefully edited tradition. Even Drexel ducked it, because he was too old to fight and too well-drilled a soldier to challenge the high command. Jean Marie had faced the question in his encyclical and this was yet another reason for suppressing it. Now the dark days were coming again. The shepherd would be struck down, the flock scattered. Who would bring them together again and hold them in love, while the rooftrees of the world toppled about them?

When the celebrant raised the host and the chalice after the Consecration, Mendelius bowed his head and made a silent, heartfelt prayer: "O God, give me light enough to know the truth, courage enough to do what will be asked of me!" Suddenly he found himself weeping, uncontrollably. Lotte reached out and took his hand. He held to her, mute and desperate, until the mass was ended and they walked out into the sunlight of the rose arbour.

Early on Monday morning, while Lotte was taking her bath, Mendelius telephoned the Salvator Mundi hospital and enquired about the progress of Senator Malagordo. He was passed, as before, from reception to the ward sister, to the security man. Finally he was told that the Senator was much improved and would like to see him as soon as possible. He made an appointment for three that same afternoon.

He was getting restless now—more and more convinced that his Wednesday meeting with Jean Marie would be some kind of turning point in his life. If he could not accept Jean Marie's revelation, their relationship would change irrevocably. If he did accept it, then he must accept the mission as well, no matter what form it might take. Either way, he must soon be gone and he wanted as few social encumbrances as possible.

He had done some research, but he was too preoccupied to concentrate on the new material, which, in any case, was fragmentary and of little importance. Tuesday would see him out with the Evangelicals. He was still irritated by the leaking of conference material to the press; but he needed to test the reaction of a Protestant audience to certain of Jean Marie's propositions. He still had to make good his promise of a news story for Georg Rainer. So far, he had no idea in the world what he would tell him.

Lotte was still bathing, so he gathered up his notes and walked out to breakfast on the terrace. Herman had left early for the Academy. Hilde was alone at the table. She poured his coffee and then announced firmly:

"Now, you and I can have a little talk. Something's bothering you, *Carlo mio*. What is it?"

"Nothing I can't deal with."

"Herman looks at pictures. I read people. And there's trouble written all over your face. Is everything all right with you and Lotte?"

"Of course."

"Then what's the matter?"

"It's a long story, Hilde."

"I'm a good listener. Tell me!"

He told her, haltingly at first, then in a rush of vivid words, the story of his friendship with Jean Marie Barette and the strange pass to which it had led him. She listened in silence; and he found it a relief to express himself without the burden of reasoning or polemic. When he had finished he said simply, "So that's it, my love. I won't know anything more until I meet Jean Marie on Wednesday."

Hilde Frank laid a soft hand on his cheek and said gently, "That's a hell of a load to carry around—even for the great Mendelius! It helps to explain some other things, too."

"What things?"

"Herman's romantic idea of living on beans and broccoli and goat cheese up in the mountains."

"Herman doesn't know what I've just told you about Jean Marie."

"Then what the devil is he talking about?"

"He's scared of a new war. We all are. He worries about you."

"And how he worries! You know his latest idea? He wants to rush off to Zurich for a hormone implant, to improve our sex life. I told him not to bother. I'm perfectly happy the way we are."

"And are you happy, Hilde?"

"Would you believe, yes! Herman's a dear and I love him. As for the sex part, the fact is I'm not really good at it myself—never have been. Oh, I love the warm snuggly part, but the rest of it—I'm not frigid but I'm slow and hard to rouse, and what I get at the end is hardly worth the bother. So you see, Herman's really got nothing to worry about."

"Then you'd better tell him as often as you can." Mendelius tried to be casual about it. "He's feeling very uncertain of himself just now."

"Forget about us, Carl. We'll work it out. I've been managing Herman ever since we married. . . . Let's get back to your story."

"I'd like to hear your reaction to it, Hilde."

"Well, first, I've lived in Italy a long time so I'm skeptical about saints and miracles and weeping virgins and friars who levitate at Mass. Second, I'm a pretty contented woman, so I've never been drawn to fortune-tellers or séances or encounter groups. I'd much rather be doing fun things. Finally, I'm pretty self-centered. So long as my little corner of the universe makes sense, I put the rest out of my mind. There's nothing I can do to change it anyway."

"Let's put it another way then. Suppose I come back on Thursday from Monte Cassino and say: 'Hilde, I've just seen Jean Marie. I believe he's had a true revelation, that the world is going to end soon and the Second Coming of Christ will occur.' What will you do?"

"Hard to say. I certainly wouldn't go rushing off to church, or hoarding food or climbing the Apennines to wait for the Saviour or watch the last sunrise. And you, Carl? How will you react?"

"I don't know, Hilde my love. I've thought about it every day, every night, since I read Jean's letter; but I still don't know."

"There's one way to look at it, of course . . ."

"What's that?"

"Well, if somebody's really going to shut down the world, everything becomes pointless. Rather than wait for the last big bang, why not buy a bottle of whisky and a big bottle of barbiturates and put ourselves to sleep? I think a lot of people would decide to do just that."

"Would you?" asked Mendelius softly. "Could you?"

She refilled their cups and began calmly buttering a croissant.

"You're damn right I could, Carl! And I wouldn't want to wake up and meet a God who incinerated His own children."

She said it with a smile; but Carl Mendelius knew that she meant every word.

As they drove out to the Salvator Mundi hospital, Domenico Francone, the garrulous one, was taciturn and snappish. When Mendelius pointed out that they seemed to be taking a complicated route, Francone told him bluntly:

"I know my business, Professor. I promise you will not be late."

Mendelius digested the snub in silence. He himself was feeling none too happy. His talk with Hilde Frank had raised more and deeper questions on the veracity of Jean Marie and the wisdom of his encyclical. It had also cast new light on the attitude of the Cardinals who deposed him.

All through the literature of apocalyptic, in the Old and the New Testament, in Essene and Gnostic documents, one special theme persisted: the elect, the chosen, the children of light, the good seed, the sheep, beloved by the shepherd, who would be separated forever from the goats. Salvation was exclusive to them. Only they would endure through the horrors of the last time, and be found worthy of a merciful judgment.

It was a perilous doctrine, full of paradoxes and pitfalls, easily appropriated by fanatics and charlatans and the wildest of sectaries. A thousand of the elect had committed ritual suicide in Guyana. Ten million of the elect made up the Soka Gakkai in Japan. Another three million were chosen to salvation in the Unification Church of the Reverend Moon. . . . All of them and other millions, in ten thousand exotic cults, believed themselves the chosen, practiced an intense indoctrination, a fierce, exclusive and fanatical bonding. . . .

In the event of a universal panic, such as the publication of Jean Marie's encyclical might raise, how would such sectaries perform? The history of every great religion offered only the gloomiest forecast. It was not so long ago that

Mahdist Moslems had occupied the Kaaba in Mecca and held hostages and spilled blood in the holiest place of Islam. It was a nightmare possibility that the Parousia might be preceded by a vast and bloody crusade of the insiders against the outlanders. Against such a horror, a swift and painless suicide might seem to many the most rational alternative.

This was the nub of the problem he must thresh out with Jean Marie. Once you invoked private revelation, reason was out the window. To which the rationalists would reply that once you invoked any kind of revelation—however hallowed by tradition—you were committed to an ultimate insanity.

Francone swung the car into the circular drive of the Salvator Mundi and stopped immediately outside the entrance. He did not get out, but simply said, "Go straight inside, Professor. Move fast."

Mendelius hesitated a split second, then opened the nearside door and went straight into the reception area. When he looked out, he saw Francone park the car in the space reserved for medical staff, get out and walk briskly to the entrance. Mendelius waited until he was inside, then asked, "What was all that about?"

Francone shrugged. "Just a precaution. We're in an enclosed space, nowhere to run. You go upstairs and see the Senator. I have a phone call to make."

An elderly nun with a Swabian accent escorted him to the elevator. On the fifth floor a security man checked his papers and passed him to the ward sister, a very brusque lady who clearly believed that the sick were best healed by the firm hands of authority. She told him he might spend fifteen minutes, no more, with the patient, who must not, in any case, be excited. Mendelius bowed his head in meekness. He, too, had suffered under the handmaidens of the Lord and knew better than to argue against their resolute virtue.

He found Malagordo propped up on his pillows, with a glucose drip strapped to his left arm. His lean, handsome face lit up with pleasure at the sight of his visitor.

"My dear Professor! Thank you for coming. I wanted so much to see you."

"You seem to be making a good recovery." Mendelius pulled a chair to the bedside. "How do you feel?"

"Better each day, thank God. I owe you my life. I understand you are now in danger because of me. What can I say? The newspapers can be so irresponsible. May I order you some coffee?"

"No, thank you. I had a late lunch."

"What do you think of my sad country, Professor?"

"It was mine, too, for a number of years, Senator. At least I understand it better than most foreigners."

"We have gone back four centuries, to the bandits and the *condottieri*! I see small hope for betterment. Like all the other Mediterraneans, we are lost tribes, squabbling on the shores of a putrid lake."

The threnody had a familiar ring to Mendelius. The Latins were great mourners of a past that never existed. He tried to lighten the conversation.

"You may be right, Senator; but I must tell you the wines are still good in Castelli, and Zia Rosa's spaghetti alla carbonara is magnificent as always. My wife and I lunched there on Sunday. The nice thing was she remembered me from my clerical days. She seemed to approve the change."

The Senator brightened immediately. "I'm told she used to be a great beauty."

"Not any longer. But she's a great cook and she rules that place with an iron fist."

"Have you been to the Pappagallo?"

"No."

"That's another very good place."

There was a moment's silence, then Malagordo said with wry humour, "We talk banalities. I wonder why we waste so much life on them."

"It's a precaution." Mendelius grinned. "Wine and women are safe topics. Money and politics lead to broken heads."

"I'm retiring from politics," said Malagordo. "As soon as I get out of here my wife and I are emigrating to Australia. Our two sons are there, doing very well in business. Besides, it's the last stop before the penguins. I don't want to be in Europe for the great collapse."

"Do you think it will collapse?" asked Mendelius.

"I'm certain of it. The armaments are nearly all ready. The latest prototypes will be operational in a year. There's not enough oil to go round. More and more governments are in the hands of gamblers or fanatics. It's the old story: if you're faced with riots at home, start a crusade abroad. Man is a mad animal, and the madness is incurable. Do you know where I was going when I got shot? To plead for the release of a woman terrorist who is dying of cancer in a Palermo jail!"

"God Almighty!" Mendelius swore softly.

"I think He'll be happy to see this race of imbeciles eliminate itself. . . ." Malagordo made a wry mouth as a sudden pain took hold of him. "I know! From a Jew that's blasphemy. But I don't believe in the Messiah anymore. He's delayed too long. And who needs this bloody mess of a world anyway?"

"Take it easy," said Mendelius. "If you get excited, they'll have me thrown out. That ward sister is a real dragon."

"A missed vocation." Malagordo was good-humoured again. "She's got quite a good body under all that drapery. Before you go . . ." He reached under his pillow and brought out a small package wrapped in bright paper and tied with a gold ribbon. "I have a gift for you."

"It wasn't necessary." Mendelius was embarrassed. "But thank you. May I open it?"

"Please!"

The gift was a small gilt box with a glass lid. Inside the box was a shard of pottery inscribed with Hebrew characters. Mendelius took it out and examined it carefully.

"Do you know what it is, Professor?"

"It looks like an *ostracon*."

"It is. Can you read the words?"

Mendelius traced them slowly with his fingertip. "I think it spells Aharon ben Ezra."

"Right! It came from Masada. I am told it is probably one of the shards which were used to draw lots when the Jewish garrison killed each other, rather than fall into the hands of the Romans."

Mendelius was deeply moved. He shook his head. "I can't take this. Truly, I can't."

"You must," said Malagordo. "It's the nearest I can get to a proper thank-you—all that's left of a Jewish hero, for the life of a lousy Senator, who isn't even a man anymore. . . . Go now, Professor, before I make a fool of myself!"

When he reached the ground floor he found Francone waiting for him. As he moved towards the exit Francone laid a restraining hand on his arm.

"We'll wait here for a few minutes, Professor."

"Why?"

Francone pointed out through the glass doors. There were two police cars parked in the driveway and four more outside in the road. Two orderlies were loading a stretcher into an ambulance under the eyes of a curious crowd. Mendelius gaped at the scene. Francone explained tersely.

"We were followed here, Professor. One car. Then a second one arrived and parked just outside the gates. They had both entrances covered. Fortunately I spotted the tail just after we left town. I telephoned the *Squadra Mobile* as soon as we arrived. They blocked both ends of the street and caught four of the bastards. One's dead."

"For God's sake, Domenico! Why didn't you tell me?"

"It would have spoiled your visit. Besides, what could you have done? Like I told you, Professor, I know how these *mascalzoni* work. . . ."

"Thanks!" Mendelius held out a damp and unsteady hand. "I hope you won't tell my wife."

"When you work for a Cardinal," said Francone with grave condescension, "you learn to keep your mouth shut."

"Dear colleagues!" Carl Mendelius, smiling and benign, adjusted his spectacles and surveyed his audience. "I begin today with a mild censure on person or persons unknown. . . .

"I know that travel is expensive. I know that ministers of the gospel are paid very little. I know that it is a common practice to supplement one's income, or one's travel allowance, by supplying conference reports to the press. I have no objection to the practice, provided it is open and declared; but I think it is an abridgment of academic courtesy to file press reports in secret and without notice to colleagues. One of our members has caused me considerable embarrassment by reporting to a senior journalist that I believed the end of the world could be imminent. True, I said so in this room; but, out of the context of our assembly and its specialist discussions, the statement could be interpreted as frivolous or tendentious. I do not ask for a confession from the reporter. I do, however, seek an assurance that what is said here today will be reported only with our full knowledge. . . . Will all those who agree please raise their hands? . . . Thank you. Any dissenters? None. Apparently we understand each other. So let us begin. . . .

"We have talked about the Doctrine of Last Things: consummation or continuity. We have expressed differing views on the subject. Now let us accept, as hypothesis, that the consummation is possible and imminent: that the world will end soon. How should the Christian respond to that event? . . . You, sir, in the third row."

"Wilhelm Adler, Rosenheim. The answer is that the Christian—or anyone else for that matter—cannot respond to a hypothesis, only to an event. This was the mistake of the schoolmen and the casuists. They tried to prescribe moral formulae for every situation. Impossible! Man lives in the here and the now, not in the perhaps."

"Good! . . . But does not human prudence dictate that he should prepare for the perhaps?"

"Could you give an example, Herr Professor?"

"Certainly. The earliest followers of Christ were Jews. They continued to live a Jewish life. They practiced circumcision. They observed the dietary laws. They frequented the synagogues and read the Scriptures. . . . Now Paul—Saul that was—of Tarsus embarks on his mission to the Gentiles, the non-Jews, to whom circumcision is unacceptable and the dietary laws are unexplainable. They see no point in bodily mutilation. They have to eat what they can get. Suddenly they are out of theory into practice. . . . The question simplifies itself. Surely salvation does not hang on a man's foreskin; nor does it depend on his starving himself to death. . . ."

They laughed at that and applauded the rabbinical humour. Mendelius went on.

"Paul was prepared for the event. Peter was not. In the absence of scriptural dictate, he had to find justification for his new position in a vision—'Take and eat'—remember?"

They remembered, and gave a murmur of approval.

"So now, our 'perhaps.' The Last Days are upon us. How prepared are we?"

They hung back now. Mendelius offered them another example.

"Some few of you here are old enough to remember the last days of the Third Reich; a country in ruins, a monstrosity of crimes revealed, a generation of men destroyed, a whole ethos corrupted, the only visible goal, survival! To those of us who remember, is it not at least a fair analogue of the millennial catastrophe? . . . But you are here today because, somewhere, somehow, faith and hope and charity survived and became fruitful again. . . . Do I explain myself?"

"Yes." The answer came back in a muted chorus.

"How then . . ." He challenged them strongly. "How do we ensure that faith and charity survive, if and when the Last Days come upon us? Forget the Last Days if you must. Suppose that, as many predict, we have atomic war within a twelvemonth, what will you do?"

"Die!" said a sepulchral voice from the back; and the room dissolved into a roar of laughter.

"Ladies and gentlemen!" Mendelius chuckled helplessly. "There speaks a true prophet! Would he like to come up here and take my place?"

No one stirred. After a few moments the laughter died into silence. More quietly now, Mendelius went on.

"I should like to read to you now an extract from a document prepared by a dear friend of mine. I cannot name him. I ask you to accept that he is a man of great sanctity and singular intelligence; one, moreover, who understands the usages of power in the modern world. After the reading I shall ask for your comments."

He paused to wipe his spectacles and then began to read from Jean Marie's encyclical: ". . . It is clear that in the days of universal calamity the traditional structures of society will not survive. There will be a ferocious struggle for the simplest needs of life—food, water, fuel and shelter. Authority will be usurped by the strong and the cruel. Large urban societies will fragment themselves into tribal groups. . . ."

He felt the words take hold of them, the tension begin to build again. When the reading was done the silence was like a wall before him.

He stepped back from the rostrum and asked simply, "Any comment?"

There was a long pause and then a young woman stood up.

"I am Henni Borkheim from Berlin. My husband is a pastor. We have two young children. I have a question. How do you show charity to a man who comes with a gun to rob you and take the last food from your children?"

"And I have another!" The young man next to her stood up. "How do you continue to believe in a God who contrives or permits so universal a calamity—and then sits in judgment on its victims?"

"So perhaps," said Carl Mendelius gravely, "we should all ask ourselves a more fundamental question. We know that evil exists, that suffering and cruelty exist, that they may well propagate themselves to extremity like cancer in the body. Can we really believe in God at all?"

"Do you, Professor?" Henni Borkheim was on her feet again.

"Yes, I do."

"Then will you please answer my question!"

"It was answered two millennia ago. 'Father, forgive them, for they know not what they do!' "

"And that's the answer you would give?"

"I don't know, my dear." He was about to add that he had not yet been crucified; but he thought better of it. He stepped down from the rostrum and walked down through the audience to where the girl was sitting with her husband. He talked calmly and persuasively.

". . . You see the problem we get when we demand a personal testimony on every issue? We do not, we cannot, know how we will act. How we *should* act, yes! But how we will, in an immediate situation, there is no way to know in advance. . . . I remember as a youth in Dresden my mother talking to my aunt about the coming of the Russians. I was not supposed to hear; but I did. My mother handed her a jar of lubricant jelly and said: 'Better relax and survive than resist and be murdered.' . . . Either way it's rape, and there is no miracle promised to prevent it; no legislation to cover the time of chaos." He smiled and held out his hand to the young woman. "Let's not contend; but discuss in peace."

There was a small murmur of approval as they joined hands; then Mendelius put another question.

"In a plural world, who are the elect? We Romans, you Lutherans, the Sunnis or the Shi'ites in Islam, the Mormons of Salt Lake City, the Animists of Thailand?"

"In respect of the individual, it is not for us to distinguish." A grey-haired pastor rose painfully to his feet. His hands were knotted with arthritis. He spoke haltingly but with conviction. "We are not appointed to judge other men by our lights. We are commanded only to love the image of God in our fellow pilgrims."

"But we are also commanded to keep the faith pure, to spread the good news of Christ," said Pastor Allman of Darmstadt.

"When you sit down at my table," said the old man patiently, "I offer you the food I have. If you cannot digest it, what should I do—choke you with it?"

"So, my friends!" Mendelius took command of the meeting again. "When the black night comes down, in the great desert, when there is neither pillar of cloud nor spark of fire to light the path, when the voice of authority is stilled, and we hear nothing but the confusion of old argument, when God seems to absent himself from his own universe, where do we turn? Whom can we sanely believe?"

He walked slowly back to the rostrum and, in a long hush, waited for someone to answer.

"I'm scared, liebchen! So damn scared, I'd like to walk out of here and take the next plane back to Germany!"

It was thirty minutes after midday and they were eating an early lunch in a quiet restaurant near the Pantheon, before Mendelius left for Monte Cassino. Two tables away, Francone shovelled spaghetti into his mouth and kept a vigilant eye on the door. Lotte leaned across to Mendelius and wiped a speck of sauce from the corner of his mouth. She chided him firmly:

"Truly, Carl, I don't know what the fuss is about! You're a free man. You're going to see an old friend. You don't have to accept any commission, any obligations, beyond this one visit."

"He's asked me to judge him."

"He had no right to demand that."

"He didn't demand—he asked, begged! Look, liebchen. I've thought round and round this thing. I've talked it up and down; and still I'm no nearer to an answer. Jean Marie's asking for an act of faith just as big as . . . as an assent to the Resurrection! I can't make that act."

"So tell him!"

"And do I tell him why? 'Jean, you're not mad; you're not a cheat; you're not deluded; I love you like a brother—but God doesn't have dialogues in country gardens about the end of the world; and I wouldn't believe it if you came complete with the stigmata and a crown of thorns!'"

"If that's what you mean, say it."

"The problem is, liebchen, I think I mean something else altogether. I'm beginning to believe the Cardinals were right to get rid of Jean Marie."

"What makes you say that?"

"It arises out of my dialogues at the Academy—and even a talk I had with Hilde Frank. The only finality people can cope with is their own. . . . Total catastrophe is beyond their comprehension and probably their capacity to deal with. It's an invitation to despair. Jean Marie sees it as a call to evangelical charity. I think it would lead to an almost complete breakdown in social communication. Who was it who said: 'The veil that hides the face of the future was woven by the hand of Mercy'?"

"Then I think," said Lotte firmly, "you have to be as honest with Jean Marie as you're trying to be with yourself. He asked you for a judgment. Give it to him!"

"I want to ask you a straight question, liebchen. Do you think I'm an honest man?"

She did not answer him directly. She cupped her chin on her hands and looked at him for a long time without speaking. Then very quietly she told him:

"I remember the first day I met you, Carl. I was with Frederika Ullman. We were walking down the Spanish Steps, two German girls on their first visit to Rome. You were there, sitting on the steps next to a lad who was painting a very bad picture. You were dressed in black pants and a black roll-necked sweater. We stopped to look at the picture. You heard us talking in German and you spoke to us. We sat down beside you, very glad to have someone to chat with us. You bought us tea and buns in the English Tea Shop. Then you invited us to go for a ride in a *carrozza*. Off we went, clip-clopping, all the way to the Campo dei Fiori. When we got there you showed us that marvellous brooding statue of Giordano Bruno and told us about his trial and how they burned him for heresy on the same spot. Then you said: 'That's what they'd like to do to me!' I thought you were drunk or a little crazy until you explained that you were a priest under suspicion of heresy. . . . You looked so lonely, so haunted, my heart went out to you. Then you quoted Bruno's last words to his judges: 'I think, gentlemen, that you are more afraid of me than I of you.' . . . I'm looking at the same man I saw that day. The same man who said: 'Bruno was a faker, a charlatan, a muddled thinker, but one thing I know: he died an honest man!' I loved you then, Carl. I love you now. Whatever you do, right or wrong, I know you'll die an honest man!"

"I hope so, liebchen!" said Carl Mendelius gravely. "I hope to God I can be honest with the man who married us!"

V

AT three-thirty precisely Francone set him down at the portals of the great Monastery of Monte Cassino. The guestmaster welcomed him and led him to his room, a plain whitewashed chamber furnished with a bed, a desk and chair, a clothes closet and a prie-dieu over which was hung a crucifix carved in olive wood. He threw open the shutters to reveal a dizzying view across the Rapido valley to the rolling hills of Lazio. He smiled at Mendelius' surprise and said:

"You see! Already we are halfway to heaven! . . . I hope you enjoy your stay with us."

He waited while Mendelius laid out his few belongings and then led him along the bare, echoing corridors to the Abbot's study. The man who rose to greet him was small and spare with a lean, weathered face and iron-grey hair and the smile of a happy child.

"Professor Mendelius! A pleasure to meet you! Please, sit down. Would you like coffee, a cordial perhaps?"

"No, thank you; we stopped for a coffee on the autostrada. It's very kind of you to receive me."

"You come with the best recommendations, Professor." There was a hint of irony in the innocent smile. "I don't want to keep you too long from your friend; but I thought we should talk first."

"Of course. You told me on the telephone he had been ill."

"You will find him changed." The Abbot chose his words carefully. "He has survived an experience that would have crushed a lesser man. Now he is going through another—more difficult, more intense, because it is an interior struggle. I counsel him as best I can. The rest of the brethren support him with their prayers and their attentions; but he is like a man consumed by a fire inside him. It may be he will open himself to you. If he does, let him see that you understand. Don't press him. I know that he has written to you. I know what he has asked. I am his confessor and I cannot discuss that subject with you, because he has not given me permission to do so. . . . You, on the other hand, are not my subject and I cannot presume to direct your conscience either."

"Perhaps then, you and I could open our minds to each other."

"Perhaps." Abbot Andrew's smile was enigmatic. "But first, I think you should talk to our friend Jean."

"Certain questions arise. Does he truly want to see me?"

"Oh, yes, indeed."

"Then why, when I wrote to you both, did he not write back as well as you? When I called on the telephone, why did you not invite him to speak with me?"

"It was not discourtesy, I promise you."

"What was it?"

The Abbot sat silent for a long moment, studying the backs of his long hands. Finally he said, slowly, "There are times when it is not possible for him to communicate with anyone."

"That sounds ominous."

"On the contrary, Professor. It is my belief, based on personal observation, that your friend Jean has reached a high degree of contemplation, that state, in fact, which is called 'illuminative,' in which, for certain periods, the spirit is totally absorbed in communication with the Creator. It is a rare phenomenon; but not unfamiliar in the lives of the great mystics. During these periods of contemplation the subject does not respond to any external stimuli at all. When the experience is over, he returns immediately to normality. . . . But I am telling you nothing you don't know from your own reading."

"I know also," said Carl Mendelius drily, "that catatonic and cataleptic states are very well known in psychiatric medicine."

"I, too, am aware of it, Professor. We are not altogether in the Dark Ages here. Our founder, Saint Benedict, was a wise and tolerant legislator. It may surprise you to know that one of our fathers is a quite eminent physician with degrees from Padua, Zurich and London. He entered the order only ten years ago after the death of his wife. He has examined our friend. He has, on my direction, consulted with other specialists on the matter. He is convinced, as I am, that we are dealing with a mystic and not a psychotic."

"Have you so informed the people who declared him a madman?"

"I have informed Cardinal Drexel. For the rest . . ." He gave a small chuckle of amusement. "They're very busy men. I prefer not to disturb them in their large affairs. Any more questions?"

"Only one," said Mendelius gravely. "You believe Jean Marie is a mystic, illuminated by God. Do you also believe that he was granted a relevation of the Parousia?"

The Abbot frowned and shook his head.

"Afterwards, my friend! After you've seen him. Then I'll tell you what I believe. . . . Come! He's waiting in the garden. I'll take you to him."

He was standing in the middle of the cloister garden, a tall slim figure in the black habit of St. Benedict, feeding crumbs to the pigeons that fluttered at his feet. At the sound of Mendelius' footfall he turned, stared for a single moment, and then hurried towards him, arms outstretched, while the pigeons wheeled in panic above his head. Mendelius caught him in midstride and held him in a long embrace, shocked to feel, even through the coarse stuff of the habit, how thin and frail he was. His first words were a stifled cry:

"Jean . . . Jean, my friend!"

Jean Marie Barette clung to him, patting his shoulder and saying over and over, *"Grâce à Dieu . . . Grâce à Dieu!"*

Then they held each other at arms' length, looking into each other's face.

"Jean! Jean! What have they done to you? You're as thin as a rake."

"They? Nothing." He fished a handkerchief from the sleeve of his habit and dabbed at Mendelius' cheeks. "Everybody's been more than kind. How are all your family?"

"Well, thank God. Lotte's here in Rome. She sends you her best love."

"Thank her for lending you to me. . . . I prayed you would come quickly, Carl!"

"I wanted to come sooner; but I couldn't leave Tübingen until end of term."

"I know . . . I know! And now I read that you are involved in a terrorist shooting in Rome. That troubles me. . . ."

"Please, Jean! It's a nine-day wonder. Tell me about yourself."

"Shall we walk awhile? It's very pleasant here. One gets the breeze from the mountains, cool and clean, even on the hottest day."

He took Mendelius' arm and they began to stroll slowly round the cloisters, making small tentative talk, as the first rush of emotion ebbed and the calm of an old friendship took hold of them.

"I am very much at home here," said Jean Marie. "Abbot Andrew is most considerate. I like the rhythm of the day; the hours of the office sung in choir, the quiet work. . . . One of the fathers is an excellent sculptor in wood. I sit in his workshop and watch. I love the smell of wood shavings! It's a feast day today. I prepared the dessert you will be having for supper. It's an old recipe my mother used. The fruit is from our own orchard. In the kitchen they have decided I'm better as a cook than as a Pope. . . . And how is life with you, Carl?"

"It's good, Jean. The children are beginning to make their own lives. Katrin is head over heels in love with her painter. Johann is brilliant in economics. He's decided he's not a believer anymore. One hopes he will grope his way back into faith; but he's a good lad just the same. Lotte and I, well, we're just beginning to enjoy being middle-aged together. . . . The new book's moving ahead. At least it was, until you put it all out of my head. . . . I don't think there's been an hour when you were absent from my thoughts. . . ."

"And you were never far from mine, Carl. It was as if you were the last spar to which I could cling after the shipwreck. I dared not let you go. I look back on those last weeks in the Vatican, with real horror."

"And now, Jean . . . ?"

"Now I am calm—if not yet at peace, because I am still struggling to divest myself of the last impediments to a conformity with God's will. . . . You cannot believe how hard it is, when it should be so simple, to abandon yourself absolutely to His designs, to say and mean it: 'Here I am, a tool in your hands. Use me any way you want.' The trust has to be absolute; but always one tries—without even knowing—to hedge the bet."

"And I was part of the hedge?" Mendelius said it with a smile and a hand's touch to soften the question.

"You were, Carl. I suppose you still are; but I believe also that you are part of God's design for me. Had you not written, had you declined to come, I would have been forced to think otherwise. I prayed desperately for strength to face the possibility of a refusal."

"It's still a possibility, Jean," said Mendelius with grave gentleness. "You asked me to judge you."

"Have you reached a verdict yet?"

"No. I had to talk to you first."

"Let's sit down, Carl. Over there, on the stone bench. That's where I was sitting when it happened. But, first, there are other things to tell you. . . ."

They settled themselves on the bench. Jean Marie scooped up a handful of pebbles from the path and began tossing them at an imaginary target. He talked casually, in a tone of wry reminiscence.

". . . Let me say outright, Carl, that in spite of all the ritual disclaimers and the public acts of humility, I really wanted to be Pope. All my life I had been a careerist in the Church. I use the word in the French sense. I was built for what I did. As a youth I fought with the Maquis. I came to the seminary a man, sure of his vocation and of his motives. More, I understood instinctively how the system works. It's like Saint Cyr or Oxford or Harvard . . . If you know the rules of the game, the averages are in your favour. There's no discredit . . . that's not what I'm saying. I simply point out that there is, there has to be, an element of ambition, an element of calculation . . . I had the ambition. I also had a good, tidy French mind. . . .

"So, I was a good priest, a good diocesan bishop. I mean that! I worked hard at it. I spent a lot of love. I held the people together, even the young. I set up social experiments. I was attracting vocations to the ministry while others were losing them. My people told me they felt a sense of unity, of religious purpose. In short, I had to be, sooner or later, a candidate for the red hat. In the end it was offered to me, on condition that I came to Rome and joined the Curia. Naturally, I accepted. I was appointed Prefect of the Secretariat for Christian Unity and Subprefect of the Secretariat for Nonbelievers. . . . These were minor offices as you know. The real power was vested in the important Congregations: Doctrine of the Faith, Episcopal and Clerical Affairs.

"Still I was very happy. I had access to the Pontiff. I had an open brief, the opportunity to travel, to make contacts far outside the Roman enclave. . . . This was when we met, Carl. You remember the excitements we shared. It was like having a box at the opera! . . . And there were good and great things to be done. . . .

"But then, slowly I began to see how very little I had accomplished—or could ever accomplish for that matter. At home, if I founded a school or a hospital, the results were there, tangible and consequential. I saw the dying comforted by the sisters. I saw the children taught in a religious tradition. . . . But as a Cardinal in Rome—what? Plans and projects and discussions and a new printing press to roll out the documents, but between me and the people a wall was thrown up. I was no longer an apostle. I was a diplomat, a politician, a go-between, and I did not like the man who walked in my shoes. . . . I liked the system even less: cumbersome, archaic, costly and full of cozy corners where slothful men could sleep their lives away and intriguers flourish like exotic plants in a hothouse.

"However, if I wanted to change it—and I did, believe me!—I had to stay inside the Curia. I had to work within the limits of my own character. I am a persuader, not a dictator. I hate rudeness. I have never pounded a table in my life! . . .

"So, when my predecessor died and the conclave was deadlocked, they chose me, Jean Marie Barette, Gregory the Seventeenth, Successor to the Prince of the Apostles!" He tossed the last pebbles onto the pathway and eased himself painfully to his feet. "Do you mind, Carl, if we go to Father Edmund's workshop? It's warmer there, and we can still be private. When evening comes I feel the cold. . . ."

Inside the workshop, amid the cheerful clutter of wood billets and shavings and tools and a shaggy Baptist half born from a block of oak, they perched themselves like schoolboys on the bench while Jean Marie continued his story.

". . . And there I was, my dear Carl, suddenly as high as man could climb in the City of God. My titles assured me of my eminence and my authority: Supreme Pontiff of the Universal Church, Patriarch of the West, Primate of Italy . . . *et patati et patata!*" He gave a laugh of genuine amusement. "I tell you, Carl, when you stand for the first time on that balcony and look across Saint Peter's Square and hear the applause of the crowd, you really believe you're someone! It's very easy to forget that Christ was a wandering prophet who slept in caves, and Peter was a fisherman from a lakeside in Galilee and John the Precursor was murdered in a prison cell.

". . . After that, of course, you learn very fast. The whole system is designed to surround you with the aura of absolute authority, and resolutely to obstruct your use of it. The long liturgical ceremonies and the public appearances are theatre pieces in which you are stage-managed like an actor. Your private audiences are diplomatic occasions. You talk banalities. You bless medals. You are photographed for the posterity of your visitors. . . .

"Meantime, the bureaucracy grinds on, filtering what comes to your desk, editing and glossing what you hand down. You are besieged by counsellors whose sole object seems to be to delay decision. You cannot act except through intermediaries. There are not enough hours in the day to digest a tenth of the information presented to you—and the language of Curial documents is as carefully designed as American officialese or the double-talk of the Marxists. . . .

"I remember speaking about this to the President of the United States and, later, to the Chairman of the People's Republic of China. Each told me the same thing in different words. The President, a very salty fellow, said: 'They geld us first and then expect us to win the Kentucky Derby.' The Chairman put it rather more politely: 'You have five hundred million subjects. I have nearly twice that number. That is why you need hellfire and I need the punishment camps—and death takes us both before the work is half done.' . . . That's the other thing, Carl, our own mortality makes us desperate; and desperate leaders are very vulnerable. We either surround ourselves with sycophants or we weary ourselves in a daily battle with men as resolute as we are. . . ."

"Or we begin to look for miracles," said Carl Mendelius quietly.

"Or we are tempted to create them." Jean Marie gave him a swift shrewd look. "The politicians have their propaganda pieces. The Pope has his wonder-workers. That's what you're really saying, isn't it, Carl?"

"It's a point at issue, Jean. I had to put it to you."

"The answer's simple. Yes, you wish for miracles. You pray for God to show His hand sometimes on this cruel planet. But to create them for yourself, or find yourself a ready-made magus, or adopt one from the annual crop of *soi-disant* saints—no, Carl! Not I! What happened to me was real, and uninvited. It was a torment and not a gift."

"But you did try to exploit it?"

"Do you believe that, old friend?"

"I ask because others believe it—still others could say it in the future."

"And I can offer no proof to the contrary."

"Precisely, Jean! To use the terms of biblical analysis, you claim a private disclosure experience, but you cannot ask for an act of faith in your unsupported testimony. Therefore, there has to be a legitimizing sign. . . . The Cardinals were scared you would get it by invoking the dogma of infallibility. They were desperate to get rid of you before you could do it. . . ."

Jean Marie frowned over the idea for a moment, then nodded agreement.

"Yes, I accept your definitions. I claim a disclosure experience. I lack a legitimizing sign which authorizes me to proclaim it . . ."

"Correction." Mendelius frowned over the phrase. ". . . which authorizes you to proclaim it as Pontiff of the Universal Church."

"But look at our Baptist here." Jean Marie ran his hand over the half-finished sculpture. "He came out of the desert, preaching that the Kingdom of God was at hand, that men should repent and be baptized. What was his patent of authority? I quote: 'The word of the Lord came to John the son of Zachary in the desert. . . .'" He smiled and shrugged. "At least there are precedents, Carl! But let me go on. . . . We were talking about power and its limitations. One thing I did have as Pope was access to information—and from the highest sources. I travelled. I talked to heads of state. They sent emissaries to me.

"All of them, without exception, faced the same dreadful dilemma. They were appointed to serve a national interest. If they failed to do that, they would be deposed. But they knew that at some point they had to compromise national interest with other interests equally imperative; and if the compromise failed, the world would be plunged into an atomic war. . . .

"They knew more, Carl, more than they ever dared to make public: that the means of destruction are so vast, so deadly, so far beyond antidote, that they can obliterate mankind and make the planet itself unfit for human habitation. . . . What these high men told me was the stuff of nightmares and I was haunted by them, day and night. Everything else became petty and irrelevant: dogmatic disputes, some poor priest hopping into bed with a housemaid, whether a woman should take a pill or carry a little card to count her lunar periods to avoid making gunfodder for the day of Armageddon. . . . Do you understand, my friend? Do you really understand?"

"I understand, Jean," said Mendelius with somber conviction. "Better than you perhaps, because I have children and you have not. On this matter we are not at odds. But I have to put it to you, that you didn't need a vision to show you the last disaster. It was already burned into your brain. You, yourself, called it the stuff of nightmares—and you can have those, waking or sleeping!"

"And the rest of it, Carl? The final deliverance, the last justification of God's redeeming plan, the Parousia? Did I dream that, too?"

"You could have." Mendelius pieced out his answer slowly. "I tell you as an historian, I tell you as a man and as a student of mankind's beliefs, the dream of the last things haunts the folk-memory of every race under the sun. It is expressed in every literature, in every art, in every death ritual known to man. The forms are different; but the dream persists, haunting our pillows in the dark, forming itself by day out of the storm clouds and the lightning flash. I share the dream with you; but when you say, as you do in your encyclical: 'I . . . am commanded by the Holy Spirit to write you these words,' then I have to ask, as your colleagues did, whether you are speaking in symbol or of fact. If of fact, then show me the rescript and the seal; prove to me that the message is authentic!"

"You know I can't do that," said Jean Marie Barette.

"Exactly," said Carl Mendelius.

"But if you admit, Carl, that catastrophe is possible and even imminent, if you admit that the Doctrine of Last Things is an authentic dream of all mankind—and a clear tradition in Christian doctrine, why should I not say so— vision or no vision?"

"Because you determine it!" Mendelius was implacable. "You determine it by circumstance, by approximate time. You demand immediate and specific preparations. You close out all hope of continuity—and you lock yourself into so narrow a doctrine of election that it will be rejected by most of the world and half our own church as well. For those who accept it the consequences may be disastrous—mass panic, public disorders, and most certainly a rash of suicides. . . ."

"My compliments, Carl!" Jean Marie gave him a smile of ironic approbation. "You've made a splendid case, better even than my Cardinals presented."

"I rest it there," said Carl Mendelius.

"And you expect me to answer it?"

"You asked me in your letter to spread the message which you could no longer proclaim. You have to prove to me that it is authentic."

"How, Carl? What evidence would convince you? A burning bush? A rod turned into a serpent? Our Baptist here, stepping alive out of this block of wood?"

Before Mendelius had time to frame an answer the monastery bell began to toll. Jean Marie slipped off the bench and dusted the sawdust from his robe.

"It's a feast day. Vespers are half-an-hour early. Are you going to join us in the chapel?"

"If I may," said Mendelius quietly. "I've run out of human answers."

"There are none," said Jean Marie Barette, and quoted softly: " '*Nisi dominus aedificaverit domum.* . . . Unless the Lord build the house, the builders labour in vain!' "

* * *

In the chapel, the ancient hierarchic order still prevailed. The Abbot sat in the place of honour with his counsellors about him. Jean Marie, lately a Pope, was seated with the juniors. Carl Mendelius was placed among the novices, with a borrowed breviary in his hands. It was a strange, poignant experience, as if he had stepped back thirty years, to the old monkish life in which he had been trained. Every cadence of the Gregorian chant was familiar. The words of the Psalms called up vivid pictures of his student days; lectures and disputations and long, painful discussions with superiors in the period before his exit.

"Ad te domine, clamabo . . ." the choir intoned. "To thee O Lord I will cry out. O my God be not silent to me, lest, if thou be silent to me, I become like those who go down into the pit. Hear O Lord the voice of my supplication when I pray to thee, when I lift up my hands to thy holy temple."

The invocations had a new meaning for him as well. The silence which had fallen between himself and Jean Marie was sinister. Suddenly they were strangers, met in a no-man's-land, each speaking a language alien to the other. The God who spoke to Jean Marie was silent to Carl Mendelius.

"According to the works of their hands . . ." the chant echoed through the vaulted nave, "render to them their reward." And the response came back, somber and menacing: "Because they have not understood the works of the Lord . . . thou shalt destroy them and not build them up."

But . . . but—against the counterpoint of the psalmody Mendelius wrestled his way through the argument—whose understanding was the right one? If the leap of faith were not a rational act, it became an insanity, to which he could not commit, even if his refusal meant the rupture of the bond between himself and Jean Marie. It was a thing sad to contemplate, late in life, when the simple abrasion of time wore out so many cherished relationships.

He was glad when the service was over and he joined the community for the feast-day meal in the refectory. He could laugh at the small community jokes, applaud Jean Marie's dessert, discuss with the father archivist the resources of the library, and with the Abbot, the quality of the wines of the Abruzzi. When the meal was over and the monks moved into the common room for evening recreation, Jean Marie approached the Abbot and asked:

"May we be excused, Father Abbot? Carl and I still have things to discuss. Afterwards we'll read Compline together, in my cell."

"Of course. . . . But don't keep him up too late, Professor! We're trying to get him to take care of himself."

Jean Marie's cell was as bare as the guest room. There were no ornaments save the crucifix, the only books were the Bible, a copy of the Rule, a book of hours and a French edition of *The Imitation of Christ*. Jean Marie took off his habit, kissed it and hung it in the closet. He pulled a woollen jersey over his shirt and sat on the bed, facing Mendelius. He said with a touch of irony:

"So here we are, Carl! No popery, no monkery; just two men trying to be honest with each other. Let me ask you some questions now. . . . Do you believe I am a sane man?"

"Yes, I do, Jean."

"Am I a liar?"

"No."

"And the vision?"

"I believe the experience you described in your letter was real to you. I believe you are totally sincere in your interpretation of it."

"But you will not commit yourself to that interpretation."

"I cannot. The best I can do is keep an open mind."

"And the service I asked of you?"

"To spread the word of the catastrophe and the Coming? I cannot do it, Jean. I will not. Some of the reasons I've explained to you; but there are others as well. You abdicated over this issue! You wore the Fisherman's ring. You held the seal of the Supreme Teacher. You surrendered them! If you could not proclaim as Pope what you believe, what do you want of me? I'm not a cleric anymore. I'm a secular scholar. I am deprived of authority to teach in the Church. What do you expect me to do? Go round forming little sects of millenarian Christians? That's been done before, as far back as Montanus and Tertullian—and the consequences have always been disastrous. . . ."

"That's not what I mean, Carl."

"It's what would happen! Like it or not, you'd have charismatic anarchy."

"There will be anarchy in any case!"

"Then I refuse to contribute to it."

"I will tell you something more, Carl! The mission you refuse now, you will one day accept. The light you cannot see will be shown to you. One day you will feel God's hand on your shoulder, and you will walk wherever it leads you."

"For the love of God, Jean! What are you? Some kind of oracle? You can't pile prophecy on prophecy and make anything but a madness. Now, listen to me! I'm Carl Mendelius, remember? You asked me to make a judgment. So I make it! I judge that you tell us too much and too little! You were the Pope. You say you had a vision. In the vision you were called by God to proclaim the imminence of the Parousia. . . . Now, face this fact. You did not proclaim it! You bent to a power group. Why did you let them silence you, Jean? Why are you silent now? You abdicated the one rostrum from which you might have spoken to the world! Why do you expect a middle-aged professor from Swabia to recover what you threw away?" Mendelius' anger and frustration vented itself in a final, bitter tirade. "Drexel tells me you've become a mystic. That's a fine, traditional thing to be—and it saves the Establishment a whole lot of trouble, because even the newspapers shy away from God-madness! But what you wrote in your encyclical signified life or death for millions on this small planet. Was it fact or fiction? We need full testimony! We can't wait around while Jean Marie Barette plays hide-and-seek with God in a monastery garden!"

The moment the words were out he was ashamed of his brutality. Jean Marie was silent for a long moment, staring down at the backs of his hands. Finally he answered with wintry restraint.

"You ask me why I abdicated. . . . The conflict between me and the Curia was more desperate than you can imagine. If I had decided to stay in office, there would almost certainly have been a schism. The Sacred College would have deposed me and elected a rival. Our claims would have been disputed for half a century. Popes and anti-popes are an old story, which could have been repeated in this case. But, to live and die with that on my conscience—no! . . . Just now you used a savage metaphor: 'Jean Marie, playing hide-and-seek with God in a monastery garden.' "

"I'm sorry, Jean. I didn't mean . . ."

"On the contrary, Carl, you meant exactly what you said; but you missed the point. I am not playing hide-and-seek. I am sitting very still, waiting for the Lord to speak again and tell me what I must do. I know the need for a legitimizing sign—but I can't give that sign myself. Again, I wait. . . . We talked about miracles, Carl—signs and wonders! You asked whether I had ever prayed for them. Oh, yes! When the Cardinals came to argue with me, day after day, when the doctors came, all grave and clinical, I prayed then: 'Give me something to show them I am not crazy, not a liar!' Before you came, I begged and begged: 'At least make my Carl believe me.' Well! . . ." He smiled and gave a very Gallic shrug. "It seems I must wait longer to be legitimized. . . . Shall we read Compline now?"

"Before we do, Jean, let me say one thing. I came as a friend. I want to leave as a friend."

"And so you shall. What do we pray for?"

"The last wish of Goethe—*Mehr Licht,* more light!"

"Amen!"

Jean Marie reached for his breviary. Mendelius sat beside him on the narrow bed and, together, they recited the psalms for the last canonical hour of the day.

In the morning it was easier to talk. The hardest words had been said. There was no ground of contention, no fear of misunderstanding. In the garden of the vision, the gardener swung his mattock. The father sacristan cut new roses for the altar bowls; while Jean Marie Barette, lately a Pope, tossed bread crumbs to the strutting pigeons and Carl Mendelius stated his own position.

". . . In the matter of your private revelation, Jean, I am agnostic. I do not know. Therefore I cannot act. But in the matter of us—old friends of the heart! —if I have little faith, I still have much love. Believe that, please!"

"I believe it."

"I cannot accept a mission in which I do not believe—and on which you have no authority to send me. But I can do something to test your ideas of an international audience."

"And how would you propose to do that, Carl?"

"Two ways. First, I could arrange with a Georg Rainer, a journalist of author-ity, to publish an accurate account of your abdication. Second, I myself would write, for the international press, a personal memoir on my friend the former Gregory the Seventeenth. In this memoir I should draw attention to the ideas expressed in your encyclical. Finally, I could ensure that the two pieces were brought to the notice of the people on your diplomatic list. . . . Understand what I am offering, Jean. It is not an advocacy, not a crusade, but an honest history, a sympathetic portrait, a clear exposition of your ideas as I have understood them . . . with a chance for total disclaimer if you don't like whatever is written."

"It's a generous offer, Carl." Jean Marie was touched.

Mendelius cautioned him. "It falls far short of what you asked. It will also expose the gaps and weaknesses in your position. For instance, even to me in this meeting you have explained very little of your spiritual state. . . ."

"What can I tell you, Carl?" The implied challenge seemed to surprise him. "Sometimes I am in a darkness so deep, so threatening, that it seems I have been stripped of all human form and damned to an eternal solitude. At other times I am bathed in a luminous calm, totally at peace, yet harmoniously active, like an instrument in the hands of a great master. . . . I cannot read the score; I have no urge to interpret it, only a serene confidence that the dream of the composer is realized in me at every moment. . . . The problem is, my dear Carl, that the terror and the calm both take me unaware. They go as suddenly as they come, and they leave my days as full of holes as a Swiss cheese. Sometimes, I find myself in the garden, or in chapel or in the library, with no idea how I came there. If that is mysticism, Carl, then God help me! I'd rather plod along in the purgative way like ordinary mortals! . . . How you explain that to your readers is your affair."

"Then you do agree to the kind of publication I suggest?"

"Let's be very precise about it." There was a mischief in his eyes. "Let's be very Roman and diplomatic. A journalist does not require my permission to speculate about current history. If you, my learned friend, choose to memorialize me or my opinions, I cannot prevent your doing so. . . . Let's leave it like that, shall we?"

"With pleasure!" Mendelius chuckled with genuine amusement. "Now, one more question. Could you, would you, consider coming to me for a vacation in Tübingen? Lotte would love to have you. For me, it would be like having a brother in the house."

"Thank you, dear friend; but no! If I asked, the Abbot would be embarrassed. The diplomatic problems would be far too delicate to handle. . . . Besides, we can never be closer than we are at this moment. . . . You see, Carl, when I was in the Vatican, I saw the world in panorama—a vast planet with its teeming millions, labouring and fearful, under the threat of the mushroom cloud. Here, I perceive everything in little. All the love and the longing and the caring that I have is concentrated on the nearest human face. At this moment it is your face, Carl; you in all and all in you. It is not easy to express—but that was the agony I experienced in the vision: the stark simplicity of things, the splendid, terrifying oneness of the Almighty—and His designs."

Mendelius frowned and shook his head.

"I wish I could share that vision, Jean. I can't. I think we have enough terrors without the God of the final holocaust. I have met good people who would prefer eternal blackness to the vision of Siva the Destroyer."

"Is that how you see Him, Carl?"

"Back in Rome," said Mendelius quietly, "there are assassins waiting to kill me. I am less afraid of them than of a God who can slam the lid on His own toy box and toss it into the fire. That's why I can't preach your millennial catastrophe, Jean . . . not if it is inevitable, a horror decreed from eternity."

"It is not God who is the assassin, Carl—not God who will press the red button."

Carl Mendelius was silent for a long moment. He took the bread crumbs from Jean Marie's hands and began pitching them to the birds. When, finally, he spoke again it was to utter a banality.

"Cardinal Drexel asked me to call him after this visit. What do you want me to say?"

"That I am content; that I bear no one any ill will; that I pray for them all each day."

"Pray for me, too, Jean. I am an arid man in a darkling desert."

"The darkness will pass. Afterwards you will see the dayspring and the well of sweet water."

"I hope so." Mendelius stood up and stretched out a hand to lift Jean Marie to his feet. "Let's not linger on the farewells."

"Write to me sometimes, Carl."

"Every week. I promise."

"God keep you, my friend."

They held to each other in a last silent embrace. Then Jean Marie walked away, a frail dark figure whose footsteps rang hollowly on the pavement of the cloister.

"You asked me a question, Professor." The Father Abbot was walking him to the monastery gate. "I told you I would give you my answer today."

"I am curious to hear it, Father Abbot."

"I do believe that our friend was granted a vision of the Parousia."

"Another question then. Do you feel obliged to do anything about it?"

"Nothing special," said the Abbot mildly. "After all, a monastery is a place where men come to terms with the last things. We watch; we pray; we hold ourselves ready, according to the commandment; we dispense charity to the community and to the voyager."

"You make it sound very simple." Mendelius was unimpressed.

"Too simple, too bland." The Abbot gave him a quick sidelong look. "That's what you really mean, isn't it? What would you suggest I do, my friend? Send my monks out into the mountain villages to preach the Apocalypse? How many do you think would listen? They'll still be watching Lazio play football when the last trumpet sounds! . . . What will you do now?"

"Finish the vacation with my wife. Go back and prepare for next year's lectures. . . . Look after Jean for me."

"I promise."

"With your permission I'll write to him regularly."

"Let me assure you your correspondence will be private."

"Thank you. May I leave an offering with the guestmaster?"

"It would be appreciated."

"I'm grateful for your hospitality."

"A word of advice, my friend."

"Yes?"

"You cannot wrestle with God. He is too large an adversary. . . . You cannot manage His universe either, only the small garden He has given you. Enjoy it while you can. . . ."

"This has been a very painful episode for you."

Drexel poured the dregs of the coffee into Mendelius' cup and handed him the last sweet biscuit.

"Yes, it has, Eminence."

"And now that it is ended . . . ?"

"That's the problem." Mendelius heaved himself out of the chair and walked to the window. "It isn't ended at all. For Jean Marie, yes! He has made the final acts of a believer: an act of submission to his own mortality, an act of faith in the continued beneficent working of the Spirit in human affairs. I have not come to that yet. God knows if I ever shall. I hated coming back to the Vatican today. I hated the pomp and the power, the historic impedimenta of Congregations and Tribunals and Secretariats, all dedicated to what? The most elusive abstraction: man's relationship to an unknowable Creator! I am glad Jean is quit of it all. . . ."

"And you, my friend." The Cardinal's tone was very gentle. "Do you want to be quit of it, too?"

"Oh, yes!" Mendelius swung round to face him. "But I cannot, any more than I be quit of my mother or my father or my furthest ancestors. I cannot dispense with the traditions that have shaped me. I cannot adopt another man's history or fabricate a new mythos for myself. I loathe what this family does, often, to its children; but I cannot leave it and I will not traduce it. So I wait. . . ."

He made a shrugging gesture of defeat, and then stood, bowed and silent, staring out at the placid garden.

"You wait . . ." Drexel pressed him, "for what, Mendelius?"

"God knows! The last dayspring before the holocaust. The fiery finger writing on the wall. I wait, that's all! Did I tell you—no, I must have forgotten—Jean Marie made a prophecy about me, too?"

"What did he say?"

"He said," Mendelius quoted the words in a flat voice, ". . . 'The mission you refuse now, you will one day accept. The light you cannot see will be shown to you. One day you will feel God's hand on your shoulder, and you will walk wherever it leads you.' "

"And did you believe him?"

"I wanted to. I could not."

"I believe him," said Drexel quietly.

Mendelius' control snapped and he challenged Drexel harshly. "Then why in God's name didn't you believe the rest of it? Why did you let the others destroy him?"

"Because I could not risk him." There was an infinite pathos in his voice. "Like you—more than you perhaps—I needed the reassurance of being what I am, a high man in an old system that has stood the test of centuries. I was afraid of the dark. I needed the calm cool light of tradition. I wanted no mysteries, only a God I could cope with, an authority to which, in good conscience, I could bend. When the moment came I was unready. I could neither repeal the past nor abdicate my function in the present. . . . Don't judge me too curtly, Mendelius! Don't judge any of us. You are more free and more fortunate."

Mendelius bowed to the reproof and said, with bleak humility, "I was rude and unjust, Eminence. I had no right to . . ."

"Please! No apologies!" Drexel stayed him with a gesture. "At least we have managed to be open with each other. Let me explain something more. In ancient days, when the world was full of mystery, it was easy to be a believer— in the spirits who haunted the grove, in the god who cast the thunderbolts. In this age we are all conditioned to the visual illusion. What you see is what exists. Remove the visible symbols of an established organization—the cathedrals, the parish church, the bishop in his miter—and the Christian assembly, for many, ceases to exist. You can talk until you're blue in the face about the abiding Spirit and Mystical Body; but even among the clergy, you'll be talking to the deaf. Subconsciously they associate these things with the cultists and the charismatics. Discipline is the safe word—discipline, doctrinal authority and the Cardinal's High Mass on Sunday! There's no place anymore for wandering saints. . . . Most people prefer a simple religion. You make your offering in the temple and carry away salvation in a package. Do you think any cleric in his right mind is going to preach a charismatic church or a Christian diaspora?"

"Probably not." Mendelius gave a small reluctant smile. "But they do have to come to terms with one fact."

"Which is?"

"We all belong to an endangered species: millennium man!"

Drexel pondered the phrase for a moment and then nodded approval. "A sobering thought, Mendelius. It merits a meditation."

"I'm glad you think so, Eminence. I propose to include it in my essay on Gregory the Seventeenth."

Drexel showed no surprise. He asked, almost as if it were a matter of academic interest, "Do you think such an essay is opportune at this moment?"

"Even if it were not, Eminence, I believe it is a matter of simple justice. The meanest functionary is memorialized on his retirement, even if only by five lines in the *Government Gazette*. . . . I hope I may be free to consult your Eminence on matters of fact—perhaps even coax you into an expression of opinion on certain aspects of recent history."

"On matters of fact," said Drexel calmly, "I am happy to assist, by directing you to appropriate sources. As for my opinions—I'm afraid they are not for publication. My present master would hardly approve. . . . But thank you for the invitation. And good luck with your essay."

"I'm glad you like the idea." Mendelius was bland as honey.

"I didn't say I liked it." Drexel's craggy face was lit by a fleeting smile. "I recognize it as an act of piety, which, morally, I am bound to commend. . . ."

"Thank you, Eminence," said Carl Mendelius. "And thank you for the protection you have afforded me and my wife in this place."

"I wish I could extend it," said Drexel gravely. "But where you are going my writ does not run. Go with God, Professor!"

It was five in the afternoon when Francone dropped him off at the apartment. Lotte and Hilde were at the hairdresser; Herman had not yet returned from the Academy; so he had time and privacy to bathe, rest and set his thoughts in order before reporting to the others his experiences at Monte Cassino. He was happy about one thing: he was no longer bound to secrecy. He could discuss the issues involved; test his opinions against those of devotees and cynics alike, talk out his puzzlements in the language of simple folk, instead of the loaded dialect of the theologians.

He was still far from satisfied by the explanations Jean Marie had given him. The description of his mystical states, which obviously others had witnessed, seemed too bland, too familiar, too—he groped for the word—too derivative from the vast body of devotional writing. Jean Marie was precise about the possibilities of catastrophic conflict. He was, even in visionary terms, vague about the nature of the Parousia itself. Most apocalyptic writings were vivid and detailed. The revelation of Jean Marie Barette was too open and general for credence.

In psychological terms there was a contradiction also, between Jean Marie's view of himself as a natural careerist and his tragic failure to exercise power in a crisis. His willingness, not to say his eagerness, to accept even a partial defense in the popular press was sad, if not faintly sinister in a man who claimed a private dialogue with Omnipotence.

And yet, and yet . . . as he stepped out into the sunset glow on the terrace Mendelius was forced to admit that Jean Marie Barette was easier to damn in absence than to demean face to face. He had not retreated one pace from his claim of a disclosure experience or from his calm conviction that the legitimizing sign would be given. Beside him, Carl Mendelius was the small man, the courier who carried secrets of state in his body belt, but had no personal convictions beyond the state of the beds and the cost of the wine in the posthouses. . . .

All this and more Mendelius talked out eagerly with Lotte and the Franks over cocktails. He was surprised that they all put him under rigid inquisition. Herman Frank was the most anxious questioner.

"Aren't you really saying, Carl, that you believe half the story at least? Discount the vision, discount the Second Coming, which is a primitive myth anyway; but the catastrophe of global war is very close to us."

"That's about the size of it, Herman."

"I don't think it is." Hilde's smile carried more than a hint of irony. "You're still a believer, Carl. So you're still plagued by the presence of a God in every proposition. You've been like that as long as I've known you—half rationalist, half poet. That's true, isn't it?"

"I suppose so." Mendelius reached for his drink. "But the rationalist says all the evidence isn't in yet and the poet says there's no time for versifying when the assassins are at the gates."

"There's something more." Lotte reached out and stroked his wrist. "You love Jean Marie like a brother. Rather than reject him outright, you are prepared to split yourself in two. . . . You've told him you will write this memoir about him. Are you sure you can do it with such a divided mind?"

"No, I'm not, liebchen. Rainer will do a good job on his part. It's a plum for any journalist—a big exclusive that will go round the world. As for my part— the personal portrait, the interpretation of Jean's thoughts—I'm not at all sure I can do it right."

"Where will you work on it?" asked Hilde. "You're welcome to stay with us as long as you like."

"We must get home to Tübingen." Lotte was a shade too anxious. "The children will be back early next week."

"Carl could stay awhile longer . . ."

"It's not necessary." Mendelius was firm. "Thanks for the offer, Hilde; but I'll work better at home. I'll talk to Georg Rainer on Friday. We'll leave on Sunday for Tübingen. This place is too seductive—I need a strong dose of Protestant common sense."

"Delivered in a Swabian accent!" said Herman with a grin. "As soon as summer's over, Hilde and I will start preparing our place in Tuscany."

"Take it easy, Herman." Hilde sounded irritable. "Nothing's going to happen that fast. Is it, Carl?"

Mendelius grinned and refused to be drawn. "I'm married, too, girl! We males have to stick together sometimes. I'd be inclined to get your place in order as soon as you can. If there's a whiff of crisis, materials and manpower will double in price overnight. Besides, you'll need to plant this winter for the next summer harvest."

"And what are you going to do, Carl?" Hilde asked pointedly. "Your friend Jean Marie is safe in his monastery. If anything happens, Germany will be the first battle zone. What are you going to do about Lotte and the children?"

"I haven't really thought about it."

"Tübingen's only a hundred and eighty kilometers from the Swiss border," said Herman. "It would pay you to have some of your royalties accumulate there."

"I refuse to talk about this anymore." Lotte was suddenly close to anger. "These are our last days in Rome. I want them to be happy ones."

"And so they shall be!" Herman was instantly penitent. "So we dine here. Afterwards we go listen to folk music at the Arciliuto. It's a quaint place. They say Raffaello kept a mistress there. Who knows? At least it proves the Roman talent for survival."

There were still loose ends to be tucked away before Lotte and he could pack and be gone. He spent all of Friday morning preparing his final tape for Anneliese Meissner: an account of his visit to Monte Cassino, a frank admission of his own perplexities and a somewhat terse envoi:

". . . You now have the full record as honestly as I can set it down. I want you to study it carefully before we meet again in Tübingen. . . . There is much more to tell; but it will keep. See you soon . . . I am sick of this febrile and inbred city. Carl."

He packed the tapes carefully and instructed Francone to deliver them to a courier service which plied daily between Rome and various German cities. Then Francone drove him to his luncheon appointment with Georg Rainer. At one o'clock, tucked into a private booth at Ernesto's, he began the ritual fencing match. Georg Rainer was a very practiced performer.

"You've been a busy man, Mendelius. It's hard to keep track of your movements. That affair at the Salvator Mundi, when the police shot one man and arrested three others . . . you were at the hospital?"

"Yes. I was visiting Senator Malagordo."

"I guessed as much. I didn't print anything because I thought you shouldn't be exposed any more."

"That was generous. I appreciate it."

"Also I didn't want to spoil today's story. . . . You do have one for me, I hope?"

"I do, Georg. But before I give it to you, I want to see if we can agree to some ground rules."

Rainer shook his head. "The rules are already in operation, my friend. What you give me I check first and then put it on the telex. I guarantee an accurate rendering of the facts and the quotes and I reserve the right to make whatever comment I choose for the guidance of my editors. . . . I can't guarantee your immunity from editorial emphasis, dramatic or misleading headlines, or distorted versions of the same story by other hands. Once we start this interview you're on the witness stand and everything you say goes into the court record. . . ."

"In this case," said Mendelius deliberately, "I'd like to see if we could agree the way the story is to be presented."

"No," said Georg Rainer flatly. "Because I can make no agreement about what happens after the copy leaves my office. I'm happy to show you what I file, and I'll gladly change any rendering that seems inaccurate. . . . But if you're thinking there's some way to control the consequences of a news release, forget it! It's like Pandora's box: once you open it, all the mischiefs fly out. . . . Why are you giving me this story anyway?"

"First, you kept your word to me; I'm trying to keep mine to you. Second, I want the truth about a friend put on public record before the mythmakers get to work. And, third, I want to do a companion piece to your story in the form of a personal memoir. I can't do that if your version goes wildly off the rails. So, let me frame my question another way. How can we get together to meet my needs and yours?"

"Tell me the name of the story first."

"The abdication of Gregory the Seventeenth."

Georg Rainer gaped at him in undisguised amazement. "The true story?"

"Yes."

"Can you document it?"

"Provided we can agree to an appropriate use or non-use of the documents, yes . . . and to save you further trouble, Georg, I've just spent twenty-four hours with Gregory the Seventeenth in the Monastery of Monte Cassino!"

"And he agrees to the disclosures?"

"He offers no impediment, and relies on my discretion in the choice of a reporter for the exclusive story. We have been close friends for a long time. So you see, Georg, I have to be very sure of the ground rules before we start."

A waiter hurried up flourishing his pad and pencil.

Georg Rainer said, "Let's order first, shall we? I hate waiters hovering around while I'm doing an interview."

They settled for a pasta, saltimbocca and a carafe of Bardolino. Then Georg Rainer laid his miniature tape recorder on the table and pushed it towards Mendelius. He said quietly:

"You handle the recording. You keep the tape until we've agreed to a final text. We'll work on it together. All out-takes will be destroyed immediately. Satisfactory?"

"Fine!" said Mendelius. "Let's begin with two documents, handwritten by Gregory the Seventeenth and delivered to me by personal messenger. The one is a letter to me describing the events which led to his abdication. The other is an unpublished encyclical which the Curia suppressed."

"Can I see them?"

"At an appropriate time, yes. Obviously I don't carry them around."

"What is the key message?"

"Gregory the Seventeenth was forced to abdicate because he claimed to have had a vision of the end of the world—the holocaust and the Second Coming. He believed he was called to be the precursor of the event." He gave a wry-mouthed grin and added, "Now you understand why I ducked the story on the end of the world. I was testing the theme on an audience of Evangelical clerics before I went to Monte Cassino. . . ."

Georg Rainer sipped at his wine and munched a crust of dry bread. Finally he shrugged, like a losing poker-player, and said, "Now of course it all makes sense. The Curia simply had to get rid of him. The man's a lunatic."

"That's the problem, Georg." Mendelius poured more wine and signalled the waiter to remove the pasta plates. "He's as sane as you or I."

"Who says so?" Rainer stabbed a finger at his chest. "You, his friend?"

"I, yes. And Cardinal Drexel and Abbot Andrew, who directs his life at Monte Cassino. These two accept him as a mystic like John of the Cross. Drexel's going through a crisis of conscience because he didn't defend him against the Curia and the Sacred College."

"You've talked to Drexel?"

"Twice. And twice to the Abbot of Monte Cassino. The odd thing is they're the believers and I'm the skeptic."

"Which is just the way they want it," said Rainer with tart humour. "They've removed a troublesome Pope—now they can afford to praise his obedient virtue. . . . You know, Mendelius, for a notable scholar you're sometimes very naïve. You even accept to be driven around by the Cardinal's chauffeur in the Cardinal's car; so Drexel knows every move you've made in Rome—including this lunch with me."

"The point is, Georg, I don't care a curse what he knows."

"Does he know you've got the documents?"

"Yes. I told him."

"And?"

"Nothing."

"You don't think he might drop a word to have them recovered—or diverted to more orthodox hands?"

"Frankly, I can't see Drexel as a spymaster or a receiver of stolen manuscripts."

"Then you're more trusting than I am." Rainer shrugged. "I read history, too, and the usages of power don't change in the Church or anywhere else. However . . . let's talk about Gregory the Seventeenth. How do you judge him?"

"I believe he's sane—and sincere in his own convictions."

"There's nobody more dangerous than a sincere visionary."

"Jean Marie recognized that. He abdicated to avoid a schism. He is silent because he has no legitimizing sign to prove his vision authentic."

"Legitimizing sign? I don't recall the expression."

"It's a term that's become popular in modern biblical analysis. Basically it means that when the prophet or the reformer claims to speak in the name of God he needs to show some patent of authority. . . ."

"Neither you nor I can give him that."

"No; but between us we should be able to guarantee him an honest publication of the facts and an enlightened interpretation of his message. We can set down the events that led to the abdication. The documents will demonstrate the why of the matter. We can record what Jean Marie Barette has told me about his alleged vision."

"So far so good. But that vision deals with mighty matters: the end of the world, the Second Coming, the Last Judgment. What can you and I tell our readers about those things?"

"I can tell them what people in the past believed and wrote about these things. I can direct their attention to the existence of millenarian sects in today's world. . . ."

"Nothing else?"

"After that, Georg, it's your turn. You're the man who writes the bulletins about the state of the nations. How close are we now to Armageddon? The world is full of prophets. Could anyone of them be the One who is to come? If you look at it in concordance with all the crazy social phenomena, Jean Marie's prediction is far from irrational."

"I agree." Rainer was thoughtful. "But to get this story into readable shape will take a hell of a lot of work. Can you stay on in Rome?"

"I'm afraid not. I have to prepare for the opening of the University. What's the chance of your spending a few days in Tübingen? You'd be very welcome to stay in my house. We could work better there. I have all my texts and filing systems."

"I need to work fast. It's my training to grab the idea, test the logic and write it for the telex the same day. . . ."

"I'm probably much slower," said Mendelius, "but I at least am prepared in the subject. . . . Anyway, I'll leave here Sunday and begin work the next day."

"I could be with you by Wednesday. I'll get a stringer to cover for me here. But I don't want to discuss this story with my editor until you and I have written it together and tested every phrase of it. . . . So I'll have to work up an excuse for a few days' absence."

"There's one thing we should discuss," said Mendelius. "You and I have to act jointly. There should be a contract between us. And I'd like to use my agent in New York to arrange our joint contracts with publishers."

"That's fine."

"Then I'll call him tonight and ask him to meet us both in Tübingen."

"Can I give you a piece of advice, Mendelius? For God's sake be careful with those documents. Lodge them in the bank. I know people who'd kill you to get hold of them."

"Jean Marie warned me of that in his letter. I'm afraid I didn't take him too seriously."

"Then you'd better be very serious from now on. This story will make you just as famous or notorious as the shooting on the Corso. Even when you're back in Tübingen, watch your step. You're still a key witness against the girl, and you've cost the underground four men. . . . These operators have long arms and long memories."

"The terrorist thing, I understand." Mendelius was genuinely puzzled. "But the documents—a private letter to me, an unpublished encyclical—I can see their news value, but they're certainly not worth a man's life."

"No? Look at it another way. The encyclical brought about a papal abdication. It could equally have brought about a schism or caused Gregory the Seventeenth to be certified insane. . . ."

"True, but . . ."

"So far," Rainer silenced him brusquely, "all you've thought about is your personal reaction to his affair, and your concern for your friend. But what about all the thousands of other people with whom Gregory the Seventeenth had dealings during his pontificate? How have they reacted? How might they react if they knew the true facts? Some of them must have had very close relationships with him. . . ."

"They did. He sent me a list . . ."

"What kind of list?" Rainer was instantly alert.

"People in high places all over the world, who he believed would be receptive to his message."

"Can you give me some of the names on it?" Mendelius thought for a moment and then recited half a dozen names, which Rainer wrote in his notebook. Then he asked, "Has any one of these tried to contact him in Monte Cassino?"

"I don't know. I didn't ask. However, they'd certainly be thoroughly screened before they got through. I was. In fact I never did speak to Jean Marie on the telephone. There were moments when I thought I was being carefully steered away from him; but Drexel was definite. There were no impediments to my visit, just a lot of official interest."

"Which is hardly likely to wane, now that they know you've talked to me."

"Let's be fair, Georg. Drexel didn't enquire what I proposed to do. He didn't make any further mention of the documents—and he took some very rough talk from me."

"So what does that prove? Nothing except that he's a patient man. And, remember, he was the one the Cardinals chose to be their messenger. Think about that! As for other friends or acquaintances of Gregory the Seventeenth, I'm going to be doing some digging on my own account before I come to Tübingen. . . . No! No! I'm paying for lunch. I'm going to make so much money out of you it's almost obscene!"

"You'll work for it, my friend." Mendelius laughed. "Two things I learned from the Jesuits were the rules of evidence and a respect for stylish writing. I want this to be the best story you've ever delivered!"

* * *

As soon as he reached the apartment, Mendelius made a guarded telephone call to his agent, Lars Larsen, in New York. Larsen's immediate reaction was a whistle of excitement and then a howl of anguish. . . . The idea was wonderful. It was worth a mint of money—but why the hell did Mendelius have to share it with a journalist? Rainer had nothing to contribute but his connection with a big German news empire. This story should be launched from America. . . .

And so on, and so on, for ten minutes of impassioned pleading, after which Mendelius explained patiently that the whole purpose of the exercise was to present a sober account of recent events and direct serious attention to the core of Jean Marie's last message. Therefore, would Lars please come to Tübingen and discuss the matter with the gravity it deserved? . . .

Lotte, listening to the one-sided conversation, tut-tutted unhappily.

". . . I warned you, Carl! All these people have personal concerns that must conflict with yours. The agent smells big money. Georg Rainer's reputation as a newsman will be enormously enhanced. But you . . . You're writing about a friend. You're treating a subject which you know has haunted man through his history. You can't let yourself be treated like an overnight film star. . . . You hold the trump card: the documents. Don't display them to anyone until you've got all the terms you need to protect yourself and Jean Marie."

Later, cradled in his arms in the big baroque bed, she mused drowsily:

". . . It's ironic really. In spite of all your skepticism, you've given Jean exactly what he asked in the first place. Because you're his friend you can't fail to give him sympathetic treatment. Because you're a scholar of world repute, your commentaries will protect him from the clowns. If Anneliese Meissner is willing to go into print with you, she'll be at least clinically honest. . . . All in all, my love, you're making a handsome payment on our debts to Jean Marie. . . . By the way, I bought a gift today for Herman and Hilde. It was rather expensive but I knew you wouldn't mind. They've been so generous with us."

"What is it, liebchen?"

"A piece of old Capo di Monte, Cupid and Psyche. The dealer said it was quite rare. I'll show it to you in the morning. I hope they'll like it."

"I'm sure they will." He was grateful for the quiet aimless talk.

"Oh, and I forgot to tell you. Katrin sent us a card from Paris. It doesn't say much except: 'Love is wonderful. Thanks to you both from both of us.' There's also a long letter and some colour prints from Johann."

"That's a surprise! I thought he'd be the one to send the postcard."

"I know. Funny, isn't it? He's quite lyrical about his vacation. They didn't get very far, though—not even into Austria. He and his friend discovered a little valley high up the Bavarian Alps. It has a lake and a few ruined cabins . . . not a soul for miles around. They've been camping there ever since, just going into town for supplies. . . ."

"It sounds wonderful. I wouldn't mind changing places with him. I don't want to see Rome again for a long, long time. I'll write to Jean Marie as soon as we get back to Tübingen. . . . By the way, we must do something for Francone. I think a gift of money would be best. I don't imagine he gets paid too much. Remind me, will you, liebchen?"

"I will. Close your eyes now and try to sleep."

"I'll drowse off in a little while. Oh, that's another thing. I have to send Cardinal Drexel a thank-you note for the use of the car and of Francone."

"I'll remind you. . . . Now go to sleep. You looked absolutely worn out tonight. I want you around for a long while yet."

"I'm fine, liebchen, truly. You mustn't worry about me."

"I do worry. I can't help it. Carl, if Jean Marie is right, if there is a last great war, what will we do? What will become of the children? I'm not being foolish. I just want to know what you think."

There was no way he could qualify the answer and he knew it. He heaved himself up on his elbow and looked down at her, glad of the dark that hid the pain in his eyes.

"This time, my love, there will be no banners and no trumpets. The campaign will be short and terrible; and afterwards no one will care where the frontiers used to be. If we survive, we'll try to hold together as a family; but you have to remember we can't dictate what our children do. If we're separated from them, then we gather some good souls together and do what we can to hold out against the assassins in the streets! That's all I can tell you."

"It's strange!" Lotte reached up to touch his cheek. "When we first talked about this, before we came away, I was afraid all the time. Sometimes I wanted to sit in a corner and cry about nothing at all. Then, while you were in Monte Cassino, I took out that little piece of pottery the Senator gave you and held it in my hands. I traced the name that was written on it. I remembered how the lots were drawn to see who would die, and who would perform the act of execution, on Masada. Suddenly I felt very calm—fortunate somehow. I understood that if you hold too tightly to anything—even to life—you become a captive. So you see, you mustn't worry about me either. . . . Kiss me good night and let's go to sleep."

As he lay wakeful through the small, cold hours, he wondered at the change in her: the air of new confidence, the curious calm with which she seemed to accept an unspeakable prospect. Had Aharon ben Ezra bequeathed a last magical courage to the potsherd which bore his name? Or was it perhaps a small wind of grace blown from the desert, where Jean Marie Barette communed with his Creator?

VI

IT was good to be home. In the countryside the harvest was safely gathered; the blackbirds were pecking contentedly over the brown stubble. The Neckar flowed silver under a summer sky. Traffic was sparse in the city, because the holiday-makers had not yet returned from their sojourn in the sun. The halls and cloisters of the University were almost empty. The rare footfalls of janitor or colleague sounded hollow in the hush. It was possible to believe—provided one read no newspapers, switched off radio and television—that nothing would ever change in this quiet backwater, that the old Dukes of Württemberg would sleep forever in peace under the floor stones of the Stiftskirche.

But the peace was an illusion, like the painted backdrop of a pastorale. From Pilsen to Rostock the armies of the Warsaw Pact were arrayed in depth: shock troops and heavy tank formations and, behind them, the rocket launchers with tactical atomic warheads. Facing them were the thin lines of the NATO forces, prepared for a fallback under the first onslaught, trusting, but none too confidently, that their own tactical warheads would hold up the advance until the big bombers came in from the British Isles and the IBM's were launched from their silos on mainland United States.

There was no mobilization yet, no call-up of reserves, because the crisis had not matured to the point where democratic governments could rely on their depressed and uneasy populations to answer a call to arms, or respond to the rhetoric of the propaganda machine. German industry still depended on guest-workers, who, deprived of tenure and citizenship, could hardly be expected to render liege service in a lost cause. At the other side of the world a new axis had been formed: industrial Japan was pouring plant and technical experts into China, in return for oil from the northern fields and the new wells in the Spratleys. Islam was in ferment from Morocco to the high passes of Afghanistan. South Africa was an armed camp, beleaguered by the black republics. . . . No leader, no junta, no parliamentary assembly could compass or control the complex geo-polity of a world haunted by depletion and the debasement of every currency of human intercourse. Reason rocked under the barrage of contradictions. The corporate will seemed frozen in a syncope of impotence.

After the first relief of homecoming, Carl Mendelius found himself tempted to the same despair. Who would hear one small voice above the babel cry of millions? What was the point of propagating ideas which would immediately be swept away like sandmotes in a tempest? What was the profit in expounding a past that would soon be as irrelevant as the magical animals of the cavemen?

This, he understood clearly, was the syndrome that produced spies, defectors, fanatics and professional destructors. Society is a stinking slum; blow it up! Parliament is a nest of nincompoops and hypocrites; destroy the filthy brood! God is dead; let's polish up Baal and Ashtaroth, call back the Witch of Endor, to make the spells we need.

The best remedy was the sight of Lotte, busy and cheerful, dusting and polishing and chatting with women friends on the telephone, knitting a winter jersey for Katrin. He had no right to trouble her with his own dark dreaming. So he retired to his study and addressed himself to the pile of work that had accumulated in his absence.

There was a stack of books, which he was begged to read and recommend. There were student reports to be assessed, revisions to be made in his lecture texts, the inevitable bills to be paid.

There was a note from the President of the University, inviting him to an informal meeting with a few senior colleagues on Tuesday forenoon. The President's "informal meetings" were well known. They were designed to pre-empt any problems before they were raised at the full meeting of the faculties in mid-August. They were also intended to persuade the gullible that they were privileged members of an inner cabinet. . . . Mendelius had small taste, but a reluctant admiration, for the President's skill in academic intrigue.

The next letter was a communication from the Bundeskriminalamt, the Federal Criminal Bureau in Wiesbaden.

> . . . We are informed by our Italian colleagues that as a result of recent incidents in Rome, you may become the target of attack, either by foreign terrorist agents or by local groups affiliated with them.
>
> We advise you, therefore, to take the precautions outlined in the enclosed pamphlet, which we circulate normally to government officials and senior executives in industry. In addition, we advise you to exercise special vigilance within the precincts of the University, where political activists may easily conceal themselves in a large congregation of students.
>
> Should you notice any suspicious activity, either in your neighbourhood or at the University, please contact the Landeskriminalamt in Tübingen without delay. They have already been apprised of your situation. . . .

Mendelius read the pamphlet carefully. It told him nothing he did not know; but the final paragraph was a chill reminder that violence was as infectious as the Black Death.

. . . These precautions should be strictly observed, not only by the subject, but by all members of his household. They, too, are under threat, because the subject is vulnerable through them. A common and concerted vigilance will reduce the risk.

There was a brutal irony in the fact that an act of mercy in a Roman street should expose a whole family to violent invasion in a provincial town in Germany. There was an even grimmer corollary: that a shot fired on the Amur River in China could plunge the whole planet into war.

Meantime, there were more pleasant thoughts to distract him. The Evangelicals had written a joint letter expressing their thanks for "your openness in discussion and your emphatic affirmation of Christian charity as the binding element in our diverse lives." There was also a second letter from Johann, addressed to him personally.

. . . Before I left on this vacation I was in deep depression. Your gentleness about my religious problem helped very much; but the rest of it I couldn't explain. I was worried about my career. I couldn't see any point to what I was doing. I didn't want to join some big company, planning the economics of a world that could blow up in our faces. I was afraid of being called up for military service in a war that would produce nothing but universal disaster. . . . My friend Fritz felt exactly the same way. We were angry with you and your generation because you had a past to look back on, while we had only a question mark before us. . . . Then we found this place—Fritz and I and two American girls we met in a *Bierkeller* in Munich.

It's a small valley, with only a footpath leading into it. There are high cliffs all around, covered with pines to the snow line. There is an old hunting lodge and a few cabins grouped around a lake, surrounded by lush meadows. There are deer in the woods and the lake is full of fish. There's an old mine tunnel that goes a long way into the mountain. . . .

Fritz, who is an amateur archaeologist, says it was worked in the Middle Ages for bloodstone. We've found broken tools and a leather jerkin, and a pewter drinking mug and a rusted hunting knife. . . .

Last time we went into town I made enquiries and found that the place is private property, owned by a very old lady, the Gräfin von Eckstein. . . . Her husband used to use it as a hunting preserve. We traced her to Tegernsee and went to see her. . . . She's a spry old girl, and after she got over her surprise at being invaded by four young people she'd never met before, she gave us English tea and cakes and told us she was happy we were enjoying the place. . . .

Then, purely on impulse, I asked her whether she'd consider selling it. She asked what for. I told her it would make a wonderful holiday place for students like us. . . . At the beginning it was just something to talk about; but she took it quite seriously. . . .

Anyway, the upshot of it all was she named a price—a quarter of a million deutschmarks. I told her there was no way we could raise money like that. . . . Then she said, if we were serious, she'd consider leasing it to us. I said we'd think about it and get back to her. . . .

I'd love to do it. It's so quiet, so remote from today; and it could be made to pay for itself. . . . It's one of the things we've talked about often in class: the small, self-contained economy where a quality of life can be preserved. When we come back I'd like to talk to you about it and see what you think.

I spend my nights by lamplight trying to set down a plan. I find it a much more satisfying exercise than the currency problems of the European community or the relations between the oil producers and the industrial economies and the agricultural nations. . . . Somehow, as Fritz says, we have to scale things down to human size again, otherwise we all go mad, or become indifferent robots in a system we can never control . . . I'm running on, I know; but this is the first time I've felt free to open myself to the father I truly love. It's a pleasant sensation. . . .

Later, as they ate supper together, Mendelius read the letter to Lotte. She smiled and nodded approval.

"That's good! He's coming out of the dark forest, at last. It isn't easy to be young these days. I'd encourage the idea, Carl; even if nothing comes of it. We can't afford money like that; but still . . ."

"We might," said Mendelius thoughtfully. "We just might. I've got some big royalties due in September; and once the new book is delivered . . . Besides, Johann isn't the only one with a private dream."

Lotte gave him a swift reproachful glance. "You wouldn't care, perhaps, to share yours with your wife?"

"Come on, liebchen!" Mendelius laughed. "You know I hate talking about things until I've got them clear in my head. This one's been simmering for a long time. What happens to elderly professors when they give up the chair? I can go on writing, I know; but I'd like to go on teaching, too, with small, selected groups of advanced students. I've had thoughts of founding a private academy, offering annual specialist courses to postgraduates. Musicians do it all the time—violinists, composers, conductors. . . . A place like the one Johann describes could be ideal."

"It could." Lotte was dubious. "Don't misunderstand me. I love your idea, Carl; but it would be a mistake to mix it up with Johann's project. Show him you're interested; but don't meddle. Let him follow his own star."

"You're right of course." Mendelius leaned across and kissed her cheek. "Don't worry! I'll keep my big hands out of the pie dish. Besides, we've got another problem to face. . . ."

He told her about the letter from the police in Wiesbaden. Lotte frowned and sighed unhappily.

"How long will we have to live like this, always looking over our shoulders?"

"God knows, liebchen! But we can't panic. We just have to make it a routine —like watching traffic lights and locking the house at night, and driving within the speed limit. After a while it will become automatic." He changed the subject abruptly. "Georg Rainer called. He's arriving Wednesday evening. Lars

Larsen arrives in the morning from Frankfurt. That gives us a chance to talk before Rainer gets here."

"Good!" Lotte nodded a vigorous approval. "You must see the terms are right before you go one step further with Rainer."

"I will. It's a promise. Do you need any extra help in the house?"

"I've got it. Gudrun Schild is coming in each day."

"Good. . . . I wonder what our noble president has in mind for Tuesday's meeting?"

"He worries me, that one." Lotte was terse. "He's a conjuror. He makes you think he's pumping wine out of his elbow. What you really get is . . ."

"I know what you get, liebchen," said Mendelius with a grin. "The trick is never to drink the stuff. . . ."

The President's notion of an informal gathering was strictly Old Empire. Each colleague was treated to a firm handshake, a solicitous enquiry about his wife and his family, a cup of coffee and a slice of apple cake, freshly baked by the President's wife and served by a maid in a starched apron.

The ceremony was a careful contrivance. With a cup of coffee in one hand and a plate in the other, the guests had to sit down. The chairs, each with a tabouret table beside it, were arranged in a semicircle facing the President's desk. The President did not sit down. He perched himself on the edge of the desk in an attitude intended to suggest informality, intimacy and openness among colleagues. The fact that he spoke from three feet above their heads and had his hands free for gestures and punctuation was only a gentle reminder of his primacy. His speech was unctuous and usually banal.

". . . I am in need of your expert advice. The—ah—responsibilities of my office preclude me from the day-to-day contact which I should like to have with the junior faculty and the students. I look to you, therefore, to interpret them to me and me to them. . . ."

Brandt, from Latin Language, leaned across to Mendelius and whispered, "He's the *fons et origo*—and we're the bloody water carriers."

Mendelius stifled a grin behind his paper napkin.

The President went on, "Last week I was invited, with the heads of other universities, to a private meeting with the Minister of Education and the Minister for the Interior, in Bonn. The purpose of the meeting was to discuss the—ah—academic implications of the present international crisis. . . ."

He paused a moment to let them consider the solemnity of the occasion in Bonn and what the—ah—academic implications might be. They were startling enough to dispel any boredom in his audience.

". . . In September this year the Bundestag will authorize full mobilization of both men and women for military service. We are asked to prepare recommendations for exempted categories of students, and to supply lists of those with specialist qualifications in physics, chemistry, engineering, medicine and related disciplines. . . . We are further asked to consider how courses in these subjects may be accelerated to meet the needs of industry and the armed services. We have also to face the depletion of students and junior staff as a result of the call-up. . . ." There was a ripple of surprise in the audience. The President hushed it with a gesture. "Please, ladies and gentlemen, let me finish! There will be time for discussion afterwards. In this matter we have no choice. We, like everyone else, will have to comply with regulations. There is, however, a more contentious issue. . . ." He paused again. This time he was obviously embarrassed and groping for the right words. ". . . It was raised by the Minister for the Interior, prompted, I believe, by pressure from our NATO allies. It is the question of internal security, of protection against subversion, espionage, and—ah—the activities of disaffected elements, in the student body. . . ." The only reaction was a hostile silence. He took a deep breath and hurried on. "In short, we are asked to cooperate with the security service by supplying them with copies of student dossiers and any other information which may be required from time to time, in the interest of public security."

"No!" The sound erupted from the gathering. Someone dropped a coffee cup, which shattered on the parquet.

"Please! Please!" The President pushed himself off the desk and raised his hands in a pleading gesture. "I have conveyed the Minister's request. It is now open for discussion."

Dahlmeyer from Experimental Physics was the first on his feet, a big shaggy fellow with a jutting jaw. He challenged the President harshly. "I think we have a right to know, sir, what response you made to the Minister."

There was a chorus of approval. The President shuffled uneasily.

"I told the Minister that while we were all conscious of the need for—ah—adequate security in a critical time, we were—ah—at least equally concerned to preserve the—ah—principles of academic freedom."

"Oh, Christ!" Dahlmeyer exploded.

There was an audible groan from Brandt. Mendelius stood up. He was white with anger but he spoke with quiet formality.

"I wish to make a personal statement, sir. I hold tenure to teach in this place. I do not hold, nor will I accept, a commission to investigate the private lives of my students. I am ready to resign rather than do so."

"I would point out, Professor"—the President was cold—"that I have conveyed a request, not a ministerial order; which would, in the present circumstances at least, be illegal. However, you must understand that in conditions of national emergency, the situation may change radically."

"In other words"—Hellman from Organic Chemistry was on his feet—"we have a threat, as well as a request."

"We are all under threat, Professor Hellman—the threat of armed conflict, when civil liberties must inevitably be curtailed in the national interest."

"There's another threat, which you should also consider," said Anneliese Meissner. "Student revolt, expressing total loss of faith in the integrity of the academic faculty. I remind you of what happened to our universities in the thirties and forties when the Nazis ran the country. . . . Do you want to see that again?"

"Do you think you will not see it when the Russians come?"

"Ah! So you have already committed yourself, sir."

"I have not." The President was fuming now. "I told the Minister I would refer the request to my staff and report their reactions."

"Which puts us all straight into the computer bank of the security service.

Well, so be it! I'm with Mendelius. If they want me to spy on my students, I'm out!"

"With respect to the President and to my esteemed colleagues." A small mousy fellow stood up. It was Kollwitz, who taught forensic medicine. "I suggest that such a situation can be avoided very simply. The President reports that his senior faculty is unanimously against the proposed measure. He does not have to give names."

"It's a good idea," said Brandt. "If the President himself stands firm with us, then we're in a strong position: and other universities may be encouraged to follow suit."

"Thank you, ladies and gentlemen." The President was obviously relieved. "As usual, you've been most helpful. I'll give some thought to—ah—an appropriate answer to the Minister!"

After that no one had very much to say and the President was eager to be rid of them. They left the coffee dregs and the last of the apple cake and straggled out into the sunlight. Anneliese Meissner fell into step beside Mendelius. She was snorting with fury.

"God Almighty! What an old humbug! . . . An appropriate answer to the Minister! . . . Balls!"

"They've got his balls in a nutcracker," said Mendelius with a sour grin. "He's only two years off retirement. You can't blame him for trying to compromise. . . . Anyway, he's got a united faculty behind him. That has to give him some courage."

"United?" Anneliese snorted again. "My God, Mendelius! How simple can you get? That was just choir practice—all of us noble souls chanting 'A Mighty Fortress Is Our God'! How many will stand firm when the security boys really put the pressure on? . . . 'Isn't it true, Professor Brandt, that you've been laying little Mary Toller? . . . And you, Dahlmeyer? Does your wife know about your Saturdays in the Love Hotel in Frankfurt? . . . And for you, Heinzl, or Willi, or Traudl, if you don't cooperate we've got some lovely filthy jobs—like sanitation scientist or bath attendant in the nut-house . . . !' Don't make any mistake, my friend. If we get three out of ten in the final count, we'll be damn lucky."

"You're forgetting the students. The moment they hear of it, they'll be up in arms."

"Some, yes! But how many will still be standing up after the first baton charge, and the tear gas and the water cannon? Not too many, Carl! And there'll be fewer still when the police cut loose with live ammunition."

"They'll never do it!"

"What have they got to lose? Once the propaganda machine starts blaring who will hear the shots in the alley? Besides, one itty-bitty atom bomb on Tübingen and the slate is wiped clean. . . . Will you have lunch with me? If I eat alone I'll probably get drunk."

"We can't have that, can we?" Mendelius hooked his arm through hers and drew her thick body close to him. "There's only one consolation, girl: every university in the world is probably facing the same pressure at this moment."

"I know! Philistines of the world, unite! The eggheads will be crushed at last! My God, Carl! Your Jean Marie wasn't too far wrong!"

"Have you listened to the tapes I sent you?"

"Over and over. I've been doing a lot of reading, too."

"And . . . ?"

"And I'm not going to say another word until I've got a big drink inside me. I'm a bitch, Carl—cynical and old and too ugly to believe in a God who makes monsters like me. . . . But now, I'm so damned scared I could cry."

"Where do you want to eat?"

"Anywhere! The first *Bierkeller* we find. Sausage and sauerkraut, beer and a double schnapps! Let's join the happy proletariat!"

He had never seen her so upset. She ate ravenously and drank with a desperate determination; but even after a liter of beer and two very large schnapps she was still cold sober. She called the waitress to clear the dishes and bring another shot of liquor, then announced that she was ready for a rational discussion.

"About you first, Carl . . ."

"What about me?"

"I understand you better now. I like you more."

"Thank you." Mendelius grinned at her. "I love you, too!"

"Don't make fun of me. I'm not in the mood for it. Those tapes shook me up. You sounded so damned desperate, trying to come to terms with the impossible."

"What about Jean Marie?"

"Well, now, that was another surprise. Your portrait of him was too vivid to be a fake. I had to accept that it was authentic . . . I saw him. I felt him."

"How did you judge him?"

"He's a very lucky man."

"Lucky?"

"Yes! . . . I spend half my life dealing with sick minds. Leaving aside organic defects, most cases boil down to a fragmentation of the personality, a loss of identity. Life—interior and exterior—is a jigsaw, with the pieces scattered all over the table. . . . The clinician spends his time trying to create a condition of self-recognition—a condition in which even the confusion makes sense. The patient has to see that the jigsaw is designed to make you work at putting it together. . . . Whatever happened to your Jean Marie had just that saving effect. I made sense of everything—conflict, failure, your rejection, even his present darkness. . . . God! If I could do that with my patients, I'd be the greatest healer in the world. If I could do it with myself, I'd be a hell of a lot happier than I am now. . . ."

"I'd say you were a pretty integrated personality."

"Would you, Carl? Look at me now—half drunk on cheap liquor, because I'm scared of tomorrow and I hate the fat frog my mother brought into the world! . . . I've learned to live with me, but not to like me—not ever!"

"I'm proud to know you, Anneliese," said Carl Mendelius gently. "You're a dear friend and a great woman."

"Thanks!" She closed up again instantly. "I told you I've been doing a lot of reading: comparative religion, the basis of mystical experience in various cults. It's still strange country to me; but the idea of salvation begins to make sense. We all experience pain, fear, injustice, confusion, death. We struggle to stay whole through the experience. Even when we fail, we try to salvage our selves out of the wreckage. We can't do it alone. We need support. We need more—a module or exemplar to show us what a whole human being looks like. . . . Hence the prophet, the Messiah, the Christ figure. The same thing applies to the communities of believers. The Church—whatever church!—says: 'Truth is here; light is here; we are the chosen; join us!' . . . Yes or no, Professor?"

"Yes," said Mendelius. "But the important question is, which module do you choose, and why?"

"I don't know yet," said Anneliese Meissner. "But I do know that the final assent is simple, as it was for your Jean Marie. The catch is that you have to be absolutely desperate before you make your submission. The patient I can help quickest is the desperate one who knows he's sick. . . . The best candidate for the cults is the person at the end of his rope."

"Which brings us to the next problem." Mendelius reached out to touch her hand. "What are we going to do, you and I, about the situation at the University? If the President sells us out to the politicos, as he probably will, if half our colleagues surrender to the witch-hunters, what then?"

"We go underground." Anneliese Meissner had no doubts on that score. "We start organizing for it now."

"You see?" Mendelius chuckled and lifted his glass in salute. "Even you, Frau Professor, are prepared to bury the sacred scrolls and take to the mountains!"

"Don't count on it, Carl. It's the drink talking. . . ."

"In vino veritas . . ." said Mendelius with a grin.

"Oh, Christ!" Anneliese Meissner glowered at him. "We've had more than enough clichés for one day! Let's walk awhile. It's stifling in here."

As he strolled homeward through the placid streets of the old town, Mendelius found himself faced with a new dilemma. In a pointless conflict, a war that would be fought to extinction, where did a man's loyalties belong? To the blasted, sterile earth that had once been a homeplace? To the men who rode the juggernaut chariot, heedless of the victims under its wheels? To the nation-state, soon to be as meaningless to the living as to the dead? To race, blood, tribe, tradition, *Gott und Vaterland?* If not to these, then to what? And when should Carl Mendelius begin to disengage himself from the system of which he had been so long a beneficiary?

Katrin and Johann would be called to the colours before the year was out. How should he advise them to answer? Yes, to the mad imperative? Or no, we will not serve, because there is no possible end but catastrophe? Once again, childhood memories rose up to haunt him: the bodies of boy soldiers hanged from lampposts in Dresden because they had given up a hopeless cause, in the last days of a crazed despot.

Now he was truly caught in the closed circuit of Jean Marie's predetermined cosmos. So long as you could still flip a coin on a 50-50 chance, you could live, at least, in hope. But once you discovered that the coin had two heads and the Creator wasn't offering any odds at all, when you were in a gull's game, and the quicker you got out, the better . . . So which do you think it is, Herr Professor? Continuity or chaos? And if you opt out of coming chaos, on what far planet and with what remnant creatures will you build your new Utopia?

It was a treadmill argument and he was soon weary of it. He needed distraction; so he turned down a narrow lane, pushed open a worm-eaten door and climbed three flights of stairs to the studio of Alvin Dolman, onetime master sergeant in the U. S. Army of the Rhine, onetime husband of the Bürgermeister's daughter, now happily divorced and working as an illustrator for a local publisher. He was a big, laughing fellow with ham fists and a game leg, the result of an accident on the autobahn. He also had a shrewd eye for old prints; and Mendelius was one of the regular clients to whom he served Rhine wine, knackwurst and gratuitous advice on women, politics and the art market.

". . . You've come at the right time, Professor. Trade is so goddam slow, I'm thinking of going into the porno business. . . . Look at these! I spotted them in a junk shop in Mannheim—three pen-and-ink drawings by Julius Schnorr von Carolsfeld. . . . See! There's the signature and the date, 1821. Beautiful draftsman, isn't he? And the models are pretty, too. . . . How about five hundred marks for the lot?"

"How about three hundred, Alvin?" Mendelius munched happily on his knackwurst.

"Four—and it's a steal!"

"Three fifty—they're foxed anyway."

"You're taking the bread out of my mouth, Professor!"

"I'll throw in a rye loaf."

"You've got a deal. Do you want 'em framed?"

"The usual price?"

"Would I steal from a friend?"

"His wife, maybe," said Mendelius with a grin. "But not his watch. How is life with you, Alvin?"

"Not bad, Professor! Not bad!" He splashed wine into his glass. "How's the family?"

"Fine! Fine!"

"That young fellow—your daughter's boyfriend—he's got the makings of a good artist. I've been giving him lessons in drypoint. He learns fast. . . . It's a shame, though, what's going to happen to these kids."

"What is going to happen, Alvin?"

"I only know what I hear, Professor. I keep in touch with our soldier boys in Frankfurt, sell 'em a print or two occasionally, when they're drunk enough. There's lots of war talk. They're filtering in fresh troops and new equipment. Back in Detroit they're switching to military vehicles. . . . I'm thinking of pulling up stakes and heading home. It's nice to be the artist-in-residence in a university town—but hell!—who wants to get his ass shot off for the sake of the *Fräuleins*! If anything happens, Tübingen will be a battle zone inside a week. But then, so will Detroit, I guess. . . . Help yourself to the wine. I want to show you something."

He rummaged in a cupboard and brought out a small square package, wrapped in oilcloth. He unpacked it carefully to reveal a small duplex portrait of a sixteenth-century nobleman and his wife. He set it on the easel and adjusted the light.

"Well, Professor, what do you say?"

"It looks like a Cranach."

"It is. Lucas Cranach the Elder. He painted it in Wittenberg in 1508."

"Where the devil did you get it?"

Dolman grinned and laid his forefinger along his nose. "I smelled it, Professor—in a woman's bedroom if you want to know. She was so happy with my company she gave it to me. I cleaned it up and—presto!—a ready-made insurance policy! No way I'm selling it in Germany though. It goes home with me. . . ."

"What about the lady? Doesn't she share the profits?"

"Hell, no! She's beautiful but dumb; and her husband's got money running out of his ears. Besides, it was a fair trade. I made her very happy."

"You're a rogue, Alvin." Mendelius chuckled.

"Aren't I though! . . . But with inflation the way it is, an army pension hardly buys pretzels!"

"If things get bad, maybe they'll pull you back into the Army."

"No way, Professor!" Dolman began rewrapping his treasure. "I'm out and I'm staying out! Next time it won't be a war, just one big firestorm and then— bingo!—I'll be back to painting buffalo on the walls of a cave!"

". . . The fear is everywhere, Jean . . ." Mendelius was at his desk writing, while Lotte sat quietly knitting in the corner and listening to a Brahms concerto, broadcast from Berlin. "It is like a dark mist rising from the marshes, spreading through the streets, permeating every dwelling place. It taints the most casual talk. It enters into the simplest domestic calculation.

"Our faculty members are now asked to report to the security service on the political affiliations of our students. So, this most elementary of relationships is corrupted and may be utterly destroyed. I have already given notice that I shall resign if the request is made an order. But you see how subtly the corruption works: if I rely on the police for personal protection, how can I, with sound reason, refuse them my cooperation in a national emergency? The answer is clear to me. It will be clear to very few others, when the propagandists raise what Churchill called 'the bodyguard of lies.'

". . . But if fear is an infection, despair is a plague. Your vision of the end of temporal things obsesses us all; but the rest of it—the final redeeming act, the ultimate demonstration of divine justice and mercy—how does one express these, in terms that will keep human hope alive? Your closed-out cosmos, my dear friend, will be a terrible place without it. . . ."

The telephone rang. Lotte laid down her knitting to answer it. Georg Rainer was on the line. When Mendelius picked up the phone Rainer launched immediately into monologue.

"I'm in Zurich. I flew up just to make this telephone call. I couldn't trust the Italian circuits. Now, listen carefully and don't make any comments at all. Do you remember, at our last meeting, we discussed a list?"

"Yes."

"Do you have it close by?"

"Upstairs. Hang on."

Mendelius hurried up to his study, unlocked the old safe and fished out Jean Marie's list. He picked up the receiver. "Right. I have it in front of me."

"Is it arranged by countries?"

"Yes."

"I'm going to mention four names from four countries. I want to know whether the names are on your list. Clear?"

"Go ahead."

"U.S.S.R. . . . Petrov?"

"Yes."

"U.K. . . . Pearson?"

"Yes."

"U.S.A. . . . Morrow?"

"Yes."

"France . . . Duhamel?"

"Yes."

"Good. That means my informant is reliable."

"You're talking in riddles, Georg."

"I sent you a letter from the General Post Office in Zurich. It will explain the riddles."

"But you're coming here on Wednesday."

"I know. But I'm a pessimist. I hope for the best and prepare for the worst. Somebody's had a tail on me since Saturday. Pia thought she spotted a change-over at the airport which means we could be under surveillance in Zurich as well. So we're going to try a little evasive action and come overland instead of by air. Can you accommodate both of us? No way I would leave Pia alone in Rome."

"Of course! This is all very sinister, Georg!"

"I warned you it might be. Sit tight and light a candle for us. *Auf wiedersehen.*"

Mendelius set down the receiver, and began absently leafing through the typewritten pages of Jean Marie's list. Right from the beginning he had accepted Anneliese Meissner's dismissive description of it as "an aide-mémoire pulled out of a filing cabinet." He had given no thought at all to the stretch and potency of friendship between high men. But Rainer had understood its importance; Rainer had opened a whole new area of investigation and was now at risk because of it. . . .

Lotte stuck her head around the door and asked, "What did Rainer want?"

"He was rather cryptic. He wanted me to confirm that four names were on this list from Jean Marie. He also wanted to tell me he was coming overland to Tübingen and bringing Pia with him."

It was on the tip of his tongue to say that Rainer was under surveillance but he thought better of it.

"Oh, dear!" Lotte was instantly the housewife. "That does make complications. I'll have to change the rooms about. Do you think we could put Lars Larsen up here in the study?"

"Whatever you want, liebchen. . . . Any chance of some coffee?"

"Chocolate," said Lotte firmly. "I don't want you tossing about all night." She kissed him and went out.

Mendelius turned back to his letter. He was tempted to make reference to Rainer's phone call and ask for further explanation of the significance of the list, but he thought better of it. Italian mails were never secure and he did not wish to be too specific.

. . . So I find myself returning again and again to your letter and annexures and I am exercised by the problem of presenting your ideas in open forum. I wonder how you would wish them presented, for example, to the people on your list. . . .

In what terms do we discuss the Parousia with a twentieth-century audience of believers and nonbelievers? I ask, my dear Jean, whether we have not corrupted its meaning out of all recognition. We talk of triumph, judgment, "the Son of Man coming on the clouds of heaven, with great power and majesty. . . ."

I wonder whether the power and the majesty and the glory may not demonstrate themselves far otherwise than we expect. I remember the phrase in your letter: "a moment of exquisite agony" and how you explained it as a sudden perception of the oneness of all things. . . . Like the dying Goethe, I cry still for more light. I am a sensual man, burdened with too much learning and too little real understanding. At the end of a long day, I know I am very content with Lotte's hot chocolate and her arms around me in the dark. . . .

Lars Larsen, brusque, dapper and voluble, arrived an hour before midday after a night flight from New York and a breakneck drive from Frankfurt. Within fifteen minutes he was closeted with Mendelius, reading him the facts of life within the literary establishment.

". . . Yes, I'll represent you and Rainer but not until I've worked out a satisfactory contract between you both—and that has to be at least sixty-forty in your favour. Before we even get that far Rainer has to disclose his arrangements with *Die Welt*. If he's a staff man, pure and simple, the Springer group can claim full ownership of anything he contributes to this project. . . . So, first I talk to Rainer alone. You stay away until I'm ready. . . . Now, don't give me any arguments, Carl. Fifty-fifty just isn't acceptable. You have to control this thing, and you can't do that unless you own the votes. . . . Besides, it's you the customers want to buy. I've got three bids for world rights to serial and book publication with a million and a half up front—and that's on your name, and your association with Gregory the Seventeenth, not on Rainer! Once I see what you've got we can probably raise the floor to two million . . . plus a whole lot of healthy spin-offs. So get it clear, Carl! You're making Rainer a wealthy man. You don't have to apologize for the terms. . . ."

"I wasn't thinking about Rainer." Mendelius was suddenly moody. "I was thinking about myself. When this story is published, a lot of people will want to discredit me as they discredited Jean Marie. Two million dollars could make me look like a very expensive Judas."

"If you do it for nothing," said Lars Larsen, "they'll think you're a schnook— too crazy to be believed. Money always smells clean. However, if it bothers you, talk to your lawyer, maybe he'll advise you to set up a benefice for fallen women! That's not my problem. The money I get you guarantees that your publishers have to get you a big readership . . . and that, in the end, is what you want. Now, can I look at the documents, please?"

Mendelius unlocked the old safe and brought out the envelope containing Jean Marie's letter and the encyclical. Larsen glanced at the documents and then asked bluntly:

"These are genuine?"

"Yes."

"You can authenticate the handwriting?"

"Of course—and I've verified them in personal discussion with the author."

"Good. I'll want a notarized deposition to that effect. I'd also like to photograph some specimen passages . . . not necessarily the important ones. For this kind of money the clients demand boiler-plate protection. And the last thing they want is a run-in with the Vatican over phony attributions."

"I've never known you so careful before, Lars."

"We're only at the beginning, Carl." Larsen was not amused. "Once this story breaks, your past and present will be under the microscope. So will Rainer's—and professionally, at least, he'd better be squeaky clean. . . . Now do you think you could get me another cup of coffee and leave me alone to study this stuff . . ."

"While you're doing it," said Mendelius with a grin, "make a few notes on the internal evidence: the handwriting, the polished French style, the quality of the reasoning and the rendering of personal emotion."

"I know about internal evidence," said Larsen tartly. "One of my earliest clients was a master plagiarist. . . . He was sued for a million and lost. I had to return my commissions. . . . Now, what about that coffee?"

When he came down to lunch at one-thirty, Larsen was a different man, shaken and subdued. He picked at his food, and talked disjointedly.

". . . I'm usually detached when I read. I have to be. . . . No one can sustain the impact of all those student personalities clamouring at you from the manuscripts. . . . But that letter, Lotte! It had me in tears. I never go to church except for weddings and funerals. But my grandfather on my mother's side was an old-fashioned Swedish Lutheran. When I was little he would sit me on his knee and read the Bible to me. . . . Upstairs, it was as if I were listening to him again. . . ."

"I know what you mean." Lotte picked up the discussion eagerly. "That's why I keep saying to Carl that this account of Jean Marie must be done with love and fidelity. . . . No one must be allowed to make it cheap or vulgar."

"How do you feel, then, about Georg Rainer?"

"I don't know him very well. He's charming and witty. I think he's very knowledgeable about Italy and the Vatican. However, I do say Carl must stay in control of this project."

"Let's be clear about this." Mendelius was suddenly edgy and irritable. "Georg Rainer arrives here this afternoon as our guest. The important thing is that he and I work happily and productively together. I don't want any arguments about money to spoil that. And I don't want to offer him a halfhearted welcome either."

"*Jawohl,* Herr Professor!" Lotte made a mocking mouth at his solemnity.

"Trust me, Carl." Lars Larsen grinned at him. "I'm a very good surgeon. I cut clean and all my patients recover! . . . Now I want to tie up your phone for a couple of hours. They're open for business in New York; and after what I've read—oh, boy!—do we have business!"

Afterwards, in the kitchen, Lotte giggled helplessly to Mendelius.

"Lars is so funny! As soon as he starts talking money, you can feel the electricity. His eyes sparkle and you almost expect his hair to stand on end. . . . I'm sure he'd be shocked if you told him; but he's like the fat man at the circus gate, shouting his head off, selling tickets for Judgment Day!"

Lars Larsen's sales campaign went on all the afternoon. At five-thirty, with the bidding at two and a quarter million, he closed the market. As he explained to Mendelius, he now had a handsome cash guarantee with which to begin discussions with Georg Rainer. But Georg Rainer was late. At seven, he called in from a roadhouse twenty miles south of Tübingen. He explained that they had been followed out of Zurich, that he had shaken the surveillance team before the border post, and then driven half the country roads in Swabia to make sure they had not been picked up again. At eight-thirty he arrived with Pia, windblown and travel-worn. An hour later, relaxed over Lotte's ample supper, he explained the melodrama.

". . . The most extraordinary thing about the abdication was the secrecy with which it was accomplished. Nobody, but nobody, was willing to talk. . . . Which prompted us in the press corps to believe that Gregory the Seventeenth must not only have made powerful enemies, but also alienated most of his friends inside and outside the Vatican. We knew him as you did, Carl, for a man of singular charm. So where had all his friends gone? . . . Then you told me about this list and it seemed to me that it must have a special importance. . . . You said it was typewritten. So it had to have come from a file. I asked myself who would know about Gregory the Seventeenth's private file. . . . I came up with his private secretary. . . . In my records he was listed as Monsignor Bernard Logue, who, in spite of his Irish name, is a Frenchman, a descendant of one of the wild geese who fled to France to fight the English. . . . I enquired what had happened to him after the abdication. . . ."

"That was clever of you, Georg. Logue was the man who denounced the encyclical to the Curia and started the whole affair. I never thought to ask how he was rewarded."

"Apparently not well. He was moved out of the papal household into the Secretariat for Public Communications. I had been told he was a rather unhappy fellow who might be prepared to air his grievances. . . . On the contrary! He was the perfect clerical functionary—precise, patronizing, absolutely convinced that the finger of God guided every scribe in Vatican City. . . . Clearly he was not about to spill secrets on my plate. So, I told him I was working on an account of the last days of Gregory the Seventeenth, in which he, Monsignor Logue, had played a key role. . . . That shook him. He asked me to define the role he was supposed to have played. I told him that he had informed the Curia of the contents of Gregory the Seventeenth's last unpublished encyclical. That really upset him. He denied any such act. He disclaimed knowledge of any encyclical. Then I mentioned the list and quoted from it the names which you had confirmed to me. He demanded to know where I had seen that document. I told him I had to protect my sources; but clearly, I might be prepared to trade some information with him. He told me he knew about the list but he had never seen it. He went on to explain Gregory the Seventeenth was a great believer in personal diplomacy. He was altogether too vulnerable to gestures of friendship. The Secretariat of State saw great dangers also in his attitude towards *Les Amis du Silence.* . . ."

"The what?" It was almost a shout from Mendelius. Rainer threw back his head and laughed.

"I thought that would get to you, Carl! It certainly did to me. Who were the Friends of Silence? I asked. But our little Monsignore realized that he had made a big blunder and urged me to forget that I had ever heard such a phrase. . . . I tried to reassure him. He refused to be comforted. The interview was over. I was left with the four names: Petrov and the others and something called *Les Amis du Silence.* . . . That night, Saturday, I took Pia to dinner at Piccola Roma and afterwards to a discothèque. We left about two in the morning. The streets were almost deserted. That was when we realized we were being followed. . . . We've been under surveillance ever since."

"But no mischief?" asked Larsen. "No violence?"

"Not yet," said Rainer dubiously. "But once they know where the list is . . ."

"Who are 'they'?" asked Lotte.

"I have no idea." Rainer's gesture was one of weary puzzlement. "Unlike Carl here, I am not surprised by anything the Vatican does. But in this case we are dealing with a single cleric, a zealot, a known informer, who was willing to topple his own master. He may be serving other interests than the Vatican. Pia has her own opinion."

"Please!" Mendelius urged her into the discussion. "We could use some fresh thoughts."

Pia Menendez hesitated for a moment and then explained quietly, "My father was a diplomat. He used to say that diplomacy was possible only between established institutions, good or bad. In a revolutionary situation you could not negotiate, only gamble. . . . Now, from what Georg has told me, Gregory the Seventeenth believed that a worldwide revolutionary situation would follow an atomic catastrophe and that he or others would have to gamble on men of goodwill inside and outside the Church. They might be presently obscure, but such as could survive into positions of power."

"Men presently obscure." Larsen seized on the phrase. "Or perhaps out of favour, or even considered dangerous to existing régimes. That would make another reason for pushing Gregory the Seventeenth off the throne."

"But it doesn't tell me who is having us shadowed," said Georg Rainer.

"Let's reason a little." Mendelius entered the talk again. "Monsignor Logue said he had never seen the list. That's possible. Once Jean Marie knew him for an informer he would obviously try to protect his documents. But Logue knew the list existed. . . . Once he knew you had access to it, Georg, whom would he tell: his present masters in the Vatican—or those other unspecified interests? Round-the-clock surveillance doesn't sound like a Vatican tactic. As Pia points out, they, above all, play the institutional game. So, my guess is the outside interest. What's your view on that, Georg?"

"None until I've read all your documents. I'd like to take them to bed with me."

"Before you go to bed," said Lars Larsen hastily, "I'd like a short chat about contracts."

"I'll save you the trouble," said Georg Rainer with a grin. "Mendelius is the Jesuit among us. If your contracts satisfy his sense of justice, I'll sign 'em."

"I'll get the stuff Jean Marie sent me," said Mendelius. "I warn you, it will keep you awake all night."

"For once," said Pia, the diplomat's daughter, "I'm happy to be sleeping alone!"

That night Mendelius lay wakeful, long into the small, sinister hours after midnight, trying, as any good historian should, to think himself back into the ancient battles of Christendom: the battle to establish a codex of belief, a constitution for the assembly and to hold them secure against the encroachments of the fantasists and the forgers.

The battles were always bitter and sometimes violent. Men of goodwill were sacrificed without mercy. Complaisant rogues flourished under the umbrella of orthodoxy. Marriages of convenience were made between Church and State. There were harsh divorcements of nations and communities from union with the elect.

The battle continued still. Jean Marie Barette, lately a Pope, was one of its casualties. He had invoked the Spirit; the Cardinals had invoked the assembly —and the assembly had won, as always, by the weight of numbers and the strength of the organization. This was the lesson the Romans had taught the Marxists: keep the codex pure and the hierarchy exclusive. With the one you smoke out the heretic; with the other you crush him.

Which brought Mendelius by swift turnabout to this question: who were The Friends of Silence? It was tempting to adopt Pia Menendez' theory of men waiting in the shadows to be called to salvage a situation of revolution or catastrophe. On the other hand, he remembered a letter from the long-ago when Jean Marie, still a Cardinal, had inveighed against elitist movements in the Church.

> . . . I distrust them, Carl! If I were Pope I should discourage actively anything that remotely resembled a secret society, a hermetic association, a privileged cadre in the Church. Of all societies, the assembly of the people of God should be the most open, the most sharing. There are enough mysteries in the universe without our fabricating any more. . . .
> But the Romans love their whispers and their gossip in the corridors and their secret archives!

It was hard to believe that the man who had written those words would set up his own elite club and give it so obvious a name. Was it not more probable that *Les Amis du Silence* was an outside group whose French title was designed to create the impression of approval by a French Pope? Years ago the Spaniards had set the example when they created their own authoritarian elite and called it *Opus Dei*—God's work.

Still restless, Mendelius began rummaging in his memory for anything that would associate with The Friends of Silence. The word friends produced some odd correlatives: from the Society of Friends, to *amicus curiae,* and the Marquis de Mirabeau's "Friend of Man." The word silence produced a greater variety of associations. In the Mamertine Prison in Rome a dusty lamp burned in memory of the "Church of Silence": the faithful denied the liberty to worship or persecuted for their adherence to the old faith. There was the Amyclean Silence, which forbade the citizens of Amyclae to speak of the Spartan threat, so that when the invasions did come, the city fell easy prey. There was the sinister Italian proverb: "Noble vengeance is the daughter of deep silence." . . .

Drowsy at last, Mendelius decided that this might be the occasion to test Drexel on his promise to supply reference points on matters of fact. Lotte stirred and reached out in the dark for reassurance. He folded himself into her warmth and lapsed swiftly into sleep.

There were unexpected problems in Georg Rainer's contract with *Die Welt,* so immediately after breakfast Lars Larsen left for Bonn and Berlin to talk with executives of the Springer group. He was jaunty and confident as always.

"They have to play ball. No agreement, no newsbreak—and Georg resigns! Leave it to me. You guys settle down and put the story together. I want to carry it back by hand to New York."

Mendelius and Rainer closed themselves in the study to set their materials in order: Rainer's files on the pontificate of Gregory XVII, Mendelius' private correspondence with him, before and during his reign, lecture notes and bibliography on the millennial tradition, and, for cornerstone to the edifice, the three most recent documents: the letter, the encyclical and the list of names. On these last Georg Rainer rendered a curt judgment.

". . . If you're not a believer—and I'm at best a vestigial Lutheran—the letter and the encyclical are like poetry, beyond rational discussion. Either you feel them or you don't. I felt the man's agony. However, for me, he was walking on the moon, far out of reach. . . . But the list of names—that was a different matter. I recognized most of them. I knew enough about them to observe certain common factors, and guess that a computer run might show even more. I want to work through the list again this morning before I commit to any conclusions. . . ."

"Can you see them as Friends of Silence?"

"No way at all. They've all been very vocal people, some of whom have suffered checks in their careers and may or may not recover."

"I'm going to try the name on Drexel."

Mendelius reached for the phone, dialled the number of Vatican City and asked to be connected with Cardinal Drexel. His Eminence sounded surprised and a little wary.

"Mendelius? You're stirring early. What can I do for you?"

"I am working on my memoir. You were kind enough to offer your assistance on matters of fact."

"Yes?"

"Who are *Les Amis du Silence?*"

"I'm sorry." Drexel was brusque. "I can give you no information at all on that question."

"Can you refer me, as you promised, to any other source?"

"That would not be opportune."

"Others have informed me that the subject may be dangerous."

"As to that, I can offer no opinion."

"Thank you, Eminence, at least for accepting my call."

"My pleasure, Mendelius. Good morning!"

Rainer was not surprised. "No luck?"

Mendelius gave a snort of disgust. "The subject is inopportune!"

"I love that word! They use it to bury all sorts of bodies. . . . Why not ring Monte Cassino and ask your friend for clarification?"

"Because I don't want him to bear any responsibility for what we write. You're the reporter. Where else can we try?"

"I suggest we forget it for the moment and block out the argument of the piece. As I see it we start with the abdication itself, a large, consequential act, the reason for which is still a mystery. We have now accumulated enough evidence to affirm that the members of the Sacred College engineered the situation. We demonstrate how it was done. Finally we come to the why; which depends on your testimony, the final three documents and your interviews with Drexel in Rome and the former Gregory the Seventeenth in Monte Cassino. I report all that and cite the evidence. Immediately our readers make judgments. The cynics say the man was mad and the Cardinals were right to get rid of him. The devout rest tranquil on the official line that whatever happened, the Holy Spirit will make it come right in the end. The curious and the critical will want to know more. . . . Which is where you take up the narrative with a portrait of the man and an examination of what he said and wrote. I know you're a very lucid writer, but this time you'll really have to spell things out in simple language—even for our sub-editors! . . . Well, do you agree the form?"

"As a beginning, yes. Let's see how it looks in typescript. . . . You make yourself comfortable. I'm going to take a walk before I start work."

As he was walking through the lounge the telephone rang. The man on the other end of the line identified himself as Dieter Lorenz, senior investigator with the Landeskriminalamt. A matter of some importance had come up; he would like to discuss it with the Herr Professor.

He arrived ten minutes later, a gangling shabby-looking fellow dressed in blue jeans and a leather jacket. While Lotte prepared coffee he displayed to Mendelius a grubby sheet of mimeograph paper on which was a line-drawn portrait of Mendelius with his name, address and telephone number. The paper was folded several times as if it had been carried in a wallet. Lorenz explained its provenance.

". . . There's a beer hall frequented by Turkish workmen from the paper factory. It's one of the centers for drug traffic in the city and among the students. Last night there was an affray between some Turks and a bunch of young Germans. A man was knifed. He was dead before they got him to hospital. We've identified him as Albrecht Metzger, onetime clerk at the paperworks, sacked six months ago for petty theft. We found that paper in his wallet."

"What does it mean?"

"In brief, Professor, it means you are under terrorist surveillance. The sketch is mimeographed, which indicates it has been circulated to a number of people. The paper is German. The drawing was probably done in Rome. It was

made from one of the photographs of you which appeared in the Italian press.
. . . The rest of the story is not yet clear. We do know that some underground
groups finance themselves by trafficking in drugs which originate in Turkey.
There are twenty thousand students at the University—so that's a highly significant market for the dealers. The dead man was not on any of our wanted
lists. However, the terrorist groups do use fringe operators, paid in cash, in
order to protect the central organization. The way things are now—with high
unemployment and social unrest—there's no trouble finding pickup labour for
jobs like this. . . ."

Lotte brought the coffee and while she served it Mendelius explained the
situation. She took it calmly enough; but her face was pale and her hand
trembled as she set down the coffeepot. Lorenz continued his exposition:

". . . You have to understand how the terrorist system works. Using people
like our deceased friend Metzger—we call them 'spotters'—they build up a
picture of the habits and movements of the intended victim. In a big city it's
more difficult; but in a small one like Tübingen and with a professional man
like yourself, it's comparatively easy. You go always to the same place of work.
You shop at the same stores. . . . You can't introduce too many variations. So
you get inattentive and careless. Then, one day, they move in a hit team—
three, four people, with a couple of vehicles, and—poof!—the thing is done."

"It's not a very hopeful picture, is it?" Lotte's voice was unsteady.

"No, dear lady, it is not." Lorenz offered no comfort at all. "We can give your
husband a pistol permit; but unless he's prepared to take small-arms training,
it's not much use. You can hire bodyguards, but they're ruinously expensive—
unless of course your students are prepared to help."

"No!" Mendelius refused flatly.

"Then the only answer is personal vigilance, and constant contact with us.
You must report even the most trivial incident that appears strange or out of
the ordinary. I'll leave you my card. . . . Call that number at any time, day or
night. There's always a man on desk duty."

"One thing I can't understand," said Lotte. "Why do they pursue Carl like
this? He made his depositions in Rome. The information is already on file.
Dead or alive he can't change that."

"You miss the point, dear lady," Lorenz explained patiently. "The whole
object of terror is to create fear and uncertainty. If the terrorist does not exact
retribution, he loses his influence. . . . It's the old idea of vendetta, which
never stops until one side is wiped out. In a settled society, our job as policemen
was easier. Now it gets harder every day—dirtier, too!"

"That's what bothers me," said Mendelius moodily. "You know, I presume,
that the University staff may be asked to supply security information on our
students?"

Lorenz gave him a swift hooded glance and nodded. "I know. . . . I gather
you don't like the idea."

"I loathe it."

"It's a question of priorities, isn't it? How much are you prepared to pay for
safety in the streets?"

"Not that much," said Carl Mendelius. "Thank you for your help. We'll keep
in touch."

He handed back the sketch. Lorenz folded it carefully and put it back in his wallet. He gave Mendelius his card and repeated:

"Remember! Anytime, day or night. . . . Thank you for the coffee, ma'am."

"I'll walk you to your car," said Mendelius. "Back in a minute, liebchen. I want to walk awhile before I begin work with Georg."

"Who is Georg?" The policeman was suddenly cautious.

"Georg Rainer. He's the Rome correspondent for *Die Welt*. We are doing a story together on the Vatican."

"Then please don't let him print this story. There's too much attention focused on you already."

As they strolled up the Kirchgasse towards the Old Market, Dieter Lorenz added a brusque afterthought to their discussion.

"I didn't want to say this in front of your wife. You've got two children. From the terrorist point of view kidnapping is an even better bargain than murder. It gives them a huge press and it puts them in funds. When your kids get back from vacation, you'd better teach them the drill, too."

"We're really getting back to the jungle, aren't we?"

"We're deep inside it," said Dieter Lorenz drily. "This used to be a nice quiet town; but if you could see some of the stuff that crosses my desk, it would make your hair stand up."

"What's the answer?"

"Christ knows. Maybe we need a good war to kill off some of the bastards and let us start clean again!"

It was a wild sad thought from an overworked man. It did nothing to allay the prickling fear that filled Mendelius as he walked down to the newsstand, that made him jump when a housewife jostled him and a boy on a motorcycle roared past him with an open exhaust. There was no Francone now to shepherd him. Point, flanks and rear, he was exposed to the silent hunters, who carried his image like a juju doll wherever they walked.

VII

RAINER was a fast worker, trained to meet daily deadlines with clean, accurate copy. Mendelius was accustomed to the ambling gait of an academic author. He finicked over points of style, argued over the refinement of a definition. He insisted on writing his copy in longhand; his corrections demanded two or three drafts of typescript.

In spite of their apparent incompatibility they produced, at the end of four days, the first and most important stage of the project—a twenty-thousand-word version for immediate serial publication in newspapers and magazines. Before handing it over to the translator—an English version being mandatory under the contracts—they had it read in turn by Lotte, Pia Menendez and Anneliese Meissner. The readings elicited some frank and unexpected comments.

Lotte tried hard to be gentle but succeeded only in devastating the scribes. ". . . There's something wrong. I can't say exactly what it is . . . or perhaps I can. I know Jean Marie. He's a warm man, complex and always interesting to a woman. I don't feel him in anything that you've written there. It's too detached, too . . . I don't know! I'm quite uninterested in the character you've described! I don't really care what happens to him."

Pia Menendez weighed in with a qualified agreement and an explanation. ". . . I think I see what has happened. I know how Georg's mind works. . . . You've always said, darling, that you're reporting from Rome for believers and unbelievers alike. You can't indulge the one, for fear of alienating the other. So you have to show a touch of the cynic. I think Professor Mendelius has fallen into the same trap. He's trying so hard to be detached from a dear friend that he sounds like a censor of morals. And he's trying so hard to be scholarly about the Doctrine of Last Things that it sounds like an exercise in higher mathematics. I don't mean to be rude, but . . ."

"Don't apologize!" Anneliese Meissner was brusque as always. "I agree with you and Lotte. We've lost the man who is, after all, the center-point, the pivot of this whole historic episode. In his discussion of a prophet Carl has abdicated poetry for pedantry. . . . I've got another complaint, too, Carl! I believe this one may be very important. In your discussion of the Last Things you duck two important questions: the nature of evil, the presence of evil in a man-made cataclysm, and the nature of the Parousia itself. What are we going to see? Or, more accurately, what do the apocalyptic prophets—Jean Marie among them —promise that we will see? What will distinguish the Christ from the Antichrist? . . . I'm your reader now, even if I'm not a believer! Once you open the box, I'm as anxious as anyone to see what's inside . . ."

Mendelius and Rainer looked at each other in dismay. Rainer grinned and made a gesture of defeat.

"If the readers don't like us, Carl, we're dead. And if we can't move them to pity and terror with this subject, we deserve to be dead."

"Back to the desk then." Mendelius began restacking the manuscript.

"Not tonight!" Lotte was very firm. "I've booked dinner for the five of us at the Hölderlinhaus. The food's good and the atmosphere seems to do something for Carl. It's the only place I've seen him tipsy enough to recite *Empedocles on Etna* with the roast and sing Schubert with the dessert. . . . Both very well, I might add!"

"I might get drunk again tonight," warned Mendelius. "I'm profoundly discouraged. I'm only glad Lars Larsen didn't read this version."

"A word of advice then," said Anneliese Meissner. "Scrap your part of the piece, Carl! Start from the beginning. Let your heart speak as it did on the tapes you sent me from Rome!"

"Bravo!" said Lotte. "And if a little drinking helps the heart to speak, I'm all in favour!"

"And what's your prescription for me?" asked Georg Rainer.

"For you it's less difficult," said Anneliese Meissner boldly. "I think you'll do better if you stick to the history of the event, leave the interpretation to Carl and then simply swing back at the end with a straight question that makes the readers judge and jury."

Georg Rainer thought about it for a moment and then nodded agreement. "You could be right. I'll try it. . . . But tell me one thing, Frau Doctor Meissner. You're a nonbeliever. You deal with the sick and the deluded. Why do you care so much about this piece of religious history?"

"Because I'm scared," said Anneliese Meissner curtly. "I read the omens in every newspaper. I hear the distant drums and the mad trumpets. . . . I think we'll have our Armageddon. I dream about it every night—and I wish I could find a faith to comfort me in the dark."

The air was still soft with summer. The Neckar flowed tranquil under the willows, while the lovers plied their lazy traffic of punts and rowboats under the windows of the Bursa and the Old Hall, where once Melanchthon had taught and the great Johannes Stöffler had lectured in astronomy and mathematics— and designed the Town Hall clock!

The Holderlinhaus was a small antique villa with a round tower that looked across the river to the botanical gardens. Friedrich Hölderlin had died there in

1843, a sad, mad genius overshadowed by his contemporary Uhland, in whom, as Goethe had prophesied, the politician would gobble up the poet.

The alleys were quiet now, because the University was still in recess; but the restaurant was busy with a dinner party for staff from the Evangelical Institute and another for a group of actors in town for rehearsals at the University theatre. Mendelius presented Georg Rainer and Pia to his colleagues, and as the meal went on and the wine flowed, there were constant exchanges of talk between the three tables.

As the well-known correspondent of a famous newspaper, Rainer was the center of attention and Mendelius noted with admiration how skillfully he drew the scholars into talk, baiting them with scraps and snippets of information about the Roman scene. Finally, in a sedulously casual aside, he asked:

"Has any of you ever heard of an organization called The Friends of Silence?" He did not use the original French phrase but the German one: *Die Freunde des Schweigens.*

He was talking to the academics; but a response came in startling fashion from the actors at the other table. A tall, cadaverous young man stood up, and in a ceremonious announcement introduced himself and his troupe.

"We," he told them, "we are the friends of silence. To understand us, you must be silent, too. We will, in silence still, tell you a tale of love and fear and pity. . . ."

And there, in the old room, where poor Hölderlin had tried to grasp the last tatters of his dreams, they played out a mimed version of the man who lost his shadow and the woman who gave it back to him again.

It was one of those strange, spontaneous encounters that turned a sober evening into a magical event, that went on with wine and singing and tale-telling until Master Stöffler's clock struck two in the morning from the tower of the Town Hall. As they were saying their good-nights an elderly colleague from the Institute tugged at Mendelius' sleeve and volunteered a suggestion.

". . . Your friend Rainer really didn't get an answer to his question. We were all distracted by those talented young people. You take the *Review of Patristic Studies*, don't you? . . . There's an article in the April issue on the Discipline of the Secret. It makes a couple of references that may help his enquiry. . . ."

"Thank you. I'll look them up in the morning."

"Oh, and there's one more thing, Mendelius . . ."

"Yes?" He was anxious to be gone. Lotte and the others were already drawing away.

"I heard about your stand on the question of student surveillance. I agree with it; but you should be warned; the President is less than happy. He claims you affronted him. My guess is he's scared of a faculty revolt—which is the last thing he needs before his retirement. Well . . . good night, my dear fellow. Walk carefully. A man can break an ankle on these damned cobbles!"

At three and at four in the morning Mendelius was still tossing restlessly between sleep and waking. At five he got up, made himself coffee and settled himself at his desk with the April edition of the *Review of Patristic Studies*. The edition had been published before the abdication and clearly had been in preparation several months before.

The article on the Discipline of the Secret was datelined Paris and signed by someone called Jacques Mandel. It dealt with a practice in the early Christian communities called *disciplina arcani*. The phrase itself was not coined until the seventeenth century; but the discipline was one of the earliest in the Christian community—a mandatory concealment of the more mysterious rites and doctrines of the Church. These were never to be mentioned to the unbeliever or even to aspirants under instruction. Any necessary reference was to be made in cryptic, enigmatical or even misleading terms. The most famous example of such language was the inscription discovered at Autun in 1839: "Take the honey-sweet food of the Saviour of the holy ones; eat and drink holding the fish in your hands." The word fish was an anagram for Jesus Christ, Son of God, Saviour. The "honey-sweet food" was the Eucharist.

The first part of Mandel's article was a scholarly assessment of evidence on the practice and the resulting scarcity of early patristic evidence on doctrinal and sacramental matters. However, there was nothing new in it beyond one or two curious sidelights on the Synod of Antioch, where the orthodox condemned the Arians for admitting catechumens and even pagans to a discussion of "the mysteries." Mendelius found himself wondering why the writer had taken the trouble to write a rehash of such old material. Then suddenly the tenor of the writing changed. Jacques Mandel, whoever he might be, was using the Discipline of the Secret as a text on which to hang a very modern argument.

He claimed that within the hierarchy of the Roman Catholic Church, there existed a powerful group who wished to stifle all debate on doctrinal matters, and impose a twentieth-century version of the Discipline of the Secret. He pointed to the suppressive action taken against certain Catholic theologians in the seventies and early eighties and the rigorist attitudes of certain contemporary bishops in France and elsewhere. He wrote:

> . . . One has heard that there exists a clandestine fraternity of these bishops, who have high friends in the Curia, and are able to bring great pressure to bear even on the Pontiff. . . . So far, Gregory XVII, himself a Frenchman, has navigated successfully between the rigorists and the innovators; but he makes no secret of his disapproval of what he calls "a freemasonry of senior clerics, the friends of silence and of darkness." The author has seen a copy of a letter from the Pontiff to a senior Archbishop in which these terms of censure are used. . . .

They were blunt words for such a sober and specialist journal; but Mendelius understood their import. Jacques Mandel was flying a kite to see who would shoot at it or who might salute it. But, clearly, he had information that explained much of the background to the abdication.

Long before the vision and the abdication, Jean Marie had been under enormous pressure. The possibility of schism had been real. Bishops were powerful men both in the religious and in the secular orders. In the one they were leaders of large congregations. In the other they were a discreet but potent force, controllers of a confessional vote on contentious issues. In the outcome—because the Cardinals would not have moved without majority support from the bishops—they had proved strong enough to topple a Pope. . . .

In the light of this new information, Georg Rainer's story of surveillance and pursuit made a certain grim sense. Not all clerics were divorced from politics. Not all were strangers to its more violent practices. History was full of shabby deals made by high men for holy purposes. And, sitting in his own high place, Jean Marie knew the mischiefs that could be concealed or condoned under the discipline of the secret or within a confraternity of silence.

Mendelius marked the relevant passages in the article and scribbled a memo for Georg Rainer.

> . . . This isn't evidence; but add it to the indiscretion of Monsignor Logue and we have a strong indicator as to the nature of The Friends of Silence. My feeling is to incorporate a reference into our story as Mandel has done and see what reactions we get. I'm going to draft a small section on another aspect of the phenomenon: that in times of acute crisis, the public leans always to dictators and juntas as the sick man leans to the reassuring doctor however incompetent he may be. . . . If I'm not here when you start work, you'll find the new stuff on my desk.

He pinned the note to Rainer's copy of the draft, then drew his own copy of the manuscript towards him, and under the heading "The Time-frame of Gregory XVII," he began to write:

> Psychic epidemics are no new phenomenon in human history. The germs which cause them lie encapsulated, like the anthrax bacillus, until conditions are ripe for their rebirth. These conditions are fear, uncertainty, the breakup of social systems too fragile for the loads imposed on them. The symptoms are as various as the illusions of mankind: the self-mutilation of the flagellants and the castrate priests, the murderous fury of the *sicarii,* the sexual perversion of the witch-hunters, the methodical madness of the inquisitors who think to confine truth in a phrase and burn any contumacious fellow who dares dissent from their definition. But the effects of the disease are always the same. The patient becomes fearful and irrational, subject to nightmare terrors, addicted to pleasurable illusions—an easy prey to peddlers of nostrums, magical incantations and the collective follies of the other afflicted ones. . . .
>
> To chart the origin and the course of the disease is one thing; to cure it is quite another. The most drastic remedy is extermination. The only problem is that you are never sure who will emerge from the slaughterhouse: the lunatics or the sane. Propaganda is another potent medicine. You pump the patients full of healing thoughts from dawn to dusk, and even through their sleeping hours. You tell them, over and over, that all is for the best in this most benign of all creations. And they will believe you too, gladly and gratefully—until the day when they first smell fire in the wind and see blood on the altar stone. Then they will turn and rend you limb from limb in a manic fury of resentment.

It was for this reason that the Sacred College decided to silence Jean Marie Barette and suppress the account of his vision. They knew that the backlash of a millennial proclamation could be enormous. Yet it was for exactly the same reason that Jean Marie proposed in his encyclical a preparation of the spirit against an inevitable period of social insanity. He wanted physicians and places of asylum already established before the epidemic took hold. And, in principle, at least, I believe he was right.

Even in ancient times asylum was a mystic word. It connoted a sacred place, a temple, a shrine, a forest grove where a criminal or a runaway slave would find sanctuary from his pursuers and sleep safe under the numen of the resident god. It was not merely the ingathering which was important. It was the outgoing, as well; the outgoing of the power, the hope, the life-thrust, which sustained the panting fugitive for the last mile as the hounds bayed closer and closer at his heels. . . .

A new thought took hold of Mendelius. He laid down his pen to meditate on it. Everything he had just written about the causes and symptoms of psychic epidemic might be applied with equal justice to Jean Marie. He had abdicated reason for the wildest revelations. He had abdicated the place from which alone power could be exercised. He offered no hope, only a cataclysm and a final judgment on the survivors. His adversaries, whatever they called themselves, had at least pragmatic common sense on their side. Traditional organizations had been tested by time and had survived the vast stresses of the centuries. Traditional interpretations commanded respect, if only for their antiquity and durability. When the roof was falling in you needed a tiler and not a prophet.

And here precisely was the weakness which Lotte, Anneliese and Pia had all found in his portrait of Jean Marie. It carried no conviction because its author had none. It excited no passion because it was bathed in the flat white light of pure reason. . . . Or perhaps, as Anneliese Meissner had warned him long ago, he was still too much the Jesuit to embarrass the family of the faith with an unpopular truth! Enough then! He picked up a red pencil and began savagely and methodically to cut his copy of the manuscript to pieces. Then he pulled a clean brief-pad towards him and began again with a simple stark testimony.

I write of a man I love. I am, therefore, a suspect witness. For this reason, if for no other, I offer only such testimony as may be accepted under the strictest rules of evidence. Where I present an opinion I call it so. I express my doubts as honestly as my certainties. But, I repeat, I am writing of a man I love, to whom I am in debt for some of the best things in my life, who is closer to me than a brother—and whose present agonies I have been unable fully to share. . . .

Suddenly, it was as if he were endowed with a grace of eloquence. He knew exactly what he must say about Jean Marie and how he must say it to touch the hearts of the most simple. When he came to expound the doctrine of last things and how closely Jean Marie adhered to it, he was lucid and persuasive. Jean Marie had been silenced without a hearing. Now, said Mendelius, the unwilling advocate, he must have open judgment.

But when he came to answer the questions which Anneliese had asked, the nature of evil and the mode of the Second Coming, he was forced to a moving admission.

> . . . I know that evil exists. I am already marked as a victim of its destructive power. I pray daily to be delivered from it. I do not know why there is evil and pain in a world designed by a beneficent creator. The vision of Gregory XVII described only the effects of that evil, it cast no light upon the mystery of its existence. So, too, with the Second Coming. He tells us nothing of the how, the when, the where of the event, which Christians believe is implicit in and irrevocably guaranteed by the doctrine of the Resurrection. . . . So it would be quite just to say that the vision of Gregory XVII tells us nothing that we do not know already. But this does not discredit the vision or the visionary, any more than a painter is discredited because he shows us light and landscape as we have never seen them before. I wish I could interpret the meaning of my friend's moment of private rapture. I cannot. The best I can do is to show how for good reasons or bad Jean Marie Barette, Pope Gregory XVII, was prevented from offering his own interpretation to the world. . . . Are we the richer or the poorer? Only time will tell.

Three days later, with the help of four typists and two translators, the thing was done. The English and the German versions were boxed for the couriers. The affidavits and the photographic copies of the documents were all attested. Lars Larsen was making a farewell toast before driving to Frankfurt to pick up his flight to New York.

". . . Always, when I've sold a big one like this, I'm scared. My head's on the block. If my judgment's discredited, I'm out of a job. If my author delivers me a turkey, what do I say to the publishers? . . . But this time, I can drop a package on the publisher's desk and swear on my mother's memory he's getting his money's worth. . . . We've got worldwide agreement. Simultaneous publication next Sunday. After that, sit tight for the backlash. But you're sturdy fellows, you'll weather it well. When the going gets rough, remember every television interview is dollars and deutschmarks and yen in the bank. . . . Georg, Carl, I take off my hat to you both. Lotte, my love, thanks for your hospitality. Pia, may your man bring you to New York. And you, Professor Meissner, it's been a pleasure to know you. When I finally crack under the strain I hope you'll undertake my treatment."

"You'll never crack." Anneliese Meissner gave him her most wolfish smile. "Not until they abolish money and go back to barter!"

"Be glad of me!" said Lars Larsen cheerfully. "I like the game, so I play it well. I hope you fellows get as much fun out of spending the money as I had getting it for you. Cheers! . . ."

It was a good exit line and Mendelius gave him full marks for it. Even Anneliese offered amends and asked whether Larsen would consent to represent her works in the American market. Georg Rainer admitted that feeling rich was a novel and pleasant experience. He was reluctant to agree with Pia that there was now no impediment to his getting married—preferably to her. He changed the subject hastily.

". . . There's a couple of matters that still bother me, Carl. We've mentioned The Friends of Silence. We've introduced Gregory the Seventeenth's list of sympathetic politicians; but we've offered no firm conclusions about either. Sooner or later we're going to be questioned in these areas. So, I'll continue digging in Rome and if I get anything new I'll call."

"I'll be more interested to know if you're still under surveillance when you get back to Rome."

"So will I. The dumbest spy has had time to trace me here. But now that the story's written and with so many copies in circulation, I don't see what anyone can do about it. I'm taking Pia to Bonn to deliver a safety copy. Even if they hijacked that, the news would still break. I'm not worried . . . just curious. I hate loose ends."

After that, there was a flurry of farewells and the inevitable anticlimax. Anneliese left to keep appointments at the clinic. Lotte was impatient to get to her housekeeping so that the place would be shining for the return of her brood. Mendelius took one look at his littered study and opted for a walk in the botanical gardens to feed the ducks and the swans.

The next day the children came home. Katrin, bubbling with happiness, arrived in the morning. She presented her mother with an expensive scarf and Mendelius with the promised picture from Franz—a fully worked canvas of the Place du Tertre. Then she took a deep breath and delivered the big news. She and Franz had decided to set up house in Paris. They would be independent and modestly prosperous. Franz had been taken up by a well-known art dealer. She herself would be employed by a German import house in Paris. Yes, she and Franz had discussed the question of marriage. They both agreed it would be wiser to wait awhile—and please! please! would Mutti and Papa try to understand!

Lotte was shaken, but managed to retain her composure. It was Mendelius who tried to reason with Katrin the problems of an unmarried couple, living in a foreign country in a period of impending disorder. Yet, somehow, the arguments lacked conviction. At bottom he was glad to see her removed from the threat which hung over them all in Tübingen. He wanted her to enjoy what happiness she could before the dark times came and the world fell apart.

In the end, it was agreed that Lotte would go with her to Paris to help her find an apartment and see her settled and that Mendelius would provide a personal capital fund which would sustain her if the love affair turned sour. All three of them were aware—though none dared put it into words—that it was at bottom a cold-blooded talk about survival, and the best terms that could be arranged to hold the family together and let the leaven of the old pieties continue to work in an unsatisfactory situation.

Afterwards, while Katrin was unpacking, Lotte wept quietly and Mendelius groped for words of comfort.

". . . I know you're disappointed, liebchen; but at least this way the family holds together and she will still turn to us in the bad times. . . . I know you'd love a white wedding and a grandchild the first year afterwards. I'm afraid I wouldn't. I'm glad to see her still free. And I'm glad we now have enough money to make her independent. . . ."

"But she's so young, Carl—and Paris seems so far away."

"The farther the better at this moment," said Mendelius bitterly. "You and I can look after each other; but the last thing I want is our children taken hostages. Dry your eyes now. Go upstairs and talk with her. She needs you just as much as you need her. . . ."

By the time Johann arrived they were all calm again and ready to interest themselves in the account of his Alpine retreat. He showed them his photographs, and enthused about the possibilities of development.

". . . The entrance is hidden at the end of a timber cutter's track. It's a long, narrow defile that opens into this strange valley, which is like an axe-cut, straight down the center of the ridge. . . . All around the lake are meadows a meter deep in good soil. . . . The woods are full of deer—but they need culling. The waterfall is here . . . and to the left of it is the entrance to the old mine workings, which are nearly half a mile long, with lots of natural passages which we didn't explore, because we're not trained and we hadn't the proper equipment. . . ."

Mendelius let him talk himself out and then put the blunt question: "Are you still interested to acquire the place and develop it?"

"Interested—sure! But it would cost a mint of money to develop. You need labour for farming and building. You need expert advice on engineering, plumbing and even on Alpine cultivation. I got out some figures. Even if we leased the place, it would still take something like three hundred thousand deutschmarks to make it a going concern. I know we can't come up with that sort of money."

"Suppose we could. What then?"

Johann considered the question and then asked another. "Have I missed something while I've been away?"

"Quite a lot," Katrin told him ruefully. "These parents of ours have been embroiled in some rather explosive affairs. You'd better tell him from the beginning, Papa."

Mendelius told him. Johann listened intently, asking few questions, masking his feelings, as he always did. Finally Mendelius came to the postscript of his tale.

"As a result of what I have written about the abdication of Gregory the Seventeenth, I've made a lot of money. Therefore we're able to think more freely about our immediate futures. . . . But there are certain things beyond our control. We may well be at war within the next twelve months. . . . You and Katrin will be liable for military call-up in September."

"If we are," said Johann grimly, "there won't be much future to discuss."

"There may be," said Mendelius with bleak humor, "if you're interested in becoming an Alpine farmer. Agricultural workers and proprietors are normally exempt from military service. . . . If you're still keen to acquire that property in Bavaria, do it now. Start to develop it immediately. It could be a refuge as well as a productive property."

"It's a hell of a price to pay for a bomb shelter." Johann was thoughtful. "Not to mention the development costs. But, yes, it bears thinking on. Mother could come there and Franz and Katrin. We need labour anyway."

"Tell him the other thing, Carl!" Lotte cut into the talk. "This can wait."

"What other thing, Father?"

"There are people who want to kill me, son. So long as we are here together in Tübingen we are all in danger. That's why I think we should disperse for a while. Your mother's going to Paris to get Katrin settled. If you take up my offer on this property that gets you out of the way."

"And you, Father? Who takes care of you?"

"I do," said Lotte, "and I've changed my mind about Paris. If Katrin's old enough to take a lover instead of a husband, she's old enough to find and furnish her own lodgings. You and I will stay here, Carl . . . Johann can make his own decisions."

"Frankly, son, I'd much rather you were out of the University." Mendelius was suddenly eager to persuade him. "Things are going to get rough. There's a move to have security dossiers on all students. Faculty members will be required to contribute information. I've refused to go along. That means sooner or later—if I survive the assassins—I'm under fire from the security boys."

"It seems to me," said Johann deliberately, "all this is predicated on a belief that war is inevitable—global war!"

"That's right. It is."

"And do you truly believe mankind will commit to that monstrosity?"

"Mankind will have very little to do or to say about it," said Mendelius. "According to Jean Marie's vision war is already written into our futures. That's why I found myself at odds with him in Rome. On the other hand, everything I see and hear tells me that the nations are hell-bent on a confrontation over fuel and resources, and that the risk of conflict grows greater every day. So, what can I say to my adult children? Your mother and I have lived the best part of our lives. We'd like to offer you free choice about the disposition of your own."

"You are part of our lives. We can't just go about our own affairs as if you both didn't exist. . . . I'm very grateful for your offer, Father, but I want to think about it very carefully. I want to talk with you, too, little sister. There are things I have to arrange with your Franz!"

"Franz is my business." Katrin was instantly defensive. "I don't want a fight between you two."

"There'll be no fight," said Johann calmly. "But I want to be sure Franz knows what he's getting into—and what he'll have to share by way of a family responsibility. . . . It would be good, for instance, if we could recruit some sort of bodyguard for Father and Mother, from within the student body."

"Absolutely not!" Mendelius was very emphatic. "That's an immediate gain for the terrorist. He has disrupted our lives, forced us to take public precautions. Therefore he is important, potent and to be feared. No! No! No! Your mother and I—and you, too, so long as you are here—will protect each other. The handbook the police gave us is very good. I want you both to read it and . . ."

The doorbell rang. Mendelius went to answer it. Johann followed him. Mendelius recited the simple drill.

". . . Always use the spyhole in the door. If you cannot identify the caller, leave the chain bolt on when you open the door. If you receive a package you are not expecting, or an especially bulky letter, call the Kriminalamt and ask for a bomb expert to examine them. You may feel foolish if the packages are harmless but it's better than opening a booby trap which will blow your face off. . . ."

This time the caller and his package were both harmless. Alvin Dolman had come to deliver the framed prints. While Mendelius poured his drink he displayed them proudly to Lotte and the family.

". . . They look good, eh? I had a fellow in my studio yesterday who offered three times the price you paid. You see, you do get favoured-nation treatment, Professor!"

"With this family, I need it, Alvin."

"Be glad of this family, Professor. I wish I had one like it. I'm getting too old for hunting in the wildwood! Which reminds me, I was at a party last night in honour of the mime troupe. Your name came up. The leading man said they had performed for you and some journalist fellow at a party in the Hölderlinhaus."

"That's right. It turned into a long night."

"Anyway, I mentioned that I knew you and your family. Everybody seemed to know about your adventure in Rome. Then this girl buttonholed me and started asking questions."

"What girl?" Mendelius frowned. "What sort of questions?"

"Her name is Alicia Benedictus. She works for the *Schwabisches Tagblatt*. She said she was writing a profile on you for the paper."

"Did she offer any identification?"

"Why should she? We were both guests at the same party. I took her at face value—and the value was pretty good, believe me!"

In spite of his concern, Mendelius laughed. The light of lechery in Alvin Dolman's eyes was beacon-bright. Mendelius repeated his query. "What sort of questions did she ask?"

"Oh, the usual stuff: what sort of man you are; how were you regarded in the town; who were your most important friends . . . that sort of thing."

"Strange! If she works for the *Tagblatt*, she has a file full of that material. I think I'd like to check her out."

"Why, for God's sake?" Dolman was completely at a loss. "This was cocktail talk. I just thought you'd be interested that someone was doing a piece on you."

"I'm very interested, Alvin. Let's call the paper now."

He leafed through the directory and made the call, while Dolman and the family looked on. The call was brief; the information negative. There was no one on the staff called Alicia Benedictus. No one had been assigned to do a feature on Carl Mendelius. Mendelius put down the receiver and told them the news. Dolman gaped at him.

"Well, how do you like that?"

"I don't like it at all, Alvin. I'm calling Inspector Dieter Lorenz in the Kriminalamt. He'll want to see us both."

"The police? Hell, Professor! I live a nice quiet life here. I'd like to keep it that way till I go home. Why do you need the police?"

"Because there's a contract out on my life, Alvin. I was a key witness to a shooting in Rome. We know the terrorists have spotters covering me and my family in Tübingen. This girl could be one of them."

Alvin Dolman shook his head as if he were trying to clear it of cobwebs. He swore softly, "Christ! Who'd have believed it? They're gunning for academics now—and in Tübingen yet! O.K., Professor, let's call the cops and get it over with."

Fifteen minutes later they were in the office of Dieter Lorenz at the Landeskriminalamt. Lorenz put Dolman through a lengthy interrogation, then settled him in an interview room with a cup of coffee, a sketch pad and an instruction to produce a likeness of the girl who called herself Alicia Benedictus. Then, back in his own office, he asked Mendelius:

"How close are you to this Dolman?"

Mendelius shrugged. "Not that close; but I've known him for years. I've had him to drinks many times but rarely to dinner. I buy prints from him. I drop in at his studio sometimes for a glass of wine and a chat. I find him an agreeable jester. Why do you ask? Do you have anything against him?"

"Nothing." Lorenz was frank about it. "But he's one of those characters who always bother a policeman in a provincial town like this. A criminal you can deal with. You can ship home a guest-worker who gets into trouble. But this type is different. You can see no good reason why he stays. He's an American. He's divorced from a local girl. He's gainfully employed but there's no way he can make a reputation or a fortune. Also he's a raffish type. When he gets bored, you find him in the boozy bars and the wilder student nightclubs. His house parties make a lot of noise, and we get complaints from neighbours. So, because he's popular and a bit rowdy and a high spender, we wonder if he's got any sidelines like hash or heroin or receiving stolen goods. To this point he's clean. . . . But I still have to ask whether he could be spotting for the group that is out to get you or whether he's connected with these mysterious folk who, you told me, were supposed to be shadowing Mr. Rainer. . . ."

"It sounds a little far-fetched to me," said Mendelius.

"It probably is," Lorenz agreed patiently. "But sometimes in this business you get nasty surprises. Dolman's an artist. We've found a sketch of you in the pocket of a dead man. Wouldn't it be odd if it were done by Alvin Dolman?"

"Impossible! I've known the man for years!"

Lorenz shrugged off the objection. "It's the impossible that happens every day. Anyway, he's making another sketch now. It will be instructive to compare the two."

Mendelius was suddenly edgy and irritable. "You've put me in an intolerable position, Inspector. I can't continue to be friendly with Dolman and not tell him what you've told me."

"I don't mind your telling him." Lorenz seemed mildly surprised. "It helps me. If he's innocent, he'll go out of his way to cooperate and he's got a lot of useful contacts in town. If he's guilty, then he'll get restless and begin making mistakes."

"Don't you ever get sick of this game, Inspector?"

"I like the game, Professor; I dislike the people with whom I have to play it. . . . Excuse me, I'll see how Dolman's coming along with his art work."

As they left the police station and strolled homewards through the warm summer air, Dolman seemed philosophic about his situation. He brushed aside Mendelius' apologies with weary humour.

". . . Don't fret about it, Professor! I understand Lorenz and his kind. I'm a fringe operator, always have been, even in the Army. The only time I'm surprised is when someone drops a coin in the blind man's hat instead of kicking him in the teeth. . . . However, just between you and me, I have no interest in getting you knocked off and no connection with any group. I'm strictly a loner —and I'm sure Lorenz is bright enough to see it. What he figures is that because I get around and meet a lot of oddballs, I might stumble on some useful information. . . . Because it's you that's involved, I'm prepared to cooperate. Also, I don't like being played for a sucker—which is what Miss Alicia Benedictus tried to do. . . . All in all, Professor, this has been one lousy day! This used to be a nice cozy town. You could wrap it round yourself like strudel pastry. Now . . . ? I don't like it anymore. I think I'll start packing very soon. . . . You go on home, Professor. I know a girl who keeps a bottle of brandy warm just for Alvin Dolman!"

He turned away and strode across the bridge, a big aggressive man thrusting heedless through the shoppers and the loiterers. Mendelius turned down the path that led to the gardens. He did not want to go home yet. He needed time and quiet to set his thoughts in order. The family needed privacy to discuss the radical proposals he had made to them.

It was a warm, bright day and the burghers of Tübingen were sunning themselves on the lawns. Down by the lake a small crowd had gathered to watch the theatrical troupe working with a group of very young schoolchildren. It was a charming scene—the youngsters wide-eyed and wondering, totally absorbed in the tale of a sad clown who blew beautiful bubbles but could never coax one of them to rest on his hand. The clown was the cadaverous fellow who had entertained them at the Hölderlinhaus. The rest of the troupe played the bubbles who mocked his efforts to catch them. . . .

Mendelius sat on the grass and watched the small, innocent opera, fascinated to see how the children, timid at first, were drawn to participate in the mimicry. After the grim and grandiose debates in which he had been engaged, this simple experience was a matter of strange joy. Unconsciously he found himself aping their smirks and bows and fluttering gestures. The clown noticed him and, a few moments later, began to mime a new story. He summoned the other players and their attendant children and conveyed to them in dumb show that a new, strange creature was in their midst. Was it a dog? No. A rabbit? No. A tiger, an elephant, a pig? No. Then they must inspect it—but very, very cautiously. Finger to lips, walking on tiptoe, he led them, single file, to examine this extraordinary animal. . . .

The audience chuckled when they saw that the butt of the joke was a middle-aged fellow running to fat. Mendelius, after a moment of uncertainty, decided to join the comedy. As the actors and the children circled him he played back to them as he had once played charades with his own children. Finally, he revealed himself as a big stork standing on one leg and looking down his long beak. The audience applauded. The children laughed excitedly at their triumph. The clown and his troupe mimed their thanks. A tiny girl caught at his hand and told him:

"I knew before anybody. I really knew you were a stork!"

"I'm sure you did, liebchen."

And as he bent to talk to the little mite, Mendelius had a sudden sickening thought of what she would look like after the first blast of radiation, or a lethal infection of anthrax.

That evening at supper Katrin and Johann dominated the talk, reading an unexpected lesson to their parents. Katrin's argument was very simple.

". . . Mother has said it. If I'm old enough to go off with a man, I'm old enough to manage my own affairs. . . . Franz and I have to improve our relationship before we can think of getting married. In spite of his success with the gallery he's still very uncertain of himself . . . and I have to find a few pieces of me, too. I'm lucky. Thanks to Papa I've got financial security. . . . But for the rest I always do better if there's no one holding my hand. . . ."

"But Franz wants to marry you," Lotte objected. "He told me he's asked you several times."

"I know he does; but he wants a *Hausfrau,* someone to make him feel safe and well nourished—and reassure him that he's a genius. I don't want that role—and I don't want him to get stuck in his dependence either. He has to learn that we're partners as well as lovers."

"And what will happen," asked Johann with a grin, "if he doesn't learn as fast as you'd like, little sister?"

"Then, big brother, I find someone else!"

Lotte and Mendelius exchanged the rueful looks of parents who find themselves left far behind in argument. Mendelius asked:

"And you, Johann? Have you given any thought to my proposal?"

"A lot of thought, Father—and I'm afraid the idea doesn't work for me."

"For any special reason?"

"One and one only. You're offering to buy me out of a situation I have to handle for myself. I hate the idea of war. I see it as a vast, horrible futility. I don't want to be conscripted for gun-fodder—but I've never felt special enough to . . . well, to be exempted from the destiny of my own peer group. I've got to stay with it, at least long enough to decide whether I belong there or in opposition. . . . I'm not explaining this very well. I appreciate your care for me; but in this case, it goes further than I want or need."

"I'm glad you can be honest with us, son." Mendelius was hard put to conceal his emotion. "We don't want to run your life. The best gift we can give you is liberty and the conscience to use it. . . . So let me ask all my family a question. Does anybody object if I buy the valley?"

"What would you use it for?" Johann stared at him in surprise.

"Your father has a dream of his own." Lotte reached out to touch Mendelius' hand. "When he retires he'd like to found an academy for postgraduate studies —a place where senior scholars can meet and share the learning of a lifetime. If he wants to try it—then I support him."

"I think it's a wonderful idea." Katrin was full of enthusiasm. "I keep saying to Franz that everybody has to keep reaching out all the time. If you get too secure you go stale and fusty."

"You've got my vote, Father." Johann looked at Mendelius with a new respect. "If I can help to get the place started, count on me. . . . And if things get too rough at the University, you can always opt for early retirement."

"I'll call the lawyers first thing in the morning. They should start negotiating with the Gräfin. Next week I'll go down and look at the property. I'd like you to come with me, Johann."

"Of course."

"What about you, Lotte? Would you like to come?"

"Later, Carl. This time you and Johann should go together. Katrin and I have our own things to do."

"I'm really excited." Mendelius expounded his plan. "I'd like to talk to a good architect—a special kind of man with an interest in the ambience of living. . . ."

"We're all being very calm and logical," said Lotte abruptly. "But I've got the terrible feeling life won't turn out quite the way you expect."

"Probably it won't, liebchen; but we have to hope and act as if it will. In spite of Jean Marie's prophecies I still believe we can influence the course of human events."

"Enough and in time to prevent a war?"

There was a hint of hidden desperation in Lotte's question. It was almost as if she expected her children to be snatched suddenly from the dinner table. Mendelius gave her a swift worried look and said, with more confidence than he felt:

"Enough and in time, yes. I'm even hopeful that the publication of our piece on Sunday will focus world attention on the urgency of new initiatives for peace."

"But," Johann objected, "half the world will never see what you've written, Father."

"All the leaders will," Mendelius persisted, if only to shake Lotte out of her black mood. "All the intelligence services will read and evaluate the material . . . Never underrate the diffusion of even the simplest news item. . . . Now, why don't we clear the table and get the wash-up done. They're doing *The Magic Flute* on television. Your mother and I would like to watch it. . . ."

Halfway through the performance the telephone rang. Georg Rainer was on the line from Berlin.

". . . Carl? I think I've made sense of our amateur spies. It's clear now that Monsignor Logue passed the word that I would be working on this story. I think the surveillance was organized just to establish that fact. Now the Vatican has decided to issue its own account of the abdication. There will be a formal statement running to about three thousand words in next Tuesday's edition of *Osservatore Romano*. That means we'll be out first, and there'll be some red faces over the mistake in timing! . . . I understand the text of the Vatican release will be made available in the secular press on Monday afternoon. I'll call you if there's anything in it that affects our position. . . ."

"How do your editors feel about our piece, Georg?"

"Everyone's excited about it. Interesting though, there's a lively betting market on the kind of reaction we'll get from the public."

"How are they phrasing the bet?"

"Who will come out best in the popularity stakes—the Vatican or the one-time Pope? Listening to the office talk, I'm not sure anymore. . . . I'll be back in Rome on Monday morning. I'll call you from there. Love to Lotte."

"And to Pia."

"Oh, I almost forgot. We've decided to become engaged. Or at least Pia did and I gave my reluctant consent."

"Congratulations!"

"I'd rather be poor and free!"

"The hell you would! Thanks for calling, Georg."

"Do you want me to place a bet for you in the papal sweepstake?"

"Ten marks on Gregory the Seventeenth. We have to support our own candidate!"

A week later the verdict was in. The Rainer/Mendelius account of the abdication was received with lively interest by the public, and by the pundits with qualified respect. There was a reluctant agreement that it "clarified many issues left diplomatically vague in the Vatican account." There was question whether the authors "may not have inflated a crisis in the religious bureaucracy to the dimension of a global tragedy."

The London *Times* provided the most judicious summing-up in a leader written by its Roman Catholic editor.

> . . . The authors, each within his own competence, have written an honest brief. Their history is carefully documented; their speculations are based on sound logic. They have illuminated some of the dark byways of Vatican politics. If they have tended to exaggerate the importance of a papal abdication in twentieth-century history, it must be said in their defence that the ruined majesty of Rome can play tricks with the soberest imagination.
>
> What they do not exaggerate, however, is the perennial power of a religious idea to rouse men's passions and incite them to the most revolutionary action. It says much for the collective wisdom of the hinge-men of the Roman Catholic Church that they were prepared to act promptly and in unity against what they saw as a revival of the ancient Gnostic heresy. It says even more for the deep spirituality of Pope Gregory XVII that he chose to retire from office rather than divide the assembly of believers.
>
> Professor Carl Mendelius is a sober scholar of world repute. His tribute to his patron and longtime friend reveals him as an ardent and loyal man with more than a touch of the poet. He is wise enough to admit that human polity cannot be directed by the visions of the mystics. He is humble enough to know that the visions may contain truths which we ignore at our peril.
>
> It was the misfortune of Gregory XVII that he seemed to be writing prematurely the epitaph of mankind. It is his fortune that the memorial of his reign has been written with eloquence and with love. . . .

Mendelius was too intelligent a man not to see the irony of the situation. With Georg Rainer's help he had raised a monument to an old friend; but the monument was a gravestone, beneath which lay buried forever the last vestiges of influence and power which Jean Marie might have exercised. No man could have served the new Pontiff and his policies better than Carl Mendelius. It was fitting that his labours should have made him a millionaire and given him a reputation far beyond the merits of his scholarship. But the most bitter irony of all was a note of thanks from Jean Marie in Monte Cassino.

> . . . I thank you both from the bottom of my heart for what you tried to do. No man could have had better advocates or more gallant friends. The truth has been told with understanding and compassion. Now the chapter can be closed and the work of the Church can proceed.
>
> So, you must not talk as though all is lost. The yeast is working in the dough; the seed, scattered on the wind, will germinate in its own time. . . . As for the money, I grudge you not a centime of it. I trust you will spend some of it happily on Lotte and the children.
>
> Be calm, dear friend, and wait for the words and the sign.
>
> Yours always in Christ Jesus,
Jean Marie

Lotte, reading the letter over his shoulder, rumpled his hair and said quietly, "Leave it now, my love! You did your best and Jean knows it. The people in this house need you, too."

"I need you also, liebchen." He took her hands and drew her round to face him. "I've meddled long enough in the big world. I'm a scholar, not a gadfly journalist. . . . I'm glad we start lectures again tomorrow."

"Have you got all your stuff together?"

"Most of it." He held up a wad of typescript and laughed. "That's the first subject for this term. Look at the title: 'The Nature of Prophecy'!"

"Talking of prophecy," said Lotte. "I'll give you one. We're going to have a great season of gossip in town when Katrin goes off to Paris with her Franz. How are we going to deal with it?"

"Tell the old girls to jump in the Neckar!" said Mendelius with a grin. "Most of them gave up their own virginity in a punt under the willows!"

Every day during term time Carl Mendelius left his house at eight-thirty in the morning, walked down the Kirchgasse to the market, where he bought himself a boutonniere from the oldest character in the square: a raw-tongued grandmother from Bebenhausen. From there it was a short two blocks to the Illustrious College, which he entered always by the southeast gate under the arms of Duke Christoph and his motto: NACH GOTTES WILLEN—According to God's Will. Once inside he went straight to his study and spent half-an-hour checking over his notes, and the daily stack of memoranda from the administration office of the University. At nine-thirty precisely he was on the rostrum in the aula with his notes stacked neatly on the lectern.

Before he left the house on this first Monday of term, Lotte reminded him of the police warning to vary his route and his procedures. Mendelius shrugged impatiently. He had three streets to choose from; and lectures always began at nine-thirty. There weren't too many permutations to be made. Anyway, at least on his first morning, he wanted to sport a flower in his buttonhole. Lotte kissed him and showed him out of the house.

The ritual of arrivals was accomplished without incident. He spent ten minutes chatting in the quadrangle with the Rector of the College, then went up to his study, which, thanks to the ministrations of the housekeeper, was immaculately tidy and smelled of beeswax and furniture polish. His gown hung behind the door. His mail was stacked on the desk. The term schedules were penned on his message rack. He felt a sudden sense of relief, almost of liberation. This was home country. He could walk it blindfold.

He unpacked his briefcase, checked the texts of his day's lectures, then addressed himself to the mail. Most of it was routine material; but there was one rather bulky envelope with the President's seal on it. The superscription was faintly ominous: "Private and Confidential—Urgent—Deliver by Messenger."

Since the faculty meeting the President had been studiously silent on all matters of contention, and it was not at all impossible that he wanted to stage a set-piece battle with every order in writing. Mendelius hesitated to open the missive. The last thing he wanted was to be distracted before the first lecture of term. Finally, ashamed of his timidity, he slipped a paper knife under the flap of the envelope.

When his students came running after the explosion, they found him lying on the floor with his hand blown off and his face a bloody mess.

———— BOOK TWO ————

The voice of one crying in the wilderness:
Prepare ye the way of the Lord, make straight
His paths.

—Isaiah 40:3

VIII

H IS Holiness Pope Leo XIV settled his bulky body deeper in the chair, propped his gouty foot on the stool under his desk and surveyed his visitor like an old and ill-tempered eagle. He announced in his harsh Aemilian accent:

"Frankly, my friend, you are a great nuisance to me."

Jean Marie Barette permitted himself a wintry smile and agreed. "Unfortunately, Holiness, it is easier to be rid of redundant kings than supernumerary Popes."

"I don't like the idea of your visit to Tübingen. I like even less the idea of your cantering around the world like some fashionable Jesuit intellectual. We made a bargain over your abdication."

"Correction," said Jean Marie curtly. "There was no bargain. I signed the instrument under duress. I put myself voluntarily under obedience to Abbot Andrew—and he has told me I must in charity visit Carl Mendelius and his family. Mendelius is critically ill. He could die at any moment."

"Yes, well . . . !" His Holiness was too seasoned a bureaucrat to court a confrontation. "I will not interfere with your Abbot's decision; but I remind you that you have no canonical mission. You are expressly debarred from public preaching or teaching. Your faculties to ordain clergy are suspended—but you are not of course prohibited from the celebration of Mass or the Sacraments."

"Why are you so afraid of me, Holiness?"

"Afraid? Nonsense!"

"Then why have you never offered to restore to me the functions of my bishopric and my priesthood?"

"Because it seemed expedient for the good of the Church."

"You realize that so far as my apostolic vocation is concerned, I am reduced to impotence. I believe I have a right to know when and in what circumstances my faculties may be restored, and I may be given a canonical mission."

"I cannot tell you that. No decision has yet been made."

"What is the reason for the delay?"

"We have other concerns, more pressing."

"With great respect, Holiness, whatever your concerns, even you are not dispensed from natural justice."

"You reprove me? Here in my own house?"

"I, too, lived here once. I never felt like an owner, but rather like a tenant—which as events proved, I was."

"Let's get to the point of this visit. What do you want of me?"

"Dispensation to live in the lay state, to travel freely and exercise my priestly functions in private."

"Impossible!"

"What is the alternative, Holiness? Surely it would embarrass you more to keep me a prisoner on my own parole at Monte Cassino."

"This whole situation is a mess!" His Holiness winced as he moved his gouty foot on the stool.

"I offer you a way out of it. Look! Rainer and Mendelius published an honest account of the abdication. They thought they were defending me; but what was the real result? Business as usual in the Church; and you settled beyond attainder in the Chair of Peter! If I tried to change that situation—which, believe me, I have no desire to do—I should make a public idiot of myself. Please! Can you not see that far from being a threat or a nuisance I may even be able to help you?"

"You can't help me by propagating these lunatic ideas about the Last Days and the Second Coming!"

"Do they look so lunatic from where you sit now?"

His Holiness shifted uneasily in his chair. He cleared his throat noisily and dabbed at his cheeks with a silk handkerchief. "Well! . . . I'll admit we're approaching a highly critical situation; but I can't give myself nightmares about it. I go on doing what falls to my hand each day and . . ."

He broke off, embarrassed by the cool scrutiny of the man he had ousted. Jean Marie said nothing. Finally His Holiness found voice again.

"Now let me see, where were we? Oh, this request of yours! . . . If your situation at Monte Cassino isn't satisfactory, if you do want to return to private life, why don't we make an interim arrangement, *in petto* as it were, without any documents or formalities. If it doesn't work out, then we both have other recourse. Does that make sense?"

"Very good sense, Holiness." Jean Marie was studiously grateful. "I shall make sure you have no cause to regret it. Presumably the arrangement begins now."

"Of course."

"Then I leave for Tübingen in the morning. I've procured myself a French passport and returned the Vatican document to the Secretariat of State."

"That wasn't necessary." His Holiness was relieved enough to be magnanimous.

"It was desirable," said Jean Marie Barette mildly. "As a man without a canonical mission I should not want to give the impression that I had one."

"What do you propose to do with yourself?"

"I'm not quite sure, Holiness." His smile was limpid as a child's. "I'll probably end up telling the good news to children at the crossroads. But, first I must visit my friend Carl."

"Do you think . . ." His Holiness seemed oddly embarrassed. "Do you think Mendelius and his family would like me to send them a papal blessing?"

"Mendelius is still critically ill; but I'm sure his wife would appreciate the gesture."

"I'll sign the scroll and have my secretary post it first thing in the morning."

"Thank you. Do I have your Holiness' leave to go?"

"You have our leave."

Unconsciously he had slipped into the antique form. Then, as if to make amends for an unnecessary formality, he struggled painfully to his feet and held out his hand. Jean Marie bent over the ring which once he had worn in his own right. For the first time Leo XIV seemed touched by a genuine regret. He said awkwardly:

"Perhaps . . . perhaps if we'd known each other better, none of this need have happened."

"If this had not happened, Holiness, if I had not reached out for support in my solitude, Carl Mendelius would now be healthy and whole in his house!"

That same evening Anton Cardinal Drexel entertained him to dinner and their talk was of a far different kind. Jean Marie explained eagerly what he had concealed so carefully in his interview with the Pontiff.

". . . When I heard what had happened to Carl, I knew beyond all shadow of doubt that this was the sign and the summons I had been waiting for. It's a terrible thought, Anton, but the sign is always of contradiction: man in agony begging to be released from it. Poor Carl! Poor Lotte! It was the son who sent me the telegram. He felt his father would wish me near him and his mother begged me to come. I was terrified that our Pontiff would refuse permission. Having gone so far in conformity I did not want a battle at this stage."

"You were lucky," said Drexel drily. "He hasn't yet seen this stuff. Georg Rainer sent it round by messenger this afternoon."

He reached behind him to the buffet and picked up a large manila envelope filled with glossy press photographs. All of them were from Tübingen. They showed a city caught in a mediaeval fervor of pageant, piety and plain riot.

In the hospital Mendelius was shown bandaged like a mummy, with only his mouth and nostrils visible, while a nurse kept vigil by the bed and armed police stood guard at the door. In the Stiftskirche and the Jakobskirche, men, women and children knelt in prayer. Students paraded on the campus carrying crude banners: No FOREIGN KILLERS! GUEST-WORKERS, GUEST-MURDERERS! WHO SILENCED MENDELIUS? WHY ARE THE POLICE SILENT TOO?

In the industrial sectors of the suburbs, local youths battled with Turkish labourers. In the marketplace a politician addressed a lunchtime crowd. Behind him a four-colour poster screamed the slogan: IF YOU WANT SAFETY IN THE STREETS, VOTE MULLER! . . . Jean Marie Barette studied the pictures in silence.

Drexel said, "Incredible, isn't it. It's almost as if they've been waiting for a martyr! And the same demonstrations are being made in other German cities."

Jean Marie shivered as if some squamous creature had touched him.

"Carl Mendelius in the role of Horst Wessel! It's a horrible thought. I wonder what the family thinks of all this?"

"I asked Georg Rainer. He told me the wife is deeply shocked. She is rarely seen. The daughter looks after her at home. The son gave an interview in which he said that his father would be horrified if he knew what was being done. He claimed that the tragedy was being stage-managed to create a social vendetta."

"Stage-managed by whom?"

"Extremists of the left and the right."

"Not very specific, is it?"

"But these"—Drexel tapped the photographs spread on the table—"these are terribly, dangerously specific. This is the old black magic of the manipulators and the demagogues."

"It is more than that." Jean Marie Barette was suddenly somber. "It is as if the evil that lurks in man has suddenly found a focus in this little provincial town. Mendelius is a good man. Yet he, in his extremity, is made the hero of this—this witches' sabbath! That's gallows humour, Anton, and it frightens me."

Drexel gave him a shrewd, sidelong look and began replacing the photographs in the envelope. He asked, casually enough, "Now that you are free and able to be anonymous, do you have any plans at all?"

"To visit old friends, to hear what they say about our sorry world—but always to wait for the hand's touch, to listen for the voice that will tell me where I am commanded to be. I know it sounds strange to you; but to me it seems perfectly natural. I am Pascal's thinking reed, waiting for the wind to bend me in its passing."

"But in the face of this evil"—Drexel tossed the package of photographs on to the bureau—"in the face of the other evils that will follow, what will you do? You cannot bend to every wind, or leave every shout unanswered."

"If God chooses to borrow my vagrant voice, he will find the words for me to use."

"You talk like an Illuminist!" Drexel smiled to take the edge off the allusion. "I'm glad our colleagues in the Congregation can't hear you."

"You should tell our colleagues." There was a ring of steel in Jean Marie's answer. "They will soon hear the battle cry of Michael the Archangel. *'Quis sicut Deus?'* Who is like to God? For all their syllogisms I wonder how many will rise to the challenge and confront the Antichrist? Has any of the Friends of Silence denounced the excesses in Tübingen and elsewhere?"

"If they have"—Drexel shrugged—"we haven't heard of it. But then, they are prudent men. They prefer to let passions cool before they speak. . . . However, you and I are too old to mourn over the follies of our brethren—and we're too old to cure them either. Tell me something, Jean. It may sound an impertinent question; but the answer is important to me."

"Ask it then."

"You're sixty-five years old. You've risen as high as a man can go. Today you've put yourself back to zero. You have no calling, no visible future. What do you really want?"

"Enough light to see a divine sense in this mad world. Enough faith to follow the light. That's the core of it all, isn't it? Faith to move mountains, to say to the cripple: 'Arise and walk!' "

"We also need some love to make the darkness tolerable."

"Amen to that!" said Jean Marie softly. "I must go, Anton. I've kept you up late."

"Before you leave . . . how are you placed for money?"

"Well enough, thank you. I have a patrimony, administered by my brother, who is a banker in Paris."

"Where are you staying tonight?"

"There's a pilgrim hostel over by Santa Cecilia. I lodged there when I first came to Rome."

"Why not stay here? I have a spare room."

"Thank you, Anton, but no! I don't belong here anymore. I have to acclimatize myself to the world. I may want to sit late in the piazza and talk to the lonely ones." He added with an odd humorous pathos: "Perhaps, in the last cold hour before the day-spring, *He* may want to talk to me. . . . Please understand and pray for me."

"I wish I could come with you, Jean."

"You were made for better company, old friend. I was born under a falling star. Almost, it feels as if I were going home." He gestured towards the lights that marked the papal apartments. . . . "Stay close to our friend upstairs. He is named for a lion but he is really a house-trained pussycat. When the bad times come he will need a strong man at his side. . . ."

A handshake, a brief farewell, and he was gone, a lean, frail figure swallowed up in the shadows of the stairwell. Anton Cardinal Drexel poured himself the last of the wine and pondered wryly on the aphorism of another Illuminist, Louis Claude de Saint-Martin: "All mystics speak the same language because they come from the same country."

The journey to Tübingen was a lesson in his own inadequacy. For the first time in forty years he wore civilian clothes and it took him half-an-hour to adjust the cravat under his summer shirt. In the monastery he had been cushioned by a familiar routine. In the Vatican his every move had been attended. Now he was totally without privilege. He had to shout for a taxi to take him to the airport, argue with the bustling Roman who claimed to have called it first. He had no small notes for the tip and the driver dismissed him with contempt. There was no one to direct him to the counter where he must pick up his ticket for Stuttgart. The girl had no change for his large bank notes, and he had never owned a credit card in all his clerical life.

In the Vatican the bodily functions of the Pope were carried on in sacred privacy. In the airport urinal he stood in line, while the drunk next to him sprayed his shoes and his trouser leg. At the bar, he was jostled and had coffee spilled on his sleeve; and, for a final indignity, the aircraft was overbooked and he had to argue his way into a seat.

On board he was faced with a question of identity. His neighbour was an elderly woman from the Rhineland, nervous and voluble. Once betrayed into speaking German, he was drowned in the torrent of her talk. Finally, she asked him what he did for a living. It took him a good ten seconds to frame the obvious answer.

"I am retired, dear lady."

"My husband's retired. He's become quite impossible. How does your wife take to having you round the house all the time?"

"I'm a bachelor."

"Strange that a handsome man like you never married."

"I'm afraid I was married to my career."

"What were you? A doctor? A lawyer?"

"Both," Jean Marie assured her solemnly—and solaced his conscience with a casuist's logic. He had indeed been a doctor of souls; and there was law enough in the Vatican to choke Justinian.

When he arrived in Stuttgart, he was met by Johann Mendelius, eager to welcome him, but somehow dour and strained like a junior officer, come from his first battlefield. He called Jean Marie "sir," avoiding all clerical titles. He drove carefully round the hill roads, taking the longer route into Tübingen because, as he put it, there were things to be explained before they arrived.

". . . Father is still desperately ill. The explosive in the letter bomb was sandwiched between wafers of aluminum and impregnated with tiny ball-bearings. Some of these are embedded in one eye socket, very close to the brain. We know he has lost the sight of that eye and may lose the other. We haven't seen his face; but it is obviously much mutilated, and, of course, he has lost his left hand. Other operations will be necessary, but not until he is much stronger. There is still a dangerous infection in the arm and the eye socket and the range of antibiotics that he can tolerate is very limited. . . . So we wait. Mother, Katrin and I visit the hospital by turns. . . . Mother is holding up extraordinarily well. . . . She has courage for all of us; but don't be surprised if she gets very emotional when she sees you. . . . We've told no one else you are coming except Professor Meissner. She's Father's closest friend on the faculty. . . . The way things are now, everyone in Tübingen is peddling some gossip or other. As soon as Father recovers—if he does—I'm moving him far away."

The undertone of anger and bitterness was not lost on Jean Marie Barette. He said, "I heard about the demonstrations. Georg Rainer sent photographs to the Vatican. Apparently feelings are running high."

"Too high!" The rejoinder was abrupt. "My father was well known and respected, yes! But he was never a very public man. These parades and demonstrations were not spontaneous; they were subtly and carefully organized."

"In so short a time?" Jean Marie was dubious. "By whom? And for what reasons?"

"As a propaganda piece to hide the real authors of the attempt on my father's life."

"If you will kindly pull in to the next parking bay," said Jean Marie Barette firmly, "we'll talk this out before we get to Tübingen. Unlike your father I have been a very public man—and I do not want to walk into any surprises!"

Half a mile farther on they parked between a meadow and a pinewood and Johann Mendelius gave his reading of the attempted assassination.

". . . We begin in Rome. By pure accident, Father is a witness to a terrorist killing. Big headlines, big warnings: there may be attempts to silence him or

exact reprisals on him and his family. All that is clear, simple and logical. . . .
Father and Mother come back to Tübingen. The criminal police contact them
with renewed warnings. A drawing of my father is found in the pocket of a man
killed in a bar brawl. More words of caution. . . . Meantime, the President of
the University tells his senior faculty to expect a military call-up, to be ready to
supply scientific specialists for the armed services and to cooperate in security
surveillance of the student body. My father objects very strongly to the surveillance. He threatens to resign if it is enforced. . . . On top of that he writes
the account of your abdication and is suddenly known all over the world. There
is a smell of politics about the question which is not lost on our German
ministries. . . . My father is no longer simply an academic—he is an international figure. In a time when the men at the top are gearing up to sell a war to
the unwary public, my father could be considered dangerous. . . ."

"And as he is already under threat from an underground group, there is
splendid cover for an officially sanctioned assassination!"

"Exactly," said Johann Mendelius. "And when the attempt is made, the
whole town is manipulated into a protest. There's a bonus, too! Demonstrations against the guest-workers hasten the day when they can be shipped home
or turned to forced labour in a wartime situation!"

"You've read me the hypothesis," said Jean Marie Barette calmly. "Now
show me the proof!"

"I don't have proof, only grounds for very deep suspicion."

"For instance?"

"You say you saw photographs of student demonstrations. I saw the demon-
strators themselves—and I'm certain most of them never saw the inside of a
lecture hall. The newspapers published a diagram of the letter bomb, supposedly supplied by the police forensic department. The real bomb was something
quite different—a highly sophisticated device fabricated with laboratory precision."

"Who told you that?"

"Dieter Lorenz. He was my father's contact in the Kriminalamt. Two days
after the event, he was promoted and transferred to Stuttgart—off the case!"

"Anything else?"

"Lots of small things; but they only make sense in the context of this special
town of ours. I'm not the only one who thinks like this. Professor Meissner
agrees with me—and she's a very bright lady. You'll meet her at our house this
evening. . . ."

"One more question. Have you said anything of this to your mother?"

"No. She has enough to worry about; and the sympathy of the townspeople
helps her."

"Your father, of course, knows nothing?"

"We have no idea how much he knows." The young man made a weary
gesture. "He can make sounds of recognition; he squeezes our hands to acknowledge what we say; but that's all. Sometimes I think death would be a
mercy for him."

"He will survive. His real work has not begun yet."

"I wish I could believe that, sir."

"Do you believe in God?"

"No."

"That does make life difficult."

"On the contrary, it simplifies it very much. However brutal the facts may be, you don't complicate them with religious fiction."

"You've just told me a story which, if it is true, is as near to pure evil as it is possible to get. Your father is mutilated, may yet die, in an assassination attempt by agents of your own country. What is your remedy against those who treat murder as a simple political expedient?"

"If you really want the answer to that, sir, I'll show it to you tomorrow. . . . May we go now?"

"Before we do, I want a favour from you, Johann."

"Ask it, please!"

"You are the son of my dear friend. Please don't call me sir. My name is Jean Marie."

For the first time the young man relaxed and his taut features twitched into a smile. He shook his head. "That won't work, I'm afraid. Mother and Father would be shocked if I used your Christian name."

"How about Uncle Jean? It will save a lot of unnecessary explanations when you introduce me to your friends."

"Uncle Jean . . ." He tested the phrase once and again, then he grinned and nodded agreement. "So, Uncle Jean, let me get you home. We are to have an early lunch because Mother wants to take you to the hospital at three this afternoon." Johann eased the car out onto the highway and slipped ahead of a big hauler with a load of pine logs. "How long will you be able to stay with us?"

"Only a day or two; but long enough, I hope, to be of some use to your father and your mother—perhaps also to make the acquaintance of the noonday devil who has come to live in your town."

"The noonday devil!" Johann Mendelius gave him a sidelong tolerant smile. "I haven't heard that since Bible class."

"But you're not afraid of him?"

"Yes, I'm afraid." His answer was swift and simple. "But not of devils and spirit adversaries. I'm frightened of us—men and women—and the terrible destructive madness that takes hold of us all. . . . If I knew for certain who did this to my father I would kill him without a second thought."

"To what end?"

"Justice—to set the balance straight again, deter the future adversary."

"It's your father who is the victim. Would he approve?"

"Wrong, Uncle Jean! Father's not the only victim. What about Mother, Katrin, me—all the folk in the town who have been infected by this single act? Nothing will ever be the same again—for any of us."

"It seems to me," said Jean Marie deliberately, "you have a very clear idea of the nature of evil—and of the evil one as adversary. . . . But what about good? How does that present itself to you?"

"Very simply!" His voice was suddenly tight and hard. "My mother is good. She's brave and she's not a woman who finds it easy to be so. She thinks of us and Father before she thinks of herself. . . . By me that's goodness. Father is good, too. You look in his face and you see a *Mensch,* and there's always enough love to get you through the bad times. . . . But you'll see what's happened to these good people! . . . And I'm glad you're coming as plain Uncle Jean; because I don't think I'd have wanted to know you as Pope. . . ."

"That's the worst piece of logic I've ever heard." Jean Marie gave a wry chuckle. "You'd have been very flattered to know me. I was a much more agreeable fellow then than I am now. When I was elected one journalist called me the most personable of modern princes! Remember, it isn't always the prince who is the evildoer. Generally he's not clever enough to be a Satan. The real adversary is the one who whispers malice in his ear and offers to do his dirty work and keep him immune from bad report. . . ."

"But whichever is the evil one, we get him because we deserve him." Johann drove with deliberate care, as if he feared the discussion might excite him to some dangerous maneuver. "We want to be always innocent and out of the reach of malice. Father took the precautions he was told to take, but no more. An excessive care was beneath his dignity. He saw it as a triumph for terror. I don't see it that way. I walk very softly. I watch, I listen—and I carry a gun that I'm not afraid to use. Does that shock you, Uncle Jean?"

"No, it doesn't. It just makes me wonder how you will feel when you kill your first human being."

"I hope I never have to do it."

"Yet you go constantly prepared for that sole act. The man who tried to kill your father did it at a distance, mechanically, like blasting rock in a quarry. But with a pistol you will kill face to face. You will hear the cry of the victim in agony. You will see death in his eyes. You will smell blood. . . . Are you ready for that?"

"As I told you," said Johann Mendelius with wintry simplicity, "I hope the moment never comes; but, yes, I am ready for it."

Jean Marie Barette said nothing. The matter was beyond argument. He hoped it was not beyond the saving power of grace. He remembered the stark empty landscape of the vision, the planet from which mankind had obliterated itself, so that there was nothing and no one left to love.

His meeting with Lotte was strange at first. There was a moment of shock, almost of disappointment, when she saw him dressed in a layman's clothes. A sudden embarrassment held her back even from a hand's touch. He had to take her arms and draw her to him. For a split second it seemed that she would reject the embrace; then her control snapped and she clung to him, sobbing quietly, while he soothed her like a child, with small and tender words.

Katrin came home at that moment. Johann presented her to Uncle Jean, and after the first flurry of embarrassed talk, they were able to be calm together. Katrin had the morning's report on her father.

". . . I saw Doctor Pelzer. He's not very happy. The fever has flared up again. Papa doesn't respond to talk as well as he did yesterday. You know how he presses your hand when he understands something? Well, this morning I could only get an occasional response. The rest of the time he seemed to be unconscious. . . . Doctor Pelzer said I could leave. If there's any sudden change, we'll be called."

Lotte nodded and turned away to busy herself with the luncheon preparations. Katrin followed her out to the kitchen.

Johann said brusquely, "This is what it's like. We're all on a seesaw: up one moment, down the next. That's why I don't want to build up false hopes for Mother or Katrin. I don't want them clutching at cobwebs."

"You're afraid I may try to give them false hope?"

"You told me Father would live."

"I'm sure he will."

"I am not sure; so I'd rather Mother and Katrin learned to live with uncertainty. There'll be grief enough whether Father lives or dies."

"I'm your guest. Of course I'll respect your wishes."

At that moment Lotte came in carrying a linen cloth and napkins. She handed them to Johann and asked him to lay the table. She took Jean Marie's arm and led him into the next room.

". . . Katrin's doing the lunch. We can be quiet for a few minutes. . . . It's funny I can't get used to seeing you like this. You always looked so grand in Rome. It's strange to hear the children calling you Uncle Jean! . . ."

"I'm afraid Johann doesn't entirely approve of me."

"He's trying so hard to be the man of the house that he gets mixed up sometimes. He can't get it out of his head that you were somehow responsible for what has happened to his father."

"He's right. I am responsible."

"On the other hand, he knows how much Carl loves you and respects you, but he can't walk on that sacred ground until you or Carl invites him in. . . . That's difficult. I understand, because it was difficult for me, too, at first. . . . Add to all that the fear of war, the resentment that he, like so many millions, will be called to fight for a cause already lost. . . . Be patient with him, Jean! Be patient with us all. Our little world is tumbling round our ears and we are groping for something solid to hold."

"Look at me, Lotte!"

"I am looking at you."

"Now close your eyes tight. Don't open them until I tell you."

He fished in his breast pocket and brought out a small jewel case in red morocco. He laid it open on the small table at Lotte's elbow. It contained three objects, wrought in gold in the style of the Florentines of the sixteenth century. There was a small round box, a tiny flagon and a cup hardly bigger than a thimble.

"Open your eyes."

"What am I supposed to see?"

He pointed to the case.

"They're beautiful, Jean. What are they?"

"One of the privileges of the Pope used to be that he could carry the Eucharist constantly on his person. That's how he did it. The box was for the consecrated host. The flask and the cup were for the wine. There's a tiny damask handkerchief folded in the lid for the cleansing of the vessels. . . . The people of my first parish gave me the set as a personal gift on the day of my election. . . . When I was leaving Rome to come here, I felt ashamed. I had nothing to bring to you who were suffering so much on my account. So I got to Fiumicino early, said a private Mass in the airport chapel, and brought the Eucharist with me for you and Carl. I'll give you both communion at the hospital today. . . ."

Lotte was deeply moved. She closed the case and handed it back to Jean Marie.

"That says it all, Jean. Thank you. I only hope Carl will be conscious enough to understand."

"Sleeping or waking, God holds him in the palm of his hand."

"Luncheon is served," said Katrin from the dining room.

As they were seating themselves Lotte explained to her children the graceful gift Jean Marie had brought. Johann said with apparent surprise:

"I thought Father had been given the last rites."

"Of course," said Lotte, "but the Eucharist is a daily thing—a sharing of food; a sharing of life. That's right, isn't it, Jean?"

"That's right," said Jean Marie. "A sharing of life with the source of life."

"Thank you." Johann acknowledged the information without comment and asked with studied politeness, "Would you like to say a blessing for us, Uncle Jean?"

At the hospital, Lotte introduced him to Dr. Pelzer. She begged the good doctor to explain the medical situation to this old friend of the family. So it came to pass that Jean Marie Barette saw Carl Mendelius first in a series of X-ray photographs. The head which had once held the history of twenty centuries was reduced to a skull-case with broken jaws, a smashed septum and a scatter of opaque pellets embedded in the bony structure and in the surrounding film of flesh and mucous tissue. Dr. Pelzer, a tall, powerful fellow with iron-grey hair and a wary diagnostic eye, gave a commentary:

"A mess, as you see! But we can't go probing for all those foreign bodies until we have the poor devil stabilized. There's more of that rubbish in the rib cage and the upper abdomen. . . . So a prayer or two would help—and don't let the family expect too much, eh? Even if we save him, he'll need a lot of supportive therapy. . . ."

His next view was of the living man, hooked up to the drip bottles, the oxygen tap and the cardio-monitor. The head was swathed in bandages. The damaged eyes were mercifully hidden. The nasal and oral cavities were open and motionless. The stump of the severed hand lay like a large cloth club on the counterpane. The good hand twitched weakly at the folds of the sheets.

Lotte lifted it and kissed it. "Carl, my dearest, this is Lotte."

The hand closed over hers. A gurgling murmur issued from the mask of bandages.

"Jean Marie is here with me. He'll talk to you while I go and give a little thank-you gift to the ward sister. I'll be back shortly."

She tiptoed from the room, closing the door behind her. Jean Marie took Mendelius' hand. It was soft as satin and so weak it seemed that if one pressed too hard, the bones might crack.

"Carl, this is Jean. Can you hear me?"

There was an answering pressure against his palm and more helpless gurgling as Mendelius tried in vain to articulate.

"Please, don't try to talk. We don't need words, you and I. Just lie quiet and hold my hand. . . . I will pray for both of us."

He said no words. He made no ritual gestures. He simply sat by the bed, clasping Mendelius' hand between his own, so that it was as if they were one organism: the whole and the maimed, the blind and the seeing man. He closed his eyes, and opened his mind, a vessel ready for the inpouring of the spirit, a channel by which it might infuse itself into the conjoined consciousness of Carl Mendelius.

It was the only way he knew, now, to express the relationship between creature and Creator. He could not make petitions. They were all summed up in the original fiat: let your will be done. He could not bargain—life for life, service for service—because there was no vestige of self left to which he attached any importance. The important thing was the body and the agonized spirit of Carl Mendelius for whom he was now the lifeline. . . .

When at last the inpouring came, it was simple and extraordinarily sweet, like a waft of perfume in a summer garden. There was light and a strange awareness of harmony as though the music were not played but written into the texture of the brain. There was a calm so powerful that he could feel the fevered pulse of the sick man subside like seawaves after a storm. When he opened his eyes, Lotte was in the room again, staring at him in fear and wonderment. She said awkwardly:

"I didn't mean to interrupt, but it's nearly five o'clock."

"So late? Would you like to receive communion now?"

"Please, yes; but I don't think Carl can swallow the wafer."

"I know; but he can take a sip from the chalice. Are you ready, Carl?"

A pressure on his palm told him that Mendelius had heard and understood. While Lotte sat by the bedside, Jean Marie laid out the small golden vessels and put a stole around his neck. After a brief prayer he handed the consecrated wafer to Lotte and then held the tiny chalice to Mendelius' mouth. As he pronounced the ritual words *"Corpus domini,"* Lotte said "Amen" and Mendelius raised his hand in a feeble salute.

Jean Marie Barette cleansed the pyx and the chalice with the damask handkerchief, folded his stole, put the case and the stole in his pocket and tiptoed out of the room.

As he stepped past the armed guards in the corridor he was accosted by a squat, ugly woman of indeterminate age, who introduced herself abruptly as Professor Meissner.

". . . We're dining together tonight at the Mendelius house; but I told Lotte I needed an hour alone with you. Will you come to my place for a drink?"

"I'd be delighted."

"Good! There's a lot to talk about."

She took his arm, bustled him into the elevator, rode the three floors down in silence, then hurried him out into the late sunshine. It was not until they were outside the confines of the clinic that she slackened her pace and began a leisurely stroll down the hill towards the old town. She was more relaxed now; but her talk was still forthright and rasping.

"You know that Carl called me in for clinical advice on your letter and your encyclical?"

"He didn't put it that way; but, yes, I knew you were involved."

"And you read my quotes in his article?"

"Yes."

"There was one they didn't use. I'm going to give it to you now. I think you're a very dangerous man. Trouble will follow you wherever you go. . . . And I understand why your colleagues in the Church had to get rid of you."

The raw brutality of the attack left him speechless for a moment. When he found voice, all he could say was, "Well . . . what do I answer to that?"

"You could tell me I'm a bitch—and I am! But it wouldn't budge me from the proposition. You are a very dangerous man!"

"I've heard the charge before," said Jean Marie quietly. "My brothers in the Vatican called me a walking time-bomb. But I'd like to know how you see the danger which I represent."

"I've thought about it a long time." Anneliese Meissner was more gracious now. "I've done a lot of reading. I've listened to a lot of tapes from colleagues who have clinical experience of religious manias and cultist influences. At the end of it all, I am forced to conclude that you are a man with a special perception of what Jung calls the collective unconscious. Therefore, you have a magical effect on people. It is as if you are privy to their most intimate thoughts, desires, fears—as indeed you are on this question of the Last Things. This subject is rooted in the deepest subsoil of the race memory. So, when you talk or write about it, people feel you inside themselves, almost as a function of their own egos. . . . As a result, everything you do or say has profound and sometimes terrible consequences. You are the giant dreaming under the volcano. When you turn in your sleep, the earth shakes."

"And what do you think I should do about this dangerous potency?"

"You can do nothing," said Anneliese Meissner baldly. "That's where your Cardinals made the mistake. Had they left you in power, the very weight of the office and its traditional methods would have damped down the magical manifestations. You would have been held at a safe distance from common folk. Now there is no damping effect at all. There is no distance. Your impact is instant— and it may become catastrophic."

"And you see no good in the power or in me?"

"Good? Oh, yes! But it's the good that comes out of disaster, like battlefield heroism, or the dedication of nurses in a pesthouse."

"You call it magic. Have you no other name for it?"

"Use any name you like," said Anneliese Meissner. "Whatever you call yourself, priest, shaman, juju man, whomever you claim to serve—the spirit of the grove, the God-man or the Eternal Oneness—you'll always be at the epicenter of an earthquake. . . . Here's where I live."

They were nearly at the top of the Burgsteige, outside an old sixteenth-century house, built of oak beams and handmade bricks. Anneliese Meissner unlocked the door and led him up two flights of stairs to her apartment, whose narrow windows looked out on the turrets of Hohentübingen and the marching pines of the Swabian uplands. She swept a pile of books off an armchair and gestured to Jean Marie to sit down.

"What will you drink? Wine, schnapps or Scotch?"

"Wine, please."

As he watched her polishing a pair of dusty glasses, uncorking a bottle of Moselle and opening a jar of nuts, he was touched by the pathos of so much intelligence, so much hidden tenderness, locked in so ugly a body. She handed him the wine and made a toast:

"To Carl's recovery."

"Prosit."

She tossed off half the wine at a gulp and set down the glass. Then she made a bald and seemingly irrelevant announcement. "At the clinic we have central monitoring of all intensive-care patients."

"Indeed?" Jean Marie was politely interested.

"Yes. All vital signs are transmitted constantly to the monitor room, where a senior nurse is on duty all the time. . . . While you were with Carl, I was in the monitor room with Doctor Pelzer."

Jean Marie Barette waited. He could not be sure whether she was embarrassed or reluctant to continue. Finally he had to prompt her.

"Please! You were in the monitor room. So . . . ?"

"When you arrived Carl had a temperature of a hundred and three degrees; a pulse rate of one twenty and a pronounced cardiac arrhythmia. You were with him nearly two hours. During all that time, except for a few opening sentences, you did not utter a single word until Lotte came back into the room. By then, Carl's temperature had dropped, the pulse rate was nearly normal and the rhythm of the heartbeat was restored. What did you do?"

"I prayed, in a fashion."

"What fashion?"

"I suppose you could call it meditation. . . . But if you are trying to attribute some kind of miracle . . . please, no!"

"I don't believe in miracles. I am, however, curious about phenomena that go beyond the norms. Besides . . ." She gave him an odd sidelong glance as if she were suddenly afraid to commit herself; then she plunged ahead. "You might as well know it; everything that touches Carl, touches me. I've been in love with him for ten years. He doesn't know it and he never will. But right now, I've got to cry on someone's shoulder—and you're elected, because you're the one who got him into this mess! . . . Carl always said you had the grace of understanding. Then, maybe, you'll understand that for me, the fairy tale was reversed. It wasn't the beautiful princess and the frog-prince. It was the girl-frog waiting for the prince to kiss her and make her beautiful. I know it's hopeless and I've learned not to care too much. I'm no threat to anyone, certainly not to Lotte. But when I see poor Carl hooked up to those life-support systems, when I know how much stuff they're pumping into him, just to keep him sedated and his body functioning, then I wish I believed in miracles."

"I believe in them," said Jean Marie gently. "And they all begin in an act of love."

"But love is terrible—the same way you're terrible. If you bottle it up too long, it can blow the top of your head off. . . . Hell! I didn't bring you here to bitch you or tell you about my love life." She poured more wine and then told him, "Johann Mendelius is in big trouble."

"What sort of trouble?"

"He's putting together an underground group of students to resist military call-up, obstruct security surveillance and provide escape routes for deserters from the armed forces."

"How do you know this?"

"He told me. His father had mentioned that I would be prepared to support an underground organization among the faculty. . . . But these kids are so naïve! They don't realize how closely they're watched, how easy it is to penetrate their ranks with spies and provocateurs. They're buying and storing arms, which is a criminal offense. . . . It's only a matter of time before the police get wind of what's going on. They may know already and be waiting until all the fuss over Carl dies down."

"Johann promised he would show me what form his protest was taking. Perhaps he's thought of taking me to a meeting of this group."

"Possibly. It's because you're a Frenchman that they've named the group the Jacquerie, to recall the French peasants' revolt during the Hundred Years' War. . . . But if you take my advice, you'll stay well away."

"I'd like to keep an open mind on that. I may be able to talk some sense into Johann and his friends."

"Don't forget what I told you at the beginning. You are a very special man. Without knowing how or why, you make a potent magic; and youth is most susceptible to the witchcraft. . . . Now I want you to listen to a tape."

"What's on it?"

"Part of a clinical interview with one of my patients. I am communicating it to you under professional secrecy as Carl communicated your material to me. Agreed?"

"Agreed."

"The woman is twenty-eight, a childless divorcee, the eldest daughter of a well-known local family. The marriage lasted three years. She has been divorced for one year. She shows acute depressive symptoms, and there have been some hallucinatory episodes which are probably the sequelae of some experiments with L.S.D. in which she admits to have taken part during her marriage. . . . This tape was made yesterday. It is part of a session that lasted an hour and twenty minutes."

"And what will it tell me?"

"That's what I want to find out. It tells me one thing. It may tell you quite another."

"My dear Professor." He gave a chuckle of genuine good humour. "If you really want a profile of my character, why not start with something simple, like a Rorschach blot?"

"Because I have your profile already." The response was curt and irritable. "I've had you in my casebook for weeks now. You're a frightening phenomenon: a resolutely simple man. You say what you believe. You believe what you say. You live in a universe permeated by an immanent God with whom you have a direct and personal relationship. I don't live in such a universe, but we are both here in this room, with this tape. I want to know your reaction to it. You'll indulge me, please?"

"At your service."

"The location is my consulting room. The time: four in the afternoon. This passage occurs after forty minutes of discursive and defensive talk by the patient. . . ."

She switched on the machine. A woman's voice, low-timbred, and with a pronounced Swabian accent, picked up what was obviously a new theme in the narration:

". . . I met him one morning in the Marktplatz. I was buying grapes. He picked one from the stall and popped it in my mouth. Even though I knew how awful he could be, it made me laugh. He asked me would I like a cup of tea. I said yes I would and he took me down to that tea shop near the Nuns-House . . . you know! . . . the place you can buy teas from all over the world, even maté from Argentina. . . . He was very pleasant. I didn't feel threatened at all. The people in the shop were in and out the whole time. I agreed to try something I'd never had before: a special infusion from Ceylon. . . . I thought it was pleasant, but nothing to rave about. We talked of this and that: his work, my parents, how he was off women for a while. . . . I wondered if he'd caught anything from the last one, who was a cheap little tart from Frankfurt. I didn't say a word, but I knew he'd read my thoughts. . . . He threw the cup of tea in my face. It splashed down my blouse. He tore the blouse off, while the people in the tea shop stood by, laughing. The next thing we all joined hands and danced round the shop singing 'Boom—boom—boom,' while the big tin tea-caddies began exploding all over the place. But it wasn't tea; it was fireworks, blue and green and lots of red! . . . Then we were out in the street. I was naked and he was dragging me behind him and telling all the people . . . 'Look what the Turks did to my wife! Monsters! Bloody rapists . . . !' But when we got to the hospital there were police at the door and they wouldn't let me in because they said I had clap and the secret service never employs people with social diseases. They said he could kill me, too, if he wanted; but he said I wasn't important enough and I started to cry. . . .

"After that he took me to my house and told me to clean myself up. I had a long hot bath, then I powdered myself and put on perfume and lay on the bed, naked, to wait for him. Only it wasn't my bed. It was a beautiful circular one, soft and comfortable and smelling of lavender. After a while he came in. He went into the bathroom and when he came out he was naked and clean like me. He kissed my breasts and excited me with his hands and then he came inside me and we had a big climax which was like the tin caddies exploding in the tea shop. . . . I always close my eyes when I have a climax. This time when I opened them he was lying beside me, all bloody. His hand was on my breast, but it was just a hand with no arm or body. I tried to scream but I couldn't. Then I saw his face, it was just empty like a big red saucer. Then the bed wasn't a bed anymore, but a big black box with both of us inside it. . . ."

Anneliese Meissner switched off the machine and said, "Well, that's it!"

Jean Marie Barette was silent for a long moment, then he asked, "Who is the man in the dream?"

"Her ex-husband. He still lives in the town."

"And you know him?"

"Not very well; but, yes, I know him."

Jean Marie said nothing. He held up his glass. She refilled it for him. Then she asked tentatively:

"Any comment on what you've just heard?"

"I'm not an expert on the decipherment of dreams; but the tape did tell me something. The woman is haunted by guilt. She has knowledge which she is afraid to share with anyone else. So she dreams it, or constructs a dream about it and tells it to you. Whatever she knows is connected in some way with the Mendelius affair. . . . How am I doing so far, Frau Professor?"

"Very well. Please go on!"

"I think," said Jean Marie deliberately, "I think that you have the same problem as your patient. You know something which you're unwilling or unable to disclose."

"I'm unwilling because I'm not sure of my conclusions. I'm unable because it involves my professional integrity. You'd have the same problem with a confessional secret."

"They're both good reasons for reticence," said Jean Marie drily.

"There are others." Now she was irritable and combative.

"Please! A moment!" Jean Marie held up a warning hand. "Let's not get heated. You invited me here. I have given you my guarantee of secrecy. If you want to tell me what's bothering you, I'll listen. If not, then let's enjoy the wine!"

"I'm sorry!" It was hard for her to express any sort of penitence. "I'm so used to playing God in the consulting room that I forget my everyday manners. . . . You're right. I'm desperately worried. I don't see what I can do about it, without opening a whole new nest of vipers. Anyway, here's item one. The woman on that tape is both vulnerable and acquisitive. A young divorcee in a university town, she's had more affairs than she knows how to cope with. One of her more serious romances was with Johann Mendelius. It was finished only this summer before he left on vacation. Fortunately, neither Carl nor Lotte got wind of it. But I knew because she was my patient and I had to listen to the whole big drama. Item two is where I stumble. Her ex-husband is a man—how shall I explain it?—a man so improbable that he has to be authentic. I have a whole series of tapes on their relationship. He's the one who's selling guns to Johann and his group; and if that tape means what I think it does, he's the one who sent the letter bomb to Carl. . . . I know it sounds absurd but . . ."

"Evil is the ultimate absurdity," said Jean Marie Barette. "It is the last sad buffoonery: man sitting in the ruins of his world, daubing himself with his own excrement. . . ."

It was nearly six-thirty when he left Anneliese's apartment. As he closed the front door behind him, his attention was caught by a plaque on the building opposite, a sturdy hostelry built in the first half of the sixteenth century where the burghers of Tübingen still came to eat and drink. The plaque announced in Gothic script: "The Old Schloss Keller. Here lived Professor Michael Maestlin of Goppingen, teacher of the astronomer Johannes Kepler."

The inscription pleased him, since it celebrated the lesser-known master before the effulgent pupil. It reminded him, too, of the fear that had haunted his predecessor: that Tübingen might become the center of a second anti-

Roman revolt. He himself had never had such fears. It had always seemed as fruitless an exercise to impeach a scholar for heresy as to hang out the bloody sheets after a bridal night. It further occurred to him that he ought to provide the wine for the evening meal. So he pushed open the heavy nail-studded door and went inside.

Half the booths were full of student drinkers, and a dozen burly countrymen propped up the bar. Jean Marie Barette made himself perfectly understood in *Hochdeutsch* but was totally confused by the names of unfamiliar vintages which the barman reeled off in dialect. Finally he settled on a pleasantly dry white from the Ammertal, bought two bottles and made for the exit. A call from a corner booth stopped him in his tracks.

"Uncle Jean! Over here! Come and join us!" Johann took the bottles and pushed his companions along the bench to make room for Jean Marie. He made the introductions briskly: "Franz, Alexis, Norbert, Alvin Dolman. This is my uncle Jean. Franz is my sister's boyfriend. Alvin's an American and a very good friend of Father's."

"I'm happy to meet you gentlemen." Jean Marie was cordiality itself. "May I buy you a drink?"

He signalled the waitress and ordered a round for the company and a glass of mineral water for himself.

Johann asked, "What are you doing up this end of town, Uncle Jean?"

"Visiting Professor Meissner. We met at the hospital. I walked home with her."

"How was Father this afternoon?"

"The doctor says he's improved. His temperature is down, his pulse steadier."

"That's great news; great!" Alvin Dolman seemed a little gone in his cups. "Let me know when I can see him, Johann. I've found something he'll like. It's a carving of Saint Christopher, Early Gothic. This he gets for free, as soon as he's sitting up and taking nourishment."

Jean Marie was instantly intrigued. "You are a collector then, Mr. Dolman?"

"No, sir, a dealer! But I've got the eye for the game. You've got to have the eye."

"Indeed, yes. You live here?"

"I live here, work here. Once I was married here—son-in-law to the Bürgermeister yet! But that didn't last. Old dogfaces like me shouldn't marry. We're reject china, you might say. . . . Matter of fact, your Professor Meissner was a great friend of my wife. Helped her to straighten out after the divorce."

"I'm glad to hear it," said Jean Marie. "And what kind of work do you do, Mr. Dolman?"

"I'm an artist—a technical illustrator, if you must spell it out. I work for educational publishers up and down the Rhine. On the side I deal in antique art . . . in a small way, of course. I don't have money for the big stuff."

"I thought the *company* supplied the funds." Jean Marie leaned ever so lightly on the word.

"Please?"

It was the minutest reaction—hardly the flicker of an eyelid; but Jean Marie had dealt with too many clerics and too many other subtle fellows to miss it. Alvin Dolman smiled and shook his head.

"The company? I'm afraid you've misunderstood me. I'm strictly free-lance. I accept commissions just like a portrait painter. No, sir! The only company I've ever worked for is good old Uncle Sam."

"Forgive me." Jean Marie smiled an apology. "One speaks a foreign language, but always one makes mistakes in the simplest things. . . . Johann, what time do we sit down for your mother's dinner?"

"No later than eight. Let's finish our drinks and I'll walk back with you. We're only five minutes away."

"I should be moving, too," said Alvin Dolman. "I've got a date in Stuttgart. While I'm there I'll see what I can do for you guys. But remember, it has to be cash on the line! *Wiedersehen* all!"

He climbed awkwardly to his feet and Jean Marie had to rise to let him out of the booth. As he moved to the door Jean Marie followed him. When they came out into the nearly deserted street he said in English:

"A word with you, Mr. Dolman."

Dolman swung round to face him. His smile was gone now. His eyes were hostile.

"Yes?"

"I know you," said Jean Marie Barette. "I know who you are, and what company employs you, and whose is the evil spirit that inhabits you. If I tell them inside, they will kill you with the same guns you have sold to them. So, keep your life and go from this place. Go now!"

Dolman stared at him for a moment and then laughed.

"Who do you think you are—God Almighty?"

"You know who I am, Alvin Dolman. You know everything that has been said and written about me. . . . And you know it is true. Now, in the name of God, go!"

Dolman spat in his face, then he turned on his heel and went limping hurriedly down the cobbled slope. Jean Marie wiped the spittle from his cheeks and went back into the Schloss Keller.

". . . Get rid of the guns! Every one of them is marked to convict you. Disband the Jacquerie. You are blown anyway. Dolman made you the victims of the classic intelligence plot: concentrate all the dissidents in one group, then knock them off at leisure. Meantime he was using you to cover up his own tracks as an assassin. . . ."

It was one in the morning and they were alone in Mendelius' study under the rooftops. Outside, the first chill wind of early autumn keened around the belfry of the Stiftskirche. On the floor below, Lotte and Katrin slept peacefully, unaware of the mystery play which had been enacted around them. Johann, for all his shame and weariness, could still not abandon the debate.

". . . But it doesn't make sense. Dolman's a huckster who'll trade you anything. He's a clown who laughs when an old lady falls from a bus and shows her drawers. But an assassin—no!"

"Dolman is the perfect agent-in-place." Jean Marie admonished him patiently. "As Professor Meissner says, he's so improbable he has to be authentic.

. . . More! As an agent of a friendly power, concerned with Germany as its
eastern frontier, he's the perfect instrument for dirty jobs like the bomb strike
on your father. . . . But that's not all! I have known men highly practiced in
violence who are not half as evil as their deeds. They are conditioned, bent like
twigs beyond straightening. In some, a key component has been lost, so that
they can never be otherwise than what they are. But Dolman is different.
Dolman knows who he is and what he is and he wants to be just that. He is,
truly, in the old phrase, a habitation of evil."

"How can you know that? You met him only once. I can understand Professor
Meissner having an opinion about him, because she's heard all the stories from
his wife. I heard them, too, many a time, in her bed; but I didn't believe them,
because Dolman knew I was having her, and he encouraged me to enjoy it—
and prepared me to get out when the fun was over. . . . But you? One meeting? I'm sorry, Uncle Jean. It doesn't make sense unless you know something
more than you're telling me."

"I know less than you about Alvin Dolman—but much, much more about the
noonday devil." He clasped his hands behind his head and leaned far back in
Mendelius' armchair. "In the high places where I used to live he was a very
frequent visitor—and most beguiling company!"

"That's too easy, Uncle Jean. I don't accept it."

"Very well. Let me put it another way. While you were playing love games
with Dolman's wife, would you have invited a child to witness them?"

"Of course not."

"Why not?"

"Well, because . . ."

"Because you recognize innocence, even if you can't define it. You recognize
evil, too; but you close your eyes to it. Why?"

"I . . . I suppose because I don't want to recognize the evil in myself either."

"At last we come to it. Now will you take some advice from your uncle Jean?"

"I'll try."

"As soon as your father can travel, move away from here. If you can complete
the purchase of the Alpine property and make it fit for habitation, go there. Try
to keep the family together: your mother and father, Katrin, her man, too, if he
will go with you. . . . Dolman is gone. He will not come back; his company will
not use him again in this region; but the company is still in business—and
always in partnership with the noonday devil!"

"And where will you go, Uncle Jean?"

"Tomorrow to Paris to see my family and arrange my financial affairs. After
that . . . who knows? I wait on the call!"

Johann was still uneasy and irritable. He objected, "So we're back to private
revelation and prophecy and all that?"

"Well?"

"I don't believe in it. That's all!"

"But you believed in a man who tried to kill your father. You didn't believe
the truths his wife told you in bed. You don't know how to smell evil from good.
Does that tell you nothing about yourself, Johann?"

"You really strike for the throat, don't you?"

"Grow up, boy!" Jean Marie Barette was implacable. "We're talking about life, death and the hereafter. No one gets an absolution from reality!"

That night Jean Marie Barette had a dream. He was walking in the Marktplatz of Tübingen. He paused by a fruit stall selling beautiful black grapes. He tasted one; it was sweet and satisfying. He asked the stall holder to weigh him out a kilo. She gaped at him, horror-struck, raised her hands in front of her face and backed away. All the people in the marketplace did the same until he stood isolated in a circle of hostile humans, holding a bunch of grapes in his hand. He spoke peaceably, asking what was the matter. No one answered. He took a few steps towards the nearest person. His way was barred by a big fellow with a butcher's knife. He stopped in his tracks and cried out:

"What's the matter? Why are you afraid of me?"

The big fellow answered, "Because you're a *Pestträger*—a plague-carrier! Get out before we kill you!"

Then the crowd began to close in, forcing him inexorably towards the mouth of the alley down which, he knew, he must turn and run for his life. . . .

In the morning, red-eyed and unrested, he had an early breakfast with Lotte and then went with her to the hospital to say his farewells to Carl Mendelius. There, in a final quiet moment, he told them both:

". . . We will meet again. I'm sure of it; but where and how, God knows! Lotte, my dear, don't cling to anything here. When Carl is ready, just pack and go! Promise me!"

"I promise, Jean! It won't be hard to leave."

"Good! When the call comes, Carl, you will be ready for it. For the present, resign yourself to a long convalescence. Help Lotte to help you. Tell her you'll do that."

Carl Mendelius raised his good hand and stroked her cheek. She drew the hand to her lips and kissed the palm. Jean Marie stood up. He traced the sign of the cross with his thumb on Mendelius' forehead and then on Lotte's. His voice was unsteady.

"I hate farewells. I love you both. Pray for me."

Mendelius clutched at his wrist to stay him. He struggled to speak. This time, painfully but clearly, he managed to articulate the words:

"The fig tree, Jean. I know now. The fig tree!"

Lotte pleaded with him. "Please, dearest, don't try to talk."

Jean Marie said soothingly, "Dear Carl, remember what we agreed! No words, no arguments. Let God make the trees grow in his own good time."

Mendelius relaxed slowly. Lotte held his hand. Jean Marie kissed her and, without another word, walked out of the room.

He was halfway to Paris, flying blind through storm clouds, when Mendelius' words made sense to him. They were an echo of the text from the Gospel of Matthew that had fallen open in his hands on the day of the vision: ". . . And from the fig tree learn a parable. When the branch is tender and the leaves come forth you know that summer is near. So, when you see all these happenings you will know that the end things are very near, yes, even at the gates!"

He felt a strange surge of relief, almost of elation. If Carl Mendelius believed at last in the vision, then Jean Marie Barette was not left utterly alone.

IX

IN Paris the dream of the plague-carrier came true. His brother, Alain Hubert Barette, silver of hair, silver of tongue, a pillar of the banking establishment on the Boulevard Haussmann, was shocked to the soles of his handmade shoes. He cherished Jean Marie. He would somehow make adequate financial provisions; but to open up a forty-year-old trust, and dismantle the most complicated international arrangements—*pas possible!* Jean had come at a most inconvenient time. It would be most difficult to lodge him with the family. They had the decorators in. Odette was in a constant state of near hysteria. And the servants—my God! However, the bank would be most happy to let him use its suite at the Lancaster until he was able to make other arrangements.

How was Odette—apart from the hysteria? Well enough, but shocked—devastated indeed—by the abdication! And, of course, when Cardinal Sancerre, Archbishop of Paris, came back from the consistory and began spreading all those odd stories—that was truly an intimate distress for the whole family.

Political contacts? Diplomatic encounters? Normally Alain Hubert Barette would have been happy to act as host to such meetings; but in this precise moment—eh!—one counselled a great discretion. One did not want to risk a snub, by too direct an approach to the President or even to the high gentlemen at the Quai d'Orsay. Why not come tomorrow night for dinner with Odette and the girls and then discuss the whole question?

Meantime, the money problem . . . The bank would grant Jean Marie a substantial credit line, guaranteed by the trust, until such time as it was possible to reconstitute the arrangements.

". . . Now, let's get some documents signed so that you can have funds immediately. I suggest—strictly between loving brothers!—that a good tailor is a first requisite and a decent shirtmaker. After all, you are still a Monseigneur and even the garments of a layman should indicate the hidden dignity."

It was one idiocy too many. It put Jean Marie in a cold, Gallic rage.

"Alain, you are a fool! You are also a snob and a tasteless, greedy little money-changer! I will not come to your house. I do not wish to have the apartment at the Lancaster. You will provide me immediately with the money I need. You will call a meeting of the trustees for ten in the morning and we will discuss in detail their past administration and their future activities. I have little time and much travel to do. I will not be inhibited by the bureaucratic nonsense of your bank. Do I make myself clear?"

"Jean, you misunderstand me. I did not intend to . . ."

"Be quiet, Alain! The less said the better. What documents do I have to sign for the immediate funds I need?"

Fifteen minutes later it was done. A very subdued Alain made the last call to summon the last trustee to the next morning's meeting. He mopped his hands with a silk handkerchief and delivered himself of a carefully modified apology.

"Please! We are brothers. We should not quarrel. You have to understand: we are all under a strain now. The money markets are going mad. We have to defend ourselves as if it were against bandits. We know there will be a war. So how do we protect the banks' assets and our own? How do we arrange our personal lives? You have been away so long, protected so long . . ."

In spite of his anger Jean Marie laughed—a gusty chuckle of genuine amusement.

"Eh-eh-eh, little brother! I bleed for you! For my part, I should not know what to do with all those trunks and strong rooms full of paper and coinage and bullion. . . . But you're right. It's too late in the day to quarrel—and it's also too late for all that silly snobbery! Why don't you see if you can get Vauvenargues on the phone for me . . ."

"Vauvenargues? The Foreign Minister?"

"The same."

"As you wish." Alain shrugged resignedly and consulted his leather-bound desk directory. He switched to a private line and tapped out a number. Jean Marie listened with cool amusement to the one-sided dialogue.

"Hullo! This is Alain Hubert Barette, Director of Halévy Frères et Barette, Banquiers. Please connect me with the Minister. . . . Apropos of the fact that an old friend of his has arrived in Paris and would like to speak with him. . . . The friend is Monseigneur Jean Marie Barette, formerly his Holiness Pope Gregory the Seventeenth. . . . Oh, I see! Then perhaps you will be kind enough to pass the message and have the Minister call back to this number. . . . Thank you."

He put down the receiver and made a grimace of distaste.

"The Minister is in conference. The message will be passed. . . . You've been there, Jean! You know the routines. Once you have to explain yourself and your current identity, you're diplomatically dead. Oh, I'm sure the Minister will return the call; but what do you want with a limp handshake and some words about the weather?"

"I'll make the next call myself." Jean Marie consulted his pocketbook and spelled out the private number of the most senior presidential counsellor, a man with whom, during his pontificate, he had maintained a constant and friendly relationship. The response came immediately:

"This is Duhamel."

"Pierre, this is Jean Marie Barette. I am in Paris for a few days on private business. I'd like to see you—and your master!"

"And I you. But it has to be in private. As to the master—my regrets, but no! The official word is out. You are untouchable."

"Where does the word come from?"

"From your principal to our principal. And the Friends of Silence have been busy at all the lower levels. Where are you staying?"

"I haven't decided yet."

"Outside the city is better. Take a taxi and drive out to L'Hostellerie des Chevaliers. It's about three kilometers this side of Versailles. I'll telephone ahead and book the accommodation for you. . . . Sign yourself as Monsieur Grégoire. They won't ask for documents. I'll call there on my way home—about eight. I must go now. *A bientôt.*"

Jean Marie put down the receiver. It was his turn to apologize.

"You're right, little brother. Diplomatically I am dead and buried. Well, I should be going. Give my love to Odette and the girls. We'll try to arrange a meal together before I leave."

"You don't want to change your mind about the Lancaster?"

"Thank you, no. If I'm a plague-carrier I'd rather not spread the infection to my family. Tomorrow at ten, eh? . . ."

The Hostellerie des Chevaliers was a pleasant surprise, a cluster of ancient farm buildings converted into an agreeable and discreet hotel. There were manicured lawns and quiet rose arbours, and a millstream that meandered under a drapery of willows.

The *patronne* was a handsome woman in her mid-fifties who waived all the formalities of registration and led him immediately to a pleasant suite with a view onto a private enclave with its own greensward and a lily pond. She pointed out that he might make his telephone calls with full security, that the refrigerator was stocked with liquor and that, as a friend of M. Duhamel, he had only to raise a finger to command the total service of the Hostellerie.

As he unpacked his one suitcase he was amused and a whit surprised to see how lightly he was travelling: one suit, a raincoat, a sports jacket and trousers, a pullover, two pairs of pajamas and half a dozen changes of shirts, underwear and socks constituted his whole wardrobe. His toiletries, his mass kit, a breviary, a missal and a pocketbook made up the rest of his impedimenta. For sustenance he had a day's supply of cash, a folder of travellers' checks and a circular letter of credit from Halévy Frères et Barette. For these he was a debtor to the bank until the trustees released some of the funds from his patrimony. At least he was free to move quickly once the call came, as it had come centuries before to John, the son of Zachary, in the desert.

What troubled him now was a growing sense of isolation and of his precarious dependence on the goodwill of friends. No matter that at the center of himself was a great pool of calm, a place, an estate, where all opposites were reconciled; he was still a man, subject to all the chemistries of the flesh, all the unstable physics of the mind.

The weapon of estrangement had been used against him in the dark and bitter days before his abdication. Now it was being used again, to render him impotent in the political arena. Pierre Duhamel, longtime counsellor to the President of the Republic, was not prone to exaggeration. If he said you were dying, it was indeed time to call the priest; if he said you were dead, the stonemasons were already carving your epitaph.

That Pierre Duhamel had been so prompt to suggest a rendezvous was itself an indication of crisis. In all the years of their acquaintance, Duhamel had observed a singular and spartan code: "I have one wife: the woman I married. I have one mistress: the Republic. Never tell me anything you do not want reported. Never try to frighten me. Never offer me a bribe. I give patronage to none and my advice only to those whom I am paid to counsel. I respect all faiths. I demand to be private about my own. If you trust me I shall never lie to you. If you lie to me, I shall understand, but never trust you again."

In the days of his pontificate, Jean Marie Barette had had many exchanges with this strangely attractive man, who looked like a prize fighter, reasoned as eloquently as Montaigne and went home to cherish a wife who had once been the toast of Paris and was now a ravaged victim of multiple sclerosis.

They had a son at Saint Cyr and a daughter somewhat older, who had earned a good reputation as a producer of programs for television. For the rest, Jean Marie made no enquiry. Pierre Duhamel was what his President claimed him to be—a good man for the long road.

Jean Marie picked up his breviary and stepped out into the garden to read the vespers of the day. It was a habit he cherished: the prayer of a man walking, at day's end, hand in hand with God in a garden. The day's psalmody began with the canticle he had always loved: *Quam dilecta*. "How lovely are thy tabernacles, O Lord of Hosts. My soul longeth and fainteth for the courts of the Lord. My heart and my flesh have rejoiced in the living God. For the sparrow hath found herself a house and the dove a nest for herself where she may lay her young ones. . . ."

It was the perfect prayer for a late-summer evening, with the shadows long, the air still and languorous with the perfume of roses. As he turned down a gravelled pathway towards another stretch of lawn, he heard children's voices, and a moment later saw a group of little girls, all dressed alike in gingham dresses and pinafores, playing a simple catching game with a pair of young teachers. On a bench nearby an older woman divided her attention between the group and a piece of embroidery.

As Jean Marie passed along the gravelled walk, one of the children broke away from the group and ran towards him. She slipped on the verge and fell almost at his feet. She burst into tears. He picked her up and carried her to the woman on the bench, who dabbed at her grazed knee and offered her a lollipop to soothe her. It was only then that Jean Marie noticed that the child was a mongol—as indeed were all the others in the group. As if sensing his shock, the woman held the child towards him and said with a smile:

"We are all from the Institute across the road. . . . This one has just come to us. She's homesick; so she thinks every man is her papa."

"And where is Papa?" There was a touch of censure in the question.

The woman shook her head. "Oh, no, it isn't what you think. He's been recently widowed. He feels, quite rightly, that she is safer here with us. . . .

We have about a hundred children in the Institute. The *patronne* lets us bring the little ones here to play. Her only child was mongoloid but it died early."

Jean Marie held out his arms. The child came to him willingly and kissed him, then sat in his lap and began playing happily with the buttons of his shirt.

He said, "She's very affectionate."

"Most are," the woman told him. "People who are able to keep them in the family group find that it is like having a new baby in the house all the time. . . . But, of course, it is when the parents age and the child comes to adolescence and maturity that the tragedies begin. The boys may become very rough and violent. The girls are easy victims to sexual invasion. The future is dark for both parents and children. . . . It's sad. I am so very fond of them."

"How do you maintain the Institute?"

"We have a grant from the government. We ask fees from parents who can pay. We solicit private charity. Fortunately we have some wealthy sponsors like Monsieur Duhamel, who lives close by. He calls the children *les petites bouffonnes du bon Dieu* . . . 'God's little clowns. . . .' "

"It's a gentle thought."

"You know Monsieur Duhamel perhaps? He's a very important man, the President's right hand, they say."

"By repute," said Jean Marie carefully.

The child slipped from his knee and began tugging his hand to make him walk with her. He asked, "May I take her down to the pond to see the fish?"

"Of course. I'll come with you."

As he moved away his breviary fell from his pocket onto the bench. The woman picked it up, glanced at the title page, then laid aside her embroidery and followed him, book in hand.

"You left your breviary, Father."

"Oh! Thank you."

He shoved it back in his pocket. The woman took the child's other hand and fell into step with Jean Marie. She said, "I have the strange feeling I've seen you somewhere before."

"I'm sure we haven't met. I've been away from France a long time."

"A missionary perhaps?"

"In a way, yes."

"Where did you serve?"

"Oh, several countries, but mostly in Rome. I'm retired now. I came home for a vacation."

"I thought priests never retired."

"Let's say I'm on retreat for a while. . . . Come on, little one! Let's go see the goldfish."

He swung the child up on his shoulder and began singing a song from his own childhood as he marched her down to the pond. The woman dropped back and stood watching them from a distance. He seemed a most pleasant man, obviously a lover of children—but when a priest, still vigorous, was retired so early, there had to be a reason. . . .

Punctually at eight, Pierre Duhamel was knocking on the door of the suite. He must be gone by eight forty-five, since he never failed to have dinner at home with his wife. Meantime he would drink a Campari and soda with Jean Marie, whom he seemed to regard with bleak amusement as a highly memorable survivor, rather like the hairy mammoth.

". . . My God! They really pegged you out and ran the steamroller over you! Frankly, I'm astonished to see you looking so healthy. . . . What have you done now that makes them lean so hard on you? Of course, that big splash in the press didn't make you any more popular with the French hierarchy. The Friends of Silence are very strong here. . . . Then I heard that your friend Mendelius had been the victim of a terrorist bomb attack. . . ."

"A bomb attack, yes. A terrorist action, no. The thing was planned and executed by an agent of the C.I.A., Alvin Dolman."

"Why the C.I.A.?"

"Why not? Dolman was their agent-in-place. I think it was a neat piece of work by the Americans for the Bundesrepublik. It was designed to rid them of an influential academic who was bound to cause trouble once the call-up for military service was implemented."

"Any proof?"

"Enough for me. Not enough to raise a public outcry."

"Very soon"—Pierre Duhamel stirred the liquor with his finger—"very soon you'll be able to boil your mother in oil on the Pont Royal—and nobody will blink an eye. What is being done to you is only a pale shadow of what is being planned for the repression of persons and the suppression of debate. The new propaganda chiefs will make Goebbels look like a schoolboy amateur. . . . You haven't been back in the world long enough to feel the impact of their methods —but my God, they're effective."

"Which means you agree with them?"

"Sad to say, I do. You see, my friend, on the premise that an atomic war is inevitable—and that's our military projection and your own prophecy, remember!—the only way we can control and offer any sort of protection to large masses of people is by an intense conditioning program. There's no way we can protect the people of Paris from blast and radiation or nerve gas or a lethal virus. If we announce that nasty fact, *tout court*, we'll have instant panic. So we have to keep the cities working as long as we can at all costs. If that means sweeping the streets with tanks twice a day we'll do it. If it means pre-dawn raids on dissidents or too vocal idealists we'll have them out in their nightshirts and shoot a few to admonish the rest. Then if we need some diversions—bread and circuses and orgies on the steps of the Sacré Coeur—we'll turn those on, too! . . . And there'll be no debate about any of it! We'll all be Friends of Silence then; and God help anyone who opens his mouth at the wrong moment. . . . That's the scenario, my friend. I don't like it any more than you do; but I recommended it to my President just the same."

"Then for pity's sake," Jean Marie pleaded with him, "don't you think you should look at the scenario I suggested? Surely anything would be better than the primitive brutality and bacchanalia you're prepared to offer."

"We've done our homework," Pierre Duhamel told him with wintry humour. "We're assured on the best psychiatric authority that the oscillation of tactics between violence and bacchic indulgence will have the effect of keeping the public both puzzled and amenable to authority—especially as the facts can only be evidenced by hearsay and not by reliable report in the press or on television. . . ."

"That's monstrous." Jean Marie Barette was furious.

"Of course it's monstrous." Pierre Duhamel gave an expressive shrug. "But consider your alternative. I have it with me."

He took out his wallet, extracted a carefully folded square of newspaper and smoothed it open. He went on, "This is you, as Gregory the Seventeenth, quoted in the Mendelius article. I have to presume the quote is authentic. This is what it says:

> ". . . It is clear that in the days of universal calamity the traditional structures of society will not survive. There will be a ferocious struggle for the simplest needs of life—food, water, fuel and shelter. Authority will be usurped by the strong and the cruel. Large urban societies will fragment themselves into tribal groups, each hostile to the other. Rural areas will be subject to pillage. The human person will be as much a prey as the beasts whom we now slaughter for food. Reason will be so clouded that man will resort for solace to the crudest and most violent forms of magic. It will be hard, even for those founded most strongly in the Promise of the Lord, to sustain their faith and continue to give witness, as they must do, even to the end. . . . How then must Christians comport themselves in these days of trial and terror?
>
> ". . . Since they will no longer be able to maintain themselves as large groups, they must divide themselves into small communities, each capable of sustaining itself by the exercise of a common faith and a true mutual charity. . . .

"Now, let's see what we have in that prescription. Large-scale disorder and chaos in social relations, to be balanced by what? Small communities of the elect, making seminal experiments in the exercise of charity and the other Christian virtues. Is that a fair summary?"

"As far as it goes, yes."

"But whatever government or leadership still exists at that time will have to take account of the barbarians first. How is it going to do that, except by the violent measures we envisage? After all, your elect—not to mention the elect of all other cults!—will take care of themselves; or the Almighty will! . . . Let's face it, my friend, that's why your own people cast you out. They couldn't argue with the principle. It's a beautiful thought: God's people planting their garden of graces, as the monks and nuns of old did in the Dark Ages of Europe. But, at bottom, your bishops are cold pragmatists. They know that if you want law and order, you must demonstrate how bad chaos can be. If you want morality back again, you have to have Satan in the streets, large as life, so you can shout him down in full view of the terrified populace. . . . In every country in the world it's the same story; because no country can prosecute a war without a willing and conforming public. Your own Church has adopted the siege mentality: no debate, back to the simple kitchen moralities, and let's have everyone at Mass on Sunday so that we give public witness against the ungodly! . . . The last thing they want is some wayward prophet howling doom among the grave-stones!"

"Even though they know the doom is coming?"

"*Because* they know it. Precisely because they know it! They cannot, any more than we, cope with the unbearable before it happens. That's the whole reason for the Friends of Silence and their counterparts in secular government!" Suddenly he was laughing. "My friend, don't look so shocked! What did you expect from Pierre Duhamel—a tranquilizer and a spoonful of soothing syrup? The Roman Catholics aren't the only ones who are opting for conformity. All the other big cults which have membership and property in the Republic have assured the government of their loyalty in the event of national emergency. . . . The reason they're all holding to the old models of experience and culture is because they have no time now to test new ones, or accustom their people to live with them."

Jean Marie was silent for a long moment. Finally he said quietly:

"I accept what you tell me, Pierre. Now answer me one question. What preparations have you, personally, made for the day when the first missiles are launched?"

Duhamel was not smiling now. He took time to frame his answer.

"This is a day in our scenario called R Day—*R* for Rubicon. If any one of half a dozen actions is taken by any major powers, then the chemistry of conflict will become irreversible. War will be declared. A global conflict will follow. On R Day I shall go home. I shall bathe my wife. I shall cook her favourite meal, open the best wine in my cellar and take a long time to drink it. Then I shall carry my wife to bed, lie down beside her and administer a poison pill to us both. . . . We're agreed. Our children know. They don't like the idea. They have other plans and other reasons; but they respect our decision. . . . My wife has suffered enough. I would not want her to endure the horrors of the aftermath —and to face them without her would be, for me, a pointless masochism."

He was being challenged and he knew it. It was the same challenge Carl Mendelius had made to him in the garden at Monte Cassino: "I have met good people who would prefer eternal blackness to the vision of Siva the Destroyer." Pierre Duhamel was an even more formidable inquisitor, because he had none of Mendelius' inhibitions. He was still waiting for his answer.

Jean Marie Barette said calmly, "I believe in free will, Pierre. I believe a man is judged by the light which has been given him. If you choose a stoic end to an intolerable situation, I may condemn the act; but upon the actor I can pass no verdict at all. I would rather trust you, as I trust myself, to the mercy of God. . . . However, I have one question."

"Ask it," said Pierre Duhamel.

"For you and for your wife, everything ends on Rubicon Day. But what about the helpless ones—your little clowns of God, for example? Oh, yes, I saw them in the garden this afternoon! I talked with their *gouvernante,* who told me you were one of their most important sponsors. So, in the bad times, what will you do? Leave them to die like chickens in a barn fire, or toss them out as playthings for the barbarians?"

Pierre Duhamel finished his drink and set down the glass. He fished out a handkerchief and dabbed at his lips. He said, with rueful formality:

"You are a very intelligent man, Monseigneur; but even you do not see the whole future. My little clowns are already provided for. Under a series of most secret political directives, persons who, by reason of insanity, incurable infirmity or other gross disability, will be a burden on the wartime state will, immediately on the outbreak of hostilities, be discreetly eliminated! Hitler gave us the blueprints for that one. We have updated them to include a compassionate rather than a brutal disposal. . . . I shock you, of course?"

"What shocks me is that you can continue to live with this secret."

"What do I do? If I try to publicize it, I am branded a madman—like you with your vision of Armageddon and the Second Coming. You see, we are both in the same sad galley."

"Then let us see how we get out of it, my friend."

"First," said Duhamel, "let's look at your problem. You are, as I said, officially untouchable. You will find it increasingly difficult to circulate. Certain countries will hesitate to give you a visa. You will be harassed at every point. Your bags will be rifled. You will have lengthy sessions with frontier officials. . . . You will be surprised at how uncomfortable life can be. So, all in all, I think we have to get you a new passport in a new name."

"Can you do that?"

"I do it all the time for people on special assignment. You are not on assignment but you are most certainly a special case. Do you have any recent photographs of yourself?"

"I have a dozen copies of the one in my present passport. I was told some countries require them for visa applications."

"Give me three of them. I'll have your passport delivered here tomorrow."

"You're a good friend, Pierre. Thank you."

"Please!" Pierre Duhamel gave him a sudden boyish grin. "My master, the President, wants you out of the country. I am instructed to do everything possible to set you on your way."

"Why should he care so much?"

"He understands theatre," said Pierre Duhamel drily. "One man walking on the water is a miracle. Two is quite ridiculous."

The image amused them both. They laughed and the tension was broken. Pierre Duhamel dropped his pose of defensive irony and began to talk more freely.

". . . When you see the battle plans laid out, it is like a vision of the inferno. No horror is absent. There are neutron bombs, poison gas, spray-borne deadly diseases. In theory of course it is all based on limited action; so that the greatest horrors are held as deterrents in reserve. But, in fact, once the first shots are fired, there will be no limit to the escalation. . . . Once you've done one murder, the rest are easy, because you have only one life in jeopardy to the hangman."

"Enough!" Jean Marie Barette stopped the conversation abruptly. "You have talked yourself and your wife into a suicide pact with a surfeit of horrors! I refuse to surrender this whole planet to evil. If we can hold one corner of it for hoping and loving then we'll do it. . . . Pierre, you hate what is being plotted. You hate your impotence in the face of the vast unreason. . . . Why not make one last act of faith and step up to the firing line with me?"

"To do what?" asked Pierre Duhamel.

"Let's shock the world into listening to us. Let's tell them first about God's little clowns and what will happen to them on Rubicon Day. You get hold of the document. I'll get Georg Rainer to arrange the press conference—and we'll face it together."

"And then?"

"Dear God! We'll rouse the conscience of the world! People always rise up against the evil done to children."

"Do they? We're nearly at the end of the century and there's still child labour in Europe, not to mention the rest of the world. There's still no effective legislation against child abuse; and women are still fighting each other and their legislators over the killing of the near-term fetus. . . . No, my dear Jean! Trust in God if you must, but never, never in man. If I did what you suggest, the press would black us out and the police would have us in the deepest *cachot* in the country inside half-an-hour. . . . I'm sorry. I am a servant of what is. When what is becomes unbearable, I make my exit. *La comédie est finie.* Give me those photographs. You'll have a new passport and a new identity tomorrow."

Jean Marie took the photographs out of his wallet and handed them over. As he did so he grasped Duhamel's hand and held it firmly.

"I won't let you go like this! You're doing a terrible thing. You're closing your ears and your heart to a clear call. It may be the last one you get."

Duhamel disengaged himself from the grip.

"You have it wrong, Monseigneur." There was a remote wraith-like sadness in his voice. "I answered my call a long time ago. When my wife fell ill and the doctor gave me the prognosis, I walked to Notre Dame and sat all alone in front of the sanctuary. I didn't pray. I gave the Almighty an ultimatum. I said: '*Eh bien!* Because she's got to wear it, I'll wear it, too. I'll make her as happy as I can for as long as she's alive. But understand, enough is enough! If you push us anymore, I'll hand back the keys to the house of life and we'll both walk out . . .' Well, He's done it, hasn't He? Even to you He didn't say, 'Tell them to reform the world or else!' You got the same message as I get every day in the presidential dispatches. Judgment Day is round the corner. There's no hope! There's no way out! So, for me, all bets are off. I'm sorry for my little clowns; but I didn't beget them and I wasn't around on creation day. I didn't mix the whole bloody explosive mess of the universe. . . . Do you understand, Monseigneur?"

"Everything," said Jean Marie Barette, "except one item. Why are you taking all this trouble over me?"

"God knows! Probably because I admire the courage of a man who can take life and all the filth of it without any conditions at all. My little clowns are like that; but only because they haven't the brains to know better. At least they'll die happy." He scribbled a number on the pad beside the phone. "That's my home telephone. If you need me, call. If I'm not available ask for Charlot. He's my majordomo and very good at improvising tactical operations. However, you should be safe here for a day or two. After that, please be very careful. People don't see them; but the dagger-men are already in the streets!"

When Duhamel had gone he fell prey to a winter fear: the prickling dread of the lone traveller who hears the wolf howls from the timberline. He could not bear the solitude of his room; so he went down to the restaurant, where the *patronne* found him a table in a quiet angle, from which he could survey the rest of the company. He ordered a piece of melon, a small entrecote, a half-bottle of the house wine, then settled down to enjoy the meal.

At least there was no menace here. The lighting was restful; there were fresh flowers on every table. The napery was spotless, the service discreet. The clients, at first glance, were affluent businessmen and bureaucrats with their assorted womenfolk. Even as he made the judgment, he caught sight of himself in a wall mirror, and realized that he, who had once worn the red of a Cardinal and the white of a Pope, was now just one more grey-haired fellow in the uniform of the bourgeoisie.

The very ordinariness of his own image reminded him of one of Carl Mendelius' earliest lectures at the Gregorian. He was explaining the nature of the Gospel parables. Many of them, he said, were records of Jesus' table talk. Their metaphors of masters and servants and meals were prompted by immediate and commonplace surroundings. Then he added a rider to the proposition: ". . . However, the familiar stories are like a minefield, full of traps and trip wires. They all contain contradictions, alienating elements, which bring the listener up short and make him see a new potential, for good or evil, in the most banal event."

In his own encounter with Pierre Duhamel, he had been quite unprepared for the finality of the man's despair. It was the more terrible because it was quite passionless. It could compass, without a tremor, the most monstrous perversities; but it would not find room for the smallest hope or the simplest joy. It was so rational a madness that one could neither cure it nor argue against it. And yet, and yet . . . there was more than one trip wire in the minefield! Pierre Duhamel might despair of himself; but Jean Marie Barette must never despair of him. He must still believe that so long as life lasted, Pierre Duhamel was still within the reach of Everlasting Mercy. Jean Marie must still make prayer for his soul, must still reach out warm hands to unfreeze his stubborn heart.

The steak was tender and the wine was smooth; but even as he savoured them, Jean Marie was preoccupied by the challenge that now presented itself. His credibility was at stake—not as a visionary, but as a simple bearer of God's good news to man. He had accused Duhamel of rejecting the good news; but was it not rather Jean Marie Barette—once a Pope and servant of the servants of God—who had failed to present it with faith and love enough? Once again, he was urged imperatively to open himself to a new inpouring of strength and authority. His reverie was interrupted by the *patronne*, who paused at his table to ask how he was enjoying the food. He complimented her with a smile.

"I've been fed like a king, madame."

"In Gascony we would say 'fed like the Pope's mule.' "

There was a gleam of mischief in her eyes, but Jean Marie was in no mood to embroider the joke. He asked, "Can you tell me, is it far from here to Monsieur Duhamel's house?"

"About ten minutes by car. If you want to go there in the morning I can have one of the staff drive you. But you should telephone first. The place is guarded like a fortress by security men and dogs."

"I am sure Monsieur Duhamel will receive me. I should like to go there immediately after dinner."

"In that case, let me call a taxi. The driver can wait and bring you back."

"Thank you, madame."

"Please! It is my pleasure." She made a show of brushing a few crumbs from the cloth and said softly, "Of course, I would much rather be feeding the Pope than his mule."

"I'm sure he'll be happy to visit you, madame—once I can assure him of your absolute discretion."

"As to that," said Madame sweetly, "all our clients trust us. We learned very quickly from Monsieur Duhamel that silence is golden! . . . For dessert may I recommend the raspberries. They come from our own garden. . . ."

He finished the meal without haste. It was almost as if he were an athlete, running with a pace-maker who would, at a given moment, hand the race over to him. His conscious attention began to shift from Duhamel to his invalid wife. It was as if she were stretching out her hand to reach him. He finished his coffee, walked to the booth and telephoned Duhamel's private number. A male voice answered.

"Who is speaking, please?"

"This is Monsieur Grégoire. I should like to speak to Monsieur Duhamel."

"I'm afraid that is not possible."

"Then will you please tell him I shall be at his house in fifteen minutes."

"That will not be convenient. Madame is very ill. The doctor is with her now; and Monsieur Duhamel is in conference with an overseas visitor."

"What is your name, please?"

"Charlot."

"Charlot, two hours ago Monsieur Duhamel named you to me as a man of confidence to whom I should turn in an emergency. This is an emergency, so will you please do exactly as I ask and let Monsieur Duhamel decide whether my visit is opportune or not? I shall be with you in fifteen minutes."

The taxi arrived in the middle of a thunderstorm. The driver was a laconic fellow who announced his contract terms for this sort of job, and once they were accepted, lapsed into silence. Jean Marie Barette closed his eyes and disposed himself to what would be demanded of him in the coming encounters.

The house of Pierre Duhamel was a large country mansion in the style of the Second Empire, set in a small park, behind a tall fence of iron spikes. The front gate was closed and a police car with two men in it was parked outside. Immediate dilemma! On the telephone he had identified himself as Monsieur Grégoire. If the police demanded his papers he would be revealed as Jean Marie Barette, a most compromising visitor. He decided to bluff it out. He rolled down the window and spoke to the nearer police officer.

"I am Monsieur Grégoire. I have an appointment with Monsieur Duhamel."

"Wait a moment!" The policeman picked up a pocket radio and called the house. "A certain Grégoire. He says he has an appointment."

Jean Marie could not make out the answer but apparently it satisfied the policeman, who nodded and said:

"You're expected. Identification, please!"

"I was instructed not to carry it on this occasion. You may check that with Monsieur Duhamel."

The policeman called again. This time there was a longish interval before clearance was given. Then, the gates opened electrically, the policeman waved him through and the gates closed again. The taxi had hardly reached the portal when the front door was opened by Pierre Duhamel himself. He was shaking with anger.

"For God's sake, man! What is this? Paulette has collapsed. There's a man from Moscow in my drawing room. What the hell do you want?"

"Where is your wife?"

"Upstairs. The doctor's with her."

"Take me to her!"

Pierre Duhamel stared at him as if he were a stranger, then he made a small shrugging gesture of surrender. "Very well! Follow me, please."

He led the way upstairs and pushed open the door of the bedroom. Paulette Duhamel, a pale, shrunken figure, was lying propped about with pillows in the big four-poster bed. The doctor stood holding her limp wrist in his hand counting the pulse-beats.

Duhamel asked, "Any change?"

The doctor shook his head. "The paraplegia has extended itself. The reflexes are weaker. There is fluid in both lungs, because the muscles of the respiratory system are beginning to fail. We may do a little for her in hospital but not much. . . . Who is this gentleman?"

"An old friend. A priest."

"Ah!" The doctor was obviously surprised but tactful. "Then I shall leave you with her for a while. She drifts in and out of consciousness. If there is any marked change, please call me instantly. I shall be just outside."

He went out.

Pierre Duhamel said with cold anger, "I want no rites, no mumbo jumbo. If she could speak she would refuse them, too."

"There will be no rites," said Jean Marie Barette gently. "I will sit and hold her hand. You can wait if you wish—unless your visitor is impatient."

"He'll be patient," said Pierre Duhamel harshly. "He needs me. He's got famine on his hands this winter."

Jean Marie said nothing. He drew a chair to the bedside, sat down, picked up the woman's slack wasted hand and held it between his own. Pierre Duhamel, standing at the foot of the bed, saw a curious transformation. Jean Marie's body became quite rigid; the muscles of his face tightened, so that, in the half-light of the sickroom, his features looked as though they had been carved from wood. Something else was happening, too, which he could not put into words. It was as if all the life inside the man were draining away from the peripheries of his body into some secret well at the center of himself. All the while Paulette lay there, a sad, shrunken wax doll, her eyes closed, her breathing shallow and full of rales, so that Duhamel wished with all his heart it would stop and she— that special and essential she whom he had loved for a lifetime—might be released like a songbird from its cage.

The wish was so poignant it seemed to put a stop on time. Whether he stood for seconds or minutes or hours Duhamel did not know. He looked again at

Barette. He was changing again—the muscles softening, the taut features relaxing into a momentary smile. Then he opened his eyes and turned to the woman on the bed. He said quite casually:

"You can open your eyes now, madame."

Paulette Duhamel opened her eyes and instantly focused them on her husband at the foot of the bed. She spoke plainly, in a weak but unwavering voice.

"Hullo, *chéri*. I seem to have been foolish again."

She raised her arms to embrace him and the first thing Duhamel noticed was that the constant tremors which characterized the late stage of the disease had ceased. He bent to kiss her. When he disengaged himself, Jean Marie Barette was standing at the open door, chatting quietly with the doctor. The doctor moved to the bed, took Paulette's pulse count and auscultated her chest once more. When he straightened up, he was smiling uncertainly.

"Well, well! I think we may all relax a little, especially you, madame. This nastiness seems to be over for the moment. However, you must stay very quiet. In the morning we can think about clearing up that respiratory problem. But for now—*grâce à Dieu!*—we are out of crisis." As he walked down the hall with Pierre Duhamel and Jean Marie he became more expansive and voluble. "With this disease one never knows. Sudden collapses are not too common, but they can happen, as you saw tonight. Then, with equal suddenness, there is remission. The patient returns to a euphoric state and the degeneration slows down. . . . I have noticed often that a religious intervention, like yours tonight, Father, or the administration of the last rites, may produce in the patient a great calm, which is in itself a therapy. . . . You will remember that on the ancient island of Cos ⁻ . . ."

Duhamel steered him diplomatically to the exit and then came back to Jean Marie. He was like a sleepwalker waking in a strange countryside. He was also most oddly humble.

"I don't know what you did or how you did it, but I think I owe you a life."

"You owe nothing to me." Jean Marie spoke with a spartan authority. "You are in debt to God; but since you are in contest with him, why not make the payment to your little clowns?"

"What made you come tonight?"

"Sometimes, like all the mad, I hear voices."

"Don't mock me, Monseigneur! I'm tired; and my night isn't half over."

"I'll be going now."

"Wait! I'd like you to meet my visitor."

"Are you sure he wants to meet me?"

"Let's ask him," said Pierre Duhamel—and walked him into the library to meet Sergei Andrevich Petrov, Minister for Agricultural Production in the U.S.S.R.

He was a short man, bulky as a barrel, part Georgian, part Circassian, who was born into the subsistence economy of the Caucasus, yet understood as if by animal instinct the problem of feeding a continent that stretched from Europe to China. He greeted Jean Marie with a bone-crushing handshake and a rough joke.

"So your Holiness is out of a job. What are you doing now? Playing grey eminence to our friend Duhamel?"

His smile took the sting out of the remark but Duhamel rounded on him sharply.

"You're out of order, Sergei."

"A bad joke! I'm sorry. But I have to have answers for Moscow. Do we eat this winter, or are we on short rations? Our discussion was interrupted; so I am sharp-tempered."

"It's my fault," said Jean Marie. "I came uninvited."

"And made me a private miracle," said Pierre Duhamel. "My wife is past the crisis."

"Perhaps he will make one for me. God knows I need it." Petrov swung round to face Jean Marie Barette. "For Russia, two bad seasons make a catastrophe. When there's no feed grain we have to slaughter the livestock. With no reserves of bread grains we have to ration civilians to feed the armed forces. Now the Americans and Canadians are cutting off supplies. Grain is classified as war material. The Australians are selling all their surplus to China. So, I'm running round the world offering gold bullion for wheat. . . . And, would you believe it, I can hardly find a bushel?"

"And if we sell it to him," Duhamel added the sour afterthought, "we are perfidious France breaching the solidarity of Western Europe, and exposing ourselves to economic sanction by the Americans."

"If I don't get it somewhere, the Army has the final excuse it needs to precipitate a war." He gave a humourless chuckle and flung out his hands in a gesture of despair. "So, there's a challenge to a miracle worker!"

"There was a time," said Jean Marie, "when my good offices might have meant something among the nations. Not anymore. If I attempted now to intervene in affairs of state, I should be written off as a crank."

"I'm not so sure," said Sergei Petrov. "The whole world's a madhouse these days. You're original enough to provide some diversion. . . . Why don't you call me tomorrow at the embassy? I'd like to talk with you before I go back to Moscow."

"Better still," said Pierre Duhamel, "why don't you call him at the Hostellerie des Chevaliers? I wouldn't trust a laundry list to your embassy switchboard—and I'm trying to protect our friend as far as I can. . . . Now, if you'll excuse us, Jean. We've got a long night ahead."

He pulled the bell rope by the fireplace and an instant later Charlot was at the door, ready to conduct the guest to his taxi. Jean Marie shook hands with the two men.

Petrov said with a grin, "If you can multiply loaves I'll give you my job tomorrow!"

"My dear Comrade Petrov," said Jean Marie Barette. "You can hardly write God out of the Communist manifesto and then expect him to show up every harvest time!"

"You asked for that, Sergei!" Pierre Duhamel laughed and said to Jean Marie, "I'll pass by tomorrow with the documents. . . . Perhaps by then I'll have found words to thank you."

"I have a meeting at my brother's bank in the morning. I expect to be back by early evening. Good night, gentlemen."

The impassive Charlot conducted him to the door. The taxi driver was drowsing in his cab. The police car was still parked at the gate. Far away in the garden he heard the baying of hounds, as the security men checking the perimeter flushed a fox out of the shrubbery.

By the time he had finished his prayers and his preparations for bed it was one in the morning. He was desperately tired; but he lay a long time, wakeful, trying to understand the strange otherworldly logic of the evening's events. Twice now—once with Carl Mendelius and again with Paulette Duhamel—he had experienced the inpouring, the offering of himself as a conduit, through which a gift of comfort was made available to others.

It was a sensation quite different from that associated with the rapture and the disclosures of the vision. Then he had been literally snatched out of himself, subjected to an illumination, endowed with a knowledge which he had in nowise solicited or desired. The effect was instant and permanent. He was marked and burdened by it forever.

The inpouring was a transient phenomenon. It began with an impulse of pity or love, or a simple understanding of another's profound need. There was an empathy—more, a mode of identity—between himself and the needy. It was himself who urged mercy upon the Unseen Father, through the merit of the incarnate Son, and he offered the same self as the vessel through which the gifts of the Spirit might be passed. There was no sense of miracle, of magic or thaumaturgy. It was an act of love, instinctive and unreasoned, through which a gift was passed or renewed.

But though the act was a free dedication of himself, the impulse that prompted it came from elsewhere. He could not say why he had offered himself as a mediator for Paulette Duhamel and not for Sergei Petrov, upon whom depended matters of vast consequence: famine and the pestilence of war. Petrov made jokes about miracles—but he wanted one desperately. Offer him half a loaf on the winter ration and he would happily sing the doxology with the Patriarch in Moscow.

So why the difference? Why the prompting towards the frail one, the facile refusal of the other? It was not an act of judgment, it was an unreasoned response—the reed bowing to the wind, the migrant goose responding to the strange primal prompting that bade him begone before the winter.

Once, a long time ago, while he was still a junior in the Sacred College, he had strolled with Carl Mendelius in a villa garden overlooking Lake Nemi. It was one of those magical days, the air vibrant with the hum of cicadas, the grapes full on the vine, the sky washed clean of clouds, the pines marching like pikemen across the ridges. Mendelius had startled him with a strange proposition:

". . . All idolatry springs from a desire for order. We want to be neat, like the animals. We mark out our territories with musk and feces. We make hierarchies like the bees and ethics like the ants. And we choose gods to set the stamp of approval on our creations. . . . What we cannot cope with is the untidiness of the universe, the lunatic aspect of a cosmos with no known beginning, no visible end and no apparent meaning to all its bustling dynamics. . . . We cannot tolerate its monstrous indifference in the face of all our fears and agonies. . . . The prophets offer us hope; but only the man-god can make the paradox tolerable. This is why the coming of Jesus is a healing and a saving event. He is not what we should have created for ourselves. He is truly the sign of peace because He is the sign of contradiction. His career is a brief tragic failure. He dies in dishonour; but then most strangely, He lives. He is not only yesterday. He is today and tomorrow. He is as available to the humblest as to the highest. . . .

"But look what we humans have done with Him. We have bloated His simple talk into a babble of philosophies. We have inflated the family of His believers into an imperial bureaucracy, justified only because it exists and cannot be dismantled without a cataclysm. The man who claims to be the custodian of His truth lives in a vast palace, surrounded by celibate males—like you and me, Jean!—who have never earned a crust by the labour of their hands, never dried a woman's tears or sat with a sick child until sunrise. . . .

"If ever they make you Pope, Jean, keep one small part of yourself for a private loving. If you don't, they'll turn you into a Pharaoh, mummified and embalmed before you're dead. . . ."

The summer landscape of the Alban hills merged into the contours of the dream country. The sound of Mendelius' voice faded behind the piping of the nightingales in the garden of the Hostellerie. Jean Marie Barette, dispenser of mysteries beyond his own frail grasp, lapsed into sleep.

X

HE woke refreshed and immediately regretted his involvement with the moneymen. He reached for the telephone to call Alain at the bank and cancel the meeting of trustees; then he thought better of it. New in the world, already in quarantine as a plague-carrier, he could not afford to lose any line of communication.

In this last decade of the century, bankers were better equipped than any other group to chart the progress of mankind's mortal disease. At every day's end their computers told the story and no amount of rhetoric could change the grim passionless text: gold up, the dollar down, rare metals booming, futures in oil and grain and soybeans climbing through the roof, equities on the seesaw, confidence eroding every week towards the panic point.

Jean Marie Barette remembered his long sessions with the financiers of the Vatican, and how bleak a picture emerged from all their cabalistic calculations. They bought gold, but sold mining shares, because, they said, that was market advice. The real story was that the black guerrillas in South Africa were strong, well trained and well armed. If they could blow up an oil refinery they could certainly explode the deep tunnels of the mines. So you bought the metal and got rid of the threatened asset. One of the most potent arguments against the publication of his encyclical had been that it would put the markets of the world in a panic and expose the Vatican itself to enormous financial loss.

Jean Marie had come out of every meeting wrestling with his conscience, because his clerical experts, like all others of their ilk, were forced to speculate, without distinction, upon the moralities and immoralities of mankind. It was one domain of the Church's life where he approved of secrecy—if only because there was no way he could justify or even explain the faint bloodstains on every balance sheet, whether they came from exploited labour, a rough bargain in the market, or a reformed villain buying a first-class ride to heaven.

The trust which his father had set up to preserve the fortune he had accumulated for his family was a substantial one. Jean Marie's share of the funds was administered in a special fashion. The capital remained untouched, the increment was at his disposal. As a parish priest and later as a bishop he had dedicated it to works connected with the welfare of his flock. As Pope he had used it for charities and gifts to people in personal crisis. He still believed that while social reform could only be accomplished by effective organizations soundly financed, there was still no substitute for the act of compassion, the secret affirmation of brotherhood in affliction. Now, he himself had to make claim for sustenance. He was sixty-five years old, statistically unemployed— and in need of a minimal liberty to spread the word that had been given to him.

There were four trustees, with whom he must deal. Each was a senior official of a major bank. Alain introduced them with appropriate ceremony; Sansom from Barclays, Winter from the Chase, Lambert from the Crédit Lyonnais, Mme. Saracini from the Banco Ambrogiano all' Estero.

They were all respectful, all a trifle wary. Money lived in strange houses; power was controlled by unlikely hands. Besides, they were being called to account for their stewardship—and they wondered how well this onetime Pope could read a balance sheet and a profit-and-loss account.

Mme. Saracini was their spokesman: a tall, olive-skinned woman in her late thirties, dressed in a suit of blue linen, with lace at her throat and wrists. Her only jewellery was a wedding band, and a gold jabot brooch set with aquamarine. She spoke French with a faintly Italianate lilt. She also had a sense of humour and was obviously prepared to exercise it. She asked innocently:

"Forgive me, but how do you like to be addressed? It can't be Holiness. Should it be Eminence or Monseigneur? It cannot possibly be Père Jean."

Jean Marie laughed. "I doubt there's any protocol. Celestine the Fifth was forced to abdicate and after his death they canonized him. I'm not dead yet so that doesn't apply. I'm certainly less than an Eminence. I've always thought Monseigneur was an unnecessary relic of monarchy. So, since I'm living as a private person, without a canonical mission, why not just Monsieur?"

"I don't agree, Jean." Alain was upset by the suggestion. "After all . . ."

"After all, dear brother, I have to live in my skin and I do like to feel comfortable. . . . Now, madame, you were going to explain the mysteries of money."

"I'm sure," said Mme. Saracini with a smile, "you understand there are no mysteries at all—only the problems of maintaining a firm capital base and an income that keeps ahead of inflation. . . . This means that there is need of an active and vigilant administration. Fortunately you have had that, since your brother is a very good banker. . . . The capital, valued at the end of the last financial year, is some eight million Swiss francs. This capital, as you will see, is divided in a fairly stable ratio: thirty percent real estate, both urban and rural, twenty percent equities, twenty percent prime bonds, ten percent in art works and antiques and the remaining twenty percent liquid in gold and short-term money. . . . It's a reasonable spread. It can be varied at fairly short notice. If you have any comments, of course . . ."

"I have a question," said Jean Marie mildly. "We are threatened with war. How do we protect our possessions?"

"So far as commercial paper is concerned," said the man from the Chase, "we all have the most modern storage and retrieval systems, triplicated and sometimes quadruplicated in strategically protected areas. We've hammered out a common code of interbank practice that enables us to protect our clients against document loss. Gold, of course, is a strong-room operation. Rural land is perennial. Urban developments will be reduced to rubble, but, again, war-risk insurance favours the big operators. Art works and antiques, like gold, are a storage job. It might interest you to know that for years now we've been buying up disused mine workings and converting them for safe deposits. . . ."

"I am comforted," said Jean Marie Barette with dry irony. "I wonder why it has not been possible to invest similar money and similar ingenuity for the protection of citizens against fallout and poison gas. I wonder why we are so much concerned with the retrieval of commercial paper and so little with the proposed mass murder of the infirm and the incompetent."

There was a moment's stunned silence and then, with cold anger, Alain Hubert answered his brother.

"I will tell you why, brother Jean! It is because we, unlike many others, keep the bargain we have made with our clients—of whom you are one. Others may do ill—monstrously ill!—but you cannot blame us because we do well! I think you owe me and my colleagues an apology!"

"You're right, Alain." Jean Marie responded gravely to the reproof. "I beg your pardon—yours, too, madame, gentlemen! . . . But I hope you will permit me to make an explanation. I was shocked yesterday, shocked to the marrow!, to learn that, in this my homeland, there are plans for the elimination of the handicapped, immediately war breaks out. . . . Do any of you know of this matter?"

The man from the Crédit Lyonnais pursed his lips as though someone had put alum on his tongue.

"One hears all sorts of rumours. Some of them are based on fact; but the facts are not fully understood. If you calculate to kill a million people with a single atomic blast, and contaminate a huge peripheral area, then you have to count on some form of mercy killing for survivors beyond hope. . . . In the general chaos, who's going to draw the lines? You have to leave it to the officer in charge of the area, whoever he turns out to be."

The man from Barclays was a mite more subtle and urbane.

"Surely, my dear sir, the scenario for chaos which you set down in your own writings is almost the same as that prepared by our secular governments. The difference is that they are called upon to provide practical remedies and they do not have the luxury of moralizing about them. Even you cannot moralize about triage in a front-line hospital. The surgeon, walking down the line of wounded, is the sole arbiter of life and death. 'Operate on this one, he will survive! This one is second on the list, he may survive. Give that one a cigarette and a shot of morphine, he will die!' . . . Now, unless you are under the enormous stress of that adjudication, I submit, sir, that you have no standing in the immediate case. . . ."

Before Jean Marie had time to rebut the argument, Mme. Saracini came to his rescue. She said with bland humour:

"You see, my dear Monsieur Barette, you have, until this moment, lived a very sheltered life. You must understand that God gave up making land millions of years ago. So, if you've got a piece of real estate you hang on to it. The oil's running out with the rest of the fossil fuels. So, you have to fight to get your share. Rembrandt's dead and so is Gauguin. So, there aren't any more of their pictures. But human beings—pouf! There are too many of us already. We're due for a little genocide; and if the overkill is exaggerated then we can soon start breeding again—with some help from the sperm banks, which are housed in our vaults."

She made such a black comedy of it that they had to laugh; then, when the tension had relaxed, she pushed straight ahead into the trustees' report, which showed that Jean Marie Barette could live like a prince on his income. He thanked them for the courtesy, apologized for his lapse of manners and told them that he would draw on them only for his personal needs and let the trust pile up until Judgment Day.

The men of Barclays and the Crédit Lyonnais and the Chase took their leave. Mme. Saracini stayed behind. Alain had invited her to make a foursome at lunch with Odette, Jean Marie and himself. While they were waiting for Odette, Alain served sherry and then left them, while he took a telephone call from London. Mme. Saracini raised her glass in a silent toast and then delivered a cool reproof.

"You really were quite unpleasant to us. Why?"

"I don't know. Suddenly I was seeing two images on a split screen: all those whirring computers in their underground caverns—and, above, the bodies of children burned in front of an ice-cream parlour."

"My colleagues won't forgive you. You have made them feel guilty."

"Will you?"

"I happen to agree with you," said Mme. Saracini, "but I can't make frontal attacks. I'm the girl who makes them laugh first and see sense afterwards— when their manhood isn't threatened."

"Is my information right or wrong?"

"About euthanasia for the incompetents? It's right, of course; but you'll never prove it; because, in a strange subconscious fashion, all Europe is consenting to the conspiracy. We want an exit for ourselves and our loved ones when things get too horrible to bear."

"Do you have any children, madame?"

"No."

"And your husband?"

"He died a year after our marriage."

"Forgive me! I didn't mean to pry."

"Don't distress yourself. I'm glad you were interested enough to ask. As a matter of fact, I believe you know my father."

"Do I?"

"He is called Vittorio Malavolti. He's serving twenty years in prison for bank fraud. As I remember, he handled a great many transactions for the Vatican— cost you a lot of money, too! . . ."

"I remember. I hope you have been able to forget."

"Please! Don't be facile with me! I don't want to forget. I love my father. He is a financial genius, and he was manipulated by a lot of men whom he still protects. I worked with him. He taught me all I know about banking. He set me up clean with clean money. I bought the Banco Ambrogiano all' Estero when it was a hole-in-the-wall in Chiasso. I cleaned it up and built it up and made some strong alliances and every year I pay five percent of my father's personal debts, so that when he comes out—if he comes out!—he'll be able to walk down the street like a man. . . . And that reminds me. Don't you dare patronize your brother! He helped me get started. He pushed me into situations like this trusteeship. If he sometimes looks like a fool, it's because he married the wrong woman. But Pope or no Pope, he put you down this morning when you deserved it! That makes for respect!"

He was startled by her vehemence. Her hand was unsteady and a little runnel of liquor slopped over the side of her glass. He gave her the handkerchief from his top pocket to mop it up. He asked mildly, "Why are you so angry with me?"

"Because you don't know how important you are—especially now that you're out of office. Those articles in the newspapers made people love you. Even those who didn't agree respected you and paid attention. Sansom, the Barclays man, quoted your writings back at you this morning—and, believe me, he hardly reads anything but the financial pages! . . . So, when you do something unpleasant, you disappoint a lot of people."

"I'll try to remember it," said Jean Marie, and added with a grin, "It's a long time since I've had my knuckles rapped."

She blushed like a schoolgirl and made an awkward apology. "I've got a sharp tongue, too—and a sort of proprietory interest."

"Have you indeed?"

"Way back in the fourteenth century both my husband's family and mine were friends and correspondents of the Benincasa and of Saint Catherine herself. They supported her in her efforts to get your namesake Gregory the Eleventh back from Avignon. . . . It's a long time ago, but we Sienese are jealous of our history—and sometimes a little mystical about it." She put down the glass, fished in her handbag and brought out a notebook. "Give me your address and telephone number. I want to talk to you again."

"About anything in particular?"

"Would my immortal soul be important enough?"

"Most certainly." He acknowledged defeat with a smile and gave her the information.

And that, for the moment, was the end of their talk. Alain came in with Odette, elegant, expensive, dropping names like summer raindrops. Alain gave Jean Marie a conspiratorial wink and then left him to carry the burden of Odette's monologue until they arrived at the restaurant. Luncheon was an uneasy meal. Odette dominated the talk, while Alain remonstrated feebly against her more obvious snobberies. Mme. Saracini left before the coffee. Odette sniffed and pronounced a disdainful valediction:

"Extraordinary woman! Quite attractive—in an Italian sort of way. One wonders what domestic arrangements she's made since her husband died."

"It's none of your business," said Alain. "Let's be family for a while. What are your plans from this point, Jean? If you propose to stay in France you'll need some kind of permanent establishment: an apartment, a housekeeper . . ."

"It's too early for that. I'm still too public a figure—and obviously embarrassing to old friends. It's best I keep moving for a while."

"You should also keep silent for a while," said Alain moodily. "You are used to making big pronouncements from the top of the ladder; but, you can't do that anymore. What you said at our meeting will be all over town by evening. That's why I attacked you. I can't afford to be associated with subversive talk. . . . It's much more dangerous than you realize."

Odette chimed in, positive and omniscient as always.

"Alain's right! I was talking to the Defense Minister the other night. He's a very attractive man; though his wife is quite impossible. He said that what we needed now was not controversy but sound, businesslike diplomacy and quiet negotiation while the armed forces prepare themselves."

"Let's all understand something," said Jean Marie Barette firmly. "I became a priest to preach the word, to tell the good news of salvation. That's not something I can be prudent about, or safe, or even kind! And I have to give you the same message as I preach to the rest of the world. The battle between good and evil is already joined; but the good man looks like a fool, while evil wears a wise man's face and justifies murder by impeccable statistics!"

"Our Cardinal doesn't say that." Odette was ready, as always, for an argument. "Last Sunday he gave the television sermon on the coin of the tribute. He said it's a matter of priorities. We obey the law as a means of serving God— and even if we make mistakes in good faith, God understands."

"I'm sure he does, my dear," said Jean Marie. "And I'm sure the Cardinal has his own reasons for being so bland—but it isn't enough! It isn't half enough!"

"We should go," said Alain diplomatically. "I have a two-thirty appointment with the Finance Minister. He's seeking our advice on the best way of launching a defense bond issue!"

He had promised himself an afternoon of simple and private pleasures—an hour of book hunting along the quais, a stroll among the artists in the Place du Tertre. He had been away so long, and this was home. Even if the family were difficult he should be able to take his ease in his own natal place.

The book hunt was rewarding. He found a first edition of Verlaine's *Fêtes galantes* with an autographed quatrain pasted inside the cover. Verlaine had always haunted him: the sad, lost drunk who wrote angel songs and lived in hell with Rimbaud, and who, if there were any justice in the universe, must be singing canticles of joy at the footstool of the Almighty.

The Place du Tertre was at first a disappointment. The painters had to eat and the tourists had to take home a piece of Paris and the canvases were cynically vulgar. But, in the least-favoured corner of the Place, he came upon a curiosity: a twisted, dwarfish girl, hardly more than twenty, dressed in a sweatshirt and jeans, etching on a glass plate with a diamond point. On the table beside her were specimens of her work: a goblet, a mirror, a punch bowl. Jean Marie picked up the goblet to examine it. The girl cautioned him roughly:

"If you drop it you pay for it!"

"I'll be very careful. It's beautiful. What does the design represent?"

She hesitated for a moment, as if afraid of mockery, then explained, "I call it a cosmos cup. The goblet's a circle, the sign of perfection. The lower part is the sea, waves and fishes. The upper is the land, wheat and vines. It's a representation of the cosmos. . . ."

"And where are the humans in the cosmos?"

"They drink from the cup."

The conceit pleased him. He wondered how far she would embellish it. He asked again, "Does God figure in the design?"

She gave him a swift, suspicious look. "Is it important?"

"It's interesting, at least."

"Are you a Christian?"

Jean Marie chuckled. "I am, even if I don't look like one."

"Then you'll know that the fish and the vine and the wheat are symbols of Christ and the Eucharist."

"How much is the piece?"

"Six hundred francs." Then she added defensively, "There's a lot of work in it."

"I can see that. I'll take it. Can you pack it safely for me?"

"Yes. It won't be elegant, but it will be safe."

She set down the work she was doing and began packing the goblet in a stained cardboard box filled with plastic pellets. Watching her, Jean Marie noticed how thin she was, and how, with the small effort, the sweat broke out on her forehead, and her hands fumbled unsteadily with the fragile piece. As he counted out the money he said:

"I'm a sentimental collector. I always like to celebrate with the artist. Will you join me for a drink and a sandwich?"

Again she gave him that wary sidelong look and said curtly, "Thanks, but you paid a good price. You don't have to do me favours."

"I was asking you to do me one," said Jean Marie Barette. "I've had a rough morning and a nervous lunch. I'd be glad of someone to talk to. Besides, it's only three steps from here to the café."

"Oh, very well."

She shoved the parcel into his hands, called to a nearby painter to watch her table, then walked with Jean Marie to the café at the corner of the Place. She had a curious, hoppity gait which slewed her almost in a half-circle with every pace. The spinal curvature was grossly pronounced, and her head, elfishly beautiful, was comically mismatched, as if set askew by a drunken sculptor.

She ordered coffee and a Cognac and a ham roll and a hard-boiled egg. She ate ravenously, while Jean Marie toyed with a glass of Vichy water and tried to keep the conversation alive.

"I had another piece of luck this afternoon: a first edition of Verlaine's *Fêtes galantes*."

"You collect books, too?"

"I love beautiful things; but these are gifts for other people. Your goblet will go to a lady near Versailles who has multiple sclerosis. I'll write and explain the symbolism to her. . . ."

"I can save you the trouble. I typed up a little piece about it. I'll give it to you before you go. . . . Strange you should ask me where God came in."

"Why strange?"

"Most people find the subject embarrassing."

"And you?"

"I gave up being embarrassed a long time ago. I accept that I'm a freak. It's easier for me, it's easier for people if I take my oddity for granted. Sometimes it's hard though. Up here on the Place you get all types. There are some weird ones who want to sleep with crippled women. That's why I was a bit sharp with you. Some of the weird ones are even older than you."

Jean Marie threw back his head and laughed till the tears ran down his face. Finally he managed to splutter, "Dear God! And to think I had to come back to France to hear it!"

"Please! Don't make fun of me! Things can get very rough up here, believe me!"

"I do believe you." Jean Marie recovered himself slowly. "Now, would you mind telling me your name?"

"It's signed on the piece—Judith."

"Judith what?"

"Just that. In the community we use only first names."

"The Community? You mean you're a nun?"

"Not exactly. There are about a dozen of us women who live together. We're all handicapped in one way or another—not all physically! We share what we earn. We look after each other. We're also a kind of refuge for young girls of the quarter who get into bother. It sounds primitive, and it is; but it's very satisfying and we feel it puts us close to the early Christian idea. After what you paid for the cosmos cup, you deserve to be remembered tonight at the meal prayer! What's your name? I like to keep a list of people who've bought my work."

"Jean Marie Barette."

"Are you anybody important?"

"Just remember me in the meal prayer," said Jean Marie. "But tell me one thing. How did this—this community of yours start?"

"That was strange. You remember some months ago the Pope abdicated and a new one was elected. Normally it wouldn't have meant very much. I've never met anyone higher than a parish priest. But that was a bad time for me. Nothing seemed to be going right. There seemed to be a connection between that event and my life. You know what I mean?"

"I know very well," said Jean Marie with feeling.

"A little while afterwards I was working in my studio. I had a little mansard apartment down the road from here. A girl I know, a model who works for some of the painters, staggered in. She was drunk and she'd been raped and punched about and her concierge had thrown her out. I sobered her up and took her to the clinic to be patched up, then I brought her back to my place. That night she turned very strange—remote and hostile and—how do I say it?—disconnected. I was frightened to be near her and yet I didn't dare to leave her. So, just to get her interested in something, I started carving a little doll out of a clothes peg. I made three altogether; then we sat down and made dresses for them, as though I were the mother and she the child. . . . That night she slept quietly in my bed, holding my hand. Next day I got two friends to share the day with her; and so it went on until she came back to normal. By then we had a little group and it seemed a pity to break it up. We worked out that we could save money and live more comfortably if we lodged as a family. . . . The religious part? Well, that seemed to come in quite naturally. One girl had been in India and had learned meditation techniques. I'd been brought up in a convent and I rather liked the idea of meeting for family prayer. Then one of the girls brought home a worker priest she'd met in a brasserie. He talked to us, lent us books. Also, if we were bothered at night we'd telephone him and he'd arrive with a couple of his friends from the factory. That was a help, I promise you! Well, after a while, we managed to work out a pattern of living that suited us. Few of us were virgins. None of us is sure whether we're ready for a long-term relationship with a man. Some of us may get married. But we're all believers and we work at trying to live by the Book. . . . So there we are! I'm sure it doesn't mean too much to you, but for us, it's a peace-giving thing. . . ."

"I'm very glad to have met you," said Jean Marie Barette. "And very proud to have your cosmos cup. Would you accept a gift from me?"

"What sort of gift?" The old wary look was back.

He hastened to dispel her fears. "The Verlaine I found today. There is a line in it that might have been written about you. It's in the poet's own handwriting." He took the small volume from his pocket and read her the quatrain pasted inside the jacket . . . " '*Votre âme est un paysage choisi*. . . .' " He asked very humbly, "Will you accept it please?"

"If you'll dedicate it for me."

"What sort of dedication?"

"Oh, the usual. Just a little word and your autograph."

He thought about it for a moment and then wrote:

> For Judith, who showed me the universe in a wine cup.
> Jean Marie Barette,
> *lately Pope Gregory XVII*

The girl stared, unbelieving, at the classic script. She looked up, searching for mockery in his smiling face. She said tremulously:

"I don't understand—I . . ."

"I don't understand either," said Jean Marie Barette. "But I think you have just given me a lesson in faith."

"I don't know what you mean," said the small, twisted girl.

"It means that what I was trying to tell the world from Vatican Hill, you have accomplished from a mansard in Paris. Let me try to explain. . . ."

. . . And when he had finished telling her the whole long story, she stretched out an emaciated hand, rough from the etcher's tools, and laid it over his. She said with an urchin grin:

"I hope I can tell it to the girls the way you've explained it to me. It would help if I could. Every so often they get fed up, because our little family seems so pointless and disorganized. I keep saying that there's one good thing about hitting rock bottom. The only place to go is up!" Her smile faded and she added gravely, "You're down there now; so you know. Would you like to come home to dinner?"

"Thank you; but no!" He was careful not to disappoint. "You see, Judith my love, you don't need me. Your own hearts have taught you better than I ever could. Already you have Christ in the midst of you."

The evening traffic was murderous; but he rode back to the Hostellerie on a white cloud of serenity. Today, if ever in his life, he had seen how the Spirit pre-empted all the plans of high men. This tiny group of women, maimed and threatened, had made themselves a family. They had asked no patent, no rescript. They had love to share and they shared it. They needed to think; they thought. They found an impulse to pray; they prayed. They found themselves a teacher in a workers' bar; and girls in trouble came to them, because they felt the warmth of the hearth fire.

The group might not be stable. It had no guarantees of continuity. There was no constitution, no sanction to give it legal identity. But what matter? It was like the campfire in the desert, lit at nightfall, quenched at dawn; but while it lasted it was a testimony to human sojourn to the God who visited man in his dreams. Once again the voice of Carl Mendelius wove itself into his reverie: ". . . The Kingdom of God is a dwelling place for men. What else can it signify but a condition in which human existence is not only tolerable but joyful —because it is open to infinity. . . ."

How better could one express the phenomenon of a small, twisted girl who engraved the cosmos on a wine glass and made a family for hurt women under the rooftops of Paris?

When he arrived at the Hostellerie his first act was to telephone Tübingen. Lotte was at the hospital but Johann was at home. He had good news.

"Father's condition is stable. The infection is under control. . . . We're still not sure about his sight; but at least we know he'll survive. Oh, another piece of news! The valley's ours. The contracts were signed today. I'm going down next week to talk to surveyors and architects and engineers. And I've been deferred from military service on compassionate grounds! How are things with you, Uncle Jean?"

"Good, very good! Will you give a message to your father? Write it down like a good fellow."

"Go ahead."

"Tell him from me: 'Today I was again given a sign. It came from a woman who showed me the cosmos in a wine glass.' Repeat that please."

"Today you were again given a sign. It came from a woman who showed you the cosmos in a wine glass."

"If ever you get a message that purports to come from me, it must carry that identification."

"Understood! What are your movements, Uncle Jean?"

"I don't know—but they may be hurried. Remember what I told you. Get your family out of Tübingen as soon as you can. My love to you all!"

"And ours to you. What's the weather like in Paris?"

"Threatening."

"Same here. We disbanded our club as you suggested."

"And got rid of the equipment?"

"Yes."

"Good! I'll be in touch whenever I can. Remember me kindly to Professor Meissner. *Auf wiedersehen.*"

He had hardly set down the receiver when Pierre Duhamel came to deliver his new passport, and a new identity card, inscribed to J. M. Grégoire, *pasteur en retraite.* He described to Jean Marie their uses and limitations.

". . . Everything is authentic, since you once bore the name Gregory. You are a minister of religion. You are pensioned off. The numbers on the documents belong to a series used for special categories of government agents—so no French immigration officer will want to ask questions. Foreign consulates will not raise too many problems about granting a visa to a retired clergyman travelling for his health. . . . However, try not to lose the documents, try not to get into trouble and have them impounded. That could be embarrassing to me. . . . Apropos of which, my dear Monseigneur, you opened your mouth very wide with the bankers this morning. The lines were buzzing as soon as they got back to their offices. . . . Once again you are named as a dangerous gadfly."

"And you, my dear Pierre, are you of the same mind about me?"

Duhamel ignored the question. He said simply:

"My wife sends you her thanks. She is in remission again and more comfortable than she has been for a long time. The curious thing is that even though she appeared to be unconscious, she remembers your visit and describes what you did, most vividly, as a 'caress of life.' Under other circumstances I could be very jealous of you."

Jean Marie ignored the tiny barb. "I bought a small gift for you both."

"There was no need." Duhamel was touched. "We are already in your debt."

Jean Marie handed him the cardboard box and made a smiling apology. "I wasn't able to have it gift-wrapped. You can open it if you want."

Duhamel snapped the string, opened the box and took out the goblet. He examined it with the care of a connoisseur.

"This is lovely. Where did you find it?"

Jean Marie recounted his meeting with Judith, the maimed one, in the Place du Tertre. He gave him the paper which explained the symbolism of the design, and told of the curious little community of women.

Pierre Duhamel listened in silence and made only a single terse comment: "You're working very hard to convert me."

"On the contrary," said Jean Marie firmly. "I'm called to give witness, to offer the gifts of faith and hope and loving. What you do with them is your most private affair. . . ." His tone changed to one of pleading and desperate persuasion. "Pierre, my friend, you've helped me. I want to help you. What your wife called the caress of life is something very real. I felt it today when this girl, who looks like a caricature of womanhood, laid her hand on mine and invited me into her special world. . . . This great stoic courage of yours is so—so barren, so desperately sad!"

"I'm in a sad business," said Pierre Duhamel with arctic humour. "I'm a funeral director, preparing the obsequies of civilization. That demands a certain grand style. . . . Which reminds me. . . . Tomorrow I shall be asked to sign a document requiring Grade A surveillance of a certain Jean Marie Barette."

"Classified as what?"

"Anti-government agitator."

"And you will sign it?"

"Of course. But I'll hold it up for a few hours so that you can make suitable arrangements."

"I'll leave here tomorrow morning."

"Before you go"—Duhamel handed him a slip of paper—"call this number. Petrov wants to talk to you."

"About what?"

"Bread, politics—and a few fantasies of his own."

"When we met in Rome I liked him. Can I still trust him?"

"Not as far as you can trust me. But you'll find him much more agreeable. . . ." For the first time he relaxed. He held the cosmos cup in his hands and turned it round and round, studying all the details of the etching. Finally he said, "We will drink from it, Paulette and I. We'll think of you and the little *bossue* on the Place du Tertre. . . . Who knows? It's good enough theatre to suspend our disbelief. . . . But, you understand, this is the bad time—the day of the black battalions. If you fall into their hands, I can't help you at all."

"What does your President think of all this?"

"Our President? For God's sake! He's the same as every other president, prime minister, party leader, duce or caudillo. He's got the flag tattooed on his back and the party manifesto on his chest. If you ask him why we have to go to war, he'll tell you that war is a cyclic phenomenon, or you can't make an omelette without breaking eggs or—God rot him in hell—war is the archetypal orgasm: agony, ecstasy, and the long, long quiet afterwards. I've often wondered why I shouldn't kill him before I kill myself. . . ."

"Why do you stay then?"

"Because if I weren't there, who else would get you your passport—and who else would tell what goes on in the madhouse? I must go now! Make sure you've gone too, before midday tomorrow!"

Jean Marie Barette reached out and clamped firm hands on Duhamel's broad shoulders. "At least, my friend, give me time to thank you."

"Don't thank me," said Pierre Duhamel. "Just pray for me. I'm not sure how much more I can take!"

When he had gone, Jean Marie dialled the number for Sergei Petrov. A woman's voice answered, in French. A moment later Petrov was on the line.

"Who is this?"

"Duhamel gave me a message to call you."

"Oh, yes! Thank you for being so prompt. We should meet and talk. We have interests in common."

"I believe we may have. Where do you suggest we meet? I may be under surveillance. Does that bother you?"

"Not greatly." The news did not seem to surprise him too much. "So, let me think! Tomorrow at eleven, does that suit you?"

"Yes."

"Then let's meet at the Hotel Meurice, Room five eighty. Come straight up. I'll be waiting for you."

"I have all that. Until tomorrow then."

But over the rest of tomorrow and all the days afterward there was still a very large question mark. Before the surveillance began, he had to find himself a bolt-hole, a place where he could sleep secure, from which he could communicate and travel quickly. Alain could help; but that relationship was already uneasy, and Odette was no model of discretion. He was still ruminating over the problem when the telephone rang. Mme. Saracini was on the line. She was cheerful and abrupt.

"I told you I wanted to talk to you again. When and where can we meet?"

Jean Marie hesitated for a moment and then told her, "I've been informed by a reliable source that as of tomorrow I shall be under Grade A surveillance as an anti-government agitator."

"That's madness!"

"It is, however, a fact. So I need a secure place to stay for a while. Can you help me?"

The answer came back without a second's hesitation. "Of course! How soon could you be ready to move?"

"In ten minutes."

"It will take me forty-five minutes to get to you. Pack your bag. Pay the bill. Be waiting at the front entrance."

Before he had time to thank her, she had rung off. He packed his few belongings, explained to the *patronne* that a sudden change in his personal situation dictated his brusque departure, paid his account, then sat down to read his breviary until Mme. Saracini arrived. He felt very calm, very trustful. Step by step he was being led to the proving ground. By a curious trick of association—Saracini, Malavolti, Benincasa, we Sienese—he was reminded of the words which the twenty-five-year-old Catherine had written to Gregory XI at Avignon: "It is no longer time to sleep, because Time never sleeps, but passes like the wind. . . . In order to reconstruct the whole, it is necessary to destroy the old, right down to the foundations. . . ."

The woman who picked him up at the entrance to the Hostellerie looked ten years younger than Mme. Saracini, president of the Banco Ambrogiano all' Estero. She wore slacks and a silk blouse and a head scarf, and drove a convertible, custom-built by the most famous Italian designer. She locked his suitcase into the trunk and whisked him away with a scream of tires, before any curious guest had time to notice the car or its owner. Once on the road, however, she drove with studious care and a sharp eye for police traps, while she instructed him briskly in her plans.

". . . The safest place in Paris for you is my house—precisely because it is a house. There are no other tenants, no concierge and I can guarantee the loyalty of my domestic staff. I entertain a lot; so there's a constant coming and going of people. Any visitors you have will pass unnoticed. You will have your own apartment—a bedroom, a study and a bathroom. It has a direct telephone line and its own private stairway to the garden. My staff are underemployed; so they can easily look after your needs."

"This is most generous of you, madame; but . . ."

"There are no buts. If the arrangement doesn't work, you leave. Simple! And would you please call me by my given name, Roberta!"

Jean Marie smiled to himself in the darkness and said, "Then, Roberta, will you let me point out that there are certain risks in harbouring me."

"I'm happy to accept them. You see, I know you have a work to do. I want to be part of it. I can help more than you realize at this moment."

"Why do you want to help?"

"That's one question I'm not prepared to answer while I'm driving; but I will answer it, when I get you home."

"Try this one then. Do you think it's good for your reputation to have a man in residence?"

"I've had others, far more scandalous," she told him bluntly. "It's twenty years since my husband died. I didn't live like a nun all that time. . . . But, things happened to make me change. My father went to prison. I went through a very bad patch with someone I loved very much and who one night went crazy in my arms and nearly killed me. Then there was you. When you were Pope, I felt the same way about you as my father used to feel about the good Pope John. You had style. You had compassion. You didn't go round shouting discipline or damnation. Even when I was living pretty wildly I always felt there was a way back, as there was with my father when I'd been a naughty girl. Then, when you abdicated and I heard some of the inside story from your brother, Alain, I was furious. I thought they'd broken you; until your friend—what's his name?—wrote that wonderful piece about you."

"Mendelius?"

"That's it! . . . And then somebody passed him a letter bomb! It was then that I began to see how things fitted together. I started to go to church again, read the Bible, pick up friends that I'd dropped in the wild days, because they seemed too earnest or stuffy. . . . But we're off the track. First we install you in your apartment; then we feed you. Afterwards we talk about the future and what you need to do."

He was tempted to chide her, tell her that, while he needed help, he was not prepared to be managed. He thought better of it. He changed the subject.

"I've been provided a second passport and an identity card in the name of Jean Marie Grégoire. It's probably best if we use that name with your staff."

"I agree. There are three altogether: a man and wife and a daily maid. They've all been with me a long time. . . . We're nearly home now. My place is just off the Quai d'Orsay."

Three minutes later she stopped in front of a porte-cochère closed by a steel gate, which opened to a radio signal. The garage was on the left of the entrance and an interior stairway led to the floors above. His suite was a pair of rooms, the one a large studio lined with books, the other a bed-sitting room with a bathroom between. Outside was a balcony from which he could look down on the central atrium, which had been converted into a rock garden with a fountain in the center.

"It's not quite the Vatican," said Roberta Saracini. "But I hope you'll be comfortable. Dinner in thirty minutes. I'll send someone to fetch you."

She came in person, dressed in a house gown of some rich brocaded material, stiff as a benediction cope. She led him into the dining room, a small but beautifully proportioned room, with a coffered ceiling and refectory furniture of Spanish mahogany. The meal was simple but exquisitely cooked, a country pâté, a filet of sole, a mousse of blueberries. The wine, he told her, was much too good to waste on M. Grégoire, *pasteur en retraite*. To which she answered that the pastor was in retirement no longer and it was time to discuss what he wanted to do.

". . . I know what I must do: spread the word that the last days are upon us and that all men of goodwill must prepare for them. I know also what I must not do: make confusions or dissensions among honest believers, or undermine the principles of legitimate authority in the Christian community. . . . So, first question: how do I resolve the problem?"

"It seems to me, you've already found the solution: a new identity. After all, it's the message that's important, not the man who proclaims it."

"Not quite. How does the messenger establish his authority?"

"He shouldn't try," said Roberta Saracini. "He should put the word about, as the early Disciples did, and trust to God to make it fruitful."

There was more than piety in the way she said it. There was a total confidence, as if she had herself made proof of the proposition.

He told her, "I agree with the principle; but how do I, a man unwelcome in his own country, deprived of a canonical mission, preach the word without a breach of the obedience which I owe to the Church?"

Roberta Saracini poured coffee and handed the cup to him across the table. She offered brandy. He refused it. She explained carefully:

"I'm a banker, as you know. As a banker I have holdings in a lot of diverse enterprises: mining, fabrication, travel, advertising, entertainment, communication. So, once you are sure of what you want to say . . ."

"I have always been sure of that."

"Then we can find a hundred ways, a thousand voices, to spread the news."

"That will cost you a fortune."

"What if it does? Who's going to keep accounts after Rubicon Day?"

"How do you know about Rubicon Day?"

"I have my sources. You don't think I gamble blind in the market?"

"I suppose not."

He was still uneasy, though the explanation made sense enough. He himself would not name his sources, even to a close friend.

"There are ample funds available for whatever you want to do. I'd like to introduce you to some of my people in publishing, television and advertising. Consider them as your voices. Tell them what you want to say. You'll be surprised what ideas emerge. . . . You're looking dubious. Why? Where would the modern papacy be without television—or the American presidency for that matter? Isn't it a moral duty to use all the gifts that are placed at our disposal?"

Once again most strongly, he was reminded of that young Sienese woman of the fourteenth century who had written to Pierre Roger de Beaufort-Turenne, Gregory XI . . . *"Siatemi uomo, virile e non timoroso . . ."* "Be a man for me, virile and not a coward!"

He was silent for a moment, considering his decision. "How soon can I meet your experts?"

"Tomorrow evening."

"And how far can I trust them?"

"The ones who sit at this table you can trust, as you trust me."

"Then, will you answer the question I asked on the way here: why do you want to help a man who is telling the end of the world?"

She did not tumble with the answer, she gave it to him, flat and unadorned.

"Because he is a man, just that! All my life I've been waiting for someone who will stride out into the storm and shout against the wind. I watched you this morning at the bank. You were so angry I thought you would burst; but you had the grace to say you were sorry for bad manners. For me that's reason enough."

"Not for me," said Jean Marie Barette. "Nobody's so strong all the time. Nobody lasts so long. The man I followed as Pope—I stood by his deathbed and watched him puking up his lifeblood and crying 'Mama, Mama, Mama!' The newspapers said he was calling on the Virgin Mary. He wasn't. He was calling for his mother in the dark. . . . Don't build on me, Roberta! Build on yourself! You're not some sad *dévote* in the middle of the menopause. I'm not some troubled priest wondering why he's wasted his whole life in celibacy."

"Tell me what you are then!" said Roberta Saracini with sudden anger. "Let's be good Jesuits and define the terms!"

"I have been given a call to proclaim the Last Things and the Coming of the Lord. I have answered the call. I seek the means to make the proclamation. You have offered me shelter and funds and experts to help me. I have accepted with gratitude; but I have nothing to give in return."

"Have I asked for anything?"

"No, but I have to warn you—and believe me it is an act of love!—you must never expect to possess any part of me—or hope to manage me in any fashion."

"For God's sake! Why do you think you have to warn me?"

"Because when we first met you talked of being mystical about your own past, about your family connection with Saint Catherine of Siena. It seemed to me a very significant prelude. You were offering me the same kind of support that she had offered Gregory the Eleventh, to bring him back from Avignon to Rome. But one can't repeat history and one can't duplicate relationships. That Gregory was a mincing man, a vacillator and a coward. I have many faults, but I am not such a man. I am called to walk a desert road. . . ." She started to protest but he stayed her with a gesture. "There is more, so please let me say it. I am not ignorant of the life and works of your little saint. I wrote my doctoral thesis on the great women mystics. I have read the *Dialogo* and the *Epistolario*. Catherine wrote much and beautifully about love, human and divine. Nevertheless, there are dark passages in her relationships that none of her biographers has wholly explained. She is too exotic for my taste; possibly because I am French and she never liked the French. But I think that once or twice she pushed the young men of her *cenacolo* too far. She was dreaming divine love when they were still struggling to make sense of the human variety —and that's when the tragedies occurred. So . . ." He smiled and shrugged. "Like good Jesuits we have defined the terms and spelled out the rules of the game. Am I forgiven?"

"Yes. But not easily." She raised her glass in a silent toast and tossed off the rest of the wine. "It's late. I have to be at work early in the morning."

"I have to go out, too. I have a meeting with the Russian Minister for Agricultural Production."

"Petrov? I've had bank dealings with him. He's tough but decent. However, he's in a desperate position. If he can't get enough grain for winter, he's a ruined man."

"And our world is one hour closer to midnight."

He rose and held back her chair. When she stood up she turned and took his hand and kissed it in the old-fashioned style.

"Good night, Monsieur Grégoire."

He accepted the gesture without comment.

"Good night, madame, and thank you for the shelter of your house!"

——————— XI ———————

I N Room 580 of the Hotel Meurice, Jean Marie Barette, once a Pope, talked with Sergei Andrevich Petrov, Minister for Agricultural Production in the U.S.S.R. Petrov looked tired and crumpled, as if he had shed his clothes on the bedroom floor and climbed into them the next morning. His eyes were red and rheumy. His voice was hoarse and his skin exuded a smell of stale liquor. Even his sense of humour was wearing thin.

". . . You think I look a wreck? I am. Twelve, fifteen hours a day for weeks now, I'm travelling, talking, pleading, squawking for husks of grain like a starving parrot! But no one wants to sell to me. So I walk down the ladder to stage two. What do I ask for now? Intervention, mediation—what they call in the trade 'good offices.' It occurred to me you might be willing to help."

"Willing, yes," Jean Marie answered without hesitation. "How useful is another matter. In the democracies the leader of the opposition still has a strong voice and a lot of bargaining power. With me it's different. I'm just a *pasteur en retraite*. Put it another way. How would you react if I came asking favours from you in Moscow?"

"Better than you think. You have much respect everywhere. Will you try to help? The position is desperate. Famine is the horror nobody understands until it happens. Look at Africa! The warnings had been there for years, but nobody paid any heed! . . . From the Sahara to the Sachel to the Horn, suddenly thousands were dying. Now that threat hangs over us—except that for us it's dearth in winter! We'll just about get through it; and then, as soon as the thaw comes, I promise you the rockets will be launched and our armies will move south towards the oil fields of the gulf, west through the great Hungarian plain, by sea towards India, the Philippines and Australia. It's like an axiom of mathematics. The only way to stave off disorder at home is to march against the enemy abroad. . . . The Western powers and the Chinese are playing that dangerous game the English call brinkmanship. Well, it's not a sport that you enjoy with an empty belly. So, once again, will you try to help?"

"Yes, of course I will try; but I can't work in a vacuum. I need a briefing. I need a list of trading points which your people are prepared to concede in return for urgent supplies. You, too, play the game on the edge of the precipice and you can be just as stupid as any in the West! So, I need a piece of script, however elementary, that gives me authority to act as broker in the market."

"That may be difficult."

"Without it, the rest is impossible. Come, Comrade Petrov! I can make press statements, sermons, appeals. I did it every Sunday in Saint Peter's Square! I made special diplomatic speeches on every tour. But that's the same as you making a May Day Speech on Marxist-Leninist ideology and the solidarity of the People's Soviets! It puts no meat in the stew! But with a brief in my hand, one that you can repudiate if I botch it—*Bien!* At least I will be received as an emissary with respect."

"Would you be prepared to come to Moscow?"

"Yes—provided I get a friendly invitation from the men at the top and I'm not harassed at every step by the K.G.B."

"That won't happen, I promise you."

"When would you want me there?"

"As soon as possible; but I have to stick my toe in the water just to see that there are no crabs waiting to bite it off. How can I get in touch with you?"

"Through my brother, Alain, at the bank, Halévy Frères et Barette." He scribbled the address on a desk pad and passed it to Petrov. "Alain won't know where I am; but I'll be in touch with him from time to time."

Petrov folded the paper and put it into his pocketbook. He said, "Would you join me in a drink?"

"Thank you, but it's a little early for me."

"I need one. I know I've been hitting it hard the last few weeks; but what's a man to do at the end of another lousy day with the begging bowl? You don't get any medals for effort in this business—just fish-eyed stares and 'Tut-tut, Comrade! There must be something constructive you can do!' I know there isn't and they know there isn't; but they're safe in the Kremlin shuffling their papers while I'm wearing out shoe leather and patience."

"I thought you had some hope with Pierre Duhamel."

"So far that's all it is—hope! He's trying to work out some complicated scheme by which we purchase cargoes while they're in transit and divert them to Baltic ports. It's the size of the operation that's the problem—unless Duhamel is playing dirty. . . . What do you think of him?"

"I think he's trying to play clean in a dirty game."

"It could be. What about that drink?"

"Suggestion," said Jean Marie Barette.

"Let's hear it."

"Forget the drink. Order coffee for two. Give me your size and I'll go down and buy you a new shirt and underwear. Then you send your suit out to be pressed and take a long, hot bath while you're waiting for it."

Petrov stared at him in disbelief.

"You're telling me I'm unclean?"

"I'm telling you, dear Comrade, that if I were under the gun as you are, I'd change twice a day, never drink till after sundown—and let it be known that anyone who thinks he can do my job better is welcome to it."

"Only one problem with that prescription."

"What's that?"

"Whoever takes my job will want my head as well—and I don't want to part with it just yet. . . . But you're right about the rest of it. I'm size forty. You go buy the clothes. I'll order the coffee. It usually takes a while to get room service anyway."

"I thought you were staying at the embassy," said Jean Marie Barette.

"I am," said Sergei Petrov. "I keep this place for—private contacts."

"Are you sure they are private?"

"As sure as I can be. I know the room is not bugged. . . . On the other hand, that scares me more than anything."

"Why?"

"Because it could mean nobody really gives a damn what I do. I could be a sitting duck, just waiting for someone to knock me off. . . . Not that it would matter very much. The whole human race has a pretty limited run anyway."

"Precisely how long do you give it?"

"Let's see. We're now in September. If I can't get grain before the winter, the Army will march immediately after the spring thaw. If I get it, then there's a breathing space, but not too long, because there's still the problem of fuels and energy, and every big nation has a plan for pre-emptive strikes if the oil fields are threatened. . . . At worst we've got six, eight months—at best, eighteen. It's not a pretty thought, is it?"

"I'll go buy the clothes," said Jean Marie. "Any preference in colours?"

Sergei Andrevich Petrov burst into a bellow of laughter.

"I wish the old comrades could see me now! Ever since the revolution the Vatican has been a burr in our breeches. Now I have the Pope buying my underwear!"

"And what's odd about that?" asked Jean Marie with bland innocence. "The first one peddled fish in Israel."

As he went about the simple business of buying socks and underwear, he was struck not only by the comedy of the situation, but by the macabre recklessness of it. Born in the mid-twenties, he had been too young for military service with the French Army, and he had been forced to flee to the mountains to avoid conscription for forced labour under the Germans. He had fought with the Maquis and begun his seminary training a year after the end of hostilities. But one of his most vivid memories was the nightmare period when the Germans began to pull out and the whole edifice of occupation began to collapse. It was like a Walpurgisnacht of drunkenness, cruelty, heroism and complicated insanities.

Now he was seeing the same thing again—the operatic disorders in Tübingen, assassination by decree, Pierre Duhamel, the trusted servant of the Republic, conniving at secret horrors in the vain hope of preventing greater ones, and now Sergei Petrov, trying to break a blockade of the grain market and drowning his despair in vodka. It was the madness-in-little which was the most sinister of all. Famine in the Horn of Africa? Eh! What was it? A natural purge of surplus population from marginal land—that is, until you picked up a child with a belly like a balloon and arms like matchsticks and hardly enough heart-beat to pump air into its lungs. Then you cursed God and cursed man, his errant creature, and primed the bombs to blast the whole mess into ob-livion!

Whereupon, with sublime irrelevance, he decided that brother Alain was right. He did need some new clothes. If he were shopping for Petrov he might just as well spend a little care on himself. There was no point in going badly dressed to one's own funeral.

That night, Roberta Saracini had three guests home to dinner. They came in work clothes and brought briefcases, an artist's folio and a video tape machine. They had the purposeful air of professionals who knew exactly what they were about and needed no advice from the unskilled. The oldest of the three was a big, florid-faced fellow with a broad smile and a shrewd eye. Roberta intro-duced him as Adrian Hennessy.

". . . No relation to the Cognac. He's American, speaks seven languages, and makes expensive sense in all of them. He arrived from New York this morning. If you and he can get along he will direct our operation."

The second guest was a mannish young woman whose features looked vaguely familiar. This one was the surprise packet.

". . . Natalie Duhamel, our expert on films and television. I believe you know her father."

"I do."

Jean Marie was nonplussed. The young woman gave him a cool smile and a well-rehearsed definition.

"My father and I have an excellent relationship. He doesn't produce my shows and I don't write his reports to the President. In matters of confidence, he doesn't ask, I don't tell—and vice versa!"

"It's a very precise arrangement," said Jean Marie Barette.

"And this"—Roberta Saracini presented her third guest, a stripling youth who might have modelled for the Delphic charioteer—"this is Florent de Basil. He designs, he paints, he makes beautiful songs."

"In short, a genius." He had the ready innocent smile of a child. He took Jean Marie's hand and kissed it. "I can't tell you how much I've wanted to meet you. I hope you'll be able to give me time to do a portrait."

"First things first, my love," said Roberta Saracini. "It's half-an-hour to dinner. Why don't we start work over cocktails?"

Adrian Hennessy opened his briefcase and brought out a tape recorder. Florent de Basil produced a sketch pad. Natalie Duhamel sat placidly watching. Hennessy took a swallow of liquor and stated categorically:

"We talk off the record first. If we don't agree the terms of reference we enjoy our dinner and call it a day. If we agree, then we start work forthwith. First item. How do we call the subject? That's you, sir. Remember, certain materials like notes and tape recorders have to be carried around, therefore, they can be lost. So, we don't want real names."

"My name is Jean Marie . . ."

"Then let's change it to American: John Doe. Next, the aim of our project. As Roberta has explained it, you have a message which you wish to deliver to the world. You are concerned, however, that you should not be seen to propagate this message as an official teacher of the Roman Catholic Church."

"That's an accurate summary. Yes."

"But it is still incomplete. It ignores the heart of the problem: that as a onetime Pope you still wear the aura of your office. There is no way you can make public declarations without coming into conflict with the present incumbent—who, by the way, is the least inspiring of orators. So the question is, how far are you prepared to risk that conflict?"

"Not by a single step," said Jean Marie Barette.

"I like a man who knows his own mind," said Hennessy with a grin. "But a message has to be delivered by someone; and that someone has to have some authority. After all, you don't read the letters of John Doe in church . . . you read Saint Paul and Saint Peter and Saint James. . . ."

"I don't agree," said Jean Marie. "I'm sorry; but I've had this argument ad nauseam. I almost ended believing it. Not now! Not ever again! Listen. . . ." Suddenly he was a man on fire. The listeners hung on his every word, and gesture. Hennessy reached forward and switched on the tape recorder. ". . . If each of us were locked in a silent room, deprived of all sensory reference, we should very soon become disoriented and, finally, insane. The person who would probably endure longest would be the one who was practiced in withdrawal, in meditation, whose life had an outside reference to God. I met several such people during my pontificate, three men and one woman who had been confined as religious agitators and tortured by sensory deprivation. . . . The fact is that we live only in communion—not only with our present but with the past and the future as well. We are haunted by a whole poetry of living, by lullabies half remembered and the sounds of train whistles in the night and the scent of lavender in a summer garden. We are haunted by grief, too, and fear, and images of childhood terror and the macabre dissolutions of age. . . . But I am sure that it is in this domain of our daily dreaming that the Holy Spirit establishes His own communion with us. This is how the gift is given, which we call grace: the sudden illumination, the sharp regret that leads to penitence or forgiveness, the opening of the heart to the risk of love. . . . Authority is irrelevant here. Authority is the one-eyed man in the kingdom of the blind! It can command us to everything except love and understanding. . . . So what am I trying to tell you?" He gave them a grin of self-deprecation. "Peter is dead and Paul is dead and James the brother of the Lord. Their dust is blown away by the winds of centuries. Were they large men, little men, fair or dark? Who knows? Who cares? The testimony of the Spirit, made through them, still endures." He quoted softly, "Though I speak with the tongues of men and of angels and have not charity, I am become like a sounding brass or a tinkling cymbal. . . ."

There was a long silence in the room. Jean Marie looked from one to the other, seeking a response. Their faces were blank, their eyes downcast. Finally it was Hennessy who spoke. He switched off the tape. He addressed himself not to Jean Marie but to his colleagues.

". . . I don't need to see the man who said that. I can read it, listen to it, and make my own image. Natalie?"

"I agree, totally. Imagine that with lights, makeup, cues—all the mechanics. He'd look like a whore playing a virgin—with all respect to you, Monseigneur! What do you think, Florent?"

The young man was curiously subdued. He said, "No images, certainly. I found myself hearing music—something very simple, like the old ballads that told about love and knightly deeds. . . . Perhaps I should modify that. The image should not be of the speaker. It could be of his audience. Can we think about it for a while?"

"I'm a banker," said Roberta Saracini. "But you gave me a thought, Adrian. You said, 'You don't read the letters of John Doe in church.' Would you read a letter from this John Doe? Would you listen if he sent you a message on tape?"

"You're damn right I would!" He scribbled a note on his pad. Then he turned to Jean Marie and made a rueful apology. "I know this must sound very impertinent—treating you like some kind of puppet to be manipulated."

"I'm used to it," said Jean Marie equably. "Our people at the Vatican are experts in high theatre; and some of our masters of ceremonies were real tyrants. Don't worry! I'll let you know when I've had enough!"

"Letters!" said Natalie Duhamel. "They used to be a very fashionable form of literature."

"Still are," said Hennessy. *"Letters of Junius, Lettres de mon Moulin, Letters to The Times!* Trouble is to find editors with guts enough to run them in spite of present censorship. We could certainly find enough book publishers to run a series. . . . Could you write them, Monseigneur?"

"I've been writing them all my clerical life," said Jean Marie. "Pastoral letters, encyclicals, letters to clergy and conventual nuns. I'd welcome a change of style."

"You could also talk them onto tape?"

"Of course."

"I'm scared," said Natalie Duhamel. "Who's going to listen to sermons?"

"Was that a sermon?" The young man pointed dramatically at the tape.

"No, but can he sustain the style? . . . Can you, Monseigneur?"

"I'm not aware of style." Jean Marie was crisp and definite. "I have things to say, about living and dying. They have to be spoken heart to heart."

"If you write letters," said Hennessy boldly, "to whom do you address them? That's where you come back to authority. The editor asks, 'Who is this fellow?' The public asks, 'What the hell does he know?' "

"And you may not be dealing with editors at all," said Natalie Duhamel. "You may have to go back to the *samizdat* and the underground press or even to the wall posters of China! But Adrian's right. A letter begins 'Dear X. . . .' Who is X in this case?"

"If you're writing about the end of everything," said Florent de Basil, "it seems a pointless self-contradictory exercise. Who can do anything about the final event?"

"You're right," Jean Marie agreed with apparent good humour.

"With whom do you correspond then—God?"

"Why not?" Jean Marie savoured the thought for a moment. "Where else do we turn at world's end? It's what a child might do: write letters to God and post them in a hollow tree. You could call them *Last Letters from a Small Planet!*"

"Stop right there!" Hennessy's command was like a whipcrack. He looked around at the small assembly. "Don't anybody say a word until I ask for it. The title is beautiful. I love it." He turned to Jean Marie and asked, "Could you write those letters?"

"Of course. It's not difficult." He made a small joke of it. "After all, I do talk to the Almighty every day. I don't have to learn a new language."

"How soon could you begin putting something on paper?"

"Tonight, tomorrow morning, whenever."

"Then please! One letter a day—a thousand to twelve hundred words—until further notice. Leave it to us to find the hollow tree—and an international distribution."

"One elementary question." It was Natalie Duhamel who asked it. "Who will be the author of these letters? What character and under what name? That's basic to our promotion."

Jean Marie offered a half-serious suggestion. "I can't be a child again; but I've often felt small. Why don't I sign myself 'Jean-not' . . . Little John?"

"It sounds a little clownish to me," said Roberta Saracini.

"Then let's go the whole way! Let's admit that there is such a thing as a divine folly. I'll sign myself 'Jeannot le Bouffon'! Johnny the Clown."

"Why demean yourself?" Roberta was still unhappy. "Why step so far out of character that no one will know who you really are?"

"Because then no one can accuse me of ambition or rebellion. . . . And, who but a child or a clown would write letters to the Almighty?"

"I agree with the man!" said Hennessy. "And if we can't make Johnny the Clown a household name around the globe, I'll blow my brains out. What do you say, Natalie?"

"I can see a way to visualize the whole thing if Florent can come up with a logo."

"A logo and the music, my love—and even a counterpoint theme: 'Johnny the Clown is so simple. Why are the rest of us so complicated? . . .'"

"Let's not talk it into the air," said Hennessy. "And let's not distract the author! He's the inspired one. We're the technicians. . . . How long to dinner, Roberta? I'm starving!"

He could not believe it was so easy to write the letters. As Pontiff he had been forced to weigh every word, lest it deviate by a hair's breadth from the definitions of ancient councils: Chalcedon, Nicaea, Trent. He could not discredit the decretals of his predecessors, however much he disagreed with them. He must not speculate; he could only hope to illuminate the traditional formulae of faith. He was the fount of authority, the final arbiter of orthodoxy, the looser and the binder—himself more stringently bound than any, a tomb-slave to the Deposit of Faith.

Now, suddenly, he was free. He was no longer *Doctor et Magister* but Johnny the Clown, wide-eyed among the mysteries. Now he could sit and smell the flowers, watch the waterspout and, the fool of God, safe in his buffoon dress, dispute with his Maker.

Dear God,

I love this funny world; but I have just heard the news that You are going to destroy it; or, worse still, You are going to sit up in heaven and watch us destroy it, like comedians wrecking a grand piano, on which great masters have played Beethoven.

I can't argue with what You do. It's Your universe. You juggle the stars and manage to keep them all in space. But please, before the last big bang, could You explain some things to me? I know this is only one tiny planet; but it's where I live and, before I leave it, I'd like to understand it a little better. I'd like to understand You, too—as far as You'll let me—but for Johnny the Clown, You'll have to make it all very simple.

. . . I've never really got it clear in my mind where you fit in. No disrespect, truly! But You see, in the circus where I work, there's an audience and there's us, the people who do the tricks, and there are the animals, too. You can't leave them out because we depend on them and they on us.

Now, the audience is wonderful. Most times they're so happy and innocent you can feel the joy coming out from them; but sometimes you can smell the cruelty, too, as if they want the tigers to attack the tamer, or the aerialist to fall from the high trapeze. So, I can't really believe You're the audience!

Then there's us, the performers. We're a mixed bunch: clowns like me, acrobats, pretty girls on horseback, the people on the high wire, the women with the performing dogs and the elephants and the lions and—oh, all of it! We're a grotesque lot really: good-hearted, yes, but sometimes crazy enough to murder each other. I could tell You tales . . . but then You know, don't You? You know us like the potter knows the vase that he's turned on his own wheel.

Some people say You're the owner of the circus and that You set up the whole show for Your own private pleasure. I could accept that. I like being a clown. I get as much fun as I give. But I can't understand why the owner would want to cut the ropes of the big top and bury us all underneath it. A mad person might do that, a vengeful villain. I don't believe You can be mad and make a rose, or vengeful and create a dolphin. . . . So You see, there is a lot of explaining to do. . . .

The more he wrote, the more he wanted to write. It was not a literary exercise. He was not teaching anyone. He was engaged in the most primitive pastime of all, the contemplation of paradox, the reasoning of a simple man with ultimate mystery. He was expressing himself with a peasant's vocabulary, far different from that of the philosophers and the theologians. He did not have to invent new symbols or new cosmogonies like the Marcians and the Valentinians. He was a man in love with old and simple things—ripe grain rubbed in the hands, apples picked fresh from the tree, the first sweet savour of spring love. They were the more precious, because they would soon be lost in the doomsday chaos. As Pope he had written for women—mandates, prescriptions, counsels. Never before, in all his clerical career, had he written so tenderly about them.

. . . They tell me their secrets because I'm a clown with big boots and baggy pants and I'm always afraid. They're not ashamed to admit that they're afraid, too. They don't feel ridiculous either—even when they've made fools of themselves with a man. I'm much more foolish than they'll ever be, with my big mouth and my crybaby eyes. They just want to love and to be loved, and nest like the birds and make beautiful children. . . . But they hear the ghostly horsemen riding in the night—war, plague, famine—and they ask why they should breed babies to die at a dry breast or burn up in a bomb flash. They cannot walk safe in the streets; so they learn to fight like men and carry weapons against rape. They watch the men making war dances and they despise them. When the men get angry, they despise them the more; and the loving becomes sour or strange.

They want to know what's gone wrong with Your world . . . and why they don't see You sometimes on the street corner where Your Son used to be centuries ago, talking to the passersby, telling the truth in fairy tales. What can I tell them? I'm just Johnny the Clown! The best I can do is make them laugh by falling flat on my face or walking slap-bang into a custard tart! . . .

Will You think about all these things and try to give me some kind of answer? I know we've talked often. Sometimes I've understood. Sometimes I haven't. But right now I'm scared and I'm tripping over my big boots to run and hide.

This letter will be posted in the hollow oak at the bottom of the meadow —right near the place where we keep the circus horses.

I'll keep writing because I have a lot more questions to ask. These may be the last letters You'll ever get from our small planet; so, please don't shut down the world before I can make some sense of it.

Your puzzled friend,
Johnny the Clown

By evening he had written five letters, twenty pages of script in all, and it was only sheer physical fatigue that made him stop. It was still early. It would be pleasant to take a stroll along the quais. Then, with a small shiver of fear, he remembered that now he was the subject of Grade A surveillance and the trackers would be casting about to pick up his scent. He could not risk compromising Roberta Saracini by a trifling act of self-indulgence. Instead he called Adrian Hennessy.

". . . If you have time this evening, I'd like you to see what I've written."

"How much have you got?"

"Five letters. Something better than six thousand words."

"My God! You are industrious. I'll be over in twenty minutes."

"Would you do me a favour? On your way, pick up a basket of flowers for Roberta and a card to go with them. I'd do it myself, but I'm not supposed to leave the house."

"Better still: let me have them delivered direct from the florist. What do you want to say on the card?"

"Just: 'To say my thanks, Jeannot le Bouffon.' "

"Got it! I'm on my way."

In eighteen minutes he was at the door, brisk, blunt and businesslike. Before he read a line of the manuscript he laid down another set of ground rules.

"This is the big game: no compliments, no concessions. If it's good I say so. If it's bad we burn it. In between? Well, we think about it."

"Very proper," said Jean Marie placidly, "except you can't burn anything you don't own!"

Hennessy glanced quickly through the manuscript.

"Good! For a start it's legible. Why don't they teach handwriting like this anymore? I want to be alone for half-an-hour. That will give you time to read vespers in the garden. You might remember me when you come to the *Domine Exaudi.*"

"With pleasure."

He was hardly out of the door before Hennessy was deep in his reading. Jean Marie chuckled quietly to himself. He felt like a sceneshifter on a Japanese play, he was dressed in black and therefore to be ignored. He did, however, make remembrance of Adrian Hennessy at the *Domine Exaudi.* He said, "Please! Let me be able to trust him! I'm not sure in my judgments anymore."

The judgment that Hennessy passed on the manuscript was brief and final.

"That's what you promised. You moved me—and I've got boiler plate around my heart."

"So what happens now?"

"I take these, have them copied and a couple of file copies sent to you. I retain the original holographs in case we have to authenticate. Natalie and Florent read them and come up with ideas for special audio-visual treatments. Meantime, I'm looking for newspaper, magazine and book outlets—in all languages. You will continue writing—and may God guide your pen! As soon as we've got concrete situations, we'll present them to you for approval. . . . Your flowers are ordered. Is there anything else I can do for you?"

"I'm under Grade A surveillance as a political agitator—or at least I will be as soon as my whereabouts are known. I'd like to get out and stretch my legs, eat in a restaurant; but my face is too well known. Any suggestions?"

"Easiest thing in the world." Hennessy consulted his pocketbook and then made a telephone call. "Rolf? Adrian Hennessy. I've got a job. . . . Immediate. Highest scale for payment. Let me see . . . I'll read him off to you. Age: sixty-five, grey hair reasonably abundant, fair complexion, features thin but fine-boned, eyes blue, very slim. Well, the point is he's anchored to the house and he'll soon be chewing the carpet. . . . Yes, he is well known, so it's a whole transformation scene . . . but not the Hunchback of Notre Dame, for God's sake! He still wants to eat in a public place. . . . Have you got a pencil? I'll read you the address. . . . How long will it take you to get here? . . . Fine, I'll wait. . . . That's right. He's one of mine—and very close!" He put down the receiver and turned to Jean Marie. "Rolf Levandow, Russian-Jewish, best makeup man in the world. He'll be here in half-an-hour with his box of tricks. When he's finished, your own mother wouldn't know you without a voice-print."

"You amaze me, Adrian Hennessy."

"I am what you see. I give what I'm paid for: total service! That's the chalk line. Nobody steps over it unless I ask them—even you, Jeannot le Bouffon!"

"Please!" Jean Marie held up his hands in protest. "I wasn't asking to hear your confession!"

"You've heard it, anyway." Adrian Hennessy was suddenly strange and far-away. "I know how to arrange any service you want, from a lipstick promotion to a liquidation. I walk some pretty wavy lines; but I don't cross up my clients, and nobody owns enough of me so that I can't toss the contract back on the desk and walk out. . . . But let's talk about you for a moment. A couple of months ago you were one of the high men, spiritual leader of half a billion people, absolute monarch of the smallest but most important enclave in the world. That's an enormous power base. With it, you had a whole, worldwide organization of clergy, monks, nuns and parochial laity. Yet you surrendered it all! . . . Now look at you! You can't go for a stroll except in disguise. You're the houseguest of a lady lion-hunter. You're depending on her to buy you print-space and air-time that once you could have had for free. I have to ask myself what sense this makes to you."

Jean Marie considered the question for a moment and then shook his head.

"Let's not play dialectic games, Mr. Hennessy. An eagle can talk sense with a canary but a canary with a goldfish, never! They live by diverse modes in diverse elements. I have had an experience which has changed me completely —for better or worse is not the question. It is simply that I am different."

"How? In what particulars?" Hennessy, cold-eyed, pressed the question. "I need to know the man I'm serving."

"I can tell you only by simile," said Jean Marie quietly. "Do you remember the gospel story of Jesus raising his friend Lazarus from the dead?"

"I remember it."

"Think about the details: the sisters in grief, in fear of what might be revealed when the tomb was opened. '*Iam foetet*,' they said. 'Already he stinks!' Then the tomb opened. Jesus called. Lazarus stepped out, still wrapped in the cerecloths. Have you ever thought how he must have felt, as he stood blinking in the sunlight, looking anew on a world from which he had taken his last leave? . . . After what happened to me in the garden at Monte Cassino, I was like Lazarus. Nothing could ever be the same as it was before."

"I think I understand," said Hennessy dubiously, "but even if you've changed, the world hasn't. Never forget that!"

"Why do you call Roberta Saracini a lion-hunter?"

"Because I'm trying to be polite." Hennessy was suddenly snappish. "In my country they use a dirtier word for women who chase male celebrities. Don't mistake me! She's a good client and you need her! But part of me is an old-fashioned Irishman and I hate to see a priest tied to a woman's apron strings."

"You have bad manners and a dirty mouth!" Jean Marie was angry and harsh. "I presume you said all this to Madame Saracini before you began taking her money?"

"I did." Hennessy was unmoved. "Because it's my job to point out the land mines before you both step on them. Since her father was put away, Roberta's got religion. She works at it, as she works at everything else. It helps her and I'm glad. But before that—and I know!—cocktails with Roberta meant break-fast in bed as well. . . . So you, Monseigneur, can very easily get caught in the slipstream of her past. You're under Grade A surveillance, because the government is looking for nails to put in your coffin. If you think I've got a dirty mouth, wait till you hear the government brand of pornography! . . . Simple example! You ordered flowers for Roberta. A gentleman's gesture to his hostess; no harm in it at all! But how would you feel if someone planted a gossip item: 'What high Catholic dignitary is sending flowers to what lady banker whose daddy once took the Vatican for a reputed fifteen million?' . . . That's only one of the risks."

"I am grateful for your care," said Jean Marie with mild irony. "But I suggest that there is no recourse against malice and evil report."

"Don't patronize me!" Hennessy was suddenly furious. "It happens I do care! I believe what you say! I want it heard! But I don't want my Church shamed in the city square."

"Forgive me!" Jean Marie made a rueful apology. "I warned you. I haven't changed for the better."

"At least you've got fire in your belly," said Hennessy with a sour grin. "Next time I'll choose my words more carefully."

The makeup man arrived—a big, swart, bearded fellow who looked like an Old Testament prophet and was just as eloquent and peremptory. Disguise, he explained at length, was a matter of illusion. Complicated makeup was for the stage or the screen. Very few women knew how to use cosmetics properly, even though they applied them every day. Rolf Levandow would certainly not trust an elderly gentleman of sixty-five to do a successful maquillage. . . . So, let's see! Head this way, head that! A pity to change the hair. It would be a kind of mutilation. Presumably Jean Marie was not entering himself for a concourse of elegance. On the other hand, he could not pass for a workman—not with those thin shoulders and flat belly and soft hands. Well then! A retired professor, a magazine critic, something in the arts! . . . Again the idea was to create a local identity; so that the man behind the bar and the girl at the newspaper kiosk and the waiter in the brasserie would swear that he was familiar and safe. Finally, Jean Marie found himself looking into a mirror at a slightly seedy scholar, who wore a Basque beret, gold pince-nez with a moiré ribbon and a pair of gum-pads that gave him a rabbit-faced look. As the makeup man explained, a literary magazine under the arm would help; an inexpensive cane was optional; and a certain air of parsimony was recommended, like counting out his coins from a little leather purse. Practice would suggest other embellishments. He should try to enjoy it as a game. If he wanted a change for any reason, then it could be arranged. Frequently one found the subject got bored with a single identity. He would leave his card . . .

"Break it up, Rolf!" said Hennessy. "My friend and I have lots of work to do. I'll walk you to the taxi rank."

When he came back Jean Marie was still studying himself in the mirror. Hennessy laughed.

"It works, doesn't it? I told you he was the best. And it would pay you to keep in touch with him—for more reasons than make-up."

"Oh?"

"He's an Israeli agent, a member of Shin Beth. This job is a useful cover. He travels a lot with film people and does regular work for French television. He recognized you instantly. He says the Israelis are well disposed towards you.

They understand prophets in exile! Who knows, you may find him helpful. I should be on my way."

"When will I hear from you?"

"As soon as there's anything to report. You keep working on the letters."

"I will. Could I ask a small service?"

"Sure!"

"Let me walk with you as far as the quai. I have to get used to this new fellow with the pince-nez and the beret!"

It was the simplest of pleasures to stroll along the river, watch the hopeful anglers and the lovers hand in hand and the tourists in the *bateaux mouches* and the sunset splendours drenching the grey pile of Notre Dame. There was a childlike fun, too, in the disguise game. He bought, for a few francs, a battered volume of *Les Trophées* and a cane with a dog's-head handle. Thus protected, as if by a cloak of invisibility, he sauntered along, happy as any literary gentleman who, even if he were pinched by inflation, still got the best out of his autumn years.

It was an agreeable fantasy and it carried him through to the last ceremony of the afternoon, when he settled himself under the awning of a sidewalk café, ordered coffee and a sweet pastry and divided his attention between the passersby and the lapidarian verse of José Maria de Hérédia. He found that the old Parnassian had worn well and that he himself could still be moved by that last poignant moment between Anthony and Cleopatra on the eve of the battle of Actium.

> Et courbé sur elle, l'ardent imperator
> Voyait dans ses yeux clairs étoilés de points d'or,
> Toute une mer immense où fuyaient des galères.

The grave and fateful beauty of the image matched his own mood of elegy. It seemed a blasphemy even to contemplate the ruin of Paris, this so human city, the extinction of all its serene beauties. And yet, come Rubicon Day, the sentence would be irrevocable—and any man who had lived in Rome knew how fragile was the fabric of the greatest empire and how quiet the dead were in their urns and catacombs. Then he heard the voice. It was close and to his left, a hearty American baritone expounding the art of *bouquinage:*

". . . You don't go at it as if you're turning out Grandmother's attic. You decide on one set of prints you'd really like to own. It doesn't matter if they're as rare as hens' teeth. That's just the starting point. It tells the man you're serious, that you've got money to spend and it will pay him to take time and show you what he's hiding under the counter. That's the way I worked in Germany and . . ."

As the monologue rolled on, Jean Marie fished for money in his wallet and turned his head slowly as if to signal a waiter. He remembered the dictum of Rolf Levandow. Disguise was illusion. Even if someone thought he recognized you, he was still put off by the unfamiliar features. You had to capitalize on that, stare him down, snub him if he greeted you.

Alvin Dolman was seated at the next table, deep in talk with a young woman dressed in bright summer cotton. As Jean Marie raised his hand to signal for the check, Dolman looked up. Their eyes met. Jean Marie remembered that he was wearing pince-nez and that, very probably, Dolman could not see his eyes. He turned away slowly; then, as if impatient to be gone, shoved a ten-franc note under the saucer, gathered up his book and cane and edged his way past Dolman's table towards the street. Mercifully Dolman had not paused in his monologue.

". . . Now you have to remember the kind of things that usually turn up on the bookstalls. I met a guy today—the one next to where you were standing—who specializes in ballet designs. That's not my line, but . . ."

. . . But the noonday devil was in Paris and Jean Marie Barette could make some disturbing guesses at his current employment. Ten paces away from the café he let his book fall to the pavement. As he bent to retrieve it, he looked back. Alvin Dolman was still deep in talk with the girl. He seemed to have made some progress. He was now holding her hand. Jean Marie Barette hoped she would be responsive enough to keep him interested—at least until he himself was safe in his own bolt-hole.

There was a message waiting for him. Madame would be late home. He should order whatever he wanted for dinner. He settled for coffee and a chicken sandwich, to be served in his room. Then he bathed, put on pajamas and dressing gown and began work on another letter. Now he was dealing with that most contentious of subjects: the divisions on matters of faith between men and women of goodwill.

> Dear God,
>
> If You're the beginning and the end of it all, why didn't You give us all an equal chance? In a circus, You know, our lives depend on that. If the riggers make a mistake, the trapeze artists die. If the man with the thunderflash doesn't do it right, I lose my eyes.
>
> But, You don't seem to look at things that way. A circus travels, so we get to see how other people live—and I mean good people who love each other and love their children and really deserve a pat on the head from You.
>
> Now, here's the thing I can't understand. You know it all. You made it all. But everyone sees You differently. You've even let Your children kill each other; just because they each have a different description of Your face at the window! . . . Why do we all use different marks to tell us we're Your children? I was sprinkled with water because my parents were Christians. Louis, the lion tamer, had a little piece cut off his penis because he's a Jew. Leila, the black girl who handles the snakes, wears an ammonite around her neck, because this is the magical snake-stone. . . . And yet, when the show is over and we all sit at the supper table, tired and hungry, do You see much difference between us? Do you care? Are you really very upset when Louis, who is getting old and scared, creeps into Leila's bed for a little comfort, and Leila, who is really quite ugly, is glad to have him?
>
> I seem to remember that Your Son enjoyed eating and drinking and chatting with people like us. He liked children. He seemed to understand women. It's a pity nobody bothered to record very much of his talk with

them—a few words with his mother, the rest was mostly with girls who were on the town, one way and another.

What I'm trying to say is that You're shutting down the world without really giving us a chance to overcome the handicaps You've given us. . . . I have to say that. I wouldn't be honest if I let the matter pass. Somewhere up near the North Pole there's an old woman sitting on an ice floe. She's not suffering. She's fading slowly away. Her family have put her there. She's content, because this is the way death has always been arranged for the old. You know she's there. I'm sure You're making it easy—more easy perhaps than for some other poor old dear in a very expensive clinic. But You've never told us very clearly which situation You prefer. I like to believe it's one with the more loving in it!

On the other hand—I have to tell You this—I sat today in a café. Next to me was a man I know to be truly inhabited by a spirit of evil. He's treacherous. He's destructive. He's a murderer. How will You judge him? How will You make the judgment known to all the rest of us? We do have a right to know. I don't have children, but if I ever had any they wouldn't be just playthings, would they? Life itself would confer rights on them—at least according to our small standards. I'd hate to believe that Yours were any lower.

So please—I know I'm pushing hard tonight, but I'm tired and I'm scared of that evil man with the happy voice and the sweet smile—please tell me how and when You're going to hear the case of Creator versus creature—or should it be the other way round? Or perhaps You could call the whole thing off and turn it into a love feast?

That's strange! I've never thought to ask before. Can You, God, change Your mind? If not, why not? And if You can, why didn't You do it before we all got into such a terrible mess? I'm sorry if I sound rude. I don't mean to be . . .

. . . Once again, without warning, he was on the high peak, among the black mountains of the dead planet. Once again he was empty, alone, prey to an unendurable sadness, a shame, as if he alone were the author of all the desolation about him. There was no respite, no appeal, no forgiveness. There would be no rapture, no fiery whirlwind, no exquisite agony of union with the Other. He himself was the dead center of a dead cosmos. He could not weep. He could not rage. He could only know that this was all there was to know: himself anchored to a barren rock in the desert of eternity.

Suddenly he felt a touch on his flesh, a tug at his dangling fingers. He looked down. It was the little girl from the Institute, the little clown of God, with her vacant, trusting smile. His heart melted to her. He snatched her up and held her close. She was his life-spark. He, her last protection against the vacancy of a cold planet.

They could not stay here on the peak. There must be caves to shelter them. He began to walk, stumbling down the dark stony slope. He felt the child's cheek against his own, her warm breath, like a tiny wind, ruffling his hair. As he walked, the well-spring of emotion began to flow again. He was aware of pity and terror and tenderness and a fierce rage against the Other who had dared to desert this tiny helpless creature in a place which was no-place.

Finally he came to the mouth of a cave, within which, most strangely, he could see a tiny light, like a star reflected in the black water of a tarn. He held the child closer and closer, as if to cover her with the armour of his own skin, and strode towards the light. It grew larger and brighter until it dazzled him and he was forced to close his eyes and stand quite still like a blind man in a new place. Then he heard the voice, strong and calm and gentle.

"Open your eyes."

He did so and saw, seated on an outcrop of rock, beside a small fire, a young man of the most extraordinary comeliness. He was naked except for a breech-cloth and sandals. His hair, golden and abundant, was caught back with a linen band. Beside him on the rock was a platter of bread and a cup of water. He held out his arms and said:

"I'll take the child."

"No!" Jean Marie felt a sudden lurch of fear and stepped back against the farther wall. He eased himself down into a sitting position and cradled the child in his arms. The young man stood up and offered the bread and the cup. When Jean Marie refused he began feeding the child morsels of the loaf and tiny sips of liquid. From time to time he stroked her cheek and smoothed the hair away from her eyes. He asked again:

"Please, let me hold her. She will come to no harm."

He took the child and made a little dance with her, until she laughed and fondled his face and kissed him. Then suddenly she was not a mongol anymore, but perfect and beautiful like a princess doll.

The young man held her up to be admired. He smiled at Jean Marie and told him:

"You see! I make all things new!"

"Where are all the rest? The flowers, the animals, the people?"

"Here!"

He held the child up above his head. She stretched out her hands. The walls of the cave dissolved into a prospect of meadows and orchards and streams, silver in the sun. The young man said chidingly:

"You have to understand. The beginning and the end are one. The living and the dying are a single act because life is renewed by death."

"Then why must the dying be so terrible?"

"Man makes his own terrors, not I."

"Who are you?"

"I am who I am."

"I've never understood that."

"You should not try. Does the flower contend with the sun, or the fish with the sea? That's why you're a clown and you break things and I have to put them together again."

"I'm sorry. I know I make a mess. I'll go now."

"Don't you want to kiss your daughter?"

"Please! May I?"

. . . But when he reached out his arms to take the beautiful child, she was not there. The man and the girl and the cave and the magical meadows were all gone. He was back in his own room. Roberta Saracini was standing by the desk with a tray in her hand.

"I saw the light under your door. I thought you'd like some hot chocolate before you went to bed. When I came in you were asleep at your desk."

"I had a big day—one way and another. What time is it?"

"Just after ten."

"Thank you for the chocolate. How was your evening?"

"Most interesting! We've been invited to share in the financing of a new industrial project in Shanghai. The Chinese financial delegation entertained us at the embassy. Ours is a mixed group: British, Swiss, American and, of course, a consortium of bankers from the European Economic Community. The Chinese are very shrewd. They want as wide a spread of investment as possible. They also believe that war is inevitable and they have crash programs for enterprises that can make military materials. . . . Your name came up in the war talk."

"How?"

"Let me see if I can remember exactly. Oh, yes. . . . The Americans were talking about danger periods and trigger incidents that could set off a war—Rubicon Day in fact! They make no secret of the fact that they regard the Chinese as their natural allies. In fact, I'm sure one or two of their delegation were intelligence people. Anyway, a man named Morrow, who used to be Secretary of State but is now with Morgan Guaranty, mentioned your prophecies and the articles about your abdication. He asked the Chinese how accurate they thought you were. One of them—a director of the Bank of China—laughed and said, 'If he is a friend of the Jesuits he is very accurate indeed.' He reminded us that it was the Jesuit Matteo Ricci who first introduced into China the sundial, the astrolabe and the method of extracting square and cube roots from whole numbers and fractions. . . . He was very interested when I told him that I knew you and was, in fact, a trustee of your estate."

Jean Marie mourned silently over the indiscretion. He wanted to say something but he was tired and the milk was already spilt anyway.

Roberta Saracini went on, "Morrow said he would like to see you again. Apparently you had dealings together at the Vatican. I told him you were in touch with me from time to time and I would pass the message."

"My dear Roberta!" He had to speak now and he could not temper the words. "I'm deeply grateful for all your help; but you have just committed a monumental folly. The French want me under surveillance. This afternoon I stood within a pace of the C.I.A. man who tried to kill Mendelius. I still don't know whether he recognized me. Now you, at a diplomatic gathering, announce that you are my trustee and I am—I quote!—in touch with you from time to time. From tomorrow your phone will be tapped and your house watched. . . . I have to move! Tonight! How long will it take to get to the airport?"

"At this hour—forty minutes. But where . . . ?"

"I don't know and it's better you don't either. First thing in the morning get in touch with Hennessy and my brother, Alain. Tell them I'll make contact as soon as I can. I've got to pack."

"But the letters, the whole project . . ."

". . . Depend on me! So I need a safe place and secure communications. Will you drive me to the airport? Taxi calls can be traced."

"At least let me say I'm sorry."

She was near to tears. He took her face in his hands and kissed her lightly on the cheek.

"I know you didn't mean it. I've put you in a dangerous game and you can't be expected to know all the rules. When I'm settled we'll find a safe way to communicate. I still need your help."

"I'll get the car out. Hurry with your packing; the last planes leave at midnight."

On the face of it, a midnight flight to London was a folly of desperation, but if he could arrive without detection he could be safe while he worked on the letters and cast about among old friends for any who might believe in his mission and be prepared to cooperate in it.

He had always admired the British, though he had never wholly understood them. The subtleties of their humour often escaped him. Their snobberies always irritated him. Their dilatory habits in commerce never failed to amaze him. Yet they were tenacious of friendships and fealties. They had a sense of history and a tolerant eye for fools and eccentrics. They could be land-greedy and money-mean and capable of extraordinary social cruelties; yet they supported great charities; they were humane to fugitives; and they counted privacy a right and not a privilege. Give them a cause they understood, put liberties they valued at risk, and they would take to the streets by thousands or walk in solitary dignity to the headsman's block.

On the other hand—and he admitted it with wry humour—as Gregory XVII, he had never been a great success with the British. They had, over the centuries, developed a working relationship with the Italians, whose arts they bought, whose fashions they aped, whose talent for high rhetoric and low-keyed compromise was akin to their own. On the other hand, they looked on the French as a prickly lot, stiff-necked, uppish and politically immoral, who lived too close by for comfort, had an uncomfortable taste for grandeur and a cynical skill in pursuing it.

So, to his singular regret and occasional irritation, Jean Marie had made good friends but exercised small influence in the British Isles. In the end, he had been happy to leave the conduct of the local Church to Matthew Cardinal Hewlett, who, as one of his Curial colleagues put it, "is probably the least risky man for the job. He has zeal without fire, intelligence without talent, never makes an argument if he can avoid one, and has no redeeming vices at all." Hewlett had never joined The Friends of Silence; but at the fateful consistory he had cast his vote for abdication and justified it with a characteristic quip. "If our Pontiff is a madman we're well rid of him. If he's a saint we won't lose him. I see no problem at all. The sooner he's out, the better!"

All in all, Matthew Cardinal Hewlett was not quite the man to call at two in the morning and ask for bed and breakfast. So, with the help of a taxi driver, Jean Marie Barette found lodging in a reasonable hotel in Knightsbridge and slept dreamlessly until noon.

——— XII ———

THERE were peacocks on the lawn and swans on the lake and the gold of early autumn in the woodlands as Jean Marie Barette walked in the manor garden with a man in whom he had confided much during his papacy, and who now was to be his first publisher in the English language: Waldo Pearson, old-time Catholic, onetime Foreign Secretary in the Conservative Cabinet, now chairman of the Greenwood Press.

Adrian Hennessy was there as well, with his folio of illustrations, recordings of the *Letters* in French and English, and fully orchestrated tapes of the theme for Johnny the Clown, composed by Florent de Basil. He had also brought a certified document from the Banco Ambrogiano all' Estero, guaranteeing an initial half-million sterling, to be spent on the promotion and exploitation of *Last Letters from a Small Planet.* Jean Marie ventured the wry comment that perhaps the money was more eloquent than the author. Waldo Pearson uttered a frosty disclaimer:

". . . We are very close to the time when money will have no meaning anymore. In a nuclear conflict, we stand to lose two-thirds of the population of these islands. No government can come to terms with that catastrophe—no Church either, as you have found! So they choose, as a matter of policy, to ignore it. In the *Letters,* you have found a way to discuss the terror that confronts us without creating panic or contention. You will be judged as a prophet and not as a banker."

"And glad I am to hear you say it, Waldo!" Hennessy put on his most syrupy brogue. "Because it's me that represents the bankers and devil a dollar will you get until you've demonstrated the quality of your own publishing and promotion!"

"I've told you before." Pearson was determined to have all his reservations on the record. "We're confident of an exceptional distribution. The advance we're paying reflects that. The newspaper serialization will help, too—and, of course, the advertising funds you're providing. But you're still asking me to fight with one hand behind my back! No television, no press interviews, no revelation at all of the author's identity! I see no sense in that."

Before Hennessy had time to answer, Jean Marie stepped into the argument.

"Please! There are good reasons. If my identity is known, I may seem to put myself in conflict with the present Pontiff. I do not want that. More: I am writing in response to what I believe to be divine command. I have to rest on that act of faith and be content that the tree be recognized by its fruits. Finally, the only thing I can control is the integrity of the published text. I cannot put myself at the mercy of interviewers who may distort my message by false, biased or incompetent report."

"In short, Waldo"—Hennessy grinned like a happy leprechaun—"no way! No how!"

Waldo Pearson shrugged. "Well, it was worth a try! When may we expect the finished manuscript?"

"In two weeks."

"Good! Is the author satisfied with the English translations?"

"I am, yes. They are both fluent and accurate. . . . May we change the subject a moment? There is something else on which I should like your advice."

"Please!"

"There are several people in England whom I received while I was in office. Could you arrange for me to meet them again—and would you permit me to have the meetings here in your house?" Before Pearson had time to answer, he went on to explain. "I live in a modest hotel under an assumed name. I cannot invite known personages to such a place; but I still believe I can be of service in the crisis that faces us all. For example, Sergei Petrov has asked me to mediate in the matter of the grain embargo. However, I have no means of knowing whether I am acceptable to any other parties. You have held cabinet rank, Mr. Pearson; how would you react to me?"

"Difficult to say." Pearson, the politician, was a more prickly animal than Pearson the publisher. He began to reason aloud. "Let's take it by debit and credit. You're a defeated leader, a Roman Catholic cleric, a Frenchman, a self-styled prophet—all handicaps for a political negotiator in today's market!"

Jean Marie laughed, but made no comment. Pearson went on with his accounting.

"On the credit side, what do we have? You're a practiced diplomat. You can have no personal ambitions; your good behaviour after the abdication did not pass unnoticed! You're a free agent. The memorial which Rainer and Mendelius wrote about you took some of the mist out of your mysticism." He chuckled over his own schoolboy pun. "So, let's sum it up. If I were Foreign Secretary I should most certainly receive you. If you told me the Russians had invited you to mediate a case with me, I'd be very skeptical. I'd reason like this. You are, prima facie, an honest broker. Conversely or obversely, I'd wonder whether the Russians had turned you, or why they hadn't picked someone with more muscle in the market. Then I'd argue that if they were desperate enough to use an outsider like you, we ought to be able to drive a hard bargain. So, all in all—yes! I'd receive you with interest—and bypass you as soon as possible!"

"That makes good sense," said Jean Marie. "Now back to my first question. Would you be willing to arrange a few meetings for me—here in your house?"

"Of course! You tell me whom you want and I'll invite them down. Please remember that you yourself are welcome here at any time."

"There's something else to remember." Hennessy was uneasy. "If you don't want to reveal yourself as the author of *Last Letters,* how are you going to explain your presence in the house of a prominent British publisher?"

"We explain nothing," Pearson cut in briskly. "I let drop the information that we're discussing a possible book . . . I'd certainly like to raise the question of an autobiography."

"I'm afraid," said Jean Marie. "that's a project for which I should have neither the taste nor the time."

"There are others that may interest you. I've been trying for years to find someone who can do me a clear and unrhetorical book on the nature of religious experience. We're seeing a phenomenon in England which deserves more notice than it's getting. While the traditional churches are losing clergy and congregations at an alarming rate, the cults are flourishing. . . . Let me show you something." He walked them round the corner of the house to where the woodland opened onto a vista of hill pasture, at the end of which, perched on a rounded knoll, was a large mansion in the Palladian style. Pearson's commentary was spirited but unhappy.

". . . That place for instance! It used to belong to a good friend of mine. Now, it's the headquarters of a group who call themselves the Family of the Holy Ones. They're a cult like the Moonies, the Soka Gakkai, the Hare Krishna. They proselytize actively. They have a very strong conditioning regimen, based on excessive labour and constant surveillance of the neophyte. Lots of young people are attracted to them. They're very rich. . . . Like some of the other groups they are now arming themselves, stockpiling food, medicines and weapons against Armageddon Day. If they survive, they and others like them could be the warring barons of the post-nuclear age. . . . That's what the Catholic hierarchy were afraid of when you wanted to publish your encyclical. Matt Hewlett brought back a copy from Rome. He came down especially to talk to me about it. He stood just where you're standing now and said, 'That's where Gregory the Seventeenth is going to lead us, whether he understands it or not. Cromwellian Christianity, pikes, muskets and all!' "

"And did you believe him?" asked Jean Marie quietly.

"At the time, yes."

"What has happened to change your mind?"

"Several things. Having been in politics and seen how hard it is to make democracy work, I've often been tempted towards dictatorships of one kind or another. As a publisher I've seen how people can be conditioned to habits and points of view. To my regret I've often been seduced into manipulative exercises in politics and commerce. . . . Then Hennessy brought me your first letters. There's a passage in the fourth one which I learned by heart . . . 'When a man becomes a clown he makes a free gift of himself to the audience. To endow them with the saving grace of laughter, he submits to be mocked, drenched, clouted, crossed in love. Your Son made the same submission when He was crowned as a mock king, and the troops spat wine and water in His face. . . . My hope is that when He comes again, He will still be human enough to shed a clown's gentle tears over the broken toys—that once were women and children.' "

Pearson broke off as if embarrassed and stood a long time staring across the green folds of the land towards the Palladian mansion. Finally he admitted with odd emotion:

"I suppose you could say that was the moment of my conversion. I've always been a communicating Christian—but only because I kept my mind resolutely shut against some of the more horrifying consequences of belief: like a universe where the animals devour each other to live, and torturers are public servants, and the best offer to agonized mankind is 'Take up your cross!' . . . But somehow your words managed to release me from that credal despair and set me wondering again, looking with new eyes at an upside-down world!"

Adrian Hennessy said nothing. He reached for a handkerchief and began to polish his spectacles vigorously.

Jean Marie Barette said with grave gentleness, "I know what you feel; but it's a very fragile joy. Don't lean on it too hard; otherwise it may snap under your weight."

Pearson gave him a swift, probing look. "You surprise me! I should have thought you'd want to share the joy, however fragile."

Jean Marie held up a hand in deprecation. "Please don't misunderstand me! I am truly happy when anyone is granted the kind of insight that gives new meaning to his profession of faith. I was simply warning you, out of my own experience, that the comfort you now feel may not last. Faith is not a matter of logic; and the moment of intuition does not always repeat itself. One has to expect long periods of darkness and, often, a destructive confusion!"

Waldo Pearson was silent for a moment; then, with surprising bluntness, he said to Hennessy, "Adrian, I want to talk privately with our friend. Why don't you leave us for a while?"

"No problem!" Hennessy seemed unperturbed. "I'll take the car and drive down to the Nag's Head for a drink with the locals! Talk anything you like except contracts. That's my business!"

Waldo Pearson led Jean Marie down to the edge of the lake, where a pair of white swans floated serenely in and out of the reedbeds. He explained himself haltingly:

"We're at the beginning of—well—a fairly intimate relationship. Author and publisher can never live satisfactorily at arm's length—at least not an author like you and a publisher like me. Just now I felt—rightly or wrongly—that something important was being left unsaid between us. . . . It seemed strange that you felt the need to utter a warning about my—my spiritual health."

"I was equally concerned with my own," said Jean Marie. "It would not take much at this moment to convince me that I am suffering from a monstrous delusion."

"I find that hard to believe. You've been so adamant in your convictions. You've given up so much. You write with such deep emotion."

"Nevertheless, it is true." Jean Marie plucked a reed from the lakeside and began to shred it restlessly as he talked. "I have been in England three weeks now. I live in a comfortable hotel that looks out on an old-fashioned square, with a garden in the middle where children play and young mothers bring their babies. I work in the morning. In the afternoon, I walk. In the evening I read and pray and go to bed early. I am very free, very relaxed. I have even made friends. There is an elderly Jewish gentleman who brings his grandson to play ball in the garden. He is a fine scholar in the Rabbinical tradition. When he found that I knew Hebrew he was ready to dance with joy. Last Friday I went to a Sabbath supper in his house. Then there is the concierge, who is Italian and talkative and always ready for a little gossip. . . . So you see, my life is pleasant and I am almost converted to this extraordinary equanimity of the British . . . some of whom really do believe that God is an Englishman of impeccable taste who never lets any mess get quite out of hand. . . . But, suddenly, I have realized that this is a quite insidious temptation. I can be silenced, not by enemies, not by authority—but by my own comfortable indifference! I can believe that just because I have written a few pages which will be widely published, I have given full witness and earned the right to dream out the rest of time until Judgment Day. That's one side of the medal. The other is equally sinister, though in a different way. As I write the *Last Letters from a Small Planet*, I am expressing myself, my relationships with God and the human family. I am not teaching a body of doctrine. I am not proposing a theological argument. I am not a pastor concerned for the well-being of his flock. I am out of office, you see; I am half-laicized; I even celebrate the Eucharist for myself alone; which really makes little sense of the sacramental act . . . Now, without warning, a pit opens under my feet. Even as I wrote the lines that so moved you I was thinking: Is this true? Is that what I really believe? . . . The end of civilization I do see as possible and proximate. But the Parousia, the Second Coming, that will make all things new? I do not know how to come to terms with the concept of a God-man, risen and glorified, presiding in eternal calm over the agonizing dissolution of our earthly dwelling place. Whenever, now, I try to reason about it, I smell blood and see demon faces from the frescoes of ancient temples. I wish, sometimes, I could forget it all and talk to my old rabbi while we watch the children play. . . ."

"And yet," said Waldo Pearson quietly, "that isn't what you write. What appears on the page is the talk of a confident child with a loving father."

"So which am I?" asked Jean Marie with an odd half-humorous pathos. "The equable Englishman, doubting Thomas, the deluded prophet, or the clown who is himself a child at heart? . . . Or, perhaps, I am none of these, but something quite different."

"What, for instance?"

Jean Marie crumpled the last shreds of the reed in his fist, tossed them into the water and watched them bobbing in the wake of the regal swans. It was a long moment before he answered the question.

"I set out to make myself a thinking reed, pliant to the wind of the Spirit; but a reed is also a hollow tube through which other men may pipe a music alien to me."

Waldo Pearson took his arm and guided him away from the lake towards an old-fashioned hothouse set against the weathered brick wall of the garden.

"Our grapes are ripe. I'm very proud of them. I'd like you to try a bunch."

"Do you make your own wine?"

"No. These are table grapes." As casually as he had slid off the subject Pearson came back to it again. "It seems to me what you are trying to explain are the symptoms of an identity crisis. I understand that. I've been through it. After twelve years in the House, five of them in cabinet, I felt lost, disoriented, empty—and, I suppose, open to manipulation. It's a little frightening; but I didn't feel, as you seem to do, that it was a situation tainted with evil."

"Did I say that?" Jean Marie swung round to face him. He was puzzled and concerned. Pearson, however, did not retreat.

"Not in so many words; but you seemed to imply it. You said 'a music alien to me.'"

"You're right, I did. That's the core of the matter. All apocalyptic literature refers to false prophets deceiving the elect. Can't you feel the horror of the idea? . . . What if I were one of them?"

"I don't believe it for an instant," said Waldo Pearson firmly. "Otherwise I would not publish your book."

"I don't believe it either," said Jean Marie. "But I do feel myself to be a battleground, still in dispute. I am drawn to a safe indifference. I am tempted to lose all faith in a loving deity. I am afraid that my new and very fragile identity may suddenly explode into fragments."

"I wonder," said Waldo Pearson as he opened the glass door of the orangery. "I wonder if your so rigid obedience isn't a mistake. Contention is healthy and necessary—even in the Church—and self-imposed silence can be very demoralizing. I found that in Cabinet. You had to speak up or be killed."

"There's a difference." Jean Marie relaxed into good humour again. "You didn't have to deal with God in the Cabinet room."

"The hell we didn't!" said Waldo Pearson. "He was sitting right there in the P.M.'s chair."

They both laughed. Pearson snipped a bunch of big black grapes, divided it and offered a handful to Jean Marie, who tasted them and nodded approval.

"I've got a proposal to make to you." Pearson was adept at swift changes of subject. "You need a forum and some access to the decision-makers in this country. I need a substitute speaker for dinner at the Carlton Club. I did have the Prime Minister but he has a summit meeting in Washington. I need someone with weight and interest. It's three weeks from now. You'll probably be finished the *Letters*. It's a closed function. Everything said is off the record—and the rules have never been broken. . . . The members all belong to what you call in France *le Pouvoir*—though they're rather less drastic in its exercise. Please? You'd do me a favour; and you can certainly propagate the message."

"What should I talk about?"

"Your abdication. The reasons and the aftermath. I want to see my colleagues' faces when you tell them that God spoke to you! I'm not joking. They all invoke Him. But you're the only man I know who claims a private revelation and has put his head on the block to give witness to it. They'll be expecting some wild-eyed zealot! Tell me you'll do it!"

"Very well. If I'm to speak in English I'll need to write a text. Will you check it for me?"

"Of course! I can't tell you how happy I am. . . . And are we agreed, the reason for your presence is that we are discussing plans for a book, possibly several books?"

"Agreed."

"Splendid! Now let me tell you about these grapes. The vine was struck from cuttings taken from the Great Vine at Hampton Court. . . ."

It was all so especially British and understated that Jean Marie missed the significance of the invitation. Because he was more interested in the folklore of Waldo Pearson's estate, he forgot to tell Adrian Hennessy about the Carlton Club until they were halfway back to London. Hennessy was so startled that he almost slewed the car off the road.

"My God! The innocence of the man! Don't you understand what's happened to you?"

"I've been invited to speak at dinner in a gentlemen's club," said Jean Marie amiably. "I assure you I'll cope with the occasion. It's not nearly so formidable as a public audience in Saint Peter's or a papal visit to Washington!"

"But it can be a hell of a lot more important for you," said Hennessy irritably. "Pearson's a shrewd old fox. He invites you to the Carlton Club, the stronghold of Conservative politics. He sets you as substitute speaker for the Prime Minister at one of the three most important political dinners of the year. That's as close as you'll ever get to canonization by the English. If you make a good speech—and if you don't fall down drunk or toss chicken bones at the chairman—you're made! You can lift a telephone and talk to anyone anytime in Whitehall or Westminster—and you won't be nearly as vulnerable as you are now! The word will be around the chanceries that in Britain you're a protected species. That will have an immediate effect in France; because whatever happens in the Carlton Club is studied very carefully on the other side of the Channel. Petrov's going to hear about it, too; and the Americans. The members of the Carlton bring the guests they want to educate."

"Hennessy, my friend, if ever I am re-elected, you'll be my Cardinal Camerlengo!"

"Not unless you change the rules on celibacy! I'd have done well in the Renaissance; but not in this day and age! . . . Which reminds me—What are you going to wear to the Carlton Club dinner?"

The question took Jean Marie by surprise.

"What am I going to wear?"

"Precisely. All the other gentlemen will wear dinner jackets and black ties. How are you going to present yourself—as a cleric or a layman? If you go as a cleric, will you wear any sign of rank? A red stock, a pectoral cross? If you go as a layman, you certainly can't go in hand-me-downs from a rental company. I see you laughing, Monseigneur; but the question's important. French protocol is clear and trenchant: tictac and you know who's who in the pecking order! But the English—God bless their cotton socks!—do it differently. You can be elegant and despised, shabby and admired, eccentric and respected. If you're a genius you can even wear last year's soup on your lapels! They'll be watching you like a hawk to see how you perform in costume drama!" He swung out to overtake a juggernaut trailer. "The fate of nations may hang on the cut of your *smoking.*"

"Then let's give it the attention it deserves," said Jean Marie Barette cheerfully. "Can you find me a good Italian tailor? I need someone with a sense of theatre."

"The best," said Hennessy. "Angelo Vittucci. He can make a fat Bacchus look like Mercury in tights! I'll take you to see him tomorrow. You know, Monseigneur . . ." He pulled the car onto the motorway and pushed down hard on the accelerator. "I'm beginning to get very fond of you! For a man of God you've got a good worldly sense of humour!"

"You know what Pascal said: *'Diseur de bons mots—mauvais caractère!'* "

"Why?" asked Hennessy with enormous gravity. "Why do bad characters make good company?"

"We're the mustard on the meat!" said Jean Marie with a grin. "It would be a dull world if nothing needed mending and nobody needed saving! We'd both be out of a job!"

"If you'll pardon the expression"—Hennessy with a clear road ahead of him was prepared to enjoy himself—"you're the one who's out of a job! I'm trying to get you gainfully employed. . . . Now sit back and listen to this song again. I really believe it could be a hit!" He slipped a cassette into the tape deck and a moment later they were hearing Florent de Basil's theme song "Johnny the Clown." The tape was designed to demonstrate several different treatments of the song. It stood up solidly under all of them. The words were simple, the rhythm catchy; but the melody had an odd plangent quality that tugged at the heartstrings.

> "Big boots, floppy clothes,
> Painted face, button nose,
> That's Johnny the Clown.
>
> "Johnny, Johnny, bounced and humbled,
> Johnny, Johnny, trounced and tumbled,
> Johnny kicked and Johnny clouted,
> Johnny chased and Johnny routed,
> Who says thanks for all the laughter,
> Gives you hugs and kisses after?
> Johnny, are you lonely too?
>
> "Comic smile, goggle eyes,
> Who knows if he laughs or cries?
> Just Johnny—Johnny the Clown!"

When the song ended, Hennessy switched off the tape and asked, "Well, how does it sound this time?"

"Still charming," said Jean Marie. "Haunting, too. How do you propose to use it?"

"We're discussing a contract now with one of the biggest recording companies. They'll do a special production with one of their singing stars and launch it just before the book is published. Then, if my guess is right, the song will be picked up by other singers and should go climbing up the charts. It will provide an immediate audio link with the visual publicity on the book."

"Our young friend Florent has a very attractive talent; perhaps instead of my speaking at the Carlton Club, we should send him to sing there."

"First lesson in show business," Hennessy admonished him. "Never pass up a good booking. You may not get asked again!"

Two days later, alerted by telephone to the change in Jean Marie's circumstances, Brother Alain arrived in London. As usual he was full of irrelevant solicitudes. Was not Jean's hotel a shade too modest? Should he not entertain some of the old Catholic nobility, like the Howards of Arundel and Norfolk? If it could be arranged for the French ambassador to be invited to the Carlton Club, the climate in Paris would change immediately.

Jean Marie listened patiently and agreed to take these momentous matters under advisement. He was grieved to hear that Odette had been stricken with the grippe, delighted that one of his nieces would soon announce her engagement and that the other had taken up with a young man of excellent prospects who worked in the Ministry of Defense. It was not until they were halfway through dinner at Sophie's—a small retreat in a cul-de-sac off Sloane Street—that Alain began to talk freely about his personal concerns.

". . . I tell you, Jean, the money markets have gone mad. There is a mountain of gold in Swiss vaults and the price has gone through the roof. We are covering commodity deals all round the globe—base metals, rare metals, mineral oils, vegetable oils, beet sugar, cane sugar, timber and coking coal. . . . There aren't enough ships to carry the stuff; so we're making loans on bottoms that should have rusted through years ago and the insurance companies are charging mad money to insure the vessels and the cargoes. Even so, how do you make the payments with currencies swinging ten percent in a day? . . . God should not hear the words I say, Jean; but we need a war, just to halt the nonsense."

"Never fear, little brother!" Jean Marie was in a winter of sadness. "We're going to have one! Paris will be a priority target. Have you thought what you're going to do about Odette and the girls?"

Alain was shocked by the question. "Nothing! We conduct our normal lives."

"Bravo!" said Jean Marie. "I'm sure you'll end with pure hearts and blank minds, still believing the blast that hit you was hot air from a hair dryer. Get out of Paris, for pity's sake, even if you have to rent a hut in the Haute Savoie!"

Alain was a picture of dignity affronted. "We can't all join the panic of the Gadarene swine!"

Once again, Jean Marie had to reproach himself for the old sibling rivalry. "I know! I know! But I love you, little brother, and I'm concerned for you and your family."

"Then you must try to understand where our concerns lie. Odette and I have had our bad years. At one stage we were seriously thinking of breaking up."

"I didn't know that."

"I took care you didn't! Somehow we both managed to hold on. We're solid now. The girls are older and they've paired off with decent fellows. That's a satisfaction, if not a triumph. So far as Odette and I are concerned, there isn't too much to interest us in a refugee life in the mountains! We'd rather enjoy what we have and take our chances with the rest of Paris."

Jean Marie shrugged agreement. "It makes sense. I should not try to pre-scribe anyone else's life."

"I think you ought to take an interest in Roberta's." He said it in so flat and peremptory a fashion that Jean Marie was startled.

"What sort of interest?"

"Compassion, for a start. Her father died three days ago in prison."

"I didn't know. Why didn't someone tell me?"

"I didn't know myself until a couple of hours before I left Paris. I didn't want to throw it at you the moment I arrived. The terrible part is that he was murdered, stabbed by another inmate. The general belief is that the killing was organized from outside, probably by accomplices in the bank fraud."

"Dear God! . . . How is she taking it?"

"According to her assistant, very badly. She'd built everything on the fact that she was paying off her father's debts and giving him a chance of an honourable life later. I think you should call her and, if you can, persuade her to come to London for a few days."

"I hardly think that's appropriate!"

"To hell with appropriate!" Alain was angry. "You owe it to her! She took you into her house. She's financing your project with her own money. She adores the ground you walk on! . . . If you can't pick her off the floor, dry her tears and play Dutch uncle for a few days, then frankly, brother Jean, you're a fraud! I've heard you say a hundred times, charity isn't collective. It's thou and I . . . one to one! And if you're worried about some kind of sex scandal at sixty-five, then all I can say is you're more fortunate than I am!"

Jean Marie gaped at him for a moment in utter disbelief. Then, without a word, he got up and walked across to the cashier's desk. He laid a ten-pound note on the counter and asked if he might make an urgent call to Paris. The girl handed him the phone. He tapped out Roberta's number. A few moments later her manservant answered. He regretted most deeply that Madame was indisposed and was accepting no calls.

"Please!" Jean Marie pleaded with him. "This is Monsieur Grégoire. I am calling from London. Will you beg her to speak with me?"

There was a long, ominous silence and finally Roberta Saracini came on the line. Her greeting was pale and distant. He told her:

"Alain is with me. He has just told me the news of your father. . . . I imagine your line may be tapped. I don't care. I know how you must be feeling. I want you to come over to London. . . . Immediately! Tonight if you can make it. I'll book you a room at my hotel. . . . Yes, the same address Hennessy gave you. . . . No, I do not agree! This is no time to be alone; and with me at least you don't have to spell the words. . . . Good! I'll wait up for you! . . . *A tout à l'heure!*"

He put down the phone, then called his own hotel to reserve a room. The cashier gave him his change. He walked back to the table and answered Alain's unspoken question.

"She's coming over tonight. I've booked her into my hotel."

"Good!" said Alain brusquely. "And don't waste too much time over the obsequies! Show her the town. She loves pictures. There seems to be some good theatre. . . ."

"Why not let me plan my own tour, little brother?"

Alain Barette seemed suddenly to have turned into a wit. He raised his glass in an ironic salute. "Well, you're not really used to going about unchaperoned, are you?"

Jean Marie burst out laughing. "You and I have a lot to learn about each other!"

"And not much time to do it." Alain was moody again. "There's something else. Petrov came to see me. He wants a talk with you. I told him you were out of the country and any meeting would have to be outside the frontiers. I offered to carry a message. This is what he told me. The project for your visit to Moscow is under consideration at the highest level. So far, reactions are favourable. Once a decision is made he will contact me and I will pass the message to you."

"How does he look?"

"Ragged! He's under enormous strain."

"I wonder how long he can hold up," said Jean Marie thoughtfully. "When you get back, arrange another face-to-face meeting with him. Tell him of my engagement to speak at the Carlton Club. Explain that it may give me an opportunity to explore the situation on the grain embargo with people in positions of influence. At least they will tell me whether it is possible to reopen a dialogue. . . . How much success has Petrov had with Duhamel?"

"He thinks it may be possible for Duhamel to divert a Canadian shipment of about a quarter of a million bushels of hard wheat, originally intended for France That's a drop in the bucket and the ship is still in mid-Atlantic. So, who knows if it's just a delaying tactic. Duhamel is a champion at that game."

"Have you spoken with Duhamel?"

"Briefly, to let him know I was coming to visit you. He sent round a note which he asked me to put into your hands."

He handed an envelope across the table. Jean Marie opened it. The message was written in Duhamel's impatient script.

My friend,

Each day we come closer to the Rubicon. Our plans for the day of the crossing are unchanged, even though Paulette's remission continues and we are able to enjoy more together. We are grateful beyond words for this privilege. We cannot, however, accept it as a bribe for an act of submission which we are not yet prepared to make.

You are still listed for Grade A surveillance in France. The Americans have also become interested in you. Our people have had requests for information from a C.I.A. operator named Alvin Dolman. He left last week for the United Kingdom. His cover is that of personal assistant to former Secretary of State Morrow, who now works for Morgan Guaranty.

I asked a friend of mine in British intelligence to run a check on Dolman, as I thought he might be a double. We know he isn't; but it helps to muddy the waters.

Paulette sends her love. Take care,

Pierre

Jean Marie folded the note and shoved it in his breast pocket. Alain watched him with somber, brooding eyes.

"Bad news?"

"I'm afraid so. The man who tried to kill Mendelius is in London. He's a C.I.A. man called Dolman. They have planted him with Morrow of Morgan Guaranty."

"I shall call Morgan Guaranty and tell them about it." He announced it so pompously that it sounded like a line of bad comedy. Jean Marie noted, with some surprise, that brother Alain was getting drunk. He said with a laugh, "Truly, little brother, I don't recommend it."

Alain's sensibilities were wounded. "I don't want to find myself sitting next to a killer at a bankers' conference."

"I wonder how often you've done it, unaware."

"*Touché.*" Alain acknowledged the point with a salute and then signalled the waiter for more wine. He asked, "And what are you going to do about the Dolman fellow, Jean?"

"Tell Hennessy and Waldo Pearson—then forget it."

"Hoping that one or the other will provide you with some protection—or remove Dolman from the scene."

"In some fashion, yes."

"So, when he is found dead in his apartment or run down by an automobile, how much guilt will you carry? Or will you turn away like Pilate and wash your hands?"

"You're playing rough games tonight."

"I'm trying to see what you're made of—after all, we haven't spent much time together these last thirty years." Again there was a surprise for Jean Marie. Brother Alain could be morose and maudlin in his cups. "You've always been the high one—parish priest, bishop, Cardinal, Pope! Even now, people defer to you because of what you used to be. I see it all the time in my business. Prince Cul de Lapin, who's never done a day's work in his life, gets better treatment than a successful tradesman with half a million francs in his account." He was having a little difficulty now, getting the words out. "What I mean is, it's like ancestor worship! Great-grandpa is the wise one, he's dead! You're not dead; but—God!—you do pronounce on a lot of things you don't really understand."

"I'm going to pronounce on you, brother mine! *T'es soûl comme une grive!* You're drunk as a thrush. I'm taking you back to the hotel."

Alain was near toppling as Jean Marie paid the check and hurried him outside. They walked two blocks before Alain was able at last to get his feet in rhythm. Back at the hotel, Jean Marie helped him to his room, undressed him down to his underthings, rolled him onto the bed and covered him with the counterpane. Alain submitted to the whole performance without a word; but, as Jean Marie was about to let himself out, he opened his eyes and announced, apropos of nothing at all:

"I am drunk; therefore I am. The only time I can prove it is when I'm away from Odette. Don't you find that curious, Jean?"

"Much too curious to debate at midnight. Go to sleep. We'll talk in the morning."

"Just one thing . . ."

"What?"

"You've got to understand Roberta's problem."

"I do."

"You don't. She had to believe her father was some kind of saint, doing penance for other people's sins. Fact is, he was a real bastard. He never had a thought for anybody but himself. He ruined a lot of people, Jean. Don't let him ruin her from the other side of the grave."

"I won't. Good night, little brother. You're going to have a beautiful hangover in the morning."

He tiptoed out and went downstairs to wait for Roberta Saracini.

Her appearance shocked him. Her skin was dry and opaque. Her eyes were red, her features pinched tight over the bone structure. Her movements were jerky, her speech hurried and voluble as if silence were a trap to be avoided at all costs.

He had reserved a small suite for her on the same floor as his own. He ordered coffee for two and waited in the salon while she freshened herself after the journey. She came back on a new floodtide of talk.

". . . You were right, of course. It's crazy to stay shut up in that big house! It's amazing the number of people who take those late-night flights. Where's Alain? How long is he staying? He's worried as we all are about the fluctuation in the currency market. I suppose he's told you that. . . ."

"He told me," said Jean Marie gravely, "that you were in deep distress. I see that you are. I want to help. Will you let me, please?"

"My father's dead—murdered! You can't change that. Nobody can. I have to get used to the idea, that's all!"

She said it defiantly, as if daring him to pity her. She was tight as a fiddle string, ready to snap under the first touch of the bow. Jean Marie poured coffee and passed her a cup. He talked on, gentling her down from the high pitch of near-hysteria.

"I was so grateful when you agreed to come. It told me you were prepared to trust me. It gave me the opportunity to say my thanks for what you are doing, also to share with you some exciting things: the last stages of the *Letters,* the speech I'm to make at the Carlton Club, and new friends I've made in London. . . . I want to go to the Tate and the Royal Academy and the Tower of London, and Cardinal Wolsey's palace at Hampton Court and oh, so many other places. We'll do it together. . . ."

She gave him an odd, wary look.

"You talk as if I were a little girl. I'm not. I'm a grown woman, whose father was stabbed in a jail corridor. That makes me bad company for man or beast."

"You're hurt and lonely," said Jean Marie firmly. "I have no practice with women; so I'm probably going about this all the wrong way. I'm not trying to pat you on the head like a bishop or give you a papal blessing—which I'm not entitled to do anyway. I'm offering you an arm to hold when you cross the street and a shoulder to cry on when you feel like it."

"I haven't shed a tear since I heard the news," said Roberta Saracini. "Does that make me an unnatural daughter?"

"No, it does not."

"But I'm glad he's dead! I hope he's burning in hell!"

"Because you've already judged him," said Jean Marie with crisp authority. "And you have no right to do that! As for burning in hell, that's always bothered me, like a pebble in my shoe. Sometimes in the press I'd read about parents maltreating little children, breaking their bones, burning them on hot stoves, for some naughtiness, real or imagined. I've never been able to imagine God our Father, or His so-human Son, damning his children to burn in eternal fire. If your father were here now for judgment, and his fate were in your hands, what would you decide for him, forever and a day?"

Roberta Saracini said nothing. She sat, tight-lipped, eyes downcast, clasping her hands together to stop their trembling. Jean Marie pressed her.

"Think of the worst crimes that have ever been committed—the massacres of the Holocaust, the genocide in Kampuchea and Brazil. . . . Can they ever be expiated, even by an infinity of similar terrors? They cannot. The prisons of this world and the next could not accommodate the malefactors. I believe— and I have been shown only the faintest glimmer of what is to be—that the final Coming and the final Judgment itself must be acts of love. If they are not, then we inhabit a chaos created by a mad spirit, and the sooner we are released from it into nothingness, the better."

Still she did not answer. He went and sat beside her on the floor. He took her hand and held it firmly in his palm and said, "You haven't been sleeping very well, have you?"

"No, I haven't."

"You should go to bed now. We'll meet at breakfast and start our holiday immediately after."

"I'm not sure I want to stay."

"Will you say a small prayer with me?"

"I'll try." The answer was low and tremulous.

Jean Marie gathered himself for a moment and then, still holding her hand, intoned the prayer for the departed.

> "God, our Father,
> We believe that your Son died and rose to life.
> We pray for our brother Vittorio Malavolti,
> Who has died in Christ.
> Raise him at the last
> To share the glory of the Risen Christ.
> Eternal rest give to him, O Lord,
> And let perpetual light shine upon him."

"Amen," said Roberta Saracini, and began to weep, quiet healing tears.

For the next five days they played tourists, gorging themselves on the simpler pleasures of London. They strolled by the Serpentine, watched the changing of the guard at Buckingham Palace, spent a morning at the Tate, an afternoon at the British Museum, an evening at a Beethoven concert in the Albert Hall. They took a river excursion to Greenwich and another to Hampton Court. They went window-shopping in Bond Street, spent a morning with Angelo Vittucci, who promised to design Jean Marie a suit "so discreet that a cherub could not be scandalized, yet so beautifully fitted you will think you have grown a new skin!"

Roberta Saracini was, at first, desperately moody—happy as a child one moment, the next, buried in a deep pit of depression. He learned quickly that logical talk made no impression on her: that gentleness, distraction and an occasional curt chiding were the best remedies. He made discoveries about himself, too: how far he had travelled from Vatican Hill, how many small joys had passed him by when he was the puzzled shepherd of a faceless flock. The *Letters,* on which he worked late at night, became more poignant, as each Arcadian day made time and tenderness and the tears of things more precious.

Roberta had decided that she would stay out the week, leaving London late on Sunday evening so that she could be back at work on Monday morning. The forecast promised fine weather—a brief extension of the Indian summer before the first frosts came in. Roberta suggested a picnic. She would hire a car, pack her luggage in the trunk. They could spend the whole day in the country. Jean Marie could drop her off at the airport on the way back to London. So, it was agreed.

Early on Sunday morning, Jean Marie said Mass at a side chapel in the Oratory Church, where the sacristan had come to know him simply as Père Grègoire, an elderly French priest who wore a beret and looked rather like a benevolent rabbit. Then, with Roberta at the wheel and a picnic basket made up by the hotel, they drove out to Oxford, Woodstock and the Cotswold country beyond.

It was still early and the Sunday traffic had not yet begun to build up; so they were able to turn off the highway and meander through small villages still rubbing the sleep out of their eyes, and rolling farmland brown with the last stubble or dark after the first plowing. Their pleasure was in the small wonders: the ribbon of mist that lay along a hillside, the grey tower of a Norman church, climbing out of the huddle of a tiny hamlet, an apple tree by the roadside laden with red-ripe fruit, free to the passerby, a child perched on an ancient milestone, nursing a doll.

Somehow, it was easier to talk while they were driving. They did not have to look at each other. There was always a new distraction to bridge the betraying silence.

Roberta Saracini touched his arm and said, "I feel so much better than when I arrived. Things make more sense. I can cope better. I have you to thank for that."

"You've been good for me, too."

"I don't know how; but I'm glad anyway."

"How do you feel about your father now?"

"I'm not sure. It's all a sad kind of mess; but I know I don't hate him."

"What holds you back?" He prompted her firmly. "You love him; no matter what he was or what he did, he paid his own price—and he gave you enough to get started too. Say it! Say you love him!"

"I love him." She resigned herself to the proposition with a smile and a sigh which might have been relief or regret. Then she added the postscript. "I love you, too, Monsieur Grégoire."

"And I love you," said Jean Marie gently. "That's good. That's what it's all about. 'My little children, love one another.'"

"I hope," said Roberta Saracini, "you didn't have to be commanded to it."

"On the contrary," said Jean Marie—and left the rest of it unsaid.

"How do you feel about women—not necessarily me, in particular? I mean, you've been a celibate all these years and . . ."

"I've had a lot of practice at it." Jean Marie was douce but very firm. "And part of the practice is that you don't flirt and you don't play dangerous games and, most important of all, you never tell lies to yourself. I feel about you as any man feels about an attractive woman. I've been happy in your company and flattered to have you on my arm. There could be more; but precisely because I love you, there won't be. We were set to walk on separate paths. We've met most pleasantly at the crossroads. We'll part, each a little richer."

"That's quite a sermon, Monseigneur," said Roberta Saracini. "I wish I could believe half of it."

He glanced across at her. She was driving steadily, eyes fixed on the road, but there were tears on her cheeks. She turned to him and asked bluntly:

"What made you become a priest in the beginning?"

"That's a long story."

"We've got all day."

"Well! . . ." Immediately he was closed-in and reluctant. "The only person to whom I've ever told that was my confessor. It's still a painful subject."

"It was tactless of me to ask. I'm sorry."

They drove the next half-mile in silence; then, without further prompting, Jean Marie began to talk, slowly, musingly, as if he were putting together in his mind the pieces of a puzzle.

". . . When I first joined the Maquis I was very young—just arrived at military age. I wasn't religious. I was baptized, communicated and confirmed in the Church; but there it stopped. There was a war; life was catch-me-if-you-can. With the Maquis I was a man overnight. I carried a rifle, a pistol and a killing knife. Unlike the older ones who could sometimes slip into town, I was forced to stay out in the hills and the countryside; because if I got picked up in a city raid I'd be shipped out to forced labour in Germany. I did courier duty at night, of course; because I was young and could move fast and outrun the curfew patrols. . . . Before, I had had girl friends and some experience of sex —just enough to make me want more. Now I was without a woman and my companions mocked me, as older men do, calling me the little virgin and the choirboy. . . . Old, bawdy stuff, harmless enough, but very difficult for a youth who knew he might never live to enjoy a manhood. . . .

"Well, one of my regular courier routes took me to a farmhouse near a main road. All troop movements in the area had to pass the place; so the farmer's wife kept a list, which we collected every three days, and passed on to Allied intelligence. I never went to the house. There was a shepherd's hut and a sheep pen about half a mile away, on the brow of a hill. I'd lie up there and tie a rag to a sapling for a signal. After dark, the woman would come up with the messages and food for me and for the boys in the hills. Her name was Adèle, she was somewhere in her thirties, childless; and her husband was missing since the first days of the *Blitzkrieg*. . . . She ran the farm with two old men and a couple of sturdy girls from nearby families. . . .

"On this particular day I arrived late. I was scared and shaken. There were lots of German patrols out and twice I was nearly picked up. To make matters worse, I'd gashed my leg on some barbed wire, and I was scared of tetanus. An hour after sunset Adèle came. I was never so glad to see anyone in my life. She, too, had had a bad day, no less than three raids with troops stamping in and turning over the place. She washed my leg with wine, and bandaged it with strips from her petticoat. Then we drank the rest of the wine and ate supper together and afterwards made love on the straw mattress. . . .

"That I remember as the most wonderful experience of my life—a mature passionate woman and a frightened youth, in a single ecstatic hour, in a world full of monsters. Whenever afterwards I have talked about charity, the love of God for man and man for God and woman for man, I have done it in the light of that single hour. From curate to Pope I have remembered Adèle every morning in my Mass. Whenever I have sat in the confessional box and heard sad people tell the sins of their love lives, I have remembered her and tried to offer my penitents the gift of knowing that she gave to me."

He fell silent. Roberta Saracini swung the car into a lay-by, from which the land dropped away into a vista of farmland, and scattered coverts and walls of weathered ashlar. She wound down the window and stared out on the tranquil scene. Not daring to look at Jean Marie, she asked with singular humility, "Do you want to tell me the rest of it? Where is Adèle now?"

"Dead. She left me before midnight. When she got home there were Germans in the house again. They were drunk on her wine. They raped her and nailed her to the table with a kitchen knife. . . . That was how I found her when, eager to renew the night's loving, I broke all the rules and crept down the hill to see her at six in the morning!

"That was the day I decided I had a debt to pay. Later, much later, I decided that the exercise of the whole office of the priesthood was the best way to do it. The passion of Christ became very real to me as a drama of brutality, love, death and living again. I have never regretted the choice; nor, in spite of the horror that followed, have I been able to regret the wonder that Adèle and I shared. My confessor, who was a wise and gentle man, helped me to that. He said, "The real sin is to be niggardly in love. To give too much is a fault, easily forgiven. What you knew, your Adèle knew, too—that you had shared a moment of strange grace. I am sure she remembered it at the end.' . . . Look at me, Roberta!"

She shook her head. She was sitting, chin on hand, eyes averted, staring out at the sun-dappled countryside. He reached out and turned her tearstained face towards him. His eyes were tender, his voice full of compassion. He admonished her gently.

"I'm old enough to be your father—so you can adopt me as a Dutch uncle if you like! For the rest, remember what I told you at the beginning. *On ne badine pas avec l'amour.* One doesn't trifle with love. It's too wonderful and too terrible! . . ."

He handed her his pocket handkerchief to dry her eyes. She accepted it, but faced him with a last blunt question.

"After all that, how is it possible that your best friend, Carl Mendelius, is a German?"

"How is it possible," asked Jean Marie, "that you and I are sitting here, because your father cheated the Vatican out of millions and was killed in a prison corridor? . . . The biggest mistake we've all made through the ages is to try to explain the ways of God to men. We shouldn't do that. We should just announce Him. He explains Himself very well!"

The day before the function at the Carlton Club he went with Adrian Hennessy to deliver the manuscript of *Last Letters from a Small Planet*. He laid it on Waldo Pearson's desk and said, "There you are. It's done. Good or bad, it's a heart-cry. I hope someone hears it."

Waldo Pearson weighed the package in his hands and said that he was sure, yes, very sure, that someone would hear the heart-cry. Then he handed Jean Marie the typescript of the English version of his speech for the Carlton Club.

Jean Marie asked him, "What do you think of it? Does it make sense?"

"It makes frightening sense. It makes wonderful sense. I cannot say how the audience will take it."

"I've read it," said Adrian Hennessy. "I love it. I'm also scared. There's still time to make changes if you will consent to them."

He glanced at Jean Marie, who nodded agreement. "I know I am talking to new people in a new idiom. Be honest with me! I am your guest at your club. If I am overstepping the proprieties of the occasion, I must know."

"There is no breach of the peace or the decencies," said Waldo Pearson. "Hold to the text!"

"Will there be questions afterward?"

"There may be. We generally allow them."

"Will you please make sure I understand them before I answer? I am fluent in English but sometimes, in moments of stress, I think in French or Italian."

"I'll see you through it. There's a lot of interest."

"Do you have a guest list?" Hennessy asked the question.

"Afraid not. When there's a big attendance, as there will be this time, the members have to ballot for guest places. I have, however, invited the Soviet ambassador—and Sergei Petrov, if he should happen to be in London. If he appears it will be a sign that he is still viable politically. I have also invited Morrow, because I knew him when he was my opposite number in Washington. I suggested he might like to bring a colleague—which leaves it open for him to present Dolman if he chooses. For the rest, it's an impressive list: members of Cabinet, diplomats, heads of industry, press barons. So you'll have a wide sampling of religions, nationalities—and moralities as well."

Hennessy added an ironic footnote. "Maybe the Holy Ghost will give you the gift of tongues."

"I used to talk about that with Mendelius." Jean Marie picked up the joke and embellished it. "He used to say that it was probably the least useful of all the gifts of the Spirit. If a man was a fool in one language, you'd never make him wise in twenty!"

They all got a laugh out of that. Waldo Pearson produced champagne. They drank a toast to *Last Letters from a Small Planet* and to a quondam Pope who was about to be tossed to the lions in the Carlton Club.

Jean Marie Barette gripped the edges of the table lectern and surveyed his audience, packed into the principal dining room at the Carlton Club. He had met only a few of them—a privileged group entertained by Waldo Pearson to sherry in the committee room. Waldo, he found, ruled the Conservative strong-hold with an iron fist. He would not have his most exotic guest mauled and put upon in the vacuous preambles of cocktail time. He had professed himself delighted with Jean Marie's choice of dress—a black jacket buttoned to the neck, with a minimal display of Roman collar and a simple silver pectoral cross. The dress expressed the import of his opening words.

". . . I stand before you a private man. I am a cleric ordained to the minis-try of the Word in the Roman Catholic Church. I have, however, no canonical mission; so that what I say to you in this assembly is my private opinion and must not be construed as either the official teaching of the Church or as a statement of Vatican policy."

He gave them a grin and a Gallic gesture to take the weight off the words.

"I am sure you will need no elaboration of this point. You are all political men, and—how do you say it in English?—a wink tells as much as a nod to a blind mule."

They gave him a small chuckle to warm him—and to tempt him, too. If he were fool enough to trust this audience, he would not be worth anyone's atten-tion in the morning. His next words jolted them out of their complacency.

"Because I am a man, I have experience of fear, love and death. Because I have been, like you, a political man, I understand the usages of power and its limitations, too! Because I am a minister of the Word, I know that I am peddling a folly in the marketplace and that I risk to be stoned for it. . . . You, too, my friends, are peddling follies—monstrous insanities!—and all of us risk to perish by them!"

There was a deadly quiet in the room. For this single moment he held them hypnotized. They understood the arts of the forum. They knew that this man was a master; but if his thought proved unworthy of his orator's talent, they would shout him down as a mountebank. Jean Marie thrust forward with his argument.

"Your folly is to promise a possible perfection in the affairs of men—an equitable distribution of resources, an equal access to seaways, airways and strategic land routes, a world, in short, where every problem can be solved by an honest broker, an inspired leader, a party apparat. You make the promise as a necessary step to power. You choose to ignore that you are playing with dynamite.

"You raise illusory hopes. You excite expectations you cannot fulfil. Then, when you see that the deluded people are turning against you—presto!—there is a new solution: a cleansing war! Now, suddenly, you are not givers of gifts. You are janissaries imposing the edicts of the sultan. If the people will not obey the dictate, then you will make them do it! You will lop them, limb by limb, like

Procrustes, until they fit the bed on which they writhe tormented. But they will never fit it. The golden age you have promised will never come. . . .

"You know it! In a most terrible act of despair you are resigned to it! Already you have counted the cost: so many millions in New York, in Moscow, in Tokyo, in China, in Europe. The aftermath, the desert which will be called peace, you have elected to ignore, because who will be left to care? Let the bandits subdue the populace. Let the casualties die. There will be a new dark age—a new Black Death. In some far-distant future there will, perhaps, be a renaissance; but who cares, because we shall never see the wonder of it.

"Do you think I exaggerate? You know I do not. If the embargo on grain is not lifted, the Soviet Union will come near to starvation this winter—and her armies will march at the first thaw. Even if they do not, a movement by any power towards the oil fields in the Middle East or the Far East will precipitate a global conflict. I do not know the battle order, as some of you do; but you will recognize that I touch close to the core of the matter. . . . I make no plea to you. If your own good sense, the promptings of your own heart when you look at your children and your grandchildren, do not move you to action to avert the holocaust, then—amen! So be it! *Ruat coelum*—let the heavens fall!

"I have sought only to define your folly; which is to believe that man can construct for himself a perfect habitat, and that every time he fails, he can destroy what he has done like a sand castle and begin again. . . . In the end the constructive impulse is overmastered by the destructive one. And all the time the tide creeps in relentlessly, to obliterate the small beach-head on which we play! . . ."

He could not tell whether they approved or disapproved. All he knew was that the silence held and their ears, if not their hearts, were still open to him. He went on, more quietly and persuasively.

"Now let me tell you of my folly, which is the reverse of yours, but which served only to compound it. When I was elected Pope, I was both humbled and elated. I believed that power had been placed in my hands, the power to change the lives of the faithful, to reform the Church, to mediate perhaps in the quarrels of nations and help to maintain the precarious peace we enjoy. All of you know the feeling. You experienced it when you were first elected to office, given your first embassy, your first cabinet post, or when you bought your first newspaper or television station. A heady moment, is it not? And the headaches are all in the future!"

There was a small chuckle of assent. They were glad of the relief. The man was more than a rhetorician. He had a saving grace of humour.

"There is a catch of course—a trap into which we all step. What we have is not power but authority—which is a horse of a different colour! Power implies that we can accomplish what we plan. Authority signifies only that we may order it to be accomplished. We pronounce—*Fiat!* Let it be done! But by the time the ordinance filters down to the peasant in the rice paddy, the miner at the coal face, the slum priest in the *favela,* it has lost most of its force and meaning. The definitions in which we enshrine our dogmas and our moralities are touchstones of orthodoxy. Whether we be Popes, ayatollahs or party preceptors, we dare not abrogate them; but their relevance to man in his extremity is minimal. What theology can I teach to a girl who is dying with a

septic abortion? All I can give her is pity, comfort and absolution. What do I say
to the boy revolutionary in Salvador whose family has been shot by the soldiers
in the village square? I can offer nothing but love, compassion and an unprovable proposition that there is a Creator who will turn all this madness into
sanity, all this sorrow into eternal joy. . . . So you see, my folly was to believe
that somehow I could exercise at once the authority which I had accepted, and
the beneficence to which my heart prompted me. It was an impossibility, of
course—just as it is impossible for a foreign minister to denounce the obscenities of a dictator who supplies his essential raw materials.

"It is in this context that I want to explain my abdication, which, painful as
it was at the time, I now neither mourn nor protest. In an experience which
came unbidden and unexpected, I was given a revelation of the Last Things. I
was given a command to announce them as imminent. I myself was and am
absolutely convinced of the authenticity of this experience; but I neither had
nor have any means of proving it. So, my brother bishops decided that I could
not legitimately hold the office of Pontiff and, at the same time, assume the
role of a prophet and proclaim an unauthenticated private revelation. I say
nothing of the means they took to procure my abdication. These are at most a
footnote to a history that may never be written.

"I do, however, say this. I am glad, now, to have no authority; I am glad to be
no longer obliged to defend the formulae of definition; because the authority is
too limited, the formulae too narrow to encompass the agony of mankind in the
last days and the magnitude of the Parousia—the promised Coming.

"It may be that there are those among you who, like me, have become
conscious of the limitations of power and the folly of mass murder. It is to these
that I m—"

Suddenly he was aware that the words he was saying were not words at all,
but a single childish sound, repeated over and over: "ma . . . ma . . . ma
. . . ma ." He felt something tugging at his trouser leg. He looked down and
saw his left hand flapping helplessly against his thigh. His vision was blurred.
He could not see the audience. Then the room canted and he lurched forward
across the table. After a certain confusion of motion and time he heard two
voices very close to him. One of them was Waldo Pearson's.

"That was quite eerie. It sounded like glossolalia. Only yesterday we'd been
talking about the gift of tongues."

"It's a typical symptom of C.V.A."

"What's C.V.A.?"

"Cerebro-vascular accident. The poor devil's had a stroke! . . . That ambulance is taking a hell of a time!"

"Midday traffic," said Waldo Pearson. "What are his chances?"

"Ask me in three days."

The words reminded Jean Marie of resurrection. Instead he lapsed into
darkness.

—————— BOOK THREE ——————

Believe not in every spirit, but test the spirits to know if they be of God; for many false prophets are about in the world.

—First Epistle of St. John 4:1

XIII

Now he was another man in a strange country. The country was very small. It had four white walls, two doors and a window. There was a bed, on which he lay, a small table beside it, a chair, a chest of drawers with a mirror above it in which the man in the bed was reflected. He had a curiously lopsided look, like a before-and-after advertisement for liver salts. One side of his face was mobile and upturned, the other dragged slightly downward into an expression of dolour or distaste. One hand lay motionless on the white counterpane. The other roved restlessly, exploring contours and textures and distances.

There was at least one other inhabitant of this new country: a rather plain young woman in a nurse's uniform who appeared often to take his pulse and his blood pressure and listen to his chest. She asked him always the same simple questions: "How do you feel? What is your name? Would you like a drink?" The strange thing was that while he understood her perfectly, she did not seem to comprehend a word he said—although she did give him a drink, holding him up so that he could suck the liquid through a plastic straw. And she held a bottle to his penis so that he could make water. When he did so, she smiled and said, "Good, very good," as if he were a baby learning the act of peeing. She always used the same exit line: "Doctor will be back to see you soon." He tried to remember who the doctor was and what he looked like; but the effort was too great, so he closed his eyes and tried to rest.

He was too disturbed to sleep; not disturbed about anything in particular, but anxious, as though he had lost something precious and were groping for it in a fog. Every so often he would feel that he was close to it and close to knowing what it was; but the moment of discovery never came. Then he would feel like a man in a cellar with the trapdoor locked above his head. Finally, the doctor arrived, a lean grey-haired fellow who displayed a kind of offhand concern.

"My name is Doctor Raven. Can you repeat it for me? Raven."

Jean Marie tried several times but succeeded only in saying, "Ra . . . Ra . . . Ra . . ."

The doctor said, "Never mind. You will do better soon. Just nod if you understand me. I am speaking English. Do you know what I am saying?"

Jean Marie nodded.

"Can you see me?"

A nod.

"Smile at me. Let me see you smile."

Jean Marie tried. He was glad he could not see the result. The doctor looked into his eyes with an ophthalmoscope, tested his reflexes with a little rubber mallet, checked his blood pressure and auscultated his chest. Then he sat on the edge of the bed and delivered himself of a small lecture. Jean Marie was reminded of the discourse with which the rector of his seminary used to greet each batch of newcomers.

". . . You are a lucky man. You are alive. You are rational and you have some of your faculties intact. It is too early to know what damage has been done inside your skull. We have to wait two or three days before we know whether this is one episode or whether others may follow. You have to trust us and try to accept that for a little while you are helpless. This is the Charing Cross Hospital. Your friends and relatives know where you are. But they know you must have no visitors and no disturbance at all until we get you stabilized. Have you understood that?"

"Ma . . . ma . . . ma . . . most," said Jean Marie, and was absurdly pleased with himself.

The doctor, too, gave him a smile and a pat of approbation. "Good! That's promising. I'll be back to see you in the morning. Tonight they'll give you something to help you sleep."

Jean Marie tried to say thank you. He found he had forgotten the words in English. In French he could only get as far as *"Mer . . ."* He struggled with it until he wept in frustration and the nurse came in to pump an opiate into his arm.

After four days it seemed he had made enough progress for them to initiate him into the games of the new country. But first they had to find him a French-speaking assistant to teach him the rules. He was having enough trouble with phonic jumbles and word blocks, without launching him into a mania of mixed tongues.

The assistant was a handsome fellow in his early thirties, trim as an athlete, with the olive skin of a Mediterranean man, and an incongruous head of golden hair that looked as though it had been inherited from some long-dead Nordic crusader. He came from what he vaguely described as the Middle East. He confessed to being fluent in English, French, Arabic, Hebrew and Greek. He had built himself a modest career in medical circles in London by acting as interpreter, male nurse and physiotherapist to the polyglot groups who inhabited the metropolis. The neurologist introduced him as Mr. Atha. Together they began a series of games, all designed to map the damage to the sensorium, the part of his brain which perceived sensations. For a man who had once been, by dogmatic definition, the infallible interpreter of God's message to men, it was shocking to find how fallible he was, and in how many simple matters.

Asked to close his eyes and raise both arms horizontally in front of him, he was amazed that only one arm obeyed him fully while the other stayed, like the hand of a stopped clock, at twenty-five minutes to the hour.

Asked to tell where he was pricked with both points of a pair of dividers, he found some of his identifications were wildly astray. Worse, he could not even find the tip of his nose with his left hand.

However, there were some hopeful signs. When his feet were tickled his toes turned in. This, Mr. Atha explained, showed that his Babinski reflex was functioning. When the inside of his thigh was tickled, his scrotal sac contracted. This, he was told, was also good because his cremaster reflex was in working order.

Then came a most unhappy moment. Mr. Atha asked him to repeat for the neurologist the words of the old song:

> "Sur le pont, sur le pont,
> Sur le pont d'Avignon."

He found, to his horror, that his mouth was full of treacle, and what came out was a burble of phonic nonsense.

Once again he began to cry. The neurologist admonished him firmly. He was lucky to be alive. He was twice lucky to have suffered so little impairment. The prognosis was hopeful, provided he was prepared to be patient, cooperative and courageous—virtues quite beyond his capacity at that moment.

Mr. Atha translated it all into more soothing French and volunteered to stay with him until he was calm again. The neurologist nodded approval of the idea, patted Jean Marie's good hand and went about his other business; which, as Mr. Atha explained, included many patients far worse off than Jean Marie.

". . . I work with them, too; so I know what I am talking about. You can swallow. You have no double vision. You have control of your bowels and your urine. . . . Eh! Think how much that means! Your speech will improve; because you and I are going to practice together. You see, with the doctor, you are trying to show that you are not damaged. You are determined to prove it by a sudden burst of oratory. When it doesn't happen, you despair. We're going to start from the fact that you are damaged. We are going to repair the trauma together. . . ."

He was not only persuasive; he had an enormous quality of repose. Jean Marie felt the weight lifting off the top of his head, the fog dissipating from inside his skull case. Mr. Atha talked on quietly.

". . . You used to be Pope, they tell me. So you must remember the Scripture: 'Unless you become as little children, you shall not enter the kingdom of heaven.' Well, you're like a child now. You have to learn simple things from the beginning. You have to admit that you can't cope with complicated ones for a long while yet. But in the end you will grow up again, just as a child does. You're in kindergarten now. As the weeks go on, you'll climb through the grades. You'll learn to dress yourself, get your bad arm and leg moving again— and above all, you'll talk. You can talk now, if you take it slowly. Let's pick something very simple: 'My name is Jean Marie.' Now, one word at a time. . . ."

Somewhere in the long night hours, when the only sounds were the footfalls of the night nurse and the only light was the beam of her torch focused on his face, he learned another lesson. If he tried to remember things, they always eluded him. If, however, he lay quietly, making no effort at all, they crept up on him, and sat about him like woodland animals in a child's picture book.

They were not always in the right order. Drexel was next to the little mongol child. Mendelius was mixed up in some bishops' conference in Mexico, Roberta Saracini was drinking out of the cosmos cup; and the little twisted girl was selling prints to Alvin Dolman. But at least they were all there. He had not lost them like an amnesiac. They were pieces of a pattern in a kaleidoscope. One day they would shake themselves into a familiar order.

There was something else, too. As with the vision in the monastery garden, he was aware of it in a fashion that escaped verbal definition. Somewhere at the deep core of himself—that sorry fortress so beset and bombarded and ruined—there was a place of light where the Other dwelt, and where, when he could withdraw to it, there was communion of love, blissful but all too brief. It was like—what was it like?—deaf Beethoven with his head full of glories, Einstein bereft of mathematics to express the mysteries he understood at the end. There was another wonder, too. He could not command his limp hand or his numb leg, and only sometimes his halting tongue; but, in this small place of light and peace, he could command himself, dispose freely of himself, as a lover to the beloved. It was here that the pact was made. "Whatever you have laid on me I accept. No questions, no conditions! But please, come Rubicon Day, give light and a taste of joy to my friend Duhamel, and his wife. He is a good one. He has been niggardly only to himself!"

The first danger point was past, the neurologist told him. Fingers-crossed-and-pray-a-little, this was a one-off episode and he should make a good recovery. There would be sequelae, of course, handicaps and inhibitions of one kind and another; but, in general, there were good hopes that he could return to a normal life. But not yet! Not nearly yet! He must be trained, harder than any athlete. Mr. Atha would not only explain, but would drive him through the exercises, hour after hour, day after day. Visitors? Well, wouldn't it be better to wait awhile, until he could display to them a certain competence? Sometimes visitors got more distressed than the patients.

". . . Besides," Mr. Atha added his own good reasons, "you're an important man. I'd like to feel proud of you the first day you go on display. I want you dressed right, talking right, moving right . . . with panache, yes?"

"Panache!" said Jean Marie, and the word came out clear as a bell note.

"Bravo!" said Mr. Atha. "Now let's get the nurse in. The first thing we have to do is teach you to sit on the edge of the bed and then stand by yourself."

It sounded so simple that he could not believe the effort and the humiliation of it. Time after time, he crumpled like a rag doll into the arms of Mr. Atha and the nurse. Time after time, they stood him up and gradually withdrew their support until he was able to remain erect for a few moments. When he was weary they sat him back on the bed and showed him how to roll himself into a recumbent position and ease himself off the pressure points where bedsores might begin.

When he had mastered the overture, they began to teach him the opera: how to walk with tiny shuffling steps, how to exercise his left hand with a rubber ball, a whole series of operations with mechanical equipment in a large gymnasium. It was here that he understood, as Mr. Atha had told him, just how fortunate he was. He noted something else, too: the boundless patience which Atha dispensed to his motley group, and how quickly they reacted to his smile and his word of encouragement.

Atha made him participate in the small, disjointed community life of the gymnasium—by tossing a ball to one, making halting conversation with another, demonstrating to a third a movement which he himself had mastered. Brief as they were, these social interludes left him exhausted; but Atha was adamant.

". . . You will renew your own resources only by sharing them. You cannot expect to spend all this time of healing in a hermetic world and then emerge a social animal. If you get tired of talking, touch people, smile, share your awareness of things—like that pair of pigeons cooing on the window ledge. It may not worry you; but half the people here are terrified that they will no longer be attractive to those who love them, that they will be sexually impotent or even, in the end, a hateful burden to their families. . . ."

"I am sorry." Jean Marie managed to get the words out "I will try to do better."

"Good!" said Mr. Atha with a smile. "You can relax now. It's massage time!"

There was one set of games which gave him real pleasure. The neurologist called them gnostic sensibility tests. In fact, they meant the recognition, by touch alone, of textures and weights, shapes flat and solid. The pleasure in this game was that the sensibilities did become perceptibly sharper and his guesses came closer to the objects that produced the sensation.

His attention span became longer, too, and he was able to enjoy the mass of letters and cards which had piled up, unread, in the top drawer of his bureau. When his concentration lapsed, Mr. Atha would read them to him and help him to frame a simple reply. He would not write it, however. Jean Marie must do that himself. Mr. Atha would supply the words and phrases that lost themselves momentarily from his vocabulary or jumbled themselves with others in some synaptic short circuit.

Now he had newspapers delivered—English and French—and enjoyed scanning them, though he retained lamentably little of what he read. Mr. Atha consoled him in his calm fashion.

". . . What do you want to retain? The bad news that tells you man is dismantling civilization brick by brick? The good news is here, right under your nose! The blind see. The lame walk. Sometimes even the dead are jolted back to life . . . and if you listen hard enough, you'll hear echoes of the good news."

"You . . . you are a . . . different man!" said Jean Marie in his halting fashion.

"You meant to say 'strange.' "

"So I did."

"Then say it now."

"Strange," said Jean Marie carefully. "You are a very strange man."

"I also bring good news," said Mr. Atha. "Next week you may begin having visitors. If you tell me whom you want to see I'll make a list and get in touch with them for you."

Brother Alain was invited first, because Jean Marie felt that the family tie should be respected and now there was no reason left for sibling jealousy. They embraced awkwardly, because of Jean Marie's useless arm. After the first verbal exchanges, Jean Marie made it plain that he would rather listen than talk; so Alain hurried through the family news until he came to where his own heart was anchored: the Bourse, with all its transactions and its rumours.

". . . Now we are in the big-scale barter business. Oil for grain, soybeans for coal, tanks for iron ingots, meat for yellow powder uranium, gold for everything! If you've got commodities we can find a buyer for them. . . . But why am I running on like this? How long do you expect to be in this place?"

"They do not say." Jean Marie had found by now that he did better with simple announcements, fabricated in advance. "I don't ask. I wait."

"When you do get out, you're welcome to come to us."

"Thank you, Alain. No! There are places for . . . for . . ." He groped for the word and almost grasped it. "Rehab . . . rehab . . ."

"Rehabilitation?"

"Right. Mr. Atha will find me one."

"Who is Mr. Atha?"

"He works here with stroke victims."

"Oh!" He was not callous or indifferent. He was simply a stranger in a strange country. "Roberta sends her love. She'll be over in a few days."

"Good. Glad to see her."

It was the most he could manage. Alain, too, was glad to be dispensed. After a few more exchanges and some long silences they embraced again and parted, each wondering why he had so little to say to the other.

The next day Waldo Pearson came. He was attended by a manservant, laden with unexpected treasures: six author's copies of *Last Letters from a Small Planet*, one leather-bound volume for the author himself, a tape recorder and two best-selling versions of "Johnny the Clown," one by a male vocalist, the other by a well-known female singer with full chorus. He also brought a bottle of Veuve Clicquot, a bucket of ice, a set of champagne glasses, a jar of fresh caviar, toast, butter and the full text of Jean Marie's speech at the Carlton Club, also bound in leather. Waldo was in his best "come-and-he-cometh-go-and-he-goeth" mood.

"My father had two strokes—they didn't call them cerebro-vascular accidents in his day!—so I know the form. Chat when you want. Be silent when you feel like it. Do you like the book? . . . Handsome, isn't it. The subscriptions are rolling in. It's the biggest thing we've had in twenty years. We're assured of rave reviews and big ones, too! I'm only sorry we can't have you at our launching party. Hennessy called. He tells me the reaction in the Americas and on the Continent is the same. He says he'll see you on his way back from New York. You've really touched a nerve. . . . And everyone's whistling the song. I even sing it in my bath. . . . Champagne? Can you manage the caviar, too? . . . That's very good! You really do cope. I was determined you'd have champagne and caviar if I had to feed it to you with an eyedropper. . . ."

"I'm very touched. Thank you." Jean Marie was surprised at his own fluency. "I'm sorry I made such a scene at the club."

"That was most curious." Pearson was instantly grave. "Some of the audience were hostile. Many were deeply moved. None was able to be neutral. I sent copies of the full text of your address to all members and to their guests. The replies, pro and con, were illuminating. Some expressed fear; others spoke of a religious impact; yet others spoke of the contrast between the power of your message and the modesty of your personal demeanor. By the way, did you hear from Matt Hewlett? He said he was going to write. He thought you might be embarrassed if he came to see you."

"He wrote. He told me he had offered nine days of masses for me. The Pontiff cabled and some members of the Curia. Drexel wrote a long . . . long . . . long . . . Forgive me. The simplest words fail me sometimes."

"Relax!" said Waldo Pearson. "I'm going to play you the song. I prefer the woman's version. See what you think."

"Can you get me a copy for Mr. Atha?"

"Of course; but who is he?"

"He's a ther . . . therapist. I can't tell you what he does for all of us. He's a god . . . godsent man! I must autograph a book for him. Does it matter now if I'm known as the author?"

"I don't believe it matters a damn anymore," said Waldo Pearson. "The charitable will find God in the book. The bigots will be sure you're stricken for your sins. So everyone will be happy."

"Did . . . did Petrov get his grain?"

"Some, but not enough."

"I've lost count of time. I can't remember events . . ."

"Be glad! The times are out of joint. Events outrun our control."

Jean Marie reached out to grasp his hand. He needed the reassurance of human contact. The thought he had been trying to grasp for weeks was finally clear to him. He pieced it out with desperate care.

"He showed me the Last Things. He told me to announce the Parousia. I gave up everything to do it. I tried. I truly tried. Before I could get the words out, He struck me dumb! . . . I don't know what He wants now. I am so confused."

Waldo Pearson held the frail hand between his palms. He said gently:

"I was confused, too. I was angry. I found myself shaking a fist in His face and demanding to know, why? Why? Then I read *Last Letters from a Small Planet* and I realized that was your testimony. It was all there in black and white. Whatever you said or failed to say at the Carlton Club was postscript and dispensable. . . . I remembered something else, too. The first precursor, John, called the Baptizer, came to a strange end. While the Messiah, whom he had announced, was still walking free in Judea, he was murdered in Herod's dungeon and his head presented on a dish to a belly dancer. All he had from his Messiah was a praise that became an epitaph. 'Among men that are born of women there is none greater than John the Baptizer. . . .' "

"I'd forgotten that," said Jean Marie Barette. "But then I forget so many things."

"Have some more champagne," said Waldo Pearson, "and let's listen to the music."

The next day, new plagues afflicted him. He was sitting in his wheelchair, scanning the headlines in the morning paper, when Mr. Atha came in to say that he would be absent for a while. He had to go abroad to deal with some of his father's affairs. Jean Marie's therapy session would be conducted by a woman assistant.

". . . And when I come back," said Mr. Atha, "I want to see a vigorous, vocal man."

Jean Marie was a prey to sudden panic. "Where . . . where are you going?"

"Oh, a number of capitals. My father's interests are extensive. . . . I'm taking your book to read on the aircraft. Come now! Don't look so glum!"

"I'm afraid!"

He blurted out the word before it eluded him. Mr. Atha would not bend to the appeal.

"Then you must confront the fear! All the work we have done together is to one end: to make you walk, talk, think and work for yourself. Courage now!"

But, the moment Mr. Atha walked out the door, his courage deserted him. Depression, black as midnight, settled over him. Even the place of light was blotted out. He could not find his way back to it. As the day went on, he found himself sinking deeper and deeper into a condition of despair. He would never get well. He would never leave the hospital. Even if he did, where would he go? What would he do? What was the point of all these efforts, if they produced nothing but the ability to put on a jacket, talk elementary inanities, shuffle along a straight line on a concrete pavement?

For the first time he began to contemplate death, not merely as a release from misery, but as a personal act of termination to an intolerable situation. The contemplation produced an extraordinary calm and a mind clear as the long, cold light of the northern latitudes. It was simple logic to proceed from the contemplation of the act to a speculation on the means by which it might be accomplished. Only when the nurse came in did he realize, with a shock of guilt, how far his morbid reverie had taken him.

He was sufficiently scared by the experience to mention it to the doctor when he looked in on his evening round. The doctor perched himself on the edge of the bed and talked round the subject.

". . . I was beginning to think you'd been lucky and sidestepped this particular crisis. It was clear to all of us that your religious background had given you resources which most people don't possess. . . . But there's no telling how, or when, a depressive illness is going to strike."

"You mean I have another sickness?"

"I mean," the neurologist explained patiently, "you have just described the classic symptoms of acute depression. If these symptoms are allowed to pass untreated, the depression will develop into a chronic condition, constantly aggravated by your present handicaps. The departure of Mr. Atha was simply a trigger incident . . . So we're going to intervene before things go too far.

We'll try you with moderate doses of a euphoric drug. If it works—fine! If not, there are other prescriptions. However, if you can beat the black devils without too much psychotropic intervention, so much the better; but don't try to be brave or bold. If you feel fearful, unable to cope, tell the nurse, tell me, immediately. Promise me!"

"I promise." Jean Marie said it firmly and clearly. "But it is hard for me to feel so dependent."

"That's also my biggest problem as a doctor. The patient is at odds with himself. . . ." He hesitated and then offered a curious question. "Do you believe man has a body and a soul, which get separated at the moment of death?"

Jean Marie pondered the question for a moment, fearful that a new fog-swirl might obscure the answer for which he was reaching; but—God be thanked!—the light held. He said with surprising fluency:

"That's the way the Greeks expressed man: spirit and matter, dual and divisible. As a module it served very well for a very long time. But, after this experience, I don't know . . . I'm not aware of myself as two elements: a musician playing a piano with notes missing, or, conversely, a Stradivarius violin played badly by a schoolboy. I'm me—one and undivided! Part of me is half-dead; part of me is totally dead and will never work again. I'm . . . de . . . de . . ."

"Defective," said the neurologist.

"Yes," said Jean Marie. "Defective."

The doctor reached for the chart clipped to the end of the bed and scribbled a prescription for remedy against the black devils.

In a rare flash of his old humour, Jean Marie said, "Don't you offer an incantation to go with the medicine?"

Against what happened to him next, no medicine and no incantation availed. Two days after Mr. Atha's departure, an hour before noon, Waldo Pearson and Adrian Hennessy came to see him. Their enquiries about his progress were solicitous but brief. Waldo Pearson offered an apology.

"I'd hoped to spare you this; but it was impossible. We have to seek injunctions in Great Britain, on the Continent, in the United States—wherever else we can get them. We need your signature on the bills of complaint."

Jean Marie looked from one to the other in puzzlement. He asked, "What am I complaining about?"

Adrian Hennessy unlocked his briefcase. "Brace yourself for a shock, Monseigneur!"

He laid on the bed a large scrapbook and a paperbound volume. The title was *The Fraud*. The author was one Luigi Marco. The jacket was stamped "Uncorrected Proof Copy." The publisher was Veritas S.p.a., Panama. Hennessy held up the book.

"This little confection has been circulated to all international press agencies. It is due to be published worldwide, in twenty languages, on the day that we publish *Last Letters* in each country. We want to get injunctions to stop publication. However—and this is the nasty one!—some of the gutter press have already picked up the serial rights and are running the juicier sections of the story. The serious newspapers and the television networks can't ignore the fact of publication. They stand on their right to comment on the material. We have to file libel suits to prevent a further spread of the scandal."

"But what is the scandal?"

Waldo Pearson took up the burden of explanation. "The book, appropriately titled *The Fraud,* purports to be the true story of your career, from your earliest youth until now. It is a careful and very skilful blend of fact, fiction and scurrilous innuendo. The author's name is, of course, a pseudonym. The whole thing is a highly professional smear job, like those so-called documentaries about spies and defectors or political scandals which rival propaganda services turn out to discredit each other. The publisher is a hollow corporation registered in Panama. The printing was done in Taiwan by one of the houses that produce such things on contract. Bound copies of the book were then airfreighted to major countries. . . . Someone has laid out a mint of money on research, writing, translation and manufacture. . . . Some of the photographs were taken with a telescopic lens, which indicates that you were under professional surveillance for a long time."

"What sort of photographs?" Again Jean Marie had to explode past the phonic block.

"Show him!" said Waldo Pearson.

Hennessy, with obvious reluctance, flipped through the press cuttings in the scrapbook. There was a shot of Jean Marie with the twisted girl in the Place du Tertre. The angle was such that his face was close to hers and it was easy to assume that they were lovers *tête-à-tête.* There were several shots of Roberta Saracini and himself arm in arm, in Hyde Park, on the riverboat, and strolling in the gardens at Hampton Court. There was one shot of himself and Alain emerging from Sophie's restaurant, looking like a pair of elderly drunks. A black fury took possession of him and he almost choked on the question.

"What . . . what about the text?"

Waldo Pearson shrugged helplessly. "What you might expect. They've done a very thorough job of research and a very clever job of muckraking, so that you show up as a thoroughly bad type who is also a little crazy. . . . On that point they've managed to get hold of two reports from doctors who examined you before your abdication. There are also various other exotic details."

"For instance." Hennessy leafed through the volume. "They found someone who served with you in the Maquis. There was some story about you and a farmer's wife who was later found raped and murdered. Of course, the locals blamed it on the Germans; but . . . They're very good with the buts. Your best friend is Carl Mendelius of Tübingen but the suggestion is that you helped to procure his release from the priesthood because of a homosexual association. The fact that you defended him against charges of heresy and officiated at his wedding only reinforces the innuendo. . . . That's the horrible thing about this kind of job. The scandalmonger doesn't have to prove anything. He just plants the dirty idea. If you kiss your mother at a railway station it has to be incest."

"What do they say about Roberta?"

Hennessy frowned with distaste. "Her father swindled the Vatican Bank out of millions. The funds were never traced. You are known to have a substantial patrimony, of which Roberta Saracini is the trustee. Trusteeships in France are a matter of public record. When you went to Paris you lodged in her house. After that you're photographed in England holding hands with her in the park —and you're living here under an assumed name. . . . Do you want any more?"

"No. Who did all this? Whose idea was it? How did they get all this information? Why?"

"Let's reason through it." Waldo Pearson tried to calm him. "Adrian and I have talked to a lot of well-informed people and we believe we've come up with an explanation that fits all the available evidence. . . . Are you sure you're up to this?"

"Yes!" Jean Marie was clearly under strain but he forced the words out. "Take no notice of me! Just talk!"

Waldo Pearson talked on in the monotone of a man who brings bad news.

"From the moment you claimed a private revelation of the Last Things and made moves to publish it in a letter to the faithful, you were a dangerous man. You know what happened in the Church, and how bitter the Friends of Silence became. But outside, where the nations were actively preparing for a nuclear war, it was much worse. You, with your visions of horror and of judgment, became an instant threat to the myth-makers.

"They were preparing the public to participate in a competition of nuclear destruction, a game, a diabolical game, in which each side commits the same butchery for the same non-reason!

"Your vision, which made you seem a madman, was, in fact, the only available sanity. You saw the horror. You told it! Before the public grasped the thought, you had to be silenced.

"But that was not so easy. You were an active contentious man. In Germany, you blew the cover of a C.I.A. operative, an important agent-in-place. In France, your own country, you were instantly in the black book, under Grade A surveillance. You were watched in England, too; but I was a fairly respectable patron; and I stood surety for you with our government.

"All the time, however, you were a burr in the breeches of the mighty; because just when the war drums were booming, you might shout out that the king had no clothes—and after the first big bang, he might not have any subjects either.

"There was a question, as both Adrian and I discovered from different sources, of having you liquidated. It was a fairly unanimous recommendation. When it was known that your book was in preparation, the decision to liquidate you was rescinded. Another plan was made: to discredit you utterly. . . . You have seen how it was done."

"How did they manage to get all this material so quickly?"

"Money!" said Adrian Hennessy brusquely. "Put enough operatives in the field at once, hand out enough spending money, and you can have anyone's secret life in a month. Given a hostile situation in the Church, given top-level cooperation from governments, the job is as easy as boiling an egg."

"But who organized it?"

"Dolman was the boy who put it together and he had a special reason for making it work. You knew he had tried to kill Carl Mendelius."

"It makes sense, all of it."

"It also raises a problem."

"Please!" said Jean Marie with absolute clarity. "Please do not hold anything back."

"Even if we get restraining injunctions," said Adrian Hennessy, "we'll have only temporary relief. We'll have to fight a series of court cases in the major countries. That will cost a lot of money. You'll have to pay most of it out of your own resources. . . . And, since we're now in the dark ages and will soon be living under emergency regulations, there's no guarantee, even in England, that you'll get a fair trial from either the jury or the judiciary!"

Jean Marie thought for a moment and then said slowly:

"I have the funds. If it takes my last sou, we must fight this obscenity on any battleground we can find! I am not so naïve as to believe we can win; but we have to be seen to fight—and with my money and no one else's. Waldo, I only hope this will not damage your publication of *Last Letters.*"

"No!" said Waldo Pearson. "If anything we'll get more press space, more lively debate. In the end it will come down to a private judgment in each reader's mind: could the author of the *Letters* possibly be the same rascal who is portrayed in this piece of garbage?"

"Meantime, we should get the documents signed." Hennessy was fishing them out of his briefcase. "Unless you want to read through a mountain of legalese, you'll have to take our word that the papers are well drawn by the best legal talent in England, France and the United States."

"I take your word." Jean Marie was already signing the first pages. "But look! To provide all the background for this libel, many people who knew me well must have supplied information."

"Obviously!" said Waldo Pearson. "But the mere fact that they gave information to an interviewer doesn't make them your enemies. You don't know what fiction was employed to make them talk. They may have thought they were doing you a favour. They could have been simple gossips. The Vatican is full of those! Hennessy and I are your allies; but we talk about you! I'm sure we've dropped phrases and opinions that found their way into this false indictment! . . . I'm afraid you just have to accept what's happened, make the best fight you can and then tell the bastards to go to hell. You can't afford to become paranoid."

"I am defective," said Jean Marie. "I am not paranoid. On the scale of the last catastrophe I am a minimal quantity. What happens to me is a non-event. I am troubled for people like Roberta, who will suffer hurt because their names are linked with mine in this libel. When I was Pope, every one I touched felt blessed. Now, I am truly a plague-carrier infecting even my closest friends. . . ."

That night, for the first time, he asked for a drug to make him sleep. In the morning he woke later than usual, but refreshed and clearheaded. At the therapy session he found that he was walking more confidently, that his damaged arm was responding quite well to messages from the motor centers. His speech pattern was consistently clear and he had rarely to grope for a word. The therapist encouraged him.

". . . This is the way it happens in cases with a good prognosis. They improve rapidly; they seem to drag for a long while; then there is another major improvement which generally continues along a regular upgrade. I'll report to your doctor. He'll probably order a series of new tests. Then . . . well, let's not rush things! The trick, now, is to enjoy the improvement, but not push yourself too hard. You're still not ready to play football; but—come to think of it!—we could start you swimming!"

Jean Marie walked back, unaided, to his room. When he got there he was tired but triumphant. Whatever terrors he had to face now, at least he could confront them on his own two feet. He wished Mr. Atha were there to share this first, real victory. He lay on his bed and made a series of telephone calls to tell the good news. He drew a blank on every one. Carl Mendelius' phone was disconnected; Roberta Saracini was in Milan; Hennessy was back in New York; Waldo Pearson was in the country for a few days. Brother Alain was available, but preoccupied. He was happy to hear of Jean Marie's progress. The family would be happy, too. Please, please, keep in touch! . . .

Which brought Jean Marie, by a round turn, face to face with the problem of his own future. However much he was improved, however small his residual disabilities, he was still a man of sixty-five, rising sixty-six, victim of a cerebral episode, liable to another at any time.

Whatever the outcome of the court cases, he would emerge discredited—more so than if he were guilty of all the misdemeanors and misfeasances attributed to him. The world was fond of rascals; it had no patience with incompetents. On the face of it, therefore, Jean Marie Barette would be exactly what his passport called him: *pasteur en retraite,* a retired priest, whose best expectation would be a chaplaincy in a hospital or a cottage in the country, where he could amuse himself with his books and his garden. By evening the black devils were at him again and the doctor had to read him a lecture on manic-depressive swings and how to handle them. The lecture ended with a surprise.

". . . I've ordered an encephalogram for the day after tomorrow. If that reads the way I hope it will, we could think about discharging you within a few days. There's not too much more we can do for you. You'll need quarterly checkups, regular exercise and, for the beginning at least, some reasonable support in your domestic situation. You might care to think about that. We'll chat again tomorrow, eh?"

When the doctor had gone, he checked the calendar in his notebook. It was the fifteenth of December. In ten days it would be Christmas. He wondered where he would spend it, and how many more Nativity Days the world might see, because Petrov had not had his grain and the Soviet armies would move at the first thaw.

He chided himself. Not five minutes ago the doctor had told him he must not sit brooding. It was nearly visiting time. He tidied himself with great care, changed into fresh pajamas—just to prove that his new skills were not an illusion—put on a dressing gown and slippers, picked up his stick and began a careful but ostentatious promenade down the corridor, waving greetings at his companions from the therapy sessions.

What was it Mr. Atha had said? We must have panache! The English always translated it as style, but it had much more flourish than mere style. Flourish! That was good! Now he was coordinating two languages. He should try to get a little practice in German, too, before he met again with Carl Mendelius. Lotte's last letter—when was it dated? What had she said about their plans and movements? He retraced his steps along the corridor, acknowledging the compliment of the night nurse: "Well! Aren't you the clever one!" and the salute from the Jamaican orderly: a hop, a step, a shuffle and the invitation "Come dancin', man!"

He rummaged in the drawer of the bureau, found Lotte's letter—a whole sequence of small movements executed without trouble!—then sat down in his wheelchair to read it. The date was December 1.

. . . Our dear Carl gets stronger every day. He has become very skilful with the prosthetic device which replaces his left hand and there is very little he cannot do for himself. Unfortunately he has lost the sight of one eye and he now wears a black patch. This, with the other damage to that side of his face, gives him the look of a very sinister pirate. We have a family joke. When we need money, we can put Papa in a television serial like "Treasure Island" or "The Spanish Main"!

Johann and Katrin and a small party of their friends have been down in the valley for a month now. They are trying to make the main buildings habitable and stock up with essential supplies before winter closes in. Carl and I will go down next week to join them. We have sold our house here, fully furnished; so all we shall have to take with us are Carl's books and the few personal things that still mean something in our lives. I thought it would be a wrench to leave Tübingen after all these years; but it isn't. Wherever we go now—Bavaria or the South Seas—it doesn't matter too much.

And how are you, dear friend? We have all your cards. We trace your progress by the handwriting—and, of course, we have the messages from your kind friend in England, Waldo Pearson. We can't wait to get a copy of your book. Carl is dying to talk to you about it but we understand why you are timid about using the telephone. I am always so, especially when foreigners are on the line. I stammer and stutter and shout for Carl.

When will they let you out of hospital? Carl insists, and so do I, that you come straight to us in Bavaria. We are your family—and Anneliese Meissner says it is most important that you move directly from hospital into a secure environment. She, too, may spend some of the winter vacation with us in Bavaria. She is very attached to Carl. They are good for each other and I have learned not to be jealous of her, as I learned not to be jealous of you. As soon as you know when you are to be discharged, send a telegram to the Bavarian address we gave you. Fly straight to Munich and we shall pick you up at the airport and bring you to the valley.

Carl gets anxious sometimes. He is afraid the frontiers may be closed before you are ready to come to us. There is great tension everywhere. More and more British and American troops are being moved into the Rhineland. One sees many military convoys. The tone of the press is frankly chauvinist and the atmosphere at the University is very strange. There is a constant recruitment of specialists and, of course, all the security surveillance which Carl and Anneliese so feared. The extraordinary thing is that so few students object. They, too, are affected by the war fever, in a way one would never have expected. It is a shock to hear all the old clichés and slogans! I thank God every day Johann and Katrin are out and away. . . . The madness infects us all. Even Carl and I find ourselves using phrases we have heard on radio or television. It is as if all the old dark Teuton deities were being called up from their caverns; but then I suppose every nation has its underground galleries of war gods. . . .

A raw, transatlantic voice interrupted his reading.

"Good evening, your Holiness!"

He looked up to see Alvin Dolman, leaning against the doorjamb and grinning down at him. Dolman, too, was dressed in pajamas and dressing gown, and he carried a package wrapped in brown paper.

For a moment Jean Marie was stunned by the sardonic insolence of the man. Then he felt a wild rage boiling up inside him. He fought it down with a brief, desperate prayer that his tongue would not fail him and leave him shamed before the enemy. Dolman moved into the room and perched himself jauntily on the edge of the bed. Jean Marie said nothing. He was in command now. He would wait for Dolman to declare himself.

"You look well," said Dolman amiably. "The ward nurse tells me you'll be discharged very soon."

Jean Marie was still silent.

"I came to bring you a bound copy of *The Fraud*," said Dolman. "Inside it you'll find a list of the people who were really happy to sell you out. I thought you might get a kick out of that. It won't help you in court; but then nothing helps in a case like this. Whatever verdicts you get, the mud will stick." He laid the package on the bedside table; then, he picked it up again and partially unwrapped it. "Just to prove it isn't booby-trapped, like the one I sent to Mendelius. There's no need for that in your case, is there? You're out of the game for good."

"Why have you come?" Jean Marie's voice was cold as hoarfrost.

"To share a joke with you," said Alvin Dolman. "I thought you'd appreciate it. The fact is, I go into surgery tomorrow morning. This was the only hospital in London that could take me in a hurry. I've got a cancer on the large bowel; so, they're going to cut out a part of my gut and give me a little bag to carry around for the rest of my life. I'm just tossing up whether it's really worth the sweat. I've got all the tools for a quick, painless exit. Don't you think it's funny?"

"I ask myself why you hesitate," said Jean Marie. "What is there in your life or in yourself that you find so valuable?"

"Not too much," said Dolman with a grin. "But we're building up to one hell of a drama—the big bang that wipes out all our past and maybe the future, too! It might be worth waiting for a grandstand seat. I can still opt out afterwards. You're the man who prophesied it. What do you think?"

"For the little my opinion is worth," said Jean Marie, "this is what I think. You are scared—so scared that you need to play this silly game of mockery! You want me to be afraid with you—of you! I am not! . . . Rather I am sad; because I know how you are feeling, how pointless everything looks—how useless a man can seem to himself! This is only the second time we have met. I know nothing about the rest of your life or what you have done to other people. But how do you feel about what you did to Mendelius and to me?"

"Indifferent!" The answer was prompt and definite. "That's line-of-duty stuff! It's what I'm trained for; it's what I do. I don't question the orders I get. I make no judgments about them—good or bad, sane or insane. If I did, I'd be in the booby hatch! Mankind is a mad tribe! There's no hope for it. I found a profession in which I could profit from the madness. I work for what is, with what is. I deliver on every contract. The only things I don't deal in are love and resurrection! But in the end, I'm at least as well off as you are. You've been peddling salvation through the Lord Jesus for two thousand years—and look at where it's got you!"

"You are here, too," said Jean Marie mildly. "And you came by your own choice. That argues more than indifference."

"Curiosity," said Alvin Dolman. "I wanted to see how you were looking. I must say you've worn pretty well!"

"Still not enough!"

"O.K. Here it is!" Dolman cocked his head to one side like a predatory bird surveying its victim. "When all this started, I was the one who recommended killing you. I put up a dozen simple plans. Everybody shied away, except the French. They've always believed in quick, painless solutions. However, Duhamel intervened. He gave you a special passport and put the word about that he'd chop anyone who tried to chop you. Once you were in England liquidation seemed a less profitable solution. When you had your stroke it was clearly unnecessary. . . . The argument was that it would be better to discredit you than to make you a martyr.

"I never thought so. When I got the news yesterday that I'd have to have surgery and that I'd be carrying around my own excrement for the rest of my life, I thought, why not kill two birds with the one stone—you first, me afterwards?

"I remembered that evening in Tübingen when you said you knew me and the spirit that dwelt in me. I don't think I've ever hated anyone so much as I hated you at that moment." He fished in the pocket of his dressing gown and brought out a gold pen. He displayed it to Jean Marie. "This is Death in one of his more elegant dresses—a capsule of lethal gas sufficient to carry us both off —unless I cover my nose like this while I blow the stuff at you."

He covered his nose and mouth with a handkerchief and extended the pen, point forward, towards Jean Marie's face.

Jean Marie sat very still, watching him. He said quietly, "I came to terms with death a long time ago. You are doing me a kindness, Alvin Dolman."

"I know." Dolman stuffed the handkerchief and the pen back in his pocket and made a comic gesture of resignation. "I guess I just needed to prove it to myself!" He reached out and picked up the half-opened packet from the table. He said with a shrug, "It was a bad joke anyway. I'll be getting back to my room."

"Wait!" Jean Marie heaved himself slowly out of his chair and stood up. "I'll walk to the elevator with you."

"Don't bother! I can find my own way."

"You lost your way a long time ago." Jean Marie's tone was somber. "You will never find it by yourself."

Dolman's face was suddenly transformed into a pale mask of rage. "I said I'd find my own way back!"

"Why are you so angry over a courtesy?"

"You should know that!" Dolman was grinning now, a rictus of silent glee that was more terrible than the laughter. "You told me in Tübingen you knew the name of the spirit that dwelt in me!"

"I do know it." Jean Marie spoke with calm authority and an odd quirky humour. "His name is Legion. But let's not overplay the drama, Mr. Dolman. You are not possessed by devils. You are a habitat of evils—too many evils for one aging man to carry inside himself!"

The taut grinning mask crumpled into a tired, middle-aged face—the face of an aging *clochard* who had used up all his chances and now had no place to go.

"Sit down, Mr. Dolman," said Jean Marie gently. "Let's treat with each other like simple human beings."

"You miss the point," said Alvin Dolman wearily. "We call up our own devils because we can't live with ourselves."

"You're still alive. You are still open to change and to God's mercy."

"You're not hearing me!" The tight, twisted grin was back again. "I may look like everyone else; but I'm not. I'm of a different breed. . . . We're killer dogs. Try to change us, try to domesticate us, we go mad and tear you to pieces. You're lucky I didn't kill you tonight."

He walked out without a word. Jean Marie went to the door and watched him limping down the long corridor with the brown-paper parcel under his arm. He was reminded of the old tale of the lame devil who roamed the city at night, lifting the roofs off houses, to display the evil that dwelt there. So far as he could remember, the lame devil never found any good anywhere. Jean Marie wondered sadly whether the lame devil was purblind or just too clear-sighted to be happy. Unless one believed in a beneficent Creator and some kind of saving grace, the world was a good place to be out of—especially if you were a middle-aged killer with a cancer in the gut.

That night he offered his Compline prayer for Alvin Dolman. Next midday he telephoned Dolman's ward nurse, only to be told that Mr. Dolman had died during the night of an unexplained cardiac arrest and that an autopsy was being arranged to establish the cause of death. His papers and his personal effects had already been retrieved by an official from the United States Embassy.

Jean Marie could not deal so curtly with a man who, however evil, was an element in the divine economy. Lives had been terminated, lives damaged, lives perhaps enriched, however momentarily, by Dolman's presence on the planet. It was not enough to pass the loveless judgment of the Puritans: "Pardon was offered; pardon was rejected; he took the inevitable walk to the Judas tree."

Jean Marie Barette—once a Pope—had too much experience of paradox to believe that the Almighty dispensed frontier justice. Whatever the Scriptures said, it was not possible to divide the world into white hats and black hats. He himself had been granted a revelation—and been reduced to a cold-eyed contemplation of suicide. He had been given a mission to proclaim the Last Things and, at the moment of announcement, had been struck dumb. So, perhaps it was not too strange to see in Dolman's suicide an act of repentance, and in his visit, a victory over the killer who lived in his skin. Were there not the tales old Grandfather Barette used to tell, of men bitten by mad dogs? They knew that death was inevitable; so, rather than infect their families, they blew their brains out with a hunting gun or locked themselves in a mountain cabin and howled themselves to death.

Once again Jean Marie was back to the dark, terrifying mystery of pain and evil and who was saved and who was not and who was ultimately responsible for the whole bloody mess. Who spawned the man who trained the killer dog? And what cosmic emperor looked down, in everlasting indifference, on the baby-child which the dog tore to pieces? . . .

It was still only noonday; but the midnight blackness enveloped him again. He wished Mr. Atha were there to walk him to the gymnasium and talk him out of the darkness towards the center of light.

XIV

MR. Atha stepped back into his life as casually as he had stepped out of it. That evening, while Jean Marie was eating supper, he walked in, looked Jean Marie up and down like an exhibit at a flower show and smiled his approval.

"I see you've made splendid progress." He laid a small package on the tray. "That's your reward."

"I missed you." Jean Marie held out both hands to greet him. "Look! Both working! Did you have a successful trip?"

"It was—busy." Mr. Atha was as evasive as ever about himself. "Travel is very difficult now. There are delays at every airport and much intervention by the police and the military. People are mistrustful and afraid. . . . Look at your present."

Jean Marie unwrapped the package and found a pouch of soft leather, inside which was a small silver box, intricately engraved.

Mr. Atha explained, "The design is made up of the invocations to Allah. There is an old man in Aleppo who used to make them. Now he is blind. His son engraved this one. Open it."

Jean Marie opened the box. Inside, nestling in a bed of white silk, was an ancient ring. The setting was gold, the stone a pale emerald with the head of a man carved on it, cameo-fashion. The stone was worn and scratched like a pebble abraded by the sea. Mr. Atha told him the story.

"This was given to me by a friend in Istanbul. He says it is certainly of the early first century and it probably comes from Macedonia. There is a half-effaced inscription in Greek on the back of the stone. You need young eyes or a magnifying glass to make it out; but it says, 'Timothy to Sylvanus. Peace!' My friend thought it might have some connection with the Apostle Paul and his two companions Sylvanus and Timothy. . . . Who knows? I had the whimsical idea that since you gave up the Fisherman's ring, you might like to have this one instead."

Jean Marie was deeply moved. Behind Mr. Atha's "whimsical idea" there was so much and so gentle a care. Jean Marie slipped the ring onto his finger. It fitted comfortably. He took it off and laid it in the silver box. He said:

"Thank you, my friend. If my blessings count for anything, you have them all." He gave a small, unsteady laugh. "I suppose one does need a certain amount of faith; but wouldn't it be wonderful if it really were a gift from Timothy to Sylvanus? They were in Macedonia together. It's clear from Paul's letter to the Thessalonians. Let me see if I can remember it. . . . 'Paul and Sylvanus and Timothy to the Church of the Thessalonians: in God the Father and the Lord Jesus Christ.' " He frowned, fumbling for the next words. . . . "Sorry, I'm blocked on the rest of it."

" '. . . Grace to you and peace!' " Mr. Atha completed the quotation. " 'We give thanks to God always for you all.' "

Jean Marie stared at him in surprise. He said, "I knew you were a believer. You had to be."

He used the French word *croyant*. Mr. Atha shook his head.

"No, I am not a believer. It happens that I was brought up in the Jewish tradition; but the act of faith is not one I personally can make. As for the passage in Thessalonians, I looked it up when my friend told me the provenance of the ring. It seemed so very appropriate: 'Grace to you and peace!' . . . Now, let us talk about you. You've had all your tests and the results are good."

"Yes, thank God! The doctors say they could discharge me immediately. However, they'd prefer I stay here for three or four more days. I can go out in the daytime and return in the evening. That way they can monitor my first reactions to physical and psychic stress."

"And you'll be surprised how much of both you'll get," said Mr. Atha.

"Will you stay with me? Take me about in London—perhaps fly with me to Munich and hand me over to my friends? I want to be with them for Christmas. I'm sure they'd be glad to have you, too. I don't want to take you away from other people who need you; but I'm out of practice in the simplest things."

"Enough!" said Mr. Atha. "You have me! I'd always intended to stay with you until you were properly recovered. You're a rather special client—in spite of your bad reputation!"

"That has to mean . . ."

"Yes, I've read the other book, too," said Mr. Atha. "It has, I understand, been suppressed by injunction in some countries; but where I've been it was freely available—and selling well! The thing is a disreputable caricature."

"Even so, it will harm a lot of people," said Jean Marie moodily. "Especially Roberta."

"Not too much," said Mr. Atha. "It will be forgotten before the year is out."

"I wish I felt so confident."

"It is not a matter of confidence, but of simple fact. Before New Year's Day we shall be at war."

Jean Marie gaped at him in total amazement. "How can you say that? Every estimate I ever heard gave us at least until spring, possibly well into the summer."

"Because," Mr. Atha explained patiently, "all the estimates were based on textbook evaluations—a conventional war by land, sea and air, escalating to a limited use of tactical nuclear weapons—with the big ones held in reserve for bargaining. The logic of history says you don't start that kind of war in the winter—certainly not between Russia and Europe or Russia and China! But I'm afraid, my friend, that the logic of history is already out the window. This time they will start with the big firecrackers, on the premise that whoever hits first wins and that the outcome will be decided in a week. . . . How little they know!"

"How much do you know?" Jean Marie was wary now. There was a sharp edge to his question. "What proof can you offer?"

"None," said Mr. Atha calmly. "But then, what proof could you offer for your vision—or even for what you wrote in *Last Letters from a Small Planet?* Believe what I tell you! It will happen—and there will be no warning. What we are seeing now—troop movements, civil defense exercises, meetings of ministers— is all grand opera. It's tradition; people expect it; so their governments are giving it to them. The reality is much different: men in concrete caverns, far below the earth, men in capsules far above it, waiting on the last fatal command. . . . Did you hear the evening news?"

"No, I missed it."

"The French President arrives here tomorrow, for emergency talks at Downing Street. Your friend Duhamel will be with him."

Jean Marie set down his fork with a clatter. "How do you know Duhamel is a friend of mine?"

"He is mentioned in *The Fraud.*"

"Oh!" Jean Marie was embarrassed. "I've never read the book. . . . I wonder if Duhamel would agree with your interpretation of global events."

"I hardly think it matters."

"It matters to me," said Jean Marie testily. Then instantly he apologized. "I'm sorry; that was rude. There's a long story between Duhamel and myself. I don't want to bore you with it."

"I am never bored," said Mr. Atha. "I am too much in love with this small world. Tell me about Duhamel."

It took a long time in the telling, from the moment of his first call from brother Alain's office, to Duhamel's resolve to end it all on Rubicon Day and the cosmos cup that was the symbol of the bond between them.

When the story was ended, Mr. Atha added his own footnote. ". . . So now you'd like it all tidy and tied with a pink ribbon: Duhamel and his wife safe in the arms of Everlasting Mercy. Yes?"

"Yes!" said Jean Marie flatly. "It would be good to know something was tidy in the economy of salvation."

"I'm afraid it never is," said Mr. Atha. "The mathematics are too complicated for human calculation. . . . I must leave you now. I'll pick you up here at ten-thirty in the morning, clothed and in your right mind!"

It was extraordinary how, in the shadow of Mr. Atha's prediction, the simplest pleasures became exquisitely precious: the sight of children playing in the park, the faces of women window-shopping, the tinsel and the glitter of Christmas decorations, even the grey drizzle that drove them to seek shelter in the snuggery of an English pub.

With Mr. Atha he felt the same kind of companionable ease that he had enjoyed in the early years of his friendship with Carl Mendelius. Yet there was a difference. With Mendelius there were always the explosive moments—of anger at an injustice, of excitement at some newly grasped idea, of emotion at a glimpse of hidden beauty. Mr. Atha, on the contrary, was inexorably calm, like a great rock in a turbulent sea. He did not communicate emotion. He understood it. He absorbed it. What he gave back was an almost physical sensation of peace and repose.

If Jean Marie were surprised, Atha would somehow enlarge the surprise to wonder, the wonder to a serene illumination. If Jean Marie were saddened—as he was by moments—at the sight of a derelict sleeping rough in an alley, a youth soliciting on a street corner, a child with the marks of cruelty or neglect, Mr. Atha would transmute the sadness into a hope which, even under the threat of Armageddon, seemed not incongruous.

". . . In poorer and simpler countries we respect beggars and honour madmen. The beggars remind us of our own good fortune and the madmen are blessed by God with visions denied to others. We experience cataclysms but see them in terms of continuity rather than of termination. . . . The strange thing is that men who have unlocked the secrets of the atom and of the spiral helix will now use those secrets to destroy themselves. . . ."

"What is in us that brings us inevitably to the precipice?"

"You were taught it from a child. Man is made in God's image. . . . That means he is a creature of almost unbelievable resources, of frightening potential."

"Which he always misuses."

"Because he will not come to terms with his mortality. Always he believes he can cheat the hangman."

"I thought you told me you were not a believer."

"Nor am I," said Mr. Atha. "Belief is impossible to me."

"Relatively or absolutely?" Jean Marie teased him with a theologian's question.

"Absolutely," said Mr. Atha. "Now, let's take a taxi. Waldo Pearson wants you at the Carlton Club at twelve forty-five precisely."

"You were invited, too."

"I know. I'm duly flattered; but I'm sure Pearson and Duhamel would like to have you to themselves."

"Duhamel? I didn't know he was going to be there."

"I suggested it," said Mr. Atha amiably. "After all, it is a farewell meal. . . . I'll pick you up at two-thirty."

It was strange to be back in the room where he had been stricken, a little embarrassing to exchange nods or greetings with the men who had witnessed his collapse. This luncheon was another moment of testimony, given in the understated English fashion, but trumpet-clear to everyone familiar with the rituals of the realm. Waldo Pearson was saying, "This man is still my friend; the things you have read about him are lies; if any of you thinks otherwise let him raise his voice and tell me so!"

The presence of Pierre Duhamel was also a potent witness to his good character. The President of the Republic was lunching at Downing Street. His most trusted counsellor was very visible at the Carlton Club, giving the lie to a libel about Jean Marie Barette. But Duhamel dismissed the issue over the soup.

". . . Pouf! A nothing! A graffito on the ruins, with no one left to read it! Don't you agree, Waldo?"

"Regrettably I do," said Waldo Pearson. "We're facing a grim Christmas and a very dubious New Year. You could be as villainous as the Borgias now, Jean, and no one would give a damn."

"I am told," said Jean Marie carefully, "that we may not see a New Year."

Pearson and Duhamel exchanged anxious glances. Duhamel asked with dry irony, "Another vision?"

"No," said Jean Marie with a shrug of deprecation. "This time it was Mr. Atha, my therapist."

"In that case," said Waldo Pearson with obvious relief, "we can enjoy lunch. I recommend the rack of lamb and a bottle of the club's Burgundy. I chose it myself and you won't get better at the President's table."

Jean Marie was not to be put off so blandly, even by Waldo Pearson. He turned to Pierre Duhamel and put the barbed question, "How far are we from Rubicon Day?"

"Not very far." Duhamel answered without hesitation. "Troops of the Warsaw Pact are already mobilized in Europe. Soviet troops are also deployed in depth along the frontiers with China, Iran, Iraq and Turkey. The dispositions and strengths correspond with their known battle order and stage two of combat readiness."

"And what is stage two?" asked Jean Marie.

"Basically it means they're ready to meet any attack during winter and can be quickly reinforced for an offensive in early spring. Which is what we all expect."

"They're following the textbook," said Waldo Pearson. "Right down to the small print."

"But just suppose there's a different textbook," said Jean Marie quietly. "The order of battle is reversed and the big bang comes first."

"The way the Russians are disposed indicates they won't do that." Waldo Pearson spoke with solid John Bull conviction.

"What if we are the ones with the different textbook?"

"No comment," said Pierre Duhamel.

The waiter presented the wine, Waldo Pearson sniffed it, tasted it, announced that he was still proud of it and ordered it to be poured. He raised his glass to toast Jean Marie.

"To your continued good health and the continued success of the book."

"Thank you."

"I read it." Pierre Duhamel was eager in his praise. "Paulette too! She laughed and wept over your little clown. Me? I began by admiring the cunning of your invention and the elegance of your style. Then I found myself arguing with your Jeannot—sometimes for him, sometimes against. In the end—well, how does one say it?—the book didn't solve the problems of this lousy twentieth century, but it did leave a good taste in my mouth . . . Like your wine, Waldo!"

"My thanks to you both." Jean Marie raised his own glass. "I am blessed in my friends."

"The lamb!" said Waldo Pearson. "We get the first cut! That's why I like to be here right on time."

Jean Marie was bemused. Pearson's insistence on the trivia of the meal table seemed odd and out of character for a man so forceful and intelligent. But when Pearson left the table to take a telephone call, Duhamel explained it with a very Parisian aside.

"So British! He knows this is good-bye. He doesn't know how to say it. So he talks about the rack of lamb! Dear loving God! What a race!"

"I'm an idiot," said Jean Marie; and to cover his embarrassment he asked hastily, "What do you hear of Roberta?"

"Nothing. She is always away."

"If you see her, give her my love."

"I will."

"And to Paulette, too."

"Jean, my friend, let me give you one last piece of advice."

"Go ahead!"

"Think of yourself! Don't worry about me, Roberta, Paulette, anyone else! We all have a telephone line to our private God—whoever He may be! If He's there, He'll talk to us. If not, the whole game's a *blague*. Here! Have some more wine! . . ."

". . . Was it a good lunch?" asked Mr. Atha.

"It was good-bye," said Jean Marie Barette. "We walked out. We shook hands. I said, 'Thank you for a pleasant meal.' Waldo said, 'Delighted to have you, my dear chap.' Duhamel said, 'What horrible exit lines!' We laughed and went our separate ways."

"It sounds appropriate," said Mr. Atha. "I've picked up our plane tickets and booked a car to take us to the airport. The flight leaves at eleven. Allowing for the normal hour's delay, we should be in Munich by two in the afternoon. When we get back this evening I'll get you to sign checks for the medical bills and for staff gratuities. That way you won't be fussed in the morning."

"And then it finishes! Another chapter of my life closed—just like that!"

Mr. Atha shrugged. "Going away is dying a little and dying is very simple. There is a saying among the desert people: 'Never wave good-bye to the caravan. You will follow it soon.' . . . Now, we have to buy you some warm clothes; otherwise you'll freeze in that Alpine valley."

It was snowing hard when they landed in Munich, the last plane in before the airport closed. There was a long queue at passport control. The frontier police were checking meticulously on all foreigners. Jean Marie wondered whether his name was listed in the black book of undesirables; but finally he was waved through the barrier into the customs hall, where there was another pile-up of harassed travellers. Mr. Atha steered him to the exit and then went back to wait for the baggage. A moment later Jean Marie was caught in a bear-hug embrace by Johann Mendelius.

"Uncle Jean! You made it! You look wonderful! Mother and Father wanted to come in but the roads are bad; so I had to bring the jeep and use chains to get through the pass."

Jean Marie held him at arm's length and looked at him. There was no boy left in him now. He was a man, all muscle and sinew. His face was weather-beaten, his hands hard and calloused. Jean Marie nodded his satisfaction.

"Yes, you'll do! You look like a real countryman!"

"Oh, I am! Peasant to the boot soles! We've had a big scramble to make the place habitable for the winter; but we did it! Don't expect anything too grand though. All we guarantee is country cooking and warm shelter."

"You'll find me easy to please," said Jean Marie.

"All your people arrived safely."

"My people?"

"You know; the ones you sent with your password: 'the cosmos in a wine glass.' There were three groups, nine people in all. They've settled in very well."

Some elemental instinct warned Jean Marie not to make a discussion about it. The mystery would explain itself as soon as he arrived in the valley. He simply nodded and said, "I'm glad they caused no trouble."

"On the contrary."

"How are your mother and father and Katrin?"

"Oh, they're fine. Mother's gone rather grey; but it suits her. Father tramps around like a captain on the quarterdeck, inspecting everything with his one good eye, and learning to hold tools with that mechanical grip of his. Katrin's two months pregnant. She and Franz decided to wait and ask you to marry them."

Mr. Atha pushed through the crowd with a trolley of baggage. Johann stared at him gape-mouthed, and then burst into laughter.

"I know you! You're the one who . . . Uncle Jean, this is quite extraordinary. This man . . ."

"Don't tell him now!" said Mr. Atha. "Save it awhile. Surprises are good for him."

"I agree!" Johann laughed again and took Jean Marie's arm. "It really is worth waiting for."

Together they shepherded Jean Marie through the crowd and out to the pickup zone. When Johann hurried off to bring the jeep from the parking area, Jean Marie faced Mr. Atha with a veiled reproof.

"I think, my friend, there are lots of things about you that need explaining."

"I know," said Mr. Atha in his easy fashion. "But I'm sure we'll find a better time and place to do it. . . . That's a fine young man!"

"Johann? Yes. He's matured so much since I last saw him." A sudden thought struck him. He groaned aloud. "It's Christmas Eve! I've been so preoccupied with myself I forgot to buy any presents for the family—or for you. I feel very bad about that."

"I don't need presents and you pay me to remember! I bought some things before we left. They're wrapped. All you have to do is write on the cards." He smiled and added, "I hope I chose the right things."

"I'm sure you did; but this time I'd rather not have any surprises. What did you buy?"

"For Frau Mendelius, head scarves and lace handkerchiefs; for the young man, a ski sweater; for the girl, perfume; for the professor, a prismatic magnifier for easy reading. Did I do right?"

"Magnificently. You have my eternal gratitude. But you are still not dispensed from explanations."

"I promise you will get them. I hope you will understand," said Mr. Atha. "Here's Johann."

They helped Jean Marie into the Jeep, bundled him up in a blanket and a sheepskin pelisse and set off along the autobahn to Garmisch.

Johann talked eagerly about the small community in the valley. ". . . Our intentions were vague. Papa had this idea of founding a postgraduate academy. I thought of it as a place where my friends and I could hide out, if we got into trouble with the authorities. You'll remember that was in the days when we were buying arms from Dolman and setting up an underground at the University. . . . Then, of course, everything changed. We had to help Papa rebuild his life and this seemed a good place to do it.

"Eight of us came down to start making the buildings habitable. We camped in the lodge and worked from sunup to sunset. The place is far off the trunk routes as you will see. So we didn't expect many visitors. But they started dribbling through—young people mostly, but some older ones. We put it down to the fact that Bavaria is full of tourists in the fall. There's the Bierfest and the opera and all the fashion shows. So we got all sorts of callers: Italians, Greeks, Yugoslavs, Vietnamese, Poles, Americans, Japanese. They said they'd like to stay and help. That was great. We were terribly short of labour. We made a simple rule: work and share. It's amazing! So far we've held together and we're quite a mixed community, as you'll see!"

"Did people offer any special reason for joining you?" asked Jean Marie.

"We don't enquire," said Johann. "If they want to talk, we listen. I suppose it would be true to say that most of them have some hidden scars."

"And they'd like to be born again without them," said Mr. Atha.

"Yes, you might put it like that," said Johann thoughtfully.

When they reached the first Alpine foothills, Johann turned south and began a long, winding ascent along a country road already deep in snow. Just before the road ran out and became a rutted timber-track through the pinewoods, there was a small wayside shrine, the usual carved wooden crucifix with a gabled canopy above it. Johann slowed the car.

"That's where we first met Mr. Atha, when we were hiking through here on our way to Austria. We asked him if he knew a good camping spot. He pointed us up the track we're taking now. . . . Hang on, Uncle Jean! It gets rough from now on!"

It was, in fact, fifteen minutes of jolting and jerking that threatened to shake the teeth loose from their heads; but when they broke out of the timber, they saw a high black wall of rock, with snow piled white in the crevices, and through it a defile, cut clean as if with a giant axe. The defile was perhaps a hundred meters long. The far end was closed with a palisade of split logs hung on huge hinges of hand-forged iron. Johann got out of the jeep, swung the palisade open and drove through it into a large saucer-shaped depression fringed with black crags that gave place, tier by tier, to pinewoods and the wilder growth of the lowlands round the lake. Johann stopped the jeep. Mr. Atha got out to close the barrier. Johann pointed down through the snow swirls.

"You can't see much in this murk. The lake is bigger than it looks from up here. The lights you can see through the trees come from the main lodge and the cabins which are strung out on either side of it. The waterfall is on the far side and the old mine entrance about fifty yards to the left. . . . There's such a lot to show you. But let's get you home. Father and Mother will be biting their fingernails! . . ."

Mr. Atha climbed into the jeep and they jolted down a deer track towards the sparse yellow lights.

"We have you to ourselves until dinnertime," Lotte told him happily. "Carl laid it down like the laws of the Medes and Persians! No reception committee! No visitors! No interruptions until we had had our own time with our own Jean Marie! Johann promised to entertain your Mr. Atha. The others are busy decorating the Christmas tree, cooking for the dinner tonight. . . . We've all had to get used to less house-room and less privacy; but, at Christmas, it's rather pleasant and tribal."

They were sitting round an old porcelain stove in what had once been the servants' sitting room in the lodge. The furniture consisted of a small pine table, piled high with books, a wooden stool and three battered armchairs. They were drinking coffee laced with brandy and nibbling on cupcakes, hot from the oven.

Lotte had aged rapidly in a few short months. The last traces of youth were gone and she was now a silver-haired matron with soft, motherly features and the ready smile of a woman at peace with herself and her world. Mendelius had slimmed down; but he was still a solid, vigorous man. One side of his face was ravaged—scarred and stained by tiny fragments which had ruptured the vesicles; but his black eye-patch gave him a raffish air and there was humour still in his lopsided smile. He professed himself not unhappy with Jean Marie Barette.

". . . The limp is a nothing! It's just enough to make you look like a distinguished war veteran! The face? Well, I wouldn't know you'd had a stroke. Would you, Lotte? Anyway, beside me, you look like Donatello's *David!* . . . Still, there's a lot of life left in us both, old friend! What do you think of this place? Of course, you can't see a thing with the snowstorm; but it's all very exciting. We've got forty people here now, including four children. You'll meet them before dinner. And it will be a good dinner, I promise you! Johann and his boys hauled in nearly fifty tons of supplies last month. The woods are full of deer. We've got four milch cows in the barn. You'll smell them tonight, because your room is right over the byres. . . . You'll say midnight Mass for us, of course. Not everybody's Christian. We get over that by what we call 'a communion of friends' at the evening meal. Anybody who feels uneasy can avoid it by coming late. The rest of us sit together and hold hands in silence. If anyone feels like saying a public prayer, he or she says it. If someone wants to make a testimony or ask for an accounting of our common day, this is the time to do it. We end with the recitation of the 'Our Father.' Most people join in. Then we dine. . . . It seems to work. There's something else you should know." Mendelius straightened up in his chair. His tone was a shade more formal. "The deeds of the valley are in my name and Lotte's, with reversion to the children. However, we felt that since most of our people are young, I was no longer appropriate as a leader; so, by common consent, Johann is the head of the community."

"It works very well," said Lotte eagerly. "There is no longer a rivalry between Carl and Johann. They respect each other. Johann constantly seeks advice from Carl and me. He listens carefully—but in the end he makes the decisions. However, we'd all like you to take the place of honour, sit at the head of the table, that sort of thing!"

"No, my dear Lotte!" Jean Marie reached out to touch her cheek. "You have it wrong. I am the servant of the servants of God. I'll sit with you and Carl—old friends, wise enough to let the young cut their teeth on the barbed wire!"

Suddenly, as if a fuse had blown, the affectionate talk was over. Mendelius reached out his good hand and gripped Jean Marie's wrist. He said grimly:

"This is all too bland, Jean! We both know it. I hear the same kind of chat every day among our people here. Everything's sweetness and light. God help us! You'd think we were young lovers building our dream houses!"

"Carl, that's not fair!" Lotte was indignant. "We talk simple things to take our minds off the terrible ones we can't control. And why shouldn't we enjoy what we're doing here? There's a lot of sweat going into this place—and a lot of love, too. Only sometimes you're too crotchety to see it!"

"I'm sorry, liebchen. I don't mean to be bad-tempered. But Jean understands what I'm trying to say."

"I understand you both," said Jean Marie. "The short answer is that all the news is bad. The best hope is that hostilities will not begin until spring. The worst prediction, made by my friend Mr. Atha, and half-confirmed by a 'No comment' from Pierre Duhamel, is that the Americans might attempt a preemptive strike with the big missiles, even before the New Year."

There was a long moment of silence. Lotte stretched out her hand to touch her husband.

Carl Mendelius said, "If that happens, Jean, then everything will be tossed into the witches' cauldron: nerve gas, germs, lasers, every weird horror in the arsenals of the world."

"True," said Jean Marie. "Even so, you could be safe here for a very long time."

"But that's not the point, is it, Jean? That's not where all this began—as a plan for mere survival. If it were, I don't think Lotte and I would have taken the trouble. I don't think you would either. We've both become familiar with Brother Death; and he's not half the terrifying fellow he's made out to be. All this began with your vision and the message they wouldn't let you proclaim: centers of hope, centers of charity for the aftermath. Well, now that you're here, what do we do?"

"Carl, he's only just arrived!" Clearly Carl Mendelius' frustrations were no new thing to Lotte. "But we can tell him what we've been doing. You said it yourself: you can't give water from an empty bucket. So we're all preparing ourselves for the services we can best offer—in no matter how small a way. Anneliese Meissner is training some of the young men and the girls in practical medicine—even in homeopathic remedies which are available from local plants. She has them fired with enthusiasm by the example of the barefoot doctors in Chinese rural areas. One of the people Johann brought in is a young engineer who is working on a scheme to use the waterfall for generating power. . . . I've started classes for the children, and Carl is working on an idea for preserving a record of what we do here and the problems we encounter. . . . I know it's all small and elementary but it's . . . it's shareable! Even if the world does fall apart, sooner or later we'll have to try to make contact with the remnants near us. When we do, we must have something to offer; otherwise hope's dead and charity's empty!"

It was the longest speech Jean Marie had ever heard her make, and the finest affirmation of all she had learned as a woman.

"Bravo, Lotte! You should be proud of this girl, Carl!"

"I am." Carl Mendelius was good-humoured again. "I just get jealous because she's so much more useful than I am. I mean it! I'm a very learned fellow. But what's it worth beside a woman who can make medicine from herbs or a man who can make electricity from a waterfall?"

"Oh, I'm sure there's some use we can make of you." Lotte stood up and kissed Mendelius on the forehead. "I'm going to see what progress they're making in the kitchen."

When she had left, Jean Marie asked him a question.

"Where would you say the name Atha comes from?"

"Atha?" Mendelius repeated the word a few times and then shook his head. "Truly, I've no idea. This is the friend who came with you?"

"Yes. He's very vague about himself—and a lot of other things as well. He says he comes from the Middle East. He was brought up in the Jewish tradition and he's a nonbeliever. . . . But, Carl, he's a unique man. He's young, as you see. He can't be older than the mid-thirties. Yet he has so much maturity, so much inner endurance. When I was at my lowest, I clung to him like a drowning man. I felt he was carrying me to safety on his back. It was very strange. He slipped so easily into my life that it was as if I had known him forever. One gets the impression of immense knowledge and most varied experience. Yet he never exposes any of it. I'll be very interested to see how you react to him."

"Atha . . . Atha . . ." Carl Mendelius was still toying with the name. "It certainly isn't Hebrew. But it does ring a faint bell somewhere. . . . I don't know why; but ever since I've been in hospital, my memory isn't nearly as good as it used to be."

"Mine isn't either," said Jean Marie. "The only consolation is that there are lots of things we need to forget!"

Mendelius pushed himself out of his chair and held out a hand to pull Jean Marie to his feet.

"Let's take a stroll and see who's around. Then you won't have to face a long line of new faces at dinnertime."

In what had once been the dining room of the lodge, a big log fire was blazing and Advent candles in their sprays of greenery were set at the windows. In one corner there was the traditional Nativity tableau: wooden figures of the Virgin, Joseph and the Christ Child with the shepherds and the animals watching about the manger. Opposite was a large Christmas tree dressed with tinsel and baubles. The rest of the room was taken up by benches and trestle tables where bustling young men and women were setting places for dinner. Mendelius, fumbling for names, settled for an offhand introduction:

"Friends, this is Father Jean Marie Barette. . . . He'll be available later for confessions, counsel—or just agreeable company! You'll have plenty of time to get to know him. . . ." In an aside to Jean he added, "I know it's a comedown; but we're too small to afford a Pope or even a bishop! And we don't want to frighten off the customers!"

Jean Marie finished the old, clerical joke for him: "Not before we collect the Christmas offerings!"

The kitchen boasted a large, ancient wood oven and a half-dozen eager cooks preparing poultry, vegetables and sweetmeats. One of them was Katrin, covered in flour to her elbows. She held up her face to be kissed and made a joke of her condition.

"Would you believe it! Me of all people! At first I was panic-stricken but now I'm really happy. So is Franz. You'll see him later. He's sawing logs in the barn. You will marry us, Uncle Jean?"

"Who else is there?"

"Well, if you hadn't come, we were going to have a kind of public binding."

"It's the same thing," said Jean Marie, "except mine comes with benefit of clergy."

In the far corner, Anneliese Meissner was mixing a concoction in a large copper pot. Jean Marie said his greetings and then stuck his fingers in the pot.

"Punch!" she told him. "My own recipe. Not to be served to anyone under eighteen or persons not covered by life insurance." She held the ladle up for him to taste. "Well? What do you think?"

"Lethal!" said Jean Marie.

"You get one small glass, no more. I hope you're doing all the things you were told." She fixed him with a shrewd professional eye. "You look pretty good. . . . Only the tiniest touch of facial paresis. Give me your left hand. Grip hard! . . . You'll do. I'll check you over tomorrow, when I've recovered from the hangover I shall undoubtedly have. It's good to see you!"

It was still snowing but Carl Mendelius was eager to keep moving. He handed Jean Marie a sheepskin coat and a pair of snow boots, then took him out to give him a quick look at the contours of the tiny settlement: the lake frozen and snow-covered, with an upturned boat on the strand, the waterfall still flowing but festooned with icicles, the mouth of the ancient mine tunnel.

"It goes in a long way," Mendelius explained. "There are still some large outcrops of bloodstone. We've got all our stores in there: canned foods, seed stocks, tools. It's the best possible protection against blast or direct radiation. . . . The fall-out, of course, depends on the winds. I would guess Munich must be the nearest big target. . . . Would you like to meet the children? They're in this cabin. Some of the women are looking after them. We don't want to spoil the surprise of the Christmas tree."

But when Mendelius pushed open the door and stood aside to let him enter the cabin, Jean Marie had his own big surprise. Mr. Atha was seated in a chair with his back to the door. He had a small child on his lap. Three others were seated on the floor in front of them and behind the children were four women, all absorbed in the story. One of them made a hushing signal with her hand. Mendelius and Jean Marie crept in on tiptoe and closed the door silently. Mr. Atha went on with his story.

". . . You haven't been there; but I have. This place where the shepherds were watching their sheep is a hillside, very bare and cold. It didn't have trees like you have here, just stones and coarse grass, hardly enough to feed the sheep. The shepherds were lonely. I've spent a lot of time in the desert and I can tell you it is very frightening at night. So, one shepherd sang a little, and the one farther away picked up the song, and then another one, until they were all singing together like angel voices. Then they saw the star. It was big—big as a melon!—and it hung so low that they could almost reach up and pick it out of the sky. It was bright too; but soft-bright, so that it didn't hurt their eyes. And it hung right over the cave where the baby had just been born. So the shepherds walked towards the star, still singing, and they were the first visitors that little family of Jesus, Mary and Joseph ever had in Bethlehem of Judah. . . ."

There was a momentary hush and a big "Ah! . . ." from the children as the story ended. Then Mr. Atha stood up and turned to greet the newcomers. The child in his arms was the little mongol from the Institute at Versailles. One of the women was the *patronne* of the Hostellerie des Chevaliers; another was Judith, the little twisted one who made the cosmos cup.

Jean Marie was struck dumb with shock. He stammered and stuttered, as he had after the palsy.

"How . . . How did you get here?"

"You sent for us," said Judith. "Mr. Atha brought the message."

Jean Marie turned to Mr. Atha. "How did you know the password? I told it to no one except Johann."

"Take the child," said Mr. Atha. "She wants you."

He handed the little girl to Jean Marie and immediately she began fondling him, gurgling with pleasure. He found voice again as he crooned to her. "Eh, my little clown!"

It was only then that he was able to greet the others, and he embraced them like a father parted too long from his family. To the *patronne* he said, "Now, madame, you really have the silly mule and not the Pope!"

Mr. Atha's voice steadied him against the rush of emotion.

"These folk are my Christmas gifts to you. I invited others, too, in the same way. You'll meet them later, but you won't know them. They were clients of mine who needed special help. I hope you don't mind my small stratagem, Professor Mendelius."

"It's Christmas." Mendelius was laughing at Jean Marie's happy discomfiture. "It's always been open house at our place!"

"Thank you, Professor."

"Your name interests me, Mr. Atha. It's not Hebrew. What is its origin?"

"Syriac," said Mr. Atha.

"Oh," said Carl Mendelius, and was too polite to ask any more questions of so laconic a guest.

* * *

Dinner began with a ceremony of children. Jean Marie carried the little clown girl in his arms to show her the Christmas tree and the Nativity stable and the sparks dancing from the big pine logs. She would not leave him; so, before the meal could begin, her high chair had to be placed next to him.

Johann stood at the head of the table with his mother on his right and Anneliese Meissner on his left. Carl Mendelius was next to Lotte; Jean Marie sat next to Anneliese with the child beside him. Opposite him on the other side of the table was Mr. Atha, with Judith on one side and Katrin Mendelius on the other. Johann opened the proceedings with a formal request.

"Will you give us a blessing, please, Uncle Jean."

Jean Marie crossed himself and recited the grace, noting as he did so that Mr. Atha did not make the sign of the cross, as some did; though he did chime in with the "Amen" at the end of the prayer.

Then the feast began, ample, cheerful and noisy, with everyone primed on Anneliese's punch and fuelled with Rhine wine. It was arranged, Johann had told Jean Marie, to come to the coffee by ten-thirty, so that the children could be got to bed and the adults have a chance to sober themselves before the Christmas Mass at midnight. By ten the assembly had settled into a sentimental mood. Johann Mendelius stood up and rapped on his glass for attention. Even in the afterglow of the wine he had an air of confidence and authority. He said:

"My friends, my family. This won't be a long speech. I want first to wish you all the best of good things for Christmas and our life afterwards in this valley. I thank you all for the hard work you did to get us ready for winter. Next, I want to welcome Uncle Jean and tell him how glad we are to have him. When I saw him last, months ago, I had reservations about all the things he stood for. Now, I'd like him to know I have fewer reservations and a lot more convictions about what makes a good man. Finally, I'd like to say thank you to Mr. Atha, who first pointed me up the track to this place and now has brought us not only our most distinguished but also our most beloved citizen." He gestured towards Jean Marie and the child in the high chair beside him. There was a small burst of applause. He went on, "From a chance remark which he made while we were chatting this afternoon, I gather that Mr. Atha is one of those unfortunate people whose birthday falls on Christmas Day. Normally he gets only one present instead of two. Well, this time, we'll make sure he gets two presents!" He held up a bottle of red wine and a bottle of white and passed them down the table with a greeting. "Happy birthday, Mr. Atha!"

There was cheering and clapping and calls for a speech. Mr. Atha stood up. In the glow of the candles and the firelight he looked like a figure from some ancient mosaic, revealed in a sudden splendour of bronze and gold. Abruptly there was silence. He spoke not at all loudly; but his voice filled the room. Even the little buffoon child was still, as if she understood every word.

"First I have thanks to give. Tomorrow is indeed my birthday and I am happy to celebrate it here with you tonight. I have promised explanations to my friend Jean Marie, and it is proper that you should hear them, too, because you are sharers in the same mystery. . . . First, you should know that you are not here by your own design. You were led here, step by step, on different roads, through many apparent accidents; but, always, it was the finger of God that beckoned you.

"You are not the only community thus brought together. There are many others, all over the world: in the forests of Russia, in the jungles of Brazil, in places you would never dream. They are all different; because men's needs and habits are different. Yet they are all the same; because they have followed the same beckoning finger, and bonded themselves by the same love. They did not do this of themselves. They could not, just as you could not, without a special prompting of grace.

"You were prompted for a reason. Even as I speak, the adversary begins to stalk the earth, roaring destruction! So, in the evil times which are now upon us, you are chosen to keep the small flame of love alight, to nurture the seeds of goodness in this small place, until the day when the Spirit sends you out to light other candles in a dark land and plant new seeds in a blackened earth.

"I am with you now; but tomorrow I shall be gone. You will be alone and afraid. But I leave my peace with you and my love. And you will love one another as I have loved you.

"Please!" He urged them to cheerfulness. "You must not be sad! The gift of the Holy Spirit is gladness of heart." He smiled and the room seemed to light up. He joked with them. "Professor Mendelius and my friend Jean Marie are puzzled about my name. So much for scholarship, my dear Professor! And how quickly even Popes forget their Scripture! You were looking for one word. There are two. You will know them when I remind you. *Maran Atha.* . . . The Lord comes!"

Jean Marie was instantly on his feet. His voice was a high challenge.

"You lied to me! You said you were a nonbeliever!"

"I did not lie. You have forgotten. You asked was I a believer. I answered that I was not. I said at another time that the act of faith was impossible for me. True?"

"True."

"And still you do not understand?"

"No."

"Enough!" Carl Mendelius spoke out, angrily in defense of Jean Marie. "The man is tired. He has been ill. He is not ready for riddles!" He turned to Jean Marie. "What he is saying, Jean, is that he cannot believe because he knows. They taught you that in first-year theology. God cannot believe in Himself. He knows Himself as he knows all the work of His hands."

"Thank you, Professor," said Mr. Atha.

Jean Marie stood silent, as the full meaning of the words dawned upon him. Once again he challenged the man across the table.

"You have called yourself Mr. Atha. What is your true name?"

"You have to tell me!"

There was, again, the odd, abrupt silence. Out of it Jean Marie spoke.

"Are you the promised one?"

"Yes, I am."

"How do we know?"

"Sit down, please!"

Mr. Atha sat down first. Without a word he drew a trencher of bread towards him and poured wine into a cup. He broke a piece off the bread and held it in his hands over the cup. He said, "Father, bless this bread, fruit of Your earth, the food by which we live." He paused and then began again. "This is my body. . . ."

Jean Marie stood up. He was calm now and respectful, but still undaunted.

"Sir, you know that these are very familiar words, most sacred to us all. You know enough of our Scriptures to remember that the early disciples recognized Jesus in the breaking of bread. You could be using that knowledge to deceive us."

"Why should I do that? Why are you so mistrustful?"

"Because our Lord Jesus himself warned us: 'There will arise false Christs and false prophets who will show great signs, so as to deceive even the chosen. . . .' I am a priest. The people ask me to show them Jesus Christ. If you are He, you must give me what you gave your first disciples, a legitimizing sign!"

"Isn't all this enough?" The gesture embraced the whole room and the valley. "Doesn't this legitimize me?"

"No!"

"Why not?"

"Because there are communities which call themselves godly, but which exploit people and twist them into hate. We are not tested yet. We do not know if the gift is true or treacherous."

There was a long silence; then the man who called himself Jesus held out his hands.

"Give me the child!"

"No!" Even as he recoiled in fear, Jean Marie knew it was all presaged in the dream.

"Please let me hold her. She will come to no harm."

Jean Marie looked around the assembly. Their faces told him nothing. He lifted the child out of the high chair and passed her across the table. Mr. Atha kissed her and sat her on his knee. He dipped a crust of bread in the wine and fed it to her, morsel by morsel. As he did so, he talked, quietly and persuasively.

"I know what you are thinking. You need a sign. What better one could I give than to make this little one whole and new? I could do it; but I will not. I am the Lord and not a conjuror. I gave this mite a gift I denied to all of you—eternal innocence. To you she looks imperfect—but to me she is flawless, like the bud that dies unopened or the fledgling that falls from the nest to be devoured by the ants. She will never offend me, as all of you have done. She will never pervert or destroy the work of my Father's hands. She is necessary to you. She will evoke the kindness that will keep you human. Her infirmity will prompt you to gratitude for your own good fortune. . . . More! She will remind you every day that I am who I am, that my ways are not yours, and that the smallest dust mote whirled in darkest space does not fall out of my hand. . . . I have chosen you. You have not chosen me. This little one is my sign to you. Treasure her!"

He lifted the child from his lap, and passed her back across the table to Jean Marie. He said gently:

"It is time to give witness, my friend. Tell me! Who am I?"

"I am not sure yet."

"Why not?"

"I am a fool," said Jean Marie Barette. "I am a clown touched in the head.
. . . Truly!" He looked around at the little company. He tapped his skull. "A
little part of me up there doesn't function anymore. I limp, like Jacob after his
wrestle with the angel. I drop things. Sometimes I open my mouth and nothing
comes out. I chase the words as a child chases bu . . . bu . . ." At the last
moment he seized on the word. "Butterflies! So you must be simple with me.
Tell me: can you really change your mind?"

"Why do you ask?"

"Abraham bargained with God for Sodom and Gomorrah. He said, 'If there
be a hundred or twenty or ten just men in the cities, will you spare them?' And
God, so the Scripture said, was very reasonable about the whole affair. Our
Jesus who was of the seed of Abraham said that whatever we ask will be given
us. We should knock at the door and clamour to be heard. But there's no point
in that if there's no one inside—or if the one inside is a mad spirit whirling
heedless with the galaxies!"

"Ask then!" said Mr. Atha. "What do you want?"

"Time." Jean Marie Barette held the child close to him and pleaded as he
had never pleaded in his life before. "Enough to hope, work, pray, reason a
little longer together. Please! If you are the Lord, do you want to march into
your world like the old barbarians on a carpet of dead bodies? That would be
surely an unworthy triumph. . . . This child is a great gift; but we need all the
children and time enough to deserve them. Please!"

"And what can you offer me in return?"

"Very little," said Jean Marie with bleak simplicity. "I am diminished now. I
have to think in small ways; but, such as I am, you can have me!"

"I accept," said Mr. Atha.

"How much time will you give us?"

"Not too much—but enough!"

"Thank you. Thank you from us all."

"Now are you ready to testify?"

"Yes, I'm ready."

"Wait!" It was Carl Mendelius who uttered the final challenge. For all his
ravages and his wounds he was still the doughty old skeptic of Rome and
Tübingen. "He has promised nothing, Jean. He has uttered only words familiar
to us for centuries. I can list their sources for you, every one! He talks as though
time is in his gift. You abdicated because you had no patent of authority for
your prophecy. Why do you accept less from this man?"

There was a murmur of approval from the small assembly. They looked first
at Mr. Atha sitting calm and composed in his place, then at Jean Marie,
clasping the child close to him and rocking back and forth in his chair. Lotte
Mendelius got up from her place to take the child from him. She said, so softly
that only he could hear:

"Whatever you decide, we love you."

Jean Marie patted her hand and surrendered the little girl. He gave Carl
Mendelius the old sidelong grin which acknowledged all the things they had

shared in the bad times in Rome. He said, "Carl, old friend, there's never enough evidence. You know that. You've been digging for it all your life. We make do with what we have. From this man I have had nothing but good. What more can I ask?"

"The answer, please." Mr. Atha prompted him firmly. "Who am I?"

"I believe," said Jean Marie Barette, and prayed for a steady tongue. "I believe you are the Anointed One, the Son of the Living God! . . . B-but . . ." He stumbled and recovered himself slowly. "I have no mission, I have no authority. I cannot speak for my friends. You will have to teach them, as you have taught me."

"No!" said Mr. Atha. "Tomorrow I shall be gone about my Father's other business. You must teach them, Jean!"

"How . . . how can I with this halter on my tongue?"

"You are a rock of a man!" said Mr. Atha. "On you I can build a small standing place for my people!"

EPILOGUE

PIERRE Duhamel stood at the window of the President's chamber and watched the snow falling over Paris. He fumbled in the pocket of his jacket and his fingers closed round the tiny enamelled comfit box, which held the two gelatin capsules: the passport to oblivion for Paulette and himself. The sensation gave him a weary kind of comfort. At least Paulette would not need to suffer anymore and he himself would be spared the sight of Paris in the aftermath. He wanted to be quit of this long, despairing deathwatch and go home to bed.

The man he had served for twenty years sat behind him at the great desk, chin propped in his hands, staring sightlessly at the documents in front of him. He asked, "What time have you got?"

"Five minutes to midnight," said Pierre Duhamel. "It's a hell of a way to spend Christmas Eve."

"The President promised to call me from the White House the moment he'd reached a decision."

"I think he's reached it already," said Pierre Duhamel. "He'll tell us just as they're pushing the last button."

"Nothing we can do about that."

"Nothing," said Pierre Duhamel.

Out of the silence that followed, the telephone shrilled. The man at the desk snatched it up. Duhamel turned back to the window. He did not want to hear the death sentence read. He heard the phone replaced and then the long exhalation of relief from his master.

"They've called it off! They think they see a breakthrough with Moscow."

"What's the next deadline?"

"They haven't set it yet."

"Thank Christ!" said Pierre Duhamel. "Thank Christ!"

Somehow it sounded like a prayer.

LAZARUS

For Joy with love,
the best of the summer wine

"I've always wondered about Lazarus.
He had walked through the gates of death.
He had seen what was on the other side.
Did he want to return to life?
Did he thank Jesus for bringing him back?
What kind of man was he afterwards?
How did the world look to him?
How did he look to the world?"

—Leo XIV Pont. Max.
Conversations

— BOOK ONE —

LAZARUS AEGROTUS

*"There was a man called Lazarus
of Bethany, who had fallen sick . . .
When Jesus arrived, he found Lazarus
had been four days in the grave."*

—John xi: 1,17

I

H E was a high man and a hard one. His great beak and his jutting jaw and his dark obsidian eyes gave him the look of an old eagle, imperious and hostile. Yet, faced with the evidence of his own mortality, he felt, suddenly, small and ridiculous.

The surgeon, his junior by a quarter of a century, stood beside the desk, drew a sketch on a sheet of crested notepaper and explained it briskly.

"These are the two arteries on the left side of your heart. They are almost blocked with plaque, which is, in effect, the detritus from your blood stream. It builds up on the walls of the arteries, like scale on a water-pipe. The angiogram which we did yesterday shows that you have about five per cent of normal blood flow on the left side. That's the reason for the chest pains, the shortness of breath, the drowsiness and fatigue you have experienced lately. The next thing that will happen is this . . ." He sketched a dark globule with an arrow indicating the direction of its flow. "A small blood clot travels along the artery. It lodges here, in the narrowed section. The artery is blocked. You have the classic heart attack. You die."

"And the risk of that happening . . . ?"

"It's not a risk. It's an inevitable event. It can happen any day. Any night. Even now as we talk." He gave a small, humourless laugh. "To the pilgrims in St. Peter's Square, you're Leo XIV, Vicar of Christ, Supreme Pontiff. To me, you're a walking time-bomb. The sooner I can defuse you, the better."

"Are you sure you can?"

"At a purely clinical level, yes. We do a double bypass, replacing the blocked arteries with a vein taken from your leg. It's a simple plumbing job—the success rate is better than ninety per cent."

"And how much life does that give me?"

"Five years. Ten. More perhaps. It depends on how you behave yourself after the operation."

"And what precisely does that mean?" His Holiness was notoriously short-tempered. The surgeon remained calm and good-humoured.

"It means you've been damaging your body for years. You're at least fifteen kilos overweight. You eat enough for a peasant farmer. You've got gout. Your blood uric acid is abnormally high, but you still drink red wine and eat spices and high-purin foods. The only exercise you get is when you pace up and down reading your breviary. The rest of your life is spent at this desk or ambling through long rituals in clouds of incense, or being whisked around in automobiles and aircraft . . . Unless you make drastic changes in your lifestyle, all my skill will be wasted. *Osservatore Romano* will record that you died in the odour of sanctity. In fact, you'll have died of self-abuse."

"You're impertinent, doctor!"

"I'm telling you a necessary truth. Unless you heed me, you'll be carried out of here in a box."

There was a sudden anger in the hooded eyes. He looked like a predator ready to strike. Then, as swiftly as it had come, the anger died. His eyes became dull, his voice weary and querulous.

"You said a moment ago, 'At a purely clinical level it's a simple plumbing job . . .' Does that imply certain reservations?"

"Reservations, no. Caveats, counsels for the patient, yes."

"Will you explain them to me, please?"

"Very well. The risk factor first. I put it at ten per cent. I hold to that. The nature of the risk? Sudden collapse, a stroke, a pericardial infection. It's like driving a car or stepping into an aircraft. You accept it and forget it. In your case, I imagine, you leave it to God to dispose the outcome."

"Not quite." A ghost of a smile twitched at the corners of the grim mouth. "I have to leave certain directives. The first is that, if a collapse occurs, you terminate the procedure and let me die. The second is that if I am brain-damaged, I be not placed on any life-support system. Neither you nor I are obliged to the officious prolongation of a vegetable life. You will receive this directive in writing over my signature and seal. What next?"

"The sequelae—the consequences, short and long term, of the surgical procedures. It is very important that you understand them, think about them, talk about them freely. You must not—and I cannot emphasise this too strongly—try to cope with them by repression, by converting them into some kind of mystical, expiatory experience: a dark night of the soul, a stigma of the spirit . . ." He shrugged and grinned disarmingly. "Somehow I don't think you're the kind of man who would do that. You might, on the other hand, be tempted to bear them in proud, dignified silence. That would be a grave mistake."

The old man's answer was barbed.

"You have not yet told me what I am expected to bear."

"I am not talking about pain. That is a controllable factor. You will be unconscious for at least forty-eight hours, perfused with potent anaesthetics. You will continue to be fed opiates and analgesics until the discomforts are within tolerable limits. However, you will suffer something else: a psychic trauma, a personality change whose dimensions still elude full explanation. You will be emotionally fragile—as prone to tears as to rage. You will be subject to depressions, sudden, black and sometimes suicidal. At one moment you will be as dependent as a child, seeking reassurance after a nightmare. The next you will be angry and frustrated by your own impotence. Your short-term memory may be defective. Your tolerance of emotional stress will be greatly reduced. You will be strongly advised by the counsellors who will be working with you not to make any important decisions, emotional, intellectual or administrative, for at least three months . . . Most of these sequelae will pass. Some will remain, diminished but always present in your psychic life. The better your physical condition, the less will be your emotional handicap. So, after the first period of convalescence, you will be put on a rigid diet to lose fifteen or twenty kilograms. You will be required to do daily exercise on a graduated scale. And if you fail to do either of those things your psychic handicap will continue and your physical condition will deteriorate rapidly. In short, the whole exercise will be a painful futility. I'm sorry to make such a huge mouthful of this, but it is absolutely necessary that you understand it. Believe me, I do not exaggerate."

"I believe you. I'd be a fool if I didn't."

The old man seemed suddenly to withdraw into himself. His eyes became dull and expressionless as if a membrane had been drawn over them. The surgeon waited in silence until the words began to flow again.

"You raise, of course, the ultimate question: whether I shall be competent to resume the duties of my office."

"True. And you will not be the only one to ask it. Your brethren in the Sacred College will have access to the same clinical information as I have just given you."

For the first time, the grim mouth relaxed into a smile of genuine humour. The dull eyes lit up and the Vicar of Christ pronounced a private heresy.

"God is a practical joker, my friend. I've always known it."

The surgeon waited for an explanation of the proposition. None came. Instead, the Pontiff asked: "How long can I wait before the operation?"

"No time at all. I want you delivered to my clinic before midday tomorrow."

"Why your clinic? Why not Gemelli or Salvator Mundi?"

"Because I work only with my own team in conditions I can guarantee. I control the post-operative and convalescent procedures. Your physician will tell you I'm the best in Italy. But once you put yourself in my care there's a contract in force. You do as you're told, or I wash my hands of you."

"Before I commit to such a contract I'd like a second opinion."

"You already have a second, and a third. Morrison from London, Haefliger from New York. Both have seen computer-enhanced images of the X-rays. They agree with my diagnosis and the surgical procedures. Morrison will fly in from London to assist at the operation."

"And who, pray, authorised that little *démarche?*"

The surgeon shrugged and smiled.

"The Dean of the College of Cardinals. Your brother bishops thought they needed an insurance policy."

"I don't doubt it!" The Pontiff gave a short, barking laugh. "Some of them would be happy to see me dead; but they daren't risk losing another pontiff under suspicious circumstances!"

"Which brings me to my last counsel. I wish I could make it an order, but I cannot . . . Do not spend your convalescence at the Vatican or even at Castel Gandolfo. Take a month, at least, to be a private person. Lodge with friends or family; communicate only with your closest executives in Rome. Summer is coming. You will not be missed too much—believe me. All the faithful need to know is that you're alive and in office. One brief appearance and two communiqués should do the trick."

"You presume, young man! This is my home. My household is the only family I have. Why should I not recuperate here?"

"Two reasons: first, the air in Rome is polluted beyond belief. It will exacerbate any respiratory problems you may have after the surgery. The second is the more important: your own house, like it or not, will also be your battleground. Your competence will be on trial every day. Your every weakness will be gossiped abroad. You will know that. You will expect it. You will put yourself in a combat stance to defend yourself. Result? Stress, hypertension, anxiety; all the things we try to avoid after cardiac surgery. If that is presumption, I beg your pardon. Your Holiness has a reputation for obstinacy and brusqueness. My prime duty under the Hippocratic oath is to keep you from harm—*primum non nocere.* So I would rather be presumptuous than delinquent. But the decision is yours. Do we have a contract?"

"We do."

"Good. I shall expect you at midday tomorrow. You will have a day and a half of preparation and premedication. You will meet and talk with the principal members of the team. We will operate on Wednesday morning at seven o'clock . . . Trust me, Holiness! Today you're in the shadow of death. A week from now you'll be like Lazarus walking out of the tomb and blinking in the sunlight."

"I've always wondered about Lazarus." The old man leaned back in his chair and smiled sardonically at the surgeon. "He had walked through the gates of death. He had seen what was on the other side. Did he want to return to life? Did he thank Jesus for bringing him back? What kind of a man was he afterwards? How did the world look to him? How did he look to the world?"

"Maybe,"—the surgeon smiled and spread his hands in deprecation— "maybe that should be Your Holiness's first discourse after his recovery!"

The brief dialogue had shocked him to the core of his being. Suddenly he was bereft of everything that had sustained him: *magisterium, auctoritas, potestas;* the office, the authority, the power to use them both. He was a man under sentence of death. Even the instrument of execution was specified: a small plug of clotted blood, sealing off the life-flow to his heart. Reprieve was offered; but he had to take it from the hands of an arrogant fellow, on his own confession a mere plumber, who presumed to lecture the Vicar of Christ because he was too fat, too self-indulgent and ate like a peasant farmer.

Why should he be ashamed? He *was* a peasant, born Ludovico Gadda, only child of share-croppers from the outskirts of Mirandola, an antique principality near Ferrara. At twelve years old he was spending his mornings at school, his afternoons doing a man's work, herding the cattle and the goats, digging the vegetable plots, raking and piling the dung that would be used for fertiliser.

One day his father dropped dead behind his plough. His mother sold out his share-cropper's rights, took service as housekeeper to a local landowner and set about educating her son to a better life.

Already his mathematics were sound and he could read any book that came his way, because Mama, who had once hoped to be a teacher, had sat with him by lamplight in the long, dark country winters and drummed into him the education she had never been able to use. Knowledge, she insisted, was the key to freedom and prosperity. Ignorance was a slave's brand on the forehead. She sent him first to the Salesians, old-fashioned pedagogues, who terrified him out of his pubescent lusts with tales of hell-fire and horrible plagues visited on the promiscuous. They crammed him with Latin and Greek and mathematics, a whole dictionary of dogmatic definitions and moral precepts, not to mention twenty centuries of the expurgated history of The Church Triumphal. They also inserted, like a bead in an oyster, the notion of "vocation"—a special call to a special soul to a special life of service to God. From such a forcing-house of piety it was a short and easy step to the seminary as a candidate for the priesthood in the Archdiocese of Ferrara.

After the harsh country life to which he had been bred, the disciplines of the urban seminary and of the scholastic life were no burden at all. He was accustomed to a rhythmic existence. He was well fed, warmly clothed. His mother was protected and content. She made no secret of the fact that she much preferred the security of a son in the cloth to a gaggle of grandchildren in another woman's kitchen. Ambition made Ludovico a good scholar. He learned early that for a man who aspired to eminence in the Church the best qualifications were an orthodox theology, a solid grasp of canon law and an instant acceptance of every directive of authority—wise, foolish or merely expedient . . .

All the reports on him said the same thing. He was good clerical material. He was not profoundly spiritual, but he had, as his rector put it, *"animam naturaliter rectam"*, a spirit of natural rectitude.

What he had practised in his own youth he rewarded in others as he rose from curate to monsignor, to suffragan bishop, to Secretary of the Congregation for the Doctrine of the Faith, first under the redoubtable Leone and then under the iron-fisted German Josef Lorenz, who had pushed him slowly but steadily upward until he became a candidate for the Sub-prefecture.

It was the Ukrainian pontiff, Kiril I, who had given him the appointment and the red hat that went with it. Kiril, who in the early years of his reign had been seen as an innovator and passionate reformer, had become latterly a compulsive traveller, totally immersed in his public role as Universal Pastor, rattling the Keys of Peter wherever he was permitted to make a landfall. But while he travelled, the cabals of the Curia took control of the administration of the Church, and its interior life, its involvement in the new dilemmas of human experience, languished for want of courageous interpreters.

Whenever the question of his successor arose, Ludovico Gadda was counted among the *papabili*—a possible candidate for election. However, when Kiril died, on a flight from Rome to Buenos Aires, the man elected to succeed him was a Frenchman, Jean Marie Barette, who took the name of Gregory XVII. This Gregory was a liberaliser, who saw little merit in the rigorist policies of surveillance, censorship and enforced silence which Cardinal Gadda had rein-stituted at the Congregation for the Doctrine of the Faith. So he moved him sideways to be Prefect of the Congregation for the Bishops, knowing that the bishops were all grown-up fellows and perfectly able to take care of themselves.

But Ludovico Gadda, always the obedient servant of the system, performed ably and discreetly and managed to make a large number of friends in the most senior ranks of the episcopate. So, in that strange portentous time when Greg-ory XVII claimed to have had a private revelation of the Second Coming and to have received a call to preach it as one of the most ancient and enduring doctrines of Christianity, Gadda was able to procure his abdication by threat of a collegial vote to depose him on the grounds of mental incompetence.

He stage-managed the whole affair so adroitly that, in the hastily summoned conclave which followed, Cardinal Ludovico Gadda was elected Pope on the first ballot and took the name of Leo XIV. With so swift and massive a man-date, there was nothing now to restrain him. Within six weeks he had pub-lished his first encyclical, "Obedient unto death . . .", a chill admonition to discipline, conformity, unquestioning submission to the dictates of papal au-thority within the Church.

The Press and a large section of the clergy and laity were stunned by its reactionary tone, its echoes of ancient thunders, its smell of old bonfires. The general inclination was to ignore it; but that was much harder than it sounded. Leo XIV had spent a lifetime learning how the machinery of the Church worked and he manipulated every thread and cog like a thumbscrew to bring pressure on the recalcitrant, clergy and laity alike.

Like every bold general, he had calculated his losses in advance and, though to many they seemed appalling, he was ready to justify them by the end result: fewer clergy, smaller congregations, but all of them fired with redemptive and reforming zeal.

It was the post-Tridentine illusion. Rally the zealots, stiffen the waverers, purge out the objectors with bell, book and candle; in the end, the elect, aided by the Grace of God, would convert the backsliders by prayer and example. Instead, more and more decent folk carried on their decent lives in a silent schism of indifference to this hardnosed pragmatist, who still believed that he could rule by fiat the consciences of a billion souls scattered across the spinning planet.

But Ludovico Gadda, the peasant from Mirandola, ran true to form. He had always believed that if you did right you were right—and if you did wrong in good conscience, it was up to God to take care of the consequences.

Now, at one stroke, he was robbed of these comforting certainties. He could die with the work unfinished. He could survive yet be in no condition to com-plete it.

To the devil with such melancholy thoughts! God would dispose matters in His own time and fashion. His servant would not, could not, sit here brooding. There was work to be done. Work and prayer were a single act. He had always sought solace in action, rather than in contemplation. He pressed the buzzer to summon his secretary and have him assemble the members of the Curia at five sharp in the Borgia chamber.

* * *

His allocution to the Curial Cardinals was almost good-humoured, but never less than precise.

"The Sala Stampa will be responsible for the announcement to the world press. The statement will be accurate in all particulars. The Pontiff is suffering from heart disease, a bypass operation is indicated. It will be undertaken at the International Clinic of Professor Sergio Salviati. The operation has a high statistical success rate. The prognosis is positive. The Pontiff will be grateful for the prayers of the faithful—even the prayers of his brethren in this assembly.

"Medical bulletins will be prepared at the clinic and sent by fax to the Sala Stampa for distribution. Our attitude to the press will be cordial and informative. Questions about negative possibilities will be answered frankly, with the assistance of the clinic.

"One question which will inevitably be raised—and which I am sure is in all your minds even as I speak—is whether or not I shall be competent, physically or mentally, to serve out the term of my pontificate. It is too early to judge that; but three months from now we should all know the truth. I wish only to affirm to you, as I have already done in writing to the Dean of the Sacred College, that, since we are now an embattled Church, I am the last man in the world who would wish her to be led by an incompetent general. My abdication is already written. I suggest only that it may be untimely and embarrassing to publish it at the moment."

They laughed at that and gave him a round of applause. The tension that had been building all day was suddenly released. It seemed their country brother was not so stubborn after all. His next words cautioned them not to expect too easy a surrender of the Papal Seal.

"The surgeon recommends strongly that I absent myself from affairs of state and public ceremonial for about three months. Common sense dictates that I follow his advice and rusticate for a while away from either the Vatican or Castel Gandolfo . . . I have not yet decided where to go, or even whether to take so long a leave, but for however long or short a time I am absent, I am still the Pontiff, and I charge you all to pursue diligently the policies I have already determined with you. There will be ample opportunity—no, daily necessity— for the exercise of your collegial discretion and authority, but the Chair of Peter is not vacant until I am dead or have consented with you, my brethren, to step down from it . . . I reserve to myself the right to reverse any decisions made in my absence which do not conform to the policies we have laboured so hard to devise."

There was an uneasy silence, broken at last by Cardinal Drexel, Dean of the Sacred College, eighty years old but still bright of eye and vigorous in argument.

"A point must be made here, Holiness. I make it because the rules disqualify a man of my age from voting in any future Papal election. Your Holiness reserves his right to reverse any decisions made by any member of the Curia, or by the Curia acting in concert, during his absence. None of us, I believe, has any problem with that. But the members of the Electoral College must equally reserve their right to decide upon Your Holiness's competence to continue in office. It would seem that the criteria applied to the abdication of His Holiness Gregory XVII might be mutually agreed, here and now, as guidelines. It was, after all, Your Holiness who drafted them as head of the Congregation for Bishops."

There was a longer silence this time. Leo XIV sat hunched in his chair, staring at some point of focus in the centre of the floor.

Drexel was the last man in the world on whom he could vent his anger. He was too old, too wise, too versed in the subtleties of the canons. It was Drexel who had persuaded Jean Marie Barette to abdicate without a struggle or a scandal, and who still maintained contact with him in his secret existence abroad. It was Drexel who had censured so bluntly his own bid for election and yet, when it succeeded, had kissed hands and served as he had always done, asking no favours, condoning none of the mistakes of his new master. Drexel made no secret of his grief and anger at the new rigorism of Church government. Like Paul of old, he withstood the Pontiff to his face, claiming that he had already lapsed into gnostic error by trying to make a Kingdom of the Pure out of the tatterdemalion assembly of the errant children of God.

He stiffened the courage of other Papal Counsellors and was quite open in his intention to create a body of opposition opinion within the Curia—"because," as he put it bluntly to the Pontiff, "Your Holiness acts sometimes like a country mule and we cannot truly tolerate that in this day and age."

But, however bitterly he fought, he kept the battle private, as he had done in the case of Jean Marie Barette. More than most in Rome, he understood how ominous were the statistics of defection and he would not by word or gesture widen the gap between Pontiff and people. So finally, Leo the Bishop answered his brother bishop.

"As I remember, I produced a draft of the norms, which were then amended and agreed by the Sacred College before being submitted to the reigning Pontiff, who consented to their application even in his own case . . . So, there is no question, I too will submit myself to the same norms, if and when it is necessary to invoke them. Now, may we deal with other essential details . . ."

The details were legion: communications, security, protocols with the Republic of Italy while the Pope was resident outside Vatican territory, a schedule of those permitted access to the clinic while he was in intensive care and at each successive stage of convalescence . . .

Finally it was done. Then, to the surprise of the whole assembly, the Pontiff made the first apology they had ever heard from his lips.

"I had hoped to say Mass with you tonight. I cannot. I find that I am at the end of my strength. However, I cannot go without asking you all to hear my confession and to offer me your common absolution. I do not repent of what I have done in this office. I must repent of what I am—stubborn, blind, arrogant, swift to anger, slow to forgive. Touched by the corruption of power? Yes. A coward? That too, because I am very much afraid of what awaits me once I leave here. I lack compassion, because ever since I was a child I have been driven to thrust myself as far away as possible from the miseries of the human condition. And yet I cannot abjure what I believe, that a simple childlike obedience to the lessons of Our Lord and Saviour, as interpreted by the Holy

See, is the only true road to salvation. If I err in this, believe me it is not for lack of goodwill, but from lack of light and understanding. So, in the presence of you all, I confess and repent and I ask our brother Drexel to absolve me in the name of God and of you all."

He thrust himself awkwardly out of the great carved chair and knelt before them. Drexel approached and gave him the ritual absolution: *"Deinde ego te absolvo a peccatis tuis in nomine Patris et Filii et Spiritus Sancti . . ."*

"And for penance?" asked Leo the Pontiff.

"From us, none. You will have pain enough. We wish you the courage to endure it." Drexel held out a hand to raise him to his feet and, in the midst of a winter silence, led him from the room.

As the Curial Cardinals dispersed in the glow of a Roman evening, MacAndrew, the Scotsman from Propaganda Fide, strolled out with Agostini, from the Secretariat of State. Together they provided an almost perfect metaphor for the nature of the Church. MacAndrew's Congregation was charged with the evangelisation of the nations, the propagation of the ancient faith among the unbelievers and the maintenance of missionary foundations. Agostini's job was to create and maintain the political relations that made such efforts possible.

MacAndrew said, in his dry, humorous fashion, "Well now, that's something we haven't seen since seminary days! Public confession, with the Rector on his knees to the community. What did you make of it?"

Agostini, always the diplomat, shrugged eloquently and quoted from the Dies Irae: *"Timor mortis conturbat me!* He's sacred. It's natural. He knows he can die under the knife. He knows he will die if he doesn't risk the operation."

"I got the impression," said MacAndrew deliberately, "that he was casting up his accounts and finding a shortfall."

"We all know there's a shortfall." Agostini's tone was sombre. "You at Propaganda Fide are in a position to know how catastrophic it is. Congregations are getting smaller, we're getting fewer candidates for the priesthood, the missions and religious life: the places where the faith is strongest seem to be those furthest from our jurisdiction or our influence! Maybe our lord and master is beginning to see that he is responsible for at least part of the mess."

"We're all responsible." MacAndrew was emphatic about it. "You, me, the whole gilded gang of us. We're the Cardinals, the hinge men of the organisation. We're also bishops, vested in our own right with Apostolic authority. Yet look at us there today. Look at us any day! We're like feudal barons with their liege lord. Worse still, sometimes I think we're like a bunch of court eunuchs. We accept the pallium and the red hat and thereafter we take everything he hands out as if it were the voice of God from the holy of holies. We watch him trying to order back the waves of millennial events, silence by fiat the murmurs of troubled mankind. We listen to him preaching about sex as if he's spent his youth with the Manichees, like Augustine, and can't get the dirty notions out of his head. We know how he's silenced theologians and philosophers who are trying to make Christian redemption intelligible in our tooth and claw universe. But how many of us are prepared to tell him he just might be wrong, or needs new spectacles, or is looking at God's truth in a distorting mirror?"

"Would he listen if we did?"

"Probably not—but he'd have to treat with us as a body. All he has to do now is divide and conquer. He trades on that. So each of us has to find a separate way to deal with him. I can count 'em off for you—manipulation, evasion, flattery, the diplomacies of a kitchen cabinet . . . Drexel seems to be the only one ready to stand toe to toe with him and face him down."

"Perhaps," suggested Agostini mildly, "perhaps Drexel has less to lose than the rest of us. He'd like nothing more than to retire completely and rusticate among his vines. Besides, so long as we are in office and in favour with the Pontiff, we can do some good. Out of it, we are impotent."

"It's a fine piece of casuistry," said MacAndrew gloomily, "but it doesn't absolve us from our own delinquencies, does it? I wonder how I'd feel tonight if I were the one looking across the razor's edge to Judgement Day?"

"I'm a diplomat." Agostini at his best had a small, vinegary humour. "I am permitted—no, obliged—to heresies which in others are most damnable. I deal not only with the perfect but with the possible, the relatively good or the acceptably evil. I'm not asked to provide doctrinal definitions, just pragmatic solutions: what is the best deal we can make between the Uniats and the Orthodox in Russia? How long can we hold our precarious position in Syria? How can I unpick the tangle with the Blue Christians in China? Our master understands that. He keeps the moralists away from my cabbage patch . . . But when you come down to it, he himself is an inquisitor born and bred. You know how close we've come several times to getting another Syllabus of Errors. You ask how you'd feel, or I. I can answer for myself. A mistaken servant perhaps. A time-server perhaps. But at least I'd be myself, without surprises. But Leo XIV is a man split clean down the middle. That confession we just heard. What did it say? My policies are dead right, even though I am as full of faults as a colander is full of holes. He'll be an absolutist to the end. He has to be, else he's nothing."

"So what do we pray for?" MacAndrew was still in gallows humour. "His speedy recovery or his happy death?"

"Whatever we pray for, we have to be prepared for what we get: Lazarus returning from the dead, confirmed in the beatific vision, or a corpse that we have to bury and a new candidate we have to find."

"Who recommended Salviati?"

"Drexel. He gave him the highest praise."

"Then whether our Lazarus lives or dies, Drexel will have a lot to answer for, won't he?"

Sergio Salviati's International Clinic was a splendid domain of parkland and pinewoods, perched high on the crater lip of Lake Nemi.

From the dawn of history it had been a sacred place, dedicated to Diana the Huntress, whose shrine in the dark woodland was served by a strange custodian called the King of the Woods. The king was a runaway slave, who was guaranteed his freedom provided he slew the custodian and took possession of the shrine. Each year, another assassin came, to attempt the ritual murder. Even Caligula, the crazed emperor, took part in the grisly game and sent one of his own young bondsmen to despatch the reigning king.

Later, much later, the Colonna family took over the place and turned it into a farm and a summer refuge from the foetid heat of Rome. Later they sold it to the Gaetani, who gave it the name it still bore, Villa Diana. During the Second World War the Germans used it as a command post and afterwards the Archbishop of Westminster bought it as a holiday house for the students and faculty of the English College. However, as vocations languished and maintenance costs climbed, it was sold again, this time to a consortium of Milanese and Torinese businessmen who were financing the foundation of a modern cardiology clinic under the direction of Sergio Salviati.

This place was ideal for the purpose. The sixteenth-century villa was refurbished as a residence for senior staff and professional visitors from abroad. The clinic itself, with its outbuildings and its auxiliary generating plant, was sited on the flat space of the original farm, where there was still enough land left to grow vegetables and fruit and provide pleasances and gardens where convalescent patients could take their exercise.

Backed by the biggest corporations in the Republic—Fiat, Pirelli, Montecatini, Italcimento, Snia Viscosa—Sergio Salviati was able to realise his life's ambition: a modern clinic with full training facilities, staffed by international talent, whose graduates were beginning to rejuvenate the archaic and cumbersome Italian hospital system.

At forty-three, Sergio Salviati was already the wonder child of Italian medicine and a peer to the best names in England, Europe and America. As a surgeon, he was passionless, precise and, in a crisis, steady as a rock. As a team leader and administrator, he was open and good-humoured, always ready to listen to a contrary opinion or an imaginative proposal. However, once the protocols were set he would accept neither slackness nor compromise. The International Clinic was run with the precision of an airliner and woe betide any staff member who fumbled an essential routine or failed to deliver smiling support and comfort to a patient.

When the Pontiff arrived, the motorcycle escort provided by the Republic peeled off at the gates of the Villa Diana, where a combined group of Italian Secret Service men and Vatican Vigilanza was already in place. Accompanied only by his valet and a domestic prelate, the Pontiff was greeted in the foyer by the administrator of the clinic and escorted immediately to his room, a bright, airy chamber that looked southward over the undulation of parklands and vineyards and hilltop towns that once had been fortified strongholds.

The valet unpacked his hospital clothing and laid out his breviary and the small Mass kit he had carried since his first day as a curate. The Pontiff signed the admission papers and the permission for the surgical procedures. The prelate handed over an envelope sealed with the papal arms, containing the personal instructions of the patient in the event of an unforeseen collapse or brain death. Then, prelate and valet were dismissed and His Holiness Leo XIV was left alone; a fat, ageing, eagle-beaked fellow in dressing-gown and slippers, waiting nervously for medical staff to attend him.

His first visitor was a woman dressed in hospital style: white coat over a tailored skirt and blouse, with a clipboard and set of notes to round out the image. He judged her to be in her early forties, married—if the wedding band were not a protective device—and, from her precise but academic Italian, probably Scandinavian. She greeted him with a smile and a handshake.

"Welcome to the Villa Diana, Your Holiness. I am Tove Lundberg, director of our counselling group."

The Pontiff flinched at the familiar greeting, then smiled at the conceit of a young matron counselling the Vicar of Christ about anything. He ventured a small irony.

"And on what do you offer counsel, Signora Lundberg?"

She laughed, openly and happily, then sat down facing him.

"First, on how to adapt yourself to this new ambience. Second, how to cope with the aftermath of the surgery. Each patient has special needs. Each develops a special set of problems. When the problems reveal themselves, my staff and I are here to help."

"I'm not sure I understand."

"For instance, a young businessman is stricken with heart disease. He is terrified. He has a wife, young children. He has debts which in normal circumstances he could easily have paid off. Now what? He is threatened at every point—in his finances, in his sex-life, in his self-esteem as a husband and father, his efficiency in the workforce . . . On the other hand, an elderly widow may be obsessed by the fear of becoming a burden to her family, ending up in a refuge for old people. The important thing is that each of these patients be able to talk out the fears and share the problems. That is where my work begins."

"And you think I may have problems too?" He was still not finished with his joke.

"I am sure you will have. They may take just a little more time to surface but, yes, you will have them. Now, may we begin?"

"Please!"

"First item. The card on your door identifies you simply as Signor Ludovico Gadda."

"I confess I had not noticed."

"There is a reason, which I shall try to explain. After the operation, you will be taken first to the intensive care unit, where normally you will spend about forty-eight hours. After that, you will be transferred to a two-bedded room with another patient who is one or two days ahead of you in treatment. We have found that, at this critical stage, the elements of company, of mutual care, are vital. Later, as you begin to walk in the corridors, you will be sharing the experiences of recovery with men and women of all ages and conditions. Titles and honorifics are an impediment to this simple communication. So, we dispense with them. Does that trouble you?"

"Of course not. I was born to common folk. I have not altogether forgotten the language!"

"Next question. Who are your next of kin?"

"Both my father's and my mother's family are extinct. I was an only child. So my family is an adoptive one—the Church, and specifically the Pontifical Family at the Vatican."

"Do you have any close friends—what the Italians call friends of the heart?"

"May I ask the reason for the question?" He was suddenly wary and withdrawn. She was swift to calm him.

"Even for so exalted a man as you, there will be moments of deep emotional distress. You will feel, as you have never felt before, the need of companionship, consolation, a hand to hold, a voice of comfort. I should like to know whom to call to your side."

The simple question underlined how solitary he really was and how much the climb to eminence had cost him. His seminary days had been spent under the old order, when the whole tenor of training was to detach the subject from worldly relationships. His mother's single-minded ambition had worked to the same end. Finally, it was like killing a nerve in a tooth. What was achieved was a permanent anaesthesia against passion and affection. Since he lacked the heart and the words to explain all that to Tove Lundberg, he told her simply: "There is no one like that. No one at all. The nature of my office precludes it."

"That's very sad."

"I have never felt it so."

"But if you should, I hope you will call me. I am trained in the sharing of grief."

"I shall remember it. Thank you." He was not joking now. He felt suddenly less a man than he would have wished to be. Tove Lundberg picked up the thread of her exposition.

"Everything we do here is designed to allay anxieties and help our patients to co-operate as calmly as possible in the healing process. It's not like the old days, when the Senior Surgeon and the Senior Physician stood next door to God and all the patient could do was bow his head and let them practise their magical skills on him . . ."

Once again, he might have embellished the commentary. That was the kind of Church he was trying to recreate: one in which the Supreme Pastor was the true Physician of Souls, the Surgeon-General lopping off diseased members. But Tove Lundberg was already ahead of him.

"Now, everything is explained to you. Your help is sought, because it is a necessary element in the therapy. Look at this . . ."

She handed him what looked like a comic book in which the process of open-heart surgery was described in a series of vivid little cartoons, each with a caption that a child could understand.

"You should read this at your leisure. If you have any questions, the surgeon or I will answer them. The notion of the book we have borrowed from the Americans. The title we invented for ourselves: *A light-hearted guide to heart surgery*. I think you will find it interesting."

"I'm sure I shall." He was less than convinced, but he had to be polite. "What happens to me next?"

"Today and tomorrow, tests: blood samples, urinalysis, electrocardiogram, chest X-rays. At the end of it all you will be purged and then shaved from head to foot." She laughed. "You are, I see, a hairy man, so that will be a big job. Finally, you will be sent to sleep with a sedative. Next morning, very early, you will be given premedication and after that you won't know anything until it's all over."

"It sounds very simple."

"It is—for us. We've seen it all hundreds of times. We know that the failure rate is very, very low. But for you, for any patient, the waiting is the worst experience, the wondering if you're going to be the one statistical disaster. Of course, for a religious man like yourself it is probably very different. I cannot tell. I am—how do you say it in Italian?—a *miscredente*. Do you not teach that belief is a gift? Well, I am one of those who missed the prize-giving. Still, what one has never had, one does not regret—yes? In this connection, you should know that there is a chaplain service for all creeds. Roman Catholic, Orthodox, Anglican, Waldensian, Jewish and lately, by courtesy of the Egyptian Government, we have an Imam who will visit Muslim patients . . . I've never understood why we make so many quarrels about the same God! I am told that at one time such a diversity of religious service would have been impossible in Rome because the Vatican forbade it. Is that true?"

"Yes." He himself had grave doubts about religious tolerance in modern society; but he would have blushed to reveal them to this woman. Fortunately, she did not press the point but simply shrugged.

"Here at least there are no disputes. At the Villa Diana we try to please everyone. If you want the Catholic chaplain, just call your nurse and she'll arrange for him to visit you. If you want to meditate, there's a quiet room near the entrance. It's open to all faiths—very restful, very calm. If you want to say Mass in the morning, you can do it here or use the quiet room. No one will mind."

"You're very thoughtful, Signora. I shall not bother to call the chaplain—I've already received the Last Rites. But that doesn't mean I'm not afraid. I am. The worst illness I've ever had in my life is gout. I was not prepared for this!"

"Now is the time to count your blessings." There was a new note of authority in her tone. "You are a very lucky man. You have millions of people to care about you and pray for you. You have no wife, no children, no dependents of any kind. So you have only to worry about yourself."

"And the God to whom I must render account of my stewardship."

"Are you afraid of Him?"

He searched her face for any hint of mockery, but found none. Yet her question demanded an answer. It took him a few moments to frame it.

"It's not God I'm afraid of; it's what I may have to endure to reach Him."

She looked at him for a long, silent moment and then admonished him gently.

"Let me reassure you. First, we are very skilful in the relief of pain. We see no point in unnecessary suffering. Second, your case was discussed in detail at the surgeon's conference last night. Everyone agrees the prognosis is excellent. As Dr. Salviati put it, you're as tough as an old olive tree. You could last another decade or two!"

"That's comforting to know. And you, too, have a gift of comfort, Signora Lundberg. I'm glad that you came to see me."

"And you will try to trust us all?"

Once again, he was wary and suspicious.

"Why should you think I would not?"

"Because you are a powerful man accustomed to command others and to control his own destiny. Here you cannot do that. You have to give up control and trust the people who are caring for you."

"It seems I am already labelled as a difficult patient."

"You are a very public man. The popular press has never been kind to you."

"I know." His smile had little humour in it. "I'm the scourge of dissidents, the hammer of sinners. The cartoonists make a whole comic opera out of this ugly beak and this nutcracker jaw!"

"I'm sure you're not half as menacing as they make you out to be."

"Don't count on it, Signora! The older I get, the uglier I become. The only time I'll look into a mirror is when I'm shaving—so most days I let my valet do that for me."

At that moment his lunch was delivered: a modest meal of broth, pasta primavera and fresh fruit. He studied it with distaste. Tove Lundberg laughed and, to his surprise, quoted scripture.

" 'Some devils are cast out only by prayer and fasting.' Obesity is one of them."

"I thought you told me you were an unbeliever."

"I am; but my father was a Lutheran pastor in Aalund. So, I have a big repertoire of Bible quotations. Enjoy your meal. I'll see you tomorrow."

When she had gone he pushed the food listlessly about the plates, then ate a pear and an apple and abandoned the rest of it. Tove Lundberg had troubled him strangely. All his conditioning—even his mother's obsessive devotion to his celibate career—had been towards alienation from women. As a priest, he had shielded himself from them behind the protective screen of the confessional and the protocols of clerical life. As bishop, he had become accustomed to their homage and he had been grievously shocked and brutally repressive when any strong-minded Mother Superior with modernist tendencies had challenged his edicts or his policies. As Pontiff he had become even more remote: the Congregation for Religious handled conventual affairs, while the Pontiff sedulously refused to open any discussions about the ordination of women or their right to a voice in the senior councils of the Church.

Yet, in less than an hour, Tove Lundberg—self-styled counsellor—had come closer to him than any other woman. She had brought him to the brink of a revelation which, so far, he had confided only to his most private diary:

"An ugly man sees an ugly world because his appearance excites derision and hostility. He cannot escape from the world, any more than he can escape from himself. So, he tries to remake it, to chisel angel-shapes out of the crude rock fused by the hand of the Almighty. By the time he understands that this is a presumption so vast that it is almost a blasphemy, it is too late . . . This is the nightmare which has begun to haunt me. I had been taught, and I had accepted with total conviction, that power—spiritual, temporal and financial—was the necessary instrument to reform the Church, the fulcrum and the lever to set the whole process in motion. I remembered my father's simple wisdom as he worked in his own smithy on the farm: 'If I don't pump up the fire and swing the hammer, then the horses are never shod, the ploughshares are never made, the sods are never turned for the planting.'

"I planned for power, I intrigued for it, I was patient for it. Finally, I achieved it. I was vigorous as Tubal Cain in his smithy. I pumped up the fire of zeal, I swung the hammer of discipline with a will. I ploughed the fields and planted the seed of the Gospel . . . But the harvests have been meagre. Year after year they have declined towards failure and famine. The people of God do not listen to me any more. My brother bishops wish me gone. I, too, am changed. The springs of hope and charity are drying up within me. I feel it. I know it. I pray for light, but I see none. I am sixty-eight years old. I am the most absolute monarch in the world. I bind and loose on earth and in heaven. Yet I find myself impotent and very close to despair. *Che vita sprecata!* What a waste of life . . ."

II

THE most complete and accurate report of those two days' proceedings in the Vatican was filed by Nicol Peters of the London *Times*. His official source was the press office of the Pontifical Commission for Social Communications. His unofficial informants ranged from Curial Cardinals to second- and third-grade officials of the Congregations and junior clerks in the Private Archive.

They trusted him because he had never betrayed a confidence, never distorted a fact, nor stepped over the invisible line that divided the honest critic from the captious headline-hunter. His old mentor, George Faber, Dean of the Press Corps under the Ukrainian Pope Kiril I, had hammered the lessons into his skull: "It's all summed up in one word, Nicki: *fiducia*—trustworthiness. It's not an Italian virtue, but, by God, they respect it when they see it. Never make a promise you can't keep, never break a promise you've made. This is an old, complicated and sometimes violent society. You don't want a man's death or even damage to his career on your conscience . . . Another thing. Rome is a small town. Scandal spreads like wildfire. The Vatican is a toy kingdom—one square mile of it, that's all—but its powerlines reach into every city on the planet. The report you file today will travel the world—and if it's a crappy piece of work, the crap will finally end back on your doorstep. First you have to make sure that your files are always up to date. The Roman Church has a billion adherents all round the world. You never know, but one day a minor bishop in exile may turn up as a cardinal *in petto!*"

Nicol Peters's files, stored on computer discs behind oak panelling in his study, were as jealously guarded as the Codices in the Vatican Library. They contained biographies of every senior prelate in the world and an updated analysis of each one's influence and importance in the affairs of the Roman Church. He had plotted their public journeys and the tortuous private paths they were following towards eminence or oblivion in the global organisation.

His information about the financial affairs of the Vatican was uncomfortably accurate.

His wife Katrina had her own sources. She ran an elegant boutique on the Via Condotti and had a sharp ear for political and ecclesiastical gossip. She entertained constantly in their apartment—the top floor of a sixteenth-century palazzo in old Rome. The guest lists for her dinner parties were among the more exotic in the city. It was she who pointed out to her husband that, although the bulletin on the Pontiff's admission to hospital was unusually frank and optimistic, there was a distinct atmosphere of unease, both inside and outside the walls of Vatican City.

"Everybody's saying the same thing, Nicki. The odds are all in favour of his recovery; but there's grave doubt about how he's going to function afterwards. It's said that he's already consented to abdicate if he comes out handicapped; but everyone says that he'd have to be pushed pretty hard to make him go. Two abdications in a row would cause a hell of a scandal."

"I doubt it, Kate. The Electoral College is already prepared for a short-notice conclave in case of the Pope's death or incapacity. The ground rules are in place. Gadda wrote them himself when he was a cardinal . . . But you're right. The whole place is on edge. Drexel talked to me this afternoon—off the record, not for attribution, the usual thing. He asked what is the quickest way to break an actor's heart? Let him do Hamlet in an empty theatre. Then he gave me a neat little discourse on what he called the Age of Indifference and on the audience which has absented itself from the Church."

"And how did he explain the absent audience?"

"He quoted St Paul. You know the text . . . 'Though I speak with the tongues of men and angels and have not charity . . .' Then he added his own gloss: 'In short, Nicki, the people turn away because they believe we no longer understand or share their concerns. They are not serfs to be disciplined. They are free people, our brothers and sisters; they need the hand's touch of compassion. When we elected this Pontiff we chose a law-and-order candidate, an old-fashioned papal imperialist to make us feel secure in a time of doubt and confusion. We didn't trust the people. We called in the gendarmerie. Well, we got what we voted for: a cast-iron man, absolutely inflexible. But we lost the people. We lost 'em, Nicki, in a vain attempt to restore the mediaeval notion of a papal monarchy, bolster that strange catch-all authority, the *magisterium*. The big gong booms, but people stop their ears. They don't want thunder. They want the saving voice that says, 'Come to me, all ye who labour and are heavily burdened—and I will refresh you.' I tell you, Kate, he was quite emotional about it. So was I. That's the piece I'm trying to write now."

"But it still doesn't fully define this edginess we're talking about. Not everybody thinks the way Drexel does. Lots of Romans like the present Pontiff. They understand him. They feel a need for his kind."

"Just as some of the old ones felt a need for Mussolini!"

"If you like, sure! It's the *Führerprinzip*, the illusion of the benevolent strongman, with the people marching behind him to death or glory. But without the people, the leader is a straw man, with the stuffing spilled out of him."

"That's it, by God!" Nicki Peters was suddenly excited. "That's the theme I've been looking for. What happens to the Pontiff who alienates the Church? I don't mean just historically, though that's an essay in itself, a bloody and violent chronicle of pontiffs under siege, in exile, dogged by assassins. I'm talking about the man himself at the moment when he realises that he is a scarecrow, battered by the storms, with the crows pecking the straw out of his ears. Of course, if he doesn't realise it, there's no story; but if he does and if he's looking down the barrel of a shotgun as Leo XIV is today, then what happens? His whole internal life must be a shambles."

"One way to find out, Nicki."

"Oh, and what's that?"

"Ask his surgeon to dinner."

"Would he come?"

"How many turn-downs have I had in ten years? I'll get him here; trust me."

"What do you know about him?"

"I'm told he's divorced, has no children, that he's Jewish and an ardent Zionist."

"That's news! Are you sure it's true?"

"I heard it from a normally reliable source, the Principessa Borromini. Salviati is a Venetian name and apparently he was born into one of the old Sephardic families who traded out of the ghetto of Venice into the Adriatic dependencies of the Republic. There are Swiss and Friulan connections too, because Borromini met him first in St. Moritz and he speaks Ladino and Venetian dialects as well as Italian. It's also said he's a Freemason, not one of the P2 brand, but old-fashioned square and compass style. If that's true, it's an interesting speculation as to who at the Vatican chose him and why. You know how stiff-necked and sensitive they are on the whole Zionist question, not to mention divorce and secret societies."

Nicol Peters took his wife in his arms, kissed her soundly and waltzed her round the tiled pavement of the *salone*.

"Kate, sweet Kate! You never cease to amaze me. Divorced, Jewish, Zionist . . . what else?"

"Fanatically devoted to his job and—again, I quote my *principessa*—to one of his senior women at the clinic."

"Do you have a name for her?"

"No. I'm sure I can get one quickly enough. But you're not going to write a scandal piece, are you?"

"On the contrary. I'm following Drexel's logic. Leo XIV has lost the people. Does he know it? If he does, what has it done to him? What will it do to him in the future? Why don't you see if you can set up a dinner for Salviati—and his girlfriend, whoever she is?"

"When?"

"As soon as you like; but I wouldn't make any calls or send out any invitations until we know the result of this operation. Even for Salviati, it's no small thing to have the life of the Vicar of Christ in your hands!"

It had been a day filled with minor humiliations. He had been pierced for blood samples, hooked up to a machine that spewed out his heart's history in scrawls and squiggles. He had been sounded, prodded, dressed in a backless gown and stood baretailed in front of an X-ray machine. All his questions had been answered in monosyllables that told him nothing.

As they wheeled him back to his room, he had a sudden, vivid recollection of those sessions at the Congregation for the Doctrine of the Faith, where a luckless divine from Notre-Dame or Tübingen or Amsterdam was quizzed obliquely on charges he had never heard, by men he had never met, and where his only defender was a cleric whose name was never revealed to him. As Sub-prefect and later Prefect of the Congregation, Ludovico Gadda had never admitted any need to change the procedures. The subject of the investigation, the central figure in the colloquy, was by definition less important than the subject of the discussion: the possible corruption of a truth, a morbidity of error which, being a disease, must be extirpated. Its old name was the Congregation of the Universal Inquisition, its later one the Holy Office and, last of all, the seemingly innocuous Doctrine of the Faith. But its competences were still the same, defined in the clearest terms: "all questions that have regard to the doctrine of the faith and of the customs and usages of the faith, examination of new teachings, the promotion of studies and conferences about these same teachings, the reprobation of those which turn out to be contrary to the principles of the faith, the examination and eventually the condemnation of books; the Privilege of the Faith, judgment of crimes against the faith."

Now he, the master of that ancient but still sinister machine, was himself under inquisition, by smiling nurses and blank-faced technicians and nodding note-takers. They were polite, as were the prelates of the Piazza del Sant'Ufficio. They were detached, impersonal. They cared not one whit for what he was or what he felt. They were interested only in the diseases that inhabited his carcass. They told him nothing of what they found. They were like his own inquisitors, dedicated to the Disciplina Arcani, the Discipline of the Secret, a cult of whispers and concealment.

By early evening he was frayed and ill-tempered. His supper pleased him no more than his luncheon. The walls of his room closed in on him like a monastic cell. He would have liked to walk out in the corridor with the other patients, but he was suddenly shy about his bulky body and the unfamiliar vestments of dressing-gown and pyjamas. Instead, he sat in a chair, picked up his breviary and began to read vespers and compline. The familiar cadences of the psalmody lulled him, as they always did, into a calm, not joyful, but close to the relief of tears which he could not remember to have shed since childhood.

> Create in me a clean heart O God
> And renew a right spirit within me
> Cast me not away from thy presence
> And take not thy holy spirit from me
> Restore unto me the joy of thy salvation . . .

The strophe hypnotised him. His eyes could not see past it. His lips refused to form the antistrophe . . .

Joy was the missed experience in his life. He had known happiness, satisfaction, triumph; but joy, that strange upswelling of delight, that tingling near-ecstasy in which every sense was like a fiddle-string, making music under the master's bow, joy had always eluded him. He had never had the chance to fall in love. He had deprived himself by a lifetime vow of the experience of bodily union with a woman. Even in his spiritual life, the agonies and exaltations of the mystics were beyond his reach. Catherine of Siena, Little Brother Francis, St. John of the Cross, St. Theresa of Avila, were alien to his mindset. The role models he chose were the great pragmatists, the orderers of events—Benedict, Ignatius of Loyola, Gregory the Great, Basil of Caesarea. His earliest spiritual director explained to him the degrees of meditative communion with God: the purgative, the illuminative, the unitive. Afterwards, he shook his head and patted his young disciple on the back and dismissed him: "But for you, Ludovico my boy, it'll be the purgative way from beginning to end. Don't fret yourself about it. You're born to the plough. Just keep plodding, left right, left right, until God decides to lift you out of the furrow Himself. If He doesn't, be grateful still. The joy of illumination, the wonder of the mystical marriage with God, bring pain as well as ecstasy. You can't have one without the other . . ." It was strange that now, at sixty-eight, he felt suddenly so deprived and cheated. The remainder of the psalm echoed his sadness:

> Uphold me with the presence of thy spirit
> For thou desirest not sacrifice, else I would give it thee.
> Thou hast no delight in burnt offerings
> The Godly sacrifice is a troubled spirit
> A broken and contrite heart thou wilt not despise . . .

He had just finished the last prayer when Salviati walked in with a lean, shambling fellow in his late fifties, whom he introduced as Mr. James Morrison of the Royal College of Surgeons in London. Morrison had a rumpled, comfortable look about him and a humorous, faintly mocking twinkle in his brown eyes. To the Pontiff's surprise, he spoke passable Italian. He explained with a grin.

"I have what you might call Italian connections. One of my ancestors led a train-band of Scots mercenaries in the service of Pius II. The Morrisons, who now call themselves Morrissone, manufacture expensive shoes in Varese."

Leo XIV gave a short, barking laugh and shrugged off the joke with a Latin tag: "Tempora mutantur . . . times change, and we with them. Thank you for coming, Mr. Morrison. May I ask your opinion on my case?"

"It differs not at all from that offered by Dr. Salviati. In fact, I have to say I have nothing new to offer. I am expensive and redundant."

"On the contrary, James, you're my insurance policy—medical and political."

Morrison picked up the little comic book from the bedside table and asked: "Have you read this, Holiness?"

"Yes. I can't say I found it amusing."

Morrison laughed. "I agree. It's a good try; but heart disease is not exactly a laughing matter. Is there anything you'd like to ask me?"

"How long will I be in hospital?"

"That's up to Dr. Salviati. The average time is about two weeks."

"And after that?"

"Six to eight weeks of convalescence while the bones in your ribcage knit. We have to cut the sternum, you see, then stitch it back with wire. There's quite a bit of discomfort attached to that part of the convalescence, but it's still pretty controllable. Also it takes time to recover from the anaesthetic. The physical and psychic traumas are great, but the procedures, thank God, are almost fail-safe. How do you feel in yourself?"

"Afraid."

"That's normal. What else?"

"Troubled."

"By what in particular?"

"Things done, things undone."

"That's normal too."

"Your counsellor came to see me this afternoon." This to Salviati.

"Tove Lundberg? I know. I read her first report this evening."

"Report?"

Salviati laughed. "Why are you shocked? Tove Lundberg is a highly trained professional. She holds doctorates in Behavioural Sciences and Psychiatric Medicine. Her information is vital to our post-operative care."

"And what does she say about me?"

Salviati considered the question for a moment and then delivered a cool, judicial answer.

"She points to two problems. The first is that a man like yourself, vested with enormous authority, resigns himself with difficulty to the dependence of illness. That's not new. We have had Arab princes in here whose tribal power is as absolute as yours. They have exactly the same problem. But they do not repress it. They rage, they protest, they make scenes. *Bene!* We can deal with that. But you, the report tells me—and my own contacts with you confirm it—have a second problem. You will repress, hold back, brood in silence, because this is both your training in clerical discipline and your notion of the comportment of the Supreme Pontiff of the Roman Church. You will also, consciously or unconsciously, react against ministration by women. This will not help your recovery, but rather delay it. To use a figure of speech, you are not made of spring steel, forged and tempered and flexible. You are iron, cast in a mould. You are strong, yes; but you are not supple. You are rigid, vulnerable to shocks. But," he shrugged and spread his hands in a dismissive gesture, "we are used to that too. We shall cope with you."

"Why," asked Leo the Pontiff flatly, "why should you care? You fix the plumbing. You pack your tools. You turn to another job."

James Morrison gave a pawky Scots smile and said: "Never tangle with the Church, Sergio! They've been playing the dialectic game for centuries!"

"I know," said Salviati tartly. "Ever since Isidore wrote his first forgeries and Gratian turned them neatly into a Code!" To the Pontiff he gave a softer answer. "Why do I care? Because I'm more than a plumber. I'm a healer. After the operation, another job begins. We have not only to retrain you to cope with what has happened. We have to educate you to ensure it doesn't happen again. We also hope to learn from your case lessons we can apply to others. This is a research and teaching institution. You, too, can learn much here, about yourself and about other people."

At that moment, Salviati's beeper sounded, a series of sharp, fast signals. He frowned and turned to Morrison.

"We have an emergency. Cardiac arrest. Come with me, James. Excuse us, Holiness!"

They were gone in an instant, leaving the Pontiff with one more ironic comment on his own impotence and irrelevance in the life and death situations of common folk.

It was this irony which had troubled him more and more in the last months, as he tried first to explain away and then to comprehend the growing rift between himself and the Christian Assembly. The reasons were various and complex; but most had to do with the spread of popular education and the speed and potency of modern communications: press, radio, television and satellite dissemination of information.

History was no longer the domain of scholars, ferreting in dusty libraries. It was relived every day, in fiction or in documentary form on television screens. It was invoked in panel discussions as a paradigm of the present, a warning for the future. It stirred in the dark pools of tribal memory, raising old ghosts and the stink of ancient battlefields.

It was no longer possible to rewrite history—the facts showed through the overwritten fiction. It was not possible to plaster over the graffiti scratched into ancient stone. The plaster flaked off or fell away under the tapping hammers of the archaeologists.

He himself had written two encyclicals: the one on abortion, the other on in vitro fertilisation. In each, the words were his own; in each, he had insisted with absolute sincerity and unaccustomed eloquence on the sanctity and the value of human life. Even as he was writing them, the prancing demons of the past mocked his noble rhetoric.

Innocent III had claimed sovereign dominion of life and death over all Christians. He had decreed that the mere refusal to take an oath was a crime worthy of death. Innocent IV had prescribed the use of torture by his inquisitors. Benedict XI had declared the inquisitors who used it absolved from blame and penalty . . . What respect for life was there in the madness of the witchcraft trials, the carnage of the Crusades against the Cathars, the persecution of the Jews down the centuries? The massacres of Montsegur and Constantinople were still remembered, like Belsen and Auschwitz. The unpaid debts were still on the books, piling up interest.

It was no longer enough to say baldly that these horrors belonged to other times, were committed by primitive or barbarous men. The acts were ordered under the same *magisterium* which he exercised. They were justified by the same logic in which he himself had been schooled. He could not establish his own probity without admitting that the logic was flawed, that the men who preceded him had been in error.

But Roman policy had long since determined that no Pope should recant or attempt to explain the mistakes of his predecessors. Silence was prescribed as the safest remedy—silence, secrecy and the incredible tolerance of believers whose need of faith was greater than their disgust for its faithless ministers. But their tolerance was wearing thin and their faith was sorely tried by the garbles and glosses of its official interpreters. For them, the only time of salvation was now.

The only hope of easement was a grand illusion; a universal amnesty, a single cleansing act of repentance, universally acknowledged. But if the man who called himself the Vicar of Christ could not contemplate a public penitence, who else would dare dream it?

Decades ago, the good Pope John had acknowledged the errors and tyrannies of the past. He had called a great Council, to open the minds of the People of God and let the wind of the Spirit blow through the assembly. For a brief while there was a surge of hope and charity, a message of peace for warring nations. Then the hope waned, and the charity cooled, and Ludovico Gadda came to power on the wave of mistrust and fear that followed. He saw himself at first as the stabiliser, the great restorer, the man who would bring unity back into a community wearied and divided by a chase after novelties.

But it had not turned out so. In the privacy of his own conscience, at this moment of close encounter with Brother Death, he had to admit defeat and default. If he could not close the widening breach between Pontiff and people, then he had not merely wasted his life, but laid waste the City of God.

He looked at his watch. It was still only eight-thirty. Desiring to be spared the humiliation of his illness, he had declined all visitors on his first night in the clinic. Now, he regretted it. He needed company, as a thirsting man needed water. For Ludovico Gadda, called Leo XIV, Bishop of Rome, Patriarch of the West, Successor to the Prince of the Apostles, it promised to be a long, restless night.

At eighty years of age, Anton Cardinal Drexel had two secrets which he guarded jealously. The first was his correspondence with Jean Marie Barette, formerly Pope Gregory XVII, now living in a secret Alpine retreat in southern Germany. The second was the pleasure of his old age, a small villa estate in the Alban hills, some fifteen minutes' drive from the Villa Diana.

He had bought it many years before from Valerio Cardinal Rinaldi, who had been Camerlengo at the time of the election of Kiril I. The purchase had been pure indulgence. Valerio Rinaldi had been a papal prince in the old mode—a scholar, a humanist, a sceptic, a man of much kindness and humour. Drexel, recently made a cardinal and translated to Rome, had envied both his lifestyle and the skill with which he navigated the shoals and over-falls of Curial life. Rinaldi had made a generous deal with him and he entered with zest and skill into his existence as an elderly anonymous gentleman retired to the country.

Then, an extraordinary thing happened. At seventy years of age, Anton Cardinal Drexel, Dean of the Sacred College, Cardinal Bishop of Ostia, fell hopelessly in love.

The manner of it was very simple. One warm spring day, dressed in country clothes, checked shirt, corded trousers and hobnailed boots, he walked the five kilometres into Frascati to discuss the sale of his wine to a local *cantina*. The orchard trees were in flower, the new grass was ankle high, the first young tendrils were greening on the vines. In spite of his years, he felt supple and limber and ready to walk as far as the road would take him.

He had always loved the old town, with its baroque cathedral, its crumbling palace and the dark, cavernous wine shops in the back alleys. Once upon a time it had been the episcopal seat of His Serene Highness, Henry Benedict Mary Clement, Cardinal Duke of York, last of the Stuarts, who had once proclaimed himself Henry IX of England. Now it was a prosperous tourist resort, filled with a weekend horror of motor vehicles and petrol fumes. But in the cobbled lanes the charm of the past still lingered, and the old-fashioned courtesies of country folk.

Drexel's destination was a deep cave hewn into the tufa rock, where great tuns of ancient oak lined the walls and the serious drinkers and buyers sat at long refectory tables, with dusty bottles and plates of green olives set in front of them. The padrone, who knew Drexel only as *il Tedesco*—the German—haggled a while over the price and the delivery, then agreed to accept a sample consignment and opened a bottle of his best vintage to seal the bargain.

After a few moments, the padrone left him to attend to another customer. Drexel sat relaxed in the half-light, watching the small passage of people on the sunlit pavement outside the entrance. Suddenly, he felt a tug at his trouser leg and heard a strange gurgling sound, like water swirling down a pipe. When he looked down he saw a cascade of blonde curls, an angelic little girl-face and a flurry of spidery legs and arms that seemed to have no co-ordinated connection with the tiny body. The voice was out of control too, but the mouth seemed to be trying to form sequential sounds. "Ma-no-no, ma-no-no . . ."

Drexel lifted the child on to the table, so that she sat facing him. Her tiny marmoset hands, soft as silk, groped at his face and hair. Drexel talked to her soothingly.

"Hullo, little one! What's your name? Do you live around here? Where is your mama?"

But all he got was the agonised twisting of the mouth and the sound gurgling out of the tiny gullet. "Ma-no-no, ma-no-no." Yet she was not afraid. Her eyes smiled at him and there was, or seemed to be, a light of intelligence in them. The padrone came back. He knew the child by sight. He had seen her before, sometimes with a mother, sometimes with a nurse. They came to Frascati for shopping. They didn't belong in town, but maybe to one of the villas in the near countryside. He had no name for them, but the mother seemed to be foreign. She was a *bionda,* like this one. He shook his head sadly.

"Poor little mite. You have to think God must be dozing when he makes mistakes like this one."

"Do you think you're a mistake, little one?" Drexel stroked the blonde curls. "I'm sure you know angel talk. I don't. What are you trying to tell me?"

"I've got fifteen grandchildren," the padrone told him. "Not a runt among 'em. A man can be lucky. What about you?"

Drexel smiled and shook his head.

"No children. No grandchildren."

"That's hard, for a wife especially. A woman always needs someone to cluck over."

"No wife," said Drexel.

"Well then!" The padrone seemed embarrassed. "Maybe you're the lucky one. Families keep you poor—and when you're dead they pick you bare like vultures. Would you like me to call the police and let them know we've got this one?"

"I could perhaps take her outside and look for the mother."

"Not a good idea!" The padrone was very firm about it. "Once you leave here with her, you're suspect. Abduction, abuse. That's the times we live in. Not our folk here, but the *forestieri,* the outsiders. You could have a hell of a time proving different. Best you sit there and let me call the cops."

"Do you have something for her to eat or drink—an *aranciata,* a biscuit perhaps? Do you like sweet things, little one?"

The tiny soft hands groped at his face and she said, "Ma-no-no, ma-no-no . . ."

The padrone produced a saucer of sweet biscuits and a glass of *aransoda.* The child slopped over the drink, but Drexel steadied her and wiped her lips with his handkerchief. He helped her to manipulate the biscuit into her mouth. A mother's voice spoke behind him.

"I'm her mother. I hope she hasn't been too much trouble to you."

"No trouble at all. We're getting along famously. What's her name?"

"Britte."

"She seems to be trying to tell me something. It sounds like Ma, no, no."

The woman laughed.

"That's as close as she can get to Nonno. She thinks you look like her grandfather. Come to think of it, you do . . . He's tall and white-haired like you."

"Aren't you worried about her being lost?"

"She wasn't lost. I was just across the street in the *salumeria.* I saw her come in here. I knew she would come to no harm. The Italians care for children."

The child scrabbled awkwardly for another biscuit. Drexel fed it to her. He asked: "What's the matter with her?"

"Cerebral diplegia. It's due to a defect of the nerve cells in the central cortex of the brain."

"Is there any cure?"

"In her case, there's hope of improvement, but no cure. We work very hard with her to establish muscular co-ordination and adequate speech. Fortunately, she's one of the special ones."

"Special?"

"In spite of the lack of muscular co-ordination and the almost incoherent speech, she has a very high intelligence. Some victims verge on idiocy. Britte could turn out to be a genius. We just have to find ways to break into this—this prison."

"I'm being very rude," said Anton Drexel. "Won't you sit down and take a glass of wine with me? Britte hasn't finished her drink or her biscuits. My name is Anton Drexel."

"I'm Tove Lundberg . . ."

And that was the beginning of the love affair between an elderly Cardinal of the Curia and a six-year-old girl-child, a victim of cerebral palsy. His enchantment was instant, his commitment total. He invited the mother and child to lunch with him at his favourite trattoria. Tove Lundberg drove him home, where he introduced the child to the married couple who cared for him, and the gardener and the cellar master who made his wines. He announced that he had been officially adopted as her *nonno* and that henceforth she would be visiting every weekend.

If they were surprised they gave no sign. His Eminence could be very formidable when he chose—and besides, in the old hill towns discretion about the doings of the clergy and the gentry was a long ingrained tradition. The child would be welcome; the signora also, whenever His Eminence decided to invite them.

Afterwards, on the *belvedere*, looking out over the fall of the land towards the hazy cupolas of Rome, confidences were exchanged while the child limped happily among the flowerbeds. Tove Lundberg was unmarried; her partner's love had not been strong enough to bear the tragedy of a maimed love-child. The break-up of the union was somehow less tragic than the damage to her own self-image and self-esteem as a woman. So, she had fought shy of new attachments and devoted herself to her career and to the care and education of the girl. Her medical training had helped. Salviati had been more than supportive. He had offered to marry her; but she was not ready yet, perhaps she would never be. One day at a time was enough . . . As for His Eminence, she would not have taken him for a sentimentalist or an impulsive man. What in fact did he have in mind when he proposed himself as a surrogate grandfather? A shade less eloquently than was his wont, Anton Cardinal Drexel explained his folly . . .

"According to some of the most ancient protocols in the western world, I am a prince—a prince of the Holy Roman Catholic and Apostolic Church. I am the most senior member of the College of Cardinals, Prefect of a Congregation, member of Secretariats and Commissions—the perfect and perfected ecclesiastical bureaucrat. At seventy-five I shall offer my resignation to the Holy Father. He will accept it, but ask me to continue working, *sine die,* so that the Church may have the benefit of my experience. But the older I get, the more I feel that I shall leave this planet the way a snowflake disappears, without a trace, without a single permanent imprint to mark my passing. What little love I have left is withering inside me like a walnut in the shell. I should like to spend the last of it on this child. Why? God knows! She took possession of me. She asked me to be her *nonno.* Every child should have two grandfathers. So far she has only one." He laughed at his own earnestness. "In another age, I'd have kept mistresses and bred my own children and called them, for decency, nephews and nieces. I would have enriched them out of the coffers of the Church and made sure my sons became bishops and my daughters married nobly. I can't do that for Britte, but I can get her whatever training and therapy she needs. I can give her time and love."

"I wonder," Tove Lundberg was suddenly withdrawn and thoughtful, "I wonder if you will understand what I am about to say."

"I can try."

"What Britte needs is the company of her peers, children who are handicapped but of high intelligence. She needs the inspiration of loving and enlightened teachers. The institute which she attends now is run by Italian nuns. They are good, they are devoted, but they have the Latin view of institutional life. They dispense charity and care by routine, old-fashioned routine . . . That works for children who are mentally handicapped and who tend to be docile and responsive. But for those like Britte, imprisoned intelligences, it is far, far from enough. I don't have the time or the money, but what I would love to see started is a group, what the Italians call a *colonia*, properly staffed with trained people from Europe and America, supported by parent groups, subsidised if possible by the State and the Church." She broke off and made a little shrugging gesture of self-mockery. "I know it's impossible, but it would be one way to getting yourself a late-life family."

"For that," said Anton Drexel, "one needs more life than I have at my disposal. However, if God has endowed me with a granddaughter, He will hardly deny me the grace to perform my duties towards her. Let's walk awhile. I'll show you what we have here, the vineyards, the farmland. Then you will choose the room where you and Britte will stay whenever you visit . . . A colonia, eh? A colony of new intelligences to grace this battered planet! I'm sure I can't afford it, but the idea is wonderful!"

And that, whenever he looked backwards, was the day he identified as the beginning of his career as a surrogate grandfather to Britte Lundberg and sixteen other girls and boys who, year by year, had taken over his villa, most of his income, and the happiest corner of his life—from which small, secret standing place he now proposed to launch the most foolhardy venture of his career.

III

I T was ten o'clock when the night nurse came in to settle the Pontiff and give him a sedative. It was nearly one in the morning before he lapsed into an uneasy sleep, haunted by a serial dream.

. . . He was at his desk in the Vatican surrounded by expectant dignitaries, the highest in the Church: patriarchs, archbishops, of every rite and nationality —Byzantine, Melchite, Italo-Greek, Malakanese, Ruthenians, Copts, Bulgars and Chaldeans. He was writing a document which he intended to read aloud to them, seeking their approval and endorsement. Suddenly, he seemed to lose control of his fingers. The pen slipped from his grasp. His secretary picked it up and handed it back to him; but now it was a goose-quill, too light to handle, which dribbled ink and moved scratchily on the paper.

For some reason, he was writing in Greek instead of Latin, because he was anxious to impress on the Byzantines that he was open to their spirit and understanding of their needs. Suddenly he blocked on a word. All he could remember was the first letter—μ. The Patriarch of Antioch reproved him gently: "It is always safer to use a translator who has the language as a mother tongue." The Pontiff nodded a reluctant agreement, but continued to grope for the word among the cobwebs that seemed to have invaded his mind.

Next, still holding the paper, he found himself walking across St. Peter's Square to the Via del Sant'Ufficio. It seemed important that he confer with the Consultors to the Congregation for the Doctrine of the Faith for an explanation of the mysterious letter. They were vigilant guardians of the ancient truth, who would first rise to salute the Vicar of Christ and then enlighten him with their wisdom.

They did nothing of the kind. When he entered the *aula* where the Consultors were assembled, they sat like mutes, while the Prefect pointed to a stool where he must sit, isolated under their hostile scrutiny. The paper was taken from his hand and passed around the assembly. As each one read it, he clucked and shook his head and mouthed the sound "Mu," so that soon the room was full of the bourdon as it were of swarming bees: Mu . . . Mu . . . Mu . . .

He tried to cry out, to protest that they were making a travesty of a most important encyclical, but the only sound he could utter was Mu . . . Mu . . . until, for very shame, he fell silent, closed his eyes and waited for their verdict. Out of the darkness a voice commanded him: "Open your eyes and read!"

When he obeyed, he found himself a boy again, in a dusty classroom, staring at a blackboard upon which was written the word which had eluded him for so long, μετανοια. A great sense of relief flooded through him. He cried out: "You see, that's what I was trying to say—Metanoia, repentance, a change of heart, a new direction." But no one answered. The room was empty. He was alone.

Then the door opened and he froze in terror at the vision that confronted him: an old, eagle-beaked man, with furrows of anger about his mouth and eyes black as volcanic glass. As the man moved towards him, silent and threatening, he screamed, but the sound would not come. It was as if a noose were knotted around his neck, cutting off air and life . . .

The night nurse and a young male orderly helped him to get up. While the orderly remade his tangled bed, the nurse walked him into the bathroom, peeled off his sodden pyjamas, sponged the sweat from his body, then brought him clean night clothes and a cool drink. When he thanked her and apologised for putting her to trouble, she laughed.

"The first night in hospital is always a bad one. You're full of fears that have to be dreamed out because you can't put them into words. The sedatives get you to sleep, but they can disturb the normal rhythms of rest and dreaming . . . You're better now. Your pulse rate's steadying down. Why don't you read for a little while? You'll probably doze off again . . ."

"What time is it, please?"

"Three in the morning."

"Then it's bad luck, isn't it?"

"Bad luck? I don't understand."

Leo the Pontiff gave a small, unsteady laugh.

"Around Mirandola—that's where I come from—the peasants say that the dreams we have after midnight are the ones that come true."

"Do you believe that?"

"Of course not. I was joking. It's an old wives' tale."

But even as he said it, he knew it was an evasion. What he had dreamed was more than half the truth and what was not yet true might well be prophecy.

He could not read. He could not sleep. He felt too arid and empty to pray. So, wakeful in the dim light of the night lamp, he gave himself up to contemplation of his very uncertain future.

The word which he had been chasing through his dreams had become very important in his latter-day thinking. It expressed accurately what he desired to convey to the Church—a penitence for the mistakes of the past, a change for the better, a future openness to the needs of the faithful and to the designs of the Almighty. But the change had to be wrought in himself first of all and he could find no sure ground on which to stand while he made it.

The whole bent of his mind, the whole thrust of his education, all the transactions of his career, had been to conserve and not to change. No matter that so many historical claims made by the Church were based on forgery and fabrication; no matter that so much canonical legislation was unjust, intrusive and hopelessly loaded against the individual and in favour of the institution; no matter that so much dubious teaching was presented from the pulpit as official doctrine on the flimsiest foundation of scripture or tradition; no matter that the reforms envisaged in the decisions of a great Council were still unrealised four decades later . . . no matter, no matter! Just so the history remained obscure, the canons unchallenged, the dubious teaching unquestioned, then each generation would make, as it always had, its own accommodation with the paradox. It was better that the unbelievers should be cast out, the sceptics silenced and the disobedient censured, than that any rent should appear in the seamless robe of Roman unity.

In this frame of reference, theologians and philosophers were a dangerous luxury, biblical scholars a tendentious nuisance, still seeking to establish an historic Jesus instead of offering Jesus Christ yesterday, today and the same for ever. As for the faithful, they were at the best of times a wayward family, easily seduced by passion or by novelty.

This attitude of magisterial expediency dated far back through the centuries to an epoch when the faithful were illiterate and uncritical and the dispensation of faith, along with the exercise of power, were the prerogatives only of the literate, the clerics who were the natural custodians of knowledge and authority. As for the aberrant ones, the speculators, the too-bold theorists, they were easily dealt with. Error had no right to exist. The errant would repent or be burned.

In the twentieth century, however, in post-revolutionary, post-conciliar societies, these attitudes had no place. They were at worst an unacceptable tyranny, at best a class snobbery that clerics, high or low, could ill-afford to practise. The faithful, up to their necks in the problems of modern living, had the need and the right and the duty to reason with their pastors, and no less a right and a duty to hold them accountable for their exercise of the *magisterium,* because if magistracy were an autarchic exercise beyond appeal, then at one stride they were back to secret denunciations, witchhunts, *autos-da-fé* and automatic excommunications. The faithful would not take that any more. They were Children of God, free agents co-operating with His divine plan. If this liberty were abridged, they would refuse the abridgement and absent themselves from the assembly to await a more propitious time or a more charitable shepherd.

In the small half-light of the hospital room, whose silence was broken only by the distant sound of a patient's call-buzzer, Leo the Pontiff saw it all clearly. No matter how bitterly he regretted his own defaults, he saw no easy way to mend them. He lacked the one essential talent which the good Pope John and Jean Marie Barette had both possessed: a sense of humour, a readiness to laugh at themselves and the egregious follies of mankind. There was not one photograph in existence of Leo XIV laughing. Even his rare smile was more like a grimace than an expression of pleasure.

Yet, in all truth, only part of the blame attached to him. The sheer size and mass of the institution created an inertia like that of a black hole in the galaxies. Enormous energy was sucked into it. The energy that emerged was constantly diminishing. The old Curial cliché "We think in centuries and plan for eternity" had turned into a doom-saying.

The great tree of the Gospel parable, in which all the birds of the air could nest, was dying back from the tips of its spreading branches. The trunk was still solid, the great mass of foliage seemed intact; but at the outer edges there were dead twigs and sere leaves, and the nourishment from the taproot flowed more and more sluggishly.

The slow curse of centralism was working in the Church, as it had worked in every empire since Alexander's. The British had succumbed to it, the Russians and the Americans were the latest to be forced into divestment of their territories and spheres of influence. The symptoms of malaise were always the same; disaffection in the outer marches, disenchantment with bureaucracy, alienation and indifference on the part of the people and, on the part of government, a growing impulse towards reaction and repression.

In religious terms, the numen of the papacy was fading, as its aura of mystery was dissipated by constant exposure on television and in the Press. Government by fiat brought small joy to folk in crisis, who yearned for compassion and for understanding of the God abiding among them. They did not reject the pastoral office. They paid ritual homage to the man who held it, but they asked how he mediated for them in the double mystery of the creative Godhead and confused humanity. For Leo the Pontiff the question was personal and immediate; but it was still unanswered when sleep claimed him again. This time, mercifully, he did not dream at all. He woke at first light to find Salviati standing beside the bed, with the night nurse a pace behind him. Salviati was counting his pulse rate.

"Nurse tells me you had a rough night."

"I was having nightmares. However, I've just had a couple of hours' good rest. How is your patient?"

"Which patient are you talking about?"

"The cardiac arrest. You and Mr. Morrison went off in a great hurry last night."

"Oh, that one . . ." Salviati shook his head. "We lost her. She'd already had two heart attacks before they brought her to see me. Her case was always a long shot. Sad though; she leaves a husband and two young children . . . If I've got the story right, the husband's one of your people."

"Mine?"

"A priest, one of the Roman clergy. Apparently he fell in love, got the girl pregnant and walked out of the ministry to marry her. He's spent the last five years trying to have his position regularised by the Vatican—which, they tell me, isn't as easy as it used to be."

"That's true," said Leo the Pontiff. "It isn't easy. Disciplines have been tightened."

"Well, it's beyond mending now. The girl's dead. He's got two kids to care for. If he's wise, he'll try to find 'em a stepmother. So the situation repeats itself; yes?"

"If you'd give me his name, I could perhaps . . ."

"I wouldn't recommend it." Salviati was studiously offhand. "I'm a Jew, so I don't understand how you Christians reason about these things; but the boy's very bitter and your intervention may be unwelcome."

"I'd still like to have his name."

"Your life is complicated enough. As from tomorrow, you begin a minimalist existence. So start now to be grateful—and let the Almighty run His own world. Open your pyjamas, please. I want to listen to your chest. Give me deep breaths now." After a few minutes of auscultation, he seemed to be satisfied. "You'll do! It's going to be a beautiful day. You should take a little stroll in the garden, get some clean air into your lungs. Don't forget to tell the nurse when you're going. You can't get lost, but we like to know where all our patients are."

"I'll take your advice. Thank you . . . I'd still like to have that young man's name."

"You're feeling guilty about him." It was more an accusation than a question.

"Yes."

"Why?"

"You gave the reason yourself. He's one of mine. He broke the law. I set the penalties he incurred. When he wanted to come back, the way was barred to him by rules I made . . . I'd like to be reconciled with him, help him, too, if he'll permit me."

"Tove Lundberg will give you his name and address. But not today, not until I say you're ready to occupy yourself with affairs other than your own survival. Do I make myself clear?"

"Abundantly," said Leo the Pontiff. "I wish my mind were half as clear as yours."

To which Sergio Salviati answered with a proverb: "Every wolf must die in his own skin."

"If you want to swap proverbs," said Leo the Pontiff, "I'll give you one from my home place: 'It's a hard winter when one wolf eats another.' "

For a moment Salviati seemed to withdraw into some dark recess of himself; then he laughed, a deep happy rumbling that went on for a long time. Finally, he dabbed at his streaming eyes and turned to the night-nurse.

"You're witnessing history, my girl! Write it down and tell it to your grand-children. Here's a Jew from Venice disputing with the Pope of Rome in his own city."

"Write this down also . . ." The Pontiff laughed as he said it. "The Pope is listening very carefully, because this time the Jew is the one with the knife in his hands! He can kill me or cure me!"

"There's a proverb for that, too," said Sergio Salviati. " 'You've got a wolf by the ears. You can't hang on and you can't let go . . .' "

On that fine spring morning there were other folk, too, who found them-selves hanging on to a wolf's ears. The Secretariat of State was swamped with enquiries from all quarters of the globe, from legates and nuncios and metro-politan archbishops, from cardinals and patriarchs, from diplomats and intelli-gence agencies of one colour or another. The burden of their questions was always the same: how serious was the Pontiff's illness; what were the odds on his recovery; what would happen if . . . ?

The Secretariat, under Matteo Cardinal Agostini, normally conducted its business with an air of Olympian detachment. Its officials were a select tribe of polyglots who maintained diplomatic—and undiplomatic—relations with every region under the sun, from Zaire to Tananarive, from Seoul to St. Andrews, from Ecuador to Alexandria of the Copts. Their communications were the most modern and the most ancient: satellites, safe-hand couriers, whispers at fashionable gatherings. They had a passion for secrecy and a talent for casuistry and discretion.

How could they be otherwise, since their competence, defined by Apostolic Constitution, was the widest of any organisation in the Church: "to help from close at hand *(da vicino)* the Supreme Pontiff, both in the care of the Universal Church and in his relations with the dicasteries of the Roman Curia." The which, as cynics pointed out, put the job of managing the Curia on a par with the care of a billion human souls!

The word dicastery had its own Byzantine coloration. It signified a tribunal, a court and, by extension, a ministry or department. It suggested a complicated protocol, an intricate web of interests, an ancient subtlety in the conduct of affairs. So when the diplomats of the Secretariat of State dealt with their secular peers or with the Dicasts of the Sacred Congregations, they were required to be quick on their feet, nimble of tongue and very, very wide awake.

Their replies to the questions that poured into their offices were bland, but not too bland. They were, after all, dealers in the marts of power. They were, for the moment, the spokesmen for the Holy See. They must make it clear that Rome was never taken by surprise. What the Holy Ghost did not reveal they supplied from their own refined intelligence services.

Yes, the medical bulletins on His Holiness could and should be taken at face value. The Holy Father had decreed an open information policy. No, the Electoral College had not been summoned, nor would it be until the Camerlengo declared that the throne of Peter was vacant. In fact, the Secretariat was actively discouraging visits to Rome by cardinals and archbishops from abroad. The Holy Father understood and commended their desire to offer support and loyalty but, frankly, he would prefer them to be about God's business in their own vineyards.

Questions about the future competence of the Pontiff were dealt with curtly. They were inopportune and unfruitful. Common decency demanded that public speculation on this delicate matter be discouraged. Time elements? The doctors advised a period of three months' convalescence before the Pontiff resumed his normal schedules. In fact, this pointed to his return after the usual summer vacation, perhaps a month or so later than Ferragosto . . . Most certainly, Excellency! His Holiness will be informed of your call. He will no doubt wish to acknowledge it in person after his recovery. Meanwhile, our compliments to Your Excellency and his family . . .

All of which was sound enough, but hardly sufficient for the hinge-men of the Church, the Papal Princes who would have to decide upon the competence of the living pope or the successor to a dead one. In the context of the third millennium, total secrecy was an impossibility and the leisure for informed decision was an antique luxury. They had to be prepared at every moment. Their groupings had to be stable, their alliances tested, the terms of their bargainings and the price-tags on their votes had to be agreed in advance. So, there was a great mass of traffic—by telephone, by fax, by safe-hand courier—which bypassed Rome altogether. Chicago talked to Buenos Aires, Seoul talked to Westminster, Bangkok talked to Sydney. Some of the talk was blunt and pragmatic: "Are we agreed . . . ?"; "Can we afford . . . ?" Some of it was in *sfumature,* hints and nuances and careful allusions which could be disclaimed or reinterpreted with any shift of events.

The question which required the greatest delicacy in discussion was the one whose answer was the least evident: How far could an ailing pontiff be trusted to direct the affairs of a global community in crisis?

Tradition, established by long-dead papal dynasts, determined that a pontiff served until he dropped. History, on the other hand, proved beyond all doubt that one who outlived his usefulness became a liability to the community of the faithful—an instant liability, because in the modern world time telescoped itself, because act and consequence were immediately conjoined. There was sound argument for a term of service fixed by canonical statute, as it was in the case of cardinals and other prelates; but the man who raised the argument might well find his own career suddenly ended.

However, the subject was touched in an early morning telephone conversation between Anton Drexel and his old friend Manfred Cardinal Kaltenborn, Archbishop of Rio de Janeiro. Each was German-born, the one in Brasilia, the other in the Rhineland. They spoke in their mother tongue and their conversation was cryptic and good-humoured. They were old friends and sturdy campaigners who knew how to spell all the words in the book.

"Can we talk freely, Anton?"

"Never quite as freely as we'd like." Drexel had a healthy respect for satellite technology and the possibilities of espionage. "But let me give you some background. Our friend is already in care. I have it on the best authority that the odds are all in favour of recovery."

"To full competence?"

"Yes; but in my view that will not be the issue."

"What then?"

"It seems to have escaped most of our colleagues that our friend is undergoing a *Gewissenskrise,* a crisis of conscience. He has tried to reform the Church. Instead, he has created a wasteland. He sees no way to make it fruitful again. He has few confidants, no emotional supports, and a spiritual life based wholly on orthopraxis . . . right conduct, according to his limited lights. He will not risk beyond that, or reason beyond it either. So he is desperately lonely and afraid."

"How have the others missed this? They're all intelligent observers."

"Most are afraid of him. They spend their lives either avoiding or managing him. I'm too old to care. He knows that. He doesn't try to intimidate me."

"So what will he do?"

"He will break or he will change. If he breaks, my guess is that he will simply surrender his hold on the office and possibly on life itself. If he is to change, he will need the experience of a charity he has never known in his life."

"We can't endow him with that. It's something we have to pray for."

"I'm proposing to work on it as well. I'm inviting him to spend part of his convalescence at my villa. It's only a stone's throw from Castel Gandolfo and an hour's drive from the Vatican . . . He's a farmer's son, he might appreciate a change to country manners. He can also meet my little tribe and see how they handle their lives."

There was a brief silence and then His Eminence from Rio de Janeiro murmured a warning.

"Some of our colleagues might not understand your intentions, Anton. They mistrust kingmakers and grey eminences."

"Then they will say so." Anton Drexel's tone was testy. "And His Holiness will decide for himself. Charity may bend that stubborn will of his. Opposition will only stiffen it."

"So, let's go one step further, Anton. Our master has his second Pentecost— tongues of fire, an infusion of the Spirit, a rush of charity like the flush of spring. What next? What does he do about it? How does he retreat from the trenches he's dug for himself—for us all? You know the way it works in Rome. Never explain, never make excuses. Never appear to hurry a decision."

"I've talked about this at length with his physician, who is as concerned as I, though for other reasons. He's a Jew. He lost relatives in the Holocaust and the Black Sabbath in Rome . . . For him, this is a moment of extraordinary irony. He holds the life of the Roman Pontiff in his hands. You see the implications?"

"Some at least I see very clearly. But how does he answer my question? What does the Holy Father do—afterwards?"

"Salviati is emphatic that the Pontiff can do nothing unless we help him. I agree. I know his family history. Subsistence farming. A father dead too early. A mother determined to lift her son and herself off the dung heap. The best, if not the only, solution was the Church. It's a sad, sterile story. The one thing he has never experienced is the human family, the quarrels, the kisses, the fairytales around the fire."

"You and I, my dear Anton, are hardly experts in that area."

"You underrate me, my friend," Anton Drexel laughed. "I have a very large adoptive progeny, sixteen boys and girls. And they all live under my roof."

"Don't teach your grandmother to suck eggs, Anton! I've got a million homeless kids in the *favelas* here! If you're ever short, I can always send you some replacements."

"Send me your prayers instead. I'm not half as confident as I sound in this affair."

"It seems to me you're juggling with a man's soul—and quite possibly with his sanity. You're also playing very dangerous politics. You could be accused of making a puppet out of a sick man. Why are you doing it, old friend?"

It was the question Drexel had dreaded, but he had to answer it.

"You know I correspond with Jean Marie Barette?"

"I do. Where is he now?"

"Still in Germany, in that little mountain commune I told you about; but he manages to be very well informed about what's going on in the big world. It was he who encouraged me in this work with the children . . . You know Jean Marie; he can make jokes like a Parisian music-hall comedian and the next moment he is discoursing deep mysteries. About a month ago he wrote me a very strange letter. Part of it was pure prophecy. He told me that the Holy Father would soon be forced to make a dangerous voyage and that I was the one marked to support him on the journey. Soon afterwards the Pontiff's disease was diagnosed; the papal physician named Salviati as the best heart surgeon in Italy—and the mother of my favourite *Enkelin* is a counsellor at his clinic. So the whole pattern of related events began to form itself around me. Does that answer your question?"

"You've left out something, Anton."

"What?"

"Why do you care so much about a man you've disliked for so long?"

"You're being rough with me, Manfred."

"Answer my question. Why do you care so much?"

"Because I'm past eighty. I am perhaps closer to judgement even than our Pontiff. I have been given many of the sweets of life. If I don't share them now, they will be like Dead Sea fruit—dust and ashes in my mouth!"

Nicol Peters sat under a pergola of vines on his terrace, sipped coffee, ate fresh pastry and watched the roof-dwellers of old Rome wake to the warm spring morning.

There was the fat fellow with striped pyjamas gaping open at the crotch, whose first care was to take the cover off his canary cage and coax the birds into a morning chorus, with trills and cadenzas of his own. There was the housewife in curlers and carpet slippers, watering her azaleas. On the next terrace, a heavy-hipped girl in a black leotard laboured through fifteen minutes of aerobic exercises to the tinny tunes of a tape machine. Over by the Torre Argentina a pair of lovers thrust open their shutters and then, as if seeing each other for the first time, embraced passionately and tumbled back into bed for a public mating.

Their nearest audience was a skinny bachelor with a towel for a loincloth, who did his own laundry and hung out every morning the shirt, the jockey shorts, the cotton vest and socks which he had just washed under the shower. This done, he lit a cigarette, watched the love-making of his neighbours and went inside to reappear a few minutes later with coffee and a morning paper . . . Above them, the first swifts dipped and wheeled around the campaniles and through the forest of antennae and satellite discs, while shadowy figures passed and repassed by open doors and casements to a growing cacophony of music, radio announcements and a rumour of traffic from the alleys below.

These folk were the theme upon which Nicol Peters was building the text for his weekly column, "A View From My Terrace". He stacked the scattered pages, picked up a pencil and began his editing.

". . . The Romans have a proprietary interest in the Pope. They own him. He is their elected Bishop. His domains are all on Roman soil. They cannot be exported, but they may in some future crisis be expropriated. There is not a single Roman citizen who will not freely admit that most of his personal income depends directly or indirectly upon the Pontiff. Who else brings the tourists and the pilgrims and the art lovers and the romantics, young and old, to clog the airport and pack the hotels and pump tourist and export currency into the city?

"The fact that they need him, however, does not compel the Romans to love him. Some do. Some don't. Most accept him with a shrug and an expressive 'Boh!', a monosyllable which defies translation but conveys a wholly Roman sentiment: 'Popes come, Popes go. We acclaim them. We bury them. You must not expect us to tremble at every proclamation and every anathema they utter.

" 'That's our way, you see. Foreigners never understand it. We make horrendous laws, load them with terrible penalties—and then water them all down with *tolleranza* and casuistry! . . .

" 'It has nothing to do with faith and only a little to do with morals. It has to do with *arrangiarsi*, the art of getting along, of managing oneself in a contradictory world. If the cogs of creation slip, that has to be due to defects in the original workmanship. So, God can't be too hard on his creatures who live on a defective planet.

" 'The Pope will tell you Christian marriages are made in heaven. They are made to last a lifetime. We're good Catholics, we have no quarrel with that. But Beppi and Lucia next door come close to murder every night, and keep us all awake. Is that Christian? Is that a marriage? Does it have the seal of heaven stamped on it? We beg leave to doubt the proposition. The sooner they break up, the sooner we'll all get some sleep; but, for pity's sake, don't stop 'em finding new mates; otherwise our lives will be disrupted again by a randy bull and a heifer in heat . . .'

"Clearly, there is no way your average Roman wants to argue this with the Pope. After all, a Pope sleeps alone and loves everybody in the Lord, so he is ill-equipped to deal with such matters. So your Roman listens politely to what he has to say, makes his own arrangements and turns up faithfully in church for marriages, christenings, funerals and first communions.

"So far, so good—for the Romans! They have no need or desire to change their capital interest in the Pope. But what about the rest of Christendom—not to mention the millions outside the pale? Their attitude is exactly the reverse. They are happy to accept the Pope—or anyone else for that matter—as a champion of good conduct, just dealing, stable family relationships, social responsibility. It's his theology which now becomes the root problem. Who, they ask, determines that the Pope sees all creation plain as day, the moment after he is elected? Who gives him the prescriptive right to create, by simple proclamation, a doctrine like the Assumption of the Virgin or to declare that it is a crime most damnable for a husband and wife to control their own breeding cycle with a pill or a condom?

"The questions, it seems to this writer, are legitimate and they deserve open discussion and answers more frank than those which have yet been given. They need something else, too—a compassion in the respondent, an openness to history and to argument, a respect for the honest doubts and reservations of his questioners. I have been unable to find the source of the following quotation, but I have no hesitation in adopting it as my own sentiment: 'There will be no hope of reform in the Roman Catholic Church, there will be no restoration of confidence between the faithful and the hierarchy, unless and until a reigning pontiff is prepared to admit and abjure the errors of his predecessors . . .' "

* * *

They were strong words, the strongest Nicol Peters had written in a long time. Given the subject and the circumstances, an ailing pontiff under threat of death, they might even be considered a gross breach of etiquette. The longer he practised his craft, the more conscious he became of the dynamic of language, of speech and writing as events in themselves. The simplest and most obvious proposition, stated in the most elementary language, could so mutate itself in the mind of the reader that it could express the opposite of what the writer had intended. What he wrote as evidence for the defence could hang the man he was defending.

Nicol Peters's credit and credibility as a commentator on the Vatican depended upon his ability to render the most complex argument into clear prose for the hurried reader. The clarity of the prose depended upon a precise understanding of the matter at issue. In this case, it was a highly delicate one. It had to do with the Roman view of orthodoxy (right doctrine) and orthopraxis (right practice), the nature of the pontiff's right to prescribe either—and his duty to recant any error that might creep into the prescription.

This was the problem which still split Christendom like an apple, and which the old-fashioned absolutism of Leo XIV had only exacerbated. It would not be solved as the Romans solved it, by cynical indifference. It would not go away like a wart or heal itself like a razor nick. It would grow and fester like a cancer, sapping the inner life of the Church, reducing it to invalidism and indifference.

Which raised quite other questions for Nicol Peters, doyen of the press corps, confidant of cardinals, comfortable in his elegant Roman domain: "Why should I care so much? I'm not even a Catholic, for God's sake! Why should I sweat blood over every shade of clerical opinion, while the hierarchs themselves sit content inside the ramparts of Vatican City and watch the decline and fall of the Roman Church?"

To which his wife Katrina, arrived with fresh coffee and her good morning smile, delivered the perfect answer: "Glum today, are we? Morning sex doesn't agree with you? Brighten up, lover boy. Spring is here. The shop's making money. And I've just had a fascinating phone call about Salviati and his girlfriend and, of all people, your friend Drexel."

IV

PRECISELY at ten that same morning, Monsignor Malachy O'Rahilly, senior private secretary to the Pontiff, waited on his master at the clinic.

His presence was a radiant one: round, glowing face, blue eyes of limpid innocence, a joyful smile, six languages tripping off his tongue with a beautiful blarneying brogue to sweeten them all. His Holiness, a cross-tempered man, depended upon his good humour and even more on his Celtic talent for smelling the winds of intrigue, which in the Curial enclaves blew hot and cold and every which way in the same moment.

Monsignor O'Rahilly's loyalties were absolute. They pointed always to magnetic north, the dwelling-place of power. Statistically, papal secretaries outlived their masters; the wise ones made sure that they had post-mortem insurance always in place. Of course, all insurance required the payment of premiums: a discreet recommendation, a file brought to the Pontiff's attention, a name dropped at the right moment. The currency might vary; but the principle was ironclad and backed by biblical mandate: make friends of the mammon of iniquity, so that when you fail (or when your patron dies, which is the same thing) they may receive you into their houses!

This morning the Monsignor was serving his alternate master, the Cardinal Secretary of State, who had admonished him firmly: "No business, Monsignore, absolutely none! Tomorrow he goes under the knife and there'll be nothing, absolutely nothing, he can do about anything!"

To the Pontiff, Malachy explained with voluble good humour: "I'm under pain of instant exile if I raise your blood pressure by a single point. I'm to tell you from Their Eminences of the Curia that everything's being handled according to your instructions and that prayers and good wishes are pouring in like water from the Fons Bandusiae . . . There's even a love note from the Kremlin and one from the Patriarch Dimitri in Moscow. Chairman Tang has sent a polite note from Beijing and the Secretariat is making a full list of all the other communications . . . Cardinal Agostini said he'll be in to see you just before lunch. Once again, it's strictly no business, as the doctor has most firmly ordered. But if there are any personal things you'd like me to take care of . . ."

"There's only one." Monsignor Malachy O'Rahilly was instantly at the ready —notebook open, pen poised in his chubby fist. "A young woman died here last night. She leaves a husband and two young children. Her husband is a priest of the Roman diocese who broke his vows and contracted a civil marriage. I am told he made a number of applications to us to laicise him and to regularise the union. The applications were all refused. I want you to get me full details of the case and copies of all the documents on the file . . ."

"Be sure, I'll get on to it right away. Does Your Holiness have a name to give me?"

"Not yet. I'm waiting to speak to the counsellor here."

"No matter. I'll dig it out somehow . . . Not that you'll be able to give it much attention for a week or two . . ."

"Nevertheless, you will treat the matter as most urgent."

"May one ask the reason for your interest in this case, Holiness?"

"Two children and a grieving husband, my dear Malachy . . . and a text that keeps running through my head: 'The bruised reed he will not break, the smoking flax he will not extinguish.' "

"First, in a messy affair like this, I'll have to find out who's got the papers— Doctrine of the Faith, the Congregation for Clerics, the Apostolic Penitentiary, the Rota. None of them will be happy about an intervention by Your Holiness."

"They're not asked to be happy. Tell them this is a matter of personal concern to me. I want the documents in my hands as soon as I'm fit to read them."

"Now that," Monsignor O'Rahilly looked very dubious, "that's going to be the nub of a lot of arguments. Who will say when Your Holiness is ready—and for what? This is a big operation for a man past middle age and it needs a longish convalescence . . . You've done a pretty effective job of concentrating power in your own hands. Now the *grossi pezzi* in the Curia will be working to claw it back. I can keep you informed, but I can't stage a pitched battle with the Prefect of a Roman Congregation."

"Are you saying you have trouble already?"

"Trouble? That's not a word I'd dare breathe to Your Holiness, especially at a time like this. I'm simply pointing out that the members of your household will be rather isolated during your absence. Authorities greater than ours will be brought into play. So we need a clear direction from the Chair of Peter."

"You already have it!" The Pontiff was suddenly his old self again, frowning and emphatic. "My reserved business and my private documents remain private. In other matters, you will represent what you know to be my views. If contrary orders are given by any member of the Curia, you will request a direction in writing before you comply. If you have a big problem, go to Cardinal Drexel and put the matter to him. Is that clear?"

"It's clear," said Monsignor O'Rahilly, "but a little surprising. I'd always felt there was a certain tension between Drexel and Your Holiness."

"There was. There is. We are very different beings. But Drexel has two great virtues: he has overpassed ambition and he has a sense of humour rare in the Germans. I disagree with him often; but I trust him, always. You can, too."

"That's good to know."

"But there's also a warning, Malachy. Don't try any of your Irish tricks on him. I'm Italian, I understand—most of the time—how your mind works. Drexel's very direct: one-two-three. Work that way with him."

Monsignor O'Rahilly smiled and bowed his head under the admonition. The Pontiff was right. The Irish and the Italians understood each other very well. After all, the great St. Patrick himself was a Roman born; but once the Celts were converted it was they who exported learning and civility to Europe while the Empire was tumbling into ruins. Besides, there was much shared experience between the son of a peat-digger from Connemara and a man who had shovelled dung on a sharefarm in Mirandola. All of which gave Malachy O'Rahilly a certain freedom to advise his high master.

"With the greatest respect, Holiness . . ." He made a careful actor's pause.

"Say it, Malachy! Say it plain, without the compliments! What's on your mind?"

"The report on the finances of the Church. It will land on your desk at the end of this month. That's definitely not a matter I can refer to Cardinal Drexel."

"There's no reason why you should. I can study the document while I'm convalescing."

"Four years' work by fifteen prelates and laymen? With every bishop in the world looking over your shoulder? And all the faithful asking themselves whether they will or they won't be donating to Peter's Pence and Propaganda Fide next year? Don't delude yourself, Holiness. Better you shouldn't open the report than that you should botch the handling of it."

"I'm perfectly capable of—"

"You're not. You won't be for some time. And I'd be a bad servant if I didn't say so! Think of all the hard-nosed fellows who've been working four years on that document. Think of all the messes they've uncovered—and the ones they'll have tried their damndest to bury . . . And you'll be just recovering from a massive surgical invasion. No way you can do a proper job of study."

"And who else is going to do it for me, Malachy? You?"

"Listen to me Holiness, please!" He was pleading now, earnestly. "I remember the day, and the hour, when you swore by all the saints in the calendar that you'd clean up the *covo di ladri* who were running the Institute for Religious Works and all its banking agencies. You were so angry that I thought you'd swell up and burst. You said: 'These bankers think they're impressing me with their money jargon. Instead, they're insulting me! They're like fairground jugglers, pumping wine out of their elbows, picking coins out of children's ears! I'm a farmer's son. My mother kept all our spare cash in a jam-jar. She taught me that if you spend more than you earn, you're bankrupt—and if you lie down in the pigpen you'll get dirty. I'll never be canonised, because I'm too bad-tempered and stiff-necked, but I promise you, Malachy, I'll be one pope they never call a crook or a friend of crooks—and if I find another financial rogue wearing the purple I'll have it off his back before he goes to bed!' Do you remember all that?"

"I do."

"Then you have to admit that this report will be your first and last chance to make good on the promise. You can't, you daren't, try to study it while your mind is skewed by anaesthetics or clouded by depressions. Salviati gave you clear warning. You must heed him. Don't forget either that you promised to call a Special Synod to consider the report. Before you confront your brother bishops you'll have to be figure-perfect and fact-perfect on the document."

"What do you suggest I do with it meanwhile?"

"Receive it. Keep it *in petto*. Lock it in your private safe. Gag all discussion. Let it be known that it's any man's career if he breaks silence before you speak. If you don't, the Curia will pre-empt you, and when you come to make your statement there'll be mantraps and spring-guns at every corner."

"Then answer me this, Malachy. Suppose that I don't survive the surgery. What will happen then?"

Monsignor O'Rahilly had the answer on the tip of his fluent tongue.

"It's elementary. The Camerlengo will take possession of it, as he'll take possession of the Ring, the Seal, your will and all your personal chattels. If past history is any guide—and if my mother's second sight is still working—sometime between burying you and installing your successor, they'll lose the document, shove it in the archive, drown it deeper than the Titanic."

"And why would they do that?"

"Because they're convinced you made a mistake in ordering the study in the first place. I thought so myself—though it wasn't my place to say it. Look! The most profound mystery in this Holy, Roman and Universal Church isn't the Trinity, or the Incarnation, or the Immaculate Conception. It's the fact that we're mired up to our necks in money. We're the biggest banking house in the world. We take in money, we lend it out, we invest it in stocks and bonds. We're part of the world community of money-folk. But money makes its own rules, as it makes its own geniuses and its own rogues—of whom we have our fair share, in the cloth or out of it. The Curia expected you to understand that because they saw you swallowing a whole lot of other indigestible facts about the place and the office. But in this matter, you didn't. For some reason you gagged on it; but they still make the valid point that if you want to have your budget balanced and your staff maintained and the whole huge fabric of the Church kept in running order, then you have to stay in the banking business. If you're in it, you play by the rules and try to embarrass your colleagues as little as possible! There's much sense in that—if not a whole lot of religion . . . And now that I've recited my little piece, how would Your Holiness like my head—on a silver dish or impaled on a pike by the Swiss Guard?"

For the first time, Leo the Pontiff smiled, and the smile turned into his strange barking laugh.

"It's a shrewd head, Malachy. I can ill afford to lose it at this time. As to your future, I'm sure you've realised that I may not be the one who determines it."

"I've thought about that, too," said Malachy O'Rahilly. "I'm not sure I'd want to stay in the Vatican—presuming I were even asked. They do say that service with one pontiff is as much as the human frame can stand."

"And with Ludovico Gadda it's already too much! Is that what you're telling me, Malachy?"

Malachy O'Rahilly gave him a small, sidelong grin and a shrug of deprecation.

"It hasn't always been easy; but for a big country boy like me there'd have been no fun sparring with a lightweight—no fun at all. I was told I mustn't stay too long. So if there's nothing else I can do for Your Holiness, I'll be on my way."

"You have our leave, Malachy. And you won't forget that other matter, will you?"

"I'll be on to it this very day. God smile on Your Holiness. I'll be offering my Mass for you in the morning . . ."

"Go with God, Malachy."

Leo the Pontiff closed his eyes and lay back on the pillows. He felt strangely bereft, a piece of human flotsam bobbing helplessly in a vast and empty ocean.

On his way out of the clinic, Malachy O'Rahilly stopped at the reception desk, gave the girl his most winning Irish smile and asked: "The young lady who died here last night . . ."

"The Signora de Rosa?"

"The same. I'm most anxious to get in touch with her husband. Do you have an address for him?"

"As a matter of fact, Monsignore, he's here now, talking with the Signora Lundberg. The undertakers have just removed his wife's body. She's being buried in Pistoia. If you'd care to wait . . . I'm sure he won't be very long."

O'Rahilly was trapped. He could not leave without making a fool of himself, yet the last thing he needed was a confrontation with a grieving and aggrieved husband. In that same instant, bells rang loudly in his head. De Rosa, Lorenzo, from Pistoia in Tuscany, his own contemporary at the Gregorian University. He'd been a handsome devil, bursting with brains and passion and charm and so much unconscious arrogance that friends and masters alike swore that one day he would turn into a Cardinal or an heresiarch.

Instead, here he was, caught up in a shabby little matrimonial tragedy which did no credit to himself or to the Church—and from which not even the Pope could take him now. Not for the first time, Malachy O'Rahilly thanked his stars for a good Irish Jansenist education which assured that, though the drink might snare him one day, no woman ever would.

Then, like a walking corpse, Lorenzo de Rosa stepped into the foyer. His skin, pale and transparent, was drawn drum-tight over the bones of his classic face. His eyes were dull, his lips bloodless. He moved like a sleepwalker. O'Rahilly would have let him pass without a word, but the receptionist sprang the trap on him.

"Signor de Rosa, there's a gentleman to see you."

Puzzled and disoriented, de Rosa stopped dead in his tracks. O'Rahilly stood up and offered his hand.

"Lorenzo? Remember me? Malachy O'Rahilly from the Greg. I happened to be visiting someone here and I heard the news of your sad loss. I'm sorry, truly sorry."

His hand flapped uselessly in front of him like an autumn leaf. He let it fall to his side. There was a long, hostile silence. The dull eyes surveyed him from head to toe like a specimen of noxious matter. The bloodless lips opened and a flat, mechanical voice answered him.

"Yes, I remember you, O'Rahilly. I wish I had never known you or any other of your kind. You're cheats and hypocrites, all of you, and the god you peddle is the cruellest cheat of all. As I remember, you became a papal secretary, yes? Then tell your master from me I can't wait to spit on his grave!"

The next moment he was gone, a dark, spectral figure out of some ancient folk-tale. Malachy O'Rahilly shivered in the sudden winter of the man's rage and despair. From somewhere in the far distance, he heard the receptionist's voice, soothing and solicitous.

"You mustn't be upset, Monsignore. The poor man's had a terrible blow; his wife was such a sweet woman. They were devoted to each other and to the children."

"I'm sure they were," said Malachy O'Rahilly. "It's all very sad."

He was tempted to go back and tell the Pontiff what had happened. Then he asked himself the classic question: *cui bono?* What good could possibly come of it? All the harm had been done centuries ago, when the law had been set above simple charity and suffering souls were counted as necessary casualties in the unending crusade against the follies of human flesh.

The rest of the Pontiff's day was a slow processional towards the merciful darkness they had promised him. He strolled alone in the garden, fragrant with the first blossom trees, the smell of mown grass and fresh-turned earth. He sat on the marble lip of the fountain which the gardener told him was the site of the ancient shrine of Diana, where the new king of the woods cleansed himself after the ritual murder. He climbed the slope to the verge of the estate to peer down into the inky depths of Lake Nemi; but when he got there, he was breathless and dizzy and there was the familiar constriction in his chest. He leaned against a pine-bole until the pain passed and he had wind enough to walk himself back to the safety of his room, where the Secretary of State was waiting for him.

Agostini's performance was, as always, impeccably rehearsed. He brought only good news: the solicitous good wishes of Royalty and of Heads of State, the prayerful greetings of members of the Sacred College and the senior hierarchy . . . the replies he had drafted for the Pontiff's approval. Everything else was working to the norms that His Holiness had approved. He declined absolutely to engage in any discussion of business or statecraft.

There was, however, one important matter. If His Holiness wished to spend part of his convalescence outside Vatican territory, in the Republic of Italy, no objection would be raised, provided that adequate security could be maintained, and the Vatican was prepared to meet the cost of a State security contingent. The only caveats were that the Republic retained its right to approve the location, and that provincial and *comune* authorities be consulted in advance on problems of traffic and public assembly.

The Secretary of State understood very well that His Holiness would not wish to make a decision until after the operation, but at least the options were open. The Pontiff thanked him. Agostini asked: "Are there any personal commissions I can execute for Your Holiness?"

"None, thank you, Matteo. I am comfortable here. I have accepted that the future is out of my hands. I stand in a quiet place—but a solitary one, too."

"One wishes it were possible to share the experience, make the solitude a little more bearable."

"It is not, my friend; but one does not come to solitude wholly unprepared. It is almost as if there were a mechanism in the mind, in the body, which prepares us for this moment. May I tell you something? As a young priest, I used to preach very ardently about the consolations of the last sacraments, the confession, the anointing, the viaticum . . . They seemed to have a special meaning for me because my father, whom I loved very dearly, had died without them. He had simply dropped dead in the furrows behind his plough. In a way, I suppose I resented that. He was a good man, who deserved better. I felt that he had been deprived of something he had truly earned . . ."

Agostini waited in silence. It was the first time he had seen the Pontiff in this mood of elegy.

"As you know, before I came in here, I had my chaplain give me the last rites. I don't know what I expected—a sense of relief, or excitement perhaps, like standing on a railway station with all one's baggage packed, waiting to board a train for some exotic place . . . It wasn't like that at all. It was—how can I explain it?—a propriety only, a thing well done but somehow redundant. Whatever had subsisted between myself and the Almighty was as it had been, complete and final. I was held, as I had always been, in the palm of His hand. I could leap out of it if I chose; but so long as I wanted to stay, I was there. I was, I am. I have to accept that it is enough. Do I embarrass you, Matteo?"

"No. But you surprise me a little."

"Why?"

"Perhaps because Your Holiness is not usually so eloquent about his own emotions."

"Or as sensitive to those of other people?"

Matteo Agostini smiled and shook his head.

"I'm your Secretary of State, not your confessor."

"So, you don't have to judge me; but you can afford to indulge me a moment longer. Ask yourself how much of what we do in Rome, how much of what we prescribe and legislate, is truly relevant in the secret life of each human soul. We've been trying for centuries to persuade ourselves and the faithful that our writ runs right up to the gates of heaven and down to the portcullis of hell. They don't believe us. At bottom, we don't believe ourselves. Do I shock you?"

"Nothing shocks a diplomat, Holiness. You know that. But I would wish you happier thoughts."

"So, Matteo! Each man comes, in the end, to his own special agony. This is mine: to know how much I have failed as a man and a pastor; not to know whether I shall survive to repair the damage. Go home now. Write to your premiers and presidents and kings. Send them our thanks and our Apostolic Benediction. And spare a thought for Ludovico Gadda, who must soon begin his night watch in Gethsemane."

The night watch, however, was preceded by a series of small humiliations. The anaesthetist came to explain the procedures, to allay his patient's fears about the pain he might expect, and then to read him a lecture about the regimen he should follow afterwards to reduce his weight, increase his exercise, keep his lungs free of fluid.

Then came the barber, a voluble Neapolitan, who shaved him, clean as an egg, from throat to crotch and laughingly promised him all sorts of exquisite discomforts when the hairs started to grow again. The barber was followed by a nurse who shoved a suppository into his rectum and warned him that he would purge rapidly and frequently for an hour or two, and that afterwards he might ingest fluids only—and nothing at all after midnight.

It was thus that Anton Drexel found him, empty of dignity, empty of belly and sour of temper, when he came to pay him the last permitted visit of the day. Drexel was carrying a leather briefcase and his greeting was brisk and direct as always.

"I can see you've had a bad day, Holiness."

"I've had better. I'm told they put me to sleep with a pill tonight. I'll be glad of it."

"If you like, I'll give you communion and read compline with you before I go."

"Thank you. You're a thoughtful man, Anton. I wonder why it's taken me so long to appreciate you."

Anton Drexel laughed.

"We're a pair of hard-heads. It takes time to beat sense into us . . . Let me move this bed-lamp a little. I have something to show you." He opened his briefcase and brought out a large photographic album, bound in tooled leather, which he laid in the Pontiff's lap.

"What is this?"

"Look at it first. I'll explain later."

Drexel busied himself laying out on the bed-table a linen cloth, a pyx, a small silver flask and a cup. Beside them, he laid his breviary. By the time he had finished the Pontiff was halfway through the volume of photographs. He was obviously intrigued.

"What is this place? Where is it?"

"It's a villa, fifteen minutes away from here. It used to belong to Valerio Rinaldi. You must have known him. He served under your predecessor, Pope Kiril. His family were old nobility, quite wealthy I believe."

"I knew him, but never well. The place looks charming."

"It's more than that. It's prosperous and profitable—farmland, vineyards and vegetable gardens."

"Who owns it now?"

"I do." Drexel could not resist a small theatrical flourish. "And I have the honour to invite Your Holiness to spend his convalescence there. That's the guest villa you're looking at now. There's room for a resident servant if you choose to use your own valet. Otherwise my staff will be delighted to serve you. We have a resident therapist and dietician. The big building is occupied by my family and the people who look after them . . ."

"I can see it's a very large family." The Pontiff's tone was dry. "I'm sure Your Eminence will explain it to me in due course. I hope he will also explain how a member of my Curia can afford an establishment like this."

"That part is easy." Drexel was obviously enjoying himself. "Rinaldi sold me the place on a low deposit and a long mortgage which was financed by the Institute for Religious Works at standard rates. There was also a proviso, that on my death the title should pass from me to a recognised work of charity. With a little good luck and good management I was able to meet the mortgage payments out of the farm revenues and my own stipend as a prelate . . . I knew it was a luxury—but I knew I could not endure to live in Rome without a place to which I could retreat, be myself. Besides," he made a small joke, "as Your Holiness knows, we Germans have a long tradition of Prince Bishops! I liked the way Rinaldi lived. I admired his old-fashioned style. I was self-indulgent enough to want to emulate it. And I did, with no spiritual merit but great human satisfaction—until I decided to found this family of mine."

"Which so far you have managed to keep secret from us all! Explain, Eminence! Explain!"

Drexel explained, eloquently and at length, and Leo the Pontiff was jealous of the joy in his voice, his eyes, his every gesture, as he told the history of his encounter in Frascati with the child Britte and how she had adopted him as her grandfather. She was sixteen years old now, he announced proudly, a talented artist who painted with a brush held between her teeth, and whose pictures were sold by a very prestigious gallery in Via Margutta.

The others? Tove Lundberg had introduced some parents of diplegic children. They had recommended others. Anton Drexel had begged money from richer colleagues in the United States and Latin America and Europe. He had improved the quality of his wine and his farm produce and doubled the income of his land. Salviati had introduced him to specialists in cerebral dysfunction and to a small cadre of money-men who helped to pay his teaching and nursing staff . . .

"So, although we've lived pretty much hand to mouth for ten years, we're educating artists and mathematicians and designers of computer programmes —but most of all we've given these children a chance to be truly human, to show forth the Divine image in which, despite their grievous afflictions, they were truly made . . . It is their invitation as much as mine, Holiness, that you should come and begin to mend yourself with us. You don't have to decide now. Just think about it. One thing I can promise you: it's a very happy family."

The Pontiff's reaction was strange. For an instant he seemed very close to tears, then his face hardened into that familiar, implacable predator's mask. His tone was harsh, accusatory and pitilessly formal.

"It seems to us, Eminence, that, however worthy this enterprise, you have paid us small compliment by concealing it for so long. We deprecate, as you know, any and all aspect of luxury in the lives of our brother bishops. But all this aside, it seems you have been guilty of certain presumptions touching our office as Vicar of Christ. We are not so ill informed or so deaf to palace gossip as people sometimes believe. We are aware, for instance, that Dr. Salviati is Jewish by race and Zionist in sympathy; that his trusted counsellor, the Signora Lundberg, is an unwed mother, and that there is talk of a liaison between them. Since neither is of our Faith, their private morals are no concern of ours. But that you should have formed this . . . this quite fictional relationship with her child and, by inference, with her, that you should have concealed it for so long and then attempted to draw us into it, for however good a reason . . . This we find quite intolerable and highly dangerous to us and to our office."

Anton Drexel had heard, in his time, some classic tirades from Leo XIV, but this one topped them all. All the man's fears, frustrations and angers had been poured into it, all the buried rages of the ploughboy who had climbed and clawed his way up to be a prince. Now, having vented it in such fury, he waited, tense and hostile, for the counter attack. Instead, Drexel replied with calm formality.

"Your Holiness makes it clear that I have a case to answer. Now is not the time to do it. Let me say only that if I have offended Your Holiness I am deeply sorry. I was offering what I believed to be a kindness and a service. But we should not part like this, in anger. Can we not pray together, like brothers?"

The Pontiff said nothing, but reached for his spectacles and his breviary. Drexel opened his book and recited the opening versicle: *"Munda cor meum . . . Cleanse my heart, O Lord, that my lips may announce your praises . . ."* Soon the rhythm of the ancient psalms took hold of them, soothing them like waves on a friendly sea. After a while the Pontiff's taut face began to relax, and the hostility died out of his dark eyes. When he read the words "Yea, though I walk in the valley of death, His rod and His staff shall comfort me . . ." his voice faltered and he began to weep quietly. It was Drexel now who carried the burden of the recitation, while his hand closed over that of his master and held it in a firm and comforting grip.

When the last Amen had been spoken, Drexel put a stole around his neck and gave the Pontiff communion, then sat silently while he made his thanksgiving. No words but prayers had been spoken between them for nearly forty minutes. Drexel began repacking his briefcase. Then, as protocol prescribed, he begged leave to go.

"Please!" It was a poignant appeal from a high, proud man. "Please stay awhile! I'm sorry for what I said. You understand me better than anyone else. You always have. That's why I fight you. You will not leave me any illusions."

"Do you know why?" Drexel was gentle with him, but he would not yield an inch.

"I would like to hear it from you."

"Because we cannot afford illusions any more. The people of God cry out for the bread of life. We are feeding them stones."

"And you think I have been doing that?"

"Ask yourself the question, Holiness."

"I have—every day, every night for months now. I am asking it tonight, before they wheel me out and freeze me and split me like a carcase of beef and put my life into syncope . . . I know things must change and I must be the catalyst of change. But how, Anton? I am only what I am. I cannot crawl back into my mother's womb and be born again."

"I am told," said Drexel slowly, "by those who have undergone this operation, that it's the nearest one can come to being reborn. Salviati and Tove Lundberg tell me the same thing. It's a new lease on life—and, perforce, a new kind of life. So the question for me, the question for the Church, is what use you're going to make of the new gift."

"And you have a prescription for me, Anton!"

"No. You already know the prescription. It's repeated over and over again in Scripture. 'My little children, love one another . . . Above all, have a constant mutual charity among yourselves . . .' The question is how you will interpret the revelation, how you will respond to it in the future."

"How have I done so until now?"

"The old Roman way! Legislation, admonition, fiat! We are the custodians of truth, the censors of morals, the only authentic interpreters of revelation. We are the binders and the loosers, the heralds of good tidings. Make straight the way of the Lord! Prepare the paths before Him!"

"And you don't agree with that?"

"No. I don't. I have been fifty-five years a priest in the Roman rite. I was trained in the system and to the system. I kept my priestly vows and I lived according to the canons. I have served four pontiffs—two as a member of the Sacred College. Your Holiness will bear witness that though I disagreed often and openly, I bowed always in obedience to the *magisterium*!"

"You did, Anton, and I respected you for it. But now you say we have failed, that I have failed."

"All the evidence says we have."

"But why?"

"Because you and I, all of us, Curia and hierarchy alike, are the nearly perfect products of our Roman system. We never fought it. We marched with it every step of the way. We cauterised our emotions, hardened our hearts, made ourselves eunuchs for the love of God!—how I've come to hate that phrase!—and somewhere along the way, very early I think, we lost the simple art of loving. If you come to think about it, we're very selfish people, we bachelor priests. We're the true biblical Pharisees. We bind heavy and insupportable burdens on men's back and we ourselves lift no finger to ease them! So, the people turn away; not to strange gods, as we like to think; not to orgies and self-indulgence that they can't afford; but in search of simplicities which we, the custodians, censors and governors, have obscured from them. They want care and compassion and love and a hand to lead them out of the maze. Does yours? Does mine? I think not. But if an honest, open, brave man sat in the chair of Peter and thought first, last and always of the people, there might be a chance. There just might be!"

"But I am not that man?"

"Today, you are not. But afterwards, given a new lease on life and the grace to use it aright, who knows but that one day Your Holiness may write the great message for which the people hunger and thirst: the message of love, compassion, forgiveness. It's a call that needs to be sounded loud and clear as Roland's horn at Roncesvalles . . ." He broke off, suddenly aware of his own fervour. "In any case, that's the reason for my invitation to spend part of your healing time with my family. You will see love in action every day. You will see people giving it, taking it, growing in the warmth of it. I can promise it will be spent on you, too, and one day you will be rich enough to return it . . . You need this time; you need this experience. I see what this office does to you—to any man! It dries the sap out of you, withers you up like a raisin in the sun. Now is your chance of renewal. Take it! Be, for once, generous with Ludovico Gadda who has been a long time away from his home-place!"

"I ask myself," said the Pontiff wryly, "why I did not make you Preacher to the Pontifical Household."

Drexel laughed.

"Your Holiness knows very well why. You would have sent me to the stake within a week." The next moment he was back to formality. "It is long past my bedtime. If Your Holiness will give me leave to go?"

"You have our leave."

"Once again, I beg forgiveness for my presumption. I hope there is peace between us at last."

"There is peace, Anton. God knows, there is no time left for quarrels and banalities. I am grateful for your counsel. Perhaps I will come to stay with you; but as you well know, there are other considerations: protocols, palace rivalries, old memories of bad times in our history. I cannot ignore these things or override them rashly. However, once I'm through the tunnel, I'll think about it. Now go home, Anton! Go home to your family and give them my blessing!"

In the last private moment left to him before the arrival of the night nurse, Leo XIV wrote what he knew might be the final entry in his diary. Even if there were to be other entries, they would be written by another Leo, a reconstructed man who had been disconnected from his life source and then set working again like a mechanical toy. So there was a certain brutal urgency in the record.

"I behaved like a country clod. I abused a man who wished me nothing but good. Why? In simple truth, I always have been jealous of Anton Drexel. At eighty, he is much healthier, happier and wiser than I have ever been. To become what I am, Supreme Pastor of the Universal Church, I have worked like a brute every day of my life. Drexel, on the other hand, is a self-indulgent man whose style and talent have brought him, almost without effort, to eminence in the Church.

"In Renaissance times, they would certainly have made him Pope. Like my namesake, Leo X, he would have set out to enjoy the experience. Whatever his imperfections as a cleric, he is the most perfect diplomat. He will always tell the truth, because it is his master, not himself, who must bear the consequences. He will argue a position in the strongest terms; but in the end he will bow to the decision of authority. Rome is a very comfortable and rewarding place for such a man.

"However, tonight it was clear that he was offering me a share in a loving experience which had transformed his life and turned even his self-indulgence to good account. I did not have the courage to tell him how much I envied the intimacy and immediacy of his love for his adopted children, while whatever love I have is diffused and diluted out of existence over a human multitude.

"Nonetheless, I felt that he was still trying to manipulate me, to regulate, however indirectly, what might remain of my life and authority as Supreme Pontiff. Even that I could tolerate, because I need him. My problem is that he has the luxury of being mistaken without too grave a consequence. I am bound by every protocol, aware of every risk. I am power personified, but power inert and in stasis.

"The cold facts are these. My policies have been proven wrong. Change, radical change, is necessary in the governance of the Church at every level. But even if I survive, how can I make the change? It was I who created the climate of rigorism and repression. It was I who recruited the zealots to impose my will. The moment I begin to hint a change, they will rally to circumvent me, by clogging my communications, confusing me with scenarios of scandal and schism, misrepresenting my views and directives.

"I cannot fight that battle alone. Already I have been warned that I shall be vulnerable for some time, emotionally fragile, subject to sudden threatening depressions. If I am already a casualty, how can I mount a campaign which may well turn into a civil war?

"It is an enormous risk; but if I am not fit to take it, then I am not fit to govern. I shall have to consider the question of abdication—and that, too, is fraught with other risks for the Church.

"Even as I write these words, I am caught up in a memory of my schooldays. My history master was trying to explain to us the Pax Romana, the period of calm and prosperity throughout the Empire under Augustus. He explained it thus: 'So long as the legions were on the march, so long as the roads they trod were maintained and extended, the peace would last, trade would flourish, the Empire would endure. But the day they pitched the last camp, threw up the last earthworks and palisades and retired behind them as garrison troops, the Pax Romana was finished, the Empire was finished, the barbarians were on the move towards the heart of Rome.'

"As I sit here now, writing these lines to distract myself from tomorrow, I imagine that last commander of that last *castra* on the outer marches. I see him making his night rounds, checking the guard-posts, while beyond the ditch and the palisades and the cleared ground, men in animal masks made their war dance and invoked the old baleful gods of woodland, water and fire.

"There was no retreat for him. There is no retreat for me. I hear the night nurse trundling her little trolley down the corridor. She will come to me last of all. She will check my vital signs, pulse, temperature, blood pressure. She will ask whether I have passed water and whether my bowels have moved. Then, please God, she will give me a pill that will send me to sleep until dawn. Strange, is it not, that I who have always been a restless man, should now court so sedulously that sleep which is the brother of death. Or perhaps not so strange, perhaps this is the last mysterious mercy, that God makes us ready for death before death is quite ready for us.

"It is time to finish now, put down the pen and lock away the book. Sufficient unto the day is the evil thereof. More than sufficient are the fears and angers and the shame I feel for Ludovico Gadda, the ugly man who lives inside my skin . . . Forgive him his trespasses, O Lord, as he forgives those who have trespassed against him. Lead him not into trials he cannot endure and deliver him from evil—Amen."

V

WHEN he returned to his lodgings in Vatican City, Monsignor Malachy O'Rahilly telephoned his colleague, Monsignor Matthew Neylan of the Secretariat of State. Matt Neylan was a tall, handsome fellow, dark as a gypsy, with a crooked, satiric grin and a loose athlete's stride that made women look twice at him and then give him one more glance to fix him in their memories and wonder what he'd look like out of uniform. His title was Segretario di Nunziature di prima classe, which, however awkwardly it translated into English, put him about number twenty in the pecking order. It also gave him access to a great deal of information on a wide range of diplomatic matters. O'Rahilly saluted him with the full brogue and blarney.

"Matt, me fine boyo! Malachy! I have a question for you."

"Then spit it out, Mal. Don't let it fester in your mouth!"

"If I were to ask you, very politely, whether you'd dine with me tonight, what would you say?"

"Well now, that would depend."

"On what?"

"On where we'd eat and who was paying—and what quid I'd be asked for O'Rahilly's quo!"

"A three-in-one answer, boyo. We eat at Romolo's, I pick up the check, and you give me a piece of advice."

"Whose car do we take?"

"We walk! It's ten minutes for a one-legged man!"

"I'm on my way already. Meet you at the Porta Angelica—oh, and bring cash; they don't like credit cards."

"That's my careful friend!"

Da Romolo, near the Porta Settimiana, had once been the house of *la Fornarina*, mistress and model to the painter Raphael. However unreliable the legend, the food was good, the wine honest and the service—in age-old Roman style—agreeably impertinent and slapdash. In winter one ate inside, warmed by a fire of olive wood in the old baker's oven. In spring and summer one dined outside under a canopy of vines. Sometimes a guitarist came, singing folk songs in Neapolitan and Romanaccio. Always there were lovers, old, young and in-between. The clergy came too, in or out of uniform, because they were as much a fixture in the Roman scene as the lovers and the wandering musicians and the jostling purse-snatchers in the alleys of Trastevere.

In true Roman style, O'Rahilly kept his question until after the pasta and the first litre of wine.

"Tell me now, Matt, do you remember a fellow called Lorenzo de Rosa at the Greg?"

"I do. Handsome as Lucifer. Had a phenomenal memory. He could recite pages of Dante at a stretch! As I remember, he was laicised a few years ago."

"He wasn't. He skipped the formalities and got himself married under the civil code."

"Well, at least he had sense enough to cut clean!"

"He didn't. That was his problem. He's been trying to tidy the whole mess. Naturally enough, nobody's been very co-operative."

"So?"

"So last night his wife died in the Salviati clinic, leaving him with two young children."

"That's tough."

"Tougher than you know, Matt. I was at the clinic tonight to see our lord and master. De Rosa was just coming out. We spoke. The poor devil's near crazed with grief. He said—and I quote: 'I can't wait to spit on your master's grave!' "

"Well. I've heard the same thought expressed by others—more civilly, of course."

"It's not a laughing matter, Matt."

"And did I say it was? What's bothering you, Mal?"

"I can't make up my mind whether he's a threat to the Holy Father or not. If he is, then I've got to do something about it."

"Like what?"

"Call our security people. Have them make contact with the Carabinieri and arrange some surveillance on de Rosa."

"They won't only put him under surveillance, Mal. They'll roast him on a spit, just to frighten him off. That's pretty rough for a man with two kids and a wife hardly cold in the ground."

"That's why I'm asking your opinion, Matt. What should I do?"

"Let's be legal first of all. He uttered a malediction, not a menace. It was a word spoken in private to a priest. So he didn't commit a crime; but if it suited them, the security boys could make it look like one at the drop of a hat. More than that, your report and their embellishments would go on his dossier—and they'd be there till doomsday. All the other circumstances of his life would be read in the light of that single denunciation. That's the way the system is designed. It's a hell of a burden to lay on an innocent man!"

"I know. I know. But take the worst scenario: the man is really a nut-case, bent on vengeance for an injustice done to him and to the woman he loved.

One summer day he goes to a public audience in St Peter's Square and shoots the Pope. How will I feel then?"

"I don't know," said Matt Neylan innocently. "How has the Man been treating you lately?"

Malachy O'Rahilly laughed.

"Not so well that I'd give him a good-conduct medal. Not so badly that I'd want to see him bumped off. You'd have to agree there's that risk."

"I don't have to agree anything of the kind. You met de Rosa. I didn't. Besides, if you wanted to eliminate every possible threat to your Sacred Person, you'd have to make pre-emptive arrests up and down the peninsula. Personally, I'd be inclined to ignore the whole thing."

"I'm the man's secretary, for God's sake! I've got a certain special duty to him."

"Wait a minute! There may be a simple way to handle this, with no extra grief to anyone. Let me think it through while you order another bottle of wine. Make it a decent red this time. This house Frascati is so thin you could keep goldfish in it."

While Malachy O'Rahilly went through his little fandango over the wine, Matt Neylan sponged up the last sauce from his pasta and then delivered his verdict.

"There's a fellow who works for our security people here in Vatican City. His name is Baldassare Cotta. He owes me a favour because I recommended his son for a clerk's job in the Post Office. He used to be an investigator for the Guardia di Finanza and I know he moonlights for a private detective agency in town. I could ask him to check out de Rosa and give me a report. It would cost you round about a hundred thousand lire. Can you touch the petty cash for that much?"

"Wouldn't he do it for love?"

"He would, but then he'd have the arm on me for another favour. Come on, Mal! How much is the Bishop of Rome worth?"

"It depends on where you're sitting," said Malachy O'Rahilly with a grin. "But it's a good idea. I'll underwrite it from somewhere. You're a good man, Matt. They'll make you a bishop yet."

"I won't be around that long, Mal."

Malachy O'Rahilly gave him a swift, appraising look.

"I do believe you're serious."

"Dead serious."

"What are you trying to tell me?"

"I'm thinking of giving the game away, just walking out, like our friend de Rosa."

"To get married?"

"Hell no! Just to get out! I'm the wrong man in the wrong place, Mal. I've known it for a long time. It's only lately I've put together enough courage to admit it!"

"Matt, tell me honestly, is there a woman in it?"

"It might be easier if there were—but no. And it isn't the other thing either."

"Do you want to talk about it?"

"After the steak, if you don't mind. I don't want to choke in the middle of my own valediction."

"You're taking this very lightly."

"I've had a long time to think about it, Mal. I'm very calm. I know exactly what Luther meant when he said, 'Here I stand, I can do no other'. All I'm trying to figure is how to make the move with as little upset as possible . . . Here's the steak now, and the wine. Let's enjoy 'em. There'll be plenty of time to talk afterwards."

The Florentine steak was tender. The wine was soft and full-bodied and for a man facing a drastic change in his life and his career, Matt Neylan was singularly relaxed. Malachy O'Rahilly was forced to contain his own curiosity until the meat dishes had been cleared away and the waiter had consented to leave them in peace to consider dessert. Even then, Neylan took a roundabout route to deliver the news.

"Where to begin? That's a problem in itself, you see. Now, it's all so simple and matter-of-fact that I can hardly believe the agonies I put myself through. You and I, Mal, had the same career, chapter and verse: school with the Brothers in Dublin, seminary at Maynooth, then Rome and the Greg. We paced it out together: Philosophy, Biblical Studies, Theology—Dogmatic, Moral and Pastoral—Latin, Greek, Hebrew and Exegetics and History. We could put together a thesis, defend it, turn it inside out like a dirty sock and make it into heresy for the next debate in the Aula. Rome was right for us, we were right for Rome. We were the bright boys, Mal. We came from the most orthodox Catholic country in the world. We just had to run up the ladder, and we did, you to the Papal Household, me to the Secretariat of State, attaché first class . . . The only thing we missed was the thing that we swore brought us into the priesthood in the first place: pastoral service, the care of the people, Mal! We didn't do any of that worth a tinker's curse! We became career clerics, old-time court *abbés* from the monarchies of Europe. I'm not a priest, Mal. I'm a goddam diplomat—a good one, too, who could hold his own in any embassy in the world —but I could have been that anyway, without forswearing women and marriage and family life."

"So now we come to it!" said Malachy O'Rahilly. "I knew we would, sooner or later. You're lonely, you're tired of a solitary bed, bored with bachelor company. No discredit in that, boyo. It comes with the territory. You're riding through the badlands just now!"

"Wrong, Mal. Wrong, wrong. Rome's the easiest place in the world to come to terms with the flesh and the devil. You know damn well you can sleep two in a bed here for twenty years, with nobody any the wiser! The point—the real, needle-sharp point, old friend—is that I'm not a believer any more."

"Would you call that one back to me, please?" O'Rahilly was very quiet. "I want to be sure I've heard aright."

"You heard me, Mal." Neylan was calm as a lecturer at the blackboard. "Whatever it is that makes for faith—the grace, the gift, the disposition, the need—I don't have it. It's gone. And the strange thing is I'm not troubled at all. I'm not like poor Lorenzo de Rosa, fighting for justice inside a community to which he's still bound, heart and soul, then despairing because he doesn't get it. I don't belong in the community because I don't believe any longer in the ideas and the dogmas that underpin it . . ."

"But you're still part of it, Matt."

"By courtesy only. My courtesy!" Matt Neylan shrugged. "I'm doing everyone a favour by not making a scandal, carrying on the job until I can arrange a tidy exit. Which will probably take the form of a quiet chat with Cardinal Agostini early next week, a very polite note of resignation and presto! I'm gone like a snowflake."

"But they won't let you go like that, Matt. You know the whole rigmarole: voluntary suspension *a sacris,* application for a dispensation . . ."

"It doesn't apply." Matt Neylan explained patiently. "The rigmarole only works when you believe in it. What have they got to bind me with except moral sanctions? And those don't apply, because I don't subscribe any longer to the codex. They don't have the Inquisition any more. The Papal States don't exist. The Vatican *sbirri* can't come and arrest me at midnight. So, I leave in my own time and in my own way."

"You'll go gladly, by the sound of it." O'Rahilly's tone was sour.

"No, Mal. There's a sadness in it—a misty, grey kind of sadness. I've lost or mislaid a large part of my life. They say that an amputee can be haunted by the ghost of a missing limb; but the haunting stops after a while."

"What will you do for a living?"

"Oh, that's easy. My mother died last year. She left me a smallholding in County Cork. And last week, on the strength of my experience of Vatican diplomacy, I've signed a two-book contract with a New York publisher for better money than I've ever dreamed of. So I have no financial worries, and the chance to enjoy my life."

"And no conscience problems either?"

"The only problem I've got, Mal—and it's too early to know how I'll adjust to it—is how I'll cope with living in neutral gear, without the creed and the codex."

"You may find it harder than you think."

"It's hard already." Matt Neylan grinned at him across the table. "Right now! Between thee and me! You're inside the Communion of Saints. I'm outside it. You're a believer. I'm a *miscredente,* an infidel. We look the same, because we wear the uniform of a pair of ship's officers on the Barque of Peter. But you're still carrying the pilot. I've dropped him and I'm steering my own ship; which is a lonely and perilous thing to do in shoal waters."

"Where are you thinking of living afterwards? The Vatican won't want you hanging around Rome. They can make things quite uncomfortable if they want, as you well know."

"The thought hadn't entered my mind, Mal. I'll go first to Ireland to settle the legacy and see that the property's well managed. Then I'll take myself round the world to see how it looks to a simple tourist with a fresh mind. Wherever I end up, I hope we can still be friends. If we can't, I'll understand."

"Of course we'll be friends, man! And to prove it, I'll let you buy me a very large brandy—which, after this shock, I damn well need!"

"I'll join you—and if it makes you any happier, I'll get you the report on de Rosa for nothing!"

"That's big of you, boyo. I'll see you get credit for it on judgement day!"

For Sergio Salviati, Italian born, a Jew by ancestry and tradition, a Zionist by conviction, surgeon extraordinary to a Roman Pontiff, judgement day had already arrived. A personage, sacred to a billion people on the planet, was committed to his custody and care. Instantly, before a scalpel had been lifted, the sacred personage was under threat—a threat as deadly as any infarct or aneurysm.

It was conveyed by Menachem Avriel, Israeli Ambassador to the Republic, who delivered it over dinner in Salviati's house.

"Late this afternoon our intelligence people informed me that an attempt may be made to assassinate the Pontiff while he is at the clinic."

Salviati weighed the information for a moment and then shrugged.

"It was always on the cards, I suppose. How good is the information?"

"Grade A-plus, first hand from a Mossad man working undercover in an Iranian group, the Sword of Islam. He says they're offering a contract—fifty thousand dollars up front, fifty thousand when the job is done. He doesn't know yet what takers they've had."

"Do the Italians know about this—and the Vatican?"

"Both were informed at six this evening."

"Their answers?"

"Thank you—and we'll take appropriate action."

"They'd better." Salviati was terse. "It's out of my hands now. I start scrubbing with the team at six in the morning. I can't cope with anything else."

"Our best judgement—that is to say, Mossad's best judgement—is that any action will be taken during the convalescent period and that the attempt will be made from inside—by tampering with drugs, medications or life-support systems."

"I've got nearly a hundred staff at the clinic. They've got eight, ten languages between them. I can't guarantee that one of them isn't an agent in place. Damn it, I know at least three are agents in place for Mossad!"

Menachem Avriel laughed.

"Now you can be glad you let me put 'em there! At least they know the routines and can direct the people we're sending in tomorrow."

"And who, pray, will they be?"

"Oh, didn't you know? The Agenzia Diplomatica got a call late this afternoon for two extra wardsmaids, two electrical maintenance technicians and two male orderlies. They'll be reporting for duty at six in the morning. Issachar Rubin will be in charge. You won't have to worry about a thing—and Mossad will pick up the bill. You can concentrate on your distinguished patient. What's the prognosis, by the way?"

"Good. Very good, in fact. The man's obese and out of condition, but as a boy he was farm-fed and farm-worked. He's also got a will of iron. That helps him now."

"I wonder if it will help us?"

"To what?"

"Vatican recognition for the State of Israel."

"You're joking!" Salviati was suddenly tense and irritable. "That's been a dead duck from day one! No way will they back Israel against the Arab world! No matter what they say officially, by tradition we're Christ-killers, accursed of God. We have no right to a homeland, because we cast out the Messiah and we in our turn were cast out! Nothing's changed, believe me. We did better under the Roman Empire than under the popes. It was they who put the yellow star on us, centuries before Hitler. During the war, they buried six million dead in the Great Silence. If Israel were dismembered again, they'd be there, scrabbling for the title-deeds to their Holy Places."

"And yet you, my dear Sergio, are going to endow this man with a new lease of life! Why you? Why not remit him to his own?"

"You know why, my friend! I want him in my debt. I want him to owe me his life. Every time he looks at a Jew I want him to remember that he owes his survival to one and his salvation to another." Suddenly aware of his own vehemence, he grinned and spread his hands in a gesture of surrender. "Menachem, my friend, I'm sorry. I'm always edgy the night before a big operation."

"Do you have to spend it alone?"

"Never, if I can help it. Tove Lundberg will come over later. She'll spend the night and drive me to the clinic in the morning. She's good for me—the best thing in my life!"

"So when are you going to marry her?"

"I'd do it tomorrow, if she'd have me."

"What's the problem?"

"Children. She doesn't want any more. She's made sure she can't have them. She says it's unfair to ask a man to wear that, even if he's willing."

"She's wise!" The Ambassador was suddenly very quiet. "You're lucky to get a good woman on such easy terms. But if you're thinking of marriage and a family . . ."

"I know! I know! Your Leah will find me a nice bright Jewish girl, and you'll both send us off to Israel for the honeymoon. Forget it!"

"I'll move it up in the calendar, but I won't forget it. Where's Tove now?"

"She's entertaining James Morrison, our visiting surgeon."

"Question: does she know about the Agenzia Diplomatica, and your other connections?"

"She knows my sympathies are with Israel. She knows the people you send me to be entertained. For the rest, she doesn't ask questions and I don't volunteer answers."

"Good! The Agenzia is very important to us, as you know. It's one of the best ideas I've had in my life . . ."

Menachem Avriel spoke no more than the truth. Long before his first diplomatic appointment, when he was still a field agent for Mossad, he had proposed the notion of a chain of employment agencies, one in each diplomatic capital, which could offer casual labour—cooks, waiters, chambermaids, nannies, nurses, chauffeurs—to diplomats on station and business families serving overseas terms. Every applicant for listing on the agency's books was screened, bonded and paid the highest rate the traffic would bear. Local employment regulations were meticulously observed. Taxes were paid. Records were accurate. The clientele expanded by recommendation. Israeli agents, male and female, were filtered into the lists and Mossad had eyes and ears at every diplomatic party and business entertainment. Sergio Salviati himself kept places open on his roster for casual staff from the Agenzia, and if he ever had misgivings about the double role he was playing, he buried it under an avalanche of bitter folk-memories: the decrees of mediaeval popes that foreshadowed the Nuremberg laws of Hitler in 1935, the infamies of ghetto existence, the Black Sabbath of 1943, the massacre of the Ardeatine Caves.

There were moments when he felt that he could be riven asunder by the forces thrusting out from the centre of himself—the monomania that made him a great surgeon and a medical reformer, the fierce attachment of every Latin to his *paese,* his home-place, the tug of ten thousand years of tribal tradition, the nostalgia of psalmodies that had become the voice of his own secret heart: "If I forget thee, O Jerusalem, let my right hand forget its cunning."

"I should be going," said Menachem Avriel. "You need an early night. Thanks for the dinner."

"Thank you for the warning."

"Try not to let it worry you."

"It won't. I work with life in my hands and death looking over my shoulder. I can't afford any distractions."

"Time was," said Menachem Avriel drily, "when a Jew was forbidden to give medical aid to a Christian—and a Christian doctor had to convert the Jew before he could offer treatment."

It was then, for the first time, that Sergio Salviati revealed the torment that was tearing him apart.

"We've learned well, haven't we, Menachem? Israel has come of age. We've got our own ghettoes now, our own inquisition, our own brutalities; and our own special scapegoats, the Palestinians! That's the worst thing the *goyim* have done to us. They've taught us to corrupt ourselves!"

In her own apartment on the other side of the courtyard, Tove Lundberg was explaining Salviati to his English colleague.

"He is like a kaleidoscope, changing every moment. He is so various that it seems he is twenty men, and you wonder how you can cope with so many—or even how he copes with himself. Then suddenly he is clear and simple as water. That is how you will see him tomorrow morning in the theatre. He will be absolutely controlled. He will not say an unnecessary word, or make a redundant gesture. I have heard the nurses say they have never seen anyone so careful with human tissue. He handles it like gossamer."

"He has respect." James Morrison savoured the last of his wine. "That's the mark of a great healer. It shows. And how's his touch for other things?"

"Careful always. Very gentle most of the time. But there are lots of angers in him that I wish he could spare himself. I never understood until I came to Italy how deep is the prejudice against Jews—even against the native born with long ancestries in the land. Sergio told me that he decided very early that the best way for him to cope with it was by studying its roots and causes. He can talk for hours on the subject. He quotes passages from Doctors of the Church, from papal encyclicals and decretals, from archival documents. It's a sad and sorry tale, especially when you think that the ghetto here in Rome was abolished and the Jewish people enfranchised by royal decree only in 1870.

"In spite of soothing noises and half-hearted verbal amends, the Vatican has never repudiated its anti-semitic stance. It has never recognised the right and title of the Jewish people to a traditional homeland . . . These things trouble Sergio. They help him, too, because they drive him to excellence, to make himself a kind of banner-bearer for his people . . . Yet the other part of him is a Renaissance man, seeing all, trying desperately to understand and pardon all."

"You love him very much, don't you?"

"Yes."

"So . . . ?"

"So sometimes I think I love him too well for my own good. One thing I'm sure of, marriage would be the wrong move for both of us."

"Because he's Jewish and you're not?"

"No. It's because . . ." She hesitated a long time over the words as if testing each one for the load it must bear. "It's because I've arrived at my own standing place. I know who I am, where I am, what I need, what I can have. Sergio is still travelling, still searching, because he will go much further and stand much higher than I could even dream. A moment will come when he will need someone else. I'll be excess baggage . . . I want to make that moment as simple as possible, for him and for me."

"I wonder . . ." James Morrison poured himself another glass of wine. "I wonder if you really know how much you mean to him?"

"I do, believe me. But there are limits to what I can provide. I've spent so much love and care on Britte, there is so much more that I shall have to spend, that there's none left for another child. I haven't grudged any of it, but my capital is used up . . . I am almost at the end of my breeding time—so that special part of my passion for a man is gone. I'm a good lover and Sergio needs that because, as you well know, James, surgeons spend so much of their lives thinking about other people's bodies, they sometimes forget the one beside them in bed. On top of all that, I'm a Dane. Marriage Italian style or Jewish style isn't for me. Does that answer your question?"

"It does, thank you. It also raises another one. How do you read our distinguished patient?"

"I rather like him. I didn't at first. I saw every objectionable feature that sixty years of clerical education, professional celibacy and bachelor selfishness can produce in a man—not to mention the greed for power that seems to afflict some elderly bachelors. He's ugly, he's cross-grained, he can be quite rude. But as we talked I caught glimpses of someone else, a man who might have been. You will laugh at this, I know, but I was reminded of the old fairy story of the Beauty and the Beast . . . remember? If only the Princess could summon up courage to kiss the Beast, he would turn into a handsome prince."

James Morrison threw back his head and laughed happily.

"I love it! You didn't try, did you?"

"Of course not. But tonight, on my way home, I called in to see him. It was a few minutes after nine. They had just given him the sedatives to settle him for the night. He was drowsy and relaxed but he recognised me. There was a lock of hair hanging down into his eyes. Without thinking, I brushed it away. He took my hand and held it for the briefest of moments. Then he said, so simply I almost wept: 'My mother used to do that. She used to pretend it was my guardian angel, brushing me with her wings.' "

"Is that what he said, *'her* wings'?"

"Yes. Suddenly I saw a little, lonely boy with a girl-angel for a ghostly play-mate. Sad, isn't it?"

"But for that one small moment, joyful. You're quite a woman, Tove Lund-berg, quite a woman! Now, I'm going to bed, before I make a fool of myself."

In the Apostolic Palace in Vatican City, the lights burned late. The Cardinal Secretary of State had summoned into conference the senior officials of his Secretariat and those of the Council for the Public Affairs of the Church. These two bodies between them dealt with all the external relations of Vatican City State and, at the same time, held together the complex and sometimes con-flicting interests within the body of the Church. In the daily conduct of Curial affairs they were a kitchen cabinet; tonight, with the safety of the Pontiff at stake, they were a very cool and quite ruthless council of war.

Agostini, the Secretary of State, summed up the situation.

"I accept the Israeli information as authentic. I accept, with considerable relief, that Mossad undercover agents will be working with normal staff around the intensive care unit and, later, on the ward occupied by His Holiness. This is an irregular and unofficial intervention, so we can take no formal notice of it. We rely upon the forces of the Republic of Italy—especially the Nucleo Cen-trale Anti-Terrorismo, who are at this moment reinforcing the perimeter pro-tection of the clinic and will be placing plainclothes guards at strategic points within the building itself. This is about as much as we can do for the physical security of the Pontiff during his illness. However, a hurried check this evening with our diplomatic contacts indicates that things may not be quite so simple as they seem. Our colleague Anwar El Hachem has something to say on the Arab-Israeli aspect of the matter."

El Hachem, a Maronite from Lebanon, delivered his report.

"Sword of Islam is a small splinter group of Iranians from Lebanon, operat-ing in Rome itself. They are not associated with the mainstream of Palestinian opinion, but are known to be able to touch large funds. Even as we speak, Italian security agents are pulling some of them in for questioning. Embassy representatives of Saudi Arabia and the North African republics, as well as the Emirates, disclaim all knowledge of the threat and offer full co-operation against what they see as a free-booting operation which can only do them harm. One or two of them raised the question as to whether the Israelis were setting up the whole thing as a provocative gesture. But I found little support for this view."

"Thank you, Anwar." The Secretary continued. "Is there any doubt at all that the contract offer of $100,000 was made by Sword of Islam?"

"None at all. But the man who made it is now in hiding."

"The Americans know nothing." Agostini hurried through the list. "The

Russians disclaim all knowledge but are happy to exchange news if they get any. The French are referring back to Paris. What about the British?"

The British were the territory of the Right Reverend Hunterson, titular Archbishop of Sirte, a senior Vatican servant for many years. His report was brief but specific.

"The British Embassy said tut-tut how distressing, promised to look into it and came back about nine with the same information as Anwar, that Sword of Islam is a shop-front title for an Iranian-backed group out of Lebanon. They do have money in the quantities suggested. They do finance hostage-taking and murder. In this instance, His Holiness presents a prominent target-of-opportunity."

"Which he wouldn't be," said the Substitute Secretary tartly, "if we'd gone to Salvator Mundi or Gemelli. We have only ourselves to blame for exposing him to a hostile environment."

"It's not the ground that's hostile." Agostini was testy. "It's the terrorists. I doubt we could provide as good security elsewhere. But it does raise one important issue. His Holiness talked of spending his convalescence outside Vatican territory, in a private villa perhaps. I don't think we can permit that."

"Can we stop it?" This from a German member of the Council. "Our master does not take kindly to opposition."

"I'm sure," said the Secretary of State, "the Republic has very good reason not to want him killed on its own soil. His Holiness, Italian born, has very good reason not to embarrass the Republic. Leave that discussion to me."

"How soon can we get him home?"

"If all goes well, ten to fourteen days."

"Let's make it ten. We could move a team of nursing sisters into Castel Gandolfo. I could talk to the Mother General of the Little Company of Mary. She could even fly in some of her best people from abroad."

"As I remember," said Archbishop Hunterson, "most nursing orders are hard put to service the hospitals they have. Most now depend on lay staff. Quite frankly, I don't understand the hurry. So long as security can be maintained, I'd leave him at the Villa Diana."

"The Curia proposes," said Agostini, with tart humour, "but the Pontiff disposes—even from his sickbed! Let me see what notions I can plant in his head while he's still amenable."

It was at this precise moment in the discussion that Monsignor Malachy O'Rahilly presented himself, in response to a beeper summons from the central communications office. He was flustered and breathless and slightly—only slightly—befuddled from the white wine and the red and the strong brandies he had taken to help him through Matt Neylan's defection from the Faith.

Neylan, too, was summoned because he was a first-class Secretary of Nunziatures and his work was to edit the news and spread it around his bailiwick. They bowed to the assembled prelates, took their seats in silence and listened respectfully while Agostini first admonished them to secrecy and then walked them through the outline of threats and remedies.

Monsignor Matt Neylan had no comment to make. His functions were predetermined. His punctual performance was taken for granted. O'Rahilly, on the other hand, with drink taken, was inclined to be voluble. As a personal assistant to the Pontiff and the bearer of a Papal commission as to the conduct of his office, his address to Agostini tended to be more emphatic than discreet.

"I already have a list of those to be given access to His Holiness at the clinic. In the circumstances, should they not be supplied with a special card of admission? After all, the security people cannot be expected to recognise faces, and a soutane or a Roman collar readily disguises a terrorist. I could have the entire set printed and distributed within half a day."

"A good idea, Monsignore." Agostini nodded approval. "If you will put the matter in hand with the printers first thing in the morning. My office will be responsible for distribution—against signatures always."

"It will be done, Eminence." Wildly elated by the commendation—rare and precious in Curial circles—O'Rahilly decided to push his luck a little further. "I talked with His Holiness earlier this evening and he asked me to make special enquiries into the case of one Lorenzo de Rosa, formerly a priest of this diocese whose wife—that is to say, under the civil code—died in the Salviati clinic yesterday. Apparently de Rosa had made repeated but unsuccessful bids to be laicised canonically and have his marriage validated, but . . ."

"Monsignore!" The Secretary of State was cool. "It would seem this matter is neither relevant to our present concerns nor opportune in the context . . ."

"Oh, but it is, Eminence!"

O'Rahilly with the bit between his teeth would have put a Derby runner to shame. In the midst of a frozen silence, he described to the assembly his personal encounter with de Rosa and his later discussion with Monsignor Matt Neylan as to whether or no the threat should be taken seriously.

". . . Matt Neylan here was of the opinion, which I shared, that the poor fellow was simply overwhelmed with grief and that to expose him to interrogation and harassment by security forces would be a great and unnecessary cruelty. However, after what we've just heard, I have to ask myself—and to ask Your Eminences—whether certain precautions, at least, should not be taken."

"They most certainly should!" The Substitute Secretary was in no doubt about it. His name was Mikhaelovic and he was a Jugoslav already preconditioned to security procedures. "The safety of the Holy Father is of paramount concern."

"That is, at best, a dubious proposition." Matt Neylan was suddenly a hostile presence in the small assembly. "With great respect, I submit that to badger and bedevil this grieving man with police inquiries would be an unconscionable cruelty. The Holy Father himself is concerned that, even before his bereavement, de Rosa may have received less than Christian justice and charity. Besides, what Monsignor O'Rahilly has omitted to mention is that I have already instituted a private inquiry into de Rosa's circumstances."

"And by so doing have exceeded your authority." Cardinal Mikhaelovic did not take kindly to correction. "The very least precaution we can take is to denounce this man to the security people. They are the experts. We are not."

"My point precisely, Eminence." Neylan was studiously formal. "The antiterrorist troops are not bound by the normal rules of police procedure. Accidents happen during their interrogations. People have their limbs broken. They fall out of windows. I would remind you also that there are two young children involved."

"Illegitimate offspring of a renegade priest!"

"Oh, for Christ's sweet sake! What kind of a priest are you?"

The blasphemy shocked them all. Agostini's rebuke was icy.

"You forget yourself, Monsignore. You have made your case. We shall give it careful consideration. I shall see you in my office at ten tomorrow morning. You are excused."

"But Your Eminence is not excused—none of you is excused—the duty of common compassion! I bid Your Excellencies good night!"

He bowed himself out of the meeting and hurried back to his small apartment in the Palace of the Mint. He was blazing with anger: at Mal O'Rahilly who couldn't keep his big Irish gob shut, but had to make a great fellow of himself with a bunch of elderly eminences and excellencies; at the eminences and excellencies themselves, because they symbolised everything that, year by year, had alienated him from the Church and made a mockery of the charity which was radical to its existence.

They were mandarins, all of them, old-fashioned imperial *Kuan,* who wore bright clothes and buttoned headgear, and had their own esoteric language and disdained all argument with the common herd. They were not pastors, ardent in the care of souls. They were not apostles, zealous for the spread of the godspell. They were officials, administrators, committee men, as privileged and protected as any of their counterparts in Whitehall, in Moscow, or the Quai d'Orsay.

To them a man like Lorenzo de Rosa was a nonperson, excommunicated, committed with a shrug to the Divine Mercy, but excluded for ever from any compassionate intervention by the human Assembly—unless it were earned by penitential humiliation and a winter vigil at Canossa. He knew exactly what would happen to de Rosa. They would delate him to the Security Services. A quartet of heavies would pick him up at his apartment, take him down town, hand the children to a police matron for custody, then bounce him off the walls for two or three hours. After that they would make him sign a deposition he would be too groggy to read. It would all be quite impersonal. They wouldn't mean any real harm. It was standard procedure, to get the facts quickly before a bomb went off, and to discourage any counteraction from an innocent suspect —but then, under the old inquisitorial system, no one was innocent until proven so in court.

And what of himself, Matt Neylan? The quiet exit he had planned for himself was impossible now. The unsayable had been said. There was no way to recall the words—and all because Mal O'Rahilly couldn't hold his liquor and had to go trailing his coat-tails at a crisis conference of the biggest bigshots in the Holy Roman Church! But wasn't that the way of it, the whole conditioning process that produced a perfect Roman clerical clone? The trigger-words in the formula had never changed since Trent—hierarchy and obedience. The effect they produced on simple priest or lordly bishop was always the same. They stood with eyes downcast, tugging their forelocks, as if listening to thunders from the Mountain of Revelation.

Well, tonight was one time too many for Matt Neylan. Tomorrow he would pack and go, without regret, without a by-your-leave. The day after, they would name him a renegade like de Rosa and strike his name out of the book of the

Elect and commit him with something just short of contempt to the God who made him.

He reached for the Rome telephone directory and ran his finger down the list of folk called de Rosa. There were six entries with the initial L. He began dialling them in sequence, trusting that a mention of the Salviati clinic would bring forth an identifying response. He hoped the man would be sane enough to accept a warning from a one-time colleague. It would be nice to set Brother Fox well on his way to a safe earth, before the hounds began baying in his tracks.

Over the compound of Salviati's house, the new summer moon rode high in a sea of stars. In the shadows of the garden a nightingale began to sing. The light and the music made an antique magic in the vaulted chamber where Salviati slept and Tove Lundberg, propped on her elbow, hovered over him like a protecting goddess.

Their loving had followed their familiar pattern: a long, tender prelude, a sudden transition to play, a swift leap to the high plateau of passion, a series of fierce orgasms, a languid recall of fading pleasures, then Sergio's sudden lapse into sleep, his classic features youthful and unlined against the pillow, the muscles of his shoulders and breast frozen into marble in the moonglow. Tove Lundberg always lay wakeful afterwards, wondering that so wild a storm could be followed by so magical a calm.

Of herself she had no clear image; but the role she was expected to play on these crisis nights was one she knew by heart. She was the servant of his body, the perfect hetaera, pouring herself out on him, asking nothing but to serve him. The why of it for him was buried deep in his unconscious and she had no desire to lug it out into the light. Sergio Salviati was the perennial alien. He had become a prince by conquest. He needed the spoils to attest his victories— the gold, the jewels, the slave girls, and the respect of the mighty in the land.

The why for her was different, and she could confront it without shame. As mother, she had delivered defective offspring; she had no wish to repeat the experience. As lover, she delivered perfect pleasure and while time might diminish her charm or her capacities as a bed-mate, it could only increase her stature and influence as a professional comrade. Best of all was Sergio's own acknowledgement: "You are the one wholly calm place in my life. You are like a deep pool in the middle of a forest and every time I come to you I am refreshed and renewed. But you never ask me for anything. Why?"

"Because," she told him, "I need nothing but what I have: work I can do well, a place where my Britte can grow to be an independent and talented woman, a man I trust and admire and love."

"How much do you love me, Tove Lundberg?"

"As much as you want, Sergio Salviati. As much as you will let me."

"Why don't you ask how much I love you?"

"Because I know already . . ."

"Do you know that I am always afraid?"

"Yes."

"Of what I am afraid?"

"That one day, at some bad moment, the healing magic will fail you, you will

misread the signs, lose the master touch. But it will not happen. I promise
you."

"Are you never afraid?"

"Only in a special way."

"What way?"

"I am afraid of needing anything so much that someone could hurt me by
taking it away."

And, she might have added, she came of old Nordic seafaring stock, whose
women waited on windswept dunes and cared not whether their men were
drunk, sober or scarred from brawling, just so that, one more time, they had
escaped the grey widow-maker.

In the small, dark hours before the false dawn, Leo the Pontiff began rolling
his head from side to side on the pillow and muttering restlessly. His gullet was
thick with mucus and his brow clammy with night-sweat. The night nurse
shifted him in the bed, sponged his face and moistened his lips with water. He
responded drowsily.

"Thank you. I'm sorry to be a trouble. I was having a bad dream."

"You're out of it now. Close your eyes and go back to sleep."

For a brief, confused moment he was tempted to tell her the dream, but he
dared not. It had risen like a new moon from the darkest places of childhood
memory; and it shed a pitiless light upon a hidden hollow in his adult conscience.

At school there was a boy, older and bigger, who bullied him continually.
One day he confronted his tormentor and asked why he did such cruel things.
The answer still echoed in his memory: "Because you're standing in my light;
you're taking away my sun." How could he, he asked, since he was so much
smaller and younger. To which the bully answered: "Even a mushroom throws a
shadow. If it falls on my boot, I kick it to pieces."

It was a rough but lasting lesson in the usances of power. A man who stood
against the sun became a dark shadow, faceless and threatening. Yet the
shadow was surrounded by light, like a halo or the corona of an eclipse. So the
shadow-man assumed the numen of a sacred person. To challenge him was a
sacrilege, a most damnable crime.

So, in the last hours before they drugged him and wheeled him off to the
operating theatre, Ludovico Gadda, Leo XIV, Vicar of Christ, Supreme Pastor
of the Universal Church, understood how, in learning from the bully, he had
himself been tipped into tyranny.

In defiance of biblical injunction, of historic custom, of discontent among
clergy and faithful, he had appointed as senior archbishops, in Europe and the
Americas, men of his own choosing, hardline conservators, stubborn defenders
of bastions long overpassed, deaf and blind to every plea for change. They were
called the Pope's men, the praetorian guard in the Army of the Elect. They
were the echoes of his own voice, drowning out the murmurs of discontented
clerics, of the faceless crowd outside the sanctuaries.

It had been a harsh encounter and a heady victory. Even as he remembered
it, his face hardened into the old raptor look. Dissenting clerics had been
silenced by a double threat: suspension from their functions and the appoint-

ment of a special apostolic administrator. As for the people, when their shepherds were silenced they, too, were struck dumb. They had no voice in the assembly. Their only free utterance was outside it, among the heretics and the infidel.

It was the childhood nightmare which shamed Leo the Pontiff into admitting the harm he had done. It was the shadow of the surgeon's knife which reminded him that he might never have the chance to repair it. As the first cocks crowed from the farmlands of the Villa Diana, he closed his eyes, turned his face to the wall and made his last desperate prayer.

"If my presence hides the light of Yours, O God, remove me! Strike me out of the book of the living. But if you leave me here, give me, I beg You, eyes to see, and heart to feel, the lonely terrors of your children!"

BOOK TWO

LAZARUS REDIVIVUS

*"He cried out in a loud voice:
'Lazarus, come here, to me!' Whereupon
the dead man came out, his hands and
feet tied with strips of linen, his
face covered with a veil. Jesus said:
'Untie him. Let him go free.'"*

—John xi: 43,44

VI

ABOUT the same hour on the same morning, Monsignor Matt Neylan finally made telephone contact with Lorenzo de Rosa, one-time priest of the Roman diocese, excommunicated, newly widowed, the father of two small children. Neylan explained himself curtly.

"There's a terrorist threat to the Pontiff, who is at this moment a patient in the International Clinic. You're a suspect, because you sounded off yesterday to Malachy O'Rahilly. So you're bound to get a visit from the anti-terrorist squad. My suggestion would be to get out of town as quickly as you can."

"And why should you care?"

"God knows. Maybe a visit from the Squadristi sounds like one grief too many."

"There's nothing they can do to us now. But thank you for calling. Goodbye."

Matt Neylan stood like a ninny with the dead receiver in his hand. Then a dark thought took hold of him and sent him racing for his car and careering like a madman through the morning traffic towards EUR.

De Rosa's house was a modest but well-kept villa in a cul-de-sac near the Via del Giorgione. There was a car in the driveway and the garden gate was unlocked. The front door was open, too. Neylan called a greeting, but there was no answer. He went inside. The ground floor was deserted. Upstairs in the nursery, two little girls lay still and waxen-faced in their beds. Neylan called to them softly. They did not answer. He touched their cheeks. They were cold and lifeless. Across the hall, in the big matrimonial bed, Lorenzo de Rosa lay beside the body of his wife, who was dressed as if for a bridal night. De Rosa's face was distorted in the last rictus of dying. There was a small cake of foam about his lips.

Matt Neylan, new to unbelief, found himself murmuring a prayer for all their sad souls. Then the prayer exploded into a blasphemy against all the hypocrisy and folly that lay at the root of the tragedy. He debated, for the briefest moment, about calling the police; decided against it, then walked out of the house into the deserted street. The only witness to his departure was a stray cat. The only person to hear of his encounter was the Cardinal Secretary of State, to whom he exposed, in the same speech, his discovery of the tragedy and his decision to leave the Church.

Agostini, the lifetime diplomat, took the news calmly. With Neylan, there was no ground of argument. As an unbeliever he belonged henceforth to another order of being. The situation with the police was even easier to arrange. Both parties had a common interest. His Eminence explained it simply.

"You were wise to leave the scene. Otherwise everybody would have been swamped with depositions and interrogations. We have advised the police of your presence in the house and your discovery of the bodies. They will accept your visit as a pastoral call, subject to confessional secrecy. They will not involve you in any further questioning."

"Which, of course, leaves everything very tidy."

"Spare me the ironies, Monsignore!" His Eminence was suddenly angry. "I am just as unhappy about this sad affair as you are. The whole thing was bungled from the start. I have no taste for zealots and bigots, no matter how high they sit in the Sacred College; but I have to work with them, with as much tolerance and charity as I can muster. You can afford your anger. You have chosen to withdraw from the community of the faithful and dispense yourself from its obligations. I don't blame you. I understand what has brought you to this decision."

"It's hardly a decision, Eminence. It's a new state of being. I am no longer a believer. My identity has changed. I have no place in any Christian assembly. So I'm separating myself as discreetly as possible. I'll move out of my office today. My apartment is on a private lease, not a Vatican one, so that's no problem. I have an Irish passport, so I'll hand you back my Vatican documents. That should leave everything tidy."

"For our purposes,"—Agostini was studiously good-humoured—"we'll formally suspend you from the exercise of priestly functions and proceed immediately to have you laicised."

"With respect, Eminence, these procedures are a matter of indifference to me."

"But I, my friend, am not indifferent to you. I have seen this coming for a long time. It was like watching a classic rose mutate slowly into hedgerow stock. The beautiful bloom is gone, but the plant is still vigorously alive. I reproved you last night; but I understood your anger and admired your courage. I must say that in that moment you looked very like a Christian to me!"

"I'm curious," said Matt Neylan.

"About what?"

"We both know the Holy Father has asked for a special report on the de Rosa affair."

"So?"

"My question: how will he react to the news of their deaths—by murder and suicide?"

"We have no intention of telling him the news—until he is strong enough to receive it."

"And then what? How will he react? Will he repent his original harshness? How will he judge de Rosa—and himself? Will he amend the legislation in the canons, or mitigate its penalties?"

"What you're really asking,"—Agostini permitted himself a small, wintry smile—"is a perennial question. Does the Church change when a pope changes his mind or his heart? In my experience, it doesn't. The inertia is too great. The whole system is geared against swift movement. Besides—and this is the nub of the matter—the Church is so centralised now that every tremor is magnified to earthquake scale. The simplest act of official tolerance can be turned into a scandal. The most innocent speculation by the most orthodox theologian on the mysteries of the Faith sets off a heresy hunt." Agostini's humour turned suddenly rueful. "Living at this altitude in this place is like being perched on the edge of the San Andreas fault. So the answer to your question: every public utterance of the Pontiff is ritually controlled. In his private life he may dress in sackcloth, powder himself with ashes, mourn like Job on his dunghill; but who will know about it? The Church has its own *omerta'*, its rule of silence, every whit as binding as that of the Mafia."

"And what would happen . . ." Matt Neylan laughed as he put the question. "What would happen if I decided to breach the wall of silence?"

"Nothing." Agostini dismissed the thought with a gesture. "Nothing at all! What authority could you invoke? You'd be called an apostate, a renegade priest. In the Church you'd be prayed for and ignored. Outside it you'd carry another stigma: a fool who let himself be gulled for half a lifetime before he quit."

"A warning, Eminence?"

"A counsel only. I am told you are seeking to make a new career as an author. You will not, I am sure, damage it by peddling scandals, or betraying professional secrets."

"I am flattered by your confidence," said Matt Neylan.

"We shall all remember you as a discreet and loyal colleague. We shall pray for your well-being."

"Thank you—and goodbye, Eminence."

So, simply and curtly, a lifetime was ended, a whole identity shucked off like a reptile's skin. He passed by the Apostolic Palace to say goodbye to Malachy O'Rahilly, but was told he was waiting at the clinic until the result of the Pontiff's surgery was known.

So, because he needed at least one stepping stone between his old life and a new one, because he needed at least one weapon against the pitiless rectitude of Vatican bureaucracy, he telephoned Nicol Peters and begged to be offered a cup of coffee.

"It's my lucky day." Nicol Peters slipped a new cassette into the tape-recorder. "Two big stories and you've given me the inside running on both of them. I'm in your debt, Matt."

"You owe me nothing." Neylan was emphatic. "I believe the de Rosa business is a scandal that should be aired . . . you can do that. I can't—at least not until I've established a new identity and authority. Which, by the way, is a problem you have to face. If I'm revealed as your informant, your story will be discredited. Drop-outs like me can be an embarrassment."

Nicol Peters shrugged off the warning.

"We agreed the ground rules. Trust me to play by them."

"I do."

"So let's go back. The assassination threat is the number one story, though I'm not sure how I can use it if it jeopardises the life of an undercover agent. Anyway, that's my problem, not yours. Let's look at the sequence of events. Mossad gets the news from an agent in place. The Israelis pass the news to the Vatican and to the Italian authorities. Those two set up a joint security operation inside and outside Salviati's clinic. The Israeli's can't participate openly; but obviously they're in it up to their necks."

"Obviously."

"So far the Pontiff knows nothing of all this?"

"Nothing. The news came in early yesterday evening. The meeting which I attended did not take place until very late. The countdown to the Pontiff's surgery had already begun. There was no point in disturbing him with the news."

"I accept that. Now let's speculate a little further. An assassin is identified before an attempt is made on the Pope's life. Who deals with him—or perhaps with her, as the case may be?"

Matt Neylan poured himself more coffee and gave a slightly parodied exposition of the argument.

"The Vatican position would be defined very simply. I've written enough position papers to give it to you verbatim. Their sole concern is the safety of the Sacred Person of His Holiness. They leave the criminal to be dealt with by the Republic. Simple! Clean hands! No imbroglios with the Muslim world. The position of the Republic of Italy is somewhat different. They have the right, the power, the sovereign authority to deal with criminals and terrorists. Do they want to? Hell no! That means more terror—hijacks, hostages, kidnappings to bring the criminals out of custody. Conclusion: though they'd never admit it, they'd love Mossad to handle the business quickly and neatly and have the body buried by sunrise. You want me to prove it? No way. You want me to swear that's what I heard in the Apostolic Palace—no way either! It wasn't said. It would never be said!"

"Methinks," said Nicol Peters amiably, "methinks the lady hath protested enough! I've got enough to frame the story and prise the rest of it out of other sources. Now let's talk about de Rosa. Here again, the sequence is clear. De Rosa quits the priesthood, beds down with a girl without benefit of clergy, has two children by her. They are happy. They want to regularise their union—a situation not without precedent, not at all impossible under the canons . . ."

"But quite contrary to present policy, which is to make things as tough as possible for offenders and damp down hopes of lenient solutions."

"Check. Now tragedy strikes. The woman dies, still unreconciled, in spite of her wish to be so. The despairing husband stages a macabre family reunion, kills his children with an overdose of sleeping pills and himself with cyanide— all this while under suspicion as a possible assassin of the same Pope who had denied him canonical relief."

"A caveat here! Until I called de Rosa in the small hours of this morning he didn't know he was a suspect. He couldn't have."

"Could your news have precipitated his decision to kill his children and himself?"

"It could have. I doubt it did. The fact that he had brought his wife's body back to the house seems to indicate that he had already decided on some kind of ceremonial exit . . . But what do I know? The whole thing is a madness—all because a bunch of clerical bureaucrats refused legitimate relief in a human situation. Let me tell you something, Nico! This is one story I want His Holiness to read, no matter what it does to his sacred blood pressure!"

"Do you really think it will matter a damn what he thinks or says about it?"

"It could. He could change a lot of lives overnight if he had the will and the courage. He could bring back compassion and clemency into what, believe me, has become a rigorist institution."

"Do you really believe that, Matt? I've lived in this town longer than you have and I don't believe it for a minute. In the Roman Catholic Church, the whole system—the hierarchy, the education of the clergy, the Curial administration, the Electoral College—is designed to perpetuate the status quo and eliminate along the way any and every aberrant element. The man you get at the top is the nearest you can come to the Manchurian Candidate, the perfectly conditioned representative of the majority interest of the Electoral College itself."

"It's a good argument," said Matt Neylan with a grin. "I'm a conditioned man myself. I know how deeply the imprint goes, how potent the trigger-words become. But, by the same token, Nico, I'm the flaw in the argument too. I've lost all the conditioning. I've become another person. I know that change is possible for good or ill—and the two most potent instruments of change are power and pain."

Nicol Peters gave him a long, searching look and then said gently: "It seems I've missed something, my friend. Would you be patient enough to tell me what it is?"

"It's nothing much, Nico. And yet, in a way, it's everything. It's why I feel so angry about what happened to de Rosa. Agostini put it very bluntly this morning. I'm labelled now—I'm an apostate, a renegade, a defector, a fool. But that isn't the nature of my experience at all. I've lost something, a capacity, a faculty—as one can lose sexual potency or the gift of sight. I am changed, irrevocably. I am back at the first day of creation, when earth was still an empty waste and darkness hung over the deep . . . Who knows? There may be wonders still to come but I do not expect them. I live in the here and now. What I see is what is. What I know is what I have experienced and—most terrifying of all, Nico!—what will be is a totally random matter! That makes the world a very bleak place, Nico. So bleak that even fear can hardly survive in it."

Nicol Peters waited a long moment before he offered a dry comment.

"At least you're at the beginning of a new world, not at the end of it. And it's not all that new either. It's the same place lots of us inhabit who have never been conditioned or gifted with the massive certainties of Christianity. We have to make do with what we get—the fleeting light, the passing storm, enough love to temper the tears of things, the rare glimpse of reason in a mad world. So don't be too dismayed, matey! It's a big club you've joined—and even Christians believe that God was a founding member!"

While the Pontiff, cold and cyanosed, festooned with tubes and electrodes, was being settled in the Intensive Care Unit, Sergio Salviati took coffee with James Morrison and wrote his first communiqué to the Vatican.

"His Holiness, Pope Leo XIV, today underwent elective bypass surgery, following a short history of angina pectoris. The operation, in which three saphenous vein grafts were inserted into the coronary circulation, was performed at the International Clinic under the direction of Professor Sergio Salviati, assisted by Mr. James Morrison of the London College of Surgeons, with the Papal Physician, Professor Carlo Massenzio, in attendance. The procedures were successfully completed in two hours and fifty minutes. His Holiness is now in the Intensive Care Unit, in a stable and satisfactory condition. Professor Salviati and the attending physician anticipate an uncomplicated convalescence and are optimistic about the long-term prognosis."

He signed the document with a flourish and handed it to his secretary.

"Please send two facsimile copies to the Vatican, the first to the Secretary of State personally, the second to the Sala Stampa. Then type the following text which our switchboard operators will use verbatim to respond to all inquiries about the Pontiff. Text begins: 'The operation on His Holiness has been successfully completed. His Holiness is still in Intensive Care. For further details, apply to the Sala Stampa, Vatican City, which will issue all future bulletins.' "

"Anything else, Professor?"

"Yes. Please ask the Chief of Hospital Staff and the two senior security officers to meet me here in thirty minutes. That's all for the moment."

When the secretary had left, James Morrison offered enthusiastic praise.

"Full marks, Sergio! You've built a great team. I've never worked with a better one."

"My thanks to you, James. I was grateful to have you with me. This was a rough one for me."

"The old buzzard should be grateful he fell into your hands!"

Salviati threw back his head and laughed.

"He is an old buzzard, isn't he? That great beak, those hooded, hostile eyes. But he's a tough bird. There's probably another decade in him after this."

"It's a moot point, of course, whether the world or the Church will thank you for that."

"True, James! Very true! But at least we've honoured the Hippocratic oath."

"I wonder if he'll offer you a Vatican decoration."

"To a Jew? I very much doubt it. I wouldn't accept it. I couldn't. Anyway, it's much too early to talk about success, let alone rewards. We still have to keep him alive until the end of his convalescence."

"Are you that worried about the assassination threat?"

"You're damn right I'm worried! No one goes in or out of the Intensive Care Unit without an identity check. No drugs are dispensed to this patient except from sealed bottles by nominated personnel. Even the goddamned scrub women are searched, and the garbage collectors!"

"But I notice you and Tove still drive back and forth to the clinic without a bodyguard. Is that wise?"

"We're not the target."

"You could be a secondary one."

"James, if I thought about all the dangers of this job, I'd lock myself in a padded cell . . . To change the subject, what are your plans now?"

"I'll take a leisurely run up north to see my Italian relatives, then I'll head back to London."

"How do you want to be paid?"

"Swiss francs in Zurich, if that's possible."

"Since the money will come from the Vatican, everything is possible. When will you leave?"

"Two days, three maybe. The British Ambassador has bidden me to dinner. He'd like to make some capital out of my presence—for which I don't blame him, because I'll be eating my own tax money. But before I leave I'd like to entertain you and Tove. You pick the place. I'll pick up the bill."

"It's a date. Do you want to stroll along with me and take a quick look at our patient? He should be settled by now. And that Irish monsignor, his secretary, insists on a personal word . . ."

Monsignor Malachy O'Rahilly was tired and low-spirited. The fine glow of liquor and righteousness which had sustained him at the Secretariat meeting had subsided into the grey ashes of remorse. He had driven to the clinic just as the Pontiff was being wheeled in for surgery and he had spent three long hours wandering the grounds under the vigilant eyes of armed men.

Even before Salviati's communiqué had been issued, he had telephoned the Secretary of State to tell him that the operation had been successful. His Eminence had returned the compliment with a brief summary of the de Rosa affair and an admonition that none of the newspaper reports—which were bound to be lurid—should be communicated to His Holiness until he was well on the road to recovery. O'Rahilly read the order as a reproof for his indiscretions, and wished there were someone like Matt Neylan to whom he could make a fraternal confession.

So, when he stood by the Pontiff's bedside with Salviati and Morrison, he felt flustered and uncomfortable. His first remark was a banality.

"The poor man looks so . . . so vulnerable."

Morrison reassured him cheerfully.

"He's in great shape. The whole procedure was a copybook exercise. There's nothing to be done now except monitor the screen and change his drips. He won't be halfway lucid for another day and a half. If I were you, I'd go home and let Professor Salviati's people look after him."

"You're right, of course." O'Rahilly still felt the need to patch up his dignity. "I wondered if I should walk through the security arrangements with you, Professor Salviati; just so I can reassure the Secretary of State and the Curia."

"Not possible, Monsignore!" Salviati was curt. "Security is not your business, or mine. We should leave it to the professionals!"

"I thought only that . . ."

"Enough, please! We are all tired. I don't tell you how to write the Pope's letters. Don't tell me how to run my clinic. Please, Monsignore! Please!"

"I'm sorry." Malachy O'Rahilly was chastened but not silenced. "I had a bad night, too. I'm sure the security is first class. I couldn't move twenty yards in the garden without looking down a gunbarrel. When may His Holiness have visitors?"

"Any time. But he won't begin to make sense for at least thirty-six hours. Even then, his attention span will be limited and his emotions barely under control. Just warn your people not to expect too much and to keep their visits short."

"Be sure I'll do that. There's just one thing you should know . . ."

"Yes?"

And that was all the prompting Malachy O'Rahilly needed to blurt out the story of de Rosa's suicide, the murder of his children and the macabre obsequies he had prepared in his house.

Morrison and Salviati heard him out in silence; then Salviati led the way out of the Intensive Care Unit and into the corridor. He was deeply shocked, but his comment was studiously restrained.

"What can I say? It's a tragic mess and a sad waste of human lives."

"We are anxious,"—Malachy O'Rahilly was happy to have the spotlight again—"we are most anxious that His Holiness should be spared this news, at least until he is strong enough to cope with it."

Salviati dismissed the notion with a shrug.

"I'm sure he won't hear it from our staff, Monsignore."

To which James Morrison added a tart reminder.

"And he's not going to be able to hold, let alone focus on, a newspaper for days yet."

"So you should look to your own gossips, Monsignore." Salviati was already on the move towards the elevators. "You must excuse us now. We've had a busy morning; and it isn't over yet."

Anton Drexel, too, was having a busy morning; but a much more relaxing one. He had risen early, made his morning meditation, said Mass in the tiny villa chapel with his cellar master for acolyte and those of his household and the colonia who wished to attend. He had breakfasted on coffee and home-baked rolls and honey from his own hives. Now, dressed in workman's clothes, with a big straw hat on his white head and a basket on his arm, he was making the rounds of the garden plots, cutting fresh artichokes, pulling lettuce and radishes, picking red tomatoes and white peaches and the big yellow persimmons that the local folk called *"kaki"*.

His companion was a skinny, shambling boy with a hydrocephalic skull, who knelt among the bean rows, clutching a tape-recorder into which from time to time he murmured some runic words of his own. Later, Drexel knew, the sounds would be transcribed into the written record of a Mendelian experiment on the hybridisation of *fave,* the broad beans which flourished in the friable soil of the foothills. The boy, Tonino, was only in his fifteenth year, but already, under the tutelage of a botanist from the University of Rome, he was deep into the principles of plant genetics.

Verbal communication with Tonino was difficult, as it was with many of the children in the colonia, but Drexel had developed a technique of patient listen-

ing and a language of smiles and gestures and approving caresses, which somehow seemed to suffice these small, maimed geniuses whose intellectual reach,
he knew, was light years further than his own.

As he went about the simple, satisfying landsman's tasks, Drexel pondered
the paradoxes, human and divine, which presented themselves to him every
precious day of his Indian summer. He saw himself very clearly as a hinge-man
of a Church in crisis, a man whose time was running out, who must soon stand
for judgement on what he had done and left undone.

His prime talent had always been that of a navigator. He knew that you
couldn't sail into the eye of the wind or buck the seas head-on. You had to haul
off and tack, take the big waves on the shoulder, run for shelter sometimes and
always be content to arrive in God's time.

He had always refused to involve himself in the battles of the theologians,
being content to accept life as a mystery, and Revelation as a torch-light by
which to explore it. For him, faith was the gift that made mystery acceptable,
while hope made it endurable and love brought joy even in the cloud of unknowing. He had no belief at all in the efficacy of *Romanita'*, the ancient Roman
habit of prescribing a juridical solution to every human dilemma, and then
stamping every solution with a sacred character under the seal of the *magisterium.*

His method of dealing with *Romanita'*—and of salving his own conscience—
had always been the same. He made his protest, plainly but in strictest protocol, he pleaded his cause without passion, then submitted in silence to the
verdict of the Pontiff or the curial majority. Had he been challenged to justify
such conformity—and not even the Pontiff wanted a head-on collision with
Anton Drexel!—he would have answered with reasonable truth that open conflict would avail nothing for him or for the Church, and that while he was
happy to resign and become a country curate, he saw no virtue in abdication,
and even less in rebellion. In his official life he followed the motto of Gregory
the Great: *"Omnia videre, multa dissumulare, pauca corrigere."* See all, keep a lot to
yourself and correct a few things!

But in his private, intimate life at the villa, with the children, their parents
and teachers, he no longer had the luxury or the protection of protocol and
obedience. In a very special sense, he was the patriarch of the family, the
shepherd of the tiny flock, to whom everyone looked for guidance and decision.
He could no longer gloss over the patent facts of a tooth and claw creation, and
the random nature of human tragedy. He could no longer signify personal
assent to the prohibition of artificial birth control, or affirm that every marriage formally contracted in the Church was, of its nature, Christian, made in
heaven, and therefore indissoluble. He was no longer prepared to pronounce a
final ethical judgement on the duty of a surgeon faced with a monster birth, or
the conscience of a woman desperate to terminate a pregnancy in order to
prevent one. He was angered when theologians and philosophers were silenced
or censured for their attempts to enlarge the understanding of the Church. He
fought a long war of attrition against the secrecies and injustices of the inquisitorial system, which still survived in the Congregation for the Doctrine of the
Faith. He found himself insisting more and more upon the liberty of enlight-

ened conscience and the constant need of every human creature for compassion, charity and forgiveness.

It was to this that he sought to persuade his friends in the senior hierarchy and ultimately the Pontiff, if and when he came to spend time with the children in the colonia. It was for this that he offered his daily Mass and his nightly prayers. It was for this that he sought to prepare mind and spirit by his musings in the summer garden. Even his harvest of the summer fruits made a text for his discourse to the children and their teachers, gathered on the lawn for morning coffee.

"You see, there is an order even in what presents itself to us as cataclysm. Lake Nemi up there was once an active volcano. This land was once covered with ash and pumice and black lava. Now it is sweet and fertile. We did not see the change happen. If we had seen it, we would not have understood what was happening. We would have tried to explain the phenomenon by myths and symbols . . . Even now, with all our knowledge of the past, we still find it hard to disentangle the historical facts from the myths, because the myths themselves are a part of history . . . This is why we must never be afraid to speculate—and never, never be afraid of those who urge us to contemplate the seemingly impossible, to examine ancient formulae for new meanings. Believe me, we are more readily betrayed by our certainties than by our doubts and curiosities. I believe that half the heresies and schisms would never have happened if Christians had been willing to listen to each other in patience and charity, and not tried to turn the Divine mysteries into geometric theorems which could be taught with compass and set-squares . . . Listen now, my friends, to what the Fathers of Vatican Council II have said about our dangerous certainties: 'If the influence of events or of the times has led to deficiencies in conduct, in Church discipline, or even in the formulation of doctrine (which must be carefully distinguished from the deposit of faith itself) these should be appropriately rectified at the proper moment.' But what am I truly trying to say with all these words? I am an old man. I hold to the old Apostolic faith. Jesus is the Lord, the Son of the Living God. He took flesh. He suffered and died for our salvation and on the third day God raised him up again. Everything I see in this garden is a symbol of that birth and death and resurrection . . . Every truth that has ever been taught within the Church flows from it. Every evil that has ever been done in the Church has been a contradiction of that saving event . . . So do not ask me to judge you, my children, my family. Just permit me to love you, as God loves us all . . ."

The talk ended as informally as it had begun. Drexel moved over to the big trestle table, where one of the women offered him coffee and a sweet biscuit. It was then that he became aware of Tove Lundberg standing a few paces away with James Morrison in attendance. Tove Lundberg presented him to Drexel. Morrison paid him a sober compliment.

"I've been deaf to sermons for a good many years, Eminence. That one moved me deeply."

Tove Lundberg explained their presence.

"Sergio wanted you to know personally that the surgery was successful . . . And I thought James should see what you are doing here for Britte and the others."

"That was kind." Drexel felt as if a great load had been lifted from his shoulders. "I presume, Mr. Morrison, that means there were no unforeseen consequences—stroke, brain damage, that sort of thing?"

"None that we can see or foresee at this moment."

"Thank God! And you clever gentlemen, too!"

"We did, however, get some sad news." Tove Lundberg told him of the de Rosa affair as reported by Monsignor O'Rahilly. Drexel was suddenly grim.

"Shocking! Absolutely disgraceful that a tragedy like this could be permitted to happen! I shall take it up with the dicasteries concerned and with the Holy Father when he is sufficiently recovered." He turned to James Morrison. "Bureaucrats are the accursed of God, Mr. Morrison. They record everything and understand nothing. They invent a spurious mathematic by which every human factor is reduced to zero . . ." To Tove Lundberg he said more calmly: "I imagine Professor Salviati was very upset."

"More than he would confess, even to me. He hates the waste of human beings. Besides, the clinic is like an armed camp just now and that's a reminder of another kind of waste."

"Come!" said Anton Drexel abruptly. "Let's be grateful for a while. I'll walk you round the villa and the vineyards—and after that, Mr. Morrison, you shall taste some of the best wine that's been grown in these parts for a long time. I call it Fontamore, and it drinks better than Frascati. I'm very proud of it . . ."

Sergio Salviati's conference with the security men lasted nearly an hour. It dealt, for the most part, with the details of personnel control: a rollcall of each oncoming shift, a check of hospital identity cards against personal documents like passports and drivers' licences, access to drug cabinets and surgical instruments, routes and times by which certain key people might enter sensitive areas, the mobile surveillance of strategic points inside and outside the building. So far, it was agreed, all staff within the compound had been accounted for and were about their normal business. Visitors could be dealt with without too much fuss. Tradesmen would be met by armed guards and the goods they delivered screened and hand searched before they passed into the storerooms. So far, so good. The security men assured the Professor that he could sleep as soundly and as safely as if he were in the crypt of St. Peter's itself.

His next caller was less comforting: a lean, sallow, cold-eyed fellow in the white jacket of a male nurse. He was one of the Mossad men in permanent residence at the clinic, an elusive figure whom everybody recognised, who was on hand for every emergency, yet whose name never appeared on any regular roster. His first words were cryptic:

"Grants and scholarships."

"What about them?"

"You give a certain number to non-Italians. How are they allotted?"

"On the basis of merit and recommendation. We accept only candidates with full nursing certificates from their countries of origin and references from their consulates or embassies in Rome. We offer them two years of specialised training in cardiac theatre and post-operative practice. The scholarships are advertised in the consulates and in professional journals in Tunisia, Saudi Arabia, Trucial Oman, Israel, Kenya and Malta. We supply board, lodging, uniforms, training and health care. The candidates or the country which sponsors them must come up with the rest. It works pretty well. We get staff eager to learn, the sponsoring countries get trained personnel capable of passing on their education. End of story . . ."

"Are any security checks made on applicants?"

"You know there are. They have to apply for visas and student sojourn permits. The Italians run their own vetting system. Your people do any unofficial check for me. So there shouldn't be any surprises."

"There shouldn't be; but this time we've got a nasty one. Recognise her?"

He tossed on the desk a small, passport-size photograph of a young woman. Salviati knew her instantly.

"Miriam Latif. She's been here a year now. She comes from Lebanon. She's working in the haematology unit. And she's damned good. What the hell could you possibly have on her?"

"She has a boyfriend."

"Most girls do—and Miriam's a very pretty one."

"The boyfriend is one Omar Asnan, designated a merchant from Tehran. He trades in tobacco, hides, spot oil and pharmaceutical opium. He also disposes of large quantities of ready cash and has a string of girlfriends, some of them even prettier than Miriam Latif. He is also a known paymaster of the Sword of Islam group."

"So?"

"So the least we can say is that he has a friend, an ally, a possible assassin, in place in the clinic . . . And if you think of it, the haematology unit is a very useful place to have her."

Sergio Salviati shook his head.

"I don't buy it. The girl's been here for twelve months. The Pontiff's operation was decided only a few days ago. The assassination threat is a matter that arose in response to the opportunity."

"And why," asked the Mossad man patiently, "why else do you have people in place, under deep cover, as sleepers—except to take advantage of unforeseen opportunities? Why the hell do you think I'm here? Think of all the famous or politically important people who pass through the clinic. This is a stage simply waiting for a drama to happen . . . And Miriam Latif could be the leading lady in a tragedy."

"So what are you going to do about her?"

"Watch her. Put one of our magic rings around her, so that she can't even go to the toilet unless we know about it. There's not much time. How long before your patient is discharged?"

"Barring complications, ten days, fourteen at the outside."

"So, don't you see, they have to move fast. But now that we're alerted, we can move faster."

"Do the Italians know this?"

"No. And we don't intend to tell 'em. We'll do whatever is necessary. One thing you have to remember. If the girl fails to show up for work, I want you to make a big song and dance about it—question the staff, inform the police, call her embassy, all that!"

"And I don't ask why you want it done like that?"

"Exactly," said the Mossad man. "You are a very wise monkey, who hears no evil, sees no evil, speaks no evil."

"But you could be wrong about Miriam Latif."

"We hope we are, Professor. None of us wants to have blood on the sidewalk! None of us wants reprisal for a lost agent."

Sergio Salviati felt himself suddenly drowning in the black waters of fear and self-loathing. Here he was, a healer, netted like a tunny in a labyrinthine trap, waiting helplessly for murder to happen. The message he had been given was clear as daylight. In the game of terror, the slaughter was serial; you kill mine, I kill yours. Now there was a new twist to the sport—make the killing but put the blame on someone else: a hit-and-run motorist, a vengeful lover, an addict in search of a fix. And so long as the blood didn't splash on his own doorstep, Sergio Salviati would be silent lest even worse things should befall.

Then, because it was nearly midday, he walked to the Intensive Care Unit to take a look at the cause of all his problems, Leo XIV, Pontifex Maximus. All the signs said that he was doing well; his breathing was regular, the atrial fibrillations were within normal limits, his kidneys were functioning and his body temperature was rising slowly. Salviati smiled sourly and made a silent apostrophe to his patient: "You are a terrible old man! I give you life and what do you give to me? Nothing but grief and death . . . Morrison was right. You're a bird of ill-omen . . . Yet—God help me!—I'm still committed to keeping you alive!"

VII

THE first drugged confusions were over: the long unstable hours when he drifted between sleep and waking, the half-seen procession of Vatican visitors murmuring solicitous courtesies, the broken nights when his thorax hurt abominably and he had to ring for the nurse to move him in the bed and give him a pill to ease him back into sleep. But neither the confusions nor the pain could mask the wonder of the prime event: he had been taken apart like a watch and put together again; he had survived. It was exactly as Salviati had promised. He was like Lazarus stepping out of the tomb to stand, blinking and uncertain, in the sunlight.

Now, every day was a new gift, every unsteady step a new adventure, every word spoken a fresh experience of human contact. At moments the newness was so poignant that he felt like a boy again, waking to that first flush of spring when all the blossom trees in Mirandola seemed to burst into flame at once. He wanted to share the experience with everyone: the staff, Malachy O'Rahilly, the cardinals who came like courtiers to kiss hands and congratulate him.

The strange thing was that when he tried to express to Salviati both the wonder and his gratitude for it, his words seemed suddenly arid and inadequate. Salviati was courteous and encouraging; but when he had gone, Leo the Pontiff felt that a most important event had slipped past him, never to be celebrated again.

This sense of loss plunged him, without warning, into a black depression and a prolonged fit of weeping which shamed him into a deeper gloom. Then Tove Lundberg appeared and sat by his bedside to hold his hand and coax him out of the dark valley and on to the sunlit slopes again. He did not withdraw from her touch but surrendered to it gratefully, knowing, however vaguely, that he needed every possible handhold to anchor him to sanity. She used her own handkerchief to wipe away his tears and chided him gently:

"You must not be ashamed. This is the way it goes with everybody—high elation, then despair, a huge swing of the pendulum. You have just been subjected to an enormous invasion. Salviati says that the body weeps for what has been done to it. He says something else, too. We all believe we are immortal and invulnerable. Then something happens and the illusion of immortality is shattered for ever. We weep then for our lost illusions. Even so, the tears are part of the healing process. So let them flow . . . My father used to remind us that Jesus wept for love and for loss, just like the rest of us . . ."

"I know that. Why, then, am I so unprepared and inadequate?"

"Because . . ." Tove Lundberg pieced out her answer with great care, "because to this moment you have always been able to dictate the terms of your life. In all the world there is no one who sits higher or more securely, because you are elected for life and no one can gainsay you. All your titles affirm, beyond question, that you are the man in control. Your whole character urges you to hold that control."

"I suppose so."

"You know so. But now you are no longer master of yourself or of events. When my father was in his last illness he used to quote us a passage from the Gospel of John. It is, I believe, part of Christ's Commission to Peter . . . How does it go? 'When you were young, you used to buckle on your belt and go wherever you wanted . . .'"

Leo the Pontiff gave her the rest of the text as if it were a response in choir.

" 'But when you are old, you will hold out your hands and another will gird you and lead you where you do not want to go . . .' For a man like me, that's a hard lesson to learn."

"How can you teach it, if you haven't learnt it?"

A ghost of a smile twitched at the corners of his bloodless lips. He said softly: "Now there's a change! The Pope is taught sound doctrine by a heretic—and a woman at that!"

"You'd probably be a whole lot wiser if you listened to both the heretics and the women!" Her laugh took the sting out of the reproof. "I must go now. I have three more patients to see before lunch. Tomorrow, we'll walk in the garden. We'll take a wheelchair so that you can rest when you feel tired."

"I'd like that. Thank you."

As a parting gesture she sprinkled cologne on a facecloth and dabbed it on his forehead and his cheeks. The gesture moved him to an unfamiliar emotion. The only woman who had ever soothed him like that was his mother. Tove Lundberg ran her fingertips over his cheek.

"You're stubbled as a wheat field. I'll send someone in to give you a shave. We can't have the Pope looking scrubby for all his important visitors."

"Please, before you go . . ."

"Yes?"

"The day I came in a woman died here. The name escapes me, but her husband used to be a priest. I asked my secretary to make enquiries about him and his family. So far he hasn't given me any information. Can you help me?"

"I'll try." The tiny hesitation seemed to escape him. "There are certain rules about confidentiality; but I'll see what I can do. Until tomorrow then."

"Until tomorrow. And thank you, signora."

"Please, would Your Holiness do me a favour?"

"Anything in my power."

"Then call me simply Tove. I am not married, though I do have a child. So I am hardly a signorina either."

"Why," he asked her gently, "why have you found it necessary to tell me this?"

"Because if I do not, others will. If I am to help you, you must be able to trust me and not be scandalised by what I am or do."

"I am grateful to you. And I already know who and what you are from Cardinal Drexel."

"Of course! I should have remembered. Britte calls him Nonno Anton even now. He is very important in both our lives."

"As you are in mine at this moment." He took her hands in his own and held them for a long moment, then he reached up and signed a cross on her forehead with his thumb.

"Peter's blessing for Tove Lundberg. It is not any different from your father's."

"Thank you." She hesitated a moment and then posed the diffident question. "Some day you must explain to me why the Roman Church will not permit its priests to marry. My father was a good man and a good pastor. My mother was his helpmeet in the Church and with the people . . . Why should a priest be forbidden to marry, to love like other men . . . ?"

"That's a big question," said Leo the Pontiff. "Bigger than I could possibly answer now. But certainly we can talk about it another time . . . For the present, just let me tell you I am glad and grateful for what you are doing for me. I need this help in a way you may never understand. I shall pray for your well-being and that of your daughter . . . Now, please send me the barber and have nurse bring me fresh pyjamas. A scrubby Pope indeed! Intolerable!"

The small tenderness she had shown him, and the rush of emotion it had produced in him, lent all the more emphasis to her question about celibate clergy and his own unanswered inquiry about Lorenzo de Rosa. This cluster of small incidents was simply a micro-image of problems which had bedevilled him for a long time and had plagued the Church for more than fifteen hundred years.

The discipline of enforced clerical celibacy in the Roman communion had proved at best questionable, at worst a creeping disaster for the community of the faithful. The attempt to equate celibacy, the unmarried state, with chastity, the avoidance of unlawful sexual intercourse, was doomed to failure and productive of a whole crop of ills, not least an official hypocrisy and a harvest of tragedies among the clergy themselves. Forbidden to marry, some found relief in secret liaisons, others in homosexual practice or, more commonly, in alcohol. Not infrequently, a promising career ended in mental breakdown.

In the mid-sixties, after the Second Vatican Council, discipline had been relaxed to permit those in distress to quit the priesthood and marry validly. There had been a sudden rush for dispensations. Tens of thousands left the ministry. New vocations slowed to a trickle. The sad truth had been revealed, that this was no happy band of brothers, joyful in the service of the Lord, but a lonely ministry of lonely men facing an old age lonelier yet.

Thenceforward every attempt to drown the problem in a flood of pious rhetoric had failed miserably. His own rigorist policy—"few but good, and for none an easy exit"—had seemed at first to succeed, with a small crop of Spartan zealots coming up each year for ordination. But even he, Leo XIV, Hammer of God, had to admit in his secret heart that the remedy was a placebo. It looked good, tasted good, but did nothing for the health of the Mystical Body. There were too few shepherds for the vast flock. The zealots—in whom he recognised his younger self—were out of touch with reality. The threadbare theology that backed a face-saving legislation was no excuse for depriving the people of the saving word.

What he could or should do about it was another matter entirely. He had—at least to this moment—no intention of going down in history as the first Pope in a thousand years to legalise a married clergy. Whatever the morals of such a move, the economics of it opened a new chapter of horrors. Meantime, the personal tragedies proliferated; the faithful gave tolerance and affection to their pastors, young and old, and made their own provisions to keep the sacred fire of the Word alive. There was nothing he could do but wait and pray for light in his own puzzled mind, and strength for his still shaky limbs.

The barber came, a new one this time, sallow and saturnine, wielding an old-fashioned cut-throat razor, who shaved him clean as a billiard ball and uttered no more than a dozen words in the process. A nurse brought him fresh pyjamas and then walked him to the shower and helped him scrub himself, because his chest and back still hurt. He was no longer humiliated or even displeased by his dependence; but he was beginning at least to make a comparison between his own circumstance and that of any ageing cleric, forced to depend upon the ministrations of women, from whom he had been exiled by decree all his life. Finally, shaved, dressed and lighter in spirit, he walked back to his room, seated himself in his chair and waited for visitors to arrive.

The first, as usual, was Monsignor Malachy O'Rahilly, who brought with him a roster of those who had applied to call on His Holiness to pay respect and to keep themselves and their business under Pontifical notice. They had always recognised in him an old-fashioned Italian traditionalist and this was the old-fashioned way of papal business: protocol, propriety, compliment and courtesy.

With his master restored to him, Malachy O'Rahilly was himself renewed, bubbling with busy good humour.

"Are they treating you well, Holiness? Is there anything you need? Any delicacy to tempt your fancy? I'll have it here for you in an hour. You know that."

"I know it, Malachy. Thank you. But there's nothing I need. Who's on your list for today?"

"Four people only. I'm holding the numbers down because once they see that bright look in your eye they'll all be wanting to talk business—and that's *verboten!* First on the list is the Secretary of State. He has to see you. Then there's Cardinal Clemens from the Congregation for the Doctrine of the Faith. He's still jumping up and down about the Tübingen Petition. There's more and more discussion in the Press and on television. His Eminence wants your consent to take immediate disciplinary action against the theologians who signed the document . . . You know his arguments, it's a direct challenge to Papal authority, it calls in question your own right to appoint bishops to local churches . . ."

"I know the arguments." The familiar predator look transformed him instantly into an adversary. "I told Clemens very plainly that we should take time to reflect before we answer. We need light, not heat, in this matter. Very well. I'll see him at four-thirty. Fifteen minutes. No longer. If he runs on, you come in and get rid of him. Who's next?"

"Cardinal Frantisek, Congregation for the Bishops. That's a courtesy call on behalf of the hierarchy. It will be brief. His Eminence is a model of tact."

"Would we had more like him, Malachy! Five-fifteen?"

"Finally, Cardinal Drexel. He's spending the day in Rome; he asks if he may call on you between seven and eight, on his way home. I'm to telephone his office if you agree."

"Tell him I'll be delighted to see him."

"And that's all, Holiness. It doesn't mean I haven't been busy. It means that the Secretary of State will have my head if I submit you to even a hint of harassment."

"I'll tell him myself you're a model chamberlain, Malachy. Now, you had some enquiries to make for me about the young woman who died the night I came here. The one who was married to a priest of the Roman diocese."

Now Malachy O'Rahilly was caught between a very large rock and a very thorny place. The Pontiff demanded information. The Secretary of State had promised to boil him in oil if he divulged it. True always to his nature, Malachy O'Rahilly decided that if he wanted to stay in his job, he must cleave to the Bishop of Rome and not to his adjutants in the Curia. So, he told the truth; but this time at least he told it penny-plain, making no mention of the newspaper cuttings in his briefcase, no reference to the security meeting in the Apostolic Palace or Matt Neylan's passionate intervention on behalf of de Rosa.

When he ended his story, the Pontiff was silent a long time. He sat bolt-upright in his chair, his hands clamped to the arm-rests, his eyes closed, his mouth a pale razor-slash across his chalk-white face. Finally, he spoke. The words issued in a harsh, strained whisper, simple and final as the deaths that prompted them.

"I have done a terrible thing. May God forgive me. May He forgive us all."

Then he began to sob convulsively, so that his whole body was racked with the pain and the grief. Malachy O'Rahilly, the perfect secretary, stood mute with embarrassment, unable to raise hand or voice to comfort him. So he tiptoed out of the room and signalled a passing nurse to tell her that her patient was in distress.

"Explanations please, Professor." The Mossad man, humourless and laconic as always, pushed a clipboard across Salviati's desk. "I know most of it, but I want to check it off with you."

"Go ahead."

"That's a specimen of the chart which is hung at the foot of every patient's bed, right?"

"Right."

"Where are the charts produced?"

"On our own copier in the clinic."

"Now would you read the column headings, please?"

"Time. Temperature. Pulse. Blood pressure. Treatment administered. Drugs administered. Nurse's observations. Physician's observations. Treatment ordered. Drugs ordered. Signature."

"Now take a look at the chart in front of you. Look at yesterday's date. How many signatures are there?"

"Three."

"Can you identify them?"

"Yes. Carla Belisario, Giovanna Lanzi, Domenico Falcone."

"Functions?"

"Day nurse, night nurse, physician on duty."

"Now look at the notations. How many different handwritings are there?"

"Six."

"How do you explain that?"

"Simple. The nurses who sign are responsible for the patient. Each has several patients. Temperature, pulse and blood pressure are taken by juniors. Dosages are administered by pharmacy personnel, treatment may be given, for example, by a physiotherapist. The system is essentially simple. The physician prescribes, the nurse supervises, the others work under direction and supervision . . . Now perhaps you can tell me what you're looking for."

"Loopholes," said the Mossad man. "How to murder a Pope in a Jewish clinic and get away with it."

"And have you found one yet?"

"I'm not sure. Look again at that chart. Is there any mention of haematology?"

"Right at the beginning, in the pre-operative stage of this patient. There's an order for a whole series of blood tests."

"Explain exactly how they would be done—in respect of the patient."

"The test is ordered on the chart. The office on this floor calls haematology and puts in the order. They send someone to take blood samples, which are taken back to the laboratory for testing."

"That someone who takes the samples. What equipment does he have? How does he proceed?"

"It's generally a she," said Salviati with a grin. "She has a small tray on which there is alcohol, cottonwool swabs, some small adhesive patches, stoppered phials with the patient's name and room number written on the labels and a sterile hypodermic needle in a sealed plastic packet. She may carry a small rubber strap to constrict circulation and pump up the vein. That's the lot."

"How does she proceed?"

"She identifies the vein in the crook of the arm, swabs the spot with alcohol, inserts the needle, draws the blood and transfers it to the phial. She staunches the puncture with cotton wool, then seals it with an adhesive patch. It's all over in a couple of minutes."

"Nobody else in the room during the procedure?"

"Not usually. Why should there be?"

"Exactly. That's the loophole, isn't it? The girl is alone with the patient. She is carrying a lethal weapon."

"Which is what, precisely?"

"An empty syringe, with which blood can be extracted from a vein, or a lethal bubble of air pumped into it!"

"That's something I hadn't thought of. But there's a big hurdle she has to jump first. Our distinguished patient has had all his blood tests. Who's going to write the order for new tests on his chart? Who's going to call up haematology?"

"That's the second loophole," said the Mossad man. "Under your very thorough system, Professor, the clipboards are brought to the office at the end of each day shift and night shift. They are hung on numbered hooks and the charge sister inspects each one before completing the diary of her tour of duty. Anyone can pass by and make a notation. I've seen it done. The girl who took the patient's temperature forgot to write down the pulse rate or the blood pressure. You know it happens, and how it happens. How many times has a nurse had to ask you whether or no a dosage is to be continued?"

Salviati rejected the whole idea out of hand.

"I don't believe it—not a single damned word! You're synthesising a fiction; how a murder might happen! You're pulling an assassin out of thin air. This girl is one of my people. I'm not going to let you frame her like this."

The Mossad man was unmoved. He announced flatly:

"I haven't finished yet, Professor. I want you to listen to something." He laid on the desk a small pocket recorder and plugged in an earpiece which he handed to Salviati. "We've had Miriam Latif bugged for days now—her room, her laboratory jacket, the lining of her pocket-book. She always uses a public phone, so she has to carry *gettoni*. The pocket-book goes with her everywhere. What you will hear is a series of brief conversations with Omar Asnan, the boyfriend. They're in Farsi, so you'll have to take my word for their meaning."

Salviati listened for a few minutes then, exasperated by his inability to follow the dialogue, took out the earpiece and handed it back.

"Translation, please."

"The first conversation was from a bar in the village. She says yes, the arrangement is possible. Asnan asks how soon. She says a few days yet. He asks why. She says because of the logic. He asks what she means by logic. She says she can't tell him now. She'll try to explain at the next call . . . The explanation comes a little later in the tape. She explains that no one is allowed access to the man without passing through the security screen. She points out it wouldn't be logical to have a blood test ordered in the middle of convalescence. It would be more normal just before the patient was due to be discharged. Asnan says it's running things very fine. He'll have to think of back-up arrangements. Her answer to that clinches matters as far as we're concerned. She says: 'Be careful. The place is crawling with vermin and I haven't identified all of them yet.' There's more, but that's the core of it."

"There's no possible doubt that she's the assassin?"

"None."

"What happens now?"

"You don't ask. We don't tell."

"Would it help—it's a long shot and I'd hate to do it—would it help if I transferred the patient to Gemelli or Salvator Mundi?"

"Would it be good for the patient?" The Mossad man seemed willing to consider the idea.

"Well, it wouldn't be the best, but he'd survive it."

"What's the point then, Professor? So far as Miriam Latif is concerned it would make no difference at all. She's identified as a killer. The Vatican doesn't want her. Because she hasn't committed a crime yet, the Italians wouldn't do more than deport her back to Lebanon. We certainly don't want her running around loose in our theatre of operations. The conclusion's obvious enough, isn't it?"

"Why," asked Sergio Salviati bitterly, "why the hell did you have to tell me?"

"It's the nature of things," said the Mossad man calmly. "You're family, this is your home place, we're protecting you and all who abide here. Besides, what's to fret about? You're a doctor. Even your most successful cases end up with the undertaker!"

Then he was gone, a sinister, bloodless ghost haunting the corridors of an underworld that ordinary folk hardly believed to exist. Now he, Sergio Salviati, was a denizen of that underworld, caught in the toils of its conspiracies like a wasp in a spider web. Now he, the healer, would be made a silent party to murder; yet if he did not consent to silence, more and bloodier murders might be done. As an Italian, he had no illusions about the underside of life in the Republic; as a Jew and a Zionist, he understood how bitter and brutal was the struggle for survival in the Fertile Crescent.

Willy-nilly, he had been for a long time a player in the game. His clinic was a listening post and a refuge for sleepers in the intelligence trade. He himself, like it or not, was playing a political role; he could not, on the same stage, play the innocent dupe. Come to think of it, if the person of the Pope were directly threatened would the Vatican security men hold fire? He knew they would not. Sergio Salviati was not asked to pull a trigger, only to be silent while the professionals went about their normal business. The fact that their target was a woman had no weight in the case. The female was as lethal an instrument as the male. Besides, if any blood splashed on Sergio Salviati's hands, he could always get rid of it when he scrubbed up for surgery. There at least and at last he had to be clean . . .

In the midst of that wintry meditation, a courier brought the invitation for Tove Lundberg and himself to dine with Mr. & Mrs. Nicol Peters at the Palazzo Lanfranco.

The Secretary of State had a tidy mind and a subtle one. He hated a clutter of trifles on his agenda; he insisted always that they be disposed of before addressing himself to major issues. So, on his afternoon visit to the clinic he spoke first with Salviati, who assured him that the Pontiff was making a normal and satisfactory recovery and that he could probably be discharged in five or six days. He also talked briefly to the Italian and Vatican officials in charge of security, careful always to avoid any questions which might suggest that His Eminence knew more than his prayers. Then he presented himself to the Pontiff and walked with him to a sheltered spot in the garden, while an attendant waited at a discreet distance with the wheelchair. His Holiness came brusquely to the nub of the matter.

"I am ill, my friend; but I am not blind. Look around you! This place is like an armed camp. Inside I am hedged and picketed wherever I move. What is going on?"

"There have been threats, Holiness—terrorist threats against your life."

"By whom?"

"An extremist Arab group, calling itself the Sword of Islam. The information is high-grade intelligence."

"I still don't believe it. The Arabs know our policies favour Islam over Israel. What have they to gain by killing me?"

"The circumstances are special, Holiness. You are a patient in a clinic run by a prominent Zionist."

"Who still treats many Arab patients."

"All the more reason to teach everyone a lesson. But however twisted the logic, the threat is real. Money is on the table—big money."

"I'll be out of here in a few days—less than a week probably."

"Which brings me to my next point, Holiness. Most of us in the Curia are strongly against your proposal to lodge with Anton Drexel. It means a new and very expensive security operation, possible danger to the children and—let me say it frankly—the last thing in the world you want: jealousies within the Sacred College itself."

"God give me strength! What are they! A bunch of schoolgirls?"

"No, Holiness. They are all grown men, who understand the politics of power —and not all of them are friends of Anton Drexel. Please, Holiness, I beg you to consider this carefully. When you go from here, go straight back to Castel Gandolfo. You will have the best of care, as you know. From there, you can visit Drexel and his little tribe whenever you choose . . ."

The Pontiff was silent for a long moment, watching Agostini with hostile, unblinking eyes. Finally, he challenged him: "There's more, isn't there? I want to hear it, now."

He did not expect evasion. He did not get it. Agostini set down the core of the argument.

"All of us are aware, Holiness, of your concern at the divisions and dissensions in the community of the faithful. Those of us who are close to you have sensed for some time that you are going through a period of . . . well, of doubt and reassessment of the policies you have pursued so vigorously during your pontificate. That state of uncertainty has been increased by your illness. There are those—and let me hasten to say I am not one of them—who believe that the same illness, the sense of urgency it provokes, may cause Your Holiness to take precipitate action which, instead of doing good for the Church, may damage it further. Here is my point: if changes for the better are to take place, you will need all the help you can get from the Curia and the senior hierarchy of the National Churches. You're one man in the world who knows how the system works and how it can be used to frustrate the most determined or the most subtle of Pontiffs . . . You trust Drexel. So do I. But he is a man in the evening of his years; he is a German; he is too impatient of our Roman follies. He is, in my view, a handicap to your plans; and if you were to put that to him, I believe he would agree with you."

"Have you yourself put it to him, Matteo?"

"No."

"And where do you stand on the question of policy?"

"Where I always stand. I'm a diplomat. I deal in possibles. I'm always afraid of hasty decisions."

"Drexel is coming to visit me this evening. I owe him the courtesy of a discussion before I decide anything."

"Of course . . . There is one other matter on which I need a personal authority from Your Holiness, otherwise it will be floating around the Congregations for months. We've lost one of our best men from the Secretariat this week, Monsignor Matt Neylan."

"Lost him? What does that mean, precisely?"

"He's left us."

"A woman?"

"No. In a way, I wish it were. He came to tell me that he is no longer a believer."

"That's sad news. Very sad."

"From our point of view, he has conducted himself with singular propriety. It's tidier to laicise him without fuss."

"Do it, and do it quickly."

"Thank you, Holiness."

"I will tell you a secret, Matteo." The Pontiff suddenly seemed to have withdrawn into a private world. "I have often wondered what it would be like to wake up one morning and find that one no longer had the faith one had professed for a lifetime. One would know it all, as one might know a matter of law or a chemical equation or a piece of history; but it would no longer have any relevance . . . What is the phrase in *Macbeth?* 'It is a tale, told by an idiot, full of sound and fury, signifying nothing.' In the old days, you know, we'd have turned away from a man like that, treated him like a leper, as if the loss were his own fault. How does anyone know that? Faith is a gift. The gift may be withdrawn, as the gifts of sight or hearing may be taken away. It could as easily happen to you or me . . . I trust you were kind to him. I know you would never be less than courteous."

"I'm afraid he wasn't very happy with me, Holiness."

"Oh, why not?"

The question took them by a single stride to the story of the final Vatican involvement in the fate of Lorenzo de Rosa and his family. This time, however, it seemed that the Pontiff had no more emotion left to spend. What he uttered was a lament for lost hopes.

"We are losing too many, Matteo. They are not happy in the family of the faithful. There is no joy in our house, because there is too little love. And it is we, the elders, who are to blame."

Once each week, at an unscheduled hour, Sergio Salviati made what he called "the white-glove round" of the clinic. He had borrowed the phrase from an elderly relative who used to extol the spacious days of sea travel under the

British flag, when the Captain, accompanied by the Commodore and the Engineering Officer, donned white gloves and inspected the vessel, stem to stern. The white gloves showed every trace of dust or grime and protected the soft hands of authority.

Sergio Salviati did not wear white gloves, but his Chief of Staff carried a clipboard and a xeroxed plan of the institution on which every shortcoming was noted for immediate remedy. It was a very un-Latin procedure; but Salviati had too much at stake in patronage and professional reputation to trust to the shifting standards of a polyglot staff. He checked everything: toolsheds, linen stocks, pharmacy, pathology, files and records, surgical waste disposal, kitchen, bathrooms. He even took micro-samples from the air-conditioning ducts, which in the hot Roman summer might house dangerous bacteria.

The inspections were always made in the late afternoon, when his stint in the operating theatre was over and his ward rounds were all complete. At this hour, too, the staff were more relaxed and open. They were coming up to the end of the day and were vulnerable to criticism and well pleased by a word of praise. It was a few moments after five on this same ominous day when he came to the Haematology Department, where blood and sera were stored and analyses made of samples brought in from the wards.

Normally there were three people on duty in the laboratory. This time there were only two. Salviati wanted to know why. He was told that Miriam Latif had asked for the afternoon off to attend to some personal business. She was expected back on duty the next day. The arrangement had been cleared with the Chief of Staff's office. People within departments covered for each other as a matter of course.

Back in his own office, Salviati summoned the Mossad man and quizzed him about the girl's absence. The Mossad man shook his head sadly.

"For an intelligent fellow, Professor, you're a very slow learner. Your own staff have told you all you need to know. Best of all, they have told you the truth. The girl was called away on personal business. She made the excuse in person. Leave it at that!"

"And the threat to our patient?"

"Her absence has removed it. Her presence would restore it. We wait and watch, as always. For tonight at least you can sleep soundly."

"And tomorrow?"

"Forget tomorrow!" The Mossad man was impatient and abrupt. "You, Professor, must make a decision today—now, this moment!"

"About what?"

"The role you want to play: the reputable healer going about his reputable business in a wicked world, or the meddler who can't keep his nose out of other people's business. We can accommodate you, either way. But if you're in, you're in up to the neck and you play by our rules. Do I make myself clear?"

"Either way," said Salviati, "it seems I'm being manipulated."

"Of course you are!" The Mossad man gave him a vinegary smile. "But there's one big distinction: as Professor Salviati you are manipulated in innocence and ignorance. The other way, you do as you're told, eyes open, mouth shut. If we want you to lie, you lie. If we want you to kill, you kill—the Hippocratic oath notwithstanding. Can you wear that, my friend?"

"No. I can't."

"End of argument," said the Mossad man. "You'll enjoy your dinner tonight and sleep a lot more soundly."

"But you don't sleep," Tove Lundberg chided him tenderly. "You don't even enjoy making love; because you're not innocent, you're not ignorant, and the guilt gnaws at you all the time."

They were sitting over cocktails on the terrace of Salviati's house, looking out at a sky full of stars, misted and blurred by the emanations of Rome: river fog, traffic fumes, dust and the exhalations of a city slowly choking itself to death. He had not wanted to share the story with her, because the mere knowledge of it put her at a certain risk. However, concealment put him at greater hazard, because it clouded his judgement, robbed him of that detachment upon which his patients' lives depended. Tove Lundberg summed up her argument.

"The problem is, my love, you know too little and want too much."

"I know Miriam Latif is going to be killed—if she's not dead already."

"You don't know it. You're surmising. You can't possibly be sure she's even missing until tomorrow."

"Then what do I do?"

"What would you do if it were another person altogether?"

"I would hear it much later than everyone else. The Chief of Staff's office would already have inquired into her absence. If she didn't show up in a reasonable time, they'd ask me to authorise a replacement. I would probably advise them to contact the police and immigration officials, because the clinic has sponsored the girl's entry and guaranteed her employment. After that, it's out of our hands."

"Which is no more or no less than your Mossad man told you at the beginning."

"But don't you see . . . ?"

"No! I don't. I can't see one step beyond the routine you have just outlined. Whom else are you going to tell? The Pope? He knows about the threat to his life. He knows about the security measures. He consents, tacitly at least, to anything that may happen as a result of those measures. If the girl is a terrorist, she herself has already accepted all the risks of the job for which she has been trained."

"But that's just the point." Salviati was suddenly angry. "All the evidence against her is circumstantial. Some of it is negative, in the sense that no other more likely candidate has shown up on the Mossad lists. So she's being condemned and executed without a trial."

"Maybe!"

"All right. Maybe!"

"Again, what can you do about it, when the Italian Government abdicates its legal authority in favour of direct action by the Israelis? That's what's happening, isn't it?"

"And the Vatican sits pat on the protocol of the Concordat. The Pope's bodyguards may protect him by force of arms if necessary; but the Vatican may not intervene in the administration of justice in the Republic."

"So why go on beating your head against your own Wailing Wall?"

"Because I'm not sure any more who I am or where my loyalties lie. The Pope's my patient. Italy is my country. The Israelis are my people."

"Listen, my love!" Tove Lundberg reached across the table and imprisoned his hands in her own. "I will not take this kind of talk from you. Remember what you told me when I first came to work for you. 'Cardiac surgery is a risk business. It depends on free choice, an acceptance of known odds, clearly stated between surgeon and patient. There can be no trading back if an unknown factor tips the odds the wrong way!' So, it seems to me you're in the same position in the case of Miriam Latif. The odds are she's a trained assassin, nominated to kill the Pope. A choice has been made: to stop her without attracting reprisals. In this case, however, the choice was made by others. Your identity is not challenged; rather, it is confirmed. You are a healer. You have no place on the killing ground. Stay away from it!"

Sergio Salviati disengaged himself from her handclasp and thrust himself up from the table. His tone was rasping and angry.

"So! It's happened at last! It always does in Rome! My loyal counsellor has become a Jesuit. She should do very well with His Holiness."

Tove Lundberg sat a long while in silence, then, with an odd, distant formality, she answered him.

"A long time ago, my dear, you and I made a bargain. We could not share our histories or our traditions. We would not try. We would love each other as much as we could, for as long as we could, and when the loving was over we would stay friends always. You know I have neither taste nor talent for cruelty games. I know you play them sometimes, when you are frustrated and afraid, but I have always believed you had too much respect to force me into them . . . So, I'm going home now. When we meet in the morning I hope we can forget this ugly moment."

The next instant she was gone, a blurred figure hurrying through the twilight towards her car. Sergio Salviati raised neither hand nor voice to stay her. He stood like a stone man, clamped to the crumbling balustrade, lonelier and more desolate than he had ever felt in his life. The valiant of Zion had rejected him with contempt. A woman of the *goyim* had probed with an unerring finger towards the hollow place in his heart. Each had acknowledged him as a healer. Both had challenged him to the impossible, to mend his damaged self.

That night, the Pontiff sat late with Anton Drexel. After the emotional storms of the day he felt a need for the calm, quiet discourse which Drexel dispensed. His answer to the objections raised against a papal sojourn at the colonia was typical of the man.

"If it raises problems, then forget the idea. It was intended as a therapy, not as a stress factor. Besides, Your Holiness needs allies and not adversaries. When all the brouhaha has died down and the risks of attack on your person have diminished, as they always do, then you can visit the children. You can invite them to visit you . . ."

"And what of your own plans for me, Anton? My education to new views and policies?"

Drexel laughed, a man at ease with himself and his master.

"My plans depend on the working of the Spirit, Holiness. Alone, I could not bend you a millimetre. Besides, your Secretary of State is right—as he is most of the time. I am too old and still too much the *Ausländer,* to be a true power-broker among the Curia. That is how Your Holiness won the battle over Jean Marie Barette. You assembled the Latins against the Germans and the Anglo-Saxons. I would never attempt the same strategy twice."

Now it was the Pontiff's turn to laugh—a painful business with little amusement at the end of it.

"So what is your strategy, Anton? And what do you hope to win from me or through me?"

"What I believe you hope for yourself—a revival in the Assembly of the Faithful, a change in the attitudes which dictate the laws which are the greatest obstacle to charity."

"Easy to say, my friend. A lifetime's work to accomplish—and I have learned how short and fragile life can be."

"If you are thinking of serial solutions—picking off problems one by one like ducks in a shooting gallery—then of course you are right. Each issue sets off a new debate, new quarrels and casuistries. Finally, weariness sets in and the kind of creeping despair that has afflicted us since the Second Vatican Council. The fire of hope that John XXIII kindled has died to grey ashes. The conservatives—yourself, Holiness, not least among them—had a whole series of pyrrhic victories and the faithful were the losers every time."

"Now tell me your remedy, Anton."

"One word, Holiness—decentralise."

"I hear you. I'm not sure I understand you."

"Then I'll try to make it plainer. What we need is not reform, but liberation, an act of manumission from the shackles which have bound us since Trent. Give back to the local churches the autonomy which is theirs by apostolic right. Begin to dismantle this creaking edifice of the Curia, with its tyrannies and secrecies and sinecures for mediocre or ambitious prelates. Open the way to free consultation with your brother bishops . . . Affirm in the clearest terms the principle of collegiality and your determination to make it work . . . One document would start it—a single encyclical written by yourself, not constructed by a committee of theologians and diplomats and then emasculated by the Latinists and bled white of meaning by conservative commentary. . . ."

"You're asking me to write a blueprint for revolution."

"As I remember, Holiness, the Sermon on the Mount was a revolutionary manifesto."

"Revolutions should be made by young men."

"The old ones write the documents, the young translate them into action. But first they have to break out of the prison in which they are kept now. Give them liberty to think and speak. Give them your confidence and a charge to use the liberty. Perhaps then we will not have so many casualties like de Rosa and Matthew Neylan."

"You're a stubborn man, Anton."

"I'm older than you are, Holiness. I have even less time."

"I promise you I'll think about what you've said."

"Think about this too, Holiness. As we stand now in the Church, the centuries-old fight for papal supremacy is won—and the penalties of that victory are costing us dearly. All power is vested in one man, yourself; but you can only exercise it through the complicated oligarchy of the Curia. At this moment, you are almost impotent. You will remain so for months yet. Meantime, the men whom you appointed to positions of power are ready to range themselves in opposition to any new policies. That's a fact. Agostini has already given you the same warning. Is that a healthy state of affairs? Is that the true image of the Church of which Christ is the head and we all are members?"

"No, it is not." Leo the Pontiff was weary now. "But there is not a single thing either of us can do about it at the moment except think and pray. Go home, Anton! Go home to your family and your vineyards. You should be picking and crushing very soon, yes?"

"Very soon. Two weeks, my man tells me."

"Perhaps I could come for that. I haven't been to a *vendemmia* since I was a child."

"You'll be very welcome." Drexel bent to kiss the Ring of the Fisherman. "And a papal blessing might do wonders for the wine of Fontamore."

Long after Drexel had gone, long after the night nurse had settled him for sleep, Leo XIV, successor of the Prince of the Apostles, lay awake listening to the night noises, trying to decipher his destiny in the shadows cast by the night light.

The argument which Drexel had put to him had a certain grand simplicity on the one hand and, on the other, a very subtle distinction between authority and power.

The concept of papal power had been given its most rigid and extreme definition by Boniface VIII in the fourteenth century and Pius V in the sixteenth. Boniface had declared *tout court* that "because of the need for salvation, every human creature is subject to the Roman Pontiff".

Pius V had elaborated the proposition with breathtaking presumption. Leo XIV, his modern successor, inheritor of his rigid will and irascible temper, could recite the words by rote: "He who reigns in heaven, to whom is given all power in heaven and on earth, gave the one Holy Catholic and Apostolic Church, out of which there is no salvation, to be governed, in the fullness of authority, to one man only, that is to say, to Peter, the Prince of the Apostles and to his successor, the Roman Pontiff. This one ruler He established as prince over all nations and kingdoms, to root up, destroy, dissipate, scatter, plant and build . . ."

This was the ultimate and most flagrant claim of an imperial papacy, discredited long since by history and by common sense; but the echoes of it still lingered in the Vatican corridors. Power was still the ultimate human prize and here resided the power to move nearly a billion people, by the ultimate sanction—*timor mortis*, the fear of death and its mysterious aftermath.

Drexel's proposal was therefore an abdication of positions held for centuries, surrendered piecemeal and then only under extreme duress. It involved not an imperial concept, but a much more primitive and radical one, that the Church was one because it possessed one faith, one baptism and one Lord, Jesus Christ, in whom all were united as branches to a living vine. It involved not power, but authority—authority founded upon free consent, free conscience, an act of faith freely made. Those who were vested with authority must use it with respect and for service. They must not pervert authority to an instrument of power. To use it rightly, they must not only delegate it, but acknowledge freely the source from which it was delegated to them and the conditions of its use. It was one of the ironies of a celibate hierarchy that when you deprived a man of one satisfaction you sharpened his appetite for others, and power was a very spicy taste in the mouth.

Even if he agreed with Drexel's plan—and he had many reservations about it, as he had about Drexel himself—the obstacles to its accomplishments were enormous. That very afternoon his quarter-hour interview with Clemens of the Congregation for the Doctrine of the Faith had gone on for nearly forty minutes. Clemens had insisted very firmly that his Congregation was the watchdog guarding the Deposit of Faith—and if it were forbidden to bark, let alone bite, then why bother to have it? If His Holiness wanted to respond directly to the protestors of Tübingen, that was his right, of course. But a word from the Pontiff was not easily recalled, nor should it be gainsaid, as it might be, by these intransigent clerics.

It was the power game again and even he, the Pontiff, depleted of strength, was not exempt from it. What chance had a rural bishop, ten thousand miles from Rome, delated from some act or utterance by the local Apostolic Nuncio? Drexel could fight, because he was Clemen's peer, older and wiser in the game. Yet this very Olympian detachment made him, in some degree, a suspect advocate.

On the other hand, a man who called himself Vicar of Christ was given, perforce, a place in history. His words and acts were cited as precedents down the centuries and their consequences weighed in the balance on his own judgement day. So, it was hardly surprising that the dreams that haunted his pillow that night were a strange kaleidoscope of scenes from the Michelangelo frescoes and of men, masked and armed, stalking their quarry through a pine wood.

VIII

OUTSIDE the enclave of the International Clinic, between the hours of five and ten, a series of trivial events took place.

A woman made a phone call and left a message; another woman boarded an aircraft which two hours later arrived at its scheduled destination. A crate, labelled diplomatic documents, was loaded on to another aircraft for another destination. In a villa on the Appia Antica a man waited for a call which never came. Then he summoned his chauffeur and had himself driven to a nightclub near the Via Veneto. At Fiumicino airport, a clerk in the office of Middle East Airlines made a photocopy of a ticket coupon, put the copy in his pocket and, on his way home, delivered it to the doorman of an apartment block. The whole cycle of small events was reported to the duty officer at the Israeli Embassy in Rome. Before he left for the clinic in the morning, the Mossad man was informed of their meaning.

The telephone call to the clinic was made at seven p.m. from the foyer of the airport. The voice was distorted and almost drowned by background noise, but the switchboard operator at the clinic claimed to have understood the message and to have logged it accurately. Miriam Latif would not be reporting for work in the morning as she had promised. Her mother was very ill. She was taking the night flight to Beirut on Middle East Airlines. If she did not return, her due salary should be paid to her account in the Banco di Roma. She regretted the inconvenience but hoped that Professor Salviati would understand.

At seven-thirty a woman, veiled in traditional style, checked in at the Middle East Airlines counter. She had a ticket to Beirut and a Lebanese passport in the name of Miriam Latif. She carried only hand baggage. Since she was leaving the Republic and not entering it, the frontier police did not require her to unveil. Three hours later the same woman disembarked at Beirut airport, presented a passport in another name and disappeared.

The crate labelled diplomatic documents was loaded on to the El Al evening flight to Tel Aviv. Inside it lay Miriam Latif, heavily drugged, wrapped in thermal blankets and ventilated by air-holes and an oxygen tank on slow release. When she arrived in Tel Aviv she was raced to the infirmary of a Mossad detention centre and registered with a number and coding that indicated special and prolonged debriefing.

In the nightclub near the Veneto, Omar Asnan, the merchant from Tehran, ordered champagne for his usual girl and stuffed a 50,000 lire note into her cleavage. The message folded in the note was delivered ten minutes later to two men drinking coffee in one of the curtained alcoves. The delivery was noted by the cigarette girl, an Israeli agent who spoke French, Italian and Arabic.

Her report completed the operation. Miriam Latif the assassin had been eliminated from the game. Mossad was in possession of a valuable hostage and a source of vital intelligence. Omar Asnan and his cohorts of the Sword of Islam were still ignorant of what had happened. All they knew was that Miriam Latif had failed to keep a rendezvous. It would take them at least twenty-four hours to put together a feasible outline of events. There was only a slim chance that they could organise another assassination attempt during the limited time of the Pontiff's convalescence.

The only problem left was to reassure Salviati and rehearse him in his testimony. The Mossad man did it with his usual brevity.

"Your switchboard operator copied the message from Miriam Latif?"

"Yes. I have it here."

"Is she usually accurate and reliable?"

"All our operators have to be. They deal with medical matters—life and death."

"What are you doing with the girl's clothes, her personal effects?"

"I've asked her room-mate to list and pack them. We'll hold them in store pending word from Miriam herself."

"Then that's the lot," said the Mossad man. "Except, I thought you should see this to set your tender conscience at rest."

He handed Salviati the photostat of the ticket coupon made out in the name of Miriam Latif. Salviati scanned it quickly and handed it back.

"You haven't seen it, of course," said the Mossad man.

"I'm a wise monkey," said Sergio Salviati sourly. "Deaf, dumb and blind."

The Mossad man, however, was not blind. He saw very clearly the new options for violence opened up by the disappearance of Miriam Latif. The operation against the Pontiff was blown sky-high, as Latif herself had warned it might be: "the place is crawling with vermin". Nevertheless, money had been paid—big money—and the rules of the killing game were very explicit: we pay, you deliver. So, someone owed the Sword of Islam a lot of money. He had to hand back the cash or a body in lieu.

There was more than money involved. There was honour, esteem, the authority of the movement over its followers. If the rules were not enforced, if the promised victim were not delivered, the followers would drift away to another allegiance.

Finally—and this was perhaps the bitterest blow of all to the professionals—once the abduction of Miriam Latif had been established, the terrorist group would disperse and all the labour of penetrating it, all the risks taken to keep an agent in place within it, would be lost overnight.

Which left the Mossad man some delicate decisions. How much should he tell the Italians. What kind of warning, if any, should he give the Vatican folk— and whether Sergio Salviati himself needed, or was worth, protection. On balance it seemed wise to keep the safety nets around him. It would be a long time before Mossad could develop a cover as deep, as useful and as authentic as the International Clinic.

In a quiet angle of the garden, sheltered from the breeze by an ancient wall and from the sun by a canopy of vines, Leo the Pontiff sat at a table of weathered stone and wrote the diary of his seventh day in hospital.

He felt much stronger now. He stood straighter, walked further. The mood-swings were less violent, though he was still easily moved to tears or to doleful anxieties. Each day a therapist worked on his back and shoulders and, although his cloven ribcage still hurt, he was beginning to sit and lie more comfortably. The one thing that bothered him more than all else was the knowledge that he was under close surveillance at every hour of the day and night. Even so, he did not speak about it, for fear of seeming crotchety and querulous.

It was Salviati himself who raised the question with him when he came to share morning coffee with his patient. The Pontiff expressed pleasure at the unusual concession. Salviati shrugged and laughed.

"I had no operations today. I thought you could use some company. These fellows . . ." His gesture took in three marksmen who encircled the area. "These fellows aren't very talkative, are they?"

"Not very. Do you really think I need them?"

"My opinion wasn't asked," said Salviati. "Nor, I imagine, was yours. Odd, when you come to think of it. You're the Pope. I run this place. But it seems there's always a moment when the Palace Guard takes over. Anyway, you won't be here much longer. I'm discharging you very soon."

"When?"

"Three days from now. Saturday."

"That's wonderful news."

"But you'll have to stick to the regimen—diet and exercise."

"I will, believe me."

"Have you decided where you'll be staying?"

"I had hoped it would be at Cardinal Drexel's villa; but my Curia doesn't approve."

"May I ask why?"

"They tell me it would require a new and expensive security operation."

"I would doubt that. I've visited the place several times with Tove Lundberg. It would probably be very easy to seal off. The perimeter wall is clearly visible from the villa itself."

"That, of course, isn't the only reason. The Vatican is a court, as André Gide once observed. And courtiers are jealous as children of their precedence and privileges."

"I thought Churchmen were above such worldly matters."

Salviati's grin took the malice out of the gibe. The Pontiff laughed.

"The habit, my friend, does not make the monk."

"And since when has the Pope been reading Rabelais?"

"Would you believe, my friend, I have never read him. My reading list was rather restricted."

"You profited well from it."

"I've learned more in the last week than I have in half a lifetime—and that's the truth, *senza complimenti!* I am deeply in your debt and I owe much to the wisdom and the gentleness of your counsellor."

"She's very good. I'm lucky to have her."

"Obviously you are very fond of each other."

"We've been close for a long time."

"No thought of marriage?"

"We've discussed it. We agree it wouldn't work for either of us . . . But let's talk about you for a moment. It's clear you're going back into the stress situation of your own household. I had hoped to defer that until you were stronger . . . You are doing very well indeed; but you must be aware that the sense of well-being is relative. Today is better than yesterday, tomorrow you will feel stronger still, but the energy is quickly spent and you are still dependent on the ministrations of our staff. With your permission, I'd like to talk to Cardinal Agostini about this. Frankly, I believe your well-being is more important than the jealousies of your Curial Cardinals. Why not override them and follow my advice?"

"I could. I would rather not."

"Then let me be your advocate. At least no one can accuse me of self-interest. My clinical opinion has to carry some weight. I'd like to talk to Cardinal Agostini."

"Then do so."

"I will."

"I want you to know, my friend, how grateful I am for your skill and your care of me."

Salviati grinned like an embarrassed schoolboy.

"I did tell you I was a very good plumber."

"You are much more than that. I see all the dedication which has gone into this place and which still holds it together. Afterwards, I should like to discuss some permanent contribution to your work—an endowment perhaps, some special equipment. You will tell me."

"You can endow me now." Salviati was direct and forceful. "Tove Lundberg and I are putting together a series of psychic profiles on post-operative cardiac patients. In all our patients we note symptoms of radical psychic change. We need to understand that better. In your counselling sessions with Tove, you have described that change with various metaphors: a snake sloughing off its old skin, a graft on an orchard tree that produces a different fruit, Lazarus walking out of the tomb, a new man in a new world . . ."

"That's the best description I have found so far. Of course I know that I did not die, but . . ."

"You came close enough," said Salviati drily. "I wouldn't argue a heartbeat or two. But here's my question. You came to this situation better equipped than most. You had a clear faith, a whole well-packed baggage of philosophy, theology and moral practice . . . How much of that baggage have you left behind? How much have you brought back?"

"I don't know yet." The words came slowly as if he were weighing each one. "Certainly not all the baggage has survived the journey and what I have brought back is much, much less than I had at the beginning. For the rest, it's too early to know or to say . . . Later, perhaps, I may be able to tell you more."

"The answer will be important to us all. You have only to look around this garden to know that the fanatics are taking over the world."

"Part of the baggage I still carry," said Leo the Pontiff, "is a set of instructions for survival. It was written by a Jew, Saul of Tarsus . . . 'Now there remain these things: faith, hope and charity. And the greatest of these is charity.' I haven't always used them very well myself; but I'm learning."

Sergio Salviati looked at him for a long moment and then a slow smile softened the saturnine lines of his face.

"Perhaps I did a better job than I thought."

"I for one will never underrate you," said Leo the Pontiff. "Go with God."

He watched Salviati striding swiftly through the garden. He saw the guards salute him as he passed. Then he opened his diary and began again the task of explaining his new self to his old one.

"In my argument with Cardinal Clemens yesterday, he made much of the dangers of 'the new theology', the rejection by certain Catholic scholars of what he called 'the classic norms of orthodox teaching'. I know what he means. I understand his suspicion of novelty, his concern that new concepts of traditional doctrines are being proposed to students in seminaries and universities before they have been proven by argument and experience against the Deposit of Faith, of which Clemens and I are appointed guardians and I am the final arbiter and interpreter.

"There! I have written it! It stares at me from the page . . . 'I am the final arbiter and interpreter.' Am I? What makes me so? Election by a college of my peers? A private colloquy with the Holy Ghost, of which I personally have no record or recollection? Would I even as Pope presume to pit myself in argument against any philosopher, or theologian, or biblical scholar from the great universities? I know I could not. I should make a fool of myself; because I could only appeal to those 'classic norms' and their traditional expression, in which I was drilled so thoroughly in another age. I was not elected for my intellectual attainments or the stretch of my intuition in spiritual matters. I am no Irenaeus, no Origen, no Aquinas. I am and always have been a man of the organisation. I know it inside out, how to service it, how to keep it running. But now the organisation is outmoded and I am not inventive enough to remodel it. I am as deficient in social physics as I am in philosophy and theology. So I am forced to admit that my arbitrations and interpretations are those of others, and that all I contribute to them is the Seal of Peter.

"So, next question: what is the real authority of those upon whose judgement I rely? Why have I chosen them above others more forward-looking, more understanding of the language, temper and symbolism of our times? The answer is that I have been afraid, as so many in this office have been afraid, to let the wind of the Spirit blow freely through the House of God. We have been garrison men, holding the ramparts of a crumbling citadel, afraid to sally out and confront the world which by-passes us on the pilgrim road.

"When I first left home to go to seminary, I was surprised to find that the commerce of the world was not carried on in the Emilian dialect of my home-place. The first step in my education was to learn the language of a larger world, the customs of a less rustic society. However, in the government of the Church which calls itself universal I have tried to anchor it to the language and the concepts of centuries past, as though in some magical fashion antiquity guaranteed security and relevance.

"Our blessed Lord used the language and the metaphors of a rural people, but his message was universal. It embraced all creatures, as the sea embraces all the denizens of the deep. I have tried to reduce it to a static compendium, to stifle speculation about its myriad meanings.

"I begin, slowly, to understand what one of my more outspoken critics meant when he wrote: 'This pontiff is like a scientist trying to run the third millennium on a textbook of Newtonian physics. The cosmos has not changed, but our understanding of how it works is greater and different . . . To that extent we have all penetrated a little more deeply into the mystery of the Godhead. Just so, in the confusions and threats of the modern world, the pedagogy of the past is not enough for us. We need a teacher who will discourse with us in terms of the world in which we are involved.'

"When I first read those lines I was outraged. I felt that the writer, a layman, was uttering an arrogant insult. Now I see it differently. I am being asked to explore boldly the mysteries of a new time, by the light of ancient truth, confident that the light will not fail . . ."

A shadow fell across the page and he looked up to see Tove Lundberg standing a pace or two away. He gave her a smile of welcome and invited her to join him at the table. As he did so, a spinal spasm hit him and he winced at the pain. Tove Lundberg moved behind him and began to massage his neck and shoulders.

"When you write your posture is wrong. So when you straighten up you get a pinch and go into spasm . . . Try to hold yourself erect."

"My old master used to scold me for the same thing. He said I looked as though I were trying to crawl into the paper like a bookworm."

"But you listen only now, because it hurts!"

"True, my dear Tove. True!"

"There now, does that feel better?"

"Much better, thank you. Can I offer you some mineral water?"

"You can offer me some advice."

"Willingly."

"Do you extend the seal of confession to unbelievers?"

"They have a specially strong seal. What's troubling you?"

"Sergio and I have quarrelled."

"I'm sorry to hear that. Is it serious?"

"I'm afraid it is. We haven't been able to exchange anything but cold courtesies since it happened. It's something that goes to the root of our relationship. Neither of us is prepared to surrender our position."

"And what precisely are your positions?"

"First, we've been lovers a long time. You probably know that."

"I guessed it."

"But you don't approve, of course?"

"I cannot read your private consciences."

"We've talked often about marriage. Sergio wants it, I don't."

"Why not?"

"My reasons are very clear to me. I'm not prepared to risk another child. I don't believe I should condemn my man—any man—to a childless marriage. Britte is completing her education at the colonia; but at a certain moment she will have to leave it and I will have to provide a home and care for her. I do not want to contemplate lodging her in an institution. She is much too intelligent for that. So that's another burden I'm not prepared to lay on a husband. As a lover, I feel the contract is more equal, if more temporary . . ."

"And Sergio Salviati? How does he feel about all this?"

"He accepts it. I think he's even relieved, because he has problems of his own, which go deeper than mine but are less easy to define. First, he's a Jew—and you, of all people, must know what it means to be a Jew, even now, in this country. Second, he's a passionate Zionist, who often feels frustrated and demeaned because he's here making money and reputation, while his people are fighting for survival in Israel. At the same time, his position involves him in all sorts of compromises. You're one of them. You're the reigning Pontiff, but you still refuse to recognise the State of Israel. The Arab sheikhs he treats here are another compromise—and the fact that this place is also an undercover post for Mossad agents working in Italy. There's nothing too secret about that. The Italians know it and profit by it. The Arabs know it and feel safe against their own factions. But all of it tears Sergio apart and when he's upset and frustrated a streak of cruelty comes out, which I find unbearable. That's what caused our argument."

"You still haven't told me what the argument was about."

"Are we still under the seal?"

"We are."

"The argument was about you."

"All the more reason to tell me."

"You don't know this; but the person who was named to assassinate you was a woman, an Iranian agent who was actually employed in this clinic. Mossad agents identified her, kidnapped her and . . . well, nobody's quite certain what happened after that. The Vatican was not involved because of jurisdictional reasons. The Italians were happy to let the Israelis handle it because they didn't want reprisals. Sergio felt very guilty, because the girl was one of his employees; he knew and liked her. He felt that the evidence against her was highly circumstantial. Even so, he could not intervene in what happened. I tried to comfort him by saying that even you had to play a passive role. You accepted armed guards, which meant that you accepted that they might kill someone to protect you. Sergio wasn't happy with that either. He said . . . it doesn't matter what he said. It was just very painful and, somehow, final."

"Say the words!"

"He said: 'It's happened at last. It always does in Rome. My loyal counsellor has become a Jesuit. She should do very well with the Pope.' "

She was near to tears. The Pontiff reached across the table and imprisoned her hands in his own. With careful gentleness he told her: "Don't be too hard on your man. Guilt is a bitter medicine to swallow. I've been sitting here trying to digest a lifetime of it . . . As for cruelty, I remember that when I was a small boy, my dog had his leg broken in a rabbit snare. When I tried to release him he bit my hand. My father explained to me that an animal in pain will snap at anyone. What other response is left to it? Your man must be hurting very badly."

"And what about me? Don't you think I'm hurting too?"

"I know you are; but you will always heal more quickly. You have learned to look outside yourself, to your daughter, your patients. Every time your Sergio goes into the operating theatre, he is engaged in a private duel with death. When he comes out, he finds that all the fears he has left outside the door lie in wait for him."

"What are you telling me to do?"

"Kiss your man and make up. Be kind to each other. There is too little love in the world. We should not waste a drop of it . . . Now, could you spare the time to walk me down to the pine wood?"

She gave him her arm and they walked slowly down the paved walk to the shelter of the pines. The guards, vigilant and edgy, fanned out to encircle them. Monsignor Malachy O'Rahilly, who had just arrived for his morning visit, was tempted to follow them. Then, watching them together, animated but relaxed, like father and daughter, he thought better of it and sat down at the stone table to await his master's return.

Katrina Peters's dinner party was staged on the terrace of the Palazzo Lanfranco, with the rooftops of old Rome for backdrop and a pergola of vines for canopy. Her waiters were hand-picked from the best agency. Her cook was borrowed from Adela Sandberg, who reported Italian fashion for the glossiest of New York fashion magazines. Her guests were chosen to indulge her own taste for exotic encounters and her husband's talent for making a commentator's capital out of them.

To confront Sergio Salviati and Tove Lundberg she had chosen the Soviet Ambassador and his wife. The Ambassador was reputed to be a formidable Arabist who had spent five years in Damascus. His wife was a concert pianist of high reputation. For a partner to Matt Neylan—who, according to Nicol, had more than earned his place at table—she had invited the latest arrival at the American Academy, an attractive thirty-year-old who had just produced a highly praised thesis on the status of women in the mystery religions. To these she added Adela Sandberg for colourful gossip, Menachem Avriel because his wife was away in Israel and he enjoyed Adela Sandberg. Then, for good measure, she added Pierre Labandie, who drew satirical cartoons for *Le Canard Enchaîné,* and Lola Martinelli, who had made rich marriages and profitable divorces into a serial art-form. The fact that she was a lawyer in her own right added a certain patina to the product.

The ceremonies opened with champagne and a *pavane* around the terrace to admire the view, identify the cupolas and turrets, black against the skyline. During this prelude, Katrina Peters moved lightly but warily among her guests, bridging awkward gaps in the talk, explaining one guest to another, plagued always by those banes of Roman intercourse, the limp handshake, the muttered introductions, the almost furtive confessions of identity and profession.

This time she was lucky. Matt Neylan, trained to diplomacy, was easy and talkative. The Russian was hearty and opinionated. They took care of Tove Lundberg and the lady of the mysteries, each of whom was an agreeable and easy talker.

Nicol Peters took the opportunity for a first quick exchange with Salviati and Menachem Avriel on the terrorist threat.

"I hear you've got almost an armed camp out there in Castelli."

"We're protected." Salviati tried to evade the discussion. "We have to be in any case, threat or no threat."

"The threat is real." Avriel was an old hand at managing the Press. "The group has been identified."

"Off the record, I understand Mossad had already penetrated the group?"

"No comment," said Avriel.

"I still can't understand the political thinking behind it. The relations between Islam and the Vatican are at least stable. What's to gain by assassinating the Pontiff?"

"A statement." Menachem Avriel gestured emphatically. "Israel is a plague carrier. Any contact or compromise means death."

"But why not knock off Salviati here? He owns the place. He's a known Zionist."

"Counterproductive. Sergio treats a lot of wealthy Arabs. He's the first and best clinic between Karachi and London . . . Why lose his services? Why make enemies of the money men in Islam?"

"It's feasible; but I feel there's something missing in the logic."

Menachem Avriel laughed.

"Haven't you learned yet that there's always a term or two missing in Farsi logic? You start off with a set of clear propositions, on flat and open ground, then—hey presto!—you're winging with the bats on Magic Mountain!"

"I'm not sure I like our own logic any better," said Sergio Salviati.

"Who cares about logic?" Adela Sandberg swept in to take control of the small conclave. "Love comes in; logic goes out the window! Kiss me, Menachem! You may kiss me, too, Sergio Salviati!"

At the far end of the terrace, the Soviet Ambassador was deep in conversation with Tove Lundberg.

"You work with this Pope . . . what is he like? How does he react with you?"

"I have to say he is, even now, a very formidable man. Sometimes I think of him as an old olive tree, gnarled and twisted, still putting out leaves and fruit . . . But inside the tree is a vulnerable, loving man trying to claw his way out before it is too late. With me he is very humble, very grateful for the simplest service. But,"—she smiled and shrugged—"it is like playing with a drowsy lion.

I have the feeling that if he woke in a bad temper he would eat me in one gulp!"

"I am told there have been threats against his life."

"That's true. The clinic is under guard day and night."

"That troubles him?"

"He is troubled for the staff, for the other patients, but for himself not at all."

"You have to understand something, Excellency." Matt Neylan, with the lady of the mysteries on his arm, drifted into their talk. "This man, Leo XIV, is an archetype, a throwback. He refuses all dialogue with today's world."

"I don't agree," Tove Lundberg challenged him brusquely. "I'm not even a believer, in spite of the fact that my father was a Lutheran pastor. But I see the man every day for post-operative counselling. I find him open, self-questioning, always preoccupied by the question of change within the Church."

"I believe you." Matt Neylan was bland as honey. "But do you have any Latin about you?"

"A little," said Tove Lundberg.

"My husband is a very good Latin scholar," said the pianist. "He is fluent in ten languages."

"Then he'll have no difficulty with this little proverb: *Lupus languebat, monachus tuncesse volebat; sed cum convaluit, lupus ut ante fuit.*"

The Ambassador laughed and rendered the proverb in heavily accented English.

"When the wolf was sick he wanted to be a monk. When he recovered he was still a wolf . . . And you are saying, Mr. Neylan, this is what will happen to your Pope?"

"I'll lay long odds on it."

"Pardon?"

"I'm sure, almost a hundred per cent sure, he'll revert to exactly what he was."

"Five thousand lire says you're wrong," said Tove Lundberg.

Matt Neylan grinned.

"You've got a bet, ma'am! And if you win I'll throw in the best dinner in this city."

"It's hard to find a really first-class restaurant nowadays." Katrina Peters slipped quietly into the group.

"It's a damned sight harder to find a first-class man!" said Lola Martinelli.

"Don't give up yet, Lola," said Katrina Peters. "Matt Neylan here has just come onto the market—mint-new and beautifully trained!"

"I got him first," said the lady of mysteries. "And we're in the same business!"

They sat, the round dozen of them, at a round table laid with Florentine linen, Venetian glass, Buccellati silver and porcelain from the house of Ginori. Nicol Peters offered a toast of welcome: "This house is your house. Whatever is said here tonight is spoken between friends, in trust and confidence. *Salute!*"

Then the food was offered and the talk began to circulate, more loudly and more freely as the evening went on. Nicol Peters watched and listened and picked up the scraps of dialogue that later would fit into the mosaic of his column, "A View From My Terrace". This was the heart of his work. This was what they paid him for. Any fool could report the news: that the Pope washed feet on Maundy Thursday, that Cardinal Clemens had censured another German theologian. But it took a bright and free-ranging fellow like Nicol Peters to read the Richter scales and say bravely that an earthquake would happen on Friday.

The man from Moscow was both industrious and entertaining. He was concentrating his attention on Matt Neylan who, launched auspiciously into the world of fashionable women, was dispensing lavish doses of Irish charm.

"So I'd like your opinion, Mr. Neylan . . . What role do you see for Russian Orthodoxy in the policies of the next decade?"

"Outside Russia," said Matt Neylan judiciously, "in the Christian communities of the West, it has to create a role for itself, in theological, philosophical, socio-political debate. That's not going to be easy. Its intellectual life has been in stasis since the Great Schism in the eleventh century. Politically, you people have held it captive since the revolution . . . In spite of that, it still remains closest to the spirit of the early Eastern fathers. It has much to offer the West. For you, it may well be the strongest buffer you have against the expansion of Islam within the Soviet Union itself . . . I'm sure I don't have to tell you the statistical extent of that expansion."

"And you dealt with these matters at the Secretariat of State?"

"Not personally. Not directly. The *peritus* in this area is Monsignor Vlasov, whom you may have met . . ."

"I have not, but I should like to do so."

"Under other circumstances I should have offered to arrange a contact. Now, as you see, I am no longer a member of the club."

"Do you regret that?"

"What's to regret?" The lady of the mysteries patted Neylan's hand approvingly. "Don't they say the late vintage makes the sweetest wine!"

Over the dessert, Nicol Peters turned suddenly to Menachem Avriel and said, apropos of nothing at all: "I'm still worried about the logic."

"And . . . ?"

"I think I've got the missing proposition."

"Which is?"

"Double-think, double-shuffle. What you called 'winging with the bats on Magic Mountain'."

"Spell it for me slowly, Nico."

"It's a fair assumption—though you can't admit it—that Mossad had penetrated the Sword of Islam."

"And what follows from that?"

"A possible scenario. The group puts out a phoney plan. The Vatican, the Republic, Mossad, all make dispositions to deal with it. Maybe they're even handed a phoney assassin who is arrested or killed. Then they don't need the Pope or Salviati. They've got what they really want—a *casus belli,* a reason to stage any public coup they want, from kidnap to hijacking an airliner. It's a thought, isn't it?"

"A damned uncomfortable one," said Sergio Salviati.

Menachem Avriel shrugged off the notion. He was, after all, a diplomat skilled in social lying. Nicol Peters let the subject drop and addressed himself to the brandy. He was after all a newsman, who understood that truth lay often at the bottom of the pool and you had to stir up the mud to reach it.

When they rose from table, he drew Sergio Salviati away from the others for a private interrogation.

"I'd like to make this as simple as I can. I get the daily bulletins on the Pope's progress. Anything you can add to them without a breach of ethics?"

"Not too much. He's making very good progress. His mental faculties are unimpaired—which I guess is what you're driving at."

"Will he be able to function fully in office?"

"If he follows the regimen, yes. He will probably function better than in the immediate past."

"Differently? I caught the tag end of the talk between Tove and Matt Neylan."

"You can't quote me on this."

"I won't."

"Tove is right. The man is greatly changed. I believe he will continue so."

"Could you call it a 'conversion' in the religious sense?"

"That's a matter of semantics. I prefer to limit myself to a clinical vocabulary . . . Now could I ask you a question?"

"Go ahead."

"Your scenario of the phoney assassin; do you believe it?"

"I think it's very feasible."

"Suppose," said Salviati carefully, "just suppose the assassin had already been identified."

"And taken out?"

"Suppose that, too, if you want."

"Anything else I could suppose?"

"That there had been no reaction from the Sword of Islam."

Nicol Peters pursed his lips and then let out a long, low whistle of surprise.

"In that case, then I would say, fasten your seat belts. You could be in for a very bumpy ride! Let me know what really happens, won't you?"

"You'll probably know it before I do," said Sergio Salviati. "The way my life runs, I never get time to read the morning papers!"

After that it was playtime. As the night mist rolled in from the Tiber, they moved into the *salone*. Matt Neylan sat down at the piano and sang Neapolitan songs in a smooth Irish tenor. Thus encouraged, the Ambassador's wife sat down and unleashed a whole torrent of music—Chopin, Liszt, Tchaikovsky. Even Katrina Peters, most critical of hostesses, had to agree that the evening had been a success. Nicol Peters was preoccupied. Even instinct told him that something was about to break. He could not for the life of him define what it was.

IX

OMAR Asnan's villa on the Old Appian Way had cost him a mint of money. Situated on the most expensive stretch of the ancient road, between the tomb of Cecilia Metella and the crossroad to Tor Carbone, it was a hotch-potch of constructions that dated from Roman times to the twentieth century.

A high blank wall, topped with broken glass, hid it from the road and from the open fields of the *campagna* behind it. The garden with its swimming-pool and tubs of flowering plants was shaded by tall cypresses and spreading pines. It was also patrolled at night by an armed watchman and a pair of Dobermans.

One special feature of the house was a square watchtower, built around a chimney, from which it was possible to survey the Appia Antica in both direc-tions, watch the shepherds grazing their herds in the *campagna* and look clear across the rooftops of other villas to the apartment blocks of EUR.

The second feature, an unexpected bonus for Omar Asnan, was the cellar, vaulted and bricked in reticulated stone, which dated back to the same period as the nearby Circus of Maxentius. There was nothing unusual about the cellar itself, but a loose slab in the floor had revealed a set of ten steps that led to a tunnel. The tunnel, dug into the friable tufa rock, ran fifty metres across the *campagna* and opened into a large, circular chamber lined with great earthen-ware pots which had once been used to store grain. The air was foul, but the place was bone dry, and it was the simplest thing in the world to install a ventilating system with intake and outlet hidden in the garden shrubbery.

So, Omar Asnan—thanks to Allah, the just and the merciful!—had found himself endowed with a storeroom for special merchandise like guns, grenades and drugs, a conference room hidden from prying eyes, and a safe house to hold friends or enemies. It was here that he met with his four most trusted lieuten-ants to discuss the disappearance of Miriam Latif from the International Clinic.

They sat on cushions set about a carpet, two on either side, with Omar

Asnan presiding. He was a small, dark man, put together as neatly as a mani-
kin, with eloquent hands and a ready smile. His speech was brisk and businesslike.

"This is what we have been able to confirm in twenty-four hours. At three in
the afternoon I myself called Miriam at the clinic to set up a meeting here. She
agreed. She said she could easily arrange the time off at the end of the day. She
would drive into Rome to do some shopping and see me on the way back."

He turned to the man on his right.

"You remember all this, Khalid. You were here with me."

"I remember."

"We arranged to have dinner here, in the villa. She never arrived."

"Clearly she was—"

"Please!" Asnan raised a warning. "Please, let us discuss what we know, not
what we think we know. Miriam never arrived here. Round about ten p.m. I
drove into the club to pass the word, that probably our operation was blown.
You all got that message, yes?"

There was a murmur of assent.

"Now let me tell you what I have since established, through our various
contacts in the police and at the airport. Miriam's car was found in the long-
term parking bay at Fiumicino. The hospital claims—and I have seen the
message taken down by the switchboard operator—that Miriam called from
the airport at seven p.m. to say that her mother was very ill and she was leaving
immediately for Beirut on Middle East Airlines. I personally have checked with
our friends in the airline office. A woman calling herself Miriam Latif did buy a
ticket, did present a Lebanese passport, did check on to the aircraft. The only
problem is that this woman was veiled in traditional style. Miriam Latif never
wore a veil . . . More than that, I have confirmed with Beirut that no one
presented Miriam Latif's passport or a landing card with her name on it.
Miriam herself made no contact with her parents, who are both in excellent
health . . . So, my friends, what are we to conclude?"

The man who called himself Khalid answered for everyone.

"I think it is obvious. She must have been under surveillance. She was
intercepted and abducted on the way into Rome. Someone else drove her car to
the airport and booked out in her name to Beirut."

"Why go to all that trouble?"

"To delay what we have now begun—the search for her."

"Is she alive or dead?"

"My guess is that she's alive."

"Reason?"

"Why go through all the charade at the airport? Much simpler to kill her and
dump the body."

"Next question: who is holding her?"

"Mossad, without a doubt."

"Why?"

"Interrogation. They know we exist. They must have had some word of our
plans; otherwise why would there be that large concentration of forces at the
clinic?"

"How would they know?"

"They would know because they were told."

"You are saying there is a traitor among us?"

"Yes."

"Precisely," said Omar Asnan. "And to unmask that traitor it was necessary to sacrifice Miriam Latif. I regret that very much."

There was dead silence in the chamber. The four men looked at each other and then at Omar Asnan, who sat calm and benign, enjoying their discomfiture. Then he reached into his breast pocket and brought out a pen and a small leather-covered notebook. He opened the notebook and took up again the thread of his discourse.

"You know how we are organised. We here are five. Below us are groups of three. Each group is self-contained. Each person within it has contact with only one person from another group. Thus treachery cannot spread easily. Only we five knew about Miriam Latif and our plans for her. Only one of you knew that I had summoned her here." In a gesture almost playful, he held the lip of the pen against Khalid's temple. "Only you, Khalid, friend of my heart!"

He pressed the clip of the pen. There was a small, sharp sound and Khalid slumped to the floor. A thin trickle of blood and fluid oozed from the hole in his head. Omar Asnan said curtly: "Pick him up. Put him in the big jar, the glazed one with the lid. Seal the lid with cement. Then spray this place. Already, it stinks of Jew! We'll meet upstairs when you've finished."

In his office at the clinic, Sergio Salviati was conferring with Cardinal Matteo Agostini, Secretary of State. After a late night and a piece of simple surgery that went suddenly and dangerously wrong, his patience was wearing thin.

"Understand me, Eminence. I am talking in clinical terms about the welfare of my patient. He has said he will abide by your judgement . . . I know you have other concerns, but these are not my affair."

"His Holiness does not need my consent to do anything."

"He wants your approval, your support against possible critics."

"Is that a clinical matter?"

"Yes it is!" Salviati was curt. "At this stage of cardiac recovery, everything is a clinical matter—every unnecessary stress, every shock or anxiety. If you don't believe me, I can show you how those things read on a monitor screen."

"I believe you, Professor." Agostini was totally at ease. "So I shall make immediate arrangements for the transfer of His Holiness to Cardinal Drexel's villa. The security there will be our affair. I take it you will still be able to provide adequate medical supervision?"

"His own physician should supervise him on a day to day basis. I am close by for ready reference. I shall, in any case, see him at the end of the month. Tove Lundberg is a constant visitor to the villa. However, I would suggest you employ a good physiotherapist to supervise His Holiness in daily exercise. I can recommend such a one."

"Thank you. Now I have questions of my own. Is His Holiness fit to resume his normal duties?"

"He will be, after an adequate convalescence."

"How long is that?"

"Eight weeks for the ribcage to heal. Six months at least of graduated activity. Remember, he is not a young man. But since he is not engaged in heavy physical work—yes, he can certainly function quite well. There are, however, a couple of caveats: no long ceremonies, Masses in St. Peter's, carrying the cross around the Coliseum, that sort of thing. I know you have to have him on stage from time to time, but get him on and off as quickly as possible. Second caution: no long-haul air travel for at least six months."

"We'll do what we can to manage him," said Agostini. "Next question: his mind? Will he be . . . stable? God knows, he's never been an easy man to deal with and we know that he is emotionally fragile at this moment."

"Fragile, yes. But he understands the condition and deals with it. Tove Lundberg is full of admiration for him. She has volunteered to stay close to the case for as long as she is needed."

"My last questions then. Is he changed? How is he changed? And how permanently?"

"Certainly he is changed. In the old days the patient underwent the 'experience of the God'—the *metanoia* which was the crisis point of the therapy. The experience, however it was engineered, certainly involved terror, trauma and the shock of survival. Your man has been through all that . . . It sounds perhaps overdramatised, but . . ."

"I see the drama," said Agostini quietly. "I wonder how it will go in public performance."

"There, I'm afraid, I can't help you." Salviati laughed and spread his hands in a gesture of helplessness. "I'm only the plumber. Prophecy is the Church's business."

"So, Anton, for better or for worse, you have me as house guest."

"I can't tell you how happy I am, Holiness."

They were seated in his favourite corner of the garden, under the pergola of vines, sipping iced lemonade which Tove Lundberg had sent out to them. Drexel was flushed with pleasure. The Pontiff seemed to have certain misgivings.

"Hold a moment, my friend! It's not only me. There's a whole retinue. Security men, valet, physiotherapist, visitors I can't refuse. Are you sure you can cope with all this?"

"Absolutely sure. You will be lodged in the villetta, the small villa at the lower boundary of the estate. It's comfortable and private, with its own garden and orchard. Also it is easy to protect. The security men have looked at it, and they see no problems. There are quarters for your valet. Your own suite has a *salone,* study and dining-room. You will have my cook. I'm bringing her up from Rome."

"Anton, I really believe you are enjoying all this fuss."

"Of course I am! Do you realise that the first and last pope to visit my villa was Clement VIII, Ippolito Aldobrandini, in 1600? His nephew Piero built that big palazzo in Frascati . . . But imagine what a papal visit must have been in those days—with carriage drivers, outriders, grooms, men at arms, courtiers and their women . . ." He laughed. "Given more time, I'm sure we could have arranged at least some pageantry for you."

"To the devil with pageants." The Pontiff rejected the notion with a gesture.

"I am coming because I want to be a countryman again. I want to shed my white cassock and put on work clothes and busy myself with simple things like rust on the tomatoes and whether the lettuce are hearting properly. I won't need a secretary, because I don't propose to open a book or a letter, though I would like to listen to some good music."

"And so you shall. I'll have a player installed and some tapes and discs sent down for you."

"And I want to talk, Anton. I want us to talk like friends, looking back on a lifetime, but looking forward, too, to the world the children will inherit. I want to share your family, though I confess that scares me somewhat. I am not sure I have the skill or the energy to cope with them."

"Please! Don't worry about that. You don't have to cope with anything. You won't have to learn anything, except how to manage yourself. You will arrive. I'll introduce you. They'll welcome you. You give them your blessing. All that is five minutes, no more. Then you forget about them . . . You will find, as I did, that they are all very intelligent creatures, anxious to be about their own affairs. When they are ready to approach you they will and they will establish the communication much more quickly than you ever could. All they need is your smile and your touch to reassure them. Remember that. Touch is very important. They are sensitive to any sign of revulsion or even of timidity. They are not timid themselves. They are brave and strong and highly intelligent."

"And they have a Nonno who loves them."

"That too, I suppose. But they give more than they get."

"I have a confession to make to you, Anton. Suddenly I am afraid of leaving this place. I am protected here against pain and discomfort. I am counselled like a novice. I know that if something goes wrong, Salviati will know exactly what to do about it . . . you understand?"

"I think so." Drexel seemed to dredge up the words from deep inside himself. "I lie awake at night and wonder how Brother Death will come for me. I pray that he will arrange the meeting decently, without mess or fuss. But if he chooses otherwise—Boh!—to whom do I turn? The children can't help. The women sleep far away from my quarters . . . So, yes! I know how you feel. It's the solitude of the aged and the ailing. But since we have been given more than most, we should bear it with more grace."

"I am reproved," said Leo the Pontiff with wry humour. "Next time I will find myself a more complaisant confessor."

"No one is better placed to do so," Drexel rounded off the joke.

"Now I need some advice." The Pontiff laid on the table two small packages wrapped in tissue. "These are gifts from me to Salviati and to Tove Lundberg. I'd like to have your opinion of them. I thought a lot about Salviati. He's a brilliant, haunted man. I wanted something that would give him a moment of joy." He unwrapped the first package to reveal, laid on a bed of silk in a velvet box, an old silver *mezuzah*. "My clever secretary O'Rahilly chose this for me. It dates from the sixteenth century and is said to have been brought back from Jerusalem. The provenance is there, written in Hebrew. Do you think it will please him?"

"I'm sure it will."

"And for Tove Lundberg, this." He brought out a disc of beaten gold, incised with runic letters and hung on a golden chain. "This, O'Rahilly tells me, came originally from Istanbul, and is attributed to the first Vikings who found their way down the river systems of Russia into Turkey."

"O'Rahilly has very good taste—and obviously a good knowledge of antiquities."

"For that he depends on the Sub-prefect of the Vatican Museum, who is also an Irishman! I am told they drink together on occasion."

"I am told," said Drexel, "that he may drink too much and too often. In your present situation, that could be more dangerous for Your Holiness than for him."

"He's a good man, a kind man. He is a very good secretary."

"But not necessarily a discreet one. You may have to ask yourself whether you can afford him."

"Or whether in fact there is anyone I can afford. Is that what you are telling me, Anton?"

"To be blunt, Holiness, yes. We are all dispensable—even you. And that is my point. When you are restored, as you will be, when you begin the battle to rebuild the city of God, you will have less to fear from your enemies than from the slothful and indifferent who will never fight you but will wait, comfortable and happy, until you are dead."

"And how do I deal with that, dear Eminence?"

"Like any good countryman, Holiness. You plough the furrow and cast the seed—and wait for God to provide the harvest!"

The departure of the Pontiff from the clinic was a much more ceremonious affair than his arrival. This time there were three limousines; one for the Pontiff, another for the Secretary of State, a third for the prelates of the Papal Household. The men of the Vigilanza had their own fast cars, at front and rear and on the flanks of the motorcade. The Polizia Stradale provided a motorcycle escort. Barricades had been erected along the route from the clinic to Drexel's villa and sharpshooters were located at danger points along the winding road.

The Pontiff's farewells to Salviati and to Tove Lundberg had been made in the privacy of his room. His gifts had pleased them both. Salviati had told him that he would save the *mezuzah* for the house he planned to build on the site of an old farmhouse he had just bought near Albano. Tove Lundberg bent her head and asked that he himself invest her with the runic talisman. When he had done so, he joined hands with both of them and said his farewells.

"I have never in my life felt so poor as I do now. I have not even the words to thank you. The best I can do is leave you God's own gift: peace on your houses. *Shalom!*"

"*Shalom aleichem,*" said Sergio Salviati.

"You aren't rid of me yet," said Tove Lundberg. "I have to introduce you to my daughter."

Then she settled him in the wheelchair and pushed him along the corridor and out into the driveway, where the staff were assembled to bid him goodbye.

As the motorcade swept through the gates and out on to the open road, he felt a sudden stifling rush of emotion. This was truly resurrection day. Lazarus was out of the tomb, freed of his graveclothes and moving among the living who were strung out along the roadside, waving flags and flowers and leafy twigs torn from the hedgerows. The cry they raised was always the same: *"Eviva il papa"*, "Long live the Pope". And the Pope devoutly hoped their wish might come true.

Because of the risk which everyone knew, the police escort set a fast pace for the motorcade and the drivers were forced to slew sharply round the bends of the hillside. The sharp motions put a strain on the Pontiff's back and chest muscles, so that by the time they reached Drexel's villa, he was sweating with pain and nausea. As he was helped from the limousine he whispered to his driver: "Don't go. Stay with me. Steady me."

The driver stood with him, holding his arm while he breathed in deep gulps of mountain air and focused his eyes on the serried ranks of orchard trees and vines and the tall cypresses marching like pike men along the contours of the hills. Drexel, tactful as always, hung back until he was ready, then led him on a quick circuit of the women of the colonia, mothers and teachers and therapists.

Then the children were brought to him, a strange shambling procession, some in wheelchairs, some walking, others supported on sticks or crutches. For a moment he felt as though his unstable emotions would betray him; but he managed to contain them and, in a display of tenderness that amazed even Drexel, he embraced each one, touching their cheeks, kissing them, letting them lead him as they wished from one to the other. The last one of all was presented by Drexel himself.

"And this is Britte. She wants me to tell you she'd like to paint your portrait."

"Tell her, tell her . . ."

His voice faltered. He could not bear the sight of that beautiful child-woman face perched on the spidery body.

"Tell her yourself." Drexel's voice steadied him like a military command. "She understands everything."

"I will sit for you every day, Britte, my dear. And when the picture is done I will take it to the Vatican and hang it in my study."

Then he reached out and drew her to him, wishing he had the faith to command the miracle that would make her whole and beautiful.

On the terraces of the Palazzo Lanfranco, Nicol and Katrina Peters were taking coffee. Nicol was sorting through the facsimile messages which had accumulated overnight on the machine.

"The Pope's being discharged from hospital this morning. His condition is satisfactory. His convalescence will be supervised by the papal physician . . . we all know that . . . Here's something odd. It comes from the Arab news agency. Reuters and Associated Press have picked it up. It's captioned: 'Mysterious Disappearance. Muslim girl feared abducted. Miriam Latif, an attractive twenty-four-year-old laboratory technician is employed at Professor Salviati's clinic in Castelli, where the reigning Pope, Leo XIV, is a patient. On Tuesday last she asked for an afternoon's leave to go shopping in Rome and then keep a dinner engagement with a friend.

" 'She did not keep the dinner date. At seven in the evening the clinic received a telephone call, supposedly from Miriam Latif. She said she was at

Fiumicino airport and was leaving immediately for Beirut because her mother was seriously ill.

" 'Police enquiries have confirmed that a woman using Miriam Latif's name did buy a ticket to Beirut on Middle East Airlines and the same woman, heavily veiled in traditional fashion, presented Miriam Latif's passport and boarded the aircraft. Arrived in Beirut, the woman used another passport to go through customs and immigration and then disappeared. Miriam Latif's parents, who live in Byblos, north of Beirut, were contacted. Both are in perfect health. They know nothing of their daughter's movements and have not heard from her.

" 'Late today, airport police discovered Miriam Latif's car in the long-term parking lot at Fiumicino. Forensic tests are being conducted on the vehicle. The director of the clinic, Professor Sergio Salviati, describes Miriam as a highly competent and valued member of his staff. He says that all members of staff take occasional short absences for shopping and personal visits to Rome. No objection is raised, provided permission is obtained and a substitute is in place. Miriam's room-mate and her friends on the staff describe her as cheerful and conscientious. Asked whether Miriam Latif had any political affiliations, Dr. Salviati said he knew of none and that in any case Miriam Latif had been vetted by Italian authorities before she was permitted to take up appointment under the training scheme run by the International Clinic.

" 'Miriam's current boyfriend, Mr. Omar Asnan, with whom she was to dine on the night of her disappearance, is deeply distressed and admits frankly that he entertains fears for her safety. Mr. Asnan is an Iranian national who runs a prosperous import-export business between Italy and the Middle East . . .'

"And that," said Nicol Peters, "tells me exactly what I wanted to know."

"Do you think you could explain it to me?"

"At the party, Salviati was dancing on eggshells, with 'suppose this . . . suppose that'. It's all here! We knew the Pope was under threat of assassination. The Sword of Islam obviously had a plant in the clinic—Miriam Latif. Mossad removed her, alive or dead—who knows? Now the Sword of Islam are beginning the 'mystery and martyr' process."

"And what good does that do them?"

"It covers their present activities and prepares a climate for whatever reprisals they're planning. And, believe me, there will be reprisals!"

"So what are you going to do about it?"

"The usual. Talk around: to the Italians, the Israelis, Salviati, the Vatican, all the Muslim Ambassadors, including the Iranians. Also I'll try this Mr. Omar Asnan, the grieving lover."

"You be careful, lover boy!"

"Am I not always? Is there any more coffee?"

Katrina Peters poured the coffee and then began her own recital of affairs, which she claimed were much more important than the politics of terror and theology. As he grew older and wiser in the ways of a very old city, Nicol Peters was inclined to agree with her.

"The Russians ask us to dine at the Embassy on the 25th. She wants me to help her choose an autumn and winter wardrobe for Rome. There's a nice little profit already! Salviati wrote a very warm note. He enjoyed himself. Tove

Lundberg sent a piece of Danish porcelain, which was sweet and unexpected. I like that woman!"

"That's a rare compliment from you!" Nicol Peters grinned at her over his coffee cup.

"However, I'm not so sure that I like Micheline Mangos-O'Hara!"

"And who might that be?"

"Our lady of the mysteries, from the American Academy. I can't believe the name either. It seems her mother was Greek, her father Irish."

"Like Lafcadio Hearn?"

"And who, pray, is he?"

"A journalist, like me, but he lived in a more spacious age. He married a Japanese. Forget it. What about Mangos-O'Hara?"

"She's giving a lecture on the mystery religions. We're invited."

"Decline!"

"I have. But she also says that Matt Neylan is the most interesting male she's met in years. His note says he found her great fun and he might well invite her to move in with him for the rest of her stay in Rome!"

"That's rushing the fences, I'd say; but he does have a lot of time to make up." Nicol's thoughts were elsewhere. "He also called me. The Russians are wooing him, obviously because of his Vatican background. He's bidden to lunch at the Embassy and the Ambassador has floated the idea of a trip to Moscow to meet members of the Orthodox hierarchy. Matt is not all that keen. He says he's had a bellyful of the God-business and wants a good long swallow of the wine of life! Which means he's likely to get a bellyful of reality. He's got a lot to learn."

"And there'll be a lot of women dying to teach him."

"Why not? He's intelligent. He's fun. He really can sing—and even after all those years in the cloth he's not a tenor castrato."

"Lola Martinelli's got her eye on him."

"How do you know that?"

"She called to ask whether I thought Matt would be interested in a job as her private secretary. I told her to ask the man himself."

"And?"

"And she did and he said in his best and sweetest brogue: 'Dear lady, I'm a gentleman of independent means, so I don't need the money. I have many talents, but I'd make a lousy secretary. But if there's anything else on offer I'd be happy to discuss it with you over dinner at a convenient time and place.'"

"Well, if it's not true, it's at least *ben trovato*. It sounds like Matt. What did Lola say?"

"She told him to go to hell. Then she rang me and told me he was just another of those ex-priests who get too big for their boots."

"Good for her!"

"That's what I thought; but let's keep Matt on the guest list. He can always sing for his supper."

"True, my love. True. Now I'd better settle down and work out a line of attack on this Miriam Latif story."

* * *

The first persons to greet the Pontiff in his new lodging were his valet, Pietro, and an apple-cheeked young woman wearing the blue veil of the Little Company of Mary. She had a broad smile and a no-nonsense humour and she introduced herself as Sister Pauline.

"His Eminence brought me up from Rome to look after you. I come from Australia, which explains my bad Italian. The first thing you're going to do is get into bed and rest for a couple of hours. You're pale and clammy and your pulse is racing with all this excitement . . . Pietro here can help you undress. I'll be back to settle you and give you some medication . . . His Eminence said you might be difficult; but you won't be, will you? I've got an infallible cure for difficult patients. I just start talking and keep talking . . ."

"I surrender." He raised a weak hand in protest. "You can stop talking now. I'm ready for bed."

Ten minutes later he was settled, with the smell of fresh linen about him, listening to the shrilling of the cicadas in the garden outside. The last sound he heard was Sister Pauline explaining to Pietro.

"Sure I can handle him! He's a pussycat. Our old parish priest would have eaten him for breakfast. He was a holy terror, that one!"

When he woke it was late afternoon. He felt calm and relaxed, eager to explore this small corner of a world from which he had been excluded for so many years. On the table beside his bed was a small silver bell. When he rang it, Pietro appeared, with towels, dressing-gown, slippers—and orders from on high.

"Sister says I'm to shave you, help you to shower and dress, then take you for a stroll. They've started harvesting the grapes. His Eminence is down in the vineyards. He suggests you might like to walk down and watch."

"Let's do that, Pietro." Suddenly he was eager as a school boy. "And Monsignor O'Rahilly told me you've brought civilian clothes for me."

"I have, Holiness." He looked faintly dubious. "I know they fit, because I gave the Monsignore the measurements. The style he chose himself."

He laid the clothes out on the bed for his master's inspection—cotton slacks, open-necked shirt, loafers and sporty-looking pullover. The Pontiff hesitated for a moment and then surrendered with a laugh.

"Who's to know, Pietro! If there's any scandal we'll blame His Eminence."

"Wait until you see how he dresses, Holiness. He looks like any old peasant."

"Perhaps that's what we should do, Pietro: turn all our princes into peasants —myself included."

When he stepped into the open air and stood looking down over the fall of the rich land, he was suddenly aware of how much of his life had been spent in cloisters and chapter rooms and corridors that smelt of carbolic and beeswax and chapels that reeked of old incense. Worse still was to think how much precious time he had wasted on paperwork and arguments worn threadbare by centuries of sterile debate. In Vatican City and in Castel Gandolfo he was a prisoner, let out for ceremonial occasions and so-called missionary journeys, where every move was plotted for him and every word written in advance . . .

Suddenly here he was, on a hillside in Castelli, watching the grape pickers moving up and down the vine-rows, tossing the fruit into baskets, emptying the baskets into the cart hitched to the yellow tractor that would haul them off to the crushing vats. Everyone was out there: the villa staff, the farm hands, teachers, therapists, Sister Pauline. Even the children were busy with whatever task they could perform. Those in wheelchairs trundled them between the vines. Those on crutches leaned against the upright stakes and picked within arm's stretch. Only Britte was not picking. She sat, perched—or was it laced?—precariously on a stool, with an easel and paintbox, sketching with a brush clamped between her teeth.

The scene was so lively, so full of human detail, that the Pontiff stood for a long while contemplating the simple wonder of it—and the bleak futility of much of his own existence. This was where the people of God were to be found. This was how they were to be found, doing everyday things to the rhythms of a workaday world.

He, Leo XIV, Bishop of Rome, once called Ludovico Gadda, what did he do? Well, he ruled the Church, which meant that most days he sat at his desk and received people, read papers, wrote papers, took part in occasional pageantry, made a speech every Sunday in St. Peter's Square—which everybody heard but nobody understood, because the echo and the feedback across St. Peter's Square made the whole thing ridiculous . . . As well, therefore, not to waste a moment of this beautiful, this specially vintaged, day . . .

With Pietro supporting him on the steps of the terraces, he walked slowly down to mingle with the pickers. They saluted him as he passed, but did not pause in their tasks. This was serious business, there was money at the end of it. One of the men offered him a swig of wine. He took the bottle, tilted it to his mouth and drank, gratefully. He wiped his mouth with the back of his hand and passed back the bottle with a word of thanks. The man grinned and settled back to work.

Finally, at the end of the third row, they came upon Drexel, sitting at the wheel of a tractor waiting to move as soon as the cart was filled with grapes. He stepped down to greet the Pontiff.

"You're looking better, Holiness."

"I should be, Anton. I had a wonderful rest this afternoon. And thank you for providing me with a nurse."

Drexel laughed.

"I've known Sister Pauline since she came to Rome. She's a real character. She's even tamed me! When I first visited the community she asked me what a Cardinal Protector was supposed to do. I told her: to protect the interests of the Congregation. She looked me straight in the eye and told me in that horrible Italian of hers: 'Well, for a start, here's a whole list of things in which we're not getting protection—and here's another list where the protection we're getting is quite inadequate!' She was right, too. We've been good friends ever since."

"What can I do to help here?"

"For the moment, nothing. Just look around and relax. You could ride with me on the tractor, but it might shake you up too much. Pietro, why don't you take His Holiness into the orchard and pick some fruit for dinner. We eat country-style tonight—and another thing! You have to meet Rosa. She's got a pocketful of medals she wants you to bless—and our dinner depends on how well you do it!"

On the way back he faltered a little and Pietro scolded him.

"Please, Holiness! This is not an Olympic race. You do not have to prove you are an athlete. You never were. You never will be. So take it easy. *Piano, piano!* One step at a time."

They halted for a while to watch Britte at work on her canvas. She was totally absorbed, as if the contorted physics of the operation permitted no break in her concentration. Yet the picture that was growing under the brush was one of quite extraordinary vigour and colour. With the brush clamped between her teeth and her head bobbing between the palette and the canvas, she looked like some grotesque bird, suddenly invaded by the spirit of a master painter. Pietro, only half aware of what he was saying, uttered the poignant plea.

"Why? Why does this have to happen? Sometimes I wonder if God gets overworked and goes crazy for a while. How else could he commit such cruelty?"

At another time in another place, Leo the Pontiff would have felt obliged to reprove him for blasphemy, or at least to read him a homily on the mysterious ways of the Almighty. This time he simply shook his head sadly.

"I don't know, Pietro. Why is an old donkey like myself allowed to survive and this one condemned to imprisonment and early death?"

"Is that what you will say to them on Sunday?"

Leo the Pontiff turned swiftly to face him.

"What do you mean?"

"Nothing, Holiness—except that on Sunday the folk here are expecting you to say a short Mass for them and give them a little sermon. A few words only, of course—His Eminence was very clear about that."

And there it was, neatly dressed up as the courtesy of the house—the first test of the new man, Lazarus *redivivus*. It was the simplest and most traditional of Christian customs: the visiting bishop presided at the Eucharistic table, spoke the homily, affirmed the unity of all the scattered brethren in the bond of common faith. As a custom he could not evade it; as a courtesy he could not refuse it.

But Pietro's question pinned him more tightly yet. All his audience, women, therapists and children alike, were faced with the same paradox. All looked to him—the infallible interpreter of revealed truth!—to explain the paradox and make it acceptable and fruitful in their lives.

Why, Holiness? Why, why, why? We live in faith and hope, we are the givers of love. Why is this torment visited upon us and upon our children? And how dare you and your celibate presbyters ask us to breed again at random or live lonely and unsolaced in the name of this God who does indeed play a cruel dice game with his creatures?

"So tell me, Pietro," The Pontiff asked the question with rare humility. "What do you think I should say to them?"

"Tell them the truth, Holiness, just as you have told it to me. Tell them you don't know, you can't know. Tell them that sometimes God gives them more light and understanding than he gives to you, and they must follow the light in peaceful conscience."

The which, Leo the Pontiff was forced to agree, was a very polite way of saying that not even a Pope is a hero to his valet.

* * *

Mr. Omar Asnan received his guest in the garden of his villa on the Appia Antica. He offered coffee and sweetmeats and free access to all the information at his disposal.

"You must understand first, Mr. Peters, that Miriam Latif is a friend, a very dear friend. I am deeply troubled by what has happened. I have consented to speak with you because I believe the matter must be made known as quickly and widely as possible."

"You do not, I take it, question Dr. Salviati's account of her disappearance."

"No, I do not. As far as it goes, his account is accurate."

"Do you suggest he knows more than he is telling?"

"Of course! He was—and is—in a very difficult position. He is a Jew, treating the Pope who, like every public man, is deemed to be constantly under threat. Salviati has mixed staff: Christians, Muslims, Jews, from all round the Mediterranean basin. I admire his policy. Let me say that plainly. I think it is enlightened and useful. However, in an atmosphere of threat and crisis such as we had while the Pontiff was in residence, staff members themselves were under a certain threat—at least to their privacy."

"How so, Mr. Asnan?"

"Well, it is a fact, is it not, that the clinic was heavily guarded by Vatican, Italian—and, I believe Israeli—security men!"

"Do you know that, Mr. Asnan? Israeli agents are not officially permitted to work in Italy. Even the Vatican Vigilanza works under very restrictive protocols."

"Nevertheless, Mr. Peters, you and I know, as a matter of pure logic, that Israeli agents were involved."

"Are you saying they were involved in the abduction of Miriam Latif?"

"Without a doubt."

"But why? Professor Salviati speaks of her in the highest terms: So far as he knows, she has no political connections."

"So far as I know also, she has none; but she has been on occasion extremely indiscreet in speech. Her brother was killed in an Israeli raid on Sidon. She has never forgotten or forgiven that."

"And yet she accepted a subsidy to work and be trained at a Jewish hospital."

"I urged her to do it. I told her she could look at it in two ways—as a healing act or as part payment of a blood-debt. She chose to regard it as the latter."

"So it's possible she could have been identified—rightly or wrongly—by the Israelis as an agent for the Sword of Islam?"

"That is what I am saying, yes."

"Where do you think she is now?"

"I hope she is still in this country. If she is not, the position may become very complicated, very dangerous."

"Can you explain that, Mr. Asnan?"

"It is, I fear, quite simple. If Miriam Latif is not returned, violence will follow. None of us wants to see it happen—I least of all, because I live a quiet life here. I enjoy good business and personal relations with Italians. I do not want those relations spoiled. But, my dear Mr. Peters, I do not control events."

"I don't either," said Nicol Peters.

"But you can and do influence them, by what you publish, even by the information you transmit between your sources. I know that you will go from here and then use what I have said to elicit a comment from someone else. I don't object to that. I have nothing to hide. You may do some good . . . But remember the most important thing I have said—trouble is brewing!"

"I'll remember," said Nicol Peters. "One final question, Mr. Asnan. What is your own connection with the Sword of Islam? Obviously you know it exists."

Omar Asnan shrugged off the question with a smile.

"I know it exists. I have no connection with it at all, Mr. Peters. Like Miriam Latif, like so many of my countrymen, I am expatriate. I try to live comfortably under the laws of the country which has received me. I do not believe in terrorism—and may I remind you the only act of terror that has been committed is the abduction of Miriam Latif. It is not impossible that the whole Sword of Islam story was a fiction cooked up by the Israelis. Have you thought of that?"

"I'm sure someone has," said Nicol Peters cheerfully. "I'm still the neutral observer, like yourself."

"Don't mistake me, Mr. Peters. I have only said that I try to live within the law. In fact, I am outraged by what has happened to Miriam Latif and I care not who knows it."

And that, Nicol Peters recorded, was about as close as one could get to a declaration of war, and it was a sentiment reiterated in all his interviews with Muslim sources around Rome. The Italians understood the sentiment and, for the record at least, expressed sympathy with it. They were bending over backwards to maintain friendly relations all round the Mediterranean rim. The Pope was problem enough—but at least they had been dealing with popes for centuries. The imams and the ayatollahs were another kettle of fish altogether.

The Israelis, however, were much more pragmatic. Menachem Avriel listened to the account of his other interviews and then introduced him to a lean, soldierly fellow with a cool eye and a thin smile and Mossad written all over him. His name—at least for the purpose of the exercise—was Aharon ben Shaul. He had a proposal.

"I'm going to give you some facts, Mr. Peters. Most of them you can't print; but it's background you'd never come by otherwise. Then I'm going to make a projection about what may happen very soon. After that, I'm going to ask your advice as a long-time resident with good connections in this city. Deal?"

"Deal."

"First item. Omar Asnan runs the Sword of Islam group in Rome."

"I rather thought he might."

"Miriam Latif is an agent of that group. She is in our hands in Israel. We have no present intention of releasing her. She cost us too much to surrender her now."

"I don't understand that."

"We had a man inside the Sword of Islam. He was very close to Omar Asnan. When we decided to pick up Miriam Latif we blew his cover. Asnan killed him, in the cellar of his villa."

"How can you be sure of that?"

"Because we have it on record. Our man was wearing a bug in the collar button of his shirt. He had also planted two others, one in the garden and another in the *salone* of the villa. So we have fragments of later conversations between Omar Asnan and other members of the group. The purport of those conversations is twofold: the assassination of the Pope has been upgraded from a target of opportunity to a target of honour. He is now the Great Shaitan who must be brought down by the Sons of the Prophet, and a woman hostage will be taken to trade off against Miriam Latif. That hostage has been named."

"Who is she?"

"Tove Lundberg, Salviati's mistress!"

"God Almighty! Do they know about this?"

"Not yet. We've got them both covered and we don't believe Asnan is ready to make his move yet."

"How can you know that?"

"Because there's a fragment on our tape which suggests that Asnan will try to use local muscle to steal the girl—Calabresi or Sicilians probably. Also he knows we're on to him, so he's more concerned to cover his own back at this moment."

"Can't you do anything about him?"

"Of course we can. We're trying to do it at the least possible cost in terms of reprisals. We know he's committed murder, we know where the body is. But if the Italians charge him for the murder of an Israeli agent, they'll make themselves and us very unpopular when the vendetta begins."

"And what about the new threat to the Pope?"

"The Secretary of State will have the evidence in his hands today."

"And where do I fit in to all this?"

"In everything I have told you, the one thing you can't print is Omar Asnan's name. The rest we'll give you—transcripts of the tapes, circumstantial details, everything. We'd like you to file the story as quickly as you can."

"And what does that buy you?"

"Action. The Vatican pressures the Italians. The Italians have to move against Asnan and his group. You reinforce them with the old battle-cry—no negotiation under terror!"

"And Miriam Latif?"

"She's ours as long as she's useful."

"Salviati?"

"He's the safest of all. Nobody wants him dead, not even Asnan."

"Tove Lundberg? She's got a handicapped child."

"We know that. It's a complication. For a while at least we have to get her off the scene. She just has to disappear . . ."

On Saturday afternoon, while the pickers were still at work and the crushers were pouring out the first murky liquor, there was a crisis conference in the garden of the villetta. Present were the Pontiff himself, the Secretary of State, Drexel, Monsignor O'Rahilly and the chief of the Vatican Vigilanza. The Secretary of State read the reports he had received from the Israelis and from the Italians. The Pontiff sat bolt upright in his chair, his jaw and beak clamped together in the old predator look. He spoke with harsh finality: "There is no doubt in my mind. I cannot indulge myself in a vacation which puts others at risk. I shall stay here tonight, say Mass as I promised for the children and the parents of the colonia. After that, I shall go to Castel Gandolfo and remain there until the end of the summer vacation . . . I am sorry, Anton. You have been put to so much trouble, and I am more disappointed than I can say."

Drexel made a gesture of resignation.

"Perhaps another time, Holiness."

"Perhaps. Now, gentlemen!" The aura of command enveloped him. He seemed to grow stronger before their eyes. "The Pope retires behind the ramparts. He leaves behind a woman who, because of her service with him, is now endangered, not only in her own person, but in that of her child. I take it this danger has not been overstated?"

The question was addressed in the first instance to the Secretary of State.

"In my view, it has not, Holiness."

The Vigilanza man confirmed the verdict.

"The threat is very real, Holiness."

The Pontiff put another question: "Is it not possible for the Italian authorities, with the resources and skills which we know they have, to guarantee protection for this woman and her child?"

"No, Holiness, it is not. In fact, it is not possible for any police force to do so."

"Is it not possible for them to terminate the threat by summary action; for example, by the arrest and detention of the known conspirators?"

"It might be, given an adequate will on the part of the Italian government; but that government itself is severely handicapped by its vulnerability to terrorist methods. Even if the law is suspended to permit or tolerate unorthodox intervention, the consequences are not always controllable, as we have seen in the present case."

"Thank you. A question for you, Anton. Has Tove Lundberg been informed of this threat?"

"Yes. She telephoned today to ask my advice on what to do about Britte."

"Where is she now?"

"At the clinic, working as usual."

"Would you ring and ask her to call in here, before she goes home?"

Drexel hesitated for a moment and then left the room. Monsignor O'Rahilly began a tentative intervention.

"May I suggest, Holiness . . ."

"No, you may not, Malachy!"

"As Your Holiness wishes."

The Pontiff was beginning to sweat. He mopped his face with a handkerchief. O'Rahilly handed him a glass of water. When Drexel came back, he was accompanied by Sister Pauline. She went straight to the Pontiff, felt his pulse and announced firmly: "This meeting is over. I want my patient in bed."

"It will take only a moment, Sister." He turned to the others and said simply: "For what has happened I am responsible, at least in part. The risk is real for Tove Lundberg and her child. The protection that can be offered is minimal. Until the threat is removed or greatly reduced, I want them both to come and live within the confines of Vatican City." He turned to the Secretary of State.

"Our good sisters can make room for them and see that they are comfortable." Then he addressed himself to Drexel. "You are the Nonno of the family, Anton. Try to persuade them both."

"I will do my best, Holiness. I can promise no more."

With the old imperious gesture, the Pontiff dismissed them.

"Thank you all. You have our leave to go. Sister Pauline, I am ready for you now."

As he walked slowly back into the house, the familiar melancholy descended on him like a black cloud. Oblivious even of Sister Pauline, he muttered to himself.

"I don't believe it. I simply don't believe it. The world wasn't always like this —or was it?"

"I'm sure it wasn't," said Sister Pauline cheerfully. "Our old parish priest used to say the madmen have taken over the asylum; but they'll get tired of it very soon and hand it back."

In the chapel of Cardinal Drexel's villa, designed, so the records said, by Giacomo della Porta, the members of the colonia were assembled: the young ones in front, parents and teachers behind them and, left standing against the rear wall, the few members of the Curia to whom Drexel, the old fox, had offered a personal compliment and a test of their sympathies. Agostini was there, and Clemens from the Doctrine of the Faith, and MacAndrew from the Propagation of the same Faith, and—a long reach from the power-base— Ladislas from the Congregation for the Oriental Churches. Few as they were, they made a crush in the chapel. They also made a sharp reversal of protocol: the people before the princes.

The Pontiff entered, with Drexel as his deacon, Sister Pauline as lector, with a spastic boy and girl as acolytes.

Some, but not all, of the ritual subtlety was lost on Sergio Salviati and Tove Lundberg, who sat, with Britte between them, in the front row of the congregation. Salviati was wearing his yarmulke. Tove was wearing a veil and carrying her father's old order of service. One of the mothers handed them a Mass-book. Salviati riffled through it and then whispered to Tove: "My God! They've stolen most of it from us!" Tove, stifling a laugh, cautioned him: "Keep an eye on your patient. This is his first appearance in public."

It was more than that—much more. It was the first time in thirty years that he had said Mass as a simple priest. It was the first time he had talked to an audience within hand's touch and heart's reach.

Knowing how quickly he tired, he began the ritual at a steady pace; but by the time he came to the readings he was glad to sit down. Sister Pauline read the lesson in her emphatic and inaccurate Italian and ended with the exhortation of Paul to the Corinthians:

"While we are still alive, we die every day for the sake of Jesus, so that, in our mortal flesh, the life of Jesus, too, may be openly shown."

Then they held the book for the Pontiff. He kissed it and in a firm, clear voice read the Gospel.

"One Sabbath day, Jesus happened to be walking through the cornfields and, as they went along, His disciples picked the ears of corn and ate them. And the

Pharisees said to Him: 'Look, why are they doing that which is forbidden on the Sabbath?' And he said to them: 'The Sabbath is made for man, not man for the Sabbath . . .' "

Pale but composed, he stepped forward to face the small assembly. Salviati watched him with a clinical eye, noting the bloodless lips, the knuckles white with tension as he grasped the edges of the lectern. Then, in the midst of an eerie calm, he began to speak.

"I looked forward to this visit with you as I have looked forward to few pleasures in my life. From the moment I arrived I felt surrounded by love. I felt love welling up in my own heart, like a miraculous spring in a desert. Now, abruptly, I am called away. My brief happy time with you is ended. I lay awake last night, asking myself what gift I could leave you to say my thanks—to you, Anton, my old adversary, who has become my dear friend; to you, Sergio Salviati, my stern but careful physician; to you, Tove Lundberg, who gave wise counsel to a man much in need of it; to you, my children; to you all who care for them with so much devotion and who have made me for these few days a privileged member of this family. Then I realised that the only gift I have is the gift of which Paul speaks, the good news that in and with and through Christ we are all of us—believers and unbelievers alike—made members of the family of God our Father.

"There are no conditions to this gift. It was given to me. I pass it to you—but you have it already and already you have shared it among yourselves and have passed it back to me. This is the mystery of our communion with the Creator. It has nothing to do with laws, prescriptions, prohibitions. And this is what our Lord Himself emphasises when he says: 'The Sabbath is made for man, not man for the Sabbath.'

"One of the great mistakes we have made in the Church, a mistake we have repeated down the centuries—because we are human and often very stupid—is to make laws about everything. We have covered the pastureland with fences, so there is no place for the sheep to run free. We do it, we say, to keep them safe. I know, because I have done it all too often. But the sheep are not safe: they languish in a confinement that was never their natural habitat . . .

"For most of my life I have been a celibate priest. Before that I was a lonely boy, brought up by my mother. What do I know of the complex and intimate relationships of married life? I confess it: nothing. You are the ones who know. You are the ones who confer the sacrament on each other, who experience the joy, the pain, the confusions. What can I, what can any one of my wise counsellors, my brother bishops, tell you that you do not know already? I am sure my friend Anton will agree with me. He did not legislate this family into being—he created it, with you, out of love.

"So what am I saying to you? You do not need me, any more than you need the vast edifice of St. Peter's, the complex organisation that takes two thousand pages of the Annuario Pontificio to describe. The Lord is present with you in this place. You are a light to the world because you live in the light of His countenance. You need no law because you live by love—and if you stumble as we all do, fall as we all do, there are loving hands to lift you up.

"If you ask me why the innocent among you, the children, are stricken, why they must carry a lifetime handicap, I cannot answer you. I do not know. The mystery of pain, of cruelty, of the jungle laws of survival, have never been explained to us. God's secrets are still God's secrets. Even his Beloved Son died in darkness, crying to know why God had abandoned him. It would be a shame to me to claim that I am wiser or better informed than my Master.

"In this, perhaps, I am most your brother. I do not know. I walk often in darkness. I ask not whose hand is stretched out to guide me. I touch it and from the bottom of my heart I am grateful . . . God keep you all!"

"Thank you," said Tove Lundberg. "Thank you for offering us a refuge; but Britte and I are agreed, we live as we are. She stays here in the colonia, Sergio and I continue working as we have always done."

Anton Drexel smiled and shrugged resignedly.

"I can't say I'm sorry. I would have hated to lose my granddaughter."

Sergio Salviati obviously felt some explanation was needed.

"At first I thought it would be a good idea to have both of them out of the way. Our people advise it anyway. Then, when we thought about it, we came back always to the same question: why should we retreat? Why should we surrender to these obscenities? So we stay."

"Then we shall see each other again. You, my prickly friend, have to keep me alive; Britte must deliver my portrait; and to you, my dear counsellor, my house is open always."

He embraced them all; then Drexel led him away for a brief private talk. He told him:

"While you were speaking, I was watching our colleagues. Clemens disapproved, Ladislas too. MacAndrew was surprised, but pleasantly so I think. Your secretary was very surprised. He was trying to read everyone's reaction."

"Agostini?"

"He was neither shocked nor surprised; but that's his style. Tell him the sun failed to rise, he'll deal with it. However, there is one thing you have to remember. From this moment on, every member of the Curia, except the few geriatrics like myself, will see himself as a potential candidate at the next Papal election. You look very tired this morning, so it's natural that people will ask whether you'll really make old bones . . . So, being human, they'll begin building alliances for the next conclave. It's a point to keep in mind when you start gathering forces for a spring-cleaning."

"I'll remember it. You still haven't told me what you thought of my sermon."

"I thanked God for the good word. I'm proud it was spoken in my house. Now I have a favour to ask of Your Holiness."

"Ask it, Anton."

"Let me go now, Holiness. Relieve me of all my duties in Rome. I am long past retirement age. I desire desperately to spend the rest of my life with my little family here." He gave a small, embarrassed laugh. "As you see, there's a lot of work to do around the place."

"I shall miss you very much; but yes, you are free. I shall be very much alone now, Anton."

"You will find others, younger and stronger. From this moment I should only be an obstacle in your path."

"And how in God's name do I reach the young ones?"

"As you did this morning. Let your own voice be heard, let your own authentic utterance be read. You can do it. You must."

"Pray for me, Anton. Have the children pray for me."

They clasped hands, two old adversaries united after a long campaign. Then the Pontiff gathered his strength, straightened up and, with Drexel beside him, walked briskly outside to the waiting prelates.

BOOK THREE

Lazarus Militans

"A man's enemies shall be the folk of his own household."

—Matt. x: 36

X

FOR the next three weeks, the only reports on the Pontiff were the medical bulletins, the gossip of the Papal household at Castel Gandolfo and the occasional garrulities of Monsignor Malachy O'Rahilly.

The bulletins were studiously uninformative: the Holy Father was making steady progress but, on the advice of his physician, he had cancelled all public appearances until the end of August. The Mass of the Assumption in St Peter's on 15 August would be celebrated by His Eminence Cardinal Clemens.

The household gossip was meagre enough. His Holiness rose late and bedded early. He said his Mass in the evening instead of the morning. He was on a strict diet and was losing weight rapidly. Every day a therapist came to supervise him in an hour of exercise. For the rest—he received visitors from ten till eleven in the morning, walked, read, rested and was in bed by nine every night. One change, however, was noted by everyone. He was less tetchy, less demanding and much more gentle in manner. How long it would last, of course, was anyone's guess. After all, an intervention like that reduces a man's vitality.

The garrulities of Monsignor Malachy O'Rahilly were much more revealing. Life at Castel Gandolfo was a bore at the best of times. There was a castle, the village and the black lake below; damn small diversion for a gregarious Celt who loved convivial company. ". . . but with the old man in this mood it's Tombstone Terrace, believe me! He won't read letters. I have to send holding notes. He's become quite obsessive about what he eats and how much exercise he does, and I wish I could drop the weight off the way he's doing. But he's very quiet. When his visitors come, he doesn't talk more than courtesies: 'Thank you and how's your father', that sort of thing. He's not fey, just distant and abstracted. He reminds me sometimes of Humpty Dumpty, trying to put the pieces of himself together again. Except he isn't fat any more—and the Pontifical tailors are working overtime to refit him before he goes back to the Vatican . . . I notice he reads a lot more than he used to, prays a lot more—which doesn't exactly leap to the eye, but you become aware of it, because he's in another world, if you take my meaning. It's as if he'd put himself in retreat, a self-imposed solitude . . .

"What is he reading? Well, now, that's interesting. He's reading the very fellows that have been in trouble with Doctrine of the Faith—the Dutch, the Swiss, the Americans. In a moment of boldness—or excessive boredom—I remarked on it. He gave me the oddest look. He said: 'Malachy, when I was young, I used to watch the test pilots streaking along the Po valley and out to sea. I used to think how wonderful it would be to risk oneself like that to discover something new about a machine or about myself. As my life settled into its pattern, I forgot the wonder. Now that my life has become less important, I am reliving it again . . . Time was when we burnt men like Giordano Bruno who speculated about plural worlds and the possibility of traveling between them. Of course, we don't burn our speculative thinkers any more. Instead, if they're clerics we silence them, remove them from their teaching posts, prohibit them from public utterance on contentious matters. All this we do in the name of holy obedience. How do you feel about that, Malachy?'

"That stumped me for a minute. I didn't want to put my foot in a cowpat, so I said something like: 'Well, Holiness, I suppose there's some kind of principle of progressive enlightenment.' To which he said: 'Malachy, you're not half the fool you try to be. Don't play games with me. I haven't the time!' Needless to say, I ducked for cover; but he didn't make a big issue of it. It's hard to know what he's really thinking. I'd love to get a look at his diary. He writes in it every evening before he goes to bed. The rest of the time it's locked in his private safe . . ."

"As a young bishop, I was asked to bless a new ship, about to be launched from the slips at La Spezia. Everyone was there: the builders, the owners, the shipwrights and their families. The tension was quite extraordinary. I asked one of the executives of the *cantiere* to explain it to me. He said: 'Once they knock the chocks away and she slides down the slipway, all our lives are riding with her. If our calculations are wrong and she broaches, we are as good as dead . . . so give us your best blessing, please Excellenza . . .' I am like that now. All my temporary supports have been taken away—Drexel, Salviati, Tove Lundberg, the staff at the clinic. I am launched. I am afloat. But I am a hulk without fittings, without crew, dead in the water . . .

"The sense of isolation weighs on me like a leaden cope. Castel Gandolfo, Vatican City—these are my empire and my prison house. Outside, I move only by the permission of others. But my confinement is not by frontiers, it is by the identity to which I was elected Bishop of Rome, Successor to the Prince of the Apostles, Vicar of Christ . . . thus and thus and thus, every title a new barricade between me and the commonality of humankind. There is another confinement too—the Lazarus syndrome. I am not, nor can I ever be again, the same as other men. I have never understood until now—how could I?—the trauma of a young woman who can no longer breed because of a surgical intervention . . . the anger and despair of the soldier maimed in a minefield. They have become as I have: irretrievably *other* . . .

"I can share these thoughts only with those who have shared the experiences; but they are not accessible to me . . . I do not see myself making the rounds of hospital wards and prison cells, patting hands and mumbling platitudes. Neither can I see myself closeted with Clemens as I have been in the past, sniffing out heresies, putting this academic and that under silence and obedience to test their faith. That is a torture more acute than the rack and the thumbscrew. I will have no more of it . . .

"Now comes the rub. Clemens is where he is because I put him there. I put him there because of what he is, because of what I was. What do I say to him now? Everything is changed because I have seen a great light? He will face me down—because he does not lack courage. He will say: 'This is the oldest heresy of all. You have no right to impose your private gnosis upon the People of God.' I will be vulnerable to that, because even now I cannot explain the change in me . . .

"And that, dear Lord, is the strangest irony of all. I procured the deposition of Jean Marie Barette because he claimed a private revelation of the last things. I cannot move forward or backward until I am convinced that I am not myself entrapped in the ancient pride of private knowing. Against this kind of evil there is no remedy but prayer and fasting. I am fasting! God knows, I am fasting! Why does the prayer refuse to frame itself on my lips? Please God, put me not to the trial of darkness. I do not think I shall be able to bear it!

"I woke this morning with this same fear hanging over me. There is no one here to whom I can communicate it, as I did to Tove Lundberg, so I must grapple with it alone. I went back to that marvellous first letter of Paul to the Corinthians, where he speaks first of offices and functions in the community: 'God has given us different positions in the Church; apostles first, then prophets, thirdly teachers; then come miraculous powers, gifts of healing, works of mercy, the management of affairs . . .' Then he speaks of the better way which transcends all others: 'Though I speak with the tongues of men and angels, and have not charity, I am like sounding brass and tinkling cymbal . . .'

"This is what I must remember every day when, after the summer vacation, I begin my personal dialogues with the Church. I must not be the man who tears it apart with contention. I must heal the grievous wounds within it."

For Nicol Peters, the tag-end of summer had settled into its somnolent routine. The Miriam Latif story was dead. The Sword of Islam was no longer a headline item. The Pope was safely home. Mr. Omar Asnan was living the agreeable life of a prosperous merchant. The Israeli Ambassador was on vacation, the Mossad man, Aharon ben Shaul, had faded back into his grey netherworld and was no longer available. This was the way life rolled in the news game. You learned to roll with the rhythm of events and non-events. You kept your story-files up to date and hoped to be ready when the next rocket went up.

Katrina was busy at the boutique. The summer visitors were out in force and the cash register was playing merry little tunes every day. The Romans had a proverb: only *cani* and *Americani*—dogs and Americans—could tolerate summer in the city. There was, however, an art to it. You worked in the morning. At midday you swam and lunched at the swimming club, where you also entertained your contacts. You worked again from five until eight, then rounded off the evening with friends at a taverna where you were well enough known to get a reasonably honest bill.

Their friendship with Sergio Salviati and Tove Lundberg was maturing slowly. Distance was a problem. It was nearly an hour's drive from Castelli to the city, longer in the peak hour traffic. The shadow of the terrorist threat still hung over them. They travelled to and from the clinic at staggered hours in a Mercedes driven by a former member of the highway police trained in evasive driving.

On Saturdays, Tove worked with the other parents at the colonia. Sundays she kept for Salviati, who was busier than ever at the clinic and more and more dependent on the brief tranquil time they spent together. It was Katrina who made the astute comment: "I wonder how long they can keep it up, both so dedicated and controlled. It's like watching a trapeze act at the circus . . . You know if one mistimes, they both go. Somehow I think she's in better shape than he is, even though she's the one under threat."

Matt Neylan had become something of a fixture in their lives. His affair with the lady of the mysteries had run its cheerful little course and ended with a touching farewell at the airport, after which Neylan drove back to Rome to lunch with his New York editor and drive her up to Porto Ercole for a weekend editorial conference.

It was all good clean fun and the book—a popular study of Vatican diplomacy and the personalities involved in it—was beginning to take hold of him. However, he was becoming more and more aware that not all the attention he was paid was due to his wit or good looks.

There was a steady trickle of invitations through his mailbox; to embassy affairs, to seminars, to art shows sponsored by this or that cultural committee, screening of obscure films, appeals for victims of sundry wars and permanent famines. It was a useful antidote to boredom, provided you were not infected— as Matt Neylan knew himself to be—with the massive cynicism of the ex-believer. Once you had renounced the Almighty and all his prophets, it was hard to pin your faith to the petty propagandists of the cocktail circuit, or the recruiters of the flyblown intelligence networks who infested the city.

So, while he took full advantage of the free food and liquor and company, Matt Neylan devoted half his days to the demanding business of authorship and the other half to the passionate pursuit of women. Since he was proficient in five languages and haltingly adequate in three others, he was offered a wide range of choices. The odd thing was that he felt obliged, sooner or later, to run them past Katrina Peters for her nod of approval. Katrina found it beguiling. Nicol was not amused.

"Don't kid yourself, sweetheart. Matt's naive but he's not stupid. You're his mother hen. He's relying on you for his sentimental education."

"I find that rather flattering, Nico darling."

"It's a warning, lover. Matt's an agreeable friend but, like a lot of men with his history, he's a user. All these years he's lived a protected and very privileged bachelor life. He's never had to worry where his next meal was coming from; his career was laid out by the Church, he didn't have to battle for it; people paid him the respect they always give to the clergy and he didn't have to dirty his hands to get it. Now that he's out—and moderately well off by all accounts —he's doing exactly the same thing: freeloading, and freeloading emotionally, too . . . I get a little bored watching the game and I get irritated when I see you involved in it. There now! I've said my piece!"

"And I've listened very politely; so now let me say mine. Everything you've said is true—not only about Matt, but half the clerics we meet here. They're like Oxford dons, living in their own very comfortable bunkers while the world goes to hell in a basket. But there's something about Matt that you're missing. He's a man with a great black hole in the middle of himself. He doesn't have faith any more and nobody's ever taught him about love. He's grabbing for sex as if it were being taken off the market; then when the girl goes home or he sends her—whichever is the scenario of the day—he's back in the black hole. So don't be too rough on him. Times are, my love, when I could strangle you with my bare hands; but I'd hate to wake up and find you weren't there!"

For Matt Neylan, there were other and more subtle problems than those diagnosed by his friends. The work he had taken on, for which his publishers had paid him a very substantial advance, was easy to outline; but to finish it required a great deal of documented research for which the most necessary source was the Vatican Archive itself where, classified in various degrees of secrecy, a thousand years of records were preserved. As an official insider he had access by right; as an outsider, a recent renegade from the ranks, he could hardly claim even the privileges granted to visiting scholars and researchers.

So, well trained in the shifts and stratagems of diplomacy, he set about building a new set of alliances and communications, with junior clerics in the Secretariat of State, with lay members of the Archive staff, with foreign academics already accredited as researchers in the Archive and in the Vatican Library itself.

In this enterprise he found help from an unexpected quarter. After several feints, the Russian Ambassador made what seemed like a straightforward proposition.

"You are a citizen of a neutral country. You have long experience in a specialised field of religious and political diplomacy. You have no present affiliations. You are continuing your studies in the same field. We should like to retain you, quite openly, on a written contract, as adviser to our Embassy here. The pay would be generous . . . What do you say, Mr. Neylan?"

"I'm flattered, of course. However, I need to think about it very carefully."

"Take all the time you need. Talk to whomever you choose. As I said, this is a matter of considerable importance in the future development of our European policy."

In the end, Matt Neylan decided to take the Ambassador at his word. He sought and obtained a meeting with the Secretary of State, who received him in the bleak conference room reserved for casual visitors. Neylan came straight to the point.

"I am offering you a courtesy, Eminence. I need a favour in return."

"So far,"—Agostini made a little spire of his fingertips and smiled at him over the top of it—"so far you are admirably clear. What are you offering me?"

"A piece of information. The Russians have invited me to advise them on what they call religious and political diplomacy. They offer good money and an open contract—presumably to save me the taint of espionage."

"Will you accept the offer?"

"I'll admit it has a certain fascination—but no. I'm turning it down. However, I think it determines for your department where certain emphases are being laid in Soviet policy."

"You could be right. It could also be that you are doing exactly what they expected. You are the bearer of a signal from them to us. Either way, I am in your debt. How can I repay you?"

"You know the work on which I've embarked?"

"Yes."

"I need access to the Archive—the same access which would normally be granted to any scholar or researcher."

Agostini was puzzled.

"Has it ever been denied you?"

"No; but I thought it more tactful not to apply so soon after my exit."

"I'll send a note to the prefect tomorrow morning. You can begin work whenever you choose."

"Thank you, Eminence."

"Thank you. How are things with you? I hear on various authorities that you are much in demand socially."

"I'm enjoying myself," said Matt Neylan. "And Your Eminence? It must be a relief to have His Holiness safe behind the ramparts."

"It is; though I do not believe the threat to him is past. That is something you could do for me. If you hear any news, any rumour of terrorist activity that makes sense to you, I should be grateful if you would contact me. Also His Holiness has personal concerns about Tove Lundberg and her child . . . This is a small town. News and rumour alike travel fast. Thank you for coming, Matt."

"Next time, Eminence," said Neylan with a grin, "could you invite me into your office? I'm not a travelling salesman."

"My apologies." Agostini was urbane as ever. "But you must admit it's a little hard to define what you are."

In his search for a sexual identity, Matt Neylan was making discoveries that to men half his age were already clichés. The first was that most of the women he met at official functions were married, divorced, dedicated to dreams of permanent union, or otherwise disqualified from listing in a bachelor's telephone directory. He had also discovered that it was sometimes less expensive and less exhausting to buy the obligatory two drinks at the Alhambra Club and watch the floor show than to waste an evening and a dinner at Piccolo Roma with a bore, a bluestocking or a featherhead.

The Alhambra Club had another advantage, too: Marta the cigarette girl, who was always ready for a laugh and a few moments of gossip when business was slow. She was small, dark, and lively and, she said, a Hungarian. When he asked her for a date, she demurred. She worked the club every night. She couldn't leave until three in the morning. However, if he felt like taking her out to lunch one day . . .

Which he did, and was happy with the experience, and they both decided to repeat it, same day, same time, same place, next week.

And that was how Matt Neylan, one time Secretary of Nunziatures in the Vatican service, author to be, heir to a prosperous little holding in the Ould Sod, came to bed once a week with Marta Kuhn, Mossad agent assigned to surveillance duty in the Alhambra Club, the contact point for members of the Sword of Islam.

At ten o'clock on a warm summer morning, Leo the Pontiff was taking coffee on the terrace and wrestling with the problem of Cardinal Clemens, a man whom he himself had appointed, who had fulfilled punctually the brief he had been given, but who now was an obstacle to his master's plans.

A flight of birds passed overhead and he looked up to see a man scrambling precariously around the dome which houses the telescope of the Vatican observatory. He recognised him as Father John Gates, the director of the observatory and superior of the small community of Jesuits who ran it. He signalled to Gates to come down and join him for coffee.

Even though the observatory was perched high in the hills, on top of the castle itself, it was almost at the end of its usefulness, because the air above Rome and its environs was so polluted that the old-fashioned equipment could hardly function. Gates and his colleagues spent most of the year at the Astrophysical Institute in Houston, Texas. If the Pontiff was in residence at Castel Gandolfo Gates presented himself to pay his respects. After that he became a figure in the landscape, like the household staff and the farmhands.

He was a sturdy man in his late forties, with a ready smile and a quiet wit. His Italian was fluent and accurate. He had the easy confidence of a man secure in himself and in his scholarship. The Pontiff, hungry for company and eager for distraction from his own dark thoughts, plied him with questions, polite and casual at first, then more and more probing.

"I've always wondered how the astronomer thinks of time, of eternity. How he conceives of the Godhead?"

Gates considered the question for a moment and then, like a good Jesuit, tried to define the terms.

"If Your Holiness is asking whether I think differently from other believers, the answer has to be yes. In science we are faced always with new revelations about the universe. We are forced therefore to entertain new hypotheses and invent new terms to express them. We are always bumping our heads on the limitations of language and of mathematics. That was the last cry of Einstein: 'I have run out of mathematics.' Goethe made the same plea in different words: 'More light!' You ask me how I conceive of the Godhead. I can't. I don't try. I simply contemplate the immensity of the mystery. At the same time, I am aware that I myself am part of the mystery. My act of faith is an act of acceptance of my own unknowing."

"Are you saying that the traditional formulae of faith have no meaning for you?"

"On the contrary. They mean much more than they can say. They are man-made definitions of the indefinable."

"Let's take one formula then." The Pontiff pressed him. "That which is at the root of our Christian faith. *'Et verbum caro factum est.* And the Word was made flesh and dwelt amongst us'. God became man. What does that mean to you?

"What it says—but also much more than it says; otherwise we should be making human words a measure of God's infinite mystery."

"I'm not sure I understand you, Father."

"I look at the heavens at night. I know that what I am witnessing is the birth and death of galaxies, light years away from ours. I look at this earth, these hills, that dark water down there. I see another aspect of the same mystery. God literally clothing himself with his own creation, working within it like yeast in a dough, renewing it every day and yet still transcending it. The Godhead clothing itself with human flesh is only part of that mystery. I find myself moving further and further away from the old dualist terms—body and soul, matter and spirit—in which much of our theology is expressed. The more the limits of knowledge recede from me, the more I experience myself as a oneness."

The Pontiff gave him a long shrewd look and then lapsed for a while into silence. When finally he spoke, his words were mild, but there was a winter chill in his voice.

"Why is it that when I hear these very personal formulations, I am uneasy. I ask myself whether our faithful recognise in them the simple gospel which we are called to preach." He tried to soften the blow. "That is not intended as a reproof, believe me. You are my guest. You honour me with your openness. I seek simply to understand."

The Jesuit smiled, took out his pen and notebook and scribbled an equation. He passed it across to the Pontiff.

"Can you tell me what that means, Holiness?"

"No, I cannot. What is it?"

"It's a mathematical expression of the Doppler effect, the change of wave-length caused by any motion of a light source along a line of sight."

The Pontiff smiled and spread his hands in despair.

"Even that description means little to me!"

"I could explain it to you; but since you have no mathematics, I would have to use metaphor. Which is exactly what Jesus did. He didn't explain God. He described what God does, what God is, in the images of a rural people in an earlier age. You and I are people of another age. We have to speak and reason in the language of our own time, otherwise we make no sense. Look! It is part of my job in America to help train men to be astronauts, space travellers. Their imagery is quite different from yours or mine or that of Jesus himself. But why, for that reason, be suspicious of it? Why in this day and age try to put the human spirit in a straight jacket?"

"Do you truly believe that is what we are trying to do?"

Father Gates shrugged and smiled.

"I'm a guest at your table, Holiness."

"So you have the privilege of a guest. Speak freely. And remember that I am supposed to be the servant of the servants of God. If I am delinquent, I deserve reproof."

"Which I am not charged to administer," said the Jesuit with surprising firmness. "Let me try to approach the question differently. I've travelled a great deal. I've lived in Asia, in South America, in Africa, here in Europe. In the end, I find that all human experience is unitive. The tragic cycle—propagation, birth, death—is always completed by a metamorphosis. The graves are covered with flowers, wheat fields flourish over ancient battlefields. The techniques of modern storage and retrieval confer a continuity which is analogous to our notions of immortality, even of resurrection. Dead beauties come to life again on the television screen. I sometimes ask myself—I know this is a thorny subject right now—what might the television cameras have seen had they been trained all night on Jesus's burial place?"

The Pontiff gave a small, relaxed chuckle.

"A pity we'll never know the answer."

"I take the opposite view. A lifetime of scientific exploration has made the act of faith much easier for me. I demand always to know more, but I am prepared to risk much more on creative ignorance."

"Creative ignorance!" The Pontiff seemed to savour the phrase. "I like that. Because we are ignorant we seek to know. Because we are in darkness, we cry for light. Because we are lonely, we yearn for love . . . I confess to you, my friend, that, like Goethe, I have great need of light. I envy your starwalkers. It must be easy to pray up there."

The Jesuit grinned happily.

"When I was a boy, I couldn't make any real sense of the Doxologies—Glory to God in the Highest, and so on. It sounded like people cheering at a football match, flattering the Creator by telling Him what a great fellow he was. But now, when I look through the telescopes and listen to the myriad signals that come to us from outer space, the prayer of praise is the only one I can utter. Even the wastage and the horror of the universe seem to make a kind of sense, though the haunting presence of evil rises always like a miasma from a swamp . . . I am talking too much. I should leave Your Holiness in peace. Thank you for the coffee."

"Thank you for coming, Father. Thank you for sharing yourself with me."

When he had gone, Leo the Pontiff asked himself an almost childish question: why he had denied himself so long the pleasure of such men at his table. Why had he not given himself—stolen if need be—the leisure to learn from them? In the mood of depression that descended upon him, he found only a sad answer: he was a peasant who had never learned to be a prince.

Katrina Peters's reading of the situation between Tove Lundberg and Sergio Salviati was very close to the truth. Each for a different reason was living under stress and the stress was evident even in that part of their lives which they shared most fully and intimately.

Salviati was deeply angered by the fact that, once again, in the country of his birth, he and those close to him were under threat simply because he was a Jew. Every time he stepped into the Mercedes, said good morning to the driver, checked the alarms on his house, monitored Tove's comings and goings, he felt a fierce resentment. This was no way for a man to live, haunted by another man he had never seen, who by all accounts lived like a pasha, doing big business under the protection of the Italian government.

His resentment was all the greater, because he knew it was beginning to affect his work. In the operating theatre he was still the cool technician, totally concentrated on the patient. Outside, on ward rounds and the "white glove" inspections, he was edgy and impatient.

Tove Lundberg was worried enough to confront him over dinner.

"You can't go on like this, Sergio. You're doing exactly what you tell your patients not to do—driving yourself, living on adrenalin. You're alienating the staff, who would do anything for you. You've got to take a break."

"And tell me, pray, how do I do that?"

"Invite James Morrison down from London. He'd come like a shot. Move young Gallico up beside him. He could use the experience with another man. The administration works pretty well anyway—and I can always keep an eye on things for you. I know how the place runs."

"You wouldn't come on vacation with me?"

"No." She was very definite. "I think you need to go alone, feel absolutely free. At this moment I'm part of your burden, precisely because I'm threatened and you feel you have to protect me. Well, I am protected, as much as I ever can be. If it would make things easier, I could take off and work full time at the colonia while you're away . . . I've got some problems of my own to work out."

"Look, my love!" Salviati was instantly penitent. "I know I'm hard to live with these days—"

"It isn't you. It's Britte. She's a young woman now. I have to work out what kind of a life I can make for her and with her. The colonia isn't the final answer, you know that. It's given her a wonderful start; but it's a small, elitist group. Once Anton Drexel dies who's going to develop it and hold it together? The property is mortgaged to the Church. I'm sure one could make some arrangement with them; but much more is needed: a plan, development funds, training of new teachers."

"Is that what you see yourself doing?"

"It isn't. That's the point. I'm thinking of something much simpler—a home for Britte and myself, a career for her. It would be a limited one, but she is a good painter."

"And what about you?"

"I don't know yet. Just now I'm living from day to day."

"But you're putting me on notice there's a change coming?"

"There has to be. You know that. Neither of us is a totally free agent."

"Then why don't we do what I've suggested before—get married, join forces, make a family for Britte?"

"Because I'd still be denying you the chance to make a family for yourself."

"Suppose I accept that."

"Then one day, sure as sunrise, you'll hate me for it. Look, my love, we're still friends, we still support each other. Let's go on doing that. But let's be honest. Things are out of our control. You got the most prominent man in the world as a patient in your clinic. It was a triumph. Everybody recognised it. Now we drive back and forth with an armed guard and pistols taped under the seats . . . Britte's an adolescent. She can't be managed like a child any longer. And you, my love, have spent so much of yourself that you're wondering just what's left . . . We have to make a change!"

Still he would not admit the need. It was as if, by admitting the process of evolution, he might suddenly call on the earthquake. There was no easy solace for either of them any more. The good taste of loving was gone, all that seemed to be left was the bitter aftertaste of lost illusions.

She tried to talk about it to Drexel, who for all his ripe wisdom had his own quirks and quiddities. He did not want to lose his little family. He did not want to consider any alienation of the villa property during his lifetime. He would happily work with Tove to extend and organise the colonia; but she would have to make a total commitment to it . . . All of which meant another set of barriers to what had once been open and affectionate communication.

Then she realised that, although he was scarcely aware of it, Drexel himself was dealing with another set of problems. Now that he was truly pensioned off, he was lonely. The rustic life for which he had longed so ardently was not nearly enough to satisfy his active mind and his secret yearning for the excitements of the power game in which he had played all his life. This was the meaning of the transparent little strategy which he proposed to Tove Lundberg.

"Britte has finished her portrait of His Holiness. Why don't I arrange for her to present it to him? I'm sure he would be happy to receive us together at Castel Gandolfo."

As it turned out the strategy was unnecessary. Next morning he received by telephone a summons to wait upon the Pontiff before midday.

"Read this!" The Pontiff slammed the flat of his hand on the pages of *Osservatore Romano* laid open on his desk. "Read it very carefully!"

The article was headed "An Open Letter to the Signatories of the Tübingen Declaration" and it was a blistering attack, in the most formal terms, on the content of the document and what it called the "arrogant and presumptuous attitudes of clerics who are entrusted with the highest duties of Christian education". It ended with the flat pronouncement: "The luxury of academic argument cannot be allowed to undermine the loyalties which all Catholics owe to Peter's successor or to obscure the clear outlines of Christ's message of salvation." It was signed Roderigo Barbo.

Drexel's first question was the obvious one: "Who is Roderigo Barbo?"

"I have asked. I am informed that he is, and I quote: 'A layman. One of our regular and most respected contributors.'"

"One has to say," observed Drexel mildly, "he has a very good grasp of the official line."

"Is that all?"

"No. If your Holiness wants me to speculate . . ."

"I do."

"Then I detect—or think I detect—the fine Gothic hand of Karl Clemens in this matter."

"I too. You know I met with him in the clinic. I told him there should be a cooling off period before any contact is made with the signatories of the Tübingen Declaration or any action taken against them. He disagreed. I over-ruled him. I believe he chose this method to sidestep my direct order."

"Can you prove that, Holiness?"

"I am not required to prove it. I shall ask him the question direct. In your presence. He is already waiting to see me."

"And what does Your Holiness expect me to do?"

"What good sense and equity tell you to do. Defend him if you think he merits it. I do not wish my judgement in this matter to be clouded by anger—and I have been very angry this morning."

He pressed a buzzer on the desk. A few moments later, Monsignor O'Rahilly announced His Eminence, Karl Emil Cardinal Clemens. The ritual greetings were exchanged. The Pontiff made a curt explanation.

"Anton is present at my behest."

"As Your Holiness pleases." Clemens was steady as a rock.

"I presume you have seen this piece in *Osservatore Romano,* signed by Roderigo Barbo."

"I have seen it, yes."

"Do you have any comment on it?"

"Yes. It is in line with other editorials published in Catholic papers around the world: in London, in New York, Sydney, Australia and so on."

"Do you agree with it?"

"Your Holiness knows that I do."

"Did you have any hand in its composition?"

"Clearly, Holiness, I did not. It is signed by Roderigo Barbo, and would have been commissioned directly by the editor."

"Did you have any influence, directly or indirectly, by suggestion or comment, upon its commissioning or publication?"

"Yes, I did. Given that Your Holiness was not in favour of official action at this moment, it seemed to me not inopportune to open the matter to public discussion by the faithful—which the authors of the original document had done in any case. In short, I believed that the other side of the case should at least be heard. I believed also that the climate should be prepared for any action that might later be taken by the Congregation."

"And you did this in spite of our discussion at the clinic, and my clear directive on the matter."

"Yes."

"How do you explain that?"

"The discussions were too short to cover the whole range of issues. The directive was a limited one. I followed it to the letter—no official action or response."

"And *Osservatore Romano* is not official?"

"No, Holiness. It is sometimes a vehicle for the publication of official announcements. Its opinions are not binding."

The Pontiff was silent for a long moment. His strange predator's face, lean now from illness and dieting, was tight and grim. He turned to Anton Drexel.

"Does Your Eminence have any comment?"

"Only this, Holiness. My colleague Karl has been very frank. He has taken a position which, though it may not be palatable to Your Holiness, is still understandable, given the temper of his mind and his concern for the maintenance of traditional authority. I believe also Your Holiness must credit him with the best of intentions in trying to spare you stress and anxiety."

It was a lifeline and Clemens grasped it as eagerly as a drowning man.

"Thank you, Anton. I should have been hard put to defend myself so eloquently. There is only one more point I should like to make, Holiness. You put me in this office. You gave me a clear commission to examine rigorously—and the word is yours—any persons or situations dangerous to the purity of the faith. You quoted to me the words of your distinguished predecessor Paul VI: 'The best way to protect the faith is to promote the doctrine.' If you find my performance unsatisfactory, I shall be happy to offer you my resignation."

"We take note of the offer, Eminence. Meantime, you will refrain from further prompting of the Press—sacred or profane—and interpret our instructions broadly, according to their spirit and not narrowly, according to the letter. Do we understand each other?"

"We do, Holiness."

"You have our leave to go." He pressed the buzzer to summon Malachy O'Rahilly. "Anton, you will wait. We have other matters to discuss."

The moment Clemens had left the room, the demeanour of the Pontiff changed. The tense muscles in his face relaxed. He folded the newspaper slowly and laid it aside. Then he turned to Drexel and asked a blunt question.

"Do you think I was too hard on him?"

Drexel shrugged. "He knew the risk. He took it . . ."

"I can forgive him. I can't trust him again."

"That is for Your Holiness to decide."

A slow smile dawned in the eyes of the Pontiff. He asked: "How does it feel to be just a farmer, Anton?"

"Less interesting than I had hoped."

"And the children?"

"There, too, I have problems which I had not foreseen." He told of his conversations with Tove Lundberg, and the question which loomed for her and for all the other parents: what future could be offered to these brilliant but terribly handicapped children? "I confess I have no answer to it—nor, I fear, are we equipped in this country to deliver one. We may have to look outside for models and answers . . ."

"Then why not do it, Anton? Why not propose that to Tove Lundberg? I would be willing to find some funds from my private purse . . . But now to other matters. You are retired. You will remain retired. You will, however, remain as a member—*in petto* as it were, private and unobserved—of the pontifical family . . . Today is the beginning of change. Clemens did a foolish thing and I am very angry with him. Yet, the more I think about it, the more clearly I see that he has done us all a great favour. He has put into my hands exactly what I need: the instruments of change, the lever and the fulcrum to get the Church moving again. I lay awake for hours last night thinking about it. I got up early this morning to say the Mass of the Holy Spirit to beg for guidance on it. I'm sure I've made the right decision."

"I hope Your Holiness will permit me to reserve judgement until I've heard it."

"Let me reason it through with you." He pushed himself out of his chair and began to pace the room as he talked. Drexel was amazed to see how much weight he had lost and how vigorously he moved so early in his convalescence. His voice was strong and clear and, best of all, his exposition did not falter. "Clemens goes. He has to go. His argument was casuistry and unacceptable. He defied authority more blatantly than the Tübingen signatories who complained publicly about the alleged misuse of it . . . So now we need a new prefect for the Congregation for the Doctrine of the Faith . . ."

"Do you have anyone in mind?"

"Not yet. But you and I know that that Congregation is the most important and the most powerful instrument in the Church. All of us bend to its demands, because its purpose is to defend that upon which the existence of the Church depends—the purity of the teaching given to us by Christ and handed down from apostolic times . . . Clemens thought I would bend too, because I am still not wholly recovered and I dare not alienate the heritage of the ancient faith. But he was wrong—as the Congregation has been wrong, grievously wrong so many times down the centuries. I am going to reform it, root and branch. I am going to abrogate the dark deeds of its history, the tyrannies of the Inquisition, the secrecy and the inequities of its procedures. It is and always has been an instrument of repression. I am going to turn it into an instrument of witness, against which not only our doctrine, but our charity as a Christian Assembly, may be judged by all."

He broke off, flushed and excited, then sat down, mopping his hands and his brow. Drexel passed him a glass of water and then asked quietly: "How do you propose to do all this, Holiness?"

"By *motu proprio*. I need your help in drafting it."

"You need more than that, Holiness." Drexel gave a little rueful laugh. "There are fourteen cardinals and eight bishops running the Congregation. You can't dismiss them all. And what will you do with Clemens? He is known as your man. You can hardly stick his head on a pike outside the Porta Angelica!"

"On the contrary. I shall draw him very close to me. I shall give him your place as Cardinal Camerlengo and make him, in addition, prefect of my household. How does that sound?"

"Very much in character," said Drexel with wry humour. "Your Holiness is obviously much recovered."

"Be glad I am." The Pontiff was suddenly grim again. "I am changed, Anton, changed to the core of my being. I am setting out to repair the damage I have done to the Church. But in one thing I have not changed. I am still a country bumpkin, a hardhead. I don't want a fight; but if I'm forced into it, I have to win or drop."

At which point Anton Drexel deemed it prudent to change the subject. He asked: "Before you return to the Vatican, may I bring Britte and her mother to see you? Your portrait is finished. It's very good . . ."

"Why don't we do it tomorrow at eleven?"

"We'll be here. And, Holiness, Tove Lundberg herself is going through a difficult time. It would help if you could encourage her to talk about it."

"By all means. You can take Britte into the garden. Leave Tove to me."

As he was driven back from Castel Gandolfo to his own villa, Drexel replayed the events of the morning. First and most dramatic was the emergence of the old Leo, the man who knew how the vast machine worked and where to put his finger on the nerve-centres that controlled it. He had shed uncertainty. The fire was alight in his belly. He would thrust forward relentlessly towards the goal he had set himself. How wisely he had decided was another matter; but there was no gain-saying the sense of history that determined his choice.

Before the sixteenth century, the affairs of the Universal Church, including doctrinal matters, were handled by the Apostolic Chancery. In 1542 Paul III, Alessandro Farnese, founded the Sacred Congregation of the Inquisition. It was in the beginning a temporary institution, replaced by secular commissions under Pius IV, Gregory XIII, Paul V. But the first stable one, with an organic plan, was set up by Sixtus V, who had himself served as an inquisitor in Venice and who, as Pope, ruled with Draconian severity; imposing the death penalty for thievery, incest, procuration, adultery and sodomy. It was he who planned with Philip II of Spain to send the Armada against England, and when the Armada was sunk, defaulted on the payments to his ally. Pius X changed the name to the Holy Office, Paul VI changed it again to Doctrine of the Faith.

But the essential character of the institution had not changed. It was still essentially authoritarian, repressive, penal, incurably secretive and, in its procedures, inequitable.

In an institution like the Roman Catholic Church, built solidly on the old imperial model, relentlessly centralised, this inquisitorial institution was not only enormously powerful, it was a symbol of all the scandals of the centuries: the witch-hunts, the persecution of Jews, the burning of books and of heretics, the unholy alliances between the Church and the colonisers.

In the post conciliar world it was identified with reaction, with the concerted attempt to hold back reform and developments which the Council had set in motion. Leo XIV had used it himself precisely for those purposes. He knew its importance. His attempt to reform it was a true measure of the change in him.

The means he had in mind were interesting, too. A *motu proprio* was a document issued by a pope on his own initiative over his own signature. It was, therefore, in a special sense a personal directive. It laid him open to challenge from the Sacred Congregations and the senior hierarchy; but it also put his pontifical authority on the line in a matter on which he held strong personal convictions.

By the time the car turned into his own driveway, Drexel was convinced that there was stormy weather ahead but that Ludovico Gadda had a reasonable chance to survive it.

XI

MATT Neylan was coasting towards the end of a very satisfactory day: a morning's work on the book, lunch, tennis and a swim, and a reconciliation dinner at Romolo's with Malachy O'Rahilly. The Papal Secretary was eloquent as always, but obviously bruised from a series of recent encounters in the service of the Lord and his Vicar on earth.

"I'm still haunted by that security meeting and what happened to poor Lorenzo de Rosa and his family. I must have been pissed out of my mind, holding forth like that with all the Eminences around. I haven't been allowed to forget it, either. This very evening, when I was coming into town, I got a little lecture from the Man himself . . . 'Malachy,' he says, 'I have no personal complaints; but little birds whisper to me what I know is half scandal and you know is half truth. The downfall of the Latins is women and the Celts tend to drown their lusts and their sorrows in alcohol. So you will be careful, won't you? And you'll promise me never to drive these mountain roads with more than a glass taken.' They're on to me, Matt. That was just a warning of things to come, a shot across the bow so to speak. So maybe it's time I made a change —or a connection with Alcoholics Anonymous. What's your advice?"

"I'm out of the club," said Matt Neylan firmly. "You and I are reasoning in different categories now. But the old rule still holds: if you can't stand the heat, get out of the boiler-room. And if you can't tolerate liquor, don't drink."

"Are you happy where you are, Matt?"

"Sure. I'm very content."

"When are you going home?"

"That I'm not sure of—probably early autumn. The manager's doing a good job with the farm. I'm happy working here—for the moment, at least."

"Are you still—you know—living alone?"

"I don't have a live-in lady, if that's what you mean. For the moment I'm doing fine with temporary help . . . And what's happening on Vatican Hill?"

"At this moment, nothing; but all my instinct tells me there's going to be fun and games when the Old Man comes back into residence. He's getting stronger every day. He had Clemens on the carpet yesterday. You know what a tough customer he can be. Well, he was only in for five minutes, but he came out like a man on his way to the gallows. Drexel's retired . . . It's like waiting for a thunderstorm. You wish the damn thing would start. Which reminds me. Drexel and the Old Man are very worried about Tove Lundberg and her child. She's the one who . . ."

"I know who she is. I've met her."

"The security people say she's on a kidnap list. She goes everywhere under protection. The Old Man offered them refuge in Vatican City. They refused. I don't blame them. They'd wonder what hit 'em in our celibate metropolis. But I had a way-out thought which I've mentioned to no one . . . You wouldn't think perhaps of inviting them as paying guests to your house in Ireland? Just until the whole thing blows over, of course!"

Matt Neylan threw back his head and laughed until the tears came.

"Malachy, my boy, you're transparent as water! I can just hear the dialogue now—'A wonderful idea, Holiness! It came to me in sleep, like the visions of Joseph. I spoke to my old friend Matt Neylan—he's a good soul, though he doesn't believe he's got a soul any more—and he's offered bed, board and refuge to mother and child!' "

"So will you do it? Will you now?"

"The refuge is for you, isn't it, Malachy? You're scared they're going to ship you home to your bishop and make you do a little pastoral work for a change. Admit it now!"

"I admit it. You don't have to rub my nose in it."

"All right, I'll do it. Tell Drexel. Tell His Holiness. If I chance to meet the lady again, I'll make the offer myself."

"You're a prince, Matt!"

"I'm a footloose infidel with time and money he's never had before. I'll wake up to myself one day . . . You're paying the check, remember?"

"How could I forget a simple thing like that?"

When Malachy O'Rahilly had left him, he crossed the river, strolled for a while in the Piazza del Popolo and then took a taxi to the Alhambra Club. This was the hour that bothered him most in his new existence, the hour of the full belly and the empty bed and the craving for a woman, any woman, to share it with him. In the Alhambra he could join all the other males in a public confession of his need and sort through the offerings with offhand bravado. There were a thousand other solutions, of course. The evening papers carried columns of advertisements for masseuses, manicurists, secretary-companions; there were a dozen other clubs like the Alhambra, the tables along the Veneto, outside Doneys and the Café de Paris. He had tried them all; but the confession they demanded was too public, the encounters too prone to accident or boredom. At the Alhambra he was known. The girls acknowledged him with a smile, vied for his attention—and Marta had assured him with a certain seriousness that they had to be clean because the management insisted on a weekly medical certification and any girl who passed on something nasty to a regular client would have something very nasty happen to her. It was cobweb insurance at best; but it gave him the sense of security and belonging which his late-flowering emotions demanded.

It was a slack night. There was time for a chat with Marta at her little booth near the entrance. The girls were waiting in little groups, ready to pounce as soon as he sat at a table, so he perched himself on a stool at the bar and started a dialogue with the barman, a cheerful fellow from Tunis, who knew how to protect a quiet drinker and a generous tipper.

Neylan was halfway through his second drink when a man took the stool beside him and asked: "May I join you? I can't cope with all these women at once."

"I know how you feel. Be my guest. What will you take?"

"Coffee please, and mineral water." He introduced himself formally. "I have seen you often. We have never spoken. I am Omar Asnan."

"Matt Neylan."

"English?"

"No. Irish."

"I myself am from Iran. You live here in Rome?"

"I have for many years. I'm a writer."

"I am something much more prosaic. I'm a merchant, import and export. And what sort of books do you write, Mr. Neylan?"

"At this moment I'm working on a study of religious and political diplomacy, with special reference to the Vatican."

"You are familiar with the Vatican, Mr. Neylan?"

"Reasonably, yes. I do a certain amount of my work in the Archive."

"How interesting. I am, of course, Muslim; but I should be fascinated to visit some time."

"There are daily tours: St. Peter's, the Museum, the usual things. You can also get permission to visit the Library and other places . . ."

"I must certainly think about it. You have contacts there. You must have of course."

"Some, yes . . ."

"I am fascinated by this idea of the totally religious society. It has, of course, taken hold again in Islamic countries, most notably in my own."

"I find I need to get away from it for a while." Matt Neylan wanted to get off the subject as quickly as possible. "That's why I come here. But it looks like a dull evening that could get expensive. I think I'll be pushing along."

"No, wait!" Asnan laid a detaining hand on his sleeve. "You are bored, so am I. We can easily remedy that. Do you know a place called Il Mandolino?"

"No."

"It's in an old house in a tiny square just behind the Piazzo Navona. Lots of people go there. Two young men and a girl make music there every night, folk songs from all over the country. You buy drinks, sit in armchairs or on a cushion, and listen. It's very simple, very restful . . . If you're looking for a woman, of course, that's not the place to be; but to relax at the tail-end of an evening . . . Would you like to try it?"

After a good dinner and a brace of brandies, Neylan was relaxed enough to welcome the idea. It was made more attractive when Omar Asnan told him that his chauffeur was waiting and would drive him home afterwards. On the way out he stopped by Marta Kuhn's booth to buy cigarettes. Neylan bade her a discreet goodnight and managed a hurried whisper to confirm their lunch date.

When they had gone she went to the public phone in the foyer and made a call to the contact number of Aharon ben Shaul.

One of the less pleasant phenomena of the Pontiff's convalescence was broken sleep. He would go to bed utterly fatigued. Three hours later he would be wide awake and lie reading for another hour until sleep claimed him for another two hours. Salviati had warned him that the syndrome was common after cardiac interventions, but had warned him also against becoming dependent on opiates. It would be much better if he could do without them until a normal and natural rest pattern re-established itself. Now he kept a book and a diary by his bedside. If his mind began to spin, as it often did, with preoccupations about his future role, he would force himself to write through them, as if the act of definition would exorcise their latent terror:

> "I was not proud of myself today. I knew, and Drexel knew, that I had slipped back into the old tactics of the power game. There was an element of fear in my handling of Clemens. He had done wrong. I felt threatened and vulnerable. I struck out hard and brutally, knowing that I might not have strength for a long combat. I regret the hurt I inflicted on him less than my own failure to behave with Christian restraint and charity. I am far from recovered, it seems. I am far from ready to pick up the full burden of office.
>
> "On the other hand, I am still firm in my conviction that I have found the starting point for reform. I am dealing with an organism within the Church whose methods and functions have been a matter of dispute and discontent for a very long time. I am setting out to remodel it. If I succeed in doing so, I shall have done what Salviati has done for me: bypassed a block in the vital blood-flow of the body of the Church.
>
> "I shall not be attacking any person. I shall not be clouding an essential doctrine of the faith. I shall not be creating confusion by seeming to reverse the decrees of earlier pontiffs—or even my own rigorous policies. I believe that I can begin the process of decentralisation in a fashion which Drexel has not foreseen.
>
> "High hopes? Very high and I must beware of them. Nevertheless, the logic makes sense. Once the rules are changed, once it is impossible to make secret denunciations of a man or a work, once an accused has the right to know in detail the charges against him, the name of the accuser, once he has the right to a competent defender and an open debate upon the issue and the free exercise of his functions until the issue is decided, then the whole picture changes and it will begin to change in other sectors.
>
> "The mediaeval traps will be taken out of juridical procedures. In marriage cases, the old principle of favouring the bond over the person is fundamentally inequitable; though I have to confess, time was when I judged otherwise. In issues which must sooner or later become urgent within the Church—a married clergy, women priests, the development of

doctrine—it will be possible to have at least open discussion between competent scholars and competent authority, and an open forum even in the dicasteries of the Church.

"This is where I believe I am being led: back to the path opened by Vatican II and by the man who convened it, John XXIII. Like him, I must expect contention—and even conspiracy—against the grand design. I must expect, too, that I myself may prove my own worst enemy. Even so, I must move forward. But not tonight, not even tomorrow . . ."

Matt Neylan's evening at Il Mandolino turned out to be a pleasant experience. The setting was an old sixteenth-century house, with vaulted underpinnings from Roman times. The walls were decorated with antique musical instruments. The *salone* where the music was dispensed held no more than thirty people, who were comfortably settled in armchairs, cushioned alcoves and banquettes. The trio were talented and their music was a pleasant hour of tune-travel round the byways of the Italian peninsula.

Omar Asnan himself was an agreeable companion, good-humoured and unobtrusive. He talked vividly of the perils, pitfalls and occasional comedies of Middle Eastern trade. He explained to Matt Neylan the phenomenon of Islamic resurgence and the conflicts between Sunni and Shiite. He was interested to hear of Matt Neylan's rejection of his natal faith and suggested, with appropriate deference, that one day he might be interested to begin a study of Islam.

Neylan for his part offered to arrange a tour of the Vatican through one of his own friends: Peter Tabni, a consultor to the Commission for Religious Relations with Islam. Omar Asnan seemed astonished that such an organisation even existed. He would be delighted to accept such an invitation whenever it was offered.

As he rode home in Asnan's limousine, he felt a sense of well-being, of having assisted at one of the minor rites of civilisation in a city that was becoming more and more barbaric. He made a note on his desk pad to call Peter Tabni, laid Omar Asnan's card beside it, and then made ready for bed. At least tonight he would not have to worry whether he had caught more than a cold. To which he added, as a last waking thought, that he really had been wasting a lot of time and money in some very sleazy hangouts.

The principal item which Monsignor Malachy O'Rahilly noted in the Pontiff's diary was his appointments with Tove Lundberg, Britte and Cardinal Drexel. This was his cue to mention his dinner with Matt Neylan. The response was cordial and interested.

"I'm glad you're keeping in touch with him, Malachy. Cardinal Agostini spoke very highly of him, in spite of his defection."

"He's bright, Holiness—and he's generous. I asked him a big favour last night."

"Indeed?"

"We were talking about Tove Lundberg and the threat she's under. As it happens, he knows her. They met at the house of a journalist friend. Anyway, it seems he has a small farm property in Ireland. I asked him whether he'd have the Lundbergs there, if they wanted to go. It seemed to me at least a viable alternative to the offer Your Holiness made. He said he'd be happy to receive them."

"That was very thoughtful of you, Malachy—and most generous of Neylan. I'll inform Tove Lundberg. If she's interested, then she can discuss it directly with Neylan. Now, Malachy, you and I must talk."

"Holiness?"

"Please, sit down. How long have you been with me, Malachy?"

"Six years, Holiness; three years as junior, the last three as principal private secretary."

"You've served me well."

"I've tried, Holiness."

"And I have never been the easiest of masters . . . I know you've told me before, you were always happiest if you had to fight a little . . . However, I think the time has come for us both to make a change."

"You are dissatisfied with my work, Holiness?"

"Your work is excellent, Malachy. It's a pleasure to have you near me. You have an excellent sense of humour. However, you have two shortcomings, which unfortunately have become apparent to senior members of the Curia. You have a loose tongue and a low tolerance for liquor. Either of these is an impediment. Both together constitute a grave danger—to me and to you."

Malachy O'Rahilly felt a small, cold finger probing at his heartstrings. He sat in silence, staring down at the backs of his big hands. Finally, with more calm than he had ever thought to command, he said: "I understand, Holiness. I regret that you have been put to the embarrassment of saying it. When do you want me to quit?"

"Not until we have moved back to the Vatican, and you have had time to move your successor into place."

"And who will that be?"

"Monsignor Gerard Hopgood."

"He's a good man, an excellent linguist. He's quite up to the job. I could hand over a week after we get back."

"I should like to find you a congenial posting."

"With great respect, Holiness, I'd rather you didn't."

"You have something in mind?"

"Yes, Holiness. I want to be suspended from all duties for three months. I'm going to put myself into a place I know in England to be detoxified. Then I want to see whether I'm fit for the priesthood and whether it's a life I can endure from here to eternity. It's a rough choice to make after all these years, and all its cost in time, money and work to turn me into a Papal Secretary. One thing I'm sure of, however; I don't want to end up a whisky-priest with soup-stains down his cassock and no one to take him in but a convent of ageing nuns!"

"I had no idea you felt like this, Malachy. Why didn't you speak to me before? I am, after all, your pastor."

"No you're not, Holiness! And with great respect, don't believe that you are. You're the successor to the Prince of the Apostles. I'm the prince's minion. You're the Supreme Shepherd, but you don't see the sheep—only a vast carpet of woolly backs stretching to the horizon! It's not your fault. It's the way this institution has grown over the centuries. Talk about the Russians or the Chinese—we're the biggest collective in the world! And until you got sick and were stripped down to the skin, that's the way you thought about it and ran it. That's why it's in the parlous state it is . . . I'm sorry! I have no right to sound off like this; but it's my life, my soul's salvation that's on the line!"

"I don't blame you, Malachy. God knows, I have enough guilts of my own. But please trust me if you can. Is there anything I can do to help?"

"Yes, there is one thing."

"Name it."

"If, at the end of my purgation—which I'm not looking forward to—I find I can't take the life any more, I want you to let me go—you personally, because you've got the power. I don't want to be besieged by compulsory counsellors, put through the meat-grinder of the tribunals. If I come in good conscience, I want a clean exit. Will Your Holiness give it to me?"

"Why do you ask now?"

"Your Holiness knows why."

"I want to hear you say it, Malachy."

"Because this time, I want to make the choice of a free man."

For the first time the Pontiff was taken aback. He had not expected so curt an answer. He asked again: "Are you saying you were not free when you entered the priesthood?"

"That's the root question, isn't it? That's what I'm going into the desert to answer. But given my background in Holy Ireland, given all the pressures and conditionings of my education since the nuns first got hold of me at four years old, I'm not sure at all. I know it's not the sort of statement that will cut much ice with the tribunal, but it's the truth; just the same as it's the truth with a lot of marriages that turn into hell on earth because they were defective from day one. But what do we do? We turn the lawyers loose on 'em and not the compassion of Christ we're supposed to dispense! I'm not sure any of this is making any sense to you. I hope it is; because I'm bleeding. You've just done what this blasted bureaucracy always does. You've fired me on an anonymous denunciation. I think I deserved better than that."

Leo the Pontiff was at first stunned by the vigour of the attack, then overwhelmed by shame and guilt. He had done exactly that: damned a faithful servant on hearsay. And, remembering his own childhood, remembering how early and how rigidly his own mindset had been formed, he knew that O'Rahilly was right. He groped for the words to express his confused emotions.

"I understand what you're telling me, Malachy. I've handled this badly. I hope you will be able to forgive me. I shall pray every day that you may be able to live in peace in your vocation. If not, then I shall release you by my own rescript. One thing I have learned the hard way: there should be no slaves in the City of God."

"Thank you, Holiness. Is there anything else?"

"No, Malachy. You may go."

It was a melancholy moment and it called up memories of Lorenzo de Rosa, the defection of Matt Neylan and, beyond those local images, the large and distant ones of empty seminaries, convents without postulants, churches with aged priests and ageing congregations, men and women of ardour and goodwill frustrated by clericalism, creating small, self-protective cells within an assembly they did not trust any more because it was ruled by fiat and not by faith.

His mood was not lightened, either, by the visit of Tove Lundberg and Britte. The portrait pleased him very much. The girl was pleased that he was pleased, but communication was difficult and he was glad when Drexel took her out to show her the pleasances of the castle. Tove herself was trying hard to turn her problems into a piece of black humour:

"Except for the fact that I'm being hunted by some mad mullahs, I'm the luckiest girl in the world. One man wants to marry me. Another wants to set me up on a farm in Ireland. Nonno Drexel wants to send me to study in America. Your Holiness wants to give me money. My daughter thinks she's ready to live away from home. I wonder why I'm not happy?"

"You're really very angry, aren't you?"

"Yes, I am."

"Why?"

"Because everyone has a private purpose for me. No one seems to have given a thought to mine."

"Do you think that's quite fair? All of us are deeply concerned for you and Britte!"

"I know that, Holiness. I am grateful for it. But my life is my own. Britte is my daughter. I have to decide what is best for us both. At this moment I'm being tugged this way and that like a rag doll. I can't take that any more. I just can't."

Suddenly she was weeping and Leo the Pontiff stood beside her, stroking her hair, comforting her as she had comforted him, with small soothing talk.

"There now! It's not nearly as bad as you think! But you mustn't shut out the people who love you. You told me that, right at the beginning. I trusted you. Can you not trust me, even a little? Why not think about this house in Ireland —even as a holiday?"

Through the tears a small uncertain smile dawned and, as she dried her eyes, she told him: "I'm not sure I should risk it."

"What's the risk?"

"Didn't you know, Holiness? The Vikings burned Dublin, centuries ago. The Irish have never forgotten it!"

There was one more visitor listed in his appointment book: the Abbot of the Byzantine monastery of St. Neilus, which lay only a few kilometres away at Grottaferrata. The Abbot Alexis, who functioned as bishop of the surrounding countryside, was an old man, still vigorous, still witty, but radiating an air of extraordinary calm and spiritual ease. His visit to Castel Gandolfo was an annual affair, made always in a private and neighbourly fashion.

The monastery had existed for a thousand years and traced its origins back to the early Hellenic communities of Calabria and Apulia. The original Greek stock was mixed with Albanian and other races from ancient Illyria who, in spite of constant difficulties and frictions, managed to preserve their rites, customs and privileges, and their union with Rome, even after the Great Schism.

The present monks were mostly Italo-Albanians; but their rite was Greek.

They had a library of valuable manuscripts. They conducted a seminary for priests of the Byzantine rite. They ran a school of palaeography, illumination and restoration. For Leo the Pontiff, the place had always had a special significance, as a possible stepping stone on the long river of time back to reunion with the Orthodox churches of the East. But somehow he had never found the inspiration to make use of its resources. Too late perhaps, he was not prepared to admit that, at his first encounter, he had found the Abbot's humour a trifle too barbed.

This was the man who, asked to compare the Greek practice of married clergy with the Roman one of clerical celibacy, had remarked: "We think ours works better. After all, if you want labourers in the vineyard, why stop them bringing their lunch?" Speaking of the Roman passion for legislation, he coined the aphorism: "It is not the Church which leads people to God. It is God who draws them to Himself, sometimes through the visible witness of his Church— and sometimes in spite of it!"

In his later years, however, the old man had become a contemplative, and there were tales abroad about his power of divining human hearts and endowing them with the gift of peace. After the stress of his recent encounter, the Pontiff found him a very easy guest. He had brought a gift—a facsimile edition of the monastery's greatest treasure, a *typikon*, or liturgical compendium of the eleventh century. With the gift was a graceful dedicatory note quoting from the Epistle of John: "Beloved, I wish above all things that thou mayest prosper and be in health."

They walked together in the garden and, as Tove Lundberg had taught him to do, the Pontiff talked without embarrassment of the problems that loomed up before him.

"There's a great irony in my situation. I see all the mistakes I have made. I see even more clearly how little time I have to make them good."

The old man laughed, a light silvery sound like the laughter of a child.

"God's people are God's business. Why don't you trust Him?"

"Would it be so simple!"

"It is. That's the point. What else do the parables tell us: 'Consider the lilies of the field. They labour not, neither do they spin . . .' It is the passion for action that destroys us all. We are so busy organising and engineering and legislating that we lose sight of God's own purposes for us and for this planet of ours. You are still frail—frailer than I, who have fifteen years on you. Give yourself more time before you start work again. Don't let them bury you under a mountain of detail, as they try to do. A word from you at the right moment will do more good than a week of flurry in the Congregations."

"The problem is that I'm having difficulty with the words. The simpler they need to be, the harder it is for me to say them."

"Perhaps," said the Abbot mildly, "perhaps because you are trying to speak two languages at once: that of the heart and that of authority."

"And which one would you have me use, my Lord Abbot?"

"May I presume a little, Holiness?"

"Please!"

"In a way which you do not and, indeed, cannot experience, I face this question every day that I am in office. I am an old man now. My strength is limited. Consider a moment. We are, like our sister monasteries in Lungro, San Demetrio, Terra d'Otranto and other places, a small group of ethnic survivors —from Greek colonies and from scattered Balkan tribes. As priests and monks, we are custodians of the cultural identity of our peoples, what is left of their language, their traditions, their iconography. In the eyes of Rome—in the old days at least—this was granted as a privilege. We held it then, and hold it now, as a right. To maintain that right we have to demonstrate that we deserve it. So I as Abbot have to keep in our community a discipline that puts us beyond criticism or challenge from the Vatican. It is not always easy for my people or for me. But I have found over the years that it is better to persuade than to impose. The difference between you and me is that I can have, all the time, a face to face dialogue. Except in your own household, that is impossible for you. You are interpreted by rhetors and officials and translated by journalists. Your authentic voice is never heard. Look at the pair of us! Except for this one day of the year, this one brief hour, you and I might be on separate planets . . ."

"One advice which has been given me," said the Pontiff slowly, "is that I should begin to decentralise, give back to local bishops their authentic apostolic authority. What do you think of that?"

"In theory it's possible and desirable. We Byzantines are a case in point. We acknowledge the authority of the Pontiff, yes. We preserve our identity and our authority as an apostolic church. It works because the barriers of language and custom save us from too much interference. But if you try to do the same thing with the Germans, the English, the French, you will find opposition from the most unexpected quarters. Look what happened in Holland all those years ago! The Dutch claimed the freedoms affirmed in the decrees of Vatican II. Immediately the prophets of doom were crying from the rooftops. Reaction set in, Rome applied the thumbscrews. The Dutch Church was split and nearly ended in schism . . . But slowly, slowly, yes, it will work, it must work. I say to my monks: 'Before you stage a revolution, think what you have to put in its place— otherwise you are left with a vacuum and seven devils rush in to take possession!' "

Their walk had brought them to a small arbour with a stone bench and table. A gardener was working a few paces away. The Pontiff called him and asked him to order coffee and mineral water from the kitchen. When they were seated, he asked simply: "My Lord Abbot, would you hear my confession?"

The old man showed no surprise.

"If Your Holiness wishes, of course."

They sat side by side, leaning on the table while Leo the Pontiff poured out, sometimes haltingly, sometimes in a rush of words, the guilts and confusions that had piled up like windblown leaves in the crannies of his conscience.

He spoke without reserve, because this time he was not asking for counsel or judging the advice given, or weighing its possible consequences. This was another act altogether; this was the completion of the *metanoia,* the purging of guilt, the acceptance of penance, the resolution to begin anew. It was an act anonymous, secret and fraternal, brother mediating for brother with the Father of all. When the act was done, Leo the penitent bowed his head and heard the old man's voice pronounce in Greek the words of absolution.

* * *

Late the same morning, Matt Neylan called Monsignor Peter Tabni, consultor to the Commission for Religious Relations with Islam. His request was couched in very cautious terms.

"Peter, there's a casual acquaintance of mine, an Iranian Muslim called Omar Asnan. He's expressed interest in a visit to the Vatican. He's a permanent resident in Rome, a merchant, obviously rich and well educated. I'm wondering if you could perhaps give him an hour or two of your time."

"Sure! I'll be happy to give him a morning. How do you want to arrange it?"

"I'll call him and tell him you'll be in touch with him. You make your own arrangements."

"You won't come?"

"Best I don't, Peter. I've been granted Archive access. I don't want to push my luck."

"I understand. You're well and happy?"

"For today, I'm both. Let me know how it goes with Asnan. I'll buy you a lunch. *Ciao, caro!*"

Next he telephoned Omar Asnan, who was effusive in his gratitude.

"You are a most punctual man, Mr. Neylan. I shall not forget your kindness. You will be joining us, of course."

"Regrettably, no, but Monsignor Tabni will take very good care of you. We'll see each other very soon at the Alhambra."

Then Malachy O'Rahilly called him from Castel Gandolfo. He was obviously distressed.

"You must have the second sight, Matt."

"How come?"

"I've been fired; just as you guessed I might be. Oh, it was all very kind and compassionate. I've got three months' leave to dry out and make a conscience decision. If I can't cut it after that, I get a quiet pass-out by private rescript."

"Malachy, I'm sorry."

"Don't be. I'm not. I'm taking the Man back to the Vatican, settling my successor in the hot seat. Then I take leave."

"If you want to hang your hat for a few days, come to my place."

"I'll think about that. Thanks anyway. And there's one other thing: Tove Lundberg. Your offer was passed on to her this morning. She's very grateful. She wants to think about it. She'll call you direct to discuss it."

"So what else is new?"

"Not much. Britte Lundberg's portrait of the Man is quite wonderful. We had the annual visit of the Abbot of St. Neilus—nice old boy, transparent as old porcelain. On his way out, he stopped by my desk and gave me a funny, sidelong smile and said: 'Don't be too angry, Monsignore! His Holiness is doing you a favour.' Then, would you believe, he quoted Francis Bacon: 'Princes are like to heavenly bodies which cause good or evil times and which have much veneration but no rest.'"

"I've never met the man. It sounds as though one should invite him to dinner."

"Invite me instead, Matt. It's your turn anyway and I'm needing a shoulder to cry on."

By then it was midday. He was just getting ready to go out when the doorbell rang. Nicol Peters was standing on the mat. Behind him were Marta Kuhn and a lean, vulpine fellow he had never seen before. Peters had obviously been named master of ceremonies.

"Do you mind if we come in, Matt? There are things to explain."

"It would seem so." He waited for a word from Marta. She said nothing.

He stood inside to let them pass into the apartment. When they were seated, he remained standing, looking from one to the other. It was Nicol Peters who made the introductions.

"Marta Kuhn you know."

"Not, it seems, as well as I thought."

"And this is Aharon ben Shaul, attached to the Israeli Embassy in Rome."

"That's the identification, Nico. I'm still waiting for the explanation."

"I'm the explanation, Mr. Neylan." Aharon ben Shaul was in command now. "I work for Israeli intelligence. Miss Kuhn works for me. Part of our job is anti-terrorist activity. You frequent the Alhambra Club. Last night you left the club with a certain Omar Asnan. Miss Kuhn reported the matter to me. This morning I had a call from the International Clinic indicating that you had offered refuge in your house in Ireland to Tove Lundberg and her child. The connection was puzzling until I discovered you had met her at the house of Mr. Nicol Peters, who filled me in on your background. That encouraged me; but still left some areas of doubt."

"About what?"

"Your political sympathies."

"Which are my own bloody business!"

"And your Roman activities, which are very much the business of the Italians, ourselves and the Vatican. Where did you go last night with Mr. Asnan?"

"We went to a little music club near Monteverde Vecchio called Il Mandolino. We stayed for an hour. We left. He dropped me off at my house."

"Why did you go with Mr. Asnan?"

"It was a casual encounter on a dull night. No more."

"But you both frequent the Alhambra."

"We had seen each other. We had never talked. I believe Miss Kuhn can confirm that."

"She already has. What did you talk about?"

"Trivia mostly. I told him I was writing a book. He told me he was a merchant. When he heard I was working in the Vatican Archive, he expressed a wish to visit the City. This morning I arranged for him to be in touch with a friend of mine, Monsignor Tabni, who runs the Commission for Religious Relations with Islam. Tabni was going to give him the ten-dollar tour. End of story."

"Not the end, Mr. Neylan, just the beginning. Mr. Omar Asnan is the leader of an extremist Muslim group called the Sword of Islam, about which our friend Nicol Peters has been writing at some length. I hate to tell you, Mr. Neylan, but you have just given an assassin the keys of Vatican City."

Matt Neylan groped for the nearest chair and slumped into it.

"God in heaven! I'm the fine Vatican diplomat! And I can't see past the end of my own nose!"

"Don't be too rough on yourself, Mr. Neylan." Ben Shaul gave him a thin smile. "You were looking for the pleasant things—not the shit we deal in. Just a month ago, Asnan murdered one of our men. We couldn't move then without blowing a much bigger operation of which the Alhambra is the centre. Marta's been the agent in residence for months. Then you showed up . . ."

"And she did a very good job of checking me out—full profile, physical and mental! Congratulations, sweetheart!"

"Hold it, Matt!" Nicol Peters thrust himself into the argument. "You were playing; the girl was risking her life."

"Let's get the priorities straight." Suddenly the Israeli took over. "Two things are about to happen: a woman's going to be kidnapped; there will be an attempt on the life of the Pope. You can help prevent both crimes. Are you willing or not?"

"Do I have a choice?"

"Yes. If you want out, we can get the Italians to deport you back to Ireland as an undesirable alien."

"On what charge?"

"You're associated with a known terrorist. You've left the Vatican Secretariat of State under a cloud. Nobody will say what it is, but we can make it look pretty black. We also have reason to suspect you might have sympathetic connections with the IRA, who often come here to shop for arms with Libyan money. How does that sound?"

"It's a load of rubbish."

"Of course it is; but it will make a hell of a *denuncia!* And you know how messy things can get after you're on the books of the security boys. On the other hand, you can join our nice exclusive club here and help us clean up this mess. So what's it to be, Mr. Neylan? Hurt pride or help for the righteous?"

In spite of himself, Matt Neylan laughed.

"That's the worst piece of salesmanship I've heard in years! . . . All right, I'm in. What do you want me to do?"

XII

"YOU'RE booked out tomorrow." In his usual peremptory fashion, the Mossad man recited the details to Salviati and Tove Lundberg. "Aer Lingus direct to Dublin, departure 1405 hours, arrival 1620 local time. Italian security will handle your transport from here to the colonia to pick up your daughter, thence to the airport. You will be taken directly to the VIP lounge, where you'll be in care of the Carabinieri until departure time. Mr. Matt Neylan will meet you there and travel with you. Your tickets will be handed to you at the airport. I wish you a safe journey and a happy return when this mess is cleared up."

Then he was gone, and Tove Lundberg and Sergio Salviati were left alone. It was a curiously dry and vacant moment, all argument over, all passion spent, each anchored in a bleak private haven of solitude. Finally, Tove asked: "Have they told you what's going to happen when I'm gone?"

"Nothing. All they've said is that things are coming to a flash-point, and they want you out."

"And you?"

"I'm the one everyone wants to keep alive—it seems even terrorists can't do without a plumber!"

"I'm more scared to be going than I ever was of staying."

She shivered involuntarily and seemed to be trying to draw an invisible cloak about herself. Salviati knelt in front of her, cupping her face in his hands.

"We've had good times, rich times. We'll have them again."

"I'm sure we will."

"And I'm writing around to colleagues in Europe and America to get the best advice we can for Britte's future."

"That's the part I'm dreading; being totally alone with her, in a strange place. There's something terrible in the sight of all that passion welling up in her with no hope of satisfaction. I see it even in the way she paints—she almost attacks the canvas!"

"Drexel's going to miss her."

"He's going to miss a lot of things. But he will never complain. He's much more passionate and proud than you would ever imagine—and in his time he's been a very powerful man."

"I'm much more fascinated by his master. I keep asking myself what kind of terrible mutation I've loosed upon the world."

"You keep using that word. I've never found him terrible."

"What are you telling me, sweetheart? That you coaxed an angel out of him?"

"No; but there were moments when it almost seemed I was dealing with my father—all that repressed affection, the compassion he could never find words to express. Anyway, I must go. The car's waiting. I've got a lot to do tonight. We have to pack for autumn and winter now." She reached out and drew his face towards her own and kissed him. "No more talk, my love. Let's cut clean. It heals quicker. You taught me that."

The next moment she was gone, and Sergio Salviati wondered why his eyes were wet and his hands were unsteady, and how the hell he would face a triple bypass at seven in the morning. He was still trying to get a grip on himself when the Mossad man came back.

"Stage one is completed. We've got them covered from now until embarkation time. We're putting the word about Rome that you and Tove have broken up and she has left for a long holiday with her family in Denmark. Her car is gone, stored in the Embassy garage. Our people in Israel are releasing Miriam Latif. She'll be delivered safe into the care of her parents in Byblos. She's given us all the useful information she's got, and she'll take some time to recover from the mind-washing, so she's out of play as well as Tove Lundberg. That forces Asnan to concentrate on his operation against the Pope and leaves us free to concentrate on him and the Sword of Islam group . . ."

"And where does that put me?"

"It allows you, my dear Professor, to continue the fiction—that Tove Lundberg is out of your life and you are beginning to be interested in other women. That, of course, confirms the fairytales we'll be spreading. So while Omar Asnan is setting up his strategy for assassination, we'll be drawing the net tighter and tighter round him and his group."

"That sounds to me like a very risky race. Who pulls the pin out of the grenade first?"

"I can think of a pleasanter metaphor," said the Mossad man. "It's a very elaborate chess game. The players both know what is going on. The art is to choose the right move and judge all its consequences."

Leo the Pontiff was already laying out in his head a different chess game.

Tomorrow, in the mid-afternoon, he would go home to the Vatican. The journey would be made by helicopter, courtesy of the Italian airforce. It would save time, risk and the expense of a public procession from the mountains to the city. The Secretary of State was giving him the situation report.

"The Sword of Islam are already moving towards an attempt on Your Holiness's life. We are mounting a combined protective operation with the Italian Government and the Israelis. You will find on your return to the Vatican that internal security measures are somewhat more stringent. Apart from that, there will be no perceptible change in your administrative routine. We have noted your appointment of a new Senior Secretary and the retirement of Monsignor Malachy O'Rahilly, which, if I may say it, was generally regarded as a prudent step."

"I am glad." The Pontiff's tone was dry and formal. "For me, it was a painful decision . . . You should know that there will be other changes when I get back."

"Perhaps we should begin to set the machinery in motion immediately."

The Secretary of State could not have been more tentative, nor the Pontiff more abrupt.

"What machinery, Eminence?"

"If Your Holiness is thinking of a Curial Consistory—a meeting of all the cardinals residing in Rome—then notices should be sent out, an agenda prepared and circulated. If it's a question of a full Synod, that's at least twelve months of preparation."

"Matteo, I have never thought of you as an obtuse man."

"I trust not, Holiness."

"Then let's be clear. I have no intention of using those procedures, which so easily can be an excuse for deferring action. I am living on borrowed time. I am driven to use every moment. Look! We have command of every modern communication. We have, unless our balance sheets lie, even a substantial stake in satellite communications. I can talk by telephone or send a facsimile letter to all our senior bishops around the world. The contact is immediate. I propose to work with these tools. My Curia has a simple choice—work with me or wait around until they can elect a more complaisant candidate. I am prepared to be open with them. They have to be open with me."

"And if they oppose you?"

"I shall respect them as the loyal opposition, take their opinions under advisement and act according to my conscience."

"Then we are back to papal absolutism and collegiality goes out the window for good and all!"

"The Curia already rejects it *de facto!*" Once again he was the raptor, poised on the topmost branch ready to dive on the prey. "Most of our brethren in the Curia want it both ways. They pay lip-service to collegiality, the consensus of the bishops as apostolic successors in union with the Bishop of Rome. But that's not what they really mean, Matteo. They want what they have, a self-perpetuating oligarchy with all real power vested in them—because the Pope can't move a metre past the barriers they put up around him! I know that. You know it. It's a set-piece game. So I will play it exactly as it is laid out. I am the Successor of Peter, Supreme Pontiff and Pastor. So I am called; so I shall act: with love, because I have learned love, Matteo, but without fear, because I have looked into the face of Brother Death and seen a smile on it. I wish, I wish so much, that you may understand me!"

"I do, Holiness, believe me. You have the same loyalty as you had the day I kissed hands as your Secretary of State."

"I have demands to make on you, too, Matteo."

"I shall do my best to meet them; but I, too, am what I am. The only art I know is the art of the possible. Come the day when you want me to swear that the impossible is the possible, I will not do it."

"I ask no more. I expected no less. But I tell you truly, I am dreading my return to duty. I feel like a prisoner being walked back to his cell after a brief hour in the sunlight."

Agostini gave him a swift, appraising look and uttered the now familiar caution: "Salviati warned you, Holiness. This is only the first stage of your recovery. You must not try to do too much."

"It is not the doing, Matteo. The real burden is the knowing. I understand the workings of the Church better than any man alive, certainly better than my two immediate predecessors. But that's the problem: I understand it too well. On the one hand, Vatican City is the Sedes Apostolica, the See of Peter; on the other, it is an apparatus of power which we try always to endow with a sacred character, to justify our own mistakes and excesses. This is propaganda, not religion. It is a political conjuring trick, which impresses the faithful less and less each year. Look at me! Look at yourself! I am dressed in the white of innocence, you in the scarlet piping of a prince. Our Master walked the dusty roads of Palestine, slept under the stars, preached from a fishing boat. I am shamed by what we have become and by my personal contribution to it. Oh, I know what you will tell me. I cannot demean my office. I cannot cancel two thousand years of history. I cannot vacate the City and turn it over to the Vandals. But the plain fact is, Matteo, we cannot afford to go on as we are, a bloated bureaucracy riddled with jealousies and intrigues. I am sure even this long-awaited study of our finances will tell us the same thing in banker's language. And that brings me back to my first proposition. I propose to act, not sit as chairman of a Curial debating society."

"In that case, Holiness, permit me to offer you the advice my father gave me. He was a colonel in the Carabinieri. He used to say: never point a gun at a man, unless you're prepared to fire it. If you fire, don't miss, because one shot is all you get."

It was the warning which Abbot Alexis had given him, expressed in other terms: "It is the passion for action that destroys us all!" Yet he could see no other way of breaking out of the blockade which he himself had imposed. Expedient and not expedient, opportune, inopportune—these were the most potent words in the lexicon of Church government. They opened the floodgates of eternal debate; they could retard any decision until judgement day, on the pretext that its ultimate consequence had not yet been explored.

And yet he understood very well what Agostini was telling him: the more questions you could leave open, the less danger there was of having your mistakes cast in bronze to endure for centuries. Which reminded him of another proposition of Abbot Alexis: "You are interpreted by rhetors and officials and translated by journalists. Your authentic voice is never heard!" He put the same proposition to the Secretary of State, who gave it only a qualified answer . . .

"It's true; but how can it be otherwise? How can you guarantee the accuracy of a translation from your Italian into all the languages under heaven? Impossible. And with every new Pontiff we get the same old comedy in the press: 'The Holy Father is a great linguist. He can say "God bless you" in twenty languages.' And then he gets ambitious and starts stumbling through his public discourses like Linguaphone lessons! Your Holiness has been wise enough to know his own limitations!"

Leo the Pontiff laughed. It was an old Vatican horror story. Eight, ten different language versions of the same six-minute *discorso* used to be given to polyglot pilgrim groups in St. Peter's Square, just to prove that the Holy Father had the gift of tongues! Then there was the other cautionary tale about himself. Suggestions had been made, very sane and sensible suggestions, that he might make a series of sub-titled cassette programmes for worldwide television. However, the final impediment was his own incurable ugliness and the habitual severity of his expression. He could still chuckle over everyone's embarrassment as they tried to tell him. Agostini profited by his good humour to add an extra caution: "Your Holiness is aware of another lesson we have learned: the debasement of currency, the over-exposure of the Pontiff just to demonstrate his concern and involvement. Even in your dealings with the Curia, nice judgements have to be made; and your first policy statement will be crucial. That's the one shot which will win or lose the war."

"So tell me, Matteo; do you really believe I can win my war?"

"If it is your war, no. You will lose it. If it is God's, you will win it—though not, perhaps, in the way you hope."

The which, as the Pontiff mused on it, cast new light on the character of Matteo Agostini, Cardinal Secretary of State, a man dedicated to the art of the possible.

In the VIP lounge at Fiumicino, Matt Neylan took custody of his temporary family. He tried to be casual and good-humoured about it, but the spectacle of Britte, with her shambling body and her angelic face and the piercing intelligence that could not assemble the words to express itself, moved him strangely. She was both scared and excited in the unfamiliar surroundings and was making frantic efforts to communicate verbally with her mother, who had her own preoccupations and was unable to concentrate enough attention on the girl. Matt Neylan himself was walking on eggs. He dared not risk an untimely gesture towards mother or daughter and he was wondering how they would rub along together in a farmhouse in County Cork, with an old-fashioned Catholic housekeeper as chaperone—and she already in grief for a spoiled priest! Then Britte's small, clawlike hand stroked his cheek and her spindly body snuggled close to him. The words sprang unbidden to his lips: "You're not scared now, are you? This place we're going to is very friendly: green meadows and old stone walls and a path that runs down to a white beach. There are cattle and horses and an apple orchard, and the house is painted white and it has a big attic where you can paint to your heart's content . . . The place is large enough so you can be private and small enough to be cosy when the winter comes. Your bedroom, and your mother's, look towards the sea. My bedroom and study are on the opposite side, There's a living-room and a dining-room and a big, old-fashioned farmhouse kitchen. Mrs. Murtagh and her husband live next-door in the cottage. He manages the farm, she's my housekeeper, and i gather they're both much scandalised because I've left the Church. Still, they'll get used to it . . . I've ordered a new car to be delivered to me at the airport and there's a Range Rover at the house, so you won't be anchored or isolated . . . I hope I'm getting through to you, young lady, because I'm talking my silly head off . . ."

"You're getting through, Mr. Neylan. And you don't have to try so hard. We're both grateful; we both trust you."

"In which case, would you mind if we used Christian names?"

"We'd both like that."

Britte made her own sound of approval and turned to kiss him. Neylan caught the swift shadow of concern on Tove's face. He stood up, drew her with him out of earshot of the girl and told her curtly: "The girl's scared. She needs assurance. What do you think I am—an abuser of children?"

"Of course not! I didn't mean . . ."

"Listen! Until I get you two settled, we're going to be living like a family in the same house. I don't have much practice at that, but I do have a lot of practice at self-control. I drink only in moderation and the men of my family have the reputation of being good to their women. So why the hell don't you relax, madam, and pay me the compliment of simple trust . . . If your daughter wants to spend a little of the warmth she's got piling up inside her, I'm probably the safest man around to spend it on. Which, by the way, is not an assurance I'm giving to you or any other woman . . . if we can be clear on that, we should all have a pleasant holiday!"

Tove Lundberg gave him a small uncertain smile and then held out her hand.

"Message received and understood. I'm relieved. For a moment I thought you were going to blame me for the burning of Dublin!"

"That's for the winter. Every night I'll recite you a litany of the wrongs of Ireland."

"I'd rather you sang to me."

"Why not? There's a piano in the house—though it probably needs tuning. We'll have a come-all-ye."

"And what's that?"

"An Irish party. An open house: all your friends, and all your neighbours, and any wandering folk who happen by. It'd be interesting to see who turns up and what they think of the infidel priest and his two women!"

Nicol Peters was sitting on his terrace watching the swifts circling the cupolas of the old city and making the last adjustments to the latest edition of "A View From My Terrace". This time it was a somewhat eccentric piece, since he had agreed, in deference to a joint request from the Italians and from Mossad, to feed into it certain factual but provocative material:

"Miriam Latif, the young laboratory technician who disappeared under mysterious circumstances from the International Clinic, has now appeared, in equally mysterious circumstances, in Lebanon. According to reports, she simply walked into her parents' house in Byblos and announced that a man and a woman had brought her there. She could give no coherent account of her previous movements. She appears to have suffered no physical ill-treatment or sexual invasion and her parents have placed her in psychiatric care for observation and treatment. They have refused to disclose her whereabouts to the press.

"Meantime, reliable intelligence sources and the Vatican Secretariat of the State confirm that terrorist threats against the Pope are being taken very seriously. Special security measures are in force. His Holiness has returned by Army helicopter from Castel Gandolfo. The Pontiff is said to be untroubled by the threat, but irked by the restrictions imposed on his public appearances and even his movements within Vatican City itself.

"However, his health continues to improve. He has lost a great deal of weight and he exercises for an hour every day under the supervision of a therapist. Although His Holiness is still on a restricted schedule of work, there are strong rumours that winds of change may soon be blowing through Vatican City. Usually reliable sources suggest that the Pontiff has been deeply affected by his recent experiences and, indeed, has taken a revisionist view of certain important current issues. A well-known Vatican prelate made a pun about it: 'They told us he was having a bypass. Now it seems he has had a complete change of heart.'

"Hard evidence is, as usual, difficult to get, but already there have been two important changes. Anton Cardinal Drexel, the Camerlengo or Papal Chamberlain, has retired to his country estate. A new appointment must be made. Monsignor Malachy O'Rahilly, Senior Private Secretary to the Pontiff, is leaving Rome. His place will be taken by an Englishman, Monsignor Gerard Hopgood.

"To ordinary folk like you and me these are clerical matters, relevant only to the strange celibate world of those 'who have made themselves eunuchs for the sake of the Kingdom of Heaven'. In fact, they may well be portents of greater happenings in the worldwide organisation.

"The most important bodies in the bureaucracy of the Roman Church are the Congregations, which function like the Departments in a normal Civil Service. However, unlike the Civil Services, the Roman Congregations are organised on what is best described as an interlocking grid system. Thus the same names pop up in a variety of appointments. The Cardinal Secretary of State heads up the Council for the Public Affairs of the Church. A senior member of this Council is also a member of the Congregation for the Doctrine of the Faith. The same man sits on the Congregation for the Bishops. So to change any key personage is like pulling a thread in a piece of knitting—the whole pattern may unravel before your astonished eyes.

"So the Roman observer has to read, not only what seems to be happening, but what is happening in reality. I find it hard to believe that a man so fixed in his ideas as Leo XIV will commit himself to any relaxation of present disciplines. Yet he cannot fail to see that the Church is bleeding at every pore—people, clerics and even financial revenues.

"Vatican finances are in a parlous state. The place is running on a deficit of at least fifty million dollars a year. It is being constantly hit with rises in the cost of living and currency depreciations in every country of the world. It has never recovered from the sorry scandals of a recent era. Donations from the faithful are notably reduced. A full report by an international firm of auditors, commissioned by the present Pontiff, is to be delivered shortly. It is not expected to offer much hope of immediate improvement.

"Now to lighter, if not happier, matters. Professor Sergio Salviati, surgeon to

His Holiness, seems likely to lose the services of his most respected colleague, Ms. Tove Lundberg, who acts as counsellor to cardiac patients. Ms. Lundberg left Rome with her daughter Britte for an extended holiday in Denmark.

"Matt Neylan, recently Monsignor Matt Neylan of the Vatican Secretariat of State, now very much a man about this town, has just signed a six-figure two-book contract with an American publisher. Subject: personalities and policies at the Vatican Secretariat of State . . . Since Matt Neylan has severed all ties, not merely with the priesthood but with the Catholic Church, the book could prove an interesting investment for publishers and readers alike.

"One final item—and a caution for autumn tourists in Rome. The Guardia di Finanza have begun a new crackdown on drugs in this city. This week they seem to be concentrating their attention on the more expensive nightclubs. Latest to be gone over with a fine toothcomb was the Alhambra, a plush and pricy resort just near the Veneto. It is much frequented by Arab and Japanese businessmen and its floor shows are as expensive and raunchy as the traffic will allow. Patrons were patted down but not bothered too much; but staff got a real going over and the hat-check-and-cigarette girl was taken into custody. Latest reports say she is still being questioned . . ."

"They are playing games with us!" Omar Asnan was furious; but his anger was masked by a glacial calm. "The Lundberg woman left Rome on an Aer Lingus flight bound for Dublin. Our airport contacts identified her and her daughter, who was taken aboard in a wheelchair. Miriam Latif has been dumped back in her parents' lap, brainwashed and full of psychotropic drugs. The raid on the Alhambra was a blind—harassment and intimidation. That cigarette girl never handled anything stronger than tobacco! My servant reports two visits from the electricity company, checking the meter and the fuse-box . . . Then I have a call from the Vatican. My guided tour was cancelled because Monsignor Tabni was down with influenza. To cap it all, my friend Mr. Matt Neylan is suddenly called out of town, but he finds it necessary to telephone me, a man with whom he has passed one evening in a lifetime . . . That little thing bothered me like a flea-bite until I decided to call the airport again. Then I discovered that Mr. Matt Neylan left on the same flight as the Lundberg woman and her daughter." He broke off and surveyed the three men seated with him in the back of the limousine, which was parked on a dirt road in the pine woods near Ostia. "The conclusion is obvious, my friends. They are trying to drive us into a trap, like one of those tuna traps the fishermen use along the coast. It is constructed like a maze. The fish get in; they can't get out. They thresh about waiting for the *mattanza,* the bloody slaughter."

"So what are we going to do about it?"

"Abdicate," said Omar Asnan calmly.

"Abandon the project?"

"No. Sub-contract it."

"To whom?"

"I'm investigating possibilities."

"We have a right to know."

"You shall, at an appropriate time. But since I am underwriting the operation, I claim the privilege of arranging it to my own specifications. Besides, if any one of you is picked up as Miriam Latif was, all four of us—and the plan itself—are compromised."

"Are you saying you would hold out longer than the rest of us?"

"Not at all. Only that I am the last one they will pick up. They know about us all from Miriam; but they know most about me——where I live, where I do business, my bank accounts, and the important fact that I make a lot of money here and I'm not going to walk away from it. So trust me, gentlemen—and have a good flight to Tunis. We'll drop you in Ostia. You can take a taxi from there to the airport."

An hour and a half later, he was back in Rome lunching at Alfredo's with a Korean businessman who bought and sold container space, financed the cargoes to fill it and guaranteed to provide any service his clients needed, anywhere in the world.

The homecoming of the Pontiff was an event limited by a protocol which he himself had prescribed a long time ago and which he now regretted, with an almost childish anguish.

"At Drexel's house there were flowers in my bedroom and in the *salone*. From the first day of my accession, I forbade them here. I wanted to impress on all my household the notions of austerity and discipline. Now I miss them. I understand, as I never did before, that I have denied the Sisters who look after me the simple pleasure of a welcoming gesture. The youngest of them, a simple country girl, blurted it out: 'We wanted to put in flowers, but Mother Superior said you didn't like them.' Which at least gave me the opportunity to make the first small retreats from my old self. I told her that was an example of how wrong even a Pope could be. I would love to have flowers in my study and on the dining table. Only afterwards did it occur to me to ask myself what pleasure I could offer to them. Their lives are so much more confined, so much more under scrutiny than those of their sisters outside the Vatican. They still wear the old-fashioned habits—my orders again!—and their housekeeping tasks are boring in the extreme. Before I think about the big changes, here is a small but necessary one, right under my pontifical nose! If I feel confined—and tonight, dear God, I feel as though I am locked in a box—how much more must they feel it, in this kingdom of professional bachelors.

"Malachy O'Rahilly has already instructed them on the routines of my convalescence. He has set my desk in order, laid down a list of priorities. He has also presented his successor, a blond, square-jawed Englishman, very reserved, very cool, totally in command of himself. His Italian is more polished than mine. He writes Ciceronian Latin and Plato's Greek. He has French and Spanish, German and Russian, and a doctorate in Ecclesiastical History.

"To make conversation, I ask him what he presented as a doctoral thesis. He tells me it was a study of Pope Julius II, Giuliano della Rovere. That takes some of the stiffness out of our first talk, because there is a curious connection between this formidable warrior-pope and my home place of Mirandola. In the Palazzo Chigi in Rome there is a strange portrait of Julius in winter armour, painted during his siege of Mirandola in 1511.

"It is a tiny footnote to history, but it helps to soften the bleakness of my homecoming. It also encourages me to believe that in place of my very companionable Malachy O'Rahilly I may have found a tough young disciple with a sense of history.

"No sooner had I sent him off with Malachy O'Rahilly than I began to feel restless, claustrophobic. I wanted desperately to be at work, even though I knew I was not capable of it. Instead, I went into my private chapel and forced myself to sit in meditation for nearly an hour.

"I focused my mind on the Psalmist's words: 'Unless the Lord build the house, they labour in vain who build it.' I was immediately reminded of Agostini's warning, so unexpected from that very pragmatical man: 'If it is God's war, you will win it, though not, perhaps, in the way you expect.' Came the sudden awareness that all my thinking recently has been in terms of conflict and confrontation. Then, soft and insinuating, like the sound of distant bells, I heard the words of Jesus: 'A new commandment I give you: that you should love one another, as I have loved you.'

"How can I, an ugly man, possessed so long by an ugly spirit, gloss or change that luminous simplicity? So be it then! This will be my first text, on which I shall build my first colloquy . . ."

Yet, for all the brave confidence of the writing, his sleep was haunted by nightmares, and he woke next morning in the grip of a black and almost suicidal depression. His Mass seemed a sterile mummery. The nun who served his breakfast was like a character out of some oafish miracle play. He flinched at the pile of papers on his desk. Then, because he dared not any longer be seen as a maimed and halting spirit, he summoned his two secretaries to his desk and issued his directives for the day.

"Monsignor Hopgood. You will reply to all my well-wishers in the Hierarchy. A short letter in your best Latin, offering my thanks, telling them they will hear from me again, very soon. You will also go through these documents from the dicasteries. Give me a thumbnail summary of each, in Italian, and a draft reply, also in Italian. If you have problems, discuss them with Malachy. If you can't solve them between you, bring me what is left. Any questions?"

"Not yet, Holiness; but it is very early in the day."

He gathered up the trays of documents and left the room. The Pontiff turned to O'Rahilly. His voice was very gentle.

"Are you still bleeding, Malachy?"

"Yes I am, Holiness. The sooner I can be gone, the better I'll be pleased. Hopgood's in place now. As you've seen, he's a fast learner and he's ten times better qualified than I am. So, will Your Holiness not make it easy for me?"

"No, Malachy, I will not!"

"In God's name, why?"

"Because, Malachy, I know that if you walk out of here in anger, you'll never come back. You'll shut your mind and lock up your heart and you'll be unhappy until the day you die. You were meant to be a priest, Malachy—not a Papal Secretary, but a pastor, an understanding heart, a shoulder for folk to cry on when the world gets too much for them. It may get too much for you—and I know that's what you're afraid of—but what if it does? You and I are imperfect men in an imperfect world. You may not believe this; but I swear it is true. When I finished Mass this morning I was in so deep a despair that I wished I had died under Salviati's knife. But here I am and here you are and this sorry old world has work for both of us. Now, please, will you help me write a letter? It may be the most important one I've written in a lifetime."

There was a long moment of silence before Malachy O'Rahilly raised his eyes to confront his master. Then he nodded a reluctant assent.

"I am still in service, Holiness; but will you permit me to tell you something? If I don't get it out now it will never be said and I'll be ashamed of that always."

"Say whatever you want, Malachy."

"Here it is then, for better or worse, richer or poorer! You're just home from a long journey, a trip to the end of time, where you nearly dropped off the edge. The wonder of that and the fear of that are still with you. You're like Marco Polo, back from far Cathay, itching to share the strangeness and the risks of the Silk Road . . . You're convinced, as he was, that you've got knowledge and experience that will change the world. It will, it can, but not by the simple telling; because, as Marco Polo found and you'll find, very few even of your own brother bishops are going to believe you!"

"And why not, Malachy?"

Malachy O'Rahilly hesitated for a moment, then gave a rueful grin and threw out his hands in despair.

"Do you know what you're asking, Holiness? My head's in the lion's mouth already!"

"Answer the question, please. Why will they not believe me?"

"You're going to write them a letter first, an eloquent personal letter explaining this experience."

"That is my intention, yes."

"Holiness, believe me, you are the world's worst letter writer. You're too commonsensical. Too . . . too concrete and orderly. It takes a lot of work to polish your style, and even then it's never emotional or eloquent enough to be more than a document. It certainly doesn't speak with the tongues of men and angels. But that's only the beginning of the problem . . . The crux of it is, you're suspect, you will be for months yet. This cardiac intervention is a commonplace now. The sequelae are well documented. All your brother bishops have been warned that, for the time being at least, there will be a lame duck administration. You won't find it anywhere in writing; no one will admit to being the source of the information; but it's out there and for the present it taints everything you do or say. Right or wrong, Holiness, that's my testimony . . ."

"And your head is still on your shoulders, is it not?"

"It feels like it, Holiness."

"So answer me one more question, Malachy. I'm a suspect leader. What should I do about it?"

"Are you seeking an opinion, Holiness—or do you just feel the need to pin my ears to the wall?"

"An opinion, Malachy."

"Well, look at it from the outsider's point of view. You've been an iron-fisted Pontiff. You've installed some iron-fisted fellows in the Curia and in the national churches. Now suddenly your Grand Inquisitor, Cardinal Clemens, is out of favour. He's put that word about, all by himself. So now there's doubt. Everybody's wondering which way the cat will jump. Fine! Let 'em wonder! Do nothing. Gerard Hopgood will keep your desk clean and demonstrate that you're working as efficiently as ever. Meantime, develop the one big *motu proprio* that says and does everything you want and when it's ready, summon a short-notice full Consistory and publish it—tic-tac!—in your old style. That way, you're not putting yourself forward as Lazarus, straight out of the tomb and shaky on his pins! In this most Christian Assembly, we hate innovators—even when they sit in Peter's Chair. You can lock a saint up in a monastery; you can sack a mere monsignor; but a modernising pope is a long-term embarrassment! Now, Holiness, I beg you, please let me go!"

Forty-eight hours later, Monsignor Malachy O'Rahilly left Rome, with ten thousand dollars in his pocket—a gift from the Pontiff's privy purse. At the same time, the Pontiff announced a private Consistory of the College of Cardinals, to be held November 1st, the Feast of All Saints. At this Consistory the Pontiff would promulgate new appointments and deliver an allocution entitled *"Christus Salvator Homo Viator"*—Christ the Savior, Man the Pilgrim.

XIII

SUMMER wore swiftly into autumn. The *maestrale* stopped blowing. The seas lay slack and listless. The mists gathered in the river valleys. The late vintages were in and the stubble was ploughed under. In Rome, the final waves of tourists arrived—the wise ones who had missed the summer heats to travel in the mild, sunny weather. The pilgrims gathered on Sundays in St. Peter's Square and the Pontiff stood at his window to bless them and recite the Angelus, because his guardians would not let him descend into the square as he had done in former times. The terrorist threat was still marked "probable" in the intelligence records.

Inside the Vatican, there was an Indian summer. His Holiness was proving a docile patient. He was still following the strict regimen of diet, rest and exercise. His physician was pleased with his progress. His surgeon did not need to see him for another six months. The work that passed across the papal desk was handled promptly and efficiently.

The new secretary was discreet, serviceable and, so rumour had it, a linguist to rival the fabulous Cardinal Mezzofanti. Most important of all, the Pontiff himself gave an impression of calm, of optimism, of lively but benevolent curiosity. He had even suggested to the Mother Superior that the nuns of the Papal Household might be more comfortable in modern dress, and that they should be given more leave time outside the precinct of the City.

For the rest, the routines of the Apostolic Palace and the Papal Household had settled back to normal. His Holiness gave audience to foreign dignataries, to bishops making their *ad limina* visits to pay homage and make the offerings of their people to the Successor of Peter. They found him thinned down, less brusque than they remembered him, more generous with his time, more searching in his enquiries. He asked, for example, how matters stood between them and Apostolic Delegates or Nuncios in their countries. Was there harmony, open communication? Did they feel spied upon? Were they given copies of reports made to Rome about the local church and clergy? Did they feel totally free to announce the Good News, interpret it to their people boldly, or did they feel constrained by fear of delation or denunciation to Rome? How well or ill did Rome understand their problems, the special conditions of their flock? And the last question of each audience was always the same: What do you need from us? What can we do for you?

Sometimes the answers were bland; sometimes they were almost brutally frank; but every night Leo the Pontiff set them down in his diary. Each day he tried to incorporate them into the allocution, which was growing slowly, page by page. It was like putting together a jigsaw puzzle as big as the world. How did the problems of bio-ethics in prosperous societies fit with the appalling toll of famine in the desert fringes? What moral definitions should be applied to the destruction of rainforests and the genocidal land-grabbers of Brazil? How boldly was he prepared to speak about a married clergy, the rights and status of women within the Christian assembly, the vexed question of a female priesthood? Then, one day, Monsignor Gerard Hopgood brought back a pile of typescript, the compilation of the Pontiff's handwritten notes. By accident or design, he found, stuck in among the pages, a scrap of paper on which was written in Hopgood's clear cursive script: "Round and round the mulberry bush! Why don't we say it plainly, once and for all? We have the message of salvation, total and complete. We do not and never will have the answer to every ethical problem that may arise . . ."

The next time Hopgood came in with letters to be signed, the Pontiff handed him the paper with an offhand remark: "I think you dropped this."

Hopgood, cool as ever, simply glanced at the torn piece of foolscap and nodded.

"Yes, I did. Thank you, Holiness."

His Holiness went on signing the letters. He spoke without raising his eyes from the paper.

"What do you think of my allocution, so far?"

"So far," said Hopgood carefully, "it seems as though you are writing your way towards a document. You are a long way from the document itself."

"As bad as that, eh?" The Pontiff went on writing assiduously.

"Neither bad nor good. It should not be judged in its present tentative form."

"Monsignor O'Rahilly told me I was the world's worst writer. Any comments?"

"None. But if Your Holiness would entertain a suggestion . . . ?"

"Make it."

"Writing as you are doing it is brutal labour. Why inflict it on yourself? If you will give me an hour a day, and talk out to me what you want to say, I'll write it for you in half the time. Then you can cut it about to suit yourself. I'm good at that sort of thing. I've written and directed theatre at Oxford; so the rhetoric of the thing is easy for me . . . Besides, I very much want this Consistory to be a success."

The Pontiff put down his pen, leaned back in his chair and studied Hopgood with dark, unblinking eyes.

"And how would you define a success?"

Hopgood considered the question for a few moments then, in his precise, donnish fashion, he answered it.

"Your audience will be men powerful in the Church. They can, if they choose, remain totally indifferent to anything you say. If they dislike it, they can obstruct you in a thousand ways. But if they go out into St. Peter's Square and look at the people and feel a new kinship with them and a new care for them . . . then your allocution will have meant something. If not, it will be wind-blown words, lost the moment they are spoken."

"You seem to me to be a very dedicated but rather reclusive young man. What is your own contact with the people?"

It was the first time the Pontiff had seen Monsignor Gerard Hopgood embarrassed. He blushed, shifted uneasily on his feet and made the surprising confession.

"I'm a runner, Holiness. I train on my days off with a club over on the Flaminia. A friend of mine is the priest there. He set up the club to keep the kids off the drug circuit and out of the thieves' kitchens. So the answer is that I do see quite a lot of the people."

"Are you a good runner, Monsignore?"

"Not bad . . . which reminds me: you've been missing your morning exercises, Holiness. You can't afford to do that, it's dangerous! If it helps, I'll do them with you."

"I am rebuked in my own house," said Leo the Pontiff. "And by my own secretary! A runner indeed!"

" 'Let us run with endurance'," said Monsignor Hopgood innocently. "St. Paul to the Hebrews. I wait on Your Holiness's decision about the allocution— and the exercises. Pesonally, I'll settle for the exercises, because they at least will keep you alive. In the end, it's the Holy Spirit who takes care of the Church."

The Pontiff signed the last of the letters. Hopgood gathered them into the file and waited for his formal dismissal. Instead, the Pontiff waved him to a chair.

"Sit down. Let us go through the text we have so far . . ."

On Matt Neylan's farm, it was another kind of autumn, warm and misty from the wash of the Gulf Stream, cloudy most days, with the air smelling of sea wrack and peat smoke and the trodden grass of the cow pastures. It was a lonely place, halfway between Clonakilty and Courtmacsherry, thirty-five acres of grazing land, with an orchard and a kitchen garden and a view across the bay to Galley Head.

The house was larger than he had remembered, with a tree-break planted against the westerlies, and central heating, and a walled garden where roses grew and pears and apples were espaliered along the walls. Inside, it was spotless. His mother's ornaments were all in place, his father's books dusted, the pictures square on the walls. There was a Barry over the mantel and a David Maclise in his study, which was a pleasant windfall to be going on with.

The welcome the Murtaghs gave them was like the climate, grey and tepid; but once Neylan had told them the story: how this brave woman had nursed and counselled His Holiness and was now threatened with kidnap and worse, and how this dear child was the ward and the adoptive granddaughter of the great Cardinal Drexel himself—then they warmed up and Mrs. Murtagh fussed around the pair like a mother hen, while Neylan and Mr. Murtagh drank Irish whiskey in the kitchen.

Which left only the problem of his own defection from the faith which, as Mr. Murtagh put it, didn't worry him too much but bothered his old woman somewhat, she having a sister in the Presentation convent at Courtmacsherry. But then—he conceded after two whiskies—a man's belief was his own business, and wasn't he giving shelter and protection to these two threatened creatures? Which prompted the next question: did Neylan think they'd be pursued to this neck of the woods? Neylan admitted that it was possible, but hardly likely. However, just in case, it might pay to pass the word around the villages that an early warning of strangers would be appreciated. And—this was Murtagh's contribution—there was a twelve-bore shotgun and a rook rifle that used to belong to his father. It would be wise to keep them oiled and clean. And, by the way, how did he want to be addressed, now that he wasn't a priest any more? And what about the ladies, Missus or Miss? Christian names, Matt Neylan told him—and wondered what it was that made a name Christian when its owner wasn't.

After that, life was easier. They were fed like kings. Britte was coddled. They explored the coast from Skibbereen to Limerick and down across the counties to Waterford. They ate well and drank well and slept warm, though separate. It was only when the first gales hit that they looked at each other and asked what the devil they were doing in this place and how did they expect to get through the winter?

Two telephone calls gave them the answer. Salviati said without hesitation: "Stay put. It hasn't begun yet." The Israeli Embassy gave them an even plainer warning: "Don't move. Keep your heads down. We'll tell you when it's safe to return!" Then for good measure they gave them a telephone number in Dublin where Mossad maintained a station to watch the arms runners from Libya and elsewhere.

So, Britte began to paint. Matt Neylan picked up his writing and Tove Lundberg fretted in silence until she read that a German manufacturer of pharmaceuticals, enjoying a tax holiday in Ireland, had decided to endow a cardiac unit at the Sisters of Mercy hospital in Cork. They would need skilled staff. She had the best possible references. Any objections? From Britte, none. Matt was working at home. The Murtaghs kept the house and the farm going. From Matt Neylan?

"What can I say? If it's a choice between going crazy here or sticking your head up a little—and who, for Christ's sake, reads about Cork in Rome?—then go to it, by all means. It's a forty-mile drive from here to Cork. They'll probably give you a room at the hospital. Why not apply?"

"You don't mind looking after Britte?"

"What's to look after? Mrs. Murtagh mothers her and does the girl things she needs. I entertain her and cart her about with me when she isn't painting. It seems to work for her. You're the one who has to be happy with the arrangements."

"What about you?"

"I'm fine. I'm in my own home. For the moment, I'm happy. I'm working well."

"And that's all?"

"No, it isn't. One day I'm going to get a twitch and an itch and I'll drive to Dublin and take a flight to somewhere and come back when I've played myself out. The Murtaghs will see to Britte. You'll be around. That's my end of the bargain. Do you have any problem with it?"

"No, Matt. But I think you have."

"Sure, I've got problems!" Suddenly the urge was on him to talk. "But they're mine. They have nothing to do with you and Britte. I looked forward to coming back—and in one way I wasn't disappointed. It's a comfortable living. It's a nice cushion to have at my back if the bad times come. But that's it! There's no future for me here, no continuity. The taproot's been cut. I don't belong to the old Catholic Ireland; I've no taste for the new rich and the tax-haveners from Europe. When the day comes that I fall in love and want to settle down with a woman, I know it isn't going to be here . . ."

"I understand how you feel."

"I believe you do."

"Don't you see? Our lives run parallel to each other. We both left an old, harsh religion, a small country, a small language, a narrow history. We both became mercenaries in a foreign service. I couldn't live in Denmark now, any more than you could live here."

"That's the country. What about marriage?"

"Out of the question for me."

"Where does that leave Salviati?"

"Where he needs to be: free to make a new start with a new woman."

"That's noble of you!"

"For God's sake! It's a selfish choice right down the line. I couldn't ask any man to share the responsibility of Britte. I don't want to risk another child at my age. And even if I had one, it would put Britte into a kind of permanent exile. I've seen it happen in many families. The normal children resent the maimed one."

"It seems to me," said Matt Neylan quietly, "you're predicating everything on a perfect world, which we both know doesn't exist. For most of us, life's a make-and-mend affair. I'm sure many of my former colleagues see me as a happy-go-lucky infidel with alley-cat morals and all the women in the world to play with. Given the headlong way I've been living lately, I don't blame them. But the real truth is something different. I'm like the camel-driver who fell asleep under a palm tree and woke to find the caravan gone and himself alone in the middle of a desert. I'm not crying about it, just trying to make a point."

"Which is?"

"Britte and I. We get along very well. We manage to communicate. We're companionable. I'm at least a useful father figure to take the place of Nonno Drexel. Inside that beautiful head and behind all that gobbledegook muttering is a mind like a razor and I know she's slicing me up every day and putting me under a microscope. Right now, we're talking about an exhibition in a good gallery in Cork or Dublin."

"I presume you were going to consult me at some stage?"

"At some stage, sure; but it's too early yet. As far as you and I are concerned . . . Oh hell! How did we get into all this?"

"I don't know; but you've got the floor, Matt. First, your speech!"

He plunged ahead recklessly.

"Then I'll say it fast and if you don't like it you can spit in my eye. You're a thousand times welcome under my roof. Whether I'm here or not, this house is your house and there's neither rent nor board to be thought of! But I sleep just across the hall and I lie awake at night wanting you and knowing I'd take you on any terms, for as long or as little time as you wanted me, because you're a very special woman, Tove Lundberg, and if I thought they'd make you happy I'd pull the stars out of the sky and toss them in your lap! There now, it's out! You'll hear no more of it. Would you join me in a drink, madam? I think I need one!"

"I'll get it," said Tove Lundberg. "You Irish make such a big mouthful of simple things. Why didn't you just ask me, instead of wasting all this time?"

Late in September, His Excellency Yukishege Hayashi, Ambassador Extraordinary and Plenipotentiary to the Holy See, received a letter from Tokyo. The letter informed His Excellency that a team of independent film-makers would be visiting Rome during October and November. Part of their assignment would be to make a two-hour documentary for Japanese television on the Vatican and its treasures. His Excellency was asked to facilitate this work and secure the good offices of the Pontifical Commission on Social Communications, through whom all the required permissions must be secured.

The letter was accompanied by a copy of a recommendation from the Pro-Nuncio Apostolic Archbishop, Paul Ryuji Arai, to the President of the Commission, requesting his personal interest in the project.

It was one of hundreds of such requests the Commissioners received during a year. Its provenance was impeccable. There were very sound reasons for extending special courtesies to the Japanese. His Excellency was assured that permissions would be issued as soon as the team arrived in Rome and had filed the usual information: number of persons in the team, subjects to be photographed, equipment and transport, thus and thus and thus.

At the same time, the President wrote personally to the Ambassador, pointing out that, on the Feast of All Saints, the whole College of Cardinals would assist at a Pontifical High Mass in St. Peter's and that the Diplomatic Corps would be invited to attend. This would seem to be a ceremony, unique in character, which would recommend itself to the film-makers, especially since His Excellency himself would be present, representing the Emperor.

The information was mentioned casually in a conversation with Nicol Peters, who had called on the Commission to discuss the announcement of the Consistory and how it fitted into the hidden subtext of Vatican affairs. On that question, the President was bland but vague. To inform himself more fully, Peters telephoned Cardinal Drexel and was promptly invited to lunch. The old man was trenchant and vigorous as ever, but admitted frankly that there was a gap in his life.

"I miss my Britte. I miss her mother too. Still, I am glad they are safe and they appear to be happy. Britte sends me sketches and watercolours and they are cheerful pieces. Tove writes regularly. She speaks very warmly of your friend Neylan and his care of them both. I never knew the man, of course. There was never any scandal about him as priest . . . However, you didn't come here to talk about my family affairs. What do you want to know?"

"This Consistory. It seems an old-fashioned, almost retrograde, step. After Vatican II the notion was always to continue and to emphasise collegiality, the role of the bishops. So far the Synods have produced more window-dressing than results; but at least the principle has been affirmed. Now this private Consistory, as I understand it, is to be limited to members of the College of Cardinals. Why?"

Drexel did not answer immediately. He sat slicing a piece of country cheese and selecting a pear to go with it. Finally, he set down his knife and explained carefully.

"You will not quote me on this. That would create jealousy and do harm, since I am retired and I must not seem to be trying to intrude into Curial affairs. On the other hand, I would like you to record very accurately what I am about to tell you. It is important. You know that this Pontiff is by nature an old-fashioned man. He is changed, profoundly changed; but instead of trying to create a new image for himself, he has chosen to live with the old one of which —you may not know this—he is often ashamed. He thinks of himself as an ugly man with an ugly nature. For a long time he was just that. Now, however, he has made a decision, a wise one I believe, not to concern himself with image, but with fact and practice in the Church today. He is also holding strictly to protocol. A Consistory, by tradition, is not a consultative assembly. It is a meeting at which the Pontiff promulgates appointments, makes known his personal sentiments on matters of concern, forewarns of his personal decisions. A Synod is another matter. It is a discussive, deliberative, deciding body of bishops in union with the Bishop of Rome. Its acts are collegial acts."

"So, on the face of it," said Nicol Peters deliberately, "Leo XIV is abrogating the collegial procedure and going straight to promulgation."

"That's what they think he will do. It's absolutely in character. He will begin by announcing changes and appointments within the Curia."

"Do you have any information on those, Eminence?"

"Some, but I cannot discuss them. After that announcement, His Holiness will deliver an allocution, an address outlining his views on matters of importance. That address will foreshadow a more formal document, the *motu proprio,* which will be issued shortly afterwards."

"Will there be debate or discussion after the speech?"

"That will depend entirely on the Pontiff."

"Will the speech be available to the press?"

"No."

"Why not?"

"Protocol again. This is a private and not a public Consistory. However, His Holiness may well direct that a summary be published by *Osservatore Romano* or distributed through the Sala Stampa . . . Try some of this cheese, it's very good. Coffee?"

"Please."

"Any more questions?"

"May we talk now, off the record?"

"If you wish."

"The policies of Leo XIV have been both rigorous and divisive."

"No comment."

"Will he reverse those policies?"

"He will try, yes."

"Will he be able to heal the rifts in the Church?"

"Some, yes. Others, no. In any case, none of it will happen overnight. You see, my friend, we call ourselves the One, Holy, Universal and Apostolic Church. We are all of those things and none of them. That's the paradox and the mystery. In and through Christ we are one, we are holy, we are brothers and sisters in a worldwide family and the word we preach is that preached by the first Apostles who heard it from the lips of the Lord. But away from Him, without Him, of ourselves only, what are we? A lost race in a tiny planetary system, vagrant in the deeps of space."

"And how does Your Eminence regard those millions who do not, and cannot, share this Faith? How does His Holiness regard them?"

"I can answer only for myself," said Anton Cardinal Drexel. "This time we have is a bridge between two eternities. This light we have has been travelling to us for uncounted years. The tongues we speak, the symbols we use, are human inventions, inadequate for anything but the uses of the moment, yet always seeking to express that ineffable mystery of a Godhead which contains and maintains and sustains us all. When you get old, my dear Nico, you are much less conscious of difference than of identity. Plant us in the ground and we all turn into daffodils!"

"Which brings me to my last question, Eminence. The threat to assassinate the Pontiff was made by an Islamic group. Is it possible that he is hated enough to be killed by one of his own?"

Anton Cardinal Drexel knew this man too well to dismiss the question. He frowned and said: "We've known each other too long to play games, Nico. What exactly is on your mind?"

"The terrorist threat has been widely publicised. I'm asking whether another group, or another person even, might take advantage of that to stage a private execution."

"It's possible. Anything is possible in this crazy world. Do you have any ideas?"

"Do you remember Lorenzo de Rosa?"

"Only too well."

"I was going through my files the other day and it occurred to me that I'd never bothered to follow up that story. De Rosa, his wife, their children, were dead. The police had taken over. *Basta!* End of story."

"Not quite. His Holiness is moving towards reforms prompted by that sad business."

"Good! But that's not what I was thinking about. There were families involved, parents, aunts and uncles, cousins. Lorenzo was Tuscan, his wife was Sicilian, old family from Palermo, lots of relatives."

"Are you telling me they have made threats?"

"No. But all of us in the Press Club got one of these and there was one pinned to the message board." He fished in his wallet and brought out one of those small obituary cards, with a black cross and a black border which friends and relatives of the deceased kept in their prayer books. There was a photograph of Lorenzo de Rosa with his wife and children, the dates of their deaths and the place of their burial. The inscription read: "God has a long memory. He demands to be paid. May these we loved rest in peace."

Drexel handed back the card and said, almost pleadingly, "Once before we called up the ghosts and look what happened. Forget it, my friend! Tear it up and forget it! We know where the real threat comes from. This is just the excuse people would use to avoid trouble with the Islamic world. We cannot bow to terror, whoever practises it."

In the most secure room at the Israeli Embassy, Menachem Avriel was in conference with the man who called himself Aharon ben Shaul. They had a decision to make. It was Aharon who laid down the terms of it.

"Do we deal with the Sword of Islam ourselves or do we leave it to the Italians?"

"Can we be sure they'll take the action we want?"

"No."

"Even with an extra push from the Vatican?"

"No again."

"Once more, please, walk me though what we've got."

"Item one. Omar Asnan is the head of the organisation in this country. Item two. His three lieutenants are no longer in Italy. Two are in Tunis, one in Malta. The other members of the group, those we've identified at the Alhambra Club and other places, are still here, though inactive. Which brings us to item three. There is strong evidence to suggest that Omar Asnan has not abandoned his operations, but sub-contracted them. It's not an uncommon practice, as you know. Terror is big business, international business. The currencies are arms, cash, drugs and the barter of facilities."

"With whom is Asnan dealing?"

"This man." He shoved a photograph across the table. "Hyun Myung Kim, a Korean who peddles shipping space and sells spot cargoes around the world. He's a travelling man, who's known for driving hard bargains but delivering what he sells. Omar Asnan met him over lunch at Alfredo's the same day his henchmen left for Tunis . . . We weren't able to bug him, but we had a camera on him. Money was passed, as you see."

"The Italians have this information?"

"Sure. We're playing strictly according to the book. Their question was: what had we really got to take to court?" Then I played them the tapes from the bugs in Asnan's house. They agreed they meant what they seemed to say, but again the question: how would they sound in court? We'd have to admit they were composites and, knowing the risks involved of reprisals against aircraft, shipping, Italian citizens travelling in Islamic countries, the Italians wouldn't buy anything but a watertight case—the smoking gun, the assassin standing over the body. They're willing to deport Asnan quietly; but that gets us nowhere. We need to sweat him for information."

"So Asnan goes scot-free."

"Unless we lift him ourselves."

"How the hell do you do that? The man's a permanent resident. He goes to Embassy functions. He maintains an expensive lifestyle . . ."

"He also killed our man and made him disappear very effectively."

"Which isn't the hardest thing in the world in that archaeological zone. There are three major catacombs and a whole series of others never opened to the public. There's even one called the Catacomb of the Jews, in case you're interested!"

"I'm very interested," said Aharon ben Shaul. "So interested that I staged a power failure at Mr. Asnan's villa and put a couple of electricians in to check the wiring. They discovered a reverse cycle air conditioner that's much too big for a villa that size, with wiring and ducting that doesn't fit the registered plan . . ."

"So?"

"So before I go back to the Italians or you decide we'll go without them, I'd like to do a real job on Mr. Asnan's villa."

"What sort of job?"

"Old-fashioned break and enter. Put the dogs and the servants to sleep, strip out the valuables. The Appia Antica is a very vulnerable area. Insurance premiums are high. And they haven't had a decent robbery for nearly three months!"

"And where will Omar Asnan be while all this is happening?"

"Good question, Mr. Ambassador. When I have the answer, I'll let you know."

"Please don't," said Avriel. "Please, don't even tell me the time of day!"

"I'm not looking forward to this session." The Pontiff sat at his desk, tapping an impatient rhythm on the documents Hopgood had laid in front of him. "Clemens will be here exactly at ten. Make sure he is not kept waiting."

"How much time shall I allow for the meeting, Holiness?"

"As long as it takes. Offer coffee when he arrives; then don't come in unless I ring."

"A suggestion, Holiness."

"Yes?"

"The leatherbound volume under your hand is the report on the financial condition of the Church; three hundred and fifty pages of it, with figures, graphics and comments on every item."

"I can't even begin to think about this today."

"With respect, Holiness, I think you should read the last ten pages before Cardinal Clemens arrives. They deal with conclusions and recommendations and they confirm the main lines of the arguments you will be presenting to His Eminence."

"Who else has seen this document?"

"Copies were delivered simultaneously yesterday evening to Your Holiness, to the Prefecture for the Economic Affairs of the Holy See, the Institute for Works of Religion and the Administration of the Patrimony of the Apostolic See. No one will have had time to read or digest it; Your Holiness should, I believe, have the advantage of a first glance. There's an old English proverb which translates quite well into Italian: 'Twice armed is he whose cause is just; thrice armed the one who gets his blow in first.' "

"And that, I would remind you, my dear Hopgood, is still the language of confrontation, which is exactly what we are trying to avoid."

"With great respect, Holiness, I doubt you'll be able to avoid it this morning."

"How long before Clemens arrives?"

"Forty minutes."

"Let me take a look at this report. I'll ring when I'm ready."

The authors of the document wrote in the dry, passionless style of money-men everywhere, but their final summation took on, perforce, a bleak eloquence.

"It is difficult to avoid the conclusion that those Catholic congregations which are expanding most rapidly in Third World countries are also the most needy, while those with a no-growth or low-growth rate are the most prosperous and the least generous in the traditional gift-giving.

"In so-called Catholic countries like the South Americas, Spain, Italy, the Philippines, where there is a traditionally wealthy and privileged class, still loyal to the Church, there is an often quite appalling disparity in social conditions, and a hostility born of fear between the privileged and the deprived, the exploiters and the exploited. The privileged use their surplus to improve or protect their position. There is no noticeable increase in the revenues available for education, works of charity or social betterment.

"It has to be said also that in those dioceses and parishes where accounts are published and expenditures thoroughly documented, the level of donations is appreciably higher than elsewhere. So far as the central administration is concerned, it suffers and will continue to suffer from pandemic secrecy and the long consequences of well known scandals and affiliation with known criminals.

"Finally, with the increasing conglomeration of large corporations with diverse interests, it is becoming more and more difficult for those who handle Church funds to find untainted investments—e.g. a chemical company that does not manufacture toxic substances; a manufacturer not connected with arms or military equipment; a pharmaceutical company which does not manufacture birth control products, which Catholics are specifically forbidden to use . . . With the best will in the world, scandal can hardly be avoided; but in the end, secrecy breeds suspicion and suspicion causes the fountain of charity to dry up very quickly . . ."

There was more, much more in the same vein, carefully cross-referenced and footnoted, but the import was the same. Needs were growing, revenue was declining. The traditional sources were drying up. The traditional methods of funding from the worldwide congregations were no longer effective, because the congregations in the affluent countries were getting smaller.

But the nub of the matter was the "why". The money-men touched only the outer skin, they could not reach down for heart's reasons. In the old days, when the faithful were lapsing into indifference or their offerings were falling off, the bishop would call in missionary preachers, fiery, eloquent men who set up a cross in the market square and preached hellfire and damnation and the love of God that snatched folk like burning brands from the pit. Some were converted, some were changed for a while, no one was quite unmoved and nine months later the birthrate showed a marked increase. But those were other times and other manners, and it was very hard for the most eloquent of men to get past the glazed eyes and numbed imaginations and atrophied reason of a genera-tion of television addicts and victims of media saturation.

He himself was faced with the same problem. He was a man framed in splendour, endowed with the mighty numen of an ancient faith and yet he rated less attention than some shouting clown with a guitar or a drunken riot at a soccer match.

Hopgood ushered in His Eminence Karl Emil Cardinal Clemens. Their greeting was cordial enough. Time had passed. Tempers had cooled. Clemens opened the talk with a compliment.

"Your Holiness looks well and very trim. At least fifteen years younger."

"I train like a footballer, Karl—and eat like a bird! No fat, no red meat . . . Never talk to me about the penitential life. I'm compelled to it. And you?"

"I'm well. A touch of gout sometimes. My blood pressure's a trifle high; but my doctor tells me I'm a hypertensive character."

"And does he tell you where that can lead?"

"Well, he gives me the usual warnings."

"If you don't heed them, Karl, you'll end up exactly where I did. At your age you can't afford to play dice games with your health. Which brings me to the reason for this morning's talk. I am moving you from the Congregation for the Doctrine of the Faith. I am appointing you head of my household: Cardinal Camerlengo. You will retain your appointments with the Congregation for the Oriental Churches and for the Propagation of the Faith. These changes will be announced at the Consistory on November first. I trust that is agreeable to you?"

"It is not agreeable, Holiness, but I bow to Your Holiness's wishes."

"You have a right to know the reason."

"I have not asked for it, Holiness."

"Nonetheless, I shall give it to you. I propose to make certain drastic changes in the constitution and the functions of the Congregation. You will not agree with them. It would be quite unfair to ask you to implement them. Further— and I want you to know this—I appointed you because I saw in you the mirror image of the man I believed myself to be: the stalwart guardian of the Faith committed to us all. You have been that. You have discharged exactly the commission I gave you. Your lapse with *Osservatore Romano* angered me; but that alone would not have brought me to this decision. The fact is, Karl, I believe I misread my own duty and gave you the wrong brief!"

Clemens gaped at him in utter disbelief.

"If Your Holiness is saying that it is no longer his duty to guard the Deposit of Faith . . ."

"No, Karl. I am not saying that. I am saying that the Congregation in its present form and function is not an appropriate instrument. As a matter of historic fact, it never has been. In my view it never can be."

"I don't see that at all."

"I know you don't, Karl. That's why I'm moving you; but you are going to hear my explanation, because it has references far beyond this present matter.

Suppose you walk me through the procedures." He laid open on his desk the large volume of the Acta Apostolicae Sedis for the year 1971. "A denunciation is made of a book or publication which is deemed contrary to the Faith. What happens?"

"First, the denunciation has to be serious and it has to be signed. If the error is obvious and—I am quoting now—'if it contains certainly and clearly an error in Faith and if the publication of that opinion would do harm to the faithful', then the Congregation may ask the bishop or bishops to inform the author and invite him to amend the error."

"Let's pause there a moment. I need to be very clear. At this stage, the author knows nothing. Someone has denounced his writing. The Congregation has judged it erroneous and asked for a correction."

"That's right."

"He hasn't been heard, offered a right to reply. He is already presumed guilty."

"Effectively, yes. But that is only so in the case of blatant error, one immediately visible."

"So, let us pass to a more complex issue. A controversial opinion is published. The Congregation is required to decide whether it is or is not—and here I quote—'in harmony with divine revelation and the *magisterium* of the Church'. Immediately, it seems to me, not only the author but we are in real trouble . . . Divine revelation is one thing. The *magisterium,* the general authority of the Church, is quite another. Under that authority, things can be and have been done quite contrary to divine revelation: witch-hunts, the burning of heretics. You see the problem?"

"I point out," said Clemens stiffly, "that these anomalies have existed for a long time and Your Holiness has never found it necessary to object to them."

"Exactly what I have told you, Karl. I see them now in a different light. I propose to exercise my authority to change them. But let us go on. The author is aware of the doubts cast on his work?"

"Not yet. But we appoint a spokesman for the author; you'll find him described in the Acts as *relator pro auctore!* His function is also described: 'To indicate in a spirit of truth the merits and positive aspects of the work; to help reach the true meaning of the author's opinions . . .' and so on and so on . . ."

"But this spokesman," the Pontiff's tone was mild, "is quite unknown to the author. He is, in fact, forbidden to communicate with him. How can he possibly give an accurate rendering of his opinions, his merits, all the rest?"

"He can do so, Holiness, because he is in exactly the same position as any member of the public reading the book. He rests on the text."

The Pontiff did not answer directly. He held up two volumes which had been lying on his desk. One was entitled *The Nature of Faith*, the other *The Word Made Flesh.*

"You yourself wrote these, Karl."

"I did."

"And you kindly inscribed them to me. I read them with interest. I did not object to them, but I marked certain passages which seemed to me to be obscure, or which could be interpreted as not quite orthodox . . . Now, let me ask you: would you like to have these works judged by the same criteria and by the same secretive, inquisitorial methods as are presently employed?"

"If Your Holiness required it, yes."

"Would you feel justice had been done or could be assumed or seen to be done?"

"There are, I admit, certain shortcomings . . ."

"Which my predecessors and I have condoned but which I can permit no longer. We can go further if you want. I have a long list of objections. Shall I recite them all?"

"It will not be necessary, Holiness."

"But it will be necessary for you to understand better, Karl. We, you and I, the rest of our brother bishops, we are the City set on a mountain-top. We cannot hide our deeds, our commission is to be witness to the world—and if we do not give witness to truth, to justice, to our free search for God's meaning in God's world, then people will call us liars and hypocrites and turn away. We are going to be living very close together, you and I. Can we not be friends?"

"Your Holiness asks me to deny something I have believed all my life."

"And what is that, Karl?"

"That the doctrine we hold is a treasure beyond price. Our martyrs died for it. Nothing and no one should be permitted to corrupt it."

"I have come, by a long road, to another point of view, Karl. The truth is great and it will prevail. We make confession of it every day. But if there are no eyes to see the truth, no ears to hear it, no hearts open to receive it . . . what then? My dear Karl, when Our Lord called his first Apostles, He said: 'Come with me and I will make you fishers of men!' Not theologians, Karl! Not inquisitors, not popes or cardinals! Fishers of men! The greatest sadness of my life is that I have understood it so late."

There was a long and deathly silence in the room. Then Karl Emil Cardinal Clemens stood up and made his own confession of Faith.

"In all that conscience allows, I am at the service of Your Holiness and of the Church. For the rest, God give me light! I beg Your Holiness's leave to go."

"You have our leave," said Leo the Pontiff. Even as he said it, he wondered how many others would walk away and how he himself would endure the solitude.

XIV

THE Old Appian Way was once an imperial highway that ran south to Naples and across the Appenines to Brindisi. The Romans, courting immortality, lined it with funerary monuments, which were gradually defaced and in part demolished by time and sundry invaders. The Belle Arti put covenants upon the surrounding land, naming it an archeological zone, where villas might be built only on the sites of existing structures. Between the battered monuments, the pines grew tall and the grass was lush, so the lovers of Rome turned it into a tail-light alley, which every morning was littered with condoms, Kleenex, assorted underwear and other debris. It was no place to make a promenade or a picnic with the children, but for a population crammed into apartments, with a minimum of privacy, it was a splendid place to make love. Even the highway police were discreet and voyeurs tended to get short and violent shrift.

It was here, just across the road from Omar Asnan's villa, that Marta Kuhn and a male Mossad agent spent ten nights of vigil, plotting the movements of the servants, the dogs and the master of the house. Asnan came home every evening at seven-thirty, driven by his chauffeur. The garage gates opened and closed electrically. A little later, the watchman came out with two big Dobermanns on leash. He did not walk them, but trotted them down the grassy verge, across Erode Attico and down the Appia, almost to the ring road. Then he turned back. The whole run took between fifteen and twenty minutes. The watchman let himself back into the villa through the front gate, using a key. Omar Asnan generally went out again at ten-thirty or eleven, returning at one or two in the morning. Agents who picked up his surveillance from the Porta Latina reported that he went to one of two places: the Alhambra Club or an expensive house of appointments on Parioli patronised by Middle Eastern tourists. The only staff at the villa were the housekeeper, the chauffeur and the watchman, who appeared to be the husband of the housekeeper. All were listed in the files of the local carabinieri as Italian residents of Iranian nationality, working under special permissions and paying full local taxes.

Armed with this and other information, Aharon ben Shaul made a personal visit to the International Clinic to talk to Sergio Salviati. He had a special and unusual request.

"I'd like to borrow your medical skills for one night."

"To do what?"

"Supervise an interrogation. There will be no violence involved; but we'll be using a new Pentothal derivative developed in Israel. It can, however, have certain side effects. In some patients it produces marked arrhythmia. We need an expert to monitor the procedure."

"Who's the subject?"

"Omar Asnan, mastermind of the Sword of Islam. We're going to lift him, question him and free him."

"Which tells me nothing."

"Our sources tell us that he's still planning the assassination of the Roman Pontiff, but that he's sub-contracting the hit to another group, probably Oriental. We've got to get detailed information on who they are and how they operate. Will you help us?"

"No!"

"Why not?"

"Because everything about the suggestion stinks to me. It reminds me of all the bloody perversions our profession has been through in this century: the torture rooms in Argentina, with the doctor standing by to keep the poor bastards alive, the medical experiments in Auschwitz, the confinement of dissidents in Soviet mental institutions, what you're doing now to the Palestinians. I want no part of it!"

"Not even to prevent the assassination of your patient?"

"Not even! I gave the man a new lease on life. After that, he's on his own like the rest of us."

"If Omar Asnan has sub-contracted, he will have covered the whole operation—including Tove Lundberg, possibly her daughter as well."

"They're out of the country. Tucked away in the Irish countryside."

"Which is an easy place to get to and where killings are planned every day of the week! Come on, Professor! What's this sudden hot flush of morality? I'm not asking you to kill anyone, just to keep a man alive so he can spill his guts about an upcoming assassination. Dammit man! We kept your distinguished patient safe. We lifted the woman who was named to kill him. You owe us—and we're taking a big discount on the payment."

Salviati hesitated and was almost lost. Then he saw the mantrap.

"Why me? Any half-baked student can monitor a heartbeat."

"Because we're doing this without the Italians. We need one of our own to help."

"You forget!" Salviati's anger boiled over. "I am Italian! Our people have been here for four centuries. I'm a Jew, but I'm not an Israeli. I'm a son of the Law but I'm not a son of your house. In Italy, we've taken all the shit that's been handed to us here down the centuries right up to the final Black Sabbath when the Nazis trucked us out of the Roman ghetto to the death camps in

Germany. But we stayed, because we belong, from antique Roman times until now. I've walked a very thin line to help you and to help Israel. Now you're insulting me, blackmailing me with Tove Lundberg. You do your own business your own way. Leave me to mine. Now get the hell out here."

Aharon ben Shaul simply smiled and shrugged.

"You can't blame me for trying! Funny though! None of this would have happened if you hadn't got caught up in all this *goyische papisterei!*"

When he had gone, Salviati had an angry conversation with Menachem Avriel, who apologised profusely and disclaimed all knowledge of the affair. Then he made a call to Ireland and spoke briefly to Tove Lundberg and, for a much longer time, to Matt Neylan.

Now another word was being bandied about the corridors of the Vatican, and in the private correspondence of the hinge-men of the Church. The word was "normative", and it had a very precise meaning: "creating or establishing a standard". Every prelate knew it. Everyone understood exactly the question which Clemens and his friends were asking: "What is now to be normative in the government of the Church: the codex of Canon Law, the Acts of the Apostolic See, the Decrees of Synods or the subjective judgements of an ailing pontiff—delivered informally and without consultation? It was a two-edged blade that cut to the heart of two issues: the value of papal authority and the power of the institution itself to enforce its own decrees. It was precisely this power which the Congregation for the Doctrine of the Faith, formerly the Holy Inquisition, had been established to preserve and reinforce.

From its earliest days the Church had been infiltrated by alien ideas, Gnostic, Manichaean, Arian. Their vestiges lingered still, colouring the attitudes of this group or that—the charismatics, the traditionalists, the literalists, the ascetics. In the first centuries the instruments of purification had been public debate, the writings of the great Fathers, the decisions of Synods and Councils. Then, when imperial power was claimed as an endowment of God through His Vicar, the Pope, all the instruments of repression were available: the crusading armies, the public executioners, the merciless inquisitors, absolute in their conviction that error had no right to exist. What was left at the end of the second millennium was a pale shadow of those powers and it seemed to many a folly to surrender them in favour of a purely humanist conception of human rights.

Leo the Pontiff was made aware of the dissension in his talks with Curial Cardinals about new appointments, but only Agostini was prepared to be totally frank.

"In purely political terms, Holiness, it is a folly for any ruler to surrender any instrument of power, even though he may never see the need to use it. I don't like what you are asking me to do—reduce the powers of Apostolic Nuncios, oblige them to make the local bishops aware of any complaints they make to Rome. I know why you are doing it. I know there are as many causes of friction as there are advantages in the present system; but as a pure matter of political practice, I don't like to let go what I have. I'm like the museum curator who would rather hang on to five pages of a valuable manuscript than see them restored to the whole book in another place!"

"At least you are open about it, Matteo." The Pontiff gave him a smile of weary approval. "For a long time I held exactly the same view. This is what Clemens will not accept; I am not, overnight, his enemy or a danger to the Church."

"He thinks you are."

"And you?"

"I think you could be," said the Secretary of State.

"Explain why and how."

"We begin with a truth. Our Act of Faith, or submission to God, our confession of Jesus as the Lord, is a free act. It is the act which gives us fellowship in the Assembly of believers. The capacity to make the act is a gift. The act is free."

"And it must remain so. We choose every day."

"But this, I believe, is where Your Holiness is mistaken. You think that men and women want to be free, that they want to exercise their right of choice. The plain fact of life is that they don't. They want to be directed, they want to be told, they want the policeman on the corner, the bishop in his mitre proclaiming the Good News with authority and certainty. That's why they get dictators. That's why your predecessors ruled like Jove's thunderbolts! They split the world and the Church, but they bespoke power. The risk you run is quite different. You hand the people the first fruits of salvation, the liberty of the Sons of God. To many, as to Clemens, it will taste like Dead Sea fruit."

"So!" There was winter chill in the Pontiff's voice. "We are back to the old catchcries: It is not expedient. It is not timely!"

"I am not saying that." Agostini was unusually vehement. "I am delivering, as I am obliged to do, a counsel and a warning. But as it happens, I agree with Your Holiness—in principle at least! I read last night, for the first time in many years, the decree of Vatican II on the Dignity of the Human Person. I made myself recite it to fix it in my memory. 'Authentic freedom is an exceptional sign of the divine image within man . . . Hence man's dignity demands that he act according to a knowing and free choice.' It may be wise to remind our brethren that this is a conciliar document and not a private papal opinion."

"One wonders why it is necessary to remind grown men of such simplicities!"

"Because, for most of their lives, they never have to address them. They are protected species, living in hot-house conditions. In this allocution, do you propose to say anything about the position of women in the Church?"

"I am working on that section now. Why do you ask?"

"Because it seems to me, Holiness, we're talking to and about only half the world. We're a patriarchal society whose dialogue with its womenfolk is becoming more and more attenuated, less and less relevant. The heads of major states are women. They are legislators and judges and heads of major business enterprises. Our only recognition of their existence is through the Pontifical Commission on the Family, on which married couples serve but which meets only once a year. Women in religious communities are still 'protected' by a Curial Cardinal, who is hardly an adequate voice for their interests or concerns. Matrimonial questions, bio-ethical ones, have to be dealt with by women themselves. The question of women priests is still a taboo subject, but it will come more and more into debate and even on biblical and traditional grounds it is hard to see that it is finally closed . . ."

"So far," said the Pontiff carefully, "I have reached a point where I admit our inadequacies and our willingness to reach out for remedies. The remedies themselves are not so easy to come by. Look at this place! We are so busy protecting our unchallenged chastity and our reputation as virtuous priests that it is impossible to have a normal conversation, let alone a stroll in the sunlight with a member of the opposite sex! Inevitably we are going to be forced to admit a married clergy in the Roman rite, as we have already admitted it among the Uniats; but even I am not bold enough to broach the question at this moment. But to answer you: yes, I shall be opening the question of women in the Church, and I shall try not to embellish it with too much Marian imagery. The Mother of Jesus was a woman of her time and of her station. That is the essence of her mystery and it needs no fairytales to decorate it."

Agostini shook his head in wonderment and disbelief.

"There is work for two lifetimes in all this. Why not settle for less and spare yourself some heartache?"

The Pontiff laughed, a free, open sound that Agostini had never heard from him before.

"Why? Because I'm a farmer's son, Matteo. You plough the ground. You harrow it. You cast the seed and what the birds don't eat and the rains don't rot and the mildew doesn't get, is what you have left to harvest. Besides, for the first time in my life, I think, I'm a truly happy man. I'm gambling everything I am and have on the Gospel truth."

Even Agostini, the pure pragmatist, had not the heart to remind him that, win or lose, the reward would be the same: they would nail him to a tree and watch him die, very slowly.

By a series of Irish progressions—Murtagh, to Murtagh's cousin on his mother's side, from his cousin's wife to her brother, who was known to have connections in the Irish Republican Army and maybe, just maybe, with the Provisionals—Matt Neylan found himself one Thursday morning sitting in the office of Constable Macmanus in the Garda station at Clonakilty.

He came as a recommended man, which meant that his story would be taken for truth—even though he'd be a fool if he took for gospel everything that was told to him. His request was quickly stated.

"I'm an unfrocked priest, as you know; but I'm looking after two ladies who are very precious to certain high persons at the Vatican. One of them's a cardinal, no less, and the other's a grade higher, you might say. I had a call from Rome to tell me we might be getting some unwelcome visitors. So first I'm looking for some advice. What sort of warning can I get if strangers come asking for me? And what can you do to stop 'em getting to me?"

Constable Macmanus was a slowish thinker, but it took him no time at all to give the answer.

"Not a lot, either way. Unless someone asks for you by name, who's to know whether they're here for the fishing or the tourism or a bit of business investment? We get all sorts in Ireland nowadays: Germans, Dutch, Japanese, the whole bloody colour chart. What can we do to stop 'em getting to you? Nothing, unless they're carrying a banner with 'Kill Neylan' printed on it, or a bazooka for which they don't have a licence. You take my point, I'm sure."

"It couldn't be plainer," said Matt Neylan agreeably. "So I'll pass to my next question. Where do I get some guns and the licence to carry and use them?"

"I notice you're using the plural. Why would that be?"

"Because there are two of us who can use 'em, Murtagh and myself. Because I think we should each have a pistol; and, if possible, I'd like a couple of semi-automatics in case there's a sudden surprise attack on the farmhouse itself."

"Which I hope there won't be. I'd hate to deal with the paperwork for a thing like that . . . Let me think now. Before we go further, you'd be prepared to pay for these items?"

"Unless the Garda wanted to donate them to the cause of law and order."

"You must be joking!"

"Then, of course, we pay."

"For the weapons and the licences—and the procurement service of course."

"One always pays for that," said Matt Neylan—and was glad the constable seemed to miss the point. "How long before delivery?"

"Do you have the cash about you, by any chance?"

"No; but I can get it at the bank."

"Then fine. We'll take a small drive into the country. You can collect the goods and take 'em home with you. And while we're about it, we should get you a dog—a big one, like a wolfhound. A friend of mine breeds 'em. He'd make you a good price."

"And the licences?"

"I'll make 'em out before we leave and fill in the particulars later. Which reminds me, can you use a typewriter?"

"Sure."

"Then sit yourself down and type me out a complaint, about person or persons unknown, for threats made against yourself and the ladies. Mention their high connections and the warnings you've just had. Lay it on as thick as you like, and sign it in your best hand."

"And what's that for?"

"It's called covering your backside, Mr. Neylan. Yours and mine. The guns are no problem. There's more than one shipment for the IRA been landed in Clonakilty Bay and there's like to be more yet, so long as the war goes on. But in this little corner of Holy Ireland bodies with bullet holes are very hard to explain. So it's as well to have all the paperwork done in advance."

"I see that," said Matt Neylan fervently. "I see it very clearly."

Tove Lundberg, on the other hand, did not see it at all. She was aghast at the thought of gun battles in the misty mornings, of blood on the pastures where the placid cattle grazed. She demanded to know: "What is this, Matt? Some cheap melodrama that is being invented for us? Let's pack tonight and go to Dublin. We can fly from there anywhere we want, change planes, cover our tracks. Who knows or cares where we are?"

"It doesn't work like that," Matt Neylan explained patiently while Britte listened, nodding and muttering with desperate eagerness to be heard. "In this game we're demonstration models. Wherever we are, we have to be eliminated to show the power of the Sword of Islam. Do you want to live all your lives in hiding?"

Britte clung to him, signalling desperately: No, no, no! Tove sat immobile, watching them both. Then she thrust herself out of the chair and grasped them both with urgent hands.

"So we fight! Good! In the morning you take me out and teach me to shoot! I refuse to be a spectator any longer!"

The raid on Omar Asnan's villa took place on the sixteenth day of October. This was the manner of it. Omar Asnan arrived home at seven-thirty. Immediately afterwards the watchman came out to run the Dobermanns. Just past Erode Attico, he was overtaken by a closed van which forced him and the leashed dogs against a stone wall. The dogs were dropped cold by anaesthetic darts. The watchman was overpowered by masked men. His eyes, mouth, wrists and ankles were taped. His keys were taken. He was driven, with the animals, to a deserted spot in the pine woods near the sea and dumped there. He was discovered late next morning by a pair of joggers. The dogs were beside him, whining and licking his face.

Meantime, Aharon ben Shaul and three assistants, dressed in black track-suits and ski masks, entered the villa, overpowered the chauffeur and the woman, drugged them both, then proceeded to deal with Omar Asnan, who was taking a bath before dinner. Naked, shivering and blindfolded, he was taken down to the cellar, laid on the carpet which covered the stone floor and injected with the Pentothal derivative. Forty-five minutes later he had revealed the murder of the Mossad agent and the existence of the underground granary where his body was entombed. He also exposed the nature of the deal with the Korean who had engaged to import one hit team to kill the Pontiff and another to kidnap or kill Tove Lundberg in Ireland. As to how or when the events would take place, Asnan knew nothing. That was the nature of the deal: half the money down, plus expenses, the rest on completion; everything left to the discretion of the hit teams, who could work without fear of betrayal.

It wasn't totally satisfactory, but it was the best they could hope for—and Omar Asnan was already in acute discomfort from the heavy dose of the drug. So they rolled back the carpet, lifted the stone that covered the entrance to the crypt and carried him into the chamber where the antique grain jars were stored. Then, single-handedly, Aharon ben Shaul lifted the small brown body, put it in one of the grain jars and closed it with the lid.

"He'll die," said one of the assistants.

"For sure," said Aharon ben Shaul. "Our friend Khalid died too. That's the law, isn't it? Life for life, limb for limb. Now let's get out of here. There's still work to do upstairs."

They closed the chamber, sealed and covered the entrance, then systematically burgled the house, carried their booty to the garage in pillowcases and stowed it in the trunk of Asnan's Mercedes. The chauffeur and the house-keeper were still sleeping. Aharon ben Shaul administered an extra shot of opiate, untaped their mouths, loosened their bonds and left them. The intruders drove away in the Mercedes, which was discovered a week later in a disused marble quarry on the road to Hadrian's Villa. Most of Asnan's possessions found their way, by devious routes, to Thieves' Market and were put up for sale to Sunday morning visitors.

The disappearance of Omar Asnan caused a brief ripple of interest among local investigators and certain confusion among his business associates. His servants were rigorously questioned. Their sojourn permits were withdrawn and they were quietly repatriated. The house and the funds in Asnan's bank and the contents of his safe were committed to the care of a procurator appointed by the Republic.

Aharon ben Shaul congratulated himself on a good night's work. He had broken a terrorist ring and eliminated its leader. The Pope could look after himself and Tove Lundberg was outside his bailiwick.

Meantime, since no mention of the proceedings was made in the Press and Hyun Myung Kim was out of the country, two highly efficient teams of hunters prepared to move on their quarry.

The schedule of events for the Consistory—commonly called the *Ordo*— was sufficiently unusual to raise comment among the participants. It would begin at the ungodly hour of eight in the morning, in the new Hall of Consistories in Vatican City. It would open with prayer, the traditional invocation of the Holy Spirit, the Illuminator. His Holiness would announce certain changes in curial appointments. These preludes would finish at eight forty-five, when the allocution would begin. This was timed at one hour. Afterwards there would be half an hour left for questions and comments. At ten-fifteen the cardinals would disperse to vest for the eleven o'clock Mass in St. Peter's which His Holiness would concelebrate with six senior cardinals in the presence of the rest of the Sacred College and members of the Diplomatic Corps accredited to the Holy See.

Since nothing was ever done in Rome without a reason, the arrangements were read as a move on the part of the Pontiff to defuse any hasty controversy over his speech, to make a large public gesture of Eucharistic unity and to hold himself available for private audiences over the ensuing days. Their Eminences were informed that His Holiness would be available from five to eight in the evening and from eight till noon on ensuing days, and those desiring audience in private or in groups should register their requests with the Cardinal Camerlengo. Certain sceptics suggested that this was a very good way of counting heads. Certain others called it just another version of *"divide et impera":* divide and rule.

The simple fact was that for the Pontiff the morning was the only part of the day when he could command a full measure of strength. After a long speech and a very long ceremonial Mass in St. Peter's he would be near to exhaustion and would have to rest for at least two or three hours. He knew beyond any doubt that every ensuing conversation with these senior princes of the Church was crucial to his plans. Even a momentary lapse of attention or a flash of irritation could do damage to the grand, but fragile, design. The full extent of his anxiety was expressed only in his diary:

"Of the hundred and forty members of the Sacred College, a hundred and twenty-two will be present at the Consistory; the others have excused themselves on the grounds of illness, age or intolerance of long air travel. All have been in personal contact with me, however briefly, and all are anxious to know the direction my address will take. I have tried to reassure them by describing it as a prologue to a fraternal colloquy on matters of concern to us all. That is what I want it to be, a beginning to open-hearted talks between brothers; but my reputation as an ill-tempered autocrat is too deeply etched in their memories to be erased so easily. So I can only pray—for light and for a golden tongue.

"Gerard Hopgood is proving a tower of strength. Though he lacks Malachy O'Rahilly's wit and bubbling good humour, he is much more solidly grounded in learning and much more confident in his dealings with me. He will not let me shirk an examination of difficult issues in the text. He will not let me take refuge in arguments about expediency and opportunity. He tells me flatly: 'It will not do, Holiness. These are all adult men. They cannot have the luxury of papering over the cracks in bad arguments. If you have found the courage to face unpleasant facts, so must they.'

"Sometimes, surrounded by pages of heavily scored manuscript, we drink coffee and he talks to me about the tribe of juvenile delinquents whom he is training as athletes. He has a healthy scepticism about his success. The best ones, he tells me, are likely to be hired as purse-snatchers by the criminal gangs who prey on women tourists in Rome; but there are others for whom he and his friend have become surrogate fathers and uncles. However, he adds a shrewd footnote: 'I don't have to be a priest to do what I'm doing. I don't have to be celibate either. In fact, it's probably better if I'm not. The point I'm making, Holiness, and I think we should take another look at it in this document, is that we need to define much more clearly the identity of a modern priest, his true vocation in the Church. Believe me, I know what I'm talking about. I know how the casualties start.'

"I believe him. I respect him. Let me say it frankly: I have come to love him as the son I never had. I am touched by the small, protective gestures he lavishes on me: Have I taken my pills? I have been sitting too long. I must stand and walk about for a while . . . 'Let's take a break and do fifteen minutes exercise. I know it's a bore, but if you don't do it, you're committing suicide . . .'

"I ask him how he sees his future in the Church. I have the secret thought that one day he will make a splendid bishop. His answer surprises me. 'I'm not sure yet. There are certain dilemmas that present themselves. There's a friend of mine, a priest like me, who works in one of the base communities in a very poor part of Brazil. He couldn't figure out why the womenfolk refused to marry—refused absolutely. They cared for their men, were faithful to them, bore them children, but marriage? No way. Finally, he found out the reason. Once they married they were in bondage. Their men could walk all over them. They could never escape. So long as they didn't marry, they had at least the freedom to walk away from cruelty and take their children with them. I have film of my friend and his bishop —who is also a cardinal, and he'll be here for the Consistory—administering Communion to these people at a festival Mass. Now I approve that. I'm happy to live and work in a Christian church that lives like that. If it doesn't, then I have to do some very serious thinking.'

"This is a revelation which I cannot let pass without comment. I ask him: 'How do you justify the administration of the sacraments to people living in formal sin?' His answer comes back instantly: 'How do we justify refusing them? And which is closer to the Christian ideal of marriage, a free and caring union in which children are loved and protected, or one that creates a slavery for woman and child?' He laughs then and apologises. 'Forgive me, Holiness. You asked. I answered. I don't suggest you make this an issue at the Consistory. You will have enough on your plate already.'

"I agree with him; and I note that the Archbishop to whom he refers may well prove a sound ally in the cause I have set myself. As for the quality of the theology involved, I doubt it would recommend itself to Clemens, but at least there must be an open forum within the Church where it can be debated freely and without censure, real or implied.

"So night falls and I am another day closer to the Feast of All Saints. I have a strange dream. I am sitting in the Hall of Consistories looking down at the assembled cardinals. I am speaking to them, although I do not hear the words I am saying. Then suddenly I notice that they have all turned to stone, like courtiers in an enchanted palace."

Menachem Avriel, Ambassador of Israel to the Republic of Italy, was having a bad day. It was not as bad as some, but in all conscience, bad enough. In the morning, he was invited to a friendly conversation with the Minister for Foreign Affairs, on matters of mutual interest. It could have been much worse. He could have been summoned. The friendly conversation could have been an urgent conference and the matters of mutual interest could have been questions of singular concern. The Minister was a very urbane man. He liked Avriel. He recognised the usefulness of Israel in Mediterranean affairs. The last thing he needed in the world was a diplomatic incident. So, with infinite tact, he proposed: "My dear Menachem, we work very well together. Let us continue to do so. This Mossad fellow—what does he call himself, Aharon ben Shaul?—is very heavy-handed. So far, he has been lucky and we have profited from that. Each time he risks a little more. Enough is enough! I would like to suggest—I, personally, not Foreign Affairs—that you ship him out as soon as possible. My friend Agostini at the Vatican agrees with this advice . . . Understand, we are not telling you how to run your business. Send us any replacement you like, provided he has more tact than this one, and we'll accept him without question. What do you say?"

"I'd say it was a very timely suggestion, which I shall take under immediate advisement and refer to my government for instructions. However, my dear Minister, he'll be out of here within forty-eight hours!"

"Please, my dear friend! We do not demand miracles. Seven days would be fine. Even thirty would be acceptable."

"Forty-eight hours," said Avriel firmly. "I always say you should leave the poker table while you're ahead. And so far we're both ahead, are we not?"

"I hope so." The Minister sounded dubious. "Will you take coffee with me?"

Back at the Israeli Embassy there was a letter waiting for him. The envelope was embossed with the papal coat of arms and the Embassy sticker noted that it had been delivered by Vatican courier. The letter was handwritten in Italian.

Excellency,

I owe you a debt for your personal care for my welfare during my recent illness.

November 1st is the feast day which we call All Saints. It celebrates in a special way the community of all Christian believers with men and women of good will everywhere.

To mark this festival, I shall be celebrating a Mass in St. Peter's Basilica at 1100 hours with the College of Cardinals and members of the Diplomatic Corps accredited to the Holy See. Unfortunately, the State of Israel is not yet accredited. However, if circumstances permit, I should like you to come as my personal guest and to take your place among the members of my pontifical household. If this invitation causes you any embarrassment, please feel free to decline it. My hope is that it may prove a first step towards a closer and more formal relationship between the State of Israel and the Holy See. Centuries of unhappy history still divide us. Today's politics ensnare us at every step. But any alliance has to begin with a handclasp.

Mindful always of protocol, my Secretary of State regrets that it is not he who is issuing the invitation, to which, however, he adds his warm personal greetings. . . .

Leo +

Menachem Avriel could hardly believe his eyes. Decades of drilling and boring and hammering had made no dent in the wall of resistance to Vatican recognition of the State of Israel. Now, for the first time, there was hope that it might be breached. Then, always the diplomat, he asked himself whether there might be any connection between the *"invito"* to the Foreign Office and that of the Pontiff. Even the simplest Roman document was a palimpsest, with texts and subtexts and indecipherable fragments laid one upon the other.

When he called Sergio Salviati to share the news, he found that a new refinement had been added to the compliment. Salviati had his own invitation to the ceremony, which he read to Avriel:

I owe you, my dear Professor, a debt that I can never repay. I write to invite you to join me in a Christian celebration, the Feast of All Saints, which celebrates not only the holy ones in our calendar, but the essential community of men and women of good will everywhere.

If the notion embarrasses you, I shall understand perfectly. If you decide to come, you will be seated, along with Ambassador Avriel, among the members of my own household. It would give me great joy to think that, in spite of the horrors of history, you and I could join in common prayer to the God of Abraham and Isaac and Jacob. Always, I wish peace upon your house . . .

Salviati sounded irritable and depressed. He demanded to know: "Do we go or don't we?"

"I go," said Menachem Avriel cheerfully. "Don't you understand what this means?"

"To you, maybe. To Israel, a very big maybe. But why should I roll over because the Pope wants to scratch my belly?"

"I don't know, Sergio!" The Ambassador seemed suddenly bored with the conversation. "I've got the smell of a big diplomatic coup! All you seem to have is a royal pain in the arse!"

To Anton Drexel, drowsing in the thin autumn sun, a package was delivered: a canvas rolled inside a cardboard tube and, inside the canvas, a letter from Tove Lundberg. The canvas claimed his attention first. It was an interior, executed in a dashing bravura style, of Tove and Matt Neylan drowsing at the fireside, with a wolfhound between them and above, reflected in the mantel mirror, Britte herself, perched on her stool, painting with the brush clenched between her teeth.

The picture told its own story, to which Tove's letter added only commentary and counterpoint.

". . . Britte wanted very much that you should have this piece. She says: 'Nonno Drexel used to say that as an artist grows up, the pictures grow too. This is a happy picture and I want him to be happy with us all!' That's a long speech for her, as you know; but she still needs to share herself with her Nonno.

"Matt has become very important in her life, though in a different fashion. He is—I am searching for the word—very comradely. He challenges her, makes her do always a little more than she is willing to attempt by herself. Before she began this picture, for instance, he sat with her for hours, turning over art books, discussing styles and periods of painting. She has always been frustrated because her disabilities prevent her from working in the finished style of the classic masters. Not that she wants to paint like that, it is a question of being deprived of the capacity. Matt understands this and insists on working through the struggle with her. What surprises me with him is that he distinguishes so clearly the sexual element in her relationship with him, and handles it with enormous care.

"Which brings me, dear Nonno, to Matt and me. I won't ask you to approve, though I know you will understand—and Britte's picture says it—we are lovers and we are good for each other. We are good, too, for Britte. What more can I say? What more, indeed, can I predict? We are still under threat. The Israelis assure us the threat is real. Matt and Murtagh are always armed and there are guns in the house. I have learned to shoot and I can hit a tin can at fifteen paces with a pistol. You see, I talk as if it were a triumph. What a mad world it is . . . Still, this kind of nonsense cannot last for ever. Britte and I look forward to the time when we can visit our Nonno again, and drink the wine of Fontamore.

"Oh, I almost forgot. We had a visit last week from Monsignor Malachy O'Rahilly, the one who used to be the Pope's secretary. Matt and he had quarrelled but they made friends again. He was just out of what he called the 'funny farm', where he was taking a cure for alcohol addiction. He looked trim and fit and very confident, though Matt says the priesthood is a dangerous road for a man like him who needs a lot of real family support. We took him touring and fishing. He asked to be remembered gently to you.

"But remembering gently is not enough for Britte or for me. She loves her Nonno very much. I love him too, because he came into our lives at a very important time and opened doors that might have been closed to us for ever . . ."

Drexel dabbed at his eyes and wiped the mist off his spectacles. Soon the children would be coming out for their morning break. They would not understand an old man's tears. He folded the letter carefully and put it in his breast pocket. He rolled up the canvas and slid it back into the tube. Then he strode out of the villa grounds and down the road to Frascati, where the Petrocellis— father and son and grandson—still made picture frames for the best galleries in Rome.

BOOK FOUR

LAZARUS REVOCATUS

"And Jesus said to them: 'The light is among you still. Finish your journey while you still have the light, before the darkness overtakes you.'"

—John xii: 35

XV

ON the twenty-ninth of October, two men and two women in a Volks-wagen campervan boarded the ferry from Fishguard in Wales to Rosslare on the south-east tip of Ireland. Their van was hired from a company which specialised in rentals to Oriental tourists.

From Rosslare they drove directly to Cork, where they lodged in a modest, old-fashioned hotel much patronised by coach tours. All that was remarked about them was that they were very polite, spoke passable English and paid in cash. They let it be known that they would use the hotel as their base for a week's tour. One of the men called telephone enquiries and asked for the number of Mr. Matt Neylan, a subscriber in the county. Once he had the number it was simple to match it to an address in the directory. A tourist map supplied the rest of the information.

Matt Neylan's address was Tigh na Kopple—Home of the Horses—Galley Head Road, Clonakilty, which put it well off the main road with nothing but open fields between the house and the sea.

So, on the thirtieth of October, in the morning, they did a trial run, identi-fied the house and drove on to Bantry for lunch. In the afternoon they came back the same way. In the garden a girl, grossly handicapped, was painting with a brush held in her mouth. The driver stopped the van. One of the women got out and began to photograph the scene. She was so intent on getting as many shots as possible that at first she did not notice the man standing in the doorway watching.

When she turned and saw him she was totally confused, blushing, stammer-ing, retreating crabwise towards the van. The man gave her a greeting with a big smile and stood waving until the van turned the corner. Then he went inside and made a telephone call to the Dublin number which the Israelis had given him.

A woman answered. She passed him to another woman who assured him she had been fully briefed on the situation, but did not see this incident as cause for panic. A tourist had stopped to take photographs of a girl painting in a garden. What did that signify?"

"Possibly nothing. But I can't afford to take any risks."

"Of course not, Mr. Neylan. On the other hand, we can't afford to have essential staff careering around the country chasing moonbeams. You do see my point?"

"I do indeed, madam; but if my people are shot up or kidnapped, what then?"

"We'll send flowers. Officially, that's all we're allowed to do anyway. If anything else untoward happens, please be in touch!"

Which led Matt Neylan to think that someone in Rome had shoved a mighty large spanner in the works. However, Constable Macmanus was rather more helpful. He would "call around and come back to yez". Which he duly did and reported that there were two Japanese couples at the Boyle Hotel in Cork. They had driven to Bantry for lunch and had passed the farm going and coming. They were normal as mashed potatoes, no threat to anyone. Four people in a campervan, Orientals at that! How could they stage a crime and get off the island? Relax boyo, relax! Trouble will find you soon enough!

But Matt Neylan was not a believer any more and especially he wasn't a believer in the facile logic of the Celts, who knew with absolute certainty how God ran His world and why it was only idiots and infidels who slipped on banana skins!

The constable was right. Four Orientals in a campervan made a very conspicuous team—so conspicuous, indeed, that everyone who had seen them would swear to it, with absolute conviction. But whether at any one moment there were two or three together, whether one was in the ladies' room or in the bar or had just stepped out to take the air . . . who would know, who would care? In one particular, however, Constable Macmanus was right. If they were planning a kidnap, how the hell would they get off the island with the victim in a campervan? On the other hand, if the kidnap plot had suddenly been upgraded to murder, then the text read quite differently—one or two killers with a back-up of two women to transport them and provide their alibi.

Matt Neylan's imagination was working in high gear. How would they come? When? How would the event be staged? He had never been to war, he had never done police or army training. How far could he trust himself with four lives—because with Britte and Tove there were also the Murtaghs in the cottage. Then he understood that, now or never, this thing must be ended. No one should be forced to live continually under threat. If the only way to end it was by killing, so be it. Let's get the dying over and be done with it. Then, suddenly, he was very angry and he knew beyond all doubt that he was prepared to step on to the killing ground and stay there until the last shot was fired, the last blow struck.

Anger was not enough, however, courage was not enough. He had to choose the killing ground and entice the enemy on to it. The farmhouse, the Murtagh's cottage, the barns and cowsheds were all close to the road, grouped in a rectangle, with the farmhouse as one long side, fronting the road. The cottage and the cow bales formed the two short ends of the rectangle, the barns and storage sheds ran parallel to the main house. The floor of the rectangle was concrete which could be hosed down every day. The buildings were stone, plastered with white stucco and roofed with slate. They were stout enough, but as a defence position they were worse than useless. The barns would burn. A stun grenade or tear gas would turn the house and the cottage into death traps.

Given that he had weapons for close or more distant engagement, they would all be safer in open ground. There were thirty-five acres between the house and the sea, undulating land divided by low stone fences and bordered by a winding path that ran along the cliff edge and down the lower ground to the inlet, where there was a boatshed, invisible from the road. The women could spend the night there while Murtagh and he kept vigil. The assassins would come during the dark, he was sure of that; round midnight or in the small sinister hour before the false dawn. They would park some distance away. The killer or killers would approach on foot.

Just at that moment, Tove and Mrs. Murtagh came in with a basket of eggs and a pail of fresh milk. Murtagh was scraping his boots at the door, waiting to be invited in for his evening whiskey. Matt Neylan gathered them round him, poured the drinks and made his announcement: "I haven't a shred of proof, but I feel in my bones that we're going to have trouble tonight. So here's what I'm proposing . . ."

In Rome, at seven o'clock that same evening, Monsignor Gerard Hopgood laid the final text of the allocution on the Pontiff's desk and announced: "That's it, Holiness. I've checked every last comma. Now, with great respect, I suggest you get out of here and give yourself a quiet evening. Tomorrow's going to be a heavy day."

"You mustn't worry, Gerard."

"I do, Holiness. It's my job to keep you on your feet, with a clear mind, a good text and an air of total confidence. By the way, I've told your valet to shave you at six-thirty in the morning and to trim your hair a little."

"And you didn't think that was presumptuous?"

"I did, Holiness; but then I thought I'd rather risk your wrath and have you looking spruce at the Consistory. If you'll pardon another presumption, we have a very elegant text and it merits a very elegant spokesman."

"And that, my dear Monsignor Hopgood, bespeaks a very worldly view."

"I know; but Your Holiness is going to be addressing some very worldly-wise people. They pay you homage and obedience; but they still remember that they are the princes who elected you and who, had you not survived, would have elected another in your place!"

It was the boldest speech he had ever uttered and there was a reproof on the tip of his master's tongue. It remained unspoken, because Hopgood himself was instantly penitent.

"I'm sorry, Holiness. That was impertinent; but I am concerned for you. I am concerned for the work which you are beginning so late in life. I'm another generation. I see the need for it, I feel the hope in it. I see how easily it can be misrepresented and hindered. Please forgive me."

"You're forgiven, my son. I know as well as you that our elders are not always our betters; and although in the past I have often exacted it, I no longer believe that obedience should be blind. Your real fault is lack of trust in God. It isn't easy to commit to Him. It's like stepping out of an aeroplane without a parachute. But when you have to do it as I did—not knowing whether I was going to live or die—suddenly it seems the most natural thing in the world. We still have anxieties, the adrenalin still pumps to make us ready, like all animals, for attack or defence. But the essential calm remains, the conviction that, alive or dead, we never fall out of the hand of the Almighty . . . What are you doing for dinner tonight?"

"I'm entertaining my friend, Father Lombardi. He's the one who runs the athletic club. He's been having a bad time lately with his parish priest, who's also having a bad time because he's getting over a stroke and his housekeeper has left . . . So Lombardi needs a little cheering up."

"Where are you eating?"

"At Mario's. It's just round the corner from the Porta Angelica. I'll leave the number with the switchboard in case Your Holiness needs me."

"I shan't. Go and enjoy yourself with your friend. I'll see you here at six in the morning."

When he had gone, the Pontiff lifted the telephone and called Anton Drexel at his villa. They had agreed that Drexel, now wholly retired, should not attend the Consistory. However, a number of the visiting prelates had already telephoned him for a private reading of the situation. The Pontiff was interested to know their frame of mind. Drexel described it.

"They are puzzled. They cannot quite come to terms with the idea of a personal change in you. Clemens, I fear, has let his ill-humour get the better of him. He has presented a picture of you as a quasi-heretic, or at least a risky eccentric, which his colleagues find equally hard to accept. So, on balance, you have the advantage. Everything now depends on your allocution. Are you circulating copies?"

"No. I thought it better not to do so. I am explaining the document as a presentation of my views, an invitation to comment on them and as a prelude to a *motu proprio* on certain of the major subjects. That has to bring responses, for and against."

"I agree. As soon as I get any comments, I'll relay them to Your Holiness."

"I appreciate that, Anton. How are you feeling?"

"Lonely. I miss my Britte. She sent me a beautiful canvas, and her mother wrote a very newsy letter. They are still under threat—which bothers me a lot; but there is nothing effective I can do. Neylan is looking after them very well. But the question does arise, Holiness: how effective is your own security?"

"About as good or bad as it ever was, Anton. St. Peter's will be filled to overflowing tomorrow morning. People will be milling around the square. Who can control a crowd like that in a building so enormous? In a sense, the token presence of security men is as effective as that of a whole detachment of armed men who couldn't use their weapons anyway. Believe me, I am very relaxed about the whole affair."

"Our children are offering their prayers for you."

"That's the best protection I can get. Thank you, Anton. Thank them, too, for me. Which reminds me. Some time in the near future, I'm going to send my new secretary out to see you, Monsignor Gerard Hopgood, the Englishman. It turns out he is a very good athlete who trains a youth club out on the Flaminia. He also has experience with athletic activities for the handicapped. If he is interested and apt for the work at the colonia, he might provide both the impulse and the means of continuity . . . I should hate to lose a good secretary; but I owe you a debt, my friend. I should like to find a suitable way to repay it."

"You owe me nothing, Holiness."

"We shall not argue about it, Anton. Pray for me tonight." He gave a small, wry chuckle. "I have just read Monsignor Hopgood a homily on trust in God. At this moment I need it more than he does!"

Just before nightfall, Murtagh put out the big milk cans for collection by the co-operative, then moved all the cattle into a paddock midway between the house and the rim of the cliff. Neylan took the women down to the boathouse and settled them with food, blankets, a kerosene heater and the wolfhound and a shotgun for company. Britte was fretful and out of sorts, complaining of the cold and a headache. Tove signalled to Neylan to leave. She would cope better without him. Then he and Murtagh dressed themselves for a cold, long night, made sandwiches and a thermos of coffee, loaded their weapons and drove the Range Rover and the new car into the shadow of the wind-break on the western edge of the property. Matt Neylan laid out his plan.

". . . which isn't a plan. It's just what we've got to do any way we can, drop 'em dead in their tracks, but on this property, not outside it. Don't have any illusions now! These are hired killers. They don't fight by Queensberry Rules. They'll know all the martial arts and they'll be fast as cats on their feet. So you can't let 'em get within reach of you . . . And we've got to get 'em all, you understand? Otherwise those that are left will keep coming after Tove and Britte. Do you read me now?"

"I read you; but for a priest you're a bloody-minded bugger, aren't you?"

"A priest I'm not; but bloody-minded, yes. Now let's try to think how they'll come and what we've got to stop 'em."

"If you're bent on total elimination, then I think I can help you."

"I'm listening, Murtagh!"

"When I was younger and sillier, and before my wife threatened to leave me, I used to do occasional jobs with the Provos—not for money, mind you, but because I believed in the cause . . . What I was good at was booby traps and ambushes. But after a while it got to me. It wasn't fun any more, just bloody dangerous. Are you understanding me now?"

"I'm understanding you, Murtagh, but I wish to God you'd come to the point."

"The point is that if you'll go draw off a few gallons of petrol from the drums in the store and then help me fiddle with the electrics, then I think we can give our visitors the surprise of their lives."

"I don't want 'em surprised," said Matt Neylan flatly. "I want 'em dead."

"They will be," said Murtagh. "The booby traps will distract 'em long enough for a killing volley. You'll be up there in the barn. I'll be in the byre."

"I hope you're not going to burn the bloody house down."

"No . . . There'll be a little scorching maybe. Nothing a dab of whitewash won't cover. But you'd better pray for a good eye and a steady hand. One burst is all you'll get to bring the buggers down . . . Are you ready?"

"As ready as I'll ever be. All I was taught was priestcraft and statecraft. Neither of them is worth a tinker's curse at this moment."

"Then think of the child and the women down in the boathouse. That'll steady your nerves. What time do you reckon the bastards will come?"

"Not till after midnight, when the pubs are closed and the roads are quiet."

"That gives us time enough. Get the petrol now. Use a couple of milk pails. Set one by your own back door, the other by the kitchen of the cottage. I'll need some flex and a pair of pliers and a screwdriver . . ."

Huddled in the boathouse, with a cold wind searching through the cracks and the surf pounding on the shingle, Tove Lundberg and Mrs. Murtagh kept vigil over the ailing Britte. She slept fitfully, tossing and mewing. Tove held her hand and wiped the clammy sweat from her face, while Mrs. Murtagh fingered her rosary and clucked helplessly.

"She needs a doctor."

"I know she does." Tove had learned long since that if you argued with Mrs. Murtagh, she would retreat like a rabbit to a burrow and you lost her for hours on end. "Matt will come for us when it's safe. Just relax now and say a prayer for us all."

Mrs. Murtagh was silent until she could bear it no longer. Then she asked: "What is it with you and Matt Neylan? Are you going to marry him? If you're not, you're wasting your life, which no woman of your age can afford to do."

"All the more reason not to make a mistake, wouldn't you say?"

"It seems to me there's been a lot of mistakes already: you with this poor child and no husband to share her with, Matt Neylan with that great career in Rome. They were expecting him to be a bishop one day. Did you know that? And now look at him! Out of the cloth! Out of the Church altogether and every day in danger of damnation!"

"I'm sure God understands him better than we do, Mrs. Murtagh."

"But to throw away all the grace he's been given! Why, only last Sunday Monsignor O'Connell—that's our parish priest at Clonakilty—was preaching on the same thing, rejection of grace. He said it's like refusing a lifebuoy in a raging sea . . ."

"My father was a pastor too, Mrs. Murtagh. He used to say: 'Men and women close the door on each other, but God's door is always open.' "

"Your father, you said?"

The notion of a married priest was too complicated for Mrs. Murtagh and in any case vaguely obscene. It was one of "those Protestant things."

"Yes indeed. His people loved him."

"But you left your church too."

"Like Matt, I found I couldn't believe—not, at any rate, in the way I'd been taught. So I did the only honest thing I could see. I walked away."

"Into a lot of trouble," said Mrs. Murtagh tartly.

"But that's not the point, is it? If the only reason you hang on to God is to keep yourself out of trouble, what sort of religion is that?"

"I don't know," said Mrs. Murtagh fervently. "But let me tell you, I'm glad I've got my beads in my hand at this moment."

Britte gave a sudden sharp cry of pain and woke up in panic. Her mother tried to soothe her, but she clapped her hands to her head and rolled from side to side, moaning. Her eyes turned inward and rolled upward in their sockets. Tove sat beside her and cradled her in her arms, while Mrs. Murtagh sponged her face and crooned over her: "There now, there! The hurt will pass soon." Outside, the wind made an eerie keening and the pounding of the surf sounded like tramping feet on the shingle.

They came an hour after midnight, all four of them, two from the east and two from the west, masked and dressed from head to toe in black, trotting silently on the thick grass of the verge. When they reached the corners of the property, they stopped to take their bearings. Then one from each pair moved towards the front of the house. The other two vaulted the front fence and moved forward until they were level with the barn. Then they turned inward and moved to face each other. When the manoeuvre was completed there was a black figure standing motionless and scarcely visible at each corner of the rectangle of buildings.

Next, they began to move slowly and silently in a clockwise direction round the perimeter. As each one came to the next corner, they all stopped. They did not speak, but signalled their observations. One pointed to the cows in the far pasture. Another noted the shadowy masses of the vehicles parked against the trees. A third pointed inward to the enclosed courtyard.

Finally, reassured that the outer perimeter was clear, they stepped into the courtyard, two moving towards the back door of the cottage, two towards the kitchen entrance to the house. Before their hands touched the woodwork the lights over both doors came on. There was a sudden billow of flame as the pails of petrol caught fire and all four were cut down by enfilading fire from the barn and the cow-byre.

Neylan went into the house to telephone Constable Macmanus. He was with them in ten minutes, but it took an hour and a half to get the Garda and an ambulance out from Cork and another hour to make the appropriate depositions and get rid of them. Murtagh drove the Range Rover down to the boat-house to collect the women. When finally they returned to the house, Britte was chattering with fever. They telephoned the local doctor, who prescribed aspirin and ice-packs and promised to call at nine in the morning. By five she was delirious and screaming with pain. They bundled her into the car and, while Tove nursed her in the back seat, Neylan drove as fast as he dared to the Mercy Hospital in Cork. By the time Britte was admitted, she was in a coma. A specialist, summoned in haste, pronounced the verdict.

"Fulminating cerebro-spinal fever. It occurs most frequently in adolescents and adults. Diplegics like your daughter fall easy victims. This form is malignant. The mercy is that it runs a swift course. Already, she is terminal."

"How long?" asked Matt Neylan.

The doctor looked at his watch.

"I doubt she'll last through midday." To Tove, standing stricken but tearless at the bedside, he offered a small crumb of comfort. "In her case there may be a special mercy. She will be spared a great deal of grief."

Tove seemed not to have heard him. She turned to Matt Neylan and said, with strange detachment:

"Nonno Drexel will be terribly upset."

Then, mercifully, the tears came, and Matt Neylan held her to him, rocking her and crooning over her. "There now! There! Cry it out. The little one's fine. She had the best of it. She'll never know the worst."

Even as he said it the irony hit him. In the old days he would have found a dozen homely words of religious comfort, the standby of grieving folk down the ages. Now they were gone from him and all the love he wanted to pour on Tove Lundberg was the poorer for it. He was finding it much harder than he had expected to come to terms with an indifferent universe.

In the Hall of Consistories, Leo the Pontiff stood to address the assembly. Now the moment was upon him he felt strangely calm. His princes had come to him one by one to offer their ritual homage. They had prayed together for light to see and courage to walk the pilgrim road together. He had read them the admonition of St. Paul to the Corinthians: "It is only through the Holy Spirit that anyone can say Jesus is the Lord. The revelation of the Spirit is made to each in a particular fashion for a good purpose . . ." Then he had announced the appointments in a simple, bald statement.

This was the old Leo speaking, the one who disposed of embarrassing business and embarrassing people in short order. As he laid the text of the allocution before him on the rostrum, he wondered how they would accept the new Leo—and, for one brief frightening moment, whether the new Leo was not, after all, an illusion, the figment of a disordered imagination. He thrust the thought away, breathed a silent prayer and began to speak.

"My brothers . . . I speak to you today in the language of the land where I was born. Indeed, you will hear sometimes in my speech the country accent of my home-place.

"I want to explain to you the man I once was, Ludovico Gadda, whom the older ones among you elected to rule the Church. I need desperately to explain the man I am now and how he is different from the old Ludovico Gadda. It is not an easy story to tell, so please be patient with me.

"I once asked a distinguished biologist to explain to me the genetic imprint, the famous double helix which differentiates one being from another. He called it 'the graffito of God', because it can never be erased. All other imprints —of memory, environment, experience—he called 'human graffiti'. Let me try to decipher for you the marks which I bear.

"I was born to poor people in a hard land. I was an only child and, as soon as I could handle a mattock and a hoe, I worked with my mother and my father. My life was a cycle of labour: school, farmwork, study by lamplight with my mother. My father dropped dead behind his plough. My mother put herself into service with a landowner to complete my education and make me ready for a career in the Church. Understand this: I make no complaints. I was loved and protected. I was trained and toughened for a life without concessions. The one thing I never truly experienced was tenderness, the gentleness of leisured intercourse.

Ambition—which is only another name for the instinct to survive—was always at my back, hurrying me forward.

"For me, life in the seminary and in the Church was an easy experience. I was accustomed both to study and the harsh disciplines of a peasant farmer's life. Even my adolescent passions were damped down by fatigue and isolation and the undemonstrative relationship between my parents. So you see, it was very easy for me to accept without question—and let me say it frankly, without critical examination—the maximalist and rigorist interpretations of law, morals and biblical exegesis which were current in the clerical education of the day.

"So there you have me, dear brothers, the paradigm of the perfect cleric, the way open before me to a bishopric, a Curial appointment, a place in the Sacred College. No scandal could be breathed about my private life. My teaching was as orthodox as Aquinas, of whom I was the most diligent copyist. Step by step, I was being initiated into the political life of the Church, the exercises that prepare a man for power and authority. Some of you here sponsored me through that initiation and finally elected me to the office which I now hold.

"But something else was happening to me and I lacked the wit to see it. The small springs of compassion in my nature were drying up. The capacity for affection and tenderness was withering like the last leaves of autumn. Worse still, the desert climate of my own spiritual life was mirrored in the condition of the Church. I do not have to describe to you what has happened, what continued to happen. You read it every day in the reports which come to your desks.

"Let me tell you how I judge my own part in the failure. I was, I thought, a good pastor. I enforced discipline among the clergy. I would not compromise with the libertine spirit of the times. I would not countenance any challenge by scholars or theologians to the traditional doctrines of the Church . . . I was elected to rule. A ruler must be master in his own house. So I thought. So I acted, as you all know. And therein was my great mistake. I had forgotten the words of our Lord: 'I have made known to you all that my Father has told me and so I have called you my friends . . .' I had reversed the order of things laid down by Jesus. I had set myself up as a master, instead of a servant. I had tried to make the Church, not a home for the people of God, but an empire for the elect and, like many another empire builder, I had turned the green land into a dusty waste from which I myself could not escape.

"What happened next, you all know. I was admitted to hospital for bypass surgery. This intervention, which is now very common, with a very high success rate, is known to have a profound psychological effect on the patient. This is the experience I wish and need to share with you. It reaches far back into my childhood and is connected with St. John's narrative of Jesus raising Lazarus from the dead. You all know the story by heart. Think, if you can, of the effect of that narrative on a small boy, brought up on the fireside ghost stories of country folk.

"As I grew up, it raised more and more questions in my mind, all of them couched in the terms of the scholastic theology in which I had been trained. I asked myself had Lazarus been judged, as we should all be judged by God at the moment of death? Did he have to risk another life and another judgement?

Had he seen God? How could he bear to be torn back from that beatific vision? How was the rest of his life coloured by the death experience?

"You see where we are, my brothers? In all but the fact of dying, I went through the Lazarus experience. I want to explain it to you. Bear with me now, I beg you. If our minds and our hearts cannot meet on a matter of life and death, then we are truly lost and wandering.

"I do not propose to weary you with sick-room reminiscences. I want to tell you simply that there comes a moment when you are aware that you are about to step out of light into darkness, out of knowing into unknowing, with no guarantee of return. It is a moment of clearness and stillness, in which you know, with strange certainty, that whatever is waiting to receive you is good, beneficent, loving. You are aware that you have been prepared for this moment, not by any action of your own, but by the gift of life itself, by the nature of life itself.

"Some in this room will remember the long process against the distinguished Jesuit, Father Teilhard de Chardin, suspected of heresy and for a long time silenced within the Church. In my zeal as a young cleric, I approved what was done to him. But—here is the strange thing—in that still clear moment before the dark, I remembered a sentence de Chardin had written: 'God makes things make themselves.'

"When, like Lazarus, I was recalled from the darkness, when I stood blinded by the light of a new day, I knew that my life could never be the same again.

"Understand me, dear brothers, I am not talking miracles or private revelations or mystical experiences. I am talking about *metanoia,* that change in the self which takes place, not in contradiction to, but precisely because of, its genetic imprint, the graffito of God. We are born to die; therefore, in some mysterious way, we are being prepared for dying. In the same fashion, we grow towards an accommodation with the greatest mysteries of our existence. Whatever I am, I know that I am not an envelope of flesh with a soul inside it. I am not Pascal's thinking reed with a ghostly wind whistling through me.

"After the change I have described, I was still myself, whole and entire, but a self renewed and changed, as the desert is changed by irrigation, as a seed is changed into a green plant in the dark earth. I had forgotten what it was like to weep. I had forgotten what it was like to surrender oneself into caring hands, to rejoice at the sight of a child, to be grateful for the shared experience of age, for the comforting voice of a woman in the dark, painful hours.

"It was then—so late in life!—I began to understand what the people need from us, their pastors, and what I, who am the Shepherd over all, had so rigidly denied them. They do not need more laws, more prohibitions, more caveats. They act most normally and most morally by the reasons of the heart. They are already imprinted with the graffito of God. They need a climate of love and compassion and understanding in which they can grow to their full promise—which, my dear brothers, is the true meaning of salvation.

"Let me tell you, without rancour, the sad reproach addressed to me by a priest who is fighting a lonely battle to remain in the ministry. 'You're the Supreme Shepherd, but you don't see the sheep—only a vast carpet of woolly backs stretching to the horizon!'

"I laughed, as you are laughing now. He was and is a very amusing man; but he was telling me a bitter truth. I was not a shepherd. I was an overseer, a herder, a judge of meat or wool, anything but what I was called to be. One night before I went to sleep I read again the first letter of St. Peter, in whose shoes I stand today:

" 'Be shepherds to the flock God has given you. Do it, as God wishes it to be done, not by constraint, but willingly, not for sordid gain, but generously, not as a tyrant, but setting an example to the flock.'

"The lesson was clear, but how I should apply it was not clear at all. Look at me! I sit here, a prisoner in one square mile of territory, shackled by history, barred by protocol, hedged by cautionary counsellors, surrounded by all the creaking machinery of government which we have constructed over the centuries. I cannot escape. So, I must work from inside my prison-house.

"After much prayer and searching of conscience, I have decided to embark on a programme to reform the Curia itself. I want to make it an instrument truly serviceable to the people of God. The appointments I announced today are the first step in that programme. The next is to set the norms by which we shall be guided. I will state them for you now. The Church is the family of believers. In a more profound symbolism, it is a body of which we are all members and of which our Lord Jesus Christ is head. Our care must be for one another in the Lord. Whatever does not contribute to that care, whatever inhibits it, must be and will be abolished.

"I propose to begin with the Congregation for the Doctrine of the Faith, whose high and holy charge is to keep pure the teaching transmitted to us from Apostolic times. The Congregation has been reformed and renamed several times by recent pontiffs. However, I am forced to conclude that it is tainted beyond remedy by its own history. It is perceived still as an inquisition, an instrument of repression, a tribunal of denunciation within the Church. Its procedures are seen to be secretive and some of them are fundamentally unjust. So long as that image exists, the Congregation does more harm than good. We have been given, all of us at baptism, the liberty of the children of God. In this family, therefore, there should be no question which it is forbidden to ask, no debate which it is forbidden to hold so be it with love and respect, because in the end we all bow ourselves under the outstretched hand of the same Lord who bade the raging seas be still, and they became quiet.

"There have been too many occasions in our history, dear brothers—too many in mine!—when we have claimed to establish a certainty where no certainty existed or indeed exists now. The last word has not been spoken by our venerable predecessor on birth control. We cannot contemplate with equanimity the explosion of human population on the earth and man's ravaging of the limited resources of the planet. It is idle and hypocritical to urge sexual control as a remedy on people living at the farthest edge of survival. We must not attempt to fabricate revelations which we do not have. We must not impose, for the sake of expediency or seeming moral order, solutions to human problems which raise more questions than they answer.

"Especially we must be deeply respectful and careful of our entry into that sacrament from which we have—for good or ill—disqualified ourselves, the sacrament of matrimony and all that pertains to it in the commerce of men and women. Often it seems to me we should rather seek counsel than give it in human sexual relations.

"These are only a few of the reasons why I wish to begin our reforms with the Congregation for the Doctrine of the Faith, because it is there that the necessary debate is inhibited and arguments taken out of the public forum and buried in a private one.

"Let me tell you, in this meeting of brothers, I hold with an iron grip to the ancient symbols of faith, those credal truths for which our martyrs died. I hold also to another certainty—the certainty of doubt, the certainty of not knowing, because the most insidious of all heresies was that of the gnostics who claimed a special pathway into the mind of God. We do not have that knowledge. We seek it in the life and teachings of the Lord, in the traditions of the Fathers and —let us be very clear on this—in our own expanding experience which we, please God, will hand down to other generations.

"We are not a fortress Church. We are a Church of witness. What we do and say must be done in the light. I know what you will tell me: that life today is lived under the scrutiny of television cameras and enquiring journalists and commentators eager for sensation. We are therefore vulnerable to misquotation and misinterpretation. So, I remind you, was our Lord and Master. It is in this spirit of openness and charity and with prudent care, that I propose to examine all the functions of the dicasteries. The process will be set in motion by *motu proprio,* which will be issued before the end of the year.

"However, there is one matter which must be settled now. It is not mentioned specifically in the *Ordo,* but time has been allowed for it. You will remember that the day before I left for the hospital, I told you that my abdication was already written and that you, the members of the Sacred College, would be free to judge whether I were competent to serve any longer as Pontiff. You have seen me. You have heard me. What I offer you is not a challenge, but a choice which you must make in good conscience. If you believe I am unfit, then you must accept my abdication. There will be no drama. I will step down at the time and in the manner you deem appropriate."

He held above his head a folded document, so that everyone could see the large pendant seal attached to it.

"This, written in my own hand, is the instrument of abdication. *Placetne fratres?* Do you accept it?"

There was a long moment of dead silence, then Cardinal Agostini gave the first answer: *"Non placet.* I do not accept."

After that there were no voices, only a long, continuous clapping; but in so large a room and so mixed a gathering, it was hard to know who was applauding and who was consenting to the inevitable.

The applause was still going on when the door opened and a prelate from the Secretariat of State summoned Agostini to the telephone.

Anton, Cardinal Drexel was calling from Castelli. His message was curt.

"Neylan called me from Ireland. In the small hours of this morning there was a terrorist attack on his farmhouse. Two men, two women, believed to be Japanese. Neylan and his manager killed them. He believes that there may be an attempt today on the Holy Father's life."

"Thank you, Anton. I'll talk immediately with the Holy Father and the Vigilanza. Anything else?"

"Yes. My Britte is dying. I've been trying to contact Professor Salviati. I'm told he's attending the Pontiff's Mass."

"I'll try to get a message to him. Also I'll tell His Holiness. Where can Neylan be contacted?"

"At the Mercy Hospital, Cork. I'll give you the number . . ."

But there was no time left for courtesy calls. The Vigilanza had to be put on red alert and the Pontiff informed. The chief of security shrugged helplessly and pointed to the swelling crowd in the Basilica.

"What do you expect me to do, Eminence? We've got fifty men here; twenty down the nave, ten in the transept, fifteen around the high altar, five on the walkway around the dome."

"There are four camera teams on scaffolding, all aiming their cameras at the High Altar. What about them?"

"All their papers are in order. They've been cleared by Social Communications. The Japanese have also been cleared by your people at the Secretariat of State. We've checked all the equipment. What more can we do?"

"Pray," said the Secretary of State. "But if anything happens don't, for God's sake, close the doors. Let 'em out; let 'em run free, otherwise this place will become a slaughter yard. Meantime, call your colleagues at the Intelligence centre and tell them the news."

"What about the Israelis?"

"They're out of the picture. The Ambassador will be here this morning as a personal guest of the Pontiff. For the rest, they'll be no help any more. Their number one Mossad man here has been shipped home."

"In that case, the Vigilanza will do its best; but you should pray very hard, Eminence! And we'd better have an ambulance standing by."

The Pontiff himself was rather more relaxed.

"At Mass I am the perfect target. Most of the time I am in the centre of the altar. But before we begin I shall tell the Master of Ceremonies that my deacons and sub-deacons must stand as far from me as possible. We can literally conduct the ceremony at two arms' length from each other. No one will notice."

"We could cancel, Holiness. There is still thirty minutes before Mass. We could begin now to clear the Basilica."

"To what purpose, Matteo? *Ut Deus vult.* It is as God wills. By the way, I have not thanked you for your vote of confidence at the Consistory."

"It was a vote for the man, Holiness; not necessarily for the policies. They still have to be tested."

"And you think they will not be? My friend, we shall be ground like wheat between the millstones; but it will be as God wills it to be."

It was only then that Agostini remembered to deliver the second part of Drexel's message.

"The child, Britte Lundberg, Anton's adopted granddaughter, is dying. We are told she will not last the day."

The Pontiff was visibly shaken. His eyes filled with tears. He reached out to Agostini and held his arm to steady himself.

"All of this, all of it, comes back to me. My life was bought with all these other lives. It's too much Matteo! Too much!"

It was mid-morning on the Feast of All Saints when Britte Lundberg died in the Mercy Hospital in Cork. Her mother's outburst of grief was terrible to see. All her controls seemed to snap at once, and she threw herself on the bed, sobbing and weeping and babbling endearments to coax the child back to life. When the nurse and one of the Sisters came in and tried to calm her, Matt Neylan waved them away.

"Leave her be! She'll work through it. I'll look after her."

Then, quite suddenly, it seemed all her grief was spent. She kissed Britte on the lips, arranged the body decently on the bed and drew the covers over it. Then she went into the bathroom. A long time later she came out, pale but composed, with her hair combed and her make-up repaired. Only her eyes betrayed her. They were unfocused, staring into desert distances. Matt Neylan held her for a long time and she seemed to be glad of the comfort, but there was no passion left in her. She asked vaguely: "What do we do now?"

"We call an undertaker," said Matt Neylan. "If you like we can bury her in the cemetery at Clonakilty. We have a family plot there. She would lie next to my mother."

"That would be nice. I think she'd like that. She loved you, Matt."

"I loved her."

"I know. Could we go for a walk?"

"Sure. I'll just stop by the desk and make a couple of phone calls. Then we'll stroll in the town."

"Another thing, Matt."

"Anything."

"Could we have a priest to bury her? Not for me, not for you, of course; but I think Nonno Drexel would like it."

"It'll be done. Let's go now. She doesn't need us any more."

Their walk took them past the post office, where they sent separate telegrams to Cardinal Drexel. Tove's read: "Dearest Nonno Drexel. Your beloved granddaughter died this morning. Her illness was mercifully short, her passing peaceful. Do not grieve too much. She would not want it. I will write later. Much, much love, Tove."

Matt Neylan's message was more formal.

"Your Eminence will wish to know that Tove is working through her grief. Britte had a happy life and her last conscious words were of her Nonno. She will be buried according to the rites of the Roman Church in my family plot at Clonakilty. If I have any problems with the parish priest, which I doubt, I shall invoke the name and rank of Your Eminence. If you would like to propose an epitaph for her headstone, I shall commission a good carver to execute it. My deepest sympathies in your sad loss. Matt Neylan."

When he had written the telegram, he turned to Tove and said: "I called the Vatican and asked them to pass on a message to Salviati, who is attending the Pope's Mass. Don't you think you should send him a personal message?"

"I should, yes."

She pulled a new form towards her and wrote swiftly.

"Dear Sergio. Britte died peacefully this morning. I am sad, confused and happy for her all at once. It is too early to say what will happen now, or where I shall go. Meantime, Matt Neylan is looking after me. He's a good man and we are comfortable together. Love, Tove."

If Matt Neylan was disappointed at such passionless praise, he gave no sign of it. The girl who accepted the telegrams pointed out that, because of the difference in time zones, they would not be delivered in Italy until the following day, which would be the Feast of All Souls, the Day of the Dead.

The Basilica was packed to the doors. The diplomats and their wives were all seated. The clergy were assembled, row on row, in their appointed places. The security men were at their posts. The camera teams were perched on their platforms, aiming and focusing on the Altar of the Confession, under the great baldacchino where the Pontiff and his senior cardinals would concelebrate the Mass of All Saints.

The air vibrated with the murmur of thousands, against which the organ tones reverberated in a thunderous counterpoint. In the sacristy the celebrants were vesting, while the Master of Ceremonies moved discreetly in the background, murmuring his last directions to the acolytes. The Pontiff himself was already clothed. They had brought him a chair and he sat, eyes closed in meditation, waiting for the ceremonies to begin.

Now, truly, he was afraid. There was no comfort against a violent death, no merciful anaesthesia, no solace of human kinship, no dignity at all. He was being stalked now, as in olden times his rivals had stalked the King of the Woods, to kill him and take possession of the shrine. The fear was not in the dying, but in the manner of it, the unknown "how", the unguessable "when", the nameless "who". He had a sudden, heart-stopping vision of his assassin standing, veiled like Lazarus, against one of the pillars of the baldacchino, waiting to offer a final greeting.

He tried to dispose himself for the encounter, and the only way he could do it was by an act of abasement to the will of the unseen Creator in whose cosmos both killer and victim had their place and purpose. He forced himself to frame the words, silently, with his lips: "*Fiat voluntas tua* . . . Let thy will be done. No matter how randomly, no matter with what seeming horror and inequity, let it be done. I surrender, because I have no other recourse."

Then, by some trick of association—or by some small mercy of distraction—he thought of Tove Lundberg, keeping the deathwatch over her child in that far, misty land which the Romans called Hibernia. Hers was another kind of agony and there were refinements to it at which he could only guess. Neylan would probably understand them better. He had found the universe so irrational a place that he had abandoned all belief in an intelligent creator. Yet he of all people was behaving with courage and dignity and compassion.

What he could not ask for himself, he could beg for them. He prayed for Drexel, too, caught in the last sad irony of age. He had opened his heart to love and now, in the twilight years, he was to be robbed of it.

There was a touch on his shoulder and the voice of the Master of Ceremonies whispered: "It is time to begin, Holiness."

* * *

From his post near the Diplomatic Corps, the Chief of Security watched every move of the Pontiff and his concelebrants at the altar and listened to the laconic reports that were radioed every minute from the strategic watch points round the Basilica. From the dome, everything looked normal; down the nave, normal; the transept, normal . . .

They were at the Preface now, the prayer that introduced the central Eucharistic acts. The choir, in full voice, chanted the doxology: "Holy, holy, holy Lord God of Hosts, heaven and earth are full of Your glory . . ." The radio reports continued: baldacchino, normal. Transept normal . . . But the big danger points in the ceremony were yet to come: the Elevation, when the Pontiff stood in the centre of the altar and raised the consecrated elements high above his head for the adoration of the faithful, and the moment just before the Communion when he raised the host again and pronounced the final words of praise.

The Master of Ceremonies was following his orders precisely, isolating the Pontiff whenever possible so that, even if he were stricken, casualties would be minimal. It was a terrible irony. Just as the ritual victim was being offered on the altar, the living, breathing target was offering himself to the assassin.

Installed among the members of the Papal Household, Sergio Salviati and Menachem Avriel managed to carry on a whispered conversation under the sound of the chanting. The Secretary of State had made contact with them both and given a hurried version of the news from Ireland. Avriel wanted to know: "What will you do about Tove now?"

"Write to her, call her."

"I thought . . ."

"So did I once. But it was over before she left. Nobody's fault. Too many ghosts in our beds, that's all."

"So take my advice. Give yourself a break. Come to Israel."

"I know the rest of it. 'We'll find you a nice, bright Jewish girl and . . .' So I'll try it. My junior surgeons are doing good work. Morrison will come down and hold their hands. Where are we now in the service?"

Menachem Avriel pointed to the place in the text and explained in a whisper.

"This is their Passover narrative."

"How do you know?"

"I read. I study the native customs, which is what diplomats are trained to do. Be quiet now. This part is very sacred."

The Pontiff was reciting the first formula of consecration: "While they were at supper, He took bread, blessed it, broke it and gave it to His disciples, saying: 'Take this, all of you, and eat it; this is my body which will be given up for you.'"

In the murmurous hush that followed, the Pontiff raised the white wafer above his head while the vast congregation bowed their heads in homage. The Chief of Security held his breath. With his arms raised high above his head, the Pontiff was a perfect target. When he lowered them, the Chief gave a long exhalation of relief. The first danger point was passed. Then the Pontiff bowed over the altar, took the gold chalice in his hands and recited the words that consecrate the wine:

"In like manner, He took the cup of wine. He gave thanks, offered the cup to

His disciples and said: 'Take this, all of you, and drink from it. This is the cup of my blood, the blood of the new and everlasting covenant which will be shed for you and for all men, so that sins may be forgiven. Do this in memory of me.' "

Again he raised his arms, displaying the consecrated element for the adoration of the people.

It was then the bullet hit him, tearing a hole in his chest, toppling him backwards so that the liquid spilled over his face and vestments, mingling with his life blood.

EPILOGUE

HIS Eminence, Karl Emil Clemens, Cardinal Camerlengo, was a very busy man. The See of Peter was vacant and until a new pontiff was elected, it was the Camerlengo who administered the office under the trusteeship of the Sacred College. This time there would be no confusions, no mistakes. He ordered a post-mortem examination and requested that it be performed by the Chief Medical Officer of the Roman Comune in the presence of three medical witnesses, among them Professor Sergio Salviati, surgeon to the Pontiff.

Their findings were unanimous. Death had been caused by a high velocity, hollow-nosed bullet of large calibre, fired from an elevated position. It had ruptured the heart and gone on to shatter itself against the vertebrae, diffusing fragments through the thoracic cavity. Death was instantaneous. This was consonant with the findings of investigators called in to assist the Vatican Corpo di Vigilanza. They found that the sound boom used by the Japanese film team was in fact an elongated rifle barrel which gave extraordinary accuracy to the projectile. However, by the time his equipment had been examined, the boom operator had disappeared. Evidence was given that he was, in fact, a Korean, born in Japan, who had been hired as a freelance. The other members of the team were held for questioning but finally released into the custody of the Japanese Ambassador, who arranged for their immediate departure.

The Pontiff's body was not exposed during the Lying-in-State. The three coffins—one of lead, which carried his coat of arms and enclosed the certificate of death, one of cypress and one of elm—were already sealed and the obsequies were abridged for fear, the newspapers said, of further episodes of violence. After the first waves of shock-and-horror stories, the memorials that were published about Leo XIV were muted, too. They spoke of him as a stern man, unbending in discipline, a model of rectitude in his private life, of zeal in his care of the pure tradition of the Faith. Even Nicol Peters noted coolly: "There were public demonstrations of reverence, but none of affection. This was a kind of Cromwell in papal history—a man of the people who failed to reach their hearts . . . There were strong rumours that after his illness he was a changed man, preparing a major shift in policy; but since, according to custom, all his papers are taken into the hands of the Camerlengo, we shall probably never know the whole truth."

Two medals were struck. One for the Camerlengo and one for the Governor of the forthcoming conclave at which the new pontiff would be elected. New Vatican coinage was minted and new stamps printed, bearing the words "sede vacante". The front page of *Osservatore Romano* carried the same words and a big black border.

Meantime, the Cardinal Camerlengo had taken possession of the papal apartments, the keys thereof and all their contents, including the Pontiff's diary, his will, his personal papers and effects, as well as the contents of his office files. Monsignor Gerard Hopgood assisted the Camerlengo in these mournful duties and, because he seemed a sensible, discreet and scholarly fellow, the Camerlengo suggested that he remain where he was until the new pontiff was elected, when he could help to induct the new staff. Meantime, he should think about another appointment, for which he could count on a very good recommendation. Which was why, on a cold and blustery Sunday in November, he took himself off to Castelli to visit Cardinal Drexel.

The old man was stooping a little now. The spring had gone out of his walk and when he made his rounds of the garden and the farmlands he carried a walking stick. Yet he still maintained his robust view of men and affairs. When Hopgood mentioned the suggestion made by the late Pontiff that he might work at the villa, Drexel brushed it aside: "Don't waste your life on it. It was a short-term affair anyway—a personal indulgence of mine, going nowhere. We did some good things, helped a single small group, but it is clear to me now that to make this into a viable enterprise one would need huge money, much public support—which is hard to come by in Italy—and a nucleus of trained staff, even harder to find. You want to use your heart and your head and your muscles? Go out to the emerging countries—Africa, South America . . . Europe is too fat and too prosperous. You will stifle here—or turn into a Vatican mouse, which would be a pity."

"I'll think about it, Eminence. Meantime, may I ask some advice?"

"On what?"

"An opinion I have: that small justice is being done to the memory of his late Holiness. Everything that is being published emphasises the reactionary period of his reign. Nobody mentions that he was on the verge of making great and historic changes, as you must have known."

"I knew it, yes." Drexel was giving nothing away.

"I should like to write a tribute to his memory, a portrait of the new man he had become. I should like"—he approached the subject very gingerly—"to publish and, indeed, interpret some of his last papers, including his address to the Consistory."

"Unfortunately," said Drexel with tart humour, "you do not have title to them."

"I believe I do." Hopgood was quite firm. "Look!"

He fished in his briefcase and brought out two volumes bound in leather.

The first and larger one consisted of handwritten notes and typescripts scrawled with corrections. The second was the text of the Pontiff's address to the Consistory. Both carried the same inscription:

TO

MY BELOVED SON IN CHRIST

GERARD HOPGOOD

WHO LENT ME THESE WORDS

TO INTERPRET MY HOPES AND MY PLANS.

LEO XIV, PONT. MAX.

"As I understand it," said Hopgood cheerfully, "copyright inheres in the author of the words and in the form of the words. And, lest it should be claimed that I wrote them as an employee or donated them as a gift, His Holiness was very careful to use the word lent."

Drexel thought for a moment, then laughed with genuine enjoyment.

"I do like a thorough man. Very well! Here is my advice. Get your appointment settled. If you're prepared to go to Brazil, I can recommend you to my friend Kaltenborn, who is Cardinal Archbishop of Rio. Then when you're far from Rome and your bishop is pleased with your work, publish your piece—and give the money to your mission, so no one can accuse you of base motives."

"Thank you, Eminence. I shall do as you say, and I should be most grateful for a recommendation to Cardinal Kaltenborn."

"Good. I'll write it before you leave. Strange how God arranges things! His Holiness gained a son. I lost a granddaughter. I'm running out of time. He had years of useful work ahead of him. I'm still here. He's dead."

"I keep asking myself"—Hopgood's tone was sombre—"how much the Church has lost by his death."

"It has lost nothing!" Drexel's voice rang, loud and startling, through the vaulted chamber. "On Vatican Hill, pontiffs have come and gone through the centuries, saints and sinners, wise men and fools, ruffians, rogues, reformers, and even an occasional madman! When they are gone, they are added to the list which began with Peter the Fisherman. The good are venerated; the bad are ignored. But the Church goes on, not because of them, but because the Holy Spirit still breathes over the dark waters of human existence as it did on the first days of Creation. That is what sustains us, that is what holds us together in faith and love and hope. Remember St. Paul! 'No man can say Jesus is Lord unless the Spirit moves him.' " He broke off as if suddenly embarrassed by his own vehemence. "Come now, you must try a glass of my own wine. I call it Fontamore. You'll stay to supper, I hope? Good friends of mine are coming in on the evening flight from Ireland. They tell me they have a pleasant surprise for me."

ABOUT THE AUTHOR

MORRIS WEST was born in Melbourne, Australia, in 1916. Before becoming a novelist, he had several careers, among them that of a radio producer and twelve years as a teaching monk. His first international acclaim as a writer came with *Children of the Sun*, followed by a succession of worldwide bestsellers including *The Devil's Advocate, Daughter of Silence, The Ambassador, The Tower of Babel, The World Is Made of Glass*, and *Masterclass*, as well as his highly acclaimed Vatican Trilogy: *The Shoes of the Fisherman, The Clowns of God*, and *Lazarus*.

His work has been published in twenty-seven languages. Recipient of many awards for his writing, Morris West has also been honored by the Australian government with the Order of Australia for his services to literature and cultural life.